THE
PUSHCART PRIZE, XXIX

AN ANNUAL SMALL PRESS READER

TWENTY-NINTH ANNIVERSARY EDITION

The

BEST OF
THE SMALL
PRESSES

PUSHCART

PRIZE

2005

PUSHCART

Edited by
Bill Henderson
with the Pushcart
Prize editors

XXIX

*PS
501
.P87
V.29*

Note: nominations for this series are invited from any small, independent, literary press in the world. Up to six nominations— tear sheets or copies, selected from work published, or about to be published, in the calendar year—are accepted by our December 1 deadline each year. Write to Pushcart Press, P.O. Box 380, Wainscott, N.Y. 11975 for more information, or see our web site www.pushcartprize.com.

Acknowledgments

Selections for *The Pushcart Prize* are reprinted
with the permission of authors and presses cited. Copy-
right reverts to authors and presses immediately after
publication.

*Distributed by W. W. Norton & Co.
500 Fifth Ave., New York, N.Y. 10110*

Library of Congress Card Number: 76–58675
ISBN: 1-888889-39-x (pb)
      1-888889-40-3 (hc)
ISSN: 0149–7863

In Memoriam: George Plimpton, Frederick Morgan

INTRODUCTION

by BILL HENDERSON

FIRST THE GOOD NEWS. Edward P. Jones, Pushcart Prize winner for "Marie" (*Paris Review*), his first published fiction and the lead story in *Pushcart Prize* XVIII, this year won not only the National Book Critics Circle Award but also The Pulitzer Prize for his novel *The Known World* (Amistad/HarperCollins). He was a finalist for The National Book Award. Recognition for Jones and *The Known World* is very heartening for all of us.

More good news—the sixty-two selections from forty-eight presses that follow in our annual celebration of little magazines and small presses, including first-timers, *Noon*, *Rivendell*, *River Teeth*, *Triplopia* and *Turnrow* (Desperation Press). The down side of this news is that we ran out of room to reprint all the extraordinary stories, poems and essays that were nominated. This was a vintage year. Because of budget constraints Pushcart has to keep the PP volumes to under 600 pages, and that very sadly excludes our reprinting of all the "Special Mention" work listed at the back of the book. We urge you to read these authors in the original. In fact subscribe to the journals that printed them. Go on, you can't afford not to.

Final good news: our Pushcart Prize Fellowships, just established to provide the series with a substantial endowment, has received enthusiastic support—gifts from ten dollars to fifteen thousand dollars have poured in. As I have mentioned here before, this celebration is published from an 8' × 8' shack in Pushcart's backyard, built with scrap lumber and windows from the dump. It receives no government or corporate funds and is sustained only by the readership and the volunteer efforts of its contributing and nominating editors. Except for minuscule honorariums for our fiction, poetry and essays editors, nobody gets paid. Reprinted authors and presses are reimbursed with copies, and copies do not generally put food on the table or wine in the cup, although they may lift the spirits, which in any case is a central idea of this project.

Our spirits can fall rather low, we have noticed, when the rest of the country clamors only for the buck and conglomerate media lies inundate us constantly. As Askold Melnyczuk, past editor of *Agni*, puts it in a recent *Agni* edition (the new editor is the esteemed Sven Birkerts), we have entered into a new age of feudalism—there's the giant corporations and the rest of us. In short, we have become serfs, 21st Century serfs, tilling the fields or occupying office cubicles for our masters, with only token power.

Melnyczuk states: ". . . a writer's job is to keep the language efficient so that it communicates. But words wear out: through misuse and overuse, they grow unmoored from meaning. When slaughter is defined as liberation, when justice is color-coded, when governments feel free to pull a bait-and-switch in a matter so serious as a war costing thousands of lives . . . then language may indeed have reached a dead end."

We hope not. And we small press editors and writers resist allowing words to be debased by the power addled.

Small is still beautiful. We will not be ground under or cubicled by the national propaganda machine. That's what the small press movement has always been about. And our endurance is rather amazing. Started in the 50's and 60's by those dubbed "hippies" with mimeograph machines publishing not only literature but political tracts as well, the movement expanded in the 70's and continues to grow today in print and on-line. Our revolution is here to stay, it seems, and it can have a real impact.

The Pushcart Prize Fellowships, by endowing the Pushcart Prize series, hopes to do what it can to champion and sustain that revolution. In our concluding pages (524–526) you will find the names of our Founding Members. If you would like to join us, write to Pushcart Press (PO Box 380, Wainscott, New York 11975) and we will tell you how.

Then there is the bad news. We miss George Plimpton, always will. He died last year at age 76, just as we were going to press with PP XXVIII. Plimpton was enormously generous to all little mags and small press authors and editors, Pushcart included. Often he opened his New York home to parties honoring this series. And, almost single-handedly he kept *The Paris Review* alive for fifty years, un-sinkable in his fund-raising and editorial enthusiasms.

The New York *Times* obituary, after a chronicle of Plimpton's life as a "participatory journalist" (he played tennis with Pancho Gonza-lez, was a third-string quarterback with the Detroit Lions and once boxed with Archie Moore—who bloodied his nose), noted: "His alter ego was as the unpaid editor of *The Paris Review*, an enduring, chronically impoverished quarterly, . . . that avoided using such typi-cal little magazine words as "zeitgeist" or "dichotomous" and pub-lished no crusty critiques about Melville or Kafka but instead printed the poetry and fiction of gifted young writers not yet popular."

My favorite George story is the night the power failed at a *Paris Review* reading in a lower east side pub. Somebody produced a lamp that worked and for an hour George alone, at an advanced age, held that lamp aloft so that the poet at the podium could make out what he had written and proclaim it. I can still see Plimpton now, his left arm raised high, refusing to grimace or give way or so much as lower the lamp a fraction, as his author read on next to the man who gave him light.

Frederick Morgan, founder and editor of *The Hudson Review* died February 20, 2004 at age 81. I remember him as another friend who was with Pushcart from day one—a small gathering at a rather fancy New York restaurant signaling the start of this series. From that day on, Morgan and his wife, Paula Deitz, who carries on as *Hudson Review*'s editor, encouraged Pushcart with nominations and support.

Morgan founded *The Hudson Review* in 1948, with Joseph Ben-nett and William Arrowsmith, to publish established and unknown writers, review books and cover news of music, theater, dance and the visual arts. With no academic affiliation, political ideology or backing beyond its founders' bank accounts—and a circulation that never climbed above 4,000 copies—Morgan, after his co-founders left in the 60's, kept his journal thriving for fifty-five years and also wrote a dozen volumes of poetry, most recently *The One Abiding* (Story Line Press), which appeared last year.

"He was a great gentleman and an elegant scholar and man of let-ters," said Alice Quinn, Executive Director of The Poetry Society of America.

We also miss Ted Weiss, editor since 1943 of the Quarterly Review of Literature Press and author of eleven books of poetry. Ted was one of the great small press survivors and champions. In moving tributes published this year in *American Poetry Review* and the *Princeton University Chronicle*, Reginald Gibbons, former *TriQuarterly* editor, remembered his teacher and friend: "Simply by example, Ted taught the modest ordinary priceless human worthiness of revering what is humane, merciful, loving, of memorializing the sufferings of others, of forgiving the failings of most people—although not of bullies in print or in person, nor of rogues' greed for their power and indifferent to the harm they do."

Ted Weiss died in April, 2003, at age 86. His wife Renée carries on the work of the press.

From Hawaii arrives a tribute by Contributing Editor Tony Quagliano, editor of *Kaimana*, for William Packard, the late founder and editor of *New York Quarterly*, the "brilliant and ornery poet" who published 58 issues before his death in 2002.

Packard was "absolutely fearless and he engaged poetry with wit, scholarship, pugnacity and a great generosity," Quagliano writes. *New York Quarterly* #59, a posthumous tribute edited by Raymond Hammond, contains new and old poems by Packard, interviews and a sample of his editorials over the years.

The lives of these editors prove that it is still possible to survive and make a big difference with a little light held high, even in the new age of feudalism.

Pushcart's thanks for this 29th celebration extend to all of the "People Who Helped" and the Founding Members of our Pushcart Prize Fellowships endowment, plus Monica Hellman, Jack Driscoll, David Means—fiction editors—and Tony Brandt, our essays referee, plus guest poetry editors for this edition, Jane Hirshfield and Dorianne Laux.

Dorianne Laux is the author of three collections of poetry from BOA Editions—*Awake* (1990), *What We Carry* (1994), a finalist for the National Book Critics Circle Award, and *Smoke* (2002). She is also co-author with Kim Addonizio, of *The Poet's Companion: A Guide To The Pleasures of Writing Poetry* (W.W. Norton & Co, 1997).

Recent work has appeared in *The Best American Poetry*, *The American Poetry Review*, *Shenandoah*, *Ploughshares*, *Barrow Street* and *Five Points*.

Among her awards are a Pushcart Prize for poetry, two fellowships from The National Endowment for the Arts and a Guggenheim Fellowship.

Laux is an Associate Professor in the University of Oregon's Creative Writing Program, and a member of The Lead Pencil Club. She lives in Eugene, Oregon with her husband, poet Joseph Millar—fondly remembered by Pushcart from long ago pub days—and her daughter Tristem.

Jane Hirshfield is the author of five books of poems, most recently *Given Sugar, Given Salt*, a finalist for the 2001 National Book Critics Circle Award and winner of the Bay Area Book Reviewers Award, published by HarperCollins in 2001. Other titles include *Alaya* (Quarterly Review of Literature Series, 1982), *Of Gravity & Angels* (Wesleyan University Press, 1988); *The October Palace* (HarperCollins, 1994), and *The Lives of the Heart* (HarperCollins, 1997).

Hirshfield is also the author of a book of essays, *Nine Gates: Entering the Mind of Poetry* (HarperCollins, 1997), and editor and co-translator of two collections of poetry by women writers of the past.

Hirshfield has received fellowships from the Guggenheim and Rockefeller Foundations, and has also held residencies at Yaddo, MacDowell, the Djerassi Foundation, and the Bellagio Center for Scholars and Artists. Her poetry and essays have appeared in *The New Yorker*, *The Atlantic*, *The Nation*, *The New Republic*, and many literary periodicals, and the *Pushcart Prize* and *Best American Poetry* anthologies.

Hirshfield's books, all of which have gone into many reprintings, have appeared on bestseller lists in San Francisco, Detroit, Canberra, and Krakow. Her poems and translations have found their way to such homes as the New York City Transit Agency's "Poetry in Motion" program, a John Adams oratorio, a Philip Glass symphony and a brass plaque at a San Francisco bus stop. She has served as judge, panelist, or guest editor for the National Book Awards, the National Poetry Series, and the National Endowment for the Arts.

My profound thanks to Jane and Dorianne and our other editors and to the presses and editors that submitted nearly 8,000 nominations for this year's *Pushcart Prize*. To select sixty-two works from so much that is excellent is, of course, impossible. Here then is our version of the impossible.

As Jane Hirshfield wrote of herself at the end of this process. "She is very very tired."

And elated.

THE PEOPLE WHO HELPED

FOUNDING EDITORS—*Anaïs Nin (1903–1977), Buckminster Fuller (1895–1983), Charles Newman, Daniel Halpern, Gordon Lish, Harry Smith, Hugh Fox, Ishmael Reed, Joyce Carol Oates, Len Fulton, Leonard Randolph, Leslie Fiedler, Nona Balakian (1918–1991), Paul Bowles (1910–1999), Paul Engle (1908–1991), Ralph Ellison (1914–1994), Reynolds Price, Rhoda Schwartz, Richard Morris, Ted Wilentz (1915–2001), Tom Montag, William Phillips (1907–2002), Poetry editor: H. L. Van Brunt.*

CONTRIBUTING EDITORS FOR THIS EDITION—*Jim Moore, Rosellen Brown, Jewel Mogan, Daniel Henry, Richard Burgin, Melinda McCollum, Dana Levin, Paul Maliszewski, D.A. Powell, Jeffrey Hammond, Sherod Santos, Jim Daniels, Philip Levine, Thomas E. Kennedy, Jim Barnes, William Heyen, Bruce Beasley, Tracy Mayor, DeWitt Henry, Nancy Richard, Paul West, Mark Wisniewski, Margaret Luongo, Marianna Cherry, Christie Hodgen, Beth Ann Fennelly, Kent Nelson, Rachel Loden, David St. John, Ted Deppe, Cleopatra Mathis, Kira Henehan, Elizabeth McKenzie, Ben Fountain III, Kristina McGrath, David Zane Mairowitz, Ryan Harty, Julie Orringer, Kristin King, Ron Tanner, Marie Sheppard Williams, Martha Collins, Judith Hall, Ellen Bass, Antonya Nelson, Lucia Perillo, Maxine Kumin, John Allman, Mark Irwin, Ed Falco, Maura Stanton, Arthur Smith, John Drury, Kathy Callaway, Jeffrey Harrison, Edward Hirsch, Michael Dennis Browne, Kay Ryan, Michael Waters, Jana Harris, Robert Boswell, Colette Inez, Pamela Stewart, Kim Addonizio, Tom Filer, Dan Masterson, Karl Elder, David Jauss, Nancy McCabe, Robert McBrearty, Katherine Taylor, David Baker,*

Carl Dennis, Joyce Carol Oates, Alice Mattison, Katherine Min, H.E. Francis, Stacey Richter, Richard Garcia, Valerie Laken, Stuart Dischell, Joe Ashby Porter, Mike Newirth, Andrea Hollander Budy, Julia Kasdorf, Michael Palma, Diann Blakely, Robert Phillips, John Kistner, George Keithley, Jim Simmerman, David Jauss, Donald Revell, Jeffrey A. Lockwood, Betty Adcock, Jessica Roeder, Terese Svoboda, Wally Lamb, Michael Bowden, Renée Ashley, Junse Kim, Robert Coover, Salvatore, Scibona, Joseph Hurka, BJ Ward, Andrew Feld, Janet Sylvester, Joan Connor, Robert Thomas, John Kulka, Eric Puchner, R.T. Smith, Claire Davis, Jane Brox, Joshua Beckman, Jennifer Atkinson, C.E. Poverman, Timothy Geiger, Maureen Seaton, Linda Gregerson, Peter Orner, Kathy Fagan, S.L. Wisenberg, Roger Weingarten, Gibbons Ruark, Eleanor Wilner, James Harms, Jane McCafferty, Jack Marshall, Linda Bierds, Ed Ochester, Matt Yurdana, Reginald Gibbons, Kenneth Gangemi, Kirk Nesset, Marianne Boruch, Donald Platt, Carolyn Alessio, Gerald Shapiro, Kevin Prufer, William Olsen, Barbara Hamby, Gary Gildner, Wesley McNair, Christina Zawadiwsky, Robin Hemley, Tony Ardizzone, Bob Hicok, Jean Thompson, Alice Schell, Len Roberts, Lee Upton, Toi Derricotte, Carl Phillips, Ralph Angel, Karen Volkman, Katrina Roberts, William Wenthe, Michael Heffernan, Rita Dove, Debra Spark, Philip Appleman, Daniel Hoffman, Tony Quagliano, Laura Kasischke, Kent Nelson, Christopher Buckley, Fred Leebron, Claire Bateman, Erin McGraw, Judith Kitchen, Melanie Rae Thon, Elizabeth Spires, Thomas Lux, Robert Cording, Charles Harper Webb, Christopher Howell, Molly Bendall, Sylvia Watanabe, Alan Michael Parker, David Rivard, Rachel Hadas, Michael Martone, Lance Olsen, Vern Rutsala, Floyd Skloot, Gerry Locklin, Richard Jackson, Grace Schulman, Susan Hahn, Brenda Miller, Dara Wier, Lloyd Schwartz, Marilyn Hacker, Sharon Dilworth, Josip Novakovich, David Kirby, Robert Wrigley, Marvin Bell, Rebecca Seiferle, Kathleen Hill, Brigit Pegeen Kelly, Sharon Solwitz, Michael Collier, Antler, Gary Fincke, Paul Zimmer, Joan Silber, Christian Wiman, Eamon Grennan, Daniel S. Libman, Kim Barnes, Emily Fox Gordon, Elizabeth Graver, Judith Taylor, E.S. Bumas, James Reiss, Stephen Corey, Ladette Randolph, Dorothy Barresi, Morton D. Elevitch, Glenna Holloway, Pat Strachan, R.C. Hildebrandt, Bonnie Jo Campbell, Len Roberts

PAST POETRY EDITORS—H.L. Van Brunt, Naomi Lazard, Lynne Spaulding, Herb Leibowitz, Jon Galassi, Grace Schulman, Carolyn

CONTENTS

THE
PUSHCART PRIZE, XXIX

IMMORTALITY

fiction by YIYUN LI

from THE PARIS REVIEW

His story, as the story of every one of us, started long before we were born. For dynasties, our town provided the imperial families their most reliable servants. Eunuchs they are called, though out of reverence we call them Great Papas. None of us is a direct descendant of a Great Papa, but traveling upstream in the river of our blood, we find uncles, brothers, and cousins who gave up their maleness so that our names would not vanish in history. Generations of boys, at the age of seven or eight, were chosen and castrated—*cleaned* as it was called—and sent into the palace as apprentices, learning to perform domestic tasks for the emperor and his family. At the age of thirteen or fourteen, they started to earn their allowances, silver coins that they saved and sent home to their parents. The coins were kept in a trunk, along with a small silk sack in which the severed male root was preserved with herbs. When the brothers of Great Papas reached the marriage age, their parents unlocked the trunk and brought out the silver coins. The money allowed the brothers to marry their wives; the wives gave birth to their sons; the sons grew up to carry on the family name, either by giving birth to more sons, or by going into the palace as cleaned boys. Years went by. When Great Papas could no longer serve the imperial masters on their wobbled knees, they were released from the palace and taken in by their nephews, who respected them as their own fathers. Nothing left for them to worry about, they sat all day in the sun and stroked the cats they had brought home from the palace, fat and slow as they themselves were, and watched the male dogs chasing the females in the alleys. In time death came for them. Their funerals were the most spectacular events in our town: sixty-four Buddhist monks in golden and red robes chanted prayers for forty-nine days to lead their souls into heaven; sixty-four Tao masters in blue and gray robes danced for forty-nine days to drive away any evils that dared to attach to their bodies. The divine moment came at the end of the forty-nine days, when the silk sacks containing their withered male roots were placed in the coffins. Now that the missing part had rejoined the body, the soul could leave without regret, to a place better than our town.

This was the story of every one of our Great Papas. For dynasties they were the most trustworthy members of the imperial family. They tended to the princesses' and the emperor's concubines' most personal tasks without tainting the noble blood with the low and dirty desires of men; they served the emperor and the princes with delicacy, yet, unlike those young handmaids who dreamed of seducing the emperor and his sons with their cheap beauties, Great Papas posed no threat to the imperial wives. There were wild rumors, though, about them serving as playthings for the princes before they reached the legal age to take concubines; and unfortunate tales of Great Papas being drowned, burned, bludgeoned, beheaded for the smallest mistakes—but such stories, as we all know, were made up to attack the good name of our town. What we believe is what we have seen—the exquisitely carved tomb-stones in our cemetery, the elegantly embroidered portraits in our family books. Great Papas filled our hearts with pride and gratitude. If not for them, who were we, the small people born into this no-name town?

The glory of our town has faded in the past century. But may I tell you one boy's story, before I reach the falling of Great Papas in history? As a tradition, the boys sent to the palace were not to be the only sons, who held the even more sacred duty of siring more boys. But the greatest among our Great Papas was an only son of his family. His father, also an only son, died young before he had the chance to plant more seeds in his wife's belly. With no uncle or brother to send them money from the palace, the boy and his widowed mother lived in poverty. At ten years old, after a fight with the neighbors' boys who had bragged about their brothers accepting gold bricks from the emperor's hands, the boy went into the cowshed and *cleaned* himself, with a rope and a sickle. According to the legend, the boy walked across the town, his male root dripping blood in his hand, and shouted to the people watching on with pity in their eyes, "Wait until I become the best servant of His Majesty!" Unable to endure the shame and the despair of living under a son-less and grandson-less roof, his mother threw herself into a well. Twenty years later the son became the master eunuch in the palace, taking under his charge 2,800 eunuchs and 3,200 handmaids. With no brothers to send his money to, he saved every coin and retired as the richest man in the region. He hired men to dig out his poor mother's coffin and gave her a second funeral, the most extravagant one ever to take place in our town. It was in the ninth month of 1904, and to this day our old people haven't stopped talking about every detail of the funeral: the huge coffin carved out of a sandalwood tree, stacks of gold bricks, trunks of silk clothes, and cases of jade bowls for her to use in the next life. Even more impressive were the four young girls the son had purchased from the poor peasants in the mountain, all of them twelve years old. They were put into satin dresses they would have never dreamed of wearing, and were each fed a cup of mercury. The mercury killed them instantly, so their peachy complexions were preserved when they were paraded in sedan chairs before the coffin. With burning incense planted in their curled fingers, the four girls accompanied the mother to the other world as her loyal handmaids.

This Great Papa's story was the brightest page in our history, like that one most splendid firework streaking the sky before darkness floods in. Soon the last dynasty was overthrown. The emperor was driven out of the Forbidden City; so were his most loyal servants, the last generation of our Great Papas. By the 1930s most of them lived in poverty in the temples around the Forbidden City. Only the smartest ones earned a fair living by showing their bodies to Western reporters and tourists, charging extra for answering questions, even more for having their pictures taken.

We have a short decade of republic; the warlords; two world wars, in both of which we fight on the winning side yet win nothing; the civil war; and finally we see the dawn of communism.

The day the dictator claims the communist victory in our country, a young carpenter in our town comes home to his newly wedded wife.

"It says we are going to have a new life from now on," the young wife tells the husband, pointing to a loudspeaker on their roof.

"New or old, life is the same," the husband replies. He gets his wife into bed and makes love to her, his eyes half-closed in ecstasy while the loudspeaker is broadcasting a new song, with men and women repeating the same lyrics over and over.

This is how the son is conceived, in a chorus of *Communism is so great, so great, and so great*. The same song is broadcast day after day, and the young mother hums along, touching her growing belly and cutting carefully the dictator's pictures from newspapers. Of course we never call him the dictator. We call him Our Father, Our Savior, the North Star of Our Lives, the Never Falling Sun of Our Era. Like most women of her generation, the mother is illiterate. Yet unlike others, she likes to look at newspapers, and she saves the pictures of the dictator in a thick notebook. Isn't she the woman with the greatest wisdom in our town? No other woman would ever think of looking at the dictator's face while pregnant with a son. Of course there has always been the saying that the more a pregnant woman studies a face, the greater the possibility of the baby owning that face. Years ago, young mothers in the cities liked to look at one kind of imported doll, all of them having the foreign name of Shirley Temple. Decades later, movie stars will be the most studied faces among the pregnant mothers. But at this time, the dictator is the only super-star in the media, so the mother has been gazing at the dictator's face for ten months before the baby's birth.

The son is born with the dictator's face, a miracle unnoticed by us at first. For the next ten years, we will avoid looking at him, for fear we will see his dead father in his face. The father was a hardworking man, nice to his neighbors, good to his wife. We would have never imagined that he would be an enemy of our newborn communist nation. Yet there are witnesses, not one, but a whole pub of evening drinkers.

What gets him killed is his comment about heroes and sows. At this time, we respect the communist power above us as our big brother. In our big-brother country, it is said, women are encouraged to produce babies for the communist cause, and those who have given birth to a certain number of babies are granted the title *mother hero*. Now that we are on the same highway to the same heaven, the dictator decides to adopt the same policy.

The young carpenter is a little drunk when he jokes aloud to his fellow drinkers, "Mother heroes? My sow has given birth to ten babies in a litter. Shouldn't she be granted a title, too?"

That's it, a malicious attack on the dictator's population policy. The carpenter is executed after a public trial. All but his wife attend the meeting, every one of us sticking our fists high and hailing the people's victory, our unanimous voice drowning out his wife's moans from her bed. We shout slogans when the bullet hits the young man's head. We chant revolutionary songs when his body is paraded in the street. When we finally lose our voices from exhaustion, we hear the boy's first cry, loud and painful, and for a moment, it is difficult for us to look into each other's eyes. What have we done to a mother and a baby? Wasn't the dead young man one of our brothers?

What we do not know, at the time, is that a scholar in the capital has been thrown in jail and tortured to death for predicting a population explosion and calling on the dictator to change the policy. Nor do we know that in a meeting with the leader of the big-brother country in Moscow, the dictator has said that we do not fear another world war or nuclear weapons: *Let the Americans drop the atomic bombs on our heads. We have five hundred million people in our nation. Even if half of us are killed, we still have two hundred and fifty million, and these two hundred and fifty million would produce another two hundred and fifty million in no time.*

Later, when we read his words in the newspaper, our blood boils. For the years to come, we will live with our eyes turned to the sky, waiting for the American bombs to rain down on us, waiting to prove to the dictator our courage, and our loyalty.

The boy grows up fast like a bamboo shoot. The mother grows old even faster. After the carpenter's death, upon her request, the Revolution Committee in our town gives her a job as our street sweeper. Every dawn, we lie in our beds and listen to the rustling of her bamboo broom. She has become a widow at the age of eighteen, as beautiful as a young widow could be, and naturally some of our bachelors cannot help but fantasize about her in their single beds. Yet none of our young men offers her another marriage. Who wants to marry a counterrevolutionary's widow, and spend the rest of his life worrying about being a sympathizer of the wrong person? What's more, even though the dictator has said that men and women are equal in our nation, we still believe a widow who wants another husband is a whore inside. Our belief is confirmed when we read in newspapers the dictator's comment about one of his close followers who has become an enemy of the nation: *A man cannot conceal his reactionary nature forever, just as a widow cannot hide her desire to be fucked.*

25

So the young mother withers in our eyes. Her face becomes paler each day, and her eyes drier. By the time the boy is ten, the mother looks like a woman of sixty. None of our bachelors bothers to lay his eyes on her face anymore.

The boy turns ten the year the famine starts. Before the famine, for three years, we have been doing nothing except singing of our communist heaven and vowing to liberate the suffering working class around the world. Farmers and workers have stopped toiling, their days spent in the pains and joys of composing yet another poem, competing to be the most productive proletarian poet. We go to the town center every day to discuss the strategy of how to conquer the world under the leadership of the dictator. When the famine catches us unprepared, we listen to the dictator's encouraging words in the loudspeakers. He calls for us to make our belts one notch tighter for our communist future, and we happily punch more holes in them. The second year of the famine, the dictator says in the loudspeakers: *Get rid of the sparrows and the rats; they are the thieves who stole our food, and brought hunger to us.*

Killing sparrows is the most festive event in the three long years of famine. After months of drinking thin porridges and eating weed roots, on the morning of the sparrow-killing day we each get two steamed buns from the municipal dining room. After breakfast, we climb to the roof of every house, and start to strike gongs and drums at the Revolution Committee's signal. From roof to roof, our arrhythmic playing drives the sparrows into the sky. All morning and all afternoon we play, in different shifts, and whenever a sparrow tries to rest in a treetop, we shoo him away with colorful flags bound to long bamboo poles. In the evening the sparrows start to rain down on us like little bombs, dying in horror and exhaustion. Kids decorated as little scarecrows run around, collecting the dead sparrows from the ground for our dinner.

The boy is trying to sneak a sparrow into his sleeve when a bigger boy snatches his hand. "He is stealing the property of the People," the big boy shouts to the town.

"My mom is sick. She needs to eat something," the boy says.

"Hey, boy, what your mom needs is not this kind of bird," a man says, and we roar with laughter. The buns in our stomachs and the sparrows in the baskets have put us in a good mood.

The boy stares at the man for a moment and smacks into him with his head.

"Son of a bitch," the man says, bending over and covering his crotch with his hands.

"Beat the little counterrevolutionary," someone says, and we swarm toward the boy with fists and feet. The famine has made us angrier each day, and we are relieved to have found someone to vent our nameless rage upon.

The mother rushes into the crowd and tries to push us away. Her presence makes us hit the boy even harder. Some of us pick up bricks and boulders, ready to knock him out. Some of us bare our teeth, ready to eat him alive.

"You all look at his face. Whoever dares to touch him one more time, I'll sue him for his disrespect for our greatest leader," the mother yells, charging at us like a crazy woman.

Our bodies freeze. We look at the boy's face. Even with his swollen face and black eyes, we have no problem telling that he has the face of the dictator, young and rebellious, just as in the illustrations in the books about the dictator's heroic childhood. The boy stands up and limps to his mother. We look at his face in awe, not daring to move when he spits bloody phlegm at our feet.

"Remember this face," the boy says. "You will have to pay for this one day." He picks up a couple sparrows and walks away with his mother. We watch them supporting each other like husband and wife.

For years we do not know if it is a blessing or a disaster that a boy with the dictator's face lives among us. We treat the boy and his mother as the most precious and fragile treasure we have, never breathing one word about them to an outsider.

"It may not be a good thing," our old people warn us, and tell us the story of one of our Great Papas, who happened to have the same nickname as the emperor and was thrown into a well to drown. "There are things that are not allowed to exist in duplicates," the old people say.

Yet none of us dares to say one disrespectful word about the boy's face. As he grows older, he looks more and more like the dictator. Sometimes, walking past him in the street, there is a surge of warmth in our chests, as if the dictator himself were with us. This is the time when the dictator becomes larger than the universe in our nation. Illiterate housewives, who have used old newspapers as wallpaper and who have, accidentally, reversed the titles with the dictator's name in them, are executed. Parents of little first-graders who have misspelled the dictator's name are sent to labor camps. With the boy living among us, we are constantly walking on a thin layer of ice above deep water. We worry about not paying enough respect to the face, an indication of our hidden hatred of the dictator. We worry about respecting that face too much, which could be interpreted as our inability to tell the false from the true, worshipping the wrong idol. In our school, the teachers never speak one harsh word to him. Whatever games the students play, the side without him is willing to lose. When he graduates from the high school, the Revolution Committee has meetings for weeks, to discuss what is an appropriate job for a young man with a face like his. None of the jobs we have in town is safe enough to be given to him. Finally we think we have come up with the best solution to the problem—we elect him as the director of the advisory board to the Revolution Committee.

The young man prospers. Having nothing to do, and not liking to kill his time over cups of tea with the old board members, he walks around town every day, talking to people who are flattered by his greetings, and watching the female sales assistants in the department store blush at his sight. His mother is in much better shape now, with more color in her face. The only inconvenience is that no girl will date the young man. We have warned our daughters that marrying him would either be the greatest fortune, or the greatest misfortune. Born into a town where gambling is genuinely disapproved of, none of us wants to marry a daughter off to a man like him.

The day the dictator dies, we gather at the town center and cry like orphans. On the only television set our town owns, we watch the whole nation howling with us. For three months, we wear black mourning armbands to work and to sleep. All entertainments are banned for six months. Even a year or two after his death, we still look sideways at those women who are growing bellies, knowing that they have been insincere in their mourning. Fathers of those children never receive respect from us again.

It is a difficult time for the young man. Upon seeing his face, some of us break into uncontrollable wails, and he himself has to spend hours crying with us. It must have tired him. For a year he stays in his own room, and the next time we see him, walking toward the town center with a small suitcase, he looks much older than his age of twenty-eight.

"Is there anything wrong?" we greet him with concern. "Don't let too much grief drag you down."

"Thank you, but I am in a fine state," the young man replies.

"Are you leaving for somewhere?"

"Yes, I am leaving."

"Where to?" We feel a pang of panic. Losing him at this time seems as unbearable as losing the dictator one year ago.

"It's a political assignment," the young man says with a mysterious smile. "Classified."

Only after he is driven away in a well-curtained luxury car (the only car most of us have ever seen in our life), do we catch the news that he is going to the capital for an audition as the dictator's impersonator. It takes us days of discussion among ourselves to figure out what words like *audition* and *impersonator* mean. In the end the only agreement we come to is that he is going to become a great man.

Now that he has disappeared from our sights, his mother becomes the only source for his stories. She is a proud mother, and every time we inquire her of his whereabouts she repeats the story of how she gazed at the late dictator's face day and night when her son was growing inside her. "You know, it's like he is the son of our great leader," she says.

"Yes, all of us are sons of our great leader," we nod and say. "But sure he is the best son."

The mother sighs with great satisfaction. She remembers how in the first few years after her son was born, women of her age produced baby after baby, putting framed certificates of mother heroes on their walls and walking past her with their eyes turned to the sky. Let time prove who is the real hero, she would think, and smile to herself.

Then she tells us about her son, every bit of information opening a new door to the world. He rode in the first-class car in a train to the capital, where he and other candidates have settled down in a luxury hotel, and are taken to the dictator's memorial museum every day, studying for the competition.

"Are there other candidates?" we gasp, shocked that she may not be the only woman to have studied the dictator's face during pregnancy.

"I am sure he is the one they want," the mother says. "He says he has total confidence, when he looks at the leader's face, that he is going to be the chosen one."

In the years to come, some among us will have the chance to go to the capital, and wait in a long line for hours to take a look at the dictator's face. After his death, a memorial museum was built in the center of our nation's capital, and the dictator's body is kept there in a crystal coffin. *Let our great leader live for ten thousand years in the hearts of a hundred generations* is what the designer has carved into the entrace of the museum. Inside the entrance, we will pay a substantial fee for a white paper flower to be placed at the foot of the crystal coffin, among a sea of white flowers. For a brief moment, some of us will wonder whether the flowers are collected from the base and resold the next day, but instantly we will feel ashamed of ourselves for thinking such impure thoughts in the most sacred place in the world. With the flowers in hand, we will walk into the heart of the memorial, in a single hushed file, and we will see the dictator, lying in the transparent coffin, covered by a huge red flag decorated with golden stars, his eyes closed as if in sleep, his mouth in a smile. We will be so impressed with this great man's body that we will ignore the unnatural red color in his cheeks, and his swollen neck as thick as his head.

Our young man must have walked the same route and looked at his face with the same reverence. What else has passed through his heart that does not occur to us? We will wonder.

He must have felt closer to the great man than any one of us. He has the right to feel so, chosen among tens of candidates as the dictator's impersonator. How he beat his rivals his mother never tells us in detail, just saying that he was born for the role. Only much later do we hear the story: our young man and the other candidates spend days in training, and those who are too short or too weakly built for the dictator's stature (even they, too, have the dictator's face) are eliminated in the first round, followed by those who cannot master the dictator's accent. Then there are the candidates who have everything except a clean personal history, like those born to the landlord class. Thanks to the Revolution Committee in our town, which has concealed the history of our young man being the son of an executed counterrevolutionary, he makes it into the final round with three other men. On the final day, when asked to do an improvised performance, the other three candidates all choose to quote the dictator announcing the birth of our communist nation (which is, as you remember, also the beginning of our young man's own journey), while he, for some unknown reason, says, *"A man cannot conceal his reactionary nature forever, just as a widow cannot hide her desire to be fucked."*

For a moment, he is horrified by his blunder, and feels the same shame and anger he once felt as a dead sparrow turned cold between his fingers. To his surprise, he is chosen, the reason being that he has caught the essence of the dictator, while the other three only got the rough shape. The three of them are sent with the rest of the candidates for plastic surgery, for, as our old men have said, there are things that are not allowed to exist in duplicate.

Our young man becomes the sole face that represents the dictator in the nation, and thus starts the most glorious years of his life. Movies about the dictator, starring our young man, are filmed by the government-run movie factories. Back in town, we cram into our only theater and watch the movies, secretly blaming our mothers or wives for not having given birth to a great face.

The marriage of the young man becomes our biggest concern. He is over thirty now, an age generally considered indecent for our young daughters. But who will care about the age of a great man? The old-style ones among us hire matchmakers for our daughters, and send with them expensive gifts to his mother. Others, more modern and aggressive, knock on his mother's door with blushing daughters trailing behind. Dazed by the choices, his mother goes to the town center and makes long-distance calls to him every other day, reporting yet another suitable candidate. But he is no longer a man of our town. He has been flying all over the nation for celebrations and movies; he has seen more attractive women than our town can provide. Through his apologetic mother, he rejects all of our offers. Accepting that our town is too shallow a basin to contain a real dragon, most of us give up and marry our daughters off to local young men. Yet some among us cling to the nonexistent hope, waiting for the days when he will realize the incomparable beauties and virtues of our daughters. For a number of years, scores of girls in our town are kept untouched by their parents. Too much looking forward makes their necks grow longer each year. It is not an unfamiliar sight to see a girl with a crane like neck walk past us in the street, guarded by her parents who have grown to resemble giraffes.

The young man is too occupied with his new role to know such

31

stories. He appears in the national celebrations for all the holidays. His most loyal audience, we sit all night long in front of the television and wait for his appearance. On the screen, men and women sing and dance with hearty smiles on their faces like well-trained kindergarteners. Children four or five years old flirt with one another, singing love songs like many joyful parrots. At such moments, those of us who think a little more than others start to feel uneasy, haunted by a strange fear that our people are growing down, instead of growing up. But the worry vanishes when our young man, the dictator's impersonator, shows up. People on the screen stand up in ovation and hold out their hands to be shaken. Young women with the prettiest faces rush to him with bouquets of flowers. Kids swarm around him and call him by the name of the dictator. Nostalgic tears fill everyone's eyes. For a moment, we believe time has stopped. The dictator is still alive among us, and we are happily living as his sons.

But time has sneaked by while we were mesmerized by our young man's face. Now we have Sony and Panasonic: we have Procter & Gamble, Johnson & Johnson. We have imported movies in which men and women hold hands freely in the street, and they even kiss each other without a trace of fear in their eyes. Our life, we realize, is not as happy as we have been taught to think. People in those capitalist countries are not waiting for us to be their liberators. They never knew of our love for them.

This must be a difficult period for our young man as well. Biographies and memoirs about the dictator appear overnight like spring grass. Unlike the books written collectively by the government-assigned writing groups, these books spell trouble the moment they appear. Soon they are decided to be illegal publications, and are confiscated and burned in great piles. Yet some of the words have spread out, bad words about the dictator. Mouth to mouth the rumors travel, how under his reign fifty million people have died from famine and political persecution. But if you looked at the number closely, you would realize it is far less than what the dictator was once willing to sacrifice to American nuclear bombs. So what is all the fuss about?

Still, we start to think about what we have been led to believe all these years. Once doubt starts, it runs rampant in our hearts like wild fire. Our young man's face appears on the television regularly, but the face has lost its aura. Those of us who have been waiting for his proposal are eager to sell our daughters to the first offer available.

The young man's mother, now a garrulous old woman, walks in the street and grabs whomever she can to tell his stories, none of which impresses us anymore. From his mother, we have learned that he is touring across the nation with our present leader, a tour designed to inspire our national belief in communism. So what? we ask, and walk away before the mother has the chance to elaborate.

The tour ends early when a protest breaks out in the capital. Thousands of people rally for democracy in the center of the capital, where the dictator's memorial museum is less and less visited. Threatened and infuriated, our present leader orders the army to fire machine guns at the protesters. Astonishing as the event is, it slips out of our memory as soon as the dead are burned to ashes in the state-supervised crematoriums. The leader has said, as we later read in newspapers, that he is willing to kill two hundred thousand lives in exchange for twenty years of communist stability. Numbed by such numbers, we will echo his words and applaud his wisdom when we are required to publicly condemn those killed in the incident.

In no time the big-brother country above us no longer exists. Then one by one, our comrades-in-arms take turns exiting the historical stage. Confused as we are, we do not know what to think of them, whether we should envy, despise or pity them.

Life is presenting a big problem to our young man at this time. Although out of habit we still call him our young man, he is no longer young but in his forties. Even worse, he is a man in his forties who has never tasted a woman in his life. Can you believe it? we will ask one another. Incredible, we will shake our heads. But it is true: our young man spent most of his twenties wanting a woman, but we were unwilling to hand our daughters to him; when we were ready, he had become a man too great for our daughters. Time passes ruthlessly. Now that none of our daughters is available anymore, he starts to fantasize about the women he should have had long ago.

Once the desire is awakened, he is no longer able to live in peace. He watches women walking in the streets, their bare arms and legs in summer dresses deliciously attractive, and wonders how it would feel to have a woman of his own. Yet which woman is worthy of his greatness? Sometimes his blood is so unruly that he feels the urge to grab anyone passing by and make her his woman. But once his desire is subdued, after successful masturbation, he is no longer driven by blind craving. At such moments, he sees his life more clearly than ever, and he knows that no woman is great enough to match him.

"But you need a wife to give birth to a son," his mother, eager for a grandson, reminds him when he calls long distance to speak to her. "Remember, the first and the foremost duty of a man is to make a son, and pass on his family name."

He mumbles indistinct words and hangs up. He knows that no woman's womb will nurture a son with a face as great as his own.

Now that the dictator's life has been explored and filmed thoroughly, our young man has more time on his hands. When there is no celebration to attend, he wanders in the street with a heavy coat, his face covered by a high collar and a pair of huge dark glasses. Sometimes he feels the temptation to walk with his face completely bare to the world, but the memory of being surrounded by hundreds of people asking for autographs stops him from taking the risk.

One day he walks across the capital, in search of something he is eager to have but unable to name. When he enters an alley, someone calls to him from behind a cart of newspapers and magazines.

"Want some books, friend?"

He stops and looks at the vendor from behind his dark glasses. "What kind of books?"

"What kind do you want?"

"What kind do you have?"

The vendor moves some magazines and uncovers the plastic sheet beneath the magazines. "Yellows, reds, whatever you want. Fifty yuan a book."

He bends over and looks from above his dark glasses. Underneath the plastic sheet are books with colorful covers. He picks one up and looks at a man and a woman, both naked, copulating in a strange position on the cover. His heart starts to beat in his chest, loud and urgent.

"That's a good yellow one," the vendor says, "as yellow as you want."

He clasps the book with his fingers. "What else do you have?"

"How about this red one?" the vendor hands him another book, the dictator's face on the cover. "Everybody loves this book."

He has heard of the book, a memoir written by the dictator's physician of thirty years, banned when it was published abroad, and smuggled into the country from Hong Kong and America.

He pays for the two books and walks back to his room. He studies the dictator's portrait, and compares it with his own face in the mirror, still perfect from every angle. He sighs and plunges into the

yellow book, devouring it like a starved man. When his erection be-
comes too painful, he forces himself to drop the book and pick up
the red one.

He feels an emptiness that he has never felt before, switching be-
tween the books when one becomes too unbearable. In the yellow
book he sees a world he has missed all his life, in which a man has an
endless supply of women, all of them eager to please him. Yet for all
he knows, the only man who could have as many women as he wants
is the dictator. He leafs through the red book one more time, looking
at the pictures of the dictator in the company of young attractive
nurses, and realizes that he has misunderstood his role all these
years. To be a great man means to have whatever he wants from the
world. Blaming himself for this belated understanding, he stands up
and goes out into the night.

He has no difficulty locating a prostitute in the dimly lit karaoke-
and-dance bar. As a precaution, he keeps his dark glasses and heavy
coat on the whole time they are bargaining. Then he goes away with
the young woman to a nearby hotel, sneaking through a side door
into a room the woman has reserved while she deals with the recep-
tionist.

What comes next is perplexing to us. All we can figure out from
the rumors is that, when he is asked to undress, he refuses to take off
either his dark glasses or his heavy coat. To be a great man means to
have a woman in whatever way he wants, our young man must be
thinking. But how is a man like him able to resist the skillful fingers
of a professional like the woman he has hired? In a confusing mo-
ment, he is as naked as the woman, his face bare and easy to recog-
nize. Before he realizes it, the woman's pimp, dressed up in police
uniform, rushes in with a pair of handcuffs and a camera. Lights flash
and snapshots are taken, his hands cuffed and clothes confiscated.
Only then does the couple recognize his face, and we can imagine
how overjoyed they must be by such a discovery. Instead of the usual
amount, they ask for ten times what others pay, on account that our
young man is a celebrity, and should pay a celebrity price for the pic-
tures.

To this day we still disagree on how our young man should have
reacted. Some of us think he should have paid and let himself go
free, money being no problem for him. Others think he did nothing
wrong by refusing to cooperate, but he should have gone to the po-
lice and reported the couple, instead of thinking such things would

pass unnoticed. After that night, rumors start to spread across the capital, vivid stories about our young man's regular visits to the illegal brothels. The pictures he has failed to secure are circulated in different circles, until everyone in the capital claims that he has seen them. None of us in town has seen the pictures. Still, our hearts are broken when we imagine his body, naked and helpless, and we try our best to keep our mind's eyes away from the familiar face in those pictures.

He is considered unsuitable to continue as the impersonator of the dictator, for, as it is put in the letter addressed to him by the Central Committee of Cultural Regulation, he has soiled the name he is representing. Never before had it occurred to him that a man like him could be fired. There is no other face as his in the world, and who would replace him, the most irreplaceable man in the nation? He goes from office to office, begging for another chance, vowing never to touch a woman again. What he does not understand is that his role is no longer needed. A new leader has come into power and claimed himself the greatest guide of our communist cause in the new millennium. Talent scouts are combing through the nation for a new perfect face different from his own.

So our no longer young man comes home on a gloomy winter day. Stricken by shame, his mother has turned ill overnight and left us before he makes his way back. The day he arrives, some of us—those who remember him as the boy with a sparrow in his hand, who have secretly wished him to be our son-in-law, who have followed his path for years as the loyal audience of his mother, and who have, despite the pains of seeing him fall, lived for the joy of seeing his face—yes, those of us who have been salvaged from our mundane lives by loving him, we gather at the bus stop and hold out our hands for him to shake. He gets off the bus and ignores our earnest smiles, his dark glasses and high collar covering his face. Watching him walk to his mother's grave, with a long shadow limping behind him, we decide we will forgive him for his rudeness. Who would have the heart to blame a son like him? No matter what has happened to him, he is still the greatest man in our history, our boy and our hero.

Trust us, it breaks our hearts when he *cleans* himself by his mother's tomb. How such a thought occurred to him we will never understand, especially since, if we are not mistaken, he is still a virgin who has so much to look forward to in life. The night it happens, we

36

hear a long howl in our sleep. We rush outside into the cold night, and find him in our cemetery. Even though we have grown up listening to the legends of our Great Papas, the scene makes us sick to our bones. We wonder what the meaning of such an act is. No one in our town—not we the small people, not our Great Papas—has reached the height that he has. Even our greatest Great Papa was only the best servant of the emperor, while he, with the face of the dictator, was once the emperor himself. Watching him roll on the ground, his face smeared with tears and blood, we remember the story of the ten-year-old boy, his male root in his hand, his face calm and proud. This is a sad moment for us, knowing that we, the children of our Great Papas, will never live up to their legends.

But lamenting aside, we still have a newly cleaned man to deal with. Some of us insist on sending him to the hospital for emergency treatment; others consider such a move unnecessary, for the act is done and there is no more harm left. Confused as we are, none of us remembers to collect the most important thing at the scene. Later, when we realize our mistake, we spend days searching every inch of our cemetery. Yet the missing part from his body has already disappeared, to whose mouth we do not want to imagine.

He survives, not to our surprise. Hadn't all our Great Papas survived and lived out their heroic stories? He is among us now, with a long barren life ahead. He sits in the sun and watches the dogs chasing each other, his face hidden behind the dark glasses and high collar of his coat. He walks to the cemetery in the dusk and talks to his mother until the night falls.

As for us, we have seen him born in pain and we will, in time, see him die in pain. The only thing we worry about is his next life. With his male root forever missing, what will we put into the silk sack to bury with him? How will we be able to send a soul to the next world in such incompleteness?

For the peace of our own minds, every day we pray for his health. We pray for him to live forever as we prayed for the dictator. He is the man whose story we do not want to end, and, as far as we can see, there will be no end to his story.

Nominated by Fred Lebron, The Paris Review

BEETLE ORGY

by BENJAMIN SCOTT GROSSBERG

from WESTERN HUMANITIES REVIEW

Bloom up from the earth, blooming and curling
like ribbon, and at semi-regular intervals
sprouting leaves: almost the border art
of a Celtic manuscript, the vines up along the fence
of this old tennis court. Amid the wreck

of the net, the cracks of the surface, the rust
along the poles still standing, the vines
are a saving delicacy. Not jarring at all,
though incongruous—except as a reminder
that the school yard will gladly take this place

back in a few untended years, that between
the vines and grass, the tennis court
will be ground into meal and digested.
I stop at one of the vine edgings caught
by even finer detail: the leaves themselves

are digested; they have been eaten to
irregular lace, and the perpetrators are still here—
five of them across one particular leaf, lined up
straight and even, like cars in a parking lot.
Beetles: their backs a lustrous green and copper,

taken hot from the kiln, thrown on a bed of saw dust
that burst into flame, then lidded over

so the vacuum could draw the metal oxides
to the surface. At first it looks like there are five,
but now I see that there are seven, no eight—

and that in three of the spaces, beetles
are doubled up, one mounting, back legs
twitching, as if running and getting no where;
and one mounted, also moving, slightly rocking
in back, close to the point of intersection—

or penetration—in any case, where the bodies
touch. And here I come to it—amid the advancing
vines and decrepit court: they're on other leaves, too,
all around—coupling in company, hundreds of them,
the rows melding to make a single metallic band.

Back in Houston, a friend had parties—
lawn bags in the living room numbered with tape
to store guest clothing; plastic drop cloths
spread out in the spare bedroom (cleared of furniture
for the occasion), a tray of lubricants, different

brands in tubes or bottles, labels black, red, and silver
—a high tea sensibility. The artifacts remained
uncollected in his apartment for days, even weeks
after, when I would drop by to find his talk
transformed, suddenly transcendental—

the communality, he told me, the freedom: not
just from the condom code (HIV negative I
was never invited) but freed of individuation—
nothing less than rapture, men more than brothers,
a generosity of giving and taking, to both give

and take greedily, that he had experienced
no where else. Could I understand that?
The room pulsing as if inhabited by
a single animal, caught up in a single sensibility.
Could I understand? I could read transformation

in his face, could see his eyes, feel him trying
to tell me something: to offer this reliable revelation—
what he always knew would come, but what always
in coming disarmed him. As he talked I looked around
the spare bedroom, attempting to see it

in terms other than lust—a couple of dozen men,
how they would have lined up, become a single
working unit on clear plastic, how their bodies
might have formed a neat chain. I looked around
and tried; couldn't I understand that?

So each beetle a tiny scarab, a dime-size jewel
that glints in the sun. I lean over and touch
their backs with the tip of my finger: running
up and down the bright, smooth surface
like piano keys, hard enough to feel resistance

but not to interject foreign music. Together they form
a band of light, a band of glaze, the gold leafing
that shadows the vines in Celtic manuscripts, a living art.
Maybe that's how it was at my friend's parties—
God leaning over the house on a casual tour

of the wreck of the world, noticing ornamentation
where it wasn't expected. Moved to add
his touch, he reaches a hand through the clouds, runs
his finger over the hard arch of their backs, covering
the length of each spine with the tip;

each man brightens at the touch, comes to know
something expected, unexpected, and tenuous—
and God, also, comes to some knowledge
as if for the first time, is distracted and pleased
by the collective brightness of human skin. . . .

Then I think of God fitting the roof back on
my friend's house, and exhaling, satisfied—
just like me as I walk away
from the tennis court, just like the men inside.

Nominated by Western Humanities Review

NOIKOKYRIO

by ALISON CADBURY

from THE GEORGIA REVIEW

ONLY THIRTY YEARS AGO, when I first lived there, the island of Paros was almost an ecologist's Utopia. Island life was not simple; it was complex in its own way, but in its great respect for and harmony with nature, the polished results of thousands of years of living and learning, it exemplified the environmentalist's dream.

Island life was neither primitive nor austere. All the villages and the *hora*, the main town, had running water and some, if not very dependable, electricity, though people in the country drew their water from wells and lit their homes with oil lamps. The villagers used the electricity sparingly, getting up in the dawn and making sure to do tasks that needed light before sunset. Work done, darkness was nothing to be feared or banished: on a summer's evening, the unlit streets would be lined with neighbors sitting outside on chairs, in their courtyards, or on the street itself, gossiping and greeting strollers in the blue-velvet dark: *"Yia sas! yia sas! Kali spera! Hiairete!"* The greetings flowed like a warm breeze.

Telephones there were also, though lines were few. In the country, public telephones were installed in houses central to each area. In the village, the few householders or shop owners with phones also took messages as a matter of course, but off-island communications depended largely on the lone operator in the small telephone company office, Kyrios Themistocles, who would take messages and yell them out the door to the coffee drinkers in the *plateia*, at least one of whom would haul himself to his feet or snag a passing child to deliver the news or call someone to the phone. Themistocles, as intermediary, was always the first to hear of births, deaths, engagements, operations, and other juicy items, and enjoyed much attention and prestige by spreading the word. When he was replaced by an automatic system, he grieved his loss of status more than any deposed monarch.

The most usual form of transportation was walking. Children walked a mile or two to school; beyond that, they might ride a donkey and leave it to graze in a field next to the school. To shop and work and visit, villagers walked everywhere, even miles into the country. There was bus service between hora and villages, but it was limited to the morning hours; the last bus left the hora at one, taking the high school students home to dinner in the villages. If you needed to go to or from the hora or another village after bus hours, perhaps to catch a boat to Piraeus, you took one of the three or four taxis, and you were not surprised or put out if the driver took on other passengers or even stopped at a house along the way to deliver a package, perhaps a prescription from the pharmacy or a kilo of lamb chops. If you had a lot of stuff to haul, if for instance you were moving out to your summer place—beds, chairs, tables, kids, and all—you contracted with one of the small, green "taxi" trucks, generally three-wheelers with motorcycle engines, which were for hire to anyone. These little trucks kept busy delivering goods off the ships to shops and homes as well as lumber and bricks to building sites. Where streets in village and hora were too narrow and winding even for the small trucks, goods for shops and homes were trundled in by handcart. Both trucks and carts, however, needed paved roads; most farms and country homes were connected by *monopatia*—narrow, rocky paths that ran alongside stone walls or dry riverbeds. Here the strong and dainty donkeys and mules were the most practical way to haul both people and goods; in every village and town they had their own shady parking lots. The only two private cars on the island, one in the hora and one in the village, belonged to two doctors.

Despite these modern conveniences, there was a strong tradition of what is called *noikokyrio*, which translates as husbandry, good housekeeping, economy, and providence that reaches beyond one's own house and becomes, in Gary Snyder's words, "earth housekeeping." One of the most complimentary epithets for someone in island society is that he is a *noikokyris*, she a *noikokyra*. No adjective is necessary. This principle of caring and sparing use was reflected in every aspect of life: the objects people used, the way they used them, the work they did, the food they ate, and their relations with their families and neighbors.

Although manufactured goods, especially plastic ones, had already by the early seventies made an appearance in the stores, the great majority of objects found in the agora and in homes consisted of simple, useful things made by hand of natural if not native materials that, like the islanders themselves, endured hard and long use, changing functions as they aged but as useful in decrepitude as in youth, and when finally outworn, decomposing gracefully in the earth or—objects only—the sea. Everyday objects—brooms and mops, baskets and roofs, washtubs and boards, jugs and casseroles, blankets and rugs, saddles and plows, to name but a few—were made from materials found in the environment—straw, cane, grapevine, agave, olive wood, stone, clay, and seaweed. And while some factory-made objects and synthetic materials have now replaced the traditional ones, these readily available, cheap or even free materials are still widely used.

Cane, *kalami*, a grass similar to bamboo, is commonly planted on the edges of orchards and fields; its flexible stems and blond-tasseled heads break the crippling and parching force of winter and summer winds and yet allow enough air to pass over the crops to prevent mold from forming. Like its oriental cousin, kalami must be annually cut back and ditched to keep it from taking over, so there is always a lot of it and always a need: tied into rafts, it makes strong but flexible roofs for verandas, ceilings for traditional houses, and supports for mattresses.

Grapevines are planted for the table fruit and wine, of course, but shoots from the vines which are pruned every spring are plaited into basket handles and burned in the fireplace or *fou-fou*, a small terra-cotta brazier, to grill meat and fish. Onto twisted grapevine, flowers and leaves are tucked and tied to make *stephania*, the wreaths and garlands which decorate the churches on their holy days, and the *mai*, the May wreath. The grapevine for the mai is called *maioksilo*, May wood, and has obscurely lascivious connotations: A man to a young woman, other males attending, on the day before May Day: "You have your maioksilo?" "Yes." (Sniggers.) "You've soaked it in water?" "Yes." (Giggles and nudges.) "Is it strong and flexible?" "Yes." (Whoops and tears of laughter.)

Olive trees are also valuable mostly for fruit and oil, but no part of

43

the tree or the olives themselves is wasted: after the olives are pressed (the first pressing is for salads, the second for cooking), the rich oily residue, called *pirina*—once burned in copper braziers to heat homes—is now fed to poultry and cattle. In the old days, housewives would save all their cooking fats—largely olive oil—and once a year boil them up with seaweed to make the marvelous green soap. Green soap, even in its present manufactured form, is itself a miracle of noikokyrio, since it gets laundry, especially the white, homespun wool favored for sweaters and bedspreads, brilliantly clean, but degrades without harm to river and sea life. When, after centuries of life, an olive tree finally dies, every bit of it is used to make tool handles, butcher blocks, mortars and pestles, and lintels and beams for houses. A country house I lived in had an angled limb of an old olive that acted as both lintel and beam. So vital is this wood that even after being cut down, sawn up, and built into a house, it often sprouts new growth.

Agave, a huge, spiky-leaved succulent, shoots up a candelabrum-shaped flower whose stem may reach five meters in a season. A New World desert plant, agave demands no water, and its fearsome spininess makes it a good cattle fence. The stalks of the flowers, when dried, become a spongy, woodlike timber useful as beams for veranda roofs or small animal sheds; the wood doesn't last many years, but it saves the farmer from buying and wasting real, always imported, pine or oak.

One plant no farm is without is bottle gourd, a quick-growing annual vine. Its large leaves create a cooling shade for summer verandas, but die back in the winter when sun is welcome. It produces a great variety of shapes and sizes of gourds, which, when dried, make excellent bird feeders, containers for next year's seeds, or a way to carry a gift of wine or milk to a neighbor. These gourds were once widely used as fishermen's floats. The fishermen would choose the most spherical gourds, paint them distinctive colors, and tie their baited lines or nets to the curly stems. When lines or nets sank beneath the surface of the sea, the floats held them up and marked the fisherman's territory. On calm days, one could look out beyond the harbor and sight lines of yellow, red, or white gourd-floats bobbing in the sea.

A sea plant, *fikia* or ribbon weed, is heaped up on the beaches by every storm that blows; when harvested, it finds use as animal bedding, mulch on fields, and, packed on top of rafts of cane, insulation for ceilings in traditional houses.

Native stone from limestone to marble to gneiss to slate is the basis for all traditional building: found stones, picked up from the surface of the land or cleared from plowed fields, have more uses than Odysseus had stratagems. Found stones are piled expertly to make dry stone walls and terraces; these walls are incalculably old—some roughly shaped boulders from the time of Homer's hero still form the bases of not a few of them. All houses and churches, stables and warehouses, shops and civic buildings were until recently built with found stones mortared with clay. This method of building is very ancient: one baking-hot day I was helping Maria, an archaeological architect, measure lines of stones on a tiny island in the bay of Laggeri, an area on the north side of Paros. Looking about, I could see rectangular shapes on the ground, only two or often one stone high. "How old are these houses?" I asked her. "Oh, pre-Classical, certainly." "And what were they like?" She looked up from her clipboard for a moment and pointed across the water to the buildings of the farm I was living on. "Like those." Simple boxes of found stone mortared with clay, roofed with cane and ribbon weed, plastered with more clay, floored with the same clay pounded to terra-cotta hardness or with slabs of slate, and completely whitewashed inside and out—the islanders had been building in the same way for at least three thousand years. Later we found evidence of an apse—the same design as the one in the little church on the farm.

The rust-colored clay, used also for pottery, is still found in the marble quarries, layered between the veins of *lychnitis*, the famous translucent white marble used by Phidias and Skopas. The marble itself, though it is no longer possible to bring out sculpture-sized pieces, is now used in large slabs for tombs, in smaller ones for window sills, in fragments for terrazzo floors, and as dust in whitewash. More opaque marble and slate, quarried in only slightly more recent times (twelfth to seventeenth centuries), still pave streets and floors of houses and churches.

Whitewash itself is a kind of miracle. It is made of limestone (of which there is almost nothing but on the island), crushed, heated, and then soaked in water. The result is the highly caustic lime. Whitewash is diluted lime thickened with plaster and sometimes, for brilliance, marble dust. It is brushed onto walls and roofs and over mortared joins in streets and floors. The tissue-thin skin both seals the wall against moisture and kills insect eggs and bacteria (a can of whitewash used to stand in every toilet). Thousands of structures all over the island, all over Greece, the Mediterranean, even the world are literally held up by layers of whitewash no thicker than a sheet of newspaper (although where it has never been stripped, centuries of whitewash may build up to the thickness of a slim volume of poetry!). But if the seal is cracked, water may get in and eventually the building will collapse; to prevent this, whitewash must be frequently applied. On this island, the custom is to whitewash everything—streets and plateias, houses and shops both inside and out during the week before Easter, so that the village, like the celebrators, wears new, clean clothes for the holy day.

The beauty of the traditional Cycladic houses, whether the single-story rural houses or the two-story village ones clustered and stair-stepping up hills—apart from the dramatically simple structure which inspired Corbusier and so many other modern architects—is that almost every bit of them can be found and gathered free, from the mountains, the fields, and the seashore. Any ruined building can also be a source of materials; many buildings in village and hora boast inscribed or carved Classical or Byzantine lintels, floors, or columns. All a householder has to pay for is windows and doors. In the old days, one could begin with a single room and over time add on others as materials were collected, as children were born and, eventually, married. All the buildings were constructed in the same way, so a stable could become a house, or conversely, a house a stable. A builder was desirable, but an averagely skilled householder could certainly build his own. The tragedy is that the architecture has come back, like a prodigal son, in an impoverished form; now pale imitations are built of concrete block finished with cement. The uninspired buildings may have the plain, block shape of the originals, but the beautiful rich texture created by the irregular stones, which softened the austere lines, is missing.

Kalami finds another use in the making of baskets, the most popular and useful containers in village and countryside. While a few farmers or farmwives on the island wove baskets, most of the baskets were, and may yet be, woven by Gypsies. About once a year, to the uneasiness of the villagers, two or three rattly pickups would debark from the ferry crowded with saucy, colorfully dressed women and children. After making a deal with a farmer, the Gypsies would set up their tents and trucks in a field, bargain for kalami and grapevine and, sitting in companionable circles behind a canebrake, proceed to turn out baskets.

The barrel-shaped basket woven of cane with a grapevine handle was and still is used in every household for shopping and, by means of a hook attached to ceiling beams, for storage of everything from extra clothes to potatoes and seed onions. A cloth stitched over the opening turns it into the most popular suitcase, seen in the hundreds on any ferry to or from Piraeus.

In the kind of fishing called *paragadi*, fishermen use a wide, shallow cane and grapevine basket into which they carefully wind multiply-hooked lines, snagging the hooks on a rim of cork attached to the braided edge. The ends of the lines are tied onto floats; when the float is tossed out to sea, the line with its baited hooks unreels neatly and safely from the basket.

Besides the common barrel-shaped and flat paragadi baskets, a highly useful basket is the *kofini*, a tall, cylindrical, handled basket used in the harvests. Grape pickers gently gather the clusters in smaller, leaf-lined baskets and, when these are full, empty them into *kofinia*, which are then roped to donkeys' saddles or slid onto trucks and taken to the *patatiri*, the stone "vat" where grapes are trampled, or to the farmers' co-op. Olives are gathered differently, being shaken down or stripped from the tree onto a canvas or wool blanket, but these are emptied into the same kofinia to be taken to the press. Baskets, like their engendering plant, allow the passage of air around the harvested fruit and do not bruise it. As well, they are lightweight and easy to clean—by rinsing them in the sea. When a basket is finally done—its bottom rotted out—it often finds its way to the sea as a fish or octopus trap. On her truck farm, my flower-loving neighbor Anna used spent baskets to start seeds of flowers and vegetables. Anna and her husband lived in Ksifara, a region named for a fluffy-headed grass that was once used to stuff mattresses and pillows.

Another basket seen in every farm household, the cheese basket, is woven from grasses. When the hot curds are ladled into the baskets, they are set on plates to drip; when reasonably whey-free, the cheeses are removed from the baskets and hung outside in a *fanari*, a screened cage, to dry in the wind. The imprint of the woven grass remains on the cheese. The cheeses, especially *mezithra*, are either eaten or sold as fresh cheese, or placed into barrels of brine or oil to cure.

Farmers whose major form of transport is donkeys or mules use another sort of basket to take fruits and vegetables to market; these are oval-shaped and made of thick slatted wood, possibly oak, and bound with osier. Roped on each side of a wooden saddle, they carry the precious cargo safely. Even today, a small truck farmer, *manavis*, rather than take his produce to the shops, may roam the streets of the village in the early morning with his donkey, calling in a melodic voice to housewives to come out and inspect his wares: *"Domates eho, angouria eho, maitano, selino fresco! Fate to aroma!* I have tomatoes, I have cucumbers, parsley, and fresh celery! Eat the aroma!" In the spring, he may have bunches of wild narcissus and wood hyacinths tucked among the spinach and peas.

Other sturdy and useful materials come from animals, mostly sheep and goats. Along with meat and milk, animals provide hides for many purposes. *Touloumia* are inside-out leather sacks for curing cheese and hauling wine. From a whole sheep or goat skin (plus a cow horn and a leg-bone "flute"), a shepherd-musician who used to play in the village had fashioned his own bagpipe. And of course, the animals give their fleece, which almost every village woman used to spin with a simple drop spindle. The spun wool was woven into blankets or knitted into socks and sweaters, especially the typical *fanella*, an underwear sweater. Sadly, little weaving is still done. "The loom is torment," an elderly woman told the poet Eleni Fortouni. She was glad to be free of the necessity of weaving all her family's clothing, bed coverings, and rugs.

The island in the seventies was by no means self-sufficient; however, many goods came from other areas of Greece where there was an abundance of specific natural resources: pottery from Siphnos, wood from Crete and Thessaly, bricks from Chios. The best kofinia came from neighboring Naxos. These goods were often brought on the inter-island cargo kaikis which took local products to sell, especially the excellent black wine. Even among the goods that arrived on the ferries from Piraeus, however, a preponderance were of natural materials: woods; steel, tin, and brass; cotton and wool—all long-lasting and, as we would say, who have had to create a word to retrieve an idea, biodegradable.

"Recycling" in those days did not consist of throwing away once-used objects to be manufactured into new ones. The life of every object was carefully prolonged: clothes or sheets were mended, collars and cuffs turned, trousers patched; and when mending was no longer useful, the cloth was stripped and woven into rag rugs and saddle blankets. The rugs were woven in two-foot widths and never joined, so they were easy to whip out into the sun to dry out winter damp. When the rugs were too faded for respectability, they were placed under mattresses to deter mildew. But that was not the end: everywhere one could see the remains of rag rugs in use, here to scrub a boat deck, there to cushion a chair seat, elsewhere to block wind or water from seeping under a door or window. As well as being flat-woven, rags were knotted onto an old piece of canvas or burlap to make a thick pile rug generally used as a saddle blanket.

Long before they became rags, however, clothes were carefully hand-washed and dried in the sun and wind. Before Tide, they were washed with the gentle but efficient green soap in sun-warmed water, either at home or in the little river that has flowed through this village without cessation since pre-Classical times. The nutritious suds (lacking phosphates) either flowed down to the sea or were emptied into potted plants. The traditional washtub, the *skafi*, made of wood, metal, or stone, has sides that slant at an angle that uses the leverage of arms but spares the back of the launderer. So easy to use is the skafi that my friend Stella, who received a washing machine as part of her dowry, goes to wash in her mother's skafi. Sadly if understandably, however, like most new mothers today, she has abandoned cloth diapers for the nondegradable Pampers.

The unique short-handled but long-strawed broom is another traditional tool with a long useful life. It takes a while to get the hang of it (it is indeed all in the wrist) but, once mastered, it is amazingly quick and efficient, faster and less clumsy than the "Hoover," and much longer lived. When new it sweeps floors, catching even sand and whitewash dust in its long, tapered fibers; when less new, washes the same floors; when eroded to half its length sweeps and scrubs the stone-flagged streets; when smaller still whitewashes them; and when reduced to a hand-sized nub fans the coals of a brazier sitting on a doorstep as it grills a fish. The beautiful, rust-velvet earth floors, even in the seventies all but vanished, were maintained to terra-cotta hardness by being daily swept and sprinkled with water by these little brooms.

In those halcyon days of noikokyrio, everything possible was used and reused until it could be used no more. Bottles—wine, beer, and soda—went back to the factories on the mainland not to be crushed

49

and recast but to be refilled. One summer sunrise, while I was drinking coffee in the harbor of Ios, a neighboring island whose mountaintop hora or main town is connected to its seafront by a mile of steep, winding, stone-flagged stairs, I began to hear a faint but exquisite music, like the jingling of a thousand silver bells, but with some sort of percussion. As I strained to listen, it became louder. The music filled the bright morning air like a celestial symphony—but of what instruments? Celeste? Too strong. Xylophone? Too high. Santouri? But there would have to be a hundred of them! As the music came closer, suddenly into the harbor trotted about twenty donkeys. Strapped to their saddles were dozens of wooden crates of pop and beer bottles, and from the shaking and clinking of the glass bottles on their way to the waiting ferry came the heavenly music.

Food was another thing that never went to waste. Few villagers owned refrigerators so they bought perishables every day in small quantities—just as much butter, say two hundred grams, as needed for a New Year's cake, just as much tomato paste, olives, vegetables, fruit, meat, or fish as were to be eaten that day. Few spoilable foods were sold in predetermined quantities. Most cooked foods, often containing acids such as lemon, vinegar, or tomato, needed no refrigeration to last a day or two. In the country, houses made use of nature to keep things cool. Milk might be placed in a terra-cotta jug in an open north window, meat hung in a dark cool *apothiki* or storeroom, eggs slid under a bed on a stone floor. A house I lived in had a bed built like a stone vat, with a raft of cane over it to hold a mattress. Into the cavity, my landlord told me, who had slept on it as a child, his father would pour the newly threshed wheat; the stone kept the wheat at a safe temperature, while the wheat warmed the mattress and the backs of the children.

Food scraps and the few leftovers were fed to chickens. My neighbor Asimi shyly asked me if I would keep my vegetable scraps for her chicks, and then showed me exactly how to cut up melon rinds for them. "Bring it fresh, understand? If the food rots, the chickens get gas." My reward for this service was a warm egg or two every once in a while. When I lived in the country, I would walk over the mountain to Stelliani's farm. Seeing me toiling up the hill, she would have ready a cool slice of melon or a peeled cucumber. After I refreshed myself, she would hand me a knife and a bowl full of scraps for me to cut up for *her* chickens.

In the bare rocky islands, wood is very precious. Foreigners with little historical knowledge commonly blame the deforestation of Greece on goats—another example of blaming the "little guy" for the depredations of international business. This island's cedar forests, probably small in any case, given the terrain, went to plank and keel the navies of the conquering and occupying Romans, beginning in the first century B.C., and from the twelfth century A.D., the conquering and colonizing Venetians. Some woods may have been uprooted to provide more land for vineyards, as wine was a major export of Venice. If there was a tree left standing, it went to the Ottoman conquerors, who also maintained an extensive navy. Whatever the practices may be in other parts of Greece, here goats are few, used one or two to a flock as "sheepdogs" to control the skittish ovines, and depredations from them are correspondingly insignificant.

In any case, the islanders I knew had great respect for wood and took good care of wooden objects. Oak barrels for wine and cheeses, rectangular wooden washtubs, as well as roughly adzed saplings for roof beams and hafts for mattocks and axes are imported from Crete and are expensive. Pine for furniture, windows, and doors comes from even farther away, the forests of Sweden or Oregon. In all my years of visiting farms, I never saw a wooden object left out in the elements. Barrels were rehooped and mended time and again; leaky washtubs found new uses as bread troughs or mangers.

In the days before Greece entered the European Community, even paper was precious. Paper of every kind was reused in many ways: when you bought butter or olives, squid or *marides*, sardines, the grocer or fishmonger twisted a cone of thin, clean oiled paper, dumped in your purchase, then wrapped the whole in newspaper. "Fish wrap" a newspaper might have been—metaphorically as well as actually—but before it found its way to the fish store, it had been read in its entirety by several people, most likely in a café. Needles, sold one by one, might be wrapped in a tiny twist of the storekeeper's child's homework. One bakery in the hora collected waste paper from the schools and government offices and fired its three-hundred-year-old beehive oven with a mix of spelling tests, tax forms, and aromatic brush. The brush—thyme, oregano, sage—gathered annually from the mountains in the fall, heated all the farm ovens as well as this village one. How crusty and delicious, how fragrant were the loaves! When eventually the baker acquired electric ovens, the bread—from the same flour and starter—was pallid and crustless. The bakeries did double duty with one firing: the residual heat from the bread baking roasted pans of *moussakas*, chicken with potatoes, orzo with octopus, or mixed vegetables that the villagers brought to the bakery in midmorning and took away in time to serve up hot and delicious at their midday meals.

These native goods—the economy of their reiterated shapes (the washtub, the manger, the bread trough: all rectangular with the same slant to the sides), the multiplicity of their uses, their ultimate ability to decompose, and the thrifty and conservative practices—all embodied the belief in and practice of noikokyrio.

It is strange that our language doesn't really reflect this concept. *Husbandry* is almost archaic. There are *thrift* and *frugality*, but these imply a dourness and lack of generosity that ill accord with Greek concepts of virtue, among which are those of hospitality and openhandedness, *philoxenia*. Noikokyrio, in fact, makes philoxenia possible; the intent is not to have more for yourself but to have enough to share. When an islander celebrates his or her name day, or the name day of a family church, it is the celebrator who is the host, dispensing hospitality to all who come to pay their respects. Material gifts are not customary. It is more blessed and practical to entertain one's friends than to receive a lot of knickknacks and dust catchers.

Noikokyrio as concept and practice is, or rather was, an assumption of most villagers. But their understanding of it would equal that of any academic ecologist. "They're tarmacing the road out to your place," I said to my farmer neighbor, Dimitris; he had just split a watermelon for us to share as we sat on the wellhead in his field. "Yes," he sighed, "and now the boys"—his thirty- and forty-year-old sons—"will make me buy a tractor and I'll have to give up the donkeys and mules." "Why is that?" I asked, carefully hoarding at his request the seeds of the "best yet" melon. "*Mor-e*," he said pityingly, "donkeys' and mules' legs are strong. Loaded, unloaded, they can manage any surface on the island—dry streambeds, soft earth, stone-flagged streets—but the tarmac ruins their knees. And if I can't use them to go to market, I can't afford to keep them just for plowing. And tractors!" Here he spat his contempt. "They leave a swath of weeds around the field, they compact the earth they plow, you have to pay money for their feed, and they shit poison. The animals plow every mite of ground clean, they leave their droppings, they grow their own food, they produce their own successors. And when you're drunk, which—" he arched his shaggy gray brows—"I am from time to time, they take you home safely." I'd seen, or rather heard, in the wee hours, Dimitris coming home, singing, after a celebration, his large intelligent mule pacing carefully so as not to dump him in the road.

Begin anywhere, with any traditional Greek object or practice, and you'll discover noikokyrio. The famous dolmades, stuffed vine leaves, are rolled up in leaves that must be thinned to allow sun to fall on the grapes. (My farmer neighbor, visiting my kitchen, noticed the green and yellow cans of grape leaves on my shelf. "*Canned* grape leaves?" he said, shocked. "In *spring?* Look!" He threw open the shutters and pointed to his vineyard that grew right up to my house wall. We went out and picked fresh ones.) Fasts in the Orthodox calendar, over a hundred days a year, consist of abstention from animal products, fish with scales, and, during the most severe, oil. These fasts seem to coincide with seasons of spawning of fish and birthing and nursing of animals, or of scarcity, as in August when the hens lay few eggs. Foods are seasoned chiefly with native herbs—oregano, rosemary, bay—that grow wild on the hills. Ouzo is flavored with wild fennel. Dozens of wild greens, *horta*, such as dandelion, rocket, and wild asparagus; *vlita*, the leaves of a shrub; the buds and seedpods of capers; even wild lily bulbs, *volvoi*, are regularly gathered and eaten. The teas many prefer to coffee are brewed from sage, oregano, chamomile, mint. These and almost all the abundant wild herbs and flowers carpeting the meadows and dotting the hills have been discovered over the millennia to have myriad uses not only as flavorings but as medicines, preservatives, cosmetics, dyes, moth repellents, and even rat poisons. In flower they give nectar to honeybees and when their season is over, the dry branches are stuffed into ovens to bake and flavor bread.

And yet even the least of these generous gifts of the earth are endangered. As the tourist economy swelled, the land—at first the rocky, nonarable land where the sheep grazed and the herbs grew in abundance and later the farmland itself—became suddenly "real estate," absurdly valuable sites for building hotels and villas. As the limestone scrabble was dynamited for foundations, bulldozed for driveways, and covered with concrete slabs, the thyme and sage which fed the bees, the thorny peterium which sweetened the air of summer nights, all the other shy and useful herbs gave way to "low maintenance" plantings of the ubiquitous, nonnative ice plant, the showy geranium. Gone the glossy mastic bush and the cyclamen hiding in its shade. Goodbye to horta, volvoi, and capers, to mint and chamomile and sage, the food and medicines of the poor—and the knowing.

There is virtually no recycling now. Beverage bottles and fast-food containers are routinely thrown into the trash (previously, if you wanted to take food out from a restaurant, you brought your own plate or pan). The thousands of summer visitors now contribute hundreds of thousands of plastic bags, plastic pop and water bottles to the metastasizing garbage dumps, and the noxious smoke of their burning taints the once-pristine air.

Another cause for lament is the rapid loss of traditional skills, some inherited from generations millennia gone, and the self-sufficiency and creativity they entailed. Even in the early seventies, wooden plows were still in use on many farms, but if one broke, it was hard to find anyone to repair it. The hora boasted a saddlemaker, but as saddles began to outnumber donkeys, he must have experienced more and more unemployment. So did shoemakers and tailors, blacksmiths and tinsmiths. Manufactured goods and clothing replaced the handmade products. The loss here was double: as craftsmen disappeared, the ability to have things repaired disappeared with them. As well, when goods and clothing were handmade to order, the process demanded knowledge not only from the craftsman but from the buyer. With no ability to participate in the design of, say, a new suit or a front door, buyers become passive consumers rather than connoisseurs of the everyday.

Perhaps the greatest loss of skills has been in the building trade. Even thirty years ago, builders who could or would build or even repair a found-stone, clay-mortared house were few and aging. Most new buildings were being made of cement block and brick; unlike the traditional houses, they were hot in summer and ice-cold in winter. When remodeling, the "modern" builders preferred to cement over the age-old stone walls and earth floors and the clay and cane roofs, which made them "permanently" waterproof, but when both renovated and new houses cracked and leaked (as inevitably in earthquake country), the house owner needed a builder to make repairs. In contrast, the traditional island houses, built in the same way for over seven thousand years (as archaeologists have proved), could be maintained by almost any householder, using inexpensive or found materials. The new cement was usually unable to hold whitewash,

54

necessitating the use of chemical paint, which has neither the smoothness and brilliance nor the sanitizing effect of whitewash. Whitewash itself began to disappear.

For a while, even as the natural and sometimes native materials began to be replaced with synthetics, the islanders continued to practice noikokyrio: fishermen replaced bottle gourd floats with empty bleach bottles, housewives stripped colorful plastic shopping bags and crocheted the strips into doormats. I remember seeing a plastic garbage can, cracked and split, carefully mended with nearly surgical sutures. But the truth about synthetic materials soon became obvious: despite their lightness and cheapness, their useful lives are short, and when they break, crack, and split, even the deftest hands cannot repair them, and neither the sea nor the earth decompose them. The hills of limestone dotted with white and pink marble and rust-colored quartz, the beautiful sere fields of purple-blooming thyme and sage where sheep once safely grazed, the rocky cliffs with their seagull nests—all became shrouded in the shreds of plastic garbage bags tossed overboard by passing ships. The few, small garbage dumps proliferated and spread in the valleys.

What the skilled islanders could not begin to repair were the appliances that came with prosperity, with the tidal wave of tourism and entrance into the European Economic Community: the electric ovens, refrigerators, dishwashers, televisions, tape recorders, and automobiles, and the washing machines for which village housewives abandoned the little river, which itself soon became polluted by seepage from new hotels. Most of these goods, cheap ones at first, came from Germany or other Common Market countries, often without manuals in Greek. When they broke down, despite efforts to prolong their usefulness, there was nothing to do with them but abandon them at the now-overflowing dumps from which stinking smoke issues constantly.

The beautiful, pristine bays also suffered from the tourist boom. Previously, seaside houses channeled household waste directly into the sea. In fact, many homes did not have toilets; people took their chamber pots to the sea or used the public ones in the harbor which opened so directly into the sea that on a stormy day, a person using the privy risked being splashed by waves. The sea easily accepted and processed the human waste of the small population, along with its food scraps, old baskets and brooms, broken chairs, and chicken feathers. But with the new hotels and *pensions* along the bays, the sea reached its limit. For years, seawater you could once have used to pickle olives was too polluted to swim in or, worse, take fish from. However, in time the community realized that the old way of waste disposal was not working, and a few years ago a sewer system was laid down and a treatment plant built. Of course, it had to be done, but, like the importation of Israeli tomatoes, another industrial process interrupted the natural reciprocity between people and nature.

Decomposition is central to Orthodox Greek belief. The Orthodox do not embalm nor cremate their dead, but allow them to decompose in the earth. The bread and wine of the Eucharist are substances that have decomposed, fermented, and undergone metamorphosis, symbolizing the transformation that human beings will undergo when, at the Second Coming of Christ, all the decomposed bodies of the world will be reassembled, molecule by molecule, bone by bone from the earth of their graves, and the dead will live again in new bodies in a world transformed. How lamentable it is that the earth herself, our mother, long the very embodiment of this cycle of death and transformation, will, at the end, be buried beneath a crust of plastic, glass, and enameled steel which feed neither worms nor fishes, but hang on for a sterile eternity.

And yet, what is truly lamentable is not just the pollution of land and water by nondegradable and even toxic materials; not just the replacement of fresh locally (and mostly organically) raised foods with frozen meat from New Zealand, two-week-old tomatoes from Israel, yogurt with "expiration dates" from factories in Athens, and irradiated milk from Germany; not just the overfishing of the once-bountiful Aegean Sea, made profitable by the tourist trade and the European Market; not alone the disappearance of time-honored skills—skills that enabled a large part of the present living population to survive seven years of Italian and German occupation and previously decades of poverty—but the death of noikokyrio, an idea, an ethic, a way of life that for over seven thousand years sustained life on this small rocky island, and now is but a memory.

It is, of course, hopelessly romantic to even think of turning back. The modernization that has resulted in such pollution and loss of skills has benefited many. Rural electrification, despite the ugliness of the poles and wires and the noise of the electric factory, means that elderly Anna and her husband Pantelis can live comfortably on

56

their farm all through the year, with an electric heater to warm the house in winter, an electric pump to water the vegetables in summer. Perhaps the most valuable innovation for the general populace is the up-to-date medical clinic in the hora; no longer must an appendicitis sufferer or accident victim lie and hope that sea or sky is calm enough for the boat to Syros or the helicopter from Athens to arrive in time.

With the advent of modern conveniences and outlooks and the jobs they have created, many emigrants have returned to their families from America and Australia, and nothing means more to Greeks than family. To serve the tripled population of the village, both a lycée and a gymnasium, high and middle schools, as well as a kindergarten have been built. Village students can now more easily go on to university and on graduating find teaching and professional jobs at home. But the returning emigrants and the new groups of resident foreigners have brought with them a mixed blessing: a strange, or stranger's, view of traditional customs, putting them in a sort of archive, removing them from ordinary people. The houses being built of stone rather than concrete block are the villas of the wealthy, mostly foreigners.

A bittersweet fruit of the sophistication of the island is the revival of traditional music. In the past, there were on the whole island only three musicians (two clarinets and a bagpipe); musicians for a wedding or a festival had to be imported from Athens, and these, with their electric instruments and trap drums, were fast drifting away from tradition. Now there are two large orchestras of perhaps thirty players of traditional instruments, who play for dance performances by several folklore groups. The performances, mostly by schoolchildren, while both masterful and authentic, are nevertheless performance. Dance was once, for millennia, a joyous activity involving the entire community—grandmothers and grandfathers, aunts and uncles, mothers and fathers, young men and women, youths, and even toddlers—but the attempt to preserve tradition, laudable though it is, has transformed dancing into a spectacle in which few, and those only the young, participate. The dances and music will not be lost— a good thing because they are beautiful—but they have been set at a distance, as though in a museum, and will no longer serve the community in the same way they did in the past. What is wasted here is the union of body and spirit, exuberance and artistry, community and individual consummated in the dance.

Why mourn? Why even indulge in nostalgia for what has passed as irrevocably as last year's winds? As some answer, I offer the words of Fazil Iskander, who wrote in his *The Gospel According to Chegem* (Vintage, 1984) of the past of his own native Abkhazia:

> In idealizing a vanishing way of life we are presenting a bill to the future. We are saying, "Here is what we are losing; what are you going to give us in exchange?" Let the future think on that, if it is capable of thinking at all.

Nominated by Jewel Mogan, The Georgia Review

BROTHER DEATH,

SISTER LIFE

by DONALD PLATT

from THE VIRGINIA QUARTERLY REVIEW

> *Laudato si' mi Signore, per sora nostra Morte corporale da la quale nullo omo vivente po' scampare.*
>
> St. Francis

         Death is my idiot
brother, who comes babbling something I don't yet
         understand and throws

his arms around me and kisses me full
         on the mouth.
I hug him back. St. Francis got it all

         wrong. Death
isn't our sister, *Laudato si', mi Signore.*
         Tom Andrews

knew it too. Death was always his brother,
         John, who kept
beckoning him from the beyond. "The dead drag

         a grappling hook
for the living. The hook is enormous," Tom said
         in his shortest

poem. Tom was the hooked rainbow trout fighting
             hard, prismatic
flash of silver muscle breaking the surface, taking the line out

             from the screeching
reel with the drag on, and finally hauled thrashing into the air,
    gasping
             for water.

Death was his true element. He swam well. Life caught him,
             then threw
him back. *Laudato si', mi Signore*. He almost jumped

             from a seven-story
parking garage, while his poetry students waited for him
             to come

to the last class of the year. The tulips bloomed late,
             as always
in Indiana, recalcitrant miserly spring that spent

             only a handful
of red petals, when it should have been prodigal
             April. Tom walked

back down. *Laudato si', mi Signore*. Did he teach
             that last class?
I never learned. A year later he visited us in Georgia and told us
    how

             one week earlier
he had piped his exhaust into the cab of the blue truck with a
    rubber hose
             but stopped

when his kittens Geoffrey and Emma crawled
             onto the windshield
and tried to climb in with him, mewing for milk, scrambling up the
    glass

and sliding
back down. When he finally went to bed, Dana and I worried
        he would kill

himself overnight. But then, at the same moment, we burst
        out laughing—
Tom was too "polite" to commit suicide

        at his friends' house.
Laudato si', mi Signore. The forsythia flamed
        like a guardian

angel with a drawn sword outside his window
                while he slept
sound. Chronic depression couldn't kill him. His hemophilia

        didn't stop
him riding motorcycles down the long flat roads of Indiana
        through cornfields

that stretched dark green to the horizon, so much sky,
        a few golden tassels
of cirrus clouds, the sun setting within reach

        on one side,
the full moon rising on the other, those two shining brass
        pans of the invisible

balance that seesaws and weighs out our nights and days. Into the
    humid dusk
        Tom cruised
at seventy miles per hour. His girl friends held on tight. *Laudato si',*

        mi Signore.
They were all at his funeral, four ex-girl friends, two ex-fiancées,
        and Carrie

his ex-wife. They sobbed and embraced each other in chorus.
        His old teacher and I
read five of his poems aloud and then shut the words

61

back in their books.
The pianist played Satie's *Gymnopédie* while sirens
                careened

past the church. Tom, you would have loved the clanging fire engine
                that interrupted
the program so that the pianist had to stop

                and wait
for all that commotion to pass. We sang "Ye Watchers and Ye Holy
    Ones." It took
                a long name, thrombotic

thrombocytopenic purpura—freak virus, "a rare, but sometimes
    deadly, blood disorder"—
                to kill you,
and five weeks in a coma while Alice your mother and Alice your
    fiancée tried

                to keep you
alive. Your brother, who died from renal failure twenty-one years
                ago, kept whispering

through your respirator's deep kiss, telling you not
                to be afraid—
"It must be a country without pain. It must be a quiet

                place where the stillness
under your wrist is entered like a field of thyme
                and peppergrass. . . ."

Laudato si', mi Signore. Today, at my parents' summer cottage,
                my own brother yanks
me by the hand and points to the forty-foot silver birches

                uprooted
and blown down by an August storm's micro-bursts. "Where baz,
    baz?" he lisps.
                "Buds?" I ask.

He jerks his head from side to side. I try again.
                    "Birds?"
He smiles and nods. He means the crows, whose black song wakes

              him every morning,
have had to leave the birches and have flown to roost in the jack
   pines. *Awe, awe*, they cry.
                    Grief is the only

note they know. *Laudato si', mi Signore*. How I'll remember
                    Tom Andrews always
is in my friend's story at the bar after the funeral—

              him flying down
the hill past her house, doing a handstand on her son Will's
                    skateboard, while

she stood petrified on her front porch with beautiful Carrie, who
   shouted
                    out only,
"Hey you, crazed bleeder jock on that skateboard,

              wanna get married?"
In the bar, eleven years later, Carrie blushed. It was her, Sister Life,
                    Tom courted

upside down, feet pointing to the sky, his body a swaying
                    exclamation
point, the skateboard beneath him rumbling hallelujah

              over the pitted
asphalt, while Carrie clapped, whistled, and called after him, "Come
   back,
                    you dummkopf. Come back!"

Nominated by Bruce Beasley, Marianne Boruch, The Virginia Quarterly Review

FAST SUNDAY

fiction by SUE STANDING

from PLOUGHSHARES

SARAH WAS NINE-ABOUT-TO-BE-TEN. The world was taking its sweet time. And she was in the world. It was Easter, but it was also Fast Sunday, because Easter had fallen on the first Sunday of the month this year, so all the meetings were in a row, Sunday school, then fast and testimony meeting, which was always longer than regular sacrament meeting, because people could get up and talk as long as they wanted, *as long as the spirit moved them.* Some year Easter would fall on her birthday, her mother had told her, it had when she was five, but this year her birthday would be two weeks after Easter. Because it was Fast Sunday, Sarah and her brothers could not eat any of the candy in their Easter baskets until after dark. On Fast Sundays, they had to fast from nightfall on Saturday to nightfall on Sunday. This was one of the commandments. Not one of the Ten Commandments, but one of the other ones. One of the many she knew by heart, like the Word of Wisdom: *Thou shalt run and not be weary, and walk and not faint.*

But when she didn't eat for a whole day, she felt faint. And her head hurt. The only thing that would pass her lips all day was the sacrament—a little piece of torn-up Wonder bread, followed by a tiny fluted paper cup of water, like the ones they had at the dentist's office—passed hand to hand down the pews by the deacons on metal trays after the priests had blessed them: *That they may have His spirit to be with them.* The priests seemed old to her, though they were only sixteen, and the deacons were twelve. They joked outside on the steps after church, but when they were passing the sacrament, they were serious. Girls couldn't be deacons or priests or elders or anything but mothers and primary or Sunday school or MIA or Relief Society teachers. When boys turned twelve, they received the priesthood. Then the boys and the girls would be in separate Sunday school classes, and the boys would go to early morning priesthood meetings.

Sarah imagined receiving the priesthood must be something like receiving the gift of the Holy Ghost, but the priesthood was conferred in secret. Only the men could see. The day after she was baptized, nearly two years ago, she had been blessed in front of the whole congregation, along with the other children who had turned eight in the past month and a few converts, who always seemed strange and too large next to the children. What would it have been like not to have been born into the church? she wondered. She felt the converts were lucky the missionaries had found them in time. Both her mother and her father had been missionaries, her father in Scotland and her mother in Mexico. It was the only time either of them had ever traveled outside the United States. The onyx bookends in the living room had come from Mexico; the sheepskin rug in her parents' bedroom had come from Scotland. Her father sometimes sang songs in a funny Scottish accent. And her mother taught her and her brothers Spanish. *Me llamo Sarah. Yo soy una hija de Dios.*

"Remember who you are: you are a child of God," her parents said repeatedly, when she left for school in the morning, when she went to a friend's house to play, when she asked why she couldn't do something she wanted to do.

"Thank you for that lovely prelude, Sister Erickson. And now, Brother Meredith, President of the Quorum of Seventies, will lead us in the opening prayer, following which we will sing hymn #194, 'There Is a Green Hill Faraway.' "

Bishop Anderson was presiding at fast and testimony meeting. Sarah always thought he looked slightly uncomfortable when he was wearing a suit and tie. His wrists hung down below his shirt cuffs. During the week, he worked as an electrician, and he always wore blue coveralls with his name, Don Anderson, in red curlicue script on his left pocket. He was a very tall man with a blond crew-cut. Usually, bishops were doctors or dentists or businessmen, but everyone said that Bishop Anderson was truly a man of the spirit.

"Heavenly Father," prayed Brother Meredith, "we are grateful to be gathered here in Thy name today in this beautiful house of worship which Thou hast provided for us. We ask that Thou wilt bless us and guide us in the path of righteousness. Bless those who will speak to us today that their mouths will be filled with Thy holy presence. In the name of the Father, and of the Son, and of the Holy Ghost, Amen."

"Amen," echoed Sarah with the rest of the congregation.

Two years ago, when her father and the other elders and high priests had stood in a circle around her and put their hands on her head to confirm her and give her the gift of the Holy Ghost, Sarah had expected that she would feel the Holy Ghost enter her body, that it would be like drinking a cold glass of milk too fast or like holding her breath too long underwater. She expected that she would feel something or see something, the way she assumed, the first time she crossed the state border from Utah into Nevada, that the states would be different colors the way they were on a map. When nothing had changed colors, when the road and the salt flats and the sage-brush looked exactly the same on one side of the state line as the other, Sarah couldn't help exclaiming, "Nevada's the same color as Utah."

"Oh, it's a little different," her father had said, "you'll see."

But it wasn't, just more sand and more road and maybe hotter. On one trip across Nevada, though, they saw a giant cloud billow up in the distance. The air was full of brilliant particles, like dust, only it wasn't dust.

"It's pretty," said her brother Drew, uncharacteristically. Usually, he was too busy poking Sarah in the ribs or tickling Danny to notice what was outside the car. "It's like Tinkerbell or angels."

"It's the Test Site," said her father. "Like Hiroshima, only in the desert, where there are no people. It's so we won't have war ever again."

This was also the day that Drew would be confirmed. As always, for Easter, her mother had stayed up all night finishing the matching outfits she made for herself and Sarah and her brothers. Dresses for her mother and Sarah, shirts for the three boys, all made out of the same material. This year the cloth was an orange-and-brown plaid, which really didn't seem like Easter colors, more like fall. Sarah knew that it must have been one of the only fabrics inexpensive enough and with enough material left on the bolt for two dresses and four shirts. Only her father, in his blue suit and maroon tie with squiggles on it, didn't match. She had thought that maybe her mother wouldn't make the Easter clothes this year, since she'd been sick so long. But when Sarah and Drew and Danny and Tyler woke up early to look for their Easter baskets, even though they knew they wouldn't be able to eat anything from them, they found the row of clothes laid out on the back of the couch from left to right, from biggest (Sarah) to smallest (Tyler), just the way they always were, so Sarah knew she couldn't say anything about not liking the color of the fabric. Or the pattern—it was too babyish; her mother had used the same pattern last year, just made it a little bigger. Sarah felt she was too old for puffed sleeves and rickrack.

Now, sitting on the pew between her mother and Danny, with Tyler on the other side of her mother, she watched Drew. He was up on the dais in the choir seats with the four other children who were about to be confirmed. Her father was also on the dais, behind a table on one side, not the sacrament table, but like it. He was the ward clerk now; he had to write everything down that was said in the meeting. Sarah knew he didn't like it, even though he had been ordained.

"Why was I called to this position?" he asked their mother frequently. "Why can't I be the Gospel Doctrine teacher?"

"This, too, shall pass," her mother always said.

She wondered if Drew would feel something when they gave him the gift of the Holy Ghost. He was a little afraid of it, she could tell. Now he would have to be good, because he had reached the age of accountability. When you were eight, you knew the difference between right and wrong. That is why you were baptized then, and not when you were a baby. She remembered how the bishop asked her, right before she was baptized, if she knew that she would be making a solemn covenant between herself and the Lord. She knew, she assured him, she knew with all her heart. But she had always been good; Drew had not. He talked back, and had his mouth washed out with soap. She had had her mouth washed out with soap once, and that was enough. Now she would bite her cheek so she wouldn't say a bad thing, but Drew would say it. He was proud of saying bad words and said he liked the taste of Ivory soap. Sometimes when their parents weren't there, he would bite off a tiny piece, fill his mouth with water, and spit small bubbles at her.

Sacrament was over. The priests folded the white lace tablecloth over the trays, and moved down to sit with the rest of the congregation. Bishop Anderson got up to say a few words. There were two babies to be blessed, before the five gifts of the Holy Ghost, so it would be a long time before the testimonies even started. This is not what Bishop Anderson said, but Sarah could see it was going to be a long Fast Sunday, not a short Fast Sunday. He said not to forget the Relief Society bazaar and potluck supper next Saturday night. He said that he hoped our special prayers would be with Sister Nelson, who had broken her hip after a fall.

Sister Nelson usually led the choir. She had dark black hair with one thick white stripe in it, starting at her forehead and going all the way down the back of her head. Sarah's mother said it was a widow's peak, but it looked like a skunk to Sarah, only the stripe wasn't right in the center the way a skunk's would be. Sister Nelson had been kind to Sarah, though; she gave her a book after she was baptized. And it wasn't even a religious book, like the other ones she got, her own leather-bound copy of the *Book of Mormon* and the *Doctrine and Covenants* and *The Pearl of Great Price*, a triple combination, or a three-in-one, it was called, like the tin of oil her mother used for the sewing machine. Sister Nelson had given her *Five Children and It*. Sarah had tried some of the spells. The one that was most successful was the one where, before you went to sleep, you concentrated really hard, and banged your head on the pillow the number of times for the hour you wanted to wake up—six for six o'clock, seven for seven o'clock. It always worked. She wanted to be like the children in English storybooks, having adventures all day in the hedgerows—she imagined the hedgerows as being a little like the tunnel she and her cousins made through the honeysuckle bushes in Grandma Hart's garden—and drinking ginger beer. She didn't know what ginger beer was, but it probably wasn't allowed, the way Coca-Cola wasn't allowed. Latter-day Saints could have root beer, though. Sometimes, after all six of them piled in the station wagon and before they would go to the drive-in movie, they would go to the Arctic Circle and have root beer floats.

Oh, she was hungry now. She shouldn't have thought about food. It was bad to think about food on Fast Sunday, not bad because it wasn't allowed, but bad because it would be too hard to get through the whole day without eating if she thought about food. On regular Sundays, they would have a big meal between Sunday school and sacrament meeting. Her mother would start a pot roast or a stewed chicken cooking before Sunday school, then they would smell it first thing when they got in the door after church. Tyler didn't have to fast, because he was only two. But when it was Fast Sunday, even he couldn't have the dry Cheerios her mother would usually bring to church to keep him quiet. Her mother had given Tyler her handkerchief to fuss with instead. He was playing peek-a-boo with Sister Holmgren in the pew behind them. Sister Holmgren had seven children, but they were all grown-up now and had children of their own.

The babies had been brought up to the front of the chapel and blessed—they hardly ever cried while they were spoken over and bounced in the men's arms, but often cried when they were given back to their mothers, Sarah noticed—and now it was almost Drew's turn to receive the gift of the Holy Ghost. Today, because it was Easter besides Fast Sunday, there were flowers in the chapel, white trumpet-shaped blossoms on tall green stems. They smelled the way Sarah imagined the Celestial Kingdom must smell. They looked the same as the flowers in one of the picture books she had seen at Grandma Hart's house, a big book with gold on the edges of the pages. The flowers were in a blue vase on a checkerboard floor between Mary—her grandmother said it was Mary-the-mother-of-Jesus—and an angel, with wings, though everyone knew angels didn't have wings.

Sarah wished there were flowers in the chapel all the time, not just Easter and Christmas and missionary farewells and funerals. In the church she went to once with her friend Emma, called St. Sebastian's, there were flowers everywhere and paintings and colored glass in the windows and candles in tall, gold candlesticks and pink velvet cushions on the seats and a smell of something burning, but sweet, and, most surprising of all, a huge wooden cross with Jesus nailed on it at the front of the church. Sarah couldn't stop looking at it. It was scary, but beautiful, too. Jesus didn't look unhappy; he looked peaceful. When she asked her mother about it later, her mother said Latter-day Saints weren't allowed to have crosses in their churches or to wear crosses, because it reminded them of the bad part of Jesus' life, and that they wanted to think of the good part, when Jesus rises out of the tomb and says, *I am the resurrection and the light.*

Latter-day Saints weren't supposed to go inside other people's churches, either, but her mother had let her go, just that once. She wished she could go there again; there were so many more things to look at there than in their own chapel, which had plain white walls, brown benches with no cushions on them, and frosted-glass windows you couldn't see through, like the ones in bathrooms, so you couldn't even see whether it had started to rain. Outside she knew the apricot trees were in blossom. *I looked out the window and what did I see: popcorn popping on the apricot tree.* Val Verde, the neighborhood where they lived, used to be all orchards, no houses, her father had told her.

The only thing she could do when she got bored at her church meetings was to play with the hymnbook. She knew practically all the hymns by heart. She would make up new words to some of them. *Cherries hurt you* instead of *Cherish virtue. God be with you till we eat again* instead of *God be with you till we meet again.* She especially liked it if they sang that one on Fast Sunday, but today unfortunately they wouldn't. Today the closing hymn would be #136, "I Know That My Redeemer Lives." The numbers of the hymns they would sing were posted on a little wooden board above her father's head. He was bent over, writing, writing, writing. He had to write down the names of everyone who was in church that day and everything that happened. Sarah wondered what happened to the black notebooks after they were full. Did they keep them in a vault somewhere? In a temple, maybe? Were they to give to God when the millennium came? But didn't He know everything already? Why did it have to be written down?

"Heavenly Father," Brother Wickham's voice boomed out. His prayers were always louder than anyone else's, and he was praying over his own daughter, Karen, so he was especially loud. Sister Spackman said that man's voice would reach all the way to heaven. Karen stood up after the blessing and adjusted the sash on her pink, embroidered, store-bought dress. Brother Wickham was a doctor, and Sister Wickham didn't have to make her own or Karen's clothes. Then it was Drew and their father's turn to come down and join the circle of men. Her father prayed "that the spirit of the Holy Ghost might guide Drew and direct him in all his endeavors throughout his life, that the still, small voice would stay his hand from evil. In the name of the Father and of the Son and of the Holy Ghost, Amen."

"Amen," the men in the circle repeated and took their hands off Drew's head. Sarah remembered that when the hands had been lifted off her head, she felt as if she might float up, the way if you pressed the backs of your hands against a door frame for long enough, when you stepped away your hands would rise up, magically, by themselves, sometimes even above your head. Drew looked a little stunned as he climbed back up on the dais.

Two more confirmations followed, then finally the testimonies began. Some people bore their testimonies every single Fast Sunday. Sarah almost knew by heart what Sister Spackman, in her pale gray, much-washed shirtwaist dress, would say when she got up: "I'm grateful for the church and my family and for the strength to live each day and to be a witness for the truth of the gospel." Sister Spackman was a widow, and her youngest son had a disease. He would always stay a child. He couldn't hold the priesthood, even though he was already old enough to be a deacon.

Sarah hoped her parents wouldn't bear their testimonies this time. They had gotten up often in the months since her mother had had her operation. The Fast Sunday after her mother had come home from the hospital, even Sarah had risen to say that she knew the church was true and that Joseph Smith was a prophet and that she was grateful her prayers had been answered and that her mother was back home. She was still frightened, though, that her mother would not be all right. Sarah found it harder to pray now, harder to have faith the way she was supposed to. She was afraid God wasn't listening to her anymore, that maybe He was looking at her, and that He didn't like what He saw.

Sarah's mother was still weak; her father did all the grocery shopping, and Sarah did most of the cooking and ironing. That was why it was so surprising that her mother had made their Easter clothes this year. Her mother looked very tired; the skin around her mouth seemed yellowish next to the red lipstick. Sarah glanced over at the bodice of her mother's dress. You couldn't tell with her clothes on. She had let Sarah hold the pad that she slipped into her bra every morning. It was surprisingly heavy. She had also shown Sarah the two long red scars, and let her touch them so she wouldn't be frightened. One started at her left armpit, curved across her chest and down almost all the way to her navel; the other started at her navel and went straight down her whole belly. The scars were flat and wide and hard and criss-crossed with marks, like bumpy railroad tracks.

Her mother would have sewn herself up more neatly than the doctors did, thought Sarah. Her mother was such a good seamstress that she even made wedding dresses and Temple clothes. She had taught

71

Sarah how to sew, too, and embroider. Sarah made a cross-stitched sampler that read "I will bring the light of the gospel into my home." Her mother had taught her how to make lots of different kinds of stitches: tacking stitch, basting stitch, running stitch, overhand stitch, blind stitch, hem stitch, seed stitch, pearl stitch, invisible stitch.

Sarah's mother was even thinner now than she used to be. She couldn't have any more children, she had told Sarah. She had wanted to have twelve, like her friend, Sister Barber, who was Mrs. Utah one year. Sarah couldn't imagine more children—three brothers were enough—though it would have been nice to have had a sister. A sister could have helped with the cooking and dishwashing, so Sarah wouldn't have to do it all by herself. She could have had secrets with a sister; they could have slept in the same bed together, the way Drew and Danny did. And when they grew up, they could go on double dates together and marry brothers, the way Annie and Abby Holmgren had. They even had their first babies at the same time.

The church was suddenly quiet. Sarah looked up. Sister Spackman had finished her testimony and sat down. A man she had seen only a few times at church was walking up the aisle. Most people just stood up to speak from where they were sitting, but some people came up to the podium on the dais. The man was tall, and had wavy brown hair and blue eyes. He looked a little bit like her oldest cousin, Shep, who was on a mission in Brazil, but he was older than Shep. This man was old enough to be a father, but as far as Sarah knew, he didn't have a wife and children. No one had ever come to church with him, and he always had left quickly after sacrament meeting, not standing around shaking hands after the service, the way the other men did. Since he had never spoken before in church, Sarah was curious. Maybe he would say something about his wife and children. Maybe they had all died in a fire. People talked about things like that in fast and testimony meeting. Sarah didn't always understand what people meant when they spoke, but usually her mother would explain things later, like when Brother Watkins moved out of his house for six months, leaving Sister Watkins and their five children behind. When he came back, he repented in front of the whole congregation.

"Brothers and sisters," the man began, his hands gripping the edges of the podium, "most of you don't know me. I have only lived in this ward for a few months. My name is John Perry. I was born in Moscow, Idaho. My great-great-grandfather Perry crossed the plains with a handcart and my great-grandfather Williams converted in England during the early days of the church."

This was like Sarah's family and most of the people she knew. She wondered if he was going to tell his whole genealogy. She knew, though no one would say much about it, that her great-grandfather on her mother's side had been a polygamist. When relatives did talk about it, they called it "living the principle." Her great-grandfather had only three wives, though. Not nearly as many as Brigham Young. But because of polygamy, Sarah did seem to have a lot of relatives, the usual aunts and uncles and cousins, but also great-aunts once removed, second cousins twice removed, and honorary uncles.

"I was raised in the church, went to Ricks College for a year, then served my mission in the Netherlands. After I returned from my mission, I went to BYU and completed my degree in business administration. Then I married my high school sweetheart in the Temple, for Time and all Eternity. We went to live in Boise, and we prospered in the Lord and were blessed with three fine children."

So far, this still sounded like the story of almost every other grown-up. But then he said something Sarah didn't expect.

"I fell in love with another woman. My wife cast me out. That is why I came back here, to Bountiful, to the heart of the church. Because here, I thought, I would find kindred souls, as it is written in Helaman, Chapter 5, Verse 14: *And they did remember his words; and therefore they went forth, keeping the commandments of God, to teach the word of God among all the people of Nephi, beginning at the city of Bountiful.* I've been watching you, in the short time I've lived in this ward, and I decided that today would be the day to tell you what I was brought to this earth to accomplish."

Bountiful, Sarah thought. She had never connected her Bountiful with the Bountiful from olden days in the *Book of Mormon.* Sarah felt her mother stir beside her. She saw her father lift his pen from the record book and look more closely at the man on the podium. Drew was putting rabbit ears behind Karen Wickham's head, so maybe he hadn't changed too much yet.

"Brothers and sisters," Brother Perry continued, *"Straight is the way and narrow the gate that leads to the Kingdom of Heaven.* I believe that the church has taken a wrong turn on the path. I believe in the continuing power of revelation, and God has revealed to me that we should return to the old covenant, that men should take unto themselves more wives, that we should prepare to enter the Celestial

73

Kingdom as God has planned by giving as many souls as possible their mortal bodies. I have seen all those spirits waiting in the pre-existence, waiting to receive their terrestrial bodies, and God has told me that we must make more bodies, soon, before the millennium. It's time, brothers and sisters, to redouble and triple our efforts. We are the Chosen People, and we cannot allow only the Gentiles to populate this terrestrial plane. Every man and every woman of child-bearing age must join together to make new temples to house the spirits waiting in the preexistence."

My body is a temple, Sarah thought. That was in a song she had learned when she was very little. *My body is a temple*. How could a body be a building? What about her mother—did the operation mean her mother's body couldn't be a temple anymore? What if her father decided to marry someone else? Her mother was clasping her hand tightly now, and Sarah, in turn, had taken Danny's hand on her left.

The man paused for a moment. Members of the congregation started to murmur and look at each other. Sarah noticed that Bishop Anderson was whispering to Brother Jenson, the first counselor, sitting on his right. "Sarah," her mother said, "maybe you shouldn't listen. Tell Danny not to listen, too. He might be bearing false witness." But Sarah had to listen, just the way she had to read everything in the World Book and all the biographies of composers in the library. Maybe he would say something that would help her make sense of what had happened to her mother, even though her mother was so very good.

"Brothers and sisters, I ask you to remember with me the tidings of 3 Nephi 11:1: *And now it came to pass that there were a great multitude gathered together of the people of Nephi, round about the temple which was in the land Bountiful; and they were marveling and wondering one with another, and were showing one to another the great and marvelous changes which had taken place.* We have the opportunity now, in Bountiful, to fulfill our great spiritual destiny, to come and be numbered with the house of Israel. I have chosen you to join with me and restore the principle we are meant to follow. All those of you who truly hunger and thirst after righteousness, come follow me now. Come follow me into the hills of Zion, and we will start a new era of brotherly and sisterly love. Come follow me or be cast down into the pit of wickedness."

The man stepped down from the dais and walked across the front of the chapel. He opened the door by the sacrament table, letting in the surprising blue light of the day, like the stone being rolled away from the tomb. He cupped his hands in front of him, like a picture Sarah had seen of Jesus speaking to the disciples. "Come follow me," he said one last time, and stepped outside.

No one moved.

Finally, Bishop Anderson got up. He said, "And now, brothers and sisters, difficult as it is, we must act. As we know from 1 Nephi 22:19, *all who fight against Zion shall be cut off,* and from Moroni 6:7, *the names of the unrighteous are blotted out.* We must never speak of John Perry again. Because he has apostatized, he will be cut off temporally and spiritually from the presence of God. And it is our duty as followers of the gospel and members of the true church to excommunicate him. After the close of testimony meeting, I ask all the elders, seventies, and high priests to meet with me in a special priesthood meeting. But now it is even more important than ever for us to continue to bear our testimonies."

Bishop Anderson bore his, then one by one, almost all the members of the congregation stood up to bear theirs. When Sarah's mother rose, she said, "I know I was put on this earth for a special purpose, and, even though my strength has been tested by illness, I love the gospel more than ever. I know this church is true and that Joseph Smith was a prophet of God and that we are guided today by a prophet, seer, and revelator."

Even Drew and Danny got up to speak. Drew sounded very grown-up when he said how grateful he was to have been baptized into the true church and to have received the gift of the Holy Ghost. He even recited part of a hymn, *"The witness of the Holy Ghost, / As borne by those who know, / Has lifted me again to thee, / O Father of my soul."* Danny simply said he was thankful for his family and glad that it was Easter.

But Sarah felt something hard inside herself, as if she had accidentally swallowed the pit of an apricot. Why couldn't she stand up like everyone else to bear her testimony? It was Easter, the holiest day of the year. Where were the words that used to come so easily?

It was dark by the time everyone finished speaking and sang the final hymn; one of the lines, *"He lives my hungry soul to feed,"* leapt out at Sarah. On a normal Fast Sunday, she and Drew might have repeated that line over and over instead of singing the rest of the hymn, or they might have giggled at *"He lives, my ever-living Head,"* but now she sang straight through, without changing any words, and it looked like Drew was singing his heart out on the dais.

After the final amen after the final prayer, Sarah rushed outside. She knew that the women would stand in the foyer and talk while the men gathered in the gospel doctrine room for the special priesthood meeting. Her mother would probably ask Sister Holmgren for a ride home, since the men might meet for hours more. Sarah wanted to see if John Perry was still around. She walked to the edge of the parking lot. Along with the scent of apricot blossoms, she could smell a faint tang of smoke from the oil refineries next to the Great Salt Lake. Down in the valley, she could see the chain of lights from Slim Olson's, the huge gas station where her father was a bookkeeper. Even in the dark, she could see the sheen of the white screen of the drive-in movie, which hadn't yet opened for the season. But no sign of John Perry. So she walked back toward the chapel. By the side of a red pickup truck, she saw him. No one else was near. She wanted to say something to him, but she didn't know what. She wanted to ask him if he knew whether her mother would ever get well again. As she walked closer, she could see he was crying. She pulled her new Easter handkerchief out of her patent-leather purse. Without a word, she gave it to him. He looked down at her. "You believe me, don't you," he said in a soft voice. "You'll know I'm right when you get older. I can see that; I can see you're a thoughtful child."

"Good luck," Sarah said, but that didn't seem quite enough, so she added, "God bless," then turned away. She knew her mother would be looking for her by now, or wondering if she'd taken a ride with Sister Spackman, who lived nearby. When she saw her mother in the foyer with Sister Holmgren, Sarah ran towards her, but stopped before hugging her. She was afraid her mother, so thin already, would dissolve at her touch. She knew she would never be able to tell her parents about seeing John Perry outside the chapel.

Sarah and her mother and brothers rode home in Sister Holmgren's big car. Drew got in the middle of the back seat right away, without even fighting Sarah for a window seat. Sarah opened the window a crack so she could smell the blossoming trees. She was hungry, so hungry, and she felt that she occupied a very small corner in the world, a corner into which no hands could reach to comfort her.

Nominated by Thomas Kennedy, Ploughshares

WONDER: RED BEANS AND RICELY

by SYDNEY LEA

from THE SOUTHERN REVIEW

He blew the famous opening figure of "West End Blues"
and then—a long pause. A long long pin-drop pause.
This sounded like nothing the four of us had been hearing out here
at the Famous Sunnybrook Ballroom in East Jesus, PA,
which was in fact a moth-eaten tent to which in summer
the big postwar bands, then fading into the '50s—
the likes of the Elgars or Les Brown and His Band of Renown—
would arrive to coax the newly middle-aged and their elders
into nostalgia and dance. My second cousin, our steadies,
and I were younger, cocksure, full of contraband beer,
but the moment I speak of knocked even us in the know-it-all
    chops.

I suddenly dreamed I could see through the vast canvas top
clear to stars as they stopped their fool blinking and planets
    standing
stock-still over cows and great-eyed deer in the moonlight
and ducks ablaze on their ponds because everything in God's world
knew this was nothing like anything they'd known before.
It's still a fantasy, that sorry tent a lantern,
transparent as glass, through which I beheld the landscape around it
as though it showed in some Low Country more-than-masterpiece
while no one danced. The crassest fat-necked burgher in the crowd

sat rapt, as did his missus, the moment being that strong.
It lingered strong, beginning to end, through the "Blues" that
   followed.

Then Velma Middleton got up to jive and bellow.
She broke the charm, her scintillant dress like a tent itself,
and people resumed the lindy and fox-trot as she and he
traded the always-good-for-laughs double meanings
of "Big Butter and Egg Man," "That's My Desire,"
and so on. And so we four, or rather we two boys,
resumed our drinking and boasting until the band took its break.
Full enough by now of the Bud°and some of the rum
that the cousin had brought, which would take him in time, too
   sadly short
a time, to another shore forever, I stood and pledged:
I'll get his autograph. It made no sense at all.

I staggered to and through the canvas's backstage hole,
the mocking jibes of cousin and sweethearts dying behind me,
and beheld four semi-tractor trucks—his equipage.
There were doors as to a house in each, and a little set
of metal steps underneath. Without a hitch, I climbed
one stair of the bunch. It made no sense except it did.
I *knew*. . . . Something had burned into my fogged brain
when that opening solo started, he would have to be
just there where he was when I knocked on one of the several doors
inside the truck, and the growl was Fate: it didn't surprise me:
Come in, he said. How could he? How could he not? I came.

It had had to be, and yet I stammered with puzzlement, shame.
I'd had a vision, yes, and yet to have the vision
there before me. . . . Wonder! Great Armstrong at his desk
in an undershirt, suspenders flapping, his face near blinding,
sweat beads charged by the gimcrack string of fluorescent lights
so that he seemed to wear an aura—it was all
one supple motion, the way he reached into a drawer,
drew out a jug of Johnny Walker, sucked it down
to the label, squared before him a sheet of paper (where
did *that* come from?), flourished a fountain pen, and wrote:
Red Beans and Ricely Yours at Sunny Brook Ballroom. Pops.

Back at the table they judged it was real enough by the looks.
"I just walked in and got it," I bragged, as if a miracle
hadn't transpired, surely as great as any I'd know.
I bragged as if my part in it all were important somehow,
and God hadn't just looked down and said, "Well OK—him."
And what remains from then? Not the paper, long since lost,
nor the lovely, silken girls, Sally and Margot,
nor the cousin, as I've said, who became the Guy with the Liver.
Nor that old, that old brash blessèd younger I. . . .
Just the heaven-struck beasts and the trees and the moon and the
    sky

below that spray of opening notes which are there forever.

Nominated by Wesley McNair, Jeffrey Harrison, The Southern Review

DUES

fiction by DALE PECK

from THREEPENNY REVIEW

FIRST OF ALL, Adam. He creaked up beside me on a bicycle that seemed welded of leftover plumbing parts. "Pull over," he said with all the authority of a keystone cop.

He was cute enough. In particular, the hair: black, thick, sticking out of his head in a dozen directions. His long thin legs straddled the flared central strut of his bicycle like denim-covered tent poles and he stared down at my own bike with eyes the color of asphalt—the old gray kind, with glass embedded in it to reflect light.

But this wasn't a pick-up.

"That is my bicycle," he announced. A trace of an accent?

"I'm sure there's some misunderstanding," I said. "I paid for this bike."

"Then you bought stolen merchandise," he said, his consonants soft, Eastern European. *Shtolen mershendise*. "I think you should show me where."

I'd gone on a tip. Benny's East Village. "You won't believe his prices," a friend had told me. "Isn't that the burrito place?" I'd said. In fact my friend had said, "They're probably all stolen, but what you don't know won't hurt you." "He steals burritos?" I'd said. "*Bicycles*," my friend said. "Come *on*."

By the time Adam and I arrived the shop had closed for the day. Adam's thin legs had labored to turn his creaking pedals, and it occurred to me I could have outrun him, but I didn't. The sun was setting at our backs and our shadows stretched out in front of us like twinned towers. I thought we were a pair. I thought we were in it to-gether.

Benny sat on a swivel chair on the sidewalk, a television propped in front of him on a pair of milk crates; a tin of rice and beans wobbled on his lap. We'd been there only a few minutes when a man half carried, half pushed a bike up the street. He held it by the seat, lifting the back wheel off the ground because it couldn't turn: it was still locked to the frame. After inspecting the bicycle, Benny paid the man from a roll of bills he pulled from the breast pocket of his T-shirt, stowed the bicycle under the grate of his store, and returned to his chair.

I turned to Adam.

"I guess I should have investigated further."

"You should have."

He was pulling the kryptonite U-lock from its frame-mounted holder, and I inferred from this action that he wanted to trade bikes. I dismounted, and was unwinding my chain from the seat post when his lock caught me in the side of the head, just behind and below my left eye. Fireflies streaked through my field of vision when the lock struck me, but I didn't actually lose consciousness until the sidewalk hit me in the forehead.

Charlie sponged the grit from my face. What was stuck to solid skin washed away easily, but the bits of gravel embedded in the gashes on my cheek and forehead resisted, had to be convinced to relinquish their berth. I closed my eyes against the water trickling from his rag.

One summer when I was seven or eight I carried cupfuls of water from a stream and poured them down chipmunk holes. The chipmunks would remain underground for as long as possible until, wobbling like drunken sailors, they staggered into the sunshine. Gently I lifted them into a tinfoil turkey tray I'd habitated with rocks, plants, a ribbed tin can laid on its side (a sleeping den, I'd thought), and then I watched as the chipmunks revived, explored their playground tentatively, and then, inevitably, hurdled the shiny wall and scrambled back down their holes.

"I'm afraid I'm going to have to use a tweezers for the last of it."

I opened my eyes. Charlie was making a face, as if performing this surgery hurt him instead of me.

He asked me if it hurt me.

I was still remembering the way the last chipmunk had lain on its side after I'd fished it from its home, eyes closed, chest fluttering as rapidly as a bee's wings. I'd dared to stroke its heaving ribs. The chipmunk curled itself into a ball around my finger, its mouth and the claws of all four paws digging at me until I flung it away and it scurried to safety.

"It hurts," I said, then caught Charlie's arm as he flinched. "My head hurts," I said. "What you're doing doesn't hurt."

Benny's East Village sold bikes every day except Sunday from eleven until seven, but seemed always to be bustling with activity. In the mornings a young woman worked on the bicycles. This was Deneisha, who seemed to live on the third floor. Every ten minutes a younger version of her leaned out the window to relay a request: "Deneisha, Mami says why you didn't get no more coffee if you used the last of it?" "Deneisha, Benny says to call him back on his cell phone *now*." "Deneisha, Eduardo wants to know when are you gonna take the training wheels off my bike so I can go riding with him?" Deneisha, her thick body covered in greasy overalls, inky black spirals of hair rubber-banded off her smooth round face, ignored these interruptions, working with Allen wrenches and oil cans and tubes of glue on gears, brakes, tires. For bicycles that still had a chain fastened to them she had an enormous pair of snips, their handles as long as her meaty arms, and for U-locks she had a special saw that threw sparks like a torch as it chewed through tempered steel.

After the shop closed there was a lull until the sun went down, and then the bicycles began to arrive. Every thief was different. Some skulked, others paraded their booty openly, offering it to anyone they passed on the sidewalk, but few spent any time bargaining with Benny. The more nervous the thief, the less interest Benny showed, the less money he pulled from the roll of bills. He seemed completely untroubled by his illicit enterprise, absorbing stolen bikes with the same equanimity with which he absorbed tins and cartons of delivered food. Only the white kids, the college-aged junkies selling off the first or the last of their ties to a suburban past, tried his patience. "I said ten bucks," I heard him say once. "Take it or leave it."

Charlie couldn't understand my obsession. We'd only been together for three months, and what I'd learned about him was that he absorbed information with a stenographer's zen. "Existence is the sum of experience," he'd shrugged that first night, as though the events of our lives were drops of water and we the puddles at the end of their runneled paths, little pools of history. When I still wouldn't let it go he prodded harder.

"Is it the coincidence that bothers you, or the fact that he hit you? Or is it that you pretended innocence of what you were getting when you bought the bike in the first place, and now it's come back and bitten you in the ass?"

At the time I couldn't answer him, and of course hindsight makes it that much less clear. I offered him words like "cleave" and "hew," words that could mean both cutting and binding, but Charlie waved my rhetoric away. "Context makes meaning clear," he said. And then, more bluntly: *"Choose."*

But I couldn't choose. My life felt splayed on either side of the incident with Adam like his long thin legs straddling the ancient bicycle which he did, in fact, leave for me. Like conjoined twins, my two selves were linked at the hip, sharing a common future but divided as to which past to claim. And so every day I rode Adam's creaking iron bike to a stoop across from Benny's and waited for something like Deneisha's saw or snips to sever my old unmolested self, leaving my new scarred body to get on with things.

At a party Charlie took me to I told the story behind the bandages on my cheek and forehead a half dozen times. By then the two bruises had joined into one, across my forehead, down my left cheek, vanishing into the hairline. The single bruise was mottled black, purple, blue, green, yellow, but, like the story I told over and over again, essentially painless, and as the night wore on Charlie added his own coda to my words. "Victim," he would say, turning my mottled left profile to the audience. "Thief," he said, showing them my right.

"Uh oh," he said at one point, "here comes trouble." Trouble was a man around our age, one hand holding shaggy bangs off his unlined forehead as though he were taking in a sight, the Grand Canyon, a caged animal. From across the room I heard his cry. "Now *where* did I leave that man?" His gaze fell on Charlie. *"There* he is."

Charlie introduced him as Fletcher. From the name I knew this to be his ex-boyfriend, who had dumped Charlie last summer after a five-year relationship that Charlie referred to by the names of various failed political unions: Czechoslovakia, Upper and Lower Egypt, the Austro-Hungarian Empire. His arms around Charlie's waist, Fletcher pulled him a few feet away, as if together they were examining my bruised face. "Is this *really* the new model," Fletcher said, "or just something you picked up at Rent-a-Wreck?" Charlie offered me a wan smile but, like the Orangeman that he was, seemed content in Fletcher's possessive embrace. Under his questions, I recited once again the story of the two bicycles, the single blow, adding this time the week of camping out across from Benny's shop. Fletcher's assessment: "I don't know why you're focusing on *him*, he's just a businessman. It was the Slav who sucker-punched you."

On the bicycle ride to Benny's, Adam had told me he came from Slovenia. He came here on a student visa, stayed on after his country seceded from the Yugoslavian republic; that was a decade ago. "Back home," he told me, "the terrain is hills and mountains but everyone rides bicycles like this." He smacked the flecked chrome of his handlebars. "Often you see people, not just grandmothers but healthy young men, pushing their bicycles up inclines too steep to pedal. I wanted a mountain bike."

He told me he was illegal, worked without a green card, had almost to live like a thief himself; he had a degree in computer science and an MBA, had emigrated to get in on the dot com boom but ended up tending bar at Windows on the World. After Fletcher's harangue I bought two books on Balkan history at a used bookstore, a novel and a book of journalism, and I read them on the stoop across from Benny's in an effort to understand what Adam meant by telling me about his stunted furtive existence, the two kinds of bicycles, the broadside with the lock. Why *did* he need a mountain bike, if he was only going to ride the swamp-flat streets of the East Village?

But then: Grace.

I was sitting on the stoop across from Benny's absorbed in the cyclical tale of centuries of avenged violence that is Balkan history. Two plaster lions flanked me, their fangs dulled beneath years of brown paint. A woman stopped in front of me and hooked a finger around one of the lion's incisors. "That is a *great* book," she said with the kind of enthusiasm only a middle-aged counter-culturalist can summon. She pointed not to the book I was reading but to the novel on the concrete beside me. Against the heat of early September she wore green plastic sandals, black spandex shorts, a halter top that seemed sewn from a threadbare bandanna. The spandex was worn and semitransparent on her thin thighs and her stomach was so flat it was concave; a ruby glowed from her navel ring, an echo of the bindi dot on her forehead. She could have been thirty or fifty. She let go of the lion's tooth and picked up the novel even as I told her I looked forward to reading it. "Like, wow," she exclaimed, and when she blinked it seemed to me her eyes were slightly out of sync. She held the book up to me, the cover propped open to the first set of endpapers. An *ex libris* card was stuck on the left-hand side with a name penned on it in black ink: *Grace* was the first name, followed by a polysyllabic scrawl ending in *-itz*. The same card adorned the book I was reading and, nervously, my index finger traced the hard shell of scab above my left eye. What she said next would have seemed no more unlikely had the lion behind her spoken it himself: "That's *my* name."

She didn't ask for her books back—they weren't stolen, she'd bought them for a class at the New School and sold them after it was over so she could afford a course in elementary Sanskrit—but I insisted she take them anyway, sensing that a drama was unfolding somewhat closer than the Balkans. In the end she accepted the novel but told me to finish the history. Over coffee I told her about Adam and the bicycle, and Grace was like, wow.

"Once I got the same cabdriver twice," she said. She blinked: her left eye and then, a moment later, her right. "I mean, I got a cabdriver I'd had before. I tried to ask him if he'd ever, you know, randomly picked up the same person twice, besides me of course, but he didn't speak English so I don't know." Her face clouded for a moment, then lit up again. Blink blink. "Oh and then once I got in the same car on the F train. I went to this winter solstice party out in Park Slope, and the kicker is we went to a bar afterward so I didn't even leave from the same stop I came out on. I think I got off at Fourth Avenue or whatever it is, and then we walked all the way to like Seventh or something, it was fucking freezing is all I remember, but whatever. When the train pulled into the station it was the same train I'd ridden out on, the same car. Totally spooky, huh?"

"How'd you know it was the same one?"

"Graffiti, duh. 'Hector loves Isabel.' Scratched into the glass with a razor blade in, like, really big letters."

"And the cabdriver?"

"His name was Jesus."
"Just Jesus?"
"Just Jesus."

The incident with Adam had been painful but finite. A city tale, one of those chance meetings leading to romance or, in this case, violence; already the bruise was fading. But the incident with Grace was more troubling, awoke in me a creeping dread. What if life was just a series of borrowed items, redundant actions, at best repetitious, at worst theft? "Those who cannot remember the past are condemned to repeat it." But what if repetition happened regardless of memory? What if we were all condemned? I felt then that I understood the history I was reading, began to sympathize with the urge to destroy something that continually reminded you of your derivative status. Like most people, I first bought used items out of poverty, but after my fortunes improved I continued to buy secondhand from a sense of a different debt. Clothes, books, bicycles: I wanted to pay my dues to history, wanted to wear it on my back, carry it in my hands, ride it through the streets. But now it seemed history had rejected my tithing, rejected it scornfully. The past can be sold, it mocked me, but it can never be bought.

Charlie was less blasé about Grace than he'd been about Adam, but ultimately dismissed it.

"It takes three events to form a narrative. Two is just a coincidence."

"But a coincidence which is made up of two coincidences. What's that?"

"Proof that New York, as someone once said, is just a series of small towns."

The first night, after cleaning and bandaging my wounds, Charlie had put me to bed and spooned himself behind me, his arms around me, the outline of his erect penis palpable through two pairs of underwear. At the time it was so familiar I didn't really notice it, but later it came to preoccupy my thoughts. It was like Adam's mountain bike, misplaced, a tool for which the pertinent scenario existed only at a remembered remove. Or Grace's *ex libris* cards, a claim of ownership on something she had no intention of keeping, like a gravestone on an abandoned grave. The night I met Grace, Charlie and I had sex for the first time since Adam had whacked me in the head, and the whole time I was unable to shake an image of Fletcher's face next to Charlie's crotch. "See this? This is *mine*." Later that night, when I was dozing off and Charlie was leafing through the book that had fallen from my hands, I suddenly sat up.

"*Fletcher.*"

"What about Fletcher?"

"You used to belong to him." Silently but victoriously, I ticked off forefinger, middle finger, ring finger. Then: "That's three."

The next day, after Charlie went to work, I stayed in the apartment. At first I wasn't aware that I was doing it. Staying in. I worked in the morning, ordered lunch from an Italian place around the corner. I read while I ate tepid fettuccini and kept reading after I'd finished my meal; all this was normal, or had been normal, if you disregarded the weeks I'd spent in front of Benny's. On a pad made up of reused sheets from early drafts of stories was written "shaving cream, milk," but after I'd finished the history I neglected my shopping and instead took a nap. I didn't wake until Charlie called that evening after he got off work.

"Dinner? There's that new French place on 12th."

"Oh," I said. "I'm sorry, I was hungry, I ordered in. Mexican."

"That's fine," Charlie said. "I've got some chicken in the fridge, and some work I really should get done. My place tonight?"

"Oh," I said again. "I'm sorry. I, um. My head's pounding. Do you mind?"

Charlie didn't say *that's fine* the second time. He said, "Sure," and it seemed to me his voice wasn't annoyed but instead relieved. "I'll give you a call tomorrow."

The next day I stayed in again, working. I'd been trying to write about Adam since I'd met him, but after I met Grace the story suddenly fell into place.

In the story I am afraid to leave my apartment. I am afraid that a stranger will stop me on the sidewalk and put their hand on my Salvation Army chest. "That's my shirt." Someone else claims my pants. Nearly naked, I skulk indoors. But not even my home is safe. A visitor runs his hand over my sofa (Housing Works, $250). "I used to *love* this couch." Another pulls open the drawers of my desk (Regeneration, $400): "What *are* the odds?" Finally someone waves their arms, taking in the time-smudged dimensions of my tiny apartment.

"This used to be *my* home." My throat is dry, and I go to the faucet for a drink. But as the water runs I wonder: how many bodies has this passed through to get to me?

But it was worse than all that. When Charlie came over that evening he glanced through the story I'd written and said, "Haven't I read this before?"

On the third day I didn't leave my apartment Charlie called me and told me a story:

"Once I wanted to hack all my hair off with a pair of scissors. But I had a crewcut at the time. So I went out and bought next year's calendar and marked the date a year hence with a big red X. For the next twelve months I didn't touch my hair, and when the day with the X came up I looked in the mirror and realized I liked my hair long. I realized that my crewcuts had been a way of hacking off my hair all along."

I said the only thing I could think of.

"Huh?"

"Your whole shut-in thing," Charlie said. "It's not real. Or it's not new. It's just a symbol of something you already do. You've already done. Think about it. Where is it you're *really* afraid to go?"

I thought about it.

"But you have a crewcut now," I said.

"Give me a break, will you? I'm going bald, it's the dignified thing to do."

When we met Charlie gave me a road map. This was on our third date. Oh, okay, our second. We'd gone back to his apartment and he spread the map out on his kitchen table (Ikea, $99). The table, like everything else in Charlie's apartment, was new and neat, but the map was old and wrinkled, a flag-sized copy of the continental U.S., post-Alaska, pre-Hawaii. Some of the creases were so worn they'd torn, or were about to.

"Now," Charlie said. "Fold it."

There were four long creases, twelve short, and folding the map proved as hard as solving Rubik's cube. I got it wrong a half dozen times before I finally got the front and back covers in the right place and, a little chagrined, handed it to Charlie.

"Did I fail?"

"You passed," Charlie said. "With flying colors. Anyone who can fold a map on the first try is far too rational for me."

"And what about people who can't fold one at all?"

In answer, Charlie pulled open the white laminate-fronted drawer of one of those nameless pieces of furniture, a "storage unit." Inside were several maps practically wadded up, as well as dozens of take-out menus and hundreds of crooked twist ties. He had to scrunch the pile down before the drawer would close again.

"Wow," I said. "The map test *and* your messy drawer. You must really like me."

Charlie grinned, sheepish but pleased. "It's about time I entered into a new alliance."

By the time I understood what that meant, I thought I was ready to sign. And then Adam came along.

On the fourth day, Grace called. When I asked her how she'd gotten my number she said, "Out of the book," and when I started to ask how she knew my last name she interrupted me and said, "Honey, I think you'd better turn on the television."

Months later, when the indemnity claims began to be discussed in the press, New Yorkers would learn that the opposing sides, the insurance companies and the property owners, differed on a crucial issue: whether the collapse of the towers constituted one event, or two. The World Trade Center, it turned out, was insured for three billion dollars, but if it was deemed that the crash of the second plane into the south tower, not quite twenty minutes after the north tower was hit, constituted a distinct historical event, the insurers would have to pay the full amount twice, in effect saying that the buildings had been destroyed not once but two times. A lot of the argument, as it turned out, was rhetorical: to the insurers, the World Trade Center was a single site—maps marked it with a single X, guidebooks gave it only one entry—that had been destroyed by a united terrorist attack. But to the property owners, the Twin Towers were, architecturally, structurally, visibly, two buildings destroyed by two separate planes, either one of which could have missed its target. Which argument began to make more and more sense to me as time went on and details about what had happened came out. Nearly three-quarters of the people who died were in the north tower, and, of those, more than ninety percent were on floors above those hit by the plane, including dozens of people attending a breakfast conference at Windows on the World. The reason why far fewer people died in the second tower, which stood for less than an hour, as opposed to the hundred minutes the north tower remained intact, is that people in the south tower saw what had happened to the north tower and evacuated their offices. Regardless of whether you considered the two plane crashes coincidence or concerted assault, the planes had struck separately—and people in the second incident had learned from the first.

The antonym to history is prophecy. Historical patterns only emerge when we look back in time; they exist in the future as nothing more than guesses. That we make such projections speaks of a kind of faith, though whether that faith is in the past or the future, the predictability of human nature, or physics, or God, is anybody's guess. But in the end, it always takes you by surprise. By which I mean that when I fought my way through the clouds of dust and crowds of dusty people to Charlie's apartment, I found Fletcher had beaten me there. Who could have foreseen that?

In the days to come, I rode my bike around the city, watched as walls and windows and trees and lampposts filled up with pictures of the missing. Dust clogged my lungs and coated the chain of Adam's creaking bicycle, making it harder and harder to turn the pedals, but it was three days before I stopped wandering aimlessly and actually started looking for him.

I found him, finally, a day and a half later, at the armory on Lexington and 26th. Indian restaurants lined that stretch of Lex, and the air was usually tinged with curry, but all the restaurants had been closed for days. There were thousands of pictures taped to the wall of the armory, hundreds of people queuing to look at them. Many of the pictures were printed by inkjets and had smeared into unrecognizable blurs after two days of thunderstorms. Where there was a television crew, dozens of people holding up Polaroids and snapshots and flyers jockeyed to get on camera.

By common will the line moved from left to right. Heads nodded up and down as feet shuffled side to side. I tried not to look in anyone's eyes, living or photographed. I did look at the living, just in case, but mostly I looked at the pictures on the wall.

Sometimes A leads to Z. But sometimes Z leads to A. What I mean is, I was looking for Adam, but I found Zach. Zach: "You won't believe his prices." Zach: "They're probably all stolen, but what you don't know won't hurt you." *"Bicycles,"* Zach had said. "Come *on.*"

I looked at his face for a long time. He hadn't been a close friend, but someone I'd known off and on for almost fifteen years, and as I looked at him I was suddenly reminded of everyone I'd known who had died of AIDS in the Eighties and Nineties, the tragic consequences of being in the wrong place at the wrong time. The memory was as unexpected as Adam's blow to my head but produced in me an odd, almost eerie sense of calm. Z had led to A, and A to Z, and Z back to A, but now it was a different A. History wasn't even a circle but a diminishing spiral, twisting into a tinier and tinier point.

And then:

"Keith? Keith, is that you?"

I didn't recognize him at first. He was shorter than I remembered, his features less fine. His eyes weren't gray but blue. But the hair was the same, thick and black and sticking out of his head in a dozen directions. It was streaked with soot now too, as if he hadn't washed in days. His T-shirt was also filthy, and pinned to his chest were three pictures which I hardly had time to take in—there were two women and one man, all smiling the hopelessly naive smiles of the doomed—before Adam grabbed me up in a huge embrace. His arms collapsed around me, one and then the other, and his tears salved the faded remnants of my wounded face.

"Oh my God, Keith!" Adam cried. "You're alive!"

Nominated by Threepenny Review

WAITING FOR THE MESSIAH

by CHANA BLOCH

from POETRY

Every year some student would claim to be the Messiah.
It was the rabbi who had to deal with them.
He had jumped, years ago, from a moving boxcar
on the way to a death camp. That jump
left him ready for anything.

This year at Pesach, a Jewish student proclaimed
Armageddon. "Burn the books! Burn the textbooks!"
he shouted to a cheerful crowd
in Harvard Square, sang Hebrew songs
to confuse the Gentiles,
dressed for the end like Belshazzar.
People stopped to whisper and laugh.

"I have a noble task to perform," the boy explained
gravely. "I am preparing myself to endure
the laughter of fools."

The rabbi was a skeptic.
Years ago he'd been taught, if you're planting a tree
and someone cries out, "The Messiah has come!"
finish planting the tree. Then
go see if it's true.

Still, he took the boy into his study
and questioned him slowly, stubbornly
as if the poor soul before him might be,
God help us, the Messiah.

Nominated by Marilyn Hacker

DOG SONG

fiction by ANN PANCAKE

from SHENANDOAH

Him. HELLING UP A HILLSIDE in a thin snow won't melt, rock-broke, brush-broke, crust-cracking snow throat felt, the winter a cold one, but a dry one, kind of winter makes them tell about the old ones, and him helling up that hill towards her. To where he sees her tree-tied, black trunk piercing snow hide, and the dog, roped, leashed, chained, he can't tell which, but something not right about the dog he can tell, but he can't see, can't see quite feel, and him helling. Him helling. His eyes knocking in his head, breath punching out of him in a hole, hah. Hah. Hah. Hah, and the dog, her haunch-sat ear-cocked waiting for him, and him helling. And him helling. And him helling. But he does not ever reach her.

This is his dream.

His dogs started disappearing around the fifteenth of July, near as he could pinpoint it looking back, because it wasn't until a week after that and he recognized it as a pattern that he started marking when they went. Parchy vanished first. The ugliest dog he ever owned, coated in this close-napped pink-brown hair, his outsides colored like the insides of his mouth, and at first, Matley just figured he'd run off. Matley always had a few who'd run off because he couldn't bear to keep them tied, but then Buck followed Parchy a week later. But he'd only had Buck a few months, so he figured maybe he'd headed back to where he'd come from, at times they did that, too. Until Missy went because Matley knew Missy would never stray. She was one of the six dogs he camper-kept, lovely mutt Missy, beautiful patches of twenty different dogs, no, Missy'd been with him seven years and was not one to travel. So on July 22nd, when Missy didn't show up for supper, Matley saw a pattern and started keeping track on his funeral-home calendar. Randolph went on August one. Yeah, Matley'd always lost a few dogs. But this was different.

He'd heard what they said down in town, how he had seventy-five dogs back in there, but they did not know. Dog Man, they called him. Beagle Boy. Muttie. Mr. Hound. A few called him Cat. Stayed in a Winnebago camper beside a househole that had been his family homeplace before it was carried off in the '85 flood, an identical Winnebago behind the lived-in one so he could take from the second one parts and pieces as they broke in the first, him economical, savvy, keen, no, Matley was not dumb. He lived off a check he got for something nobody knew what, the youngest of four boys fathered by an old landowner back in farm times, and the other three left out and sold off their inheritance in nibbles and crumbs, acre, lot, gate and tree, leaving only Matley anchored in there with the dogs and the househole along the tracks. Where a tourist train passed four times a day on summer weekends, and even more days a week during leaf colors in fall, the cars bellied full of outsiders come to see the mountain sights—"farm children playing in the fields," the brochure said, "A land that time forgot"—and there sits Matley on a lawn chair between Winnebagos and househole. He knew what they said in town, the only person they talked about near as often as Muttie was ole Johnby, and Johnby they discussed only half as much. They said Mr. Hound had seventy-five dogs back in there, nobody had ever seen anything like it, half of them living outside in barrels, the other half right there in the camper with him. It was surely a health hazard, but what could you do about it? that's what they said.

But Matley never had seventy-five dogs. Before they started disappearing, he had twenty-two, and only six he kept in the camper, and one of those six was Guinea who fit in his sweatshirt pocket, so didn't hardly count. And he looked after them well, wasn't like that one woman kept six Pomeranians in a Jayco Popup while she stayed in her house and they all got burned up in a camper fire. Space heater. The outside dogs he built shelters for, terraced the houses up the side of the hill, and, yes, some of them were barrels on their sides braced with two-by-four struts, but others he fashioned out of scrap lumber, plenty of that on the place, and depending on what mood

95

took him, sometimes he'd build them square and sometimes he'd build them like those lean-to teepees where people keep fighting cocks. Some dogs, like Parchy, slept in cable spools, a cable spool was the only structure in which Parchy would sleep. Matley could find cable spools and other almost doghouses along the river after the spring floods. And he never had seventy-five dogs.

Parchy, Buck, Missy, Randolph, Ghostdog, Blackie, Ed. Those went first. That left Tick, Hickory, Cese, Muddy Gut, Carmel, Big Girl, Leesburg, Honey, Smartie, Ray Junior, Junior Junior, Louise, Fella, Meredith and Guinea. Junior Junior was only a pup at the time, Smartie was just a part-time dog, stayed two or three nights a week across the river with his Rottweiler girlfriend, and Meredith was pregnant. Guinea was at the end of the list because Guinea was barely dog at all.

They could tell you in town that Matley was born old, born with the past squeezing on him, and he was supposed to grow up in that? How? There was no place to go but backwards. His parents were old by the time he came, his brothers gone by the time he could remember, his father dead by the time he was eight. Then the flood, on his twenty-third birthday. In town they might spot Matley in his '86 Chevette loaded from floorboards to dome light with twenty-five pound bags of Joy Dog food, and one ole boy would say, "Well, there he goes. That ruint runt of Revie's four boys. End piece didn't come right."

Another: "I heard he was kinda retarded."

"No, not retarded exactly . . . but he wasn't born until Revie was close to fifty. And that explains a few things. Far as I'm concerned. Old egg, old sperm, old baby."

"Hell, weren't none of them right," observed a third.

"There's something about those hills back in there. You know Johnby's from up there, too."

"Well," Said the last. "People are different."

Matley. His ageless, colorless, changeless self. Dressed always in baggy river-colored pants and a selection of pocketed sweatshirts he collected at yard sales. His bill-busted sweat-mapped river-colored cap, and the face between sweatshirt and cap as common and un-memorable as the pattern on a sofa. Matley had to have such a face, given what went on under and behind it. The bland face, the con-stant clothes, they had to balance out what rode behind them or

Matley might be so loose as to fall. Because Matley had inherited from his parents not just the oldness, and not just the past (that gaping loss) and not just the irrational stick to the land—even land that you hated—and not just scraps of the land itself, and the collapsed buildings, and the household, but also the loose part, he knew. Worst of all, he'd inherited the loose part inside (you got to hold on tight).

Now it was a couple years before the dogs started disappearing that things had gotten interesting from the point of view of them in town. They told. Matley's brother Charles sold off yet another plat on the ridge above the household, there on what had always been called High Boy until the developers got to it, renamed it Oaken Acre Estates, and the out-of-staters who moved in there started complaining about the barking and the odor, and then the story got even better. One of Dog Man's Beagle Boy's Cat's mixed breed who-knows-what got up in there and impregnated some purebred something-or-other one of the imports owned, "and I heard they had ever last one of them pups put to sleep. That's the kind of people they are, now," taking Matley's side for once. Insider vs. outsider, even Muttie didn't look too bad that way.

Matley knew. At first those pureblood dog old people at Oaken Acre Estates on High Boy appeared only on an occasional weekend, but then they returned to live there all the time, which was when the trouble started. They sent down a delegation of two women one summer, and when that didn't work, they sent two men. Matley could tell they were away from here from a distance, could tell from how they carried themselves before they even got close and confirmed it with their clothes. "This county has no leash ordinance," he told that second bunch, because by that time he had checked, learned the lingo, but they went on to tell him how they'd paid money to mate this pureblood dog of some type Matley'd never heard of to another of its kind, but a mongrel got to her before the stud, and they were blaming it on one of his. Said it wasn't the first time, either. "How many unneutered dogs do you have down here?" they asked, and, well, Matley never could stand to have them cut. So. But it wasn't until a whole year after that encounter that his dogs started disappearing, and Matley, of course, had been raised to respect the old.

The calendar was a free one from Berger's Funeral Home, kind of calendar has just one picture to cover all the months, usually a picture of a blonde child in a nightgown praying beside a bed, and this calendar had that picture, too. Blonde curls praying over lost dog marks, Matley almost made them crosses, but he changed them to question marks, and he kept every calendar page he tore off. He kept track, and for each one, he carried a half eulogy/half epitaph in his head:

Ed. Kind of dog you looked at and knew he was a boy, didn't have to glimpse his privates. You knew from the jog-prance of those stumpylegs, cock-of-the-walk strut, all the time swinging his head from side to side so as not to miss anything, tongue flopping out and a big grin in his eyes. Essence of little boy, he was, core, heart, whatever you want to call it. There it sat in a dog. Ed would try anything once and had to get hurt pretty bad before he'd give up, and he'd eat anything twice. That one time, cold night, Matley let him in the camper, and Ed gagged and puked up a deer liver on Matley's carpet remnant, the liver intact, though a little rotty. There it came. Out. Ed's equipment was hung too close to the ground, that's how Mr. Mitchell explained it, "his dick's hung too close to the ground, way it almost scrapes stuff, would make you crazy or stupid, and he's stupid," Mr. Mitchell'd say. Ed went on August tenth.

Ghostdog. The most mysterious of the lot, even more so than Guinea, Ghostdog never made a sound—not a whimper, not a grunt, not a snore. A whitish ripple, Ghostdog was steam moving in skin, the way she'd ghost-coast around the place, a glow-in-the-dark angel cast to her, so that to sit by the household of a summer night and watch that dog move across the field, a luminous padding, it was to learn how a nocturnal animal sees. Ghostdog'd give Matley that vision, she would make him understand, raccoon eyes, cat eyes, deer. And not only did Ghostdog show Matley night sight, through Ghostdog he could also see smells. He learned to see the shape of a smell, watching her with her head tilted, an odor entering nostrils on breeze, he could see the smell shape, "shape" being the only word he had for how the odors were, but "shape" not it at all. Still. She showed him. Ghostdog went on August nineteen.

Blackie was the only one who ever came home. He returned a strange and horrid sick, raspy purr to his breath like a locust. Kept crawling places to die, but Matley, for a while, just couldn't let him go, even though he knew it was terribly selfish. Blackie'd crawl in a place, and Matley'd pull him back out, gentle, until Matley finally fell asleep despite himself, which gave Blackie time to get under the bed and pass on. September second. But Blackie was the only one who came home like that. The others just went away.

Before Mom Revie died, he could only keep one dog at a time. She was too cheap to feed more, and she wouldn't let a dog inside the house until the late 1970's; she was country people and that was how they did their dogs, left them outside like pigs or sheep. For many years, Matley made do with his collection, dogs of ceramic and pewter, plastic and fake fur, and when he was little, Revie's rules didn't matter so much, because if he shone on the little dogs his heart and mind, Matley made them live. Then he grew up and couldn't do that anymore.

When he first started collecting live dogs after Mom Revie was gone, he got them out of the paper, and if pickings there were slim, he drove around and scooped up strays. Pretty soon, people caught on, and he didn't have to go anywhere for them, folks just started dumping unwanteds along the road above his place. Not usually pups, no, they were mostly dogs who'd hit that ornery stage between cooey-cute puppyhood and mellow you-don't-have-to-pay-them-much-mind adult. That in-between stage was the dumping stage. The only humans Matley talked to much were the Mitchells, and more than once, before the dogs started disappearing, Mrs. Mitchell would gentle say to Matley, "Now, you know, Matley, I like dogs myself. But I never did want to have more than two or three at a time." And Matley, maybe him sitting across the table from her with a cup of instant coffee, maybe them in the yard down at his place with a couple of dogs nosing her legs, a couple peeing on her tires, Matley'd nod, he'd hear the question in what she said, but he does not, could not, never out loud say . . . .

How he was always a little loose inside, but looser always in the nights. The daylight makes it scurry down, but come darkness, nothing tamps it, you never know (hold on tight). So even before Matley lost a single dog, many nights he'd wake, not out of nightmare, but worse. Out of nothing. Matley would wake, a hard sock in his chest, his lungs a-flutter, his body not knowing where it was, it not knowing, and Matley's eyes'd ball open in the dark, and behind the eyes: a galaxy of empty. Matley would gasp. *Why be alive?* This was what it told him. *Why be alive?*

There Matley would lie in peril. The loose part in him. Matley opened to emptiness, that bottomless gasp. Matley falling, Matley down-swirling (you got to hold), Matley understanding how the loose part had given, and if he wasn't to drop all the way out, he'd have to find something to hold on tight (Yeah, boy. Tight. Tight. Tighty tight tight). Matley on the all-out plummet, Matley tumbling head over butt down, Matley going almost gone, his arms outspread, him reaching, flailing, whopping . . . . Until, finally. Matley hits dog. Matley's arms drop over the bunk side and hit dog. And right there Matley stops, he grabs holt and Matley . . . stroke. Stroke, stroke. There, Matley. There.

Yeah, the loose part Matley held with dog. He packed the emptiness with pup. Took comfort in their scents, nose-buried in their coats, he inhaled their different smells, corn chips, chicken stock, meekish skunk. He'd listen to their breathing, march his breath in step with theirs, he'd hear them live, alive, their sleeping songs, them lapping themselves and recurling themselves, snoring and dreaming, settle and sigh. The dogs a soft putty, the loose part, sticking. There, Matley. There. He'd stroke their stomachs, fingercomb their flanks, knead their chests, Matley would hold on, and finally he'd get to the only true pleasure he'd ever known that wasn't also a sin. Rubbing the deep velvet of a dog's underthroat.

By late August, Matley had broke down and paid for ads in the paper, and he got calls, most of the calls from people trying to give him dogs they wanted to get rid of, but some from people thinking they'd found dogs he'd lost. Matley'd get in his car and run out to wherever the caller said the dog was, but it was never his dog. And, yeah, he had his local suspicions, but soft old people like the ones on the ridge, it was hard to believe they'd do such a thing. So first he just ran the road. Matley beetling his rain-colored Chevette up and down the twelve-mile-long road that connected the highway and his once-was farm. Holding the wheels to the road entirely through habit, wasn't no sight to it, sight he couldn't spare, Matley squinting into trees, fields, brush, until he'd enter the realm of dog mirage. Every rock, dirt mound, deer, piece of trash, he'd see it at first and think "Dog!" his heart bulging big with the hope. Crushed like an egg when he recognized the mistake. And all the while, the little dog haunts scampered the corners of his eyes, dissolving as soon as he turned to see. Every now and then he'd slam out and yell, try Revie's different calling songs, call, "Here, Ghostdog, here! Come, girl, come!" Call "Yah, Ed, yah! Yah! Yah! Yah!" Whistle and clap, cluck and whoop. But the only live thing he'd see besides groundhogs and deer, was that ole boy Johnby, hulking along.

Matley didn't usually pay Johnby much mind, he was used to him, had gone to school with him even though Johnby was a good bit older. Johnby was one of those kids who comes every year but don't graduate until they're so old the board gives them a certificate and throws them out. But today he watched ole Johnby lurching along, pretend-hunting, the gun, everyone had to assume, unloaded, and why the family let him out with guns, knives, Matley wasn't sure, but figured it was just nobody wanted to watch him. Throughout late summer, Mrs. Mitchell'd bring Matley deer parts from the ones they'd shot with crop-damage permits; oh, how the dogs loved those deer legs, and the ribcages, and the hearts. One day she'd brought Johnby along—Johnby'd catch a ride anywhere you'd take him—and Matley'd looked at Johnby, how his face'd gone old while the mind behind it never would, Johnby flipping through his wallet scraps, what he did when he got nervous. He flipped through the wallet while he stared gape-jawed at the dogs, gnawing those deer legs from hipbone to hoof. "I'm just as sorry as I can be," Mrs. Mitchell was saying, talking about the loss of the dogs. "Just as sorry as I can be." "If there's *any*thing," Mrs. Mitchell would say, "*Any*thing we can do. And you know I always keep an eye out."

Matley fondled Guinea in his pocket, felt her quiver and live. You got to keep everything else in you soldered tight to make stay in place the loose part that wasn't. You got to grip. Matley looked at Johnby, shuffling through his wallet scraps, and Matley said to him, "You got a dog, Johnby?" and Johnby said, "I got a dog," he said. "I got a dog with a white eye turns red when you shine a flashlight in it," Johnby said. "You ever hearda that kinda dog?"

What made it so awful, if awfuller it could be, was Matley never got a chance to heal. Dogs just kept going, so right about the time the wound scabbed a little, he'd get another slash. He'd scab a little, then it would get knocked off, the deep gash deeper, while the eulogies piled higher in his head:

Cese. Something got hold his head when he was wee little, Matley never knew if it was a big dog or a bear or a panther or what it was, but it happened. Didn't kill him, but left him forever after wobbling around like a stroke victim with a stiff right front leg and the eye on the same side wouldn't open all the way, matter always crusted in that eye, although he didn't drool. Cese'd only eat soft food, canned, favored Luck's pinto beans when he could get them, yeah, Matley gave him the deluxe treatment, fed him on top of an old chest of drawers against the propane tank so nobody could steal his supper. Cese went on September ninth.

Leesburg. Called so because Matley found him dumped on a Virginia map that must have fallen out of the car by accident. Two pups on a map of Virginia and a crushed McDonald's bag, one pup dead, the other live, still teeny enough to suck Matley's little finger, and he decided on the name Leesburg over Big Mac, more dignity there. When that train first started running, Leesburg would storm the wheels, never fooled with the chickenfeed freight train, he knew where the trouble was. Fire himself at the wheels, snarling and barking, chasing and snap, and he scared some of the sightseers, who slammed their windows shut. Although a few threw food at him from the dining coach. Then one afternoon Matley was coming down the tracks after scavenging spikes, and he spotted a big wad of fur between two ties and thought, "That Missy's really shedding," because Missy was the longest-haired dog he had at the time, and this was a sizeable hair hunk. But when he got home, here came Leesburg wagging a piece of bloody bone sheathed in a shredded tail. Train'd took it, bone sticking out that bloody hair like a half-shucked ear of corn, and Matley had to haul him off to Dr. Simmons, who'd docked it down like a Doberman. Leesburg went on the thirtieth of September.

That sweet, sweet Carmel. Bless her heart. Sure, most of them, you tender them and they'll tender you back, but Carmel, she'd not just reciprocate, she'd soak up the littlest love piece you gave her and return it tenfold power. She would. Swan her neck back and around, reach to Matley's ear with her tiny front teeth and air-nibble as for fleas. Love solidified in a dog suit. Sometimes Matley'd break down and buy her a little bacon, feed it to her with one hand while he rump-scratched with his other, oh, Carmel curling into U-shaped bliss. That was what happiness looked like, purity, good. Matley knew. Carmel disappeared five days after Cese.

Guinea he held even closer, that Guinea a solder, a plug, a glue. Guinea he could not lose. Now Guinea wasn't one he found, she came from up at Mitchell's, he got her as a pup. Her mother was a slick-skinned beaglish creature, a real nervous little dog, Matley saw the whole litter. Two pups came out normal, two did not, seemed the genes leaked around in the mother's belly and swapped birthbags, ended up making one enormous lumbery retarded pup, twice the size the normal ones, and then, like an afterbirth with fur and feet, came Guinea. A scrap of leftover animal material, looked more like a possum than a dog, and more like a guinea pig than either one, the scrap as bright as the big pup was dumb, yes, she was a genius if you factored in her being a dog, but Matley was the only one who'd take her. "Nobody else even believes what she *is*!" Mrs. Mitchell said. From the start, Guinea craved pockets, and that was when Matley started going about in sweatshirts with big muff-like pockets in front, cut-off sleeves for the heat, and little Guinea with him always, in the pocket sling, like a baby possum or a baby 'roo or, hell, like a baby baby. Guinea luxuring in those pockets. Pretending it was back before she was born and came out to realize wasn't another creature like her on earth. Matley understood. Guinea he kept close.

Columbus Day weekend. Nine dogs down. Matley collapsed in his lawn chair by the househole. Matley spent quite a bit of time in his lawn chair by the househole, didn't own a TV and didn't read much besides *Coonhound Bloodlines* and *Better Beagling* magazines; Matley would sit there and knuckle little Guinea's head. Fifteen years it had been since the house swam off, the househole now slow-filling with the hardy plants, locust and cockleburs and briar, the old coal furnace a-crawl with poison ivy. Fifteen years, and across the tracks, what had been the most fertile piece of bottom in the valley, now smothered with the every-year-denser ragweed and stickweed and mock orange and puny too-many sycamore saplings. Matley could feel the loose part slipping, the emptiness pitting, he held Guinea close in his pocket. Way up the tracks, the tourist train, mumbling. Matley shifted a little and gritted his teeth.

The Mitchells had ridden the train once when they had a special price for locals, they said the train people told a story for every sight. Seemed if there wasn't something real to tell, they made something up, and if there was something to tell, but it wasn't good enough, they stretched it. Said they told that the goats that had run off from Revie decades ago and gone feral up in the Trough were wild mountain goats, like you'd see out West. Said they told how George Washington's brother had stayed at the Puffinburger place and choked to death on a country-ham sandwich. Said they pointed to this tree in Malcolms' yard and told how a Confederate spy had been hanged

103

from it, and Mr. Mitchell said, "That oak tree's old, but even if it was around a hundred and forty years ago, wasn't big enough to hang a spy. Not to mention around here they'd be more likely to hang a Yankee." Matley couldn't help wondering what they told on him, but he didn't ask. He'd never thought much about how his place looked until he had these train people looking at him all the time. He was afraid to ask. And he considered those mutt puppies, sleeping forever.

By that time, he'd made more than a few trips to Oaken Acre Estates despite himself (how old soft people could do such a thing). He'd sneak up in there and spy around, never following the new road on top of the ridge, but by another way he knew. A path you picked up behind where the sheep barn used to be, the barn now collapsed into a quarter-acre sprawl of buckled rusty tin, but if you skirted it careful, leery of the snakes, there was a game path above the kudzu patch. He usually took four or five dogs, Hickory and Tick—they liked to travel—and Guinea in his pocket, of course Guinea went. They'd scramble up into the stand of woods between househole and subdivision, Matley scuttling the path on the edges of his feet, steep in there, his one leg higher than the other, steadying Guinea with one hand. Matley tended towards clumsy and worried about falling and squashing Guinea dead. This little piece of woods was still Matley's piece of woods, had been deeded to him, and Matley, when he moved on that little land, could feel beyond him, on his bare shoulders and arms, how far the land went before. Matley angled along, keen for any dog sign, dog sound, dog sight, yeah, even dead-dog odor. But there was nothing to see, hear, stink.

Then they'd come out of the woods to the bottoms of the slopey backyards, shaley and dry with the struggling grass where the outsiders played at recreating those Washington suburbs they'd so desperately fled. Gated-off, security-systemed, empty yard after empty yard after empty, everything stripped down past stump, no sign of a living thing up in there, nor even a once-live thing dead. Hickory and Tick and whoever else had come would sniff, then piss, the lawns, been here, yeah, me, while Matley kept to the woods edge, kept to shelter, kept to shade. Guinea breathing under his chest. He had no idea where the pureblood-dog people lived, and they left no sign—no dogs, no pens, no fences—and although the ridge was full of look-alike houses, garages, gazebos, utility sheds, a swimming pool, it was the emptiest place he'd ever felt. How you

104

could kill a piece of ground without moving it anywhere. And Matley'd watch, he'd listen, he'd sniff best he could. But no dog sights, no dog sounds, no smells, and nothing to feel but his own sticky sweat. Matley'd never discover a thing.

Matley tensed in his lawn chair, nine dogs gone, Guinea in his pocket, Junior Junior cranky in his lap. He listened to that train creak and come, the train was coming and coming—it was always coming and you would never get away. The train slunk around the turn and into sight, its bad music an earbeat, a gutbeat, ta TA ta TA ta TA, locomotive slow-pulling for the sightseers to better see the sights, and how did they explain Matley? Plopped between Winnebagos and householc with some eighteen doghouses up his yard. How did he fit into this land that time forgot? ta TA ta TA ta TA, the beat when it passed the joints in the rails, and the screee sound over the rail beat, and even over top of that, a squealing, that ear-twisting song, a sorry mean ear-paining song. Starers shouldered up in open cars with cameras bouncing off golf-shirted bellies, and from the enclosed cars, some would wave. They would only wave if they were behind glass. And Matley would never wave back.

He comes to know. In the dream, he is a younger man than young he ever was, younger than he was born, and the hillside he hell-heaves, it's hill without end. The leaves loud under snow crust, his boots busting, ground cracking, the whole earth moanering, and him, him helling. Snow lying in dapples, mottles, over hillside, ridgeside, dog-marked like that, saddles, white snow saddles, see, his side seizing, breath in a blade, and the dog. Who he dream-knows is a girl dog, he knows that, the dog haunch-sat waiting pant, pant. His hill pant, her dog pant, the blade in his ribs, who pants? say good dog "good dog" good, him helling and the dog roped leashed tethered to a cat-faced red oak black against the snow blank, dog a darker white than the snow white and. He cannot ever reach her.

Eventually it trickled down to them in town. A few had seen. The fuel oil man. The UPS. Gilbert who drove the school bus to the turn-around where the road went from gravel to dirt. Dog Man blundering in bushes, whistling and yodeling some chint-chant dog-call, when few people besides the Mitchells had ever heard Muttie speak beyond shopping grunts. Of course, there were the lost ads, too, and although Matley wouldn't spend the extra dollar to print his name, just put a phone number there, well, the swifter ones put it together for those who were slow. Then somebody cornered Mr. Mitchell in the Super Fresh, and he confirmed it, yeah, they were vanishing off, and right away the story went around that Muttie was down twenty-seven dogs to a lean forty-eight. The UPS driver said he didn't think those old people out in Oaken Acre Estates were hard enough for such a slaughter, but then somebody pointed out the possibilities of poison, "people like that, scared of guns, they'll just use poison," a quiet violence you didn't have to see or touch. Yeah. A few speculated that the dogs just wised up, figured out Cat was crazy and left, and others blamed it on out-of-work chicken catchers from Hardy County. One (it was Mr. Puffinburger, he didn't appreciate the ham sandwich story) suspected the train people. Who knew to what lengths they'd go, Mr. Puffinburger said, the househole, the campers, the doghouses and Mr. Hound, that scenery so out of line with the presentation, so far from the scheme of decoration. Who knew how they might fix ole Beagle Boy and his colony of dogs. He'd heard they tried to organize the 4-H'ers for a big trash clean-up. Then a sizeable and committed contingent swore Matley had done it himself and ate 'em, and afterwards either forgot about it or was trying to trick people into pity, "I wouldn't put anything past that boy."

"I wouldn't, either, now. He's right, buddy. Buddy, he. Is. Right."

"Hell, they were all of them crazy, you could see it in their eyes."

"And I heard Charles lives out in Washington State now, but he won't work. Say he sits around all day in a toolshed reading up on the Indians."

"Well," the last one said. "People are different."

Matley standing at his little sink washing up supper dishes, skillet-sized pancakes and gravy from a can. His dogs have took up a dusk-time song. An I'm gonna bark because I just want to song, a song different from an I'm barking at something I wanna catch song or I'm barking at somebody trying to sneak up song or I'm howling because I catch a contagion of the volunteer fire department siren-wailing different from I'm barking at a trainfull of gawkers song. A sad sad song. The loose parts in him. Daylight puts a little hold down on it, but with the dark, nothing tamps it, you never know. You got to hold tight. He'd seen Johnby again that morning, humping along through the ditch by the road, and now, behind his eyes, crept Johnby, hulking and hunching to the time of the song. Dogs sought

106

Johnby because Johnby wasn't one to bathe much and dogs liked to pull in his scents, Johnby could no doubt bait dogs to him, Matley is thinking. The way Johnby's lip would lift and twitch. Muscles in a dead snake moving. Tic.

Matley stepped out, pulled Guinea from his pocket and took a look. As sometimes happened, for a second he was surprised to see her tail. The dog song made a fog around them, from sad to eerie, Matley heard the music go, while Matley counted those dog voices, one two three to twelve. Matley hollowing under his heart (the part slipping), the fear pimpling his skin, and then he called, moany, a whisper in his head: *come out come out come out come out.*

He breathed the odor the place made of an evening, a brew of dropping temperature, darkness and househole seep. A familiar odor. The odor of how things fail. Odor of ruin in progress, of must and stale hay, spoiling silage, familiar, and mildew and rotting wood and flaked paint; twenty-year-old manure, stagnant water, decaying animal hides, odor of the househole and what falls in it, the loss smell, familiar, the odor of the inside of his head. And Matley stroked little Guinea, in full dark now, the dog song dimming, and he heard Mrs. Mitchell again ("but I never did want to have more than two or three"), the not-question she used to ask, him not thinking directly on it, but thinking under thinking's place, and he knows if you get a good one, you can feel their spirits in them from several feet away, right under their fur, glassy and clear and dew-grass smelling. If you get a good one. You can feel it. No blurriness to the spirit of a dog, no haze, they're unpolluted by the thinking, by memories, by motives, you can feel that spirit raw, naked bare against your own. And dogs are themselves and aren't nothing else, just there they are, full in their skins and moving on the world. Like they came right out of it, which they did, which people did, too, but then people forget, while dogs never do. And when Matley was very young he used to think, if you love them hard enough, they might turn into people, but then he grew up a little and knew, what good would that be? So then he started wishing, if you loved one hard enough, it might speak to you. But then he grew up even more and knew that wasn't good, either, unless they spoke dog, and not just dog language, but dog ideas, things people'd never thought before in sounds people'd never heard, Matley knew. And Matley had studied the way a dog loved, the ones that had it in them to love right, it was true, not every one did, but the ones that loved right, Matley stroking, cup, cradle and

107

hold, gaze in dog eyes, the gentle passing. Back and forth, enter and return, the gentle passing, passing between them, and Matley saw that love surpass what they preached at church, surpass any romance he'd heard of or seen, surpass motherlove loverlove babylove, he saw that doglove simple. Solid. And absolutely clear. Good dog. Good dog, now. Good. Good.

Meredith. Was just a couple weeks shy of dropping her pups, no mystery there, she was puffed out like a nail keg, and who in their right mind would steal a pregnant Lab/Dalmatian mix? it could only be because they were killing them, if Matley'd ever doubted that, which he had. Which he'd had to. Meredith'd been a little on the un-brightish side, it was true, had fallen into the househole more than once in broad day, the spots on her head had soaked through and af-fected her brain, but still. And it was her first litter, might have made some nice pups, further you got from the purebloods, Matley had learned, better off you'll be. Meredith went on October seventeenth.

Muddy Gut. A black boy with a soft gold belly, and gold hair sprouting around his ears like broom sedge, soft grasses like that, he had the heaviest and most beautiful coat on the place, but the coat's beauty the world constantly marred, in envy or spite. Muddy Gut drew burrs, beggar's lice, devil's pitchforks, ticks, and Matley'd work tirelessly at the clobbed-up fur, using an old currycomb, his own hairbrush, a fork. Muddy Gut patient and sad, aware of his glory he could not keep, while Matley held a match to a tick's behind until it pulled out its head to see what was wrong. A constant grooming Mat-ley lavished over Muddy Gut, Matley forever untangling that lovely spoiled fur, oh sad sullied Muddy, dog tears bright in his deep gold eyes. Muddy Gut went on October twenty-first.

Junior Junior. Matley'd known it was bound to happen, Ray Junior or Junior Junior one. Although they were both a bit ill-tempered, they were different from the rest, they were Raymond descendants several generations down. Junior Junior was Ray Junior's son, and Ray Junior was mothered by a dog across the river called Ray Ray, and Ray Ray, Mr. Mitchell swore, was fathered by the original Ray-mond. In Junior Junior there was Raymond resemblance, well, a lit-tle anyway, in temperament for sure, and Matley didn't stop to think too hard about how a dog as inert as Raymond might swim the river to sow his oats. Raymond was the dog who came when Matley could no longer make the toy dogs live and who stayed until after the flood, and for a long time, he was the only dog Matley had to love. They'd found Raymond during a Sunday dinner at Mrs. Fox's Homestead Restaurant when Matley had stretched out his leg and hit something soft under the table, which surprised him. Was a big black dog, bloodied around his head, and come to find out it was a stray Mrs. Fox had been keeping for a few weeks, he'd been hit out on 50 that very morning and had holed up under the table to heal himself. Later, Revie liked to tell, "Well, you started begging and carrying on about this hit dog, and Mrs. Fox gave him up fast—I don't believe she much wanted to fool with him anyway—and here he's laid ever since, hateful and stubborn and foul-smelling. Then after we got done eating, Mrs. Fox came out of the kitchen, and she looked at our plates, and she said, 'You would of thought finding that hit dog under your table would of put a damper on your appetites. But I see it didn't!' It was a compliment to her cooking, you see." Junior Junior was Raymond's great-great grandson, and he disappeared on Halloween.

Matley in the bunk at night. He'd wake without the knowledge. He'd lose the loss in his sleep, and the moments right after waking were the worst he'd ever have: finding the loss again and freshly knowing. The black surge over his head, hot wash of saw-sided pain, then the bottom'd drop out. Raw socket. Through the weeks, the loss rolling, compounding, just when he'd think it couldn't get worse, think a body couldn't hold more hurt, another dog would go, the loss an infinity inside him. Like how many times you can bisect a line. They call it heartbreak, but not Matley, Matley learned it was not that clean, nowhere near that quick, he learned it was a heartgrating, this forever loss in slow-motion, forever loss without diminishment of loss, without recession, without ease, the grating. And Matley having had in him always the love, it pulsing, his whole life, reaching, for a big enough object to hold this love, back long before this crippling mess, he reached, and, now, the only end for that love he'd ever found being taken from him, too, and what to do with this love? Pummelling at air. Reaching, where to put this throat-stobbing surge, where, what? the beloved grating away. His spirit in his chest a single wing that opens and folds, opens and folds. Closing on nothing. Nothing there. And no, he says, no, he says, no, he says, no.

Come November, Matley was still running his ads, and he got a call from a woman out at Shanks, and though he doubted a dog of his would travel that far, he went anyway. The month was overly warm, seasons misplaced like they'd got in recent years, and coming home right around dusk, he crested High Boy with his windows half-down. At first, he wasn't paying much mind to anything except rattling the Chevette over that rutty road, only certain ways you could take the road without tearing off the muffler. But suddenly it came to him he didn't see no dogs. No dogs lounging around their houses, and no dogs prancing out to meet him. No dogs squirting out the far corners of the clearings at the sound of the car, even though it was dog-feeding time. No Guinea under the camper, no Hickory and Tick fighting over stripped-down deer legs, no welcome-home dog bustle. Not a dog on the place. None.

A panic began in the back of Matley's belly. Fizzing. He pushed it down by holding his breath. He parked the car, swung out slow, and when he stood up (hold on tight) there between the car seat and door, he felt his parts loosen. A rush of opening inside. He panic-scanned Winnebago and househole, sunken barns and swaying sheds, his head cocked to listen. Doghouses, tracks, bottom and trees, his eyes spinning, a vacuum coring his chest, and then he heard himself holler. He hollered "Here!" and he hollered "Come!" and he hollered "Yah! Yah! Yah!" still swivelling his head to take in every place. Him hollering "Here, Fella! Tick, C'mon now! Yah, Big Girl, Yah," his voice squawling higher while the loose part slipped. Matley hollered, and then he screamed, he clapped and hooed, he whistled until his mouth dried up. And then, from the direction of the sheep barn, way up the hill, he spied the shape of Guinea.

Little Guinea, gusting over the ground like a blown plastic bag. Matley ran to meet her. Guinea, talking and crying in her little Guinea voice, shuttling hysterical around his shins and trying to jump, and Matley scooped her up and into his pocket, stroking and trembling, and there, Guinea. There. And once she stilled, and he stilled, Matley heard the other.

Dog cries at a distance. Not steady, not belling or chopping, not like something trailed or treed. No, this song was a dissonant song. Off beat and out of tune. A snarling brutal song.

Matley wheeled. He charged up the pasture to the sheep barn there, grass tearing under his boots. He leaned into the path towards the subdivision, despite dark was fast dropping, and he hadn't any light. He pounded that game path crazy, land tilted under his feet,

110

his sight swinging in the unfocus of darkened trees, and the one hand held Guinea while the dead leaves roared. He was slipping and catching his balance, he was leaping logs when he had to, his legs bendy and the pinwheel of his head, and the parts inside him, unsoldering fast, he could feel his insides spilling out of him, Matley could no longer grip, he was falling. This land, this land under him, you got to grip, tight, Guinea crying, and now, over top the dry leaves' shout, he heard not only yelping, but nipping and growling and brush cracking, and Matley was close.

It was then that it came to him. He dreamed the dream end awake. Him helling up that endless hillslope, but the slope finally ends, and he sees the white dog tree-tied ear-cocked patient waiting, but still, Matley knows, something not right he can't tell. Black trees unplummetting out of white snow skiff, and Matley helling. Him helling. Him. Helling. He reaches, at last he reaches her, a nightmare rainbow's end, and he's known all along what he has to do, he thrusts his hand behind her to unleash her, free her, and then he understands, sees: behind the live dog front, she is bone. Her front part, her skin and face, a dog mask, body mask, and behind that, the not right he's always sensed but could not see, bone, and not even skeleton bone, but chunky bone, crumbled and granular and fragrant, the blood globbed up in chunks and clots, dry like snow cold day skiff and Matley moaning, he'd broke free of the woods and into a little clearing below the subdivision, ground rampant with sumac and dormant honeysuckle and grape and briar. It truly darkening now, and the way it's harder to see in near dark than it is in full dark, how your eyes don't know what to do with it, and Matley was stopped, trembling, loose, but he could hear. A house-sized mass of brush, a huge tangle of it making like a hill itself, dense looped and layered, crowned with the burgundy sumac spears. That whole clump asound with dog, and Matley felt himself tore raw inside, the flesh strips in him, and Matley started to yell.

He stood at a short distance and yelled at them to come out, come out of there, he knew inside himself not to dare go in, he knew before seeing what he couldn't bear to see. But nary a dog so much as poked its head out and looked at Matley, he could hear them snarling, hear bones cracking, see the brush rattle and sway, but to the dogs Matley wasn't there, and then he smelled it. Now the smell of it curled to him on that weird warm wind, as it had no doubt curled down to the househole and lured the dogs up, and he was screaming now, his voice scraping skin off his throat, ripping, and Matley, with the single ounce of gentle still left in his hand, pulled out Guinea and set her down. Then he stooped and plunged in.

Now he was with them, blundering through this confusion of plant, and he could see his dogs, saw them down through vine branch and briar. Louise, the biggest, hunkered over and tearing at it, growling if another dog got close, she held her ground, and Ray Junior writhing in it on her back, and Honey lavering his neck in dried guts. Big Girl drawn off to the side crunching spine, while Hickory and Tick battled over a big chunk, rared up on their hind legs and wrestling with their fronts, and Matley pitched deeper, thorns tearing his hands. Matley tangled in vine and slim trunk, the sumac tips, that odor gusting all over his head, and he reached for Tick's tail to break up the fight. But when he touched Tick, Tick turned on him. Tick spun around gone in his eyes, and he drew back his lips on Matley and he bared his teeth to bite, and Matley, his heart cleaved in half, dropped the tail and sprang back. And the moment he did, he saw what he'd been terrified he'd see all along. Or did he see? A sodden collar still buckled around a rotting neck, did he? The live dogs eating the dead dogs there, what he'd suspected horrified all along, did he? And then Matley was whacking, flailing, windmilling looney, beating with his hands and arms and feet and legs the live dogs off the dead things because he had nothing else to beat with, he was not even screaming any longer, he was beyond sound, Matley beyond himself, Matley reeling, dropping dropped down until Guinea was there. Against him. Hurtling up to be held. And Matley took her, did hold her. He stroked her long guinea hair, whispering, good girl, Guinea. Good.

Matley stood in the midst of the slaughter, shaking and panting, palming little Guinea's head. Most of the beat dogs had slunk off a ways to wait, but the bolder ones were already sneaking back. And finally Matley slowed enough, he was spent enough, to squint again through the dim and gradual understand.

There were no collars there.

Slowly.

These colors of fur, these shapes and sizes of bones. Were not dogs. No.

Groundhogs, squirrels, possums, deer.

Then he felt something and turned and saw: Johnby crouched in the dead grass, rifle stock stabbed in the ground and the barrel grooving his cheek. Johnby was watching.

Somehow it got going around in town that it had been a pile of dead dogs, and some said it served Muttie right, that many dogs should be illegal anyway. But others felt sad. Still other people had heard it was just a bunch of dead animals that ole Johnby had collected, Lord knows if he'd even shot them, was the gun loaded? his family said not; could have been roadkill. Then there were the poison believers, claimed it was wild animals and dogs both, poisoned by the retirees in Oaken Acre Estates, and Bill Bates swore his brother-in-law'd been hired by the imports to gather a mess of carcasses and burn 'em up in a brush pile, he just hadn't got to the fire yet. Mr. Puffinburger held his ground, he felt vindicated, at least to himself, because this here was the lengths to which those train people would go, this here was how far they'd alter the landscape to suit themselves. What no one was ever certain about was just how many'd been lost. Were they all gone? had any come back? was he finding new ones? how many were out there now? Fred at the feed store reported that Muttie wasn't buying any dog food, but the UPS truck driver had spied him along a creek bed with a dog galloping to him in some hillbilly Lassie-come-home.

Despite all the rumors, it must be said that after that, they didn't talk about Dog Man much anymore. Even for the skeptics and the critics, the subject of Matley lost its fun. And they still saw Muttie, although he came into town less often now, and when they did see him, they looked more closely, and a few even sidled up to him in the store in case he would speak. But the dogless Matley, to all appearances, was exactly like the dogful one.

These days, some mornings, in the lost-dog aftermath, Matley wakes in his camper having forgot the place, the year, his age. He's always had such spells occasionally, losses of space and time, but now it's more than ever. Even though when he was a kid, Mom Revie'd only allow one live dog at a time and never inside, they did have for some years a real dog named Blanchey, some kind of wiener-beagle mix. And now, these mornings, when Matley wakes, believing himself eight in the flood-gone house, he hears Mom Revie's dog-calling song.

Oh, the way that woman could call a dog, it was bluegrass operatic.

113

"Heeeeeere, Blanchey! Heeeeeeere, Blanchey, Blanchey, Blanchey," she'd yodel off the back porch, the "here" pulled taut to eight solid seconds, the "Blanchey" a squeaky two-beat yip. Then "You, Blanchey! C'mere, girl! 'mon!" fall from high-octave "here's" to a businesslike burr, and when Blanchey'd still not come, Revie'd switch from cajole to command. "Yah, Blanchey, Yah! Yah! Yah! Yah!" a bellydeep bass; while the "Here's" seduced, the "Yah's" insist, oh, it plunged down your ear and shivered your blood, ole Mom Revie's dog-calling song. And for some minutes, Matley lets himself hover in that time, he just lies abed and pleasures in the tones. Until she cuts loose in frustration with a two-string riff—"comeoutcomeout-comeoutcomeout"—rapid banjo plinkplunk wild, and Matley wakes enough to know ain't no dogs coming. To remember all the dogs are gone but one.

He crawls out of the bunk and hobbles outside. Guinea pokes her head from his pocket, doesn't like what she sniffs, pulls back in. It is March, the train season is long over, but Matley hears it anyway. Hears it coming closer, moaning and sagging like it's about to split. Hears the haunty music that train plays, haunty like a tawdry carnival ride. Train moving slow and overfull, passing the joints in the rails, beat beat, and the screee sound over the railbeat, he hears it shriek-squeal over steel. And Matley stands there between househole and Winnebago, the morning without fog and the air like glass, and he understands he is blighted landscape now. He is disruption of scenery. Understands he is the last one left, and nothing but a sight. A sight. Sight, wheel on rail click it on home, Sight. Sight. Sight. Then Matley does not hear a thing.

Nominated by David Jauss, Shenandoah

SOMEONE NAKED AND ADORABLE

by DAVID KIRBY

from SOUTHERN POETRY REVIEW

When I see the sign that says Nude Beach,
                I scuttle right over, though when I get there,
all I see is three guys who look like me,
                two in baggy K-Mart-type bathing suits
and one in a "banana hammock" of the type favored
        by speed racers and the lesser European nobility,

and as they wait for the naked people to appear,
                all three scowl at the sand, the water,
the very heavens themselves, the clouds
                as raw as the marble from which Bernini
carved the *Apollo and Daphne* whose bodies rang like bells
        when the restorers touched them,

like the bells of Santa Croce that summer
                that woke me and Barbara every morning
in Florence, which we called, not "Florence,"
                but "Guangdong Province," because
Hong Kong was in the news a lot in those days,
        and Hong Kong is near Guangdong Province,

and the bells would go *guang! dong!* as though
                a drunken priest were swinging from the bellrope.

115

Now surely that is "the music of the spheres"
                    (Sir Thomas Browne) as opposed to
"the still, sad music of humanity" (Wordsworth),
            which is just some guy playing a violin in the corner.

Or four guys: a string quartet, and not a good one, either,
                    one that meant well but hadn't practiced
very much, or maybe one that hadn't even
                    meant well, that just wanted to get paid,
maybe meet a scullery maid or two,
            perhaps a nymphomaniacal marchioness.

What the hell do people want, anyway?
                    Why does Barbara adore the cameo I gave her
that depicts Leda and the swan, an episode
                    in interspecies relationships that just gives me
the creeps? There must be something there
            about being, not dominated, but overcome—

about allowing oneself to be mastered
                    by a force greater than oneself
or just another person who has taken on
                    temporary godlike powers,
for life has a sting in its tail, like a chimera,
            and you can no more draw that sting yourself

than you can tickle yourself,
                    whereas another person can do both.
Why, in the "cabinet of secrets"
                    of the Archeological Museum in Naples,
I saw a bell in the shape of a gladiator at war
            not with another warrior but with his own *Schwanz!*

It had rolled back up on its back,
                    if a penis can be said to have a back,
and was clawing and snapping at its master
                    with the nails and teeth of a lion!
And in turn he, the gladiator, was slashing back
            with broadsword in one hand and some kind

116

of lion slapper or *Schwanz* slapper in the other!
                    Slap, slap, slice, slap! That would sting,
wouldn't it? And it's a bell, remember,
                    so the whole was meant to be struck
and struck hard, be it by angry bachelor
            or vengeful wife! Dong! And given the choice

of which part of the bell to strike,
                    who wouldn't strike the pecker-penis,
the ravening lion of unrequited desire?
                    As if to say, *you're* the one who's causing
all the problems, *you're* the one body part
            who's making trouble for all the others!

No, no, we want something else altogether,
                    for, as wise old Mr. Emerson says in
A Room With a View, Love is not the body
                    but is of the body, the one we are waiting for
there on the beach, rooted in the sand like shore birds,
            our every atom tingling with desire.

Nominated by Jim Daniels, Ed Falco, Southern Poetry Review

RAGING WATERS

by BRENDA MILLER

from WITNESS

ABOVE ME, the loudspeakers croon *All I need is the air that I breathe and to love you.* In this particular hour, at Raging Waters in Salt Lake City, everyone seems to believe it: the many children, and the adults who trot behind them, all of them wet and smiling, their bare legs and arms and belly buttons flashing through the heat. Some of them hoist pink rafts onto their shoulders; some drag blue tubes behind them; some have no rafts at all, just their damp feet slapping on the asphalt, their arms flung high as they slide down the chutes, through the fountains, tumbling into the frothy water. The crowd neither walks nor runs, but moves like one organism with many limbs; it undulates in all directions around the water slides, toward the snack bar, into the wave pool. A flock of boys scatters at the edge of the pool; teenage girls skitter by, the skin of their thighs and bellies radiant. Bathing suits punctuate this expanse of flesh like mere afterthought.

From where I've chosen to sit in the shade, in my black Land's End, Kindest-Cut tank, I have a clear view of the splashdowns from Shotgun Falls, The Terminator, and several loop-de-loop affairs that wind down from on high, their sources impossible to decipher. One slide drops vertically into a pool; the riders tuck themselves onto yellow sleds and plummet down, then bounce across the surface of the water like skipped rocks. For an hour, I watch people zoom out of tunnels and plunge over waterfalls, their legs and arms akimbo, one person after another, skimming around curves, flying, arcing, descending, their screams merging into a pleasant, discordant harmony, like jazz.

Though hundreds of children roam the crowd, carrying with them the opportunity for any number of altercations, I hear no cries, no parents shouting, no slaps, no whines. In the line to the snack bar (hamburgers $2.50; pretzels $1.00), the children can have whatever they want; they clutch damp dollars in their fists and hop from foot to foot, towels draped over their shoulders, or tucked around their waists.

My charges have already melded into the crowd. Hannah and Sarah are not my children, though I've come to use the word "my" when I speak of them; they are my boyfriend's girls, and I agreed, reluctantly at first, to take them on this outing to give their father a break. I've known them for two years, but I have only a few weeks more to spend with them; I'll be moving to another state, leaving them behind with promises not to forget. Though I know we will, all of us. Already, I can hardly remember their faces, here in this crowd where all the children begin to look alike—their skin slick, their hair one damp color, their bathing suits askew on bodies that take no notice.

With Sarah, who is six, I've already been to Dinosaur Pond, and swum among its sighing palms, slid through the primordial waters. We put our raft into the wave pool ("Utah's Beach") and rode the crest of the waves into shore. With the strength of someone twice her size, she tugged the raft back into deep water. Though she can't yet swim, she showed no fear as the waves broke over her head; she emerged from each one, her eyes wide, her mouth sputtering, her hands splayed at her sides. She staggered and fell back, like someone intoxicated; I lunged for her, but already she was up, laughing, her bathing-suit straps down around her elbows. Her eyes, laser-bright, no longer looked out on this earthly world. I shouted her name, but she had eyes only for the water, searching the waves, baiting them to engulf her once again. Looking at her, I could imagine her face the day she was born: her mouth a puckered exclamation of wonder, her eyes gazing back to a place I'd never be able to fathom. I reached for her again, and she was slippery as a fish, or a newborn, sliding out of my grasp.

I think I could stay cheerfully on the lawn for the rest of the day, but Hannah, the nine-year-old, issues a challenge. *White Lightning*. She knows I'm afraid to go down the slides, we've discussed this. Before we came, I told her I'd had a bad experience on a crude water slide

119

as a child; I've said there's no way I'm going down. But now she stands over me on the grass, her bikini dripping, her hands gripping her shoulders. She knows she has me; her face is alight. She reminds me that I've told her to face her fears head on, to try whatever you think is impossible.

The first, and only, time I've been on a water slide was almost thirty years ago, when I was twelve years old. I remember the tall slide in an abandoned field outside L.A. No ponds, no dinosaurs, no carefully engineered drops: only a trickle of water splashing down a Plexiglas slope, with three plateaus spaced at irregular intervals. It reminded me of a vertical slip-'n-slide; the riders careened off onto a wet, plastic drop cloth spread over the grass.

I wore a bikini with a halter top whose straps cut into the skin at the base of my neck. It was a hot summer night, the air stagnant and thick, the vapor lights of a distant air field shimmering through the smog. I climbed the ladder with my brother and his friends, those boys from the basketball team who made me breathless with a vague desire. I was aware of my body in the bikini as I climbed, the boys close behind me; I knew my legs were the finest part of me then, slender and long and tanned. I laughed carelessly as we reached the top, and turned to say something witty, but the boys pushed past me to grab their mats and hurtle down the slide, whooping. I watched them go, some of them head first, and in moments they became small distant bodies strewn across the grass. I paused a moment. My brother handed me a mat. "Go," he said, jerking his head. I crouched. He pushed me off, and I was sliding down, fast. Too fast.

No one had said anything about technique. No one had said this task required any finesse at all. I made the mistake of leaning forward at first, off balance, and as I gripped my mat, I *flew* down the side of that mountain, lifting off at each plateau and slamming down on my tailbone, bouncing up, skidding down. My body no longer belonged to me; it uncoiled into space, leaving me behind. At the bottom, when I finally veered off onto land, I was sobbing. Not whimpering in a sad, ladylike way, but crying big, snotty tears I wiped off with the flat of my hand. My brother and his friends already scrambled to go back up, but they hesitated, looking at me with their heads cocked to the side, as if I were a strange animal they'd never before encountered. They looked to my brother. I saw his lips twist with embarrassment as he held out his hand to help me. "It's supposed to be *fun*," he hissed, then let me go. The boys turned away en masse, their boxer shorts barely hugging their bony hips, their hairy calf muscles bulging as they climbed the ladder again.

It's supposed to be fun. All my life, it seems now, I've murmured that phrase to myself in the most unlikely places: on the playground as a child, at the mall as a teenager, even—as I've grown into middle age—during lovemaking with men both sweet and kind. I've said it with both wonder and despair, as if "fun" were a foreign term I've yet to fully comprehend. Now, nearly thirty years later, I stand with Hannah on the steps to White Lightning. I don't think I've ever seen her so happy, and thus so beautiful; her entire body seems incandescent, lit up with her triumph at getting me here at all, on the wooden stairs high above Raging Waters. Her hair is plastered to her head, outlining the bones so perfectly joined; her belly, midway between a child's and an adolescent's, distends just slightly between the top and bottom halves of her bathing suit. She clutches the front end of our raft, leaning toward the next step up, and the next. We have a view of the entire Salt Lake Valley from here. A haze obscures the Wasatch Front and below us golfers tee off on the 18th hole.

Hannah and I watch slider after slider go down Blue Thunder, the slower of the two rides on this platform, the one most people choose. I look to the left, at White Lightning, at the tight curves and the three sharp descents, the waterfall roaring off the end. "Why isn't anyone going down this one?" I ask, trying to be casual, but my voice squeaks up a little, and Hannah grins. "It's *fast*," she says. "That's why."

Finally we're at the top. A Raging Waters "Guest Assistant," in her white polo shirt and royal-blue shorts, watches us with lazy boredom through her sunglasses. No expression mars her placid face as I situate the raft in the starting gate, no expression of warning or respect. I sit in the back of the raft, with Hannah between my legs, and I look up at the girl a moment, wanting *something* from her—a benediction, perhaps—but she gives us only a little push with her sneaked foot, and we're off.

We enter the first curve fast, sliding up on one wall then the other, straightening out for the first drop where we lift off, *oh god*, into the air, and we bump down hard, but no pain and no time to think of pain, the water rushing us through a tunnel and into the next drop, *please*, and the next; I'm holding on to Hannah and leaning back, *yes!*, as we're spit out into the waterfall. We're sailing over it. My body no longer seems linked to me; it's lifted free of gravity and become only motion and speed and liquid as Hannah and I splash down into the pool.

I'm laughing now, not crying, but laughing so hard I can barely speak. The waters roil and dump us off the raft. Hannah hops out of the pool. She stands taut on the edge, looking down at me, eagerness trembling in all her limbs. There is so much I want to say, so much I *could* say, but all I manage to sputter is: *"That* was so much *fun."*

Hannah nods, smug in her knowledge of what fun is, satisfied to be the one teaching *me* a lesson. She pulls the raft from the water, raises her lovely eyebrows. "Again?" she asks. I look up at her. The chlorine burns my eyes, but I can see Hannah more clearly than I ever have before. Unlike my vision of Sarah in the wave pool, which rocketed her back to an infant, I imagine Hannah far into the future, as a young woman, gazing with this same intensity at a horse, at a man, at her own child sleeping in her arms. The water magnifies everything about her—her brave lips, her high cheekbones, her capable hands—and makes me believe beyond all reason that I really will know her forever.

Other sliders release into the pool, all hallelujahs and hosannas, splashing me off my feet. So I hoist my heavy body onto the cement. I sit there a moment, catching my breath, and the crowd throbs around me. It's grown larger but no less unified, feet slapping in every direction, voices raised in one keen avowal of fun. But Hannah is the only one to notice me here, a baptized convert in the midst of the masses. She's waiting for my answer. The tape on the loudspeaker has looped around full circle to *All I need is the air that I breathe and to love you.* I can only nod my head yes, when what I mean is: yes, my love, we'll do it again, and again, until the hours have spilled from this day and our time here is finally done.

Nominated by Kim Barnes, Bruce Beasley, Witness

QUELQUECHOSE

by DANA LEVIN

from RIVENDELL

You want to get in and then get out of the box.

form breakage form

—

I was in the fish shop, wondering why being experimental means
        not having a point—

        why experimentation in form is sufficient unto itself
                        (is it)

But I needed a new way to say things:
        sad tired I with its dulled violations, lyric with loss in its
    faculty den—

Others were just throwing a veil over suffering:
        glittery interesting I-don't-exist—

All over town, I marched around,
        ranting my jeremiad.

Thinking, What good is form if it doesn't *say anything*—

And by 'say' I meant wake somebody up.

Even here at the shores of Lake Champlain
        mothers were wrenching small arms out of sockets.

Not just the mothers. What were the fathers doing,
        wrenching small arms out of bedside caches—

How could I disappear into language when children were being
    called
        'fuckers'—
                    by their mothers—

        who were being called 'cunts' by their boyfriends—

        who were being called 'dickheads' behind their backs—

It wasn't that I was a liberal democrat, it was that
                        bodies had been divested of their souls—

        like poems—

Trying to get in or out of the box.

And the scallops said, "Pas des idees mais dans les choses."

And I said, "I'll have the Captain's Special with wedges instead of
    fries."

And everywhere in the fish shop the argument raged, it's baroque
    proportions,
        the conflict between harmony and invention.

But then a brilliance—

The movement of her gloved hands as she laid the haddock out
        one by one—

The sheered transparency of her latexed fingers,
        in and out of the lit display case as if they were yes, fish—

Laying haddock out in a plastic tub on a bed of ice,
      her lank brown hair pulled back from her face with a
  band—

Yes it was true she had to do this for the market
      but there was such beauty in it––

      she was the idea called Tenderness—

she was a girl who stood under fluorescent lights making
      six bucks an hour—

and she looked up at me and held out a haddock with both her
  hands,
      saying it was the best of the morning's catch.

Nominated by Rivendell

I AM NOT YOUR MOTHER

fiction by ALICE MATTISON

from PLOUGHSHARES

BEFORE THEY HAD EVER LIVED in the house, somebody's useless cow had sickened and died in the shed next door. The shaggy rope that tethered her still lay in a corner, so when Sonia figured out that her older sister, Goldie, was having to do with a boy, she got up in the night, disentangled the rope, and tied Goldie to a leg of their bed.

Goldie never sneaked out at night. The town was dark even during the day. Wooden sheds, shops, and houses leaned into one another, creating attenuated triangles of shadow that met and crossed and made further overlapping triangles: layers of deeper shadow. It wasn't hard for Goldie to meet the boy—who was tall and chubby, with a laugh that flung droplets onto her cheeks and made her ears tingle—during what was known as day.

In the morning, Goldie's leg jerked sideways when she turned to put her feet on the floor, and she laughed at her sister's trick, then untied the rope and tied up Sonia, who was still sleeping. The rope's rough fibers had hurt Sonia's fingers. When she felt Goldie's touch on her ankle, in her sleep, her sore hand went to her mouth. Sonia, at fourteen, still sucked her thumb.

Goldie became pregnant. Their parents were frightened. Nothing like this had happened in either of their families before. They hadn't known about the tall boy—who had gone to America. (Everyone wanted to leave if possible.) The parents never spoke of Goldie's big belly, but at last Aunt Leah, the mother's sister, came to see them. "Reuben and I have money for the ship," she said. "Give us the baby." Leah and Reuben had no children. Goldie screamed in childbirth and for days after, bleeding in the bed, but the baby, a girl, was taken the day of her birth. Goldie's breasts were hot. They felt as if they were about to explode. "Suck me, suck me," she cried to Sonia at night.

Aunt Leah was religious. She went to the ritual bath; when she married, she'd cut off her hair, and now wore a dusty wig. Goldie cried, "She'll shave my baby's head!" Sonia was impressed that her sister could imagine the bald baby they'd barely seen (whose ineffective kicks and arm-swats Sonia couldn't forget) as a grown girl with hair, getting married. Maybe in New York life would be different, Sonia told Goldie.

Aunt Leah, Uncle Reuben, and the baby, Rebecca (who was theirs, they told people), emigrated promptly. Goldie recovered quickly from childbirth, but she looked voluptuous from then on. A man who worked on the roads married her, though Sonia disliked him. He talked loudly in the presence of their still-frightened parents, but going to America was easy for him. He couldn't imagine things the rest of them feared, and didn't understand how faraway and wide the ocean was. Everyone had letters from relatives about the horrors of the passage, the trials of Ellis Island—but he didn't believe. Goldie, who could read a little, tried to show him a map in a schoolbook, but he tore out the page, saying, "Nothing like that." Sonia couldn't read but had some respect for print. She was shocked, but her angry brother-in-law, whose name was Aaron, was making a point: his experience—simpler than other people's—never did resemble what people who spoke in detail described, not to mention the subtleties reportedly found in books. In a moment he uncrumpled the map. "All right, we'll go to that place," he said, waving at half of North America.

They followed a cousin of his to Chicago. Goldie had mixed feelings. She would never have been permitted to tell Rebecca the truth. Aaron knew about the laughing boy and the baby, but didn't believe in them, either. In Chicago, nothing turned out as Goldie expected it to; Aaron's habit of doubt felt reasonable. Hardest was losing her daughter, but now Goldie was also separated from her parents and from Sonia, who couldn't even write a letter. Goldie remembered Sonia's shy mouth on her breasts in the middle of the night, her sister's tongue mastering the unfamiliar technique, her teeth held back but just grazing the nipple, giving relief and a terrible pleasure.

When Goldie had a baby boy, the old secret made her laugh and cry when he nursed.

She reared her boy, then three more, with spurts of pleasure at the time of the holidays—which she celebrated primarily with food—or when she'd hear indirectly of her sister. Best of all for Aaron and Goldie was sex, which was excellent, but second best was going out. They went to band concerts and parades, vaudeville and the Yiddish theater, then films. They ate out before anyone they knew. Aaron made a reasonable amount of money, not working on the roads here but selling fruit off a pushcart and later in a store. Goldie sometimes watched her husband when he didn't see her, across the street from his pushcart or outside his store, observing him with a customer. His big mouth opened wide when he spoke, and sometimes she thought she could hear his loud voice—dismissing, denying, doubting—even when she should have been out of earshot.

Sonia married a man who whispered respectfully to her parents. They couldn't always hear him, but they liked him. She soon had a girl and a boy. When her husband, Joseph, left for America alone, he announced his plans in such hushed conferences that nobody was surprised when he did what he said he'd do: he secured a job in New York and after two years sent money for his wife's passage, his children's, and his in-laws'. His own parents were dead. But Sonia's mother had something wrong with her eyes and was afraid she'd be turned back at Ellis Island. Saying goodbye at the train, Sonia and her parents pretended that their only important task was to make sure the children were warm enough. Their grandmother wrapped them in so many shawls, wiping her eyes with the corners, that the children could scarcely move.

On the trip to New York, Sonia thought only of her mother and father, whom she'd never see again. She was afraid she wouldn't find Goldie, and she couldn't remember why she cared about Joseph, but he met her in New York and had not lost his distinctive smell or sound; he had a quizzical way of speaking, as if he found himself a bit foolish, and in turn found that discovery amusing. The babies who were no longer babies made him shake his head in silence. When they were settled, Joseph wrote letters to Goldie for Sonia. The second summer, Goldie and Aaron and—by then—three boys came overnight on the train to visit. Sonia had had another daughter.

One day when Joseph was at work and Aaron was engrossed in a game of pinochle taking place in the street—not shouting, for once—the sisters and their children called on Aunt Leah, who lived at the end of a trolley ride. Goldie trembled when Leah's sturdy daughter kissed her gravely. Rebecca took little interest in the cousin from Chicago and her boys, but asked to hold Sonia's baby. Aunt Leah was quiet, and they quickly returned on the trolley to Sonia's house, not talking, busying themselves with the children. The next night, Aaron insisted that the women leave the children with a neighbor, and they all went to a boisterous performance at the theater. The actors' shouts, their stylized and exaggerated gestures, seemed to calm Aaron. Otherwise he was constantly restless; Sonia didn't know what he wanted and that made her feel like a bad hostess. She wondered what it was like to be Aaron, and got far enough to sense his relief when something was vacant, when nothing was inscribed on an object or a moment, so he didn't have to deny whatever others discerned in it.

Rebecca knew Sonia as a cousin, and Sonia's children—the boy, Morris, and, eventually, five sisters (Clara, Sophie, Sylvia, Bobbie, Minnie)—as slightly more distant cousins. At nine Rebecca scolded Cousin Sonia for insufficient attention to the Passover restrictions, and Sonia spoke sharply, then touched Rebecca's arm apologetically. Rebecca began taking the trolley herself to help Sonia with the children. She took good care of them, but was too strict about keeping them clean and quiet. She had unruly curly hair and a neat little nose rather like Reuben's, not that her father ever looked up from the Talmud to notice her. Cousin Rebecca didn't laugh, Morris and the girls complained. They sat her down and played her their favorite of a pile of records that their father had brought home one night, along with a Victrola: it was called "No News but What Killed the Dog," and told a story Rebecca found sad, though the others shrieked with laughter.
Rebecca finished high school and found a job typing. It was a Jewish company, and they gave her Saturday off, or she wouldn't have done it. Sonia's children didn't see her as often once she was working, but sometimes she'd come on Sundays. "Can I help, Cousin Sonia?" Rebecca would say, walking into the preparation of a meal or the bathing of small children. She said it so often that "Can I help, Cousin Sonia?" became a household joke, and the girls said it to one another whenever anybody picked up a dishrag or a paring knife.
Sonia had never learned to read—Sylvia tried to teach her, but Sonia's eyes became red and watery, and the project was aban-

129

doned—but the children read Goldie's letters out loud to her, and she dictated replies. Sonia mentioned Rebecca only occasionally in her letters, not wanting to make her children wonder or make Goldie sad. Rebecca stared when Sonia's girls talked about Aunt Chicago, as they called Goldie: Aunt Chicago ate in restaurants, went to plays, and wrote letters containing sentences about the bedroom.

One day Sophie screamed because she'd read ahead in a letter from Goldie to her mother. Sonia screamed, too, before she even knew what had happened. Aaron had disappeared: one day he had taken his shoes to the shoemaker's for new heels, and had never returned. The shoemaker said he didn't remember Goldie's husband or his shoes, and that was that. Goldie's oldest son had been talking about quitting school and going to work. Now he did so, and Goldie took a job in a dress factory.

Sonia pictured her brother-in-law, in shoes run down at the heel, walking into nothing—finding, at last, some fragment of life where for some reason nobody told him about what he couldn't believe in. "It's a disease," she told her family. "He can't remember where he lives. The police will bring him home when they figure it out."

Goldie wrote, "At last it's quiet around here, but I miss you-know-what."

Joseph sent Goldie money. He had worked in a furniture store for years, and now he was part-owner.

Several years after Rebecca graduated from high school, a friend married and quit her job, a *good* job: selling and keeping the books in a store that sold musical instruments and sheet music. The friend told the two bosses (who never yelled, she said) about Rebecca, who was hired after an interview, even though they were not Jewish and she said she wouldn't work on Saturdays. "I understand," said Mr. Hardy, the younger boss, nodding respectfully.

The store was called Stevens and Hardy. Mr. Stevens was an elderly man who could repair any musical instrument, while polite Mr. Hardy, who knew little about music, talked to customers. He was a widower in his forties, with two daughters. The third week Rebecca worked in the store, she was straightening the racks of music in the evening, after Mr. Stevens had left and they'd closed, when she was suddenly gripped around the legs. She looked down, alarmed. A little girl whose hair needed combing had seized Rebecca's skirt and was hiding her face in it.

"What's wrong?" Rebecca said.

"Mama died." Mama had not just died, but that was what was wrong. The little girl, Mr. Hardy's younger daughter, Charlotte, was playing a private game with Rebecca or her skirt. At the moment she was not grieving. Nonetheless, Rebecca bent compassionately and touched the child's hair, figuring out who she was.

A tall woman appeared. "I'm sorry, miss," she said. "Charlotte, get up."

Charlotte stayed where she was. The woman was Mr. Hardy's sister. She and Rebecca spoke politely, and then Mr. Hardy came out and introduced them.

The girl still knelt at Rebecca's feet, still with Rebecca's hand on her hair. Facing the child's father and aunt—two well-dressed, blond, self-confident Americans, descendants of George Washington, for all Rebecca knew—Rebecca felt for a moment like a participant in an unfamiliar religious rite such as she imagined took place at a church she passed (all but averting her eyes) on her way to work.

"Get up, Charlotte," said Mr. Hardy. Charlotte stood at last, flushed and laughing, and Rebecca's feeling passed. Rebecca swept the floor while Mr. Hardy replaced the trumpets and saxophones that customers had examined in the course of the day, and rechecked lists he'd made, as he did every night—sitting in his tiny office with the door open, singing jazz melodies extremely softly and slowly. When everyone left that evening, Mr. Hardy's sister and Charlotte went out first. Mr. Hardy held the door for Rebecca so as to lock it behind her, and he turned and looked at her in a way that seemed expectant. "Your daughter is pretty," Rebecca said.

Mr. Hardy's cheeks reddened, and then—standing in his coat, holding his hat at his side—he changed suddenly. He seemed to grow slightly shorter and wider; his limbs seemed rounder. It was as if a clever mechanical model of a human being had been replaced by a live person, inevitably less precisely assembled. Mr. Hardy was a gentile, but when he grasped the brass doorknob, Rebecca realized, it felt round and hard to him, exactly as it did to her. She suddenly pictured his arm, under his coat and shirt, full of tangled veins. "How did your wife die, Mr. Hardy?" Rebecca said. "If it's all right to ask."

"It's all right," he said. "She had a ruptured appendix."

"I'm sorry."

"Thank you."

A few weeks later, after Rebecca had found herself having occa-

131

sional strange thoughts about Mr. Hardy—not just about the veins on his arm but other parts of his body—he invited her to come for a walk. It was spring, and still light when they closed the store. They walked to a German bakery, where they drank tea and ate coffee cake. Rebecca, who brought her lunch in a bag, didn't object. The bakery wasn't kosher, but Mr. Hardy was such a conscientious person that she knew he didn't understand, and she didn't want to make him feel bad. The walk was repeated.

Her parents didn't ask why Rebecca came home from work later and less hungry. Everything about the music store baffled them; there was no point in inquiring. But Rebecca was surprised at how readily she ate at the bakery, just because poor Mr. Hardy was a widower, a man to be pitied—as if the kosher laws had an exception for tea with the grieving. She asked him questions about his daughters, about his own life. Rebecca was well-behaved, but not shy. At last, on a day when she was particularly enjoying Mr. Hardy, enjoying the look of his neck coming out of his shirt collar, she blurted out, "I'm not supposed to eat at a place like this."

"Even though it's not pork?"

"Yes."

"Your parents mind? Why didn't you tell me?"

"They don't know."

Timothy Hardy was not accustomed to concealing his behavior or feeling ashamed of it. He'd assumed she understood he was courting her, and that her parents would, too. Before asking Rebecca to walk, he'd decided he probably would marry her. He planned to give up pork and to accompany her to the Jewish church on Saturdays. He thought her parents would be doubtful at first—he was not Jewish, he had been married, he had children—but they would be reassured when they realized what an upright and serious-minded son-in-law he'd be.

Rebecca had liked Timothy Hardy's seriousness from the start. He reminded her a little of Cousin Sonia's husband, Joseph, who'd parcel out a small chicken with scrupulous fairness to his many children, making ironic, self-deprecating comments, sometimes inaudible except for their tone. Timothy Hardy was not ironic. Irony alarmed him because he couldn't endure the risk of being misunderstood, yet Rebecca had misunderstood him completely. She had not guessed he wanted to marry her. Rebecca didn't know gentiles could marry Jews.

"Tell them," Timothy Hardy now began to urge her, though he still

132

didn't mention marriage. "Tell your mother I've asked you to drink tea. Let me visit her."

"What will you talk about?"

"I'll tell her I'd like to take you to a concert. She'll see that I'm not young, but that isn't so bad."

"I don't think I can do that," said Rebecca. She tried to imagine her mother, who was engaged these weeks in embroidering a Torah cover for the shul, putting down her work and rising to greet Timothy Hardy. It wasn't just that Leah would object to him. She would be as alarmed by his interest in her daughter as if Rebecca reported that the streetcar or the lamppost on the corner wanted to visit her at home.

Mr. Hardy stopped asking her to take walks. He'd spoken of his mother, now dead, with a warmth Rebecca envied, and she knew he wouldn't allow himself to lead a young person into disobedience to her parents. "Whenever I went to see my mother," Timothy had confided one afternoon, "she'd insist she had known just when I'd get there. At last I went to visit her at six in the morning, and she said, 'Well, Timothy, I am surprised to see you!' " After that story he blinked several times, smiling hard, his dimples showing and his mustache looking stretched. Rebecca understood how daring—how loving—it had been for him to go so far as to play a trick.

After taking some walks by herself in a different direction, Rebecca knew that she loved Timothy Hardy, and that he'd given her up because she was too cowardly to tell her mother about him. If she was in love, she thought she ought to be brave enough to tell Leah, even though she was now sure that Timothy Hardy would never take her for a walk or to a concert or anywhere. When she looked at her broad face in the mirror, with heavy curls falling over her forehead—the alert face of someone about to follow instructions carefully—she was astonished to discover that it could be the face of someone in love. She thought she'd like to die saving the lives of Timothy Hardy's children.

One evening, Leah was alone, embroidering near the window, when Rebecca came back from visiting her cousins. The day was fading, and it was time to stop and light the lamp, but Leah had kept working, making neat silvery lines and loops, soothed and enchanted by her own skill. When Rebecca came in, Leah smiled apologetically. "I should have more light," she acknowledged. Leah's eyesight wasn't as good as it had been.

It was unusual for Leah to sound apologetic or tentative. She was a firm, vigorous person who followed the elaborate dictates of her religion precisely, picturing herself as a small but muscular horse pulling a sledge. Leah had had a deeply pious father, and now she had a deeply pious husband. She was grateful to both of them, feeling obscurely that if they hadn't taught her to be quite so scrupulous, something bad would have been freed in her. Her father and husband didn't seem to experience something Leah had known from childhood, a slightly exhilarating, slightly nauseating awareness that truths might also be false. Sometimes a compelling, hateful picture appeared uncontrollably in Leah's mind: the embroidered Torah cover, for example, smeared with feces. Leah knew how to keep her head down when that happened, whisper a prayer, and keep embroidering. She'd brought up her daughter carefully.

Rebecca lit the lamp. Her mother looked up and smiled, and Rebecca thought that Leah looked surprisingly young at that moment, with her double chin and the bags under her eyes momentarily in shadow. A look of query passed over Leah's face, and it was almost as if she'd invited her daughter's confidence, and so Rebecca, still in her coat, slid into a chair, rather than seating herself properly, and said, "Mama, I think I love Mr. Hardy."

"I think" was a lie, Rebecca's bow to convention, her effort to sound as she thought she should. She had always been so good that she'd had no practice speaking of hard subjects. Everything she'd said up to now had been something she knew her parents wanted to hear.

Leah looked up, so startled she thought for an instant that she must have imagined rather than heard her daughter's words, and her hand went to her mouth. "Sha!" she said involuntarily, though nobody could hear them.

"But I do."

Rebecca suddenly grinned at her mother like a baby, and her wide face glowed. Leah's hands prickled. She saw herself sitting in her chair, the Torah cover in her lap, as if she were someone else: she had a sensation of disconnection from herself, which she'd had only once before, when someone told her that her father was dead. She said, "He won't . . ."

"He did. I think he's changed his mind, so there's nothing to worry about, but I want to tell him I love him, just so he'll know. He's a good man, Mama. Sometimes when we walk together, he says just what I'm thinking. It's as if he's Jewish."

"Shhh." Leah shook her head hard. It was beyond consideration. They would have to hold a funeral. "You must stop talking like this." It was her fault. Leah should have thought about men. She should have pointed Rebecca toward a man at shul, or spoken to a friend. In Europe it would have been simple. "Rebecca," she said, "would you bring me a glass of water?"

Rebecca hurried out, still in her coat, and brought it, stretching her arm and the glass of water toward her mother when she was still halfway across the room. Leah started to rise and accept the glass, but its surface was slippery, or Rebecca, with new recklessness, let go too soon. The glass did not fall for a moment. Somehow it seemed to rise, and the water—Rebecca had filled it too full—rose in a circle as well, as if a heavy fish had dived, making a wave that broke over the hands and arms of Rebecca and her mother, and the Torah cover that was still in Leah's other hand. For a moment the water resembled feeling, pure and intense. Then it was just water, and the conversation ended with mopping, broken glass, apologies, and consultations about damp embroidery.

Just after the front door of the store had been locked the next evening, Rebecca stood in front of Timothy Hardy's desk as if she wanted to request permission to buy ink for the ledger. He looked at her over the rims of his glasses. "I would like to tell you that I love you," said Rebecca. "I know you don't want to take me walking anymore, and of course we couldn't . . . I told my mother—"

Timothy sprang up, letting his glasses fall to the desk and slide onto the floor. He seized her by the shoulders. "Marry me," he said. "I will become a Jew."

"You can't."

"I mean I'll convert."

"I don't think . . ."

"Your mother will change her mind when I convert."

She shook her head tearfully. He kissed her.

Timothy went to a synagogue he'd noticed on the Lower East Side. He knew enough to go on Saturday, but he couldn't read the Hebrew letters saying what time the service began. He thought ten a.m. would be fine, and when he arrived he saw men coming out and going in, so he walked in behind them and sat down. All around him, men were swaying and murmuring, stopping to converse, swaying and murmuring again. Eventually the scrolls in their silk cover were brought out, and Timothy was amazed to see something lavish and colorful in this drab setting. The service went on for hours. When it was over, Timothy approached the rabbi, hat in hand. "Excuse me," he said, "I would like to become Jewish." He wondered if the rabbi spoke English.

"Put on your hat," the rabbi said, and Timothy took that as a dismissal, apologized, and left. Maybe he could find a different synagogue.

Rebecca noticed that her mother looked frightened for weeks after their conversation, and she worried that she'd damaged Leah's health with her surprising admission. She didn't mention Mr. Hardy again. When they were alone in the store, she and Timothy planned their life. She couldn't resist these conversations. She would care for his children, and they'd have more. "Maybe you'd better come see the furniture," he said. "You might not like Lucy's taste." Lucy was his dead wife.

"We're keeping Lucy's furniture," said Rebecca, sounding like her mother.

"You are the bride."

"Bride shmide." She'd found her true work and wanted to get busy. She'd learn to laugh so Timothy and his daughters could laugh. Her cousins could teach her jokes. She'd get them to explain what was so funny about that record, "No News but What Killed the Dog," which consisted of a recital of disasters.

One evening Timothy told her that the rabbi who was preparing him to become Jewish, after discouraging him several times, had explained an unexpected next step. It was necessary for Timothy to be circumcised. He looked at Rebecca with love and some embarrassment, and she slowly took in what he was saying. Rebecca had allowed herself, for a few seconds at a time, alone in her bed, to consider that Timothy had a penis, but now it was as if lights had been turned on in a room that should be dark. Staring into Timothy's face, Rebecca acquired a rapid education. Her father must have a penis, too, as well as Cousin Joseph and his son, Morris. When they were little Jewish babies, their little penises had been cut. She had been to a bris more than once. She knew all about mohels and what they did, but she had never allowed herself to think the thoughts she thought now, that baby boys grew into men, that their penises grew, too, that men who were not Jewish had different penises, that a different penis hung at this moment in Timothy's trousers. Involun-

136

tarily she glanced down, and then she glanced down frankly. "It will hurt."

"They do something . . ."

"When are you going to do it?"

"Next week. There's a man who does it."

"A mohel."

"Yes."

There would be a sharp knife, slender and very bright. "Shall I come with you?"

"If you would walk to the building with me . . ."

"And wait?"

He hesitated. It was late fall, and Timothy was wearing thick trousers. He stood firmly on his two big legs, which he tended to separate a little. His tweed jacket was thick, too. It seemed to her that his clothing was fur; he was naked in the way an animal is. Rebecca knew she wanted to do something, but at first she didn't know what. Then she pulled her broadcloth blouse free of her skirt. As she pushed it up toward her neck, she knew the gesture was clumsy, that she must look more foolish than alluring, with crushed cloth bunched under her chin. Holding the sturdy material in place, she tried to push aside her slip, which came up high on her chest, with a brassiere under it. Rebecca's breasts were large, and she wore underwear with good support. She took Timothy's hand, which trembled, and drew it under her clothes. He pushed the cloth aside, leaned over her, found and released her breast, and put his mouth on it. He seemed to be crying. "Walk there with me, but then go away," he said.

"But won't you need someone, later?" Her voice had a sob in it, because of the pleasure of his touch on her breast.

"Jews are used to trouble," Timothy said. He was making a joke, the second of his life.

She loved his joke. "Are you really Jewish?" she said.

He stepped back from her and held out his hands, turning them as if the answer was written on them, maybe on his palms, maybe on the backs of his hands. "*Shema Yisrael* . . . ," he began, and though the vowels were flat, Rebecca recognized what he was saying. Her cheeks grew warm, and she straightened her clothes.

All night—shamed, throbbing—Timothy was enraged with himself and with all Jews. He wondered if a cruel trick had been played on

137

him, and if years from now he might discover that circumcision was rare among Jews, and that the rabbi had put him through such an experience as punishment for desiring one of their women. First his wife had died, and now, when he had miraculously fallen in love again, this hideously ludicrous requirement had been placed upon him. A religion that required him to expose himself, that required blood and pain . . . They gave him whiskey, but it just caused a headache. In bed, he tried not to think of his view of the knife, just before the job had been done, despite the mohel's courteous effort to place his black-clothed self between Timothy and the table where it lay. Now his penis felt as large as a melon. If it were infected, he would die and be buried a Jew, to the consternation of his Protestant relatives. Timothy began to pray in Hebrew. Then he prayed in English, to Jesus, the Jew he'd betrayed. As the pain lessened a little, as he began to think he might want to touch his penis to someone else's body again, he imagined the future, in which he and Rebecca would endure derision and shame. Timothy and Rebecca, the well behaved. That was what they had in common, good behavior and the discovery that it meant nothing: it originated in no excellence, afforded no ease or safety.

Timothy wanted to be present when Rebecca told her parents that he had become a Jew, but she refused. Three days after his conversion, she helped her mother cook supper, though her hands shook and she dropped the potatoes. "Stir," Leah said, and Rebecca stirred the soup and skimmed the fat. It was Shabbos. Rebecca waited until her father came into the dining room, then until her mother had spoken the blessing and lit the candles. She still couldn't speak. Once she did, there would be no more eating, and there was no reason to waste the food and leave everyone hungry.

When the plates were almost empty, she put down her fork. "Mama, Papa, I have to tell you something," she said.

Her mother drew her hand to her mouth so abruptly that Rebecca knew she had thought incessantly of their last conversation. Rebecca said, "Mr. Hardy wants to marry me." Her father sat back quickly; obviously Leah hadn't told him. "He has become a Jew," Rebecca continued. Then she started to cry. "Because he loves me. He . . . he went to the mohel. He was cut."

Her father stared. "You didn't tell me?" he said. "Rebecca?"

It hadn't occurred to her how he'd feel. He didn't look angry, as she had expected. He pushed his chair back, looking pinched and fearful, as if he'd been exiled. She'd never seen her father look that way.

Leah had kept her hand on her mouth, and now she bit it and pulled it away quickly and then put it on the table. Rebecca could see tooth marks. "Rebecca," said Leah quietly, her voice unsteady, "I am not your mother."

In a rush, Rebecca heard the mumbled story of Goldie the difficult and shameless, who she thought must somehow remind Leah of Timothy—but that wasn't the point. It became clear why Papa, by now, was backing his chair toward the window. The knob at the top of the chair made a star-crack in the glass that nobody noticed until next morning, by which time Rebecca, who'd cried all night, no longer thought of it as her window, or in any sense her responsibility. Yet she felt for the poor broken pane a nostalgia that made her weep some more. For calamity had not made Leah's speech extravagant and hyperbolical. Leah was not Rebecca's mother.

She was not Rebecca's mother, Reuben was not her father, but they loved her like parents. They didn't hold a funeral because Rebecca wasn't their daughter and, by means of some chicanery, she was not marrying a gentile. Leah continued embroidering Torah covers and following the laws, but sitting in her chair in the late afternoons, she felt as if the sides of her house had fallen away from the roof, that the furniture around her had slid down slides made by the fallen walls, that the wind blew on her without obstacle.

Sonia's children were amazed, full of whooping and obstreperousness. Rebecca was their first cousin, and Sonia, who seemed incapable of secrecy but had known all along, was Rebecca's aunt. After the first hard night, Rebecca had taken the trolley, Shabbos or not, to her cousins' house. "Mama says she's not my mama."

Sonia started and sucked in her breath. "Aunt Chicago is your mama."

Nobody remembered Goldie very well. "Aunt Chicago whose husband walked out."

"That Aaron, the rat."

Five years earlier, when Aaron had left, Rebecca had been dismayed to think of a cousin who couldn't keep track of her husband. "She wasn't married when she had me?"

"She was a girl. What did she know?"

Rebecca got on a bus and went to Chicago, where she located her mother in a tenement that seemed from the outside much like the one where she'd grown up, but was different inside. Rebecca had not thought to telephone Goldie; she'd simply taken the address from Sonia, packed a bag, had a tearful, stubborn conversation at the store with Timothy, and set forth. When Aunt Chicago—who had long gray-brown hair that she hadn't yet braided that morning—opened the door in her bathrobe, a dog pressed past her, wagging her tail and barking. Goldie and Rebecca looked at each other, listening to the dog. Finally Goldie said, "Who?"

"Rebecca."

"From Aunt Leah?"

"She told me."

"They wouldn't let me say anything," said Goldie, before she began to scream so loudly that the neighbors, not knowing whether they heard joy or anguish, came running. Suddenly Rebecca belonged to twenty people and a dog she had never known about: half-brothers, friends. The rejoicing involved food, dancing, drink, talk, shouts. Goldie said, "I lost that worthless Aaron, but I got my baby back." When Rebecca told her about Timothy, Goldie asked, "What if he can't still do it, from the cutting?"

"It's healing."

"Thank God."

Goldie and the boys needed her as much as Timothy and his girls, but nobody could imagine moving. Changing a religion was one thing, leaving New York or Chicago something else. Rebecca and Goldie wrote letters from then on, and shouted on the telephone. When Aaron had been gone seven years, Goldie had him declared dead. She married a widowed neighbor, a man who was gentle with her. In the end everyone moved to Florida and ran in and out of each other's apartments, but that wasn't until the fifties or sixties, when they began to grow old. Goldie had been so young when Rebecca was born that they grew old together. Timothy was the oldest, but he outlived them all, weeping and praying in a Florida synagogue in his old age, when he looked more Jewish. People asked him what his name was changed from. He thanked God for the happiness he'd had in his life. He and Rebecca, Goldie and her second husband, would all go dancing at a big hotel in Miami Beach. Rebecca always looked like a demure young girl, even as she grew gray, but she learned lightheartedness. At the wedding of one of Goldie's sons, she walked to the microphone in a slinky green satin dress and wished her half-brother "every kind of happiness, including with no clothes on." It was Rebecca's closest approximation to a dirty joke. But nothing Rebecca did could be dirty, Timothy thought, remembering—as he drove a big white convertible to the synagogue in the Florida sun—the way she had offered him her breast that first time, drawing his hand under her clothes. How happy he'd been, then and later, bending his head and pressing it into her neck, putting his mouth on Rebecca's breasts.

Nominated by Wally Lamb, Jessica Roeder, Lloyd Schwartz, Debra Spark, Ploughshares

CHAIR

by DONNA MASINI

from AMERICAN POETRY REVIEW

The moment I saw it—the rows of holes across the back—
it reminded me of a confessional, the way the screen would slide
   and I'd begin,

kneeling on my cushion, shut in the oak box, the whisper, my litany
   of sins. I'm lying
on my bed, on a phone session with my shrink. She's talking about
   dissociation,

the ways I leave myself. I am thinking about this chair my husband
and I carried home before the separation, when *husband* was a
   word

that made me feel safe, and the word—*auger* is it?—for the tool
   that makes holes
in wood. In fact (I look it up) it's an *awl* that cuts the wood. You
   split

yourself, my shrink is saying. I slide the dictionary back in its slot,
put my finger to a hole the awl made.

When I was a kid we knelt, my sister and I, on either side of the
   kitchen chair,
and one would be the priest and one would be the sinner. The
   sinner

would whisper through the chair-back holes not her list of
    offenses—*I*
lied five times, I ate meat on Friday—sins she might tick off

in a box to the priest, his profile through the screen, hand to
    forehead,
leaning forward, shielding his eyes but looking

as if he had a headache—not lists, but stories: *I watched a boy*
peeing behind the Vandeveer projects. That green book with the
    picture

of Mother Cabrini, my father's pen with the naked lady—I stole
    them.
I threw out my liverwurst sandwich. I thought about the starving

but Claire Haggerty sat on it at morning Mass. It was a relief
to tell the whole story now no one was instructing us to keep it
    brief.

The priest doesn't want your excuses, Sister Agnes said. He's busy.
He doesn't want to hear about the tear in your dress, how beautiful
    the cake looked

before you stuffed it in your mouth. I am a glutton
he wants to hear. And your contrition. But my sister

wanted stories and I would tell them (most of the time I was the
    sinner)
I'd glory in it, making up plots, characters, dramatic and precise

as the punishments Sister Agnes elaborated, *(for this lie*
a girl was struck dumb . . . for showing off her bare arms Our Lord
    turned

a girl like yourself into a leper), specific as hell with its particular
shrieking, its headless burning flesh. My friend Daniel tells that joke

about the Woman Taken in Adultery. *Let he who is without*
sin, Jesus says, *cast the first stone.* A huge rock shoots past,

143

knocks the woman down. Jesus looks up. *Mom*, he says,
I was trying to make a point. I love the literal. I loved holding the
   body

of Christ in my mouth imagining his long legs and forgiving smile. I
   loved
kneeling with my sister at that kitchen chair, peeking, watching the
   pleasure

my story gave. Once, in the confessional, the word *why?* shot back
through the screen. Because, I said, my mother forgot it was Friday.
   She made

Pork and Beans. God knew, she said, we didn't have money to
   waste.
I had to choose between one sin and my mother, the joke would go.
   I ate the beans.

Now, the priest said, I had my mother's sin, too, on my soul. I
   absolve you,
my sister would say, at the end of my stories. We'd stand, knees
   aching, unable

to look at one another, and spin, as Sister Agnes said God made the
   world spin—quickly—
to keep us still, then we'd fall, panting on the floor, breathing in the
   collaborating dark.

Nominated by Debra Spark, Joyce Carol Oates, Pamela Stewart, Jim Simmerman,
American Poetry Review

PHYSICS AND GRIEF

by PATRICIA MONAGHAN

from FOURTH GENRE

> In nature nothing remains constant. Everything is in a perpetual state of trans-
> formation, motion, and change. However, we discover that nothing simply
> surges up out of nothing without having antecedents that existed before. Like-
> wise, nothing ever disappears without a trace, in the sense that it gives rise to
> absolutely nothing existing in later times.
>
> —David Bohm

"ACTUALLY," DAN SAID, "I've been reading a lot of physics." He
looked down at his empty paper plate and shrugged one shoulder,
then the other. "I don't suppose that makes any sense."

Dan had not spoken to me in almost a year. We'd seen each other
occasionally; we had too many common friends for that not to hap-
pen. But when it did, Dan made certain to stay on the other side of
the room, to find himself in need of a drink when I came near, to
turn suddenly away when I tried to catch his eye.

That was the year when I was a new widow, and Dan was about to
become one, his partner, Steve, descending into a hell of lesions and
pneumonia and fungal invasions of the brain. Even in the blur of my
loss, I felt no anger toward Dan—though anger is so predictable a
part of grief—for avoiding me. I knew the cause: I already was what
he most feared to become.

Six months after I was widowed, Dan joined me in that state.
Steve gave up his obdurate struggle to remain alive, asking to be kept
home when the next crisis hit. It was only a week. Friends told me
that Steve's death was gentle and that Dan bore up as well as could

145

be expected. Dan dropped from sight for a time, disappearing into memories and pain.

Now it was summer, and we were sitting under blue canvas at an outdoor festival. Dan had approached me with an apology for his actions. I had embraced him with understanding. We were sitting companionably together, catching up on each other's lives, when I asked him what most helped him deal with his grief.

Physics.

Dan met my eyes, and his brows came together, then raised. "Relativity. Quantum mechanics. Bell's Theorem. You know?" I think he expected me to be surprised. But I was not. It had been the same for me.

To explain how physics came to be important on my journey of grief, I have first to describe the problem with my keys. There were five of them, bound together with a wide steel ring: a big silver skeleton key, for the embossed brass Victorian lock on the front door; a round-headed key that opens the more modern deadbolt; a little golden key to the garage; an institutional "do not duplicate" key to my office; and a black-headed key to the Ford station wagon.

I remember the day—the hour—that the keys disappeared. It was late spring, less than three months after Bob died. Walking out the door to go shopping, I had reached into my jacket pocket, where I always kept my keys.

They weren't there.

At the instant, it seemed inconsequential. I'd mislaid keys before; hasn't everyone? I was inside the house, so I had used the keys to enter. They were, therefore, somewhere in the house with me. I merely had to look carefully and I would find them.

I was unperturbed. I did what I did whenever I had mislaid something. I looked in all the logical places: in my coat's other pocket; on the shelf near the front door; next to the telephone; in the kitchen near the sink. Nothing.

I was still not overly concerned. I must have been distracted when I entered, I reasoned with myself; I must have put the keys in some unlikely spot. So I began methodically searching the house. Entry hall. Living room. Pulling out furniture, looking under pillows. Nothing. Dining room. Kitchen. Opening cabinets, reaching to the back of shelves. Nothing.

Okay, then, I must have carried them upstairs. Guest room. Bathroom. Moving around each room slowly, looking especially in places where keys were unlikely to be. Behind pictures. In rarely-opened drawers. Study. Nothing. Linen closet. Nothing.

In my bedroom, I suddenly grew frustrated. I needed my keys! The only key to my car was on that ring; I could not go to work without it. What would I do without my keys?

I started to cry.

I had been crying for months, ever since Bob had finally died, fighting cancer to the last. The six months before his death were exhausting. For three months I was his sole caregiver; then, during his final hospitalization, I visited him two, three, even four times each day. Economics forced me to continue working, so I had neither physical strength nor emotional resources left when he died.

In the days before Bob's death, I had been with him constantly, telling him stories of the future we should have had, praising his work and his son to him, reminiscing for him about happy times when he could no longer speak. I did not sleep for perhaps forty-eight hours as I held vigil by his bedside, leaving only for necessary moments, for he had been shatteringly fearful of being alone at the moment of death. And so I was with him when that moment came, holding his hand as his breathing slowed, singing old songs to him, stroking his face through its paralysis.

It was the hardest thing I have ever done, witnessing as he "departed from this strange world a little ahead of me," as Einstein said when his oldest friend, Michele Besso, died. When I left that hospital room, bearing with me the amaryllis that had bloomed only the day before, I felt that I was leaving all happiness behind, that my world had changed unutterably, and only for the worse.

I lived the months afterward in a trance of grief. There was a memorial service that I planned, I remember that. I remember a brick meeting hall with red tulips, a jazz pianist, readings from Bob's novels, visitors from many states. For the rest, I barely recall anything. I apparently kept working, and doing laundry, and feeding the dogs, and planting the garden. My body kept moving through the Midwestern spring. But my soul was in the desert, in winter.

That day in May, the loss of my keys reduced me to tears, though of course I was weeping for my greater loss, which every other loss would now reflect. Possibly I wept for hours; I did such things at that time. Finally the storm passed. I got up and set determinedly about to find the keys. To survive, I had to work. I needed to drive to my office. I could not manage without my keys. I would find them. I had to.

147

And so I repeated my search. I must have missed the keys the first time, I told myself. I started again at the front door and scoured the downstairs. Living room: no. Kitchen: no.

And so it went. After an hour or so, I found myself again in the bedroom, still keyless.

I began to weep again. This time, my desolation seemed endless. I could not stop crying. I lay on the bed, sobbing and flailing my arms. I soaked several handkerchiefs. I buried my head in pillows and drenched them with tears.

Then I became enraged. I got up from the bed and began to scream at Bob, furious at him for dying and leaving me so helplessly besieged by grief. I screamed that he was cruel and heartless, that I'd been there in his hour of need, and where was he when I needed him? I raged and wept, wept and raged.

I had not, before Bob's death, spent much time thinking about the question of whether or not there is an afterlife. I had been brought up with a conventional picture of heaven and hell. And I had studied enough other religions to realize that many wiser than I believed in some kind of survival after death. I had read believable-enough accounts of those who claimed to have been contacted by the dead. But the possibility of an afterlife was not something I dwelt upon. I did not wish to make moral decisions by weighing the possibilities of future reward or punishment for myself. Nor did the survival of my own small person seem especially important in comparison with the universe's vast majesty. So, for myself, what happened or did not happen after death was not a very important question.

Bob, by contrast, had been quite clear about his beliefs. A natural mystic, he had practiced Zen for twenty years. But he was also an unrelentingly hard-headed empiricist who believed the universe to be a mechanistic place in which consciousness was only a byproduct of the body's functions. Thus, when the body died, consciousness ceased as well. Bob believed, as Fred Alan Wolf put it in describing the Newtonian worldview, that mind—or soul, or spirit, whatever you call it—was just "a convenient by-product of the physiology of . . . the mechanisms of the brain, down to the remarkable electrical and mechanical movements of the nerve firings and blood flows."

He never changed his belief once he entered the hospital that final time, even though I, desperate for some reassurance that our love could continue after he faded from this life, talked to him about reincarnation and other possible survivals. But Bob would be no foxhole convert; he marched gamely toward that abyss which he saw as the likely end of his being. Death was painful to him; he had much to live for; but he would not grasp at hope of continued life just to ease his pain. Unless he had time to ponder, unless he could become completely convinced, he would believe as he always had. Happy lies held no appeal for him.

One thing I loved about Bob was this: he had more integrity than any person I'd ever met. That integrity remained to the end. He met his death with his long-held beliefs intact. He was frightened, but he was very, very brave.

Because I had no personal convictions on the subject, I held true to Bob's beliefs after he was gone. It was a way of remaining close to him. I, too, would refuse to grasp at imaginary straws just to ease my pain. If Bob believed that all traces of his consciousness would evaporate at his death, that only his physical works would remain, then I would loyally uphold that belief.

And so I lived in the desert. Life has never seemed so dry and meaningless to me as it did then. I would watch lovers kiss in a coffee shop and a whirlpool of pain would open beneath me, as I thought of one of them holding the other as they parted forever. I would stare at parents playing with their children near the lake and imagine sudden illnesses and accidents, wondering how life could create such joy only to obliterate it. I wept constantly: when I heard beautiful music, when I saw painful news, when I saw new flowers, when I went to bed, when I woke up.

But I adamantly refused to settle for those happy visions that religion held out, of dreamy heavens full of harps, of other lives to come, of eventual reunion in some cosmic void. I even rejected nonreligious spiritualism. When friends said they had dreamed of Bob, or felt him near, I received the information in silent disbelief. It was their need of solace, I told myself, that caused these apparitions. They had just imagined them. I, loyal to Bob's beliefs, would not settle for such self-deluding comfort. I would tough it out, looking reality right in its cruel face.

But the day I lost my keys, I could not be brave like Bob, not any longer. Seeing those loving eyes go dim had been the single most painful moment of my life. The idea that the universe could so wantonly create beauty, could bestow upon our lives the kind of love that seems like ultimate meaning, only to destroy it in a breath, had finally become too much for me.

149

I wanted so desperately to believe that Bob, and Bob's love for me, still existed somewhere in the universe, that in my furious pain I flung down a challenge. Standing in the middle of the bedroom, I demanded that he come back. Find my keys, I insisted. Find my damned keys! If there's anyone there, if there's any love left in this universe for me, find my keys!

After the fury had passed, I felt mortified. I had been screaming at a dead man. Standing in my room alone, screaming at a dead man.

Worse, it was all so trivial. If I were going to throw down the gauntlet to the universe about whether there is life after death, couldn't I have chosen something more important as proof? World peace? Personal economic security? A beatific vision?

But I'd spoken. I'd insisted that Bob prove his continuing existence by finding my keys.

Even writing about that day, I feel embarrassment cover me. It was such an excess of emotion about such a small matter, about such a minor inconvenience. Why had I broken down over such a silly thing? Why had I challenged the universe over something as unimportant as a key-ring?

But break down I had, and challenge the universe I had. And I could not bear the answer to be silence, negation, the absence of Bob forever, anywhere. Now I truly had to find the keys. So I resolutely began, yet again, to search. I started once more in the front hallway. But this time, I took a new tack. I might as well do spring-cleaning, I decided. I'd clean the entire house, front door to attic, and in doing so I would certainly find the keys.

There was more than a bit of desperation about all this. If I did not find the keys, all was indeed lost. If I did not find the keys, there was no vestige of Bob in the world. If I did not find the keys, I was alone in the cruelest universe imaginable.

Three days later, I was back in the bedroom. Except for that one room, the house was now clean, ammonia-and-paste-wax clean. I had taken down curtains and washed them, cleaned out closets, pulled up rugs. I had upended sofas and searched their bowels. I had repotted plants. I had pulled books from shelves and dusted both.

The house sparkled, indeed.

But I had not found the keys.

The bedroom was the final outpost of possibility. From the first corner around to the last, then spiraling in to the center, I cleaned and searched. I opened drawers and rearranged them, shaking out their contents on the floor. I moved pictures and dusted their frames. I worked slowly, with mounting despair, for the keys had still not appeared. I moved the bed and polished the floor under it. I shook out the bedclothes and aired out the mattress.

Finally, I was finished.

There were no keys.

I collapsed. This time my grief truly knew no bounds. I had asked for an answer from the universe, and I had—I believed—received one. Bob had been right. Consciousness was a byproduct of our body's functioning, and now that the ashes of Bob's body sat on the bookshelf in a white box, there was nothing, anywhere, left of the curiosity and passion and brilliance and love that had been him.

The depression that began that day incapacitated me. I was unable to work for nearly a week. Finally, however, I called the car dealership and got new car keys. I found the spare house keys. I began to reconstruct the openings to my life. I knew now that I was indeed alone, that I could not call upon Bob for help, that he was no longer present anywhere, in any form. It was a bleak and cruel universe, but at least I knew the truth of it.

What I experienced during that next year was more than simple grief and certainly more than emotional depression, although I suffered from both as well. It was stark existential despair. Life had no meaning, much less any savor. I tried to find what comfort I could in friendship, in earthly beauty, in art, in learning. But at my center was an abyss of meaninglessness. I could as easily have gambled all my resources away as built a garden; as easily have crashed my car as driven it safely across the Midwest; as easily have drunk slow poison as cocoa for breakfast. That I did one thing rather than another seemed only an arbitrary choice.

At last, however, I began to awaken from my coma of sorrow. I began to argue with Bob in my mind. As I gardened, I noticed again the resilient connection of matter and energy, how nature never destroys but only transforms. As I walked in the woods with my dog, I saw spring flowers emerging from the withered leaves of autumn. What hubris, I began to think, to imagine that human consciousness is the only thing this universe cares to obliterate. Surely we are not that important.

But these were fleeting thoughts, unconvincing, evanescent, ideas which did not in any case reach to the root of my grief. It was easy to accept that Bob's body would eventually nourish other beings,

151

through the cycle of decomposition and recomposition. But it was Bob's self that I'd loved—not only his body, though certainly that. And although I knew and accepted, with piercing pain, what had happened to his body, that told me nothing about where the unique energy went that had invigorated it.

Every once in a while, I would think of the lost keys and sigh. I had, after all, asked for a sign, and I had been given one.

That was when I began reading books on physics. I had been reading a lot of spiritual literature, looking for answers to the appalling questions life presented. But I only grew more isolated, angry at the serenity that seemed forever beyond my grasp, despairing at my continuing inability to find any sense in death's senselessness. It was not that the answers which spiritual literature offered seemed implausible or incorrect; it was simply that I could not believe them, could not make the leap into not-doubting. The more rigidly codified the religious insight, the more it seemed to exclude—even to mock—my anguished confusion.

I can't remember exactly which book, which author, brought me to physics. Most likely one that pushed the boundaries of science to include spirituality. Fritz Capra, perhaps, or Gary Zukov. One of those wild minds who saw bridges where others saw barricades. But it wasn't the spirituality that gripped my attention. It was the science.

Where religion had failed me, being so certain of itself, physics offered paradoxes and complexities so bizarre that my hatred and fear of the universe began to be replaced with what can only be called awe. I'd known Newtonian physics before, from my days as a science reporter, but I had never ventured into quantum mechanics. There I found the most astonishing ideas, ones which smashed the clockwork universe just as Bob's death had torn apart mine. Ideas that read like Bob's beloved Zen koans, statements that strained the limits of my linear thinking. "Our universe seems to be composed of facts and their opposites at the same time," I read in Louis de Broglie's work, and "everything happens as though it did not exist at all."

Such statements seemed eminently sensible, reasonable, even straightforward. Yes, I responded passionately. Yes, the universe was that strange, that indescribable. Death is not an equal and opposite reaction to life; consciousness is not some strange form of inertia. I needed a new physics to describe the wild movements of my grieving soul. And a new physics I found.

Like my friend Dan, I found quantum theory immeasurably consoling. With an uncertainty-loves-company kind of logic, I lost myself in Heisenberg and the reassurances of the Uncertainty Principle. If we cannot conceivably know everything about the physical universe, then the abyss of doubt whereon I stood was as good a standpoint as any from which to view life. If we cannot know something as simple as two aspects of a subatomic particle's motion simultaneously, how can we know for certain that there is no life after death—or that there is? If our measurements may alter the reality that we measure, could not consciousness be a form of measurement, subtly altering the universe?

My deepest consolation, however, was not in speculating about whether a consciousness suffused, as mine was, with grief altered the world in a different way than one flooded with happiness. Rather, I drew solace from the dumbfounding absoluteness of Heisenberg's theory. We could not know everything, not ever, because in the moment of such knowing we may change what we know. I could not know—I could never know—if or where Bob existed, for each time I sought for him—each time I measured this universe in terms of Bob's existence or nonexistence—I was perhaps changing the conditions of the very universe through which I sought. It was as though Heisenberg, by enshrining uncertainty at the center of perception and knowledge, made anything and everything both possible and impossible at once.

Suddenly the world seemed to make sense again, although in a deeply paradoxical way. Where religion's certainties had left me bitterly bereft of comfort, quantum uncertainty allowed for unimaginable possibilities. Whatever measurement I took of the universe, I understood now, could be only partial. There would always be something that eluded my grasp. This was an enormous comfort.

It was not only uncertainty that captured me. Because this new physics was all about time and space, Einstein spoke to me like a voice from a burning bush. I, who lived in a time and space from which my love had disappeared, found respite in considering the ways that time and space were linked. "Any two points in space and time are both separate and not separate," David Bohm said. What salvation that seemed! As incomprehensible as this new spacetime was, it was more lively with possibilities than linear and planar realities. My separateness from Bob was real, but in some way, we were also still together.

In some way—this was most important to me. For this was not a metaphoric togetherness, a trick of language. This was science, after all. And not just science but the queen of sciences, physics. Physics which did not ask me to believe, did not ask me to have faith. Physics which observed and experimented. Physics which offered a description of the world, admittedly bizarre but as accurate as blundering language could make it.

I did not have to believe. I only had to wonder.

The fact that, as Max Born pointed out, the quantum world is utterly unvisualizable presented no problem to me. Visions of the sub-atomic world were metaphors, whose richness and limitations I amply understood. But unlike religion, which seemed hypnotized by its own articulations of the ineffable, physics acknowledged that any picture we hold of the subatomic world is by definition inaccurate, limited, inexact. No one has ever seen a quark, much less a Higgs boson. But they act; we see their traces. Such quantum strangeness spoke to my condition. I had witnessed something deeply incomprehensible when Bob died. Studying what Bohm called the "unanalyzable ways of the universe" mirrored that experience.

My grief did not disappear, for grief is a chronic disease which exists in the body. My body would still regularly writhe with sudden memories: when I automatically reached for Bob's favorite juice at the Jewel, when I passed the lake where we had taken our last walk, when someone uttered a phrase he had relished. The tape-loop of his last hours ran constantly in my mind, so that I would see the doctor, my friends Natalie and Barbara arriving, Bob's son Michael leaving, the amaryllis, Bob's paralyzed face, the doctor, Natalie, the amaryllis, the doctor. . . .

Because of the power of these death-watch memories, relativity especially absorbed me. The paradoxes of time preoccupied me for days on end. Einstein had seen the connection between the study of time and awareness of death's approach, arguing that death really means nothing because "the distinction between past, present and future is only a stubbornly persistent illusion." I envisioned those points in the universe where radio waves of Bob's voice, from a long-ago interview, were still new and bright. I invented scenarios in which I stretched time out like taffy, making Bob's last days as eternal as they had subjectively seemed. I relished that consoling insight that Einstein's equations were time-reversible, that perhaps time does not move in one direction but can flow backward as well as forward. I imagined moving backward through time, intersecting with a healthy

Bob and recreating our life, always hopping back on the time machine before the diagnosis, living those happy times over and over and over. I knew these were fantasies, but I also knew that I no longer knew what time really was. There, once again, were limitless possibilities.

If my grief did not disappear, that crazed existential doubt did. Life no longer was so utterly senseless. It made sense again, but in a more marvelous way than I'd ever imagined. I found myself staring at graphs of the Schroedinger wave collapse, imagining a cat alive, dead, alive, dead, all at the same time—imagining Bob's continued existence as such a wave. I pondered the complementarity between particles and waves, especially the way an observer seems implicated in the emergence into reality of each. Particles dancing and leaping in a virtual world, flickering in and out of measurable existence. Or perhaps they were not even particles at all, but what Henry Sapp called "sets of relationships that reach outward to other things." To David Bohm, too, particles exist not so much as nuggets of virtual and actual matter, but as "on-going movements that are mutually dependent because ultimately they merge and interpenetrate."

Matter disappeared, at this scale, into flashing energy, particles into momentarily observable comets of being. Bob had been composed of these miraculous particles, these miraculous relationships reaching outward toward me, these mutually dependent and interpenetrating movements. And perhaps he still was, in some way, in some unmeasurable place. Our lives together had been lived in a space and a time, within a universe through which the mighty and unfathomable river of spacetime flows. Were we still connected, as Bell's Theorem hints, in some intricate and inexpressible way? Was I somehow still affected by the changes that he experienced—in whatever state those blinking-into-existence particles that had been Bob were now? And did my changes affect him still as well?

Far from compelling me toward certainty about where and how Bob still existed, quantum theory removed from me any urge toward stapling down reality within one interpretation. In the quantum world, Nick Herbert has pointed out, there are at least eight possible pictures of reality, any of which is more consoling than the Newtonian vision of the universe. Maybe there is an "ordinary reality," as de Broglie and Einstein believed; in that case the hard stuff that made up Bob is somewhere still in existence, and even now I am breathing atoms that had been part of him during his life. But the Copenhagen hypothesis of Bohr and Heisenberg questions whether there is any such "reality" at all. In their view, Bob and I had lived something like a dream together, and that dream had as much reality without him as it had with him. An alternative reading of the Copenhagen hypothesis is that we create our own realities, that reality exists only as we observe it doing so; in that case, I could create the reality of his continued existence by believing strongly enough.

These were only some of the possibilities. There was David Bohm's theory of the implicate order, which argues that there is an undivided wholeness that could wrap both Bob and me, in our varying current states, in what he called "indivisible quantum processes that link different systems in an unanalyzable way." There was the fantastic many-world hypothesis, which permitted me to envision that Bob and I still lived happily in another spacetime, after he had survived cancer; in that reality, we are writing an essay together, perhaps this very one.

Or possibly, the quantum world is based upon no logic that we would recognize. In that case, life's either/or does not exist, and Bob's apparent lack of existence is no more true than his apparent existence had been. Or perhaps I created him, or he me; perhaps neither of us existed before we met, we came into being complete with memories when we created each other, and thus he continues in me, his creation. Perhaps, as Fred Alan Wolf has argued, the mind does not "exist in the physical universe at all. It may be beyond the boundaries of space, time and matter. It may use the physical body in the same sense that an automobile driver uses a car."

Or maybe all of this is simultaneously true. Maybe this world is so full of mystery that we cannot ever grasp its actual probabilities and probable actualities.

I pondered these extraordinary possibilities as I moved through my ordinary life. Slowly, the pain of my loss began, not to diminish, but to find its place in my life. If I did not feel joy, at least my pain had become a familiar companion. I continued reading physics, but with less crazed compulsion. I even began to accept the cruel existence of thermodynamics, with its arrow of time that threatened my happy time-travel imaginings, once I realized how connected to the richness of chaos it was.

Every once and again, I thought of the lost keys. In the fall, as I was raking the front yard, I imagined that perhaps I had gone to the car for something, that spring day, and had dropped my key-ring into the crowded bed of hosta by the door. But no. In winter, when I decided to move the piano, I thought that perhaps I had missed the hidden keys during my frenzied cleaning by not moving that massive upright. But no. That next spring, after preparing for a dinner party, I sat in Bob's recliner and noticed a side pocket I had missed. There? But no: the keys were not there either. The seasons passed, and the keys remained lost.

Each time this happened, I thought to myself that finding the keys no longer mattered. That I had moved beyond the challenge I had flung out to Bob, to the universe, on that wild sad day. That unless the keys found their way back to me in some utterly strange way, I could not regard it as an answer to my desperate plea. I said to myself that finding the keys would be—just finding the keys. That if I found them in some ordinary way, it would prove nothing, one way or the other: I lost the keys, I found them, there was no connection.

And then I found the keys.

Friends were coming to dinner, and I was sitting in my study feeling sad, as I often did, and thinking of Bob, which I always did. I wishfully imagined him being with us, thought how much he would have enjoyed it. I felt my loss again, but poignantly this time, as a sad melody rather than as painful cacophony.

Then, for no special reason, I looked at the door of my study. It was open after having been closed all day. I kept it closed to keep my dog out and to keep visitors from wandering into my private space. That door had been opened and closed scores of times in the preceding year. When I entered, nothing unusual had caught my eye.

My study door is decorated. There is a Celtic knocker in the shape of a squirrel, a St. Bridget cross made of Irish rushes, and a poster. The poster, mounted on heavy blue cardboard, is a memento from the publication of my first book. Issued by my publisher for promotional parties, it shows the book's cover, my name, and the huge black words "it's here!"

The door is one of those old wooden doors with six deep panels. The poster is tacked tightly to the middle of the door, covering the two center panels and resting on the lower. The edges of the poster are flush against the door, especially at top and bottom, with the exception of two areas on each side, halfway down the cardboard, where small gaps exist.

157

From one of these gaps, I noticed a key coyly poking out. I walked to the door and pulled sharply. Immediately, out tumbled the entire missing set.

I held the keys loosely in my hand and stared at them. I looked up at the poster, with its emphatic proclamation. And then I smiled and said aloud, "You always did have a great sense of humor, Bob Shea."

It would make a good story to say that everything suddenly fell into place, that all my questions dissolved, that I was somehow transported to a place of certainty and confidence in life's meaning. That I no longer felt that the universe was a place of uncertainty and chaos. That I recognized and accepted the proof of Bob's continuing existence.

But that would not be true. What I felt was bafflement and curiosity, together with a startled amusement. This could not be the answer to my crazed prayer. No. There had to be some other, more commonsense answer. The keys were behind the poster: effect. Someone must have put them there: cause. I had been alone when the keys disappeared. Ergo, I had put the keys behind the poster. I did not remember doing so; it must have happened accidentally. Somehow, it was clear, I must have dropped the keys behind that poster, that day a year previously when I'd lost them.

I set out to prove my thesis. I tried to drop the keys behind the poster. I stood at the door, held the keys up in my right hand, and dropped them on the door. They caught at first on the cardboard's edge, then bounced off the door mounding and slid down to the floor.

I tried throwing the keys at the poster from a few feet away. The same thing happened: they slid down and did not hold. I tried walking past the door with the keys dangling from my hand, to see if they would catch in the poster and hold. They did not catch and hold.

There was only one way to get the keys into the position I had found them. I had to pull the poster forward, push the keys along a little groove in the door, and shove the poster back in place. Anything else would result in the keys either not lodging behind the poster at all, or dropping out as soon as the door was moved.

I spent a half-hour trying to make the keys stay behind that poster. Natalie, when I told her the mystery of the found keys, did the same. We stood in the green-carpeted upstairs hallway, two grown women flinging keys at a door, over and over. Thinking of more and more peculiar ways that the keys might have wound up resting on that hidden shelf. Unwilling at first to accept that only careful, conscious effort could bring the keys to rest as they had been, but unable to find any other way to make the keys stay in that place.

A year previously, the answer that I had wanted was a simple one: that Bob still existed and, hearing my call for help, would return my keys to me. But once this particular and peculiar miracle had occurred, I resisted accepting it as an answer to that crazy challenge. I attempted to catalog all possibilities. I had gone into a fugue state, placed the keys behind the poster, and forgotten all about them. A visitor had found the keys and whimsically placed them behind the poster. A worker—the plumber, say—had found the keys and hid them rather than giving them to me.

These scenarios are possible, though fairly unlikely. Were this a court of law, I would argue that there was no motive for anyone else to hide the keys, and no evidence that I have either before or since gone into a state of mindless fugue. That my beloved Bob had somehow answered my request seems as likely as any of these interpretations. Also: Bob had a unique sense of humor, and he tended to procrastinate. So it would be in character for him to have taken a year to get around to giving me the keys back, and then it would be in a suitably clever fashion.

I have, many times since the keys reappeared, asked myself how I would have responded had I found the keys, in exactly the same place, during my original frenzy of grief. I would, I think, have accepted it as a dramatic proof of Bob's continued existence. Look, I would have said to myself, he returned to me in my hour of need. He loved me still; I could still call upon him and rely upon him; there was life after death. In retrospect, I am glad that I did not find the keys then. Although my pain might have been greatly lessened at the start, I would have been left with only an odd anecdote which, over time, would have grown less and less vital, would have held less and less consolation.

Instead, the loss of the keys had propelled me into discovering a way to live with the unresolvability of our most basic questions. During my period of grief, I became familiar—even comfortable—with relativity and uncertainty. Indeed, those theories polished the world so that it shone with a strange and compelling luster. The world could never again be ordinary once I had plummeted through the rabbit-hole of quantum mechanics. If there was uncertainty at the basis of the universe, there was also a ravishing mystery.

After the keys reappeared, as I considered the various possibilities for how they got where they did, I did not feel compelled to prove any one or another. I did not call every visitor and worker who had entered the house in the previous year; I did not have myself examined for unsuspected fugue states. Neither did I convince myself that I had proof of life after death. I was, and I am, willing to live with all the possibilities. I will never know exactly how those keys got on my door, but it does not matter. The loss of the keys did not pose a question to me; it set me on a journey. Finding the keys was not an answer to my question; it was just another station on the way.

I once asked a techno-junkie friend where my email is stored. I think I pictured a huge computer somewhere, where I had the electronic equivalent of a little mailbox. I think I pictured that mailbox sometimes full with mail, sometimes empty. But where on earth was the mailbox?

My friend guffawed. "There's no big computer," she said, "it's all in the fiber-optic network."

This answer was utterly mysterious to me. In the fiber-optic network? Where is that? How can messages be in a network, rather than in a place? My mind boggled.

But quantum theory teaches us that this is not, ultimately, a universe of hard mechanistic reality where mail has to rest in mailboxes. It is a universe of connections and relations, of particle-waves in spacetime where order explicates itself in form and enfolds itself in pattern. The universe is not a great machine, Jeans said, but a great thought. A great thought that expresses itself in matter and energy, ceaselessly changing places.

Whatever part of that great thought once appeared as Bob Shea still exists, I now believe, somewhere in the network of this universe. He has only "departed from this strange world a little ahead of me." Perhaps, as Einstein said, "That means nothing. People like us, who believe in physics, know that the distinction between past, present and future is only a stubbornly persistent illusion." If I cannot access the codes to find Bob in the universal network, it does not mean that he has ceased to be. But "being" in that other world must surely be something beyond our imagining in this one, something as different as messages surging through networks are from little metal envelope-filled boxes.

I am comforted by having my keys again. We live in story, and the story of the keys now has a pleasing symmetry. But I do not know

160

what that story means. Or, rather: I know that it can mean many things, some contradictory, but perhaps all true at the same time nonetheless. And I am most deeply comforted by knowing that I cannot ever truly know, that the universe is so far beyond our understanding that miracles, even peculiar and rather silly ones like this one, are very likely to keep occurring.

Nominated by Fourth Genre

LANDSCAPE WITH

HUNGRY GULLS

by LANCE LARSEN

from GRAND STREET

If I said burial, if I said a lovely morning
    to prepare the body, who would I startle?
Not this pair of teenage girls in matching swimsuits
    making a mound of their brother.
And not the boy himself, laid out like a cadaver
    on rye, who volunteered for interment.

In the language of skin, he knows that sand rhymes
    with patience, and that patience worketh
a blue sky dotted with gulls, if only he remains
    still enough. And he does, his face a cameo
dusted with sparkling grains. Meanwhile, my son
    brings me offerings he has dug up—

a jawbone, a pair of vertebrae, ribs like planks, three teeth.
    At my feet, an ancient horse assembles.
A lesson in calcification? A beginner's oracle kit?
    If the seagulls canvassing the beach
are questions, then the pelican riding the dihedral breeze
    above the buoys is an admonition, but to what?

The sisters are at work again, making a giant
    Shasta daisy of their brother's face,

six pieces of popcorn per petal, his eyes blinking.
    Now they scatter leftover kernels across the mound
like sextons scattering lime. To my left,
    ankle-deep in shallows, my son catches minnows.

No, not minnows, damselfly larvae,
    which swim like minnows but have six legs.
He places them in a moat, so they can swim freely.
    Soon enough they will climb this castle wall.
Soon enough they will shed their syntax and leave
    one language for another, like a good translation.

The sisters have moved farther down the beach
    in hopes that the seagulls will gently
nibble their brother. So many motives. Theirs: to dress
    a body in the sands of is as though tomorrow isn't.
His: to taste the world, mouth to beak.
    The gulls draw closer, to peck at his heart.

I am trying to pretend the body is only an idea.
    I watch the pelican. I have to keep reminding myself.
A pelican is not a pterodactyl with feathers.
    A pelican is not doing moral reconnaissance.
A pelican does not know my name.
    I close my eyes long enough to drift up and up.

Poor man, napping there, far below, who looks
    and smells like me, but is stuck in a beach chair.
Quick, someone teach him to bank and hover.
    And this horse my son is decorating the moat with,
broken into pieces so small and various and eloquent—
    why do I worry whether it has enough to eat?

Nominated by Jim Barnes

THE IRISH MARTYR

fiction by RUSSELL WORKING

from ZOETROPE: ALL STORY

NADIA FIRST SAW THE FOREIGNER on her third day in al-Arish, as she and Ghaada went to swim. The Awar girls came here with their parents every August—just the four of them, now that their older sister was married and their brother remained in Cairo running a small chain of pizza parlors that Papa owned—but Nadia had never seen this stranger, or, for that matter, any foreigner in this Mediterranean town, with its litter-blown beaches and donkeys hauling carts of olives or apricots. He was wiry and ruddy, with angular limbs and a hollow where his sternum met his throat. The girls passed him as he returned from a swim. He was dripping wet and wearing gym shorts, nothing more, and although his torso was almost hairless and milky in color, sunburn and a grotesque pox of freckles stained his face and forearms. He had not shaved that morning. He was blue-eyed and handsome, or would have been without the freckles. He stared at the sisters, surprised, it seemed, to see young women heading out to swim while wearing long dresses and Islamic head scarves. At the last instant before he passed, he winked. Nadia looked away. Ghaada suffocated her giggles.

They waded into the shallow waves, as salty as bouillon, and their dresses billowed in the spume, so that someone swimming under the roiling surface could have seen the teal and purple of their bathing suits. "He likes you," Ghaada said, and she gathered her garments around her and submerged before Nadia could answer. At fourteen—two years younger than Nadia—Ghaada had already joined the legions of conservative girls who had concluded that there was no point in keeping one's weight down when even the most general outlines of one's body are hidden from the eyes of men, so they ate with the appetites of field hands and paraded the streets like blimps in raincoats. For Nadia, however, baklava and Wagon Wheels did not provide the escape they did Ghaada, and so she had grown up willowy, with a figure she would admire in the bathroom mirror as she emerged from the shower: she would let the towel slip away, revealing the volumes of her body, the breasts, the shapely belly with its ant-like trail of hair, the spiral of a navel, the shorn triangle where her legs met. Even on the streets in her formless dresses, she felt men's eyes when the wind blew and the fabric clung to her.

When Ghaada surfaced, Nadia splashed her. "You're an idiot. He's obviously an infidel."

"So? I saw how he looked at you. I wonder what he's doing here."

"He's probably one of those crazy cyclists heading from Istanbul to Cairo. Or maybe he was traveling to Sharm el-Sheikh, and he got on the wrong bus. Anyway, he'll leave soon, God willing. What's there to do in Arish?"

But the stranger did not seem to be headed anywhere. He settled on the patio on the beachside of his cottage, a flat-roofed stucco "villa" as they were advertised, that sat beside an identical one the Awars were renting. A walkway half a meter wide separated the buildings. By the time the girls returned from their swim, the foreigner had pulled on a T-shirt that read, in English, H-BLOCK MARTYRS—the fabric a faded green that reassumed its original color below his waistband, where it adhered to his swimsuit. He sprawled in a lawn chair thumbing through a copy of the *Middle East Times* and drinking a bottle of Stella beer, even at this hour, not yet one in the afternoon. As they washed their feet at the saltwater tap, Nadia sneaked another look. The man was watching her, and her gaze fell to a crack in the concrete that channeled the runoff into a hydra-headed delta on the sand. Was he still looking? She dared not check. Such a man was probably used to eyeing topless blondes shivering on the windswept beaches of Europe, and Nadia imagined that he could discern things about her in her wet garments.

Papa—a stout man, prematurely elderly at fifty-three, with wood-colored teeth that had rotted to fangs, like a shark's—stepped out for a smoke and noticed the foreigner. "Hello," the stranger said in Arabic, but Papa did not understand the man's pronunciation. He glowered, and the stranger sat up a little, alert. Then it dawned on him that Papa was directing his lightning bolts of wrath at the bottle, which now stood on a low wall, and shaking his head, the stranger took the bottle indoors. Moments later he returned carrying a coffee mug topped off with froth, as if porcelain disguised his sin in the eyes of the Omniscient One, Most Beneficent, Most Merciful.

By the time the girls had changed, Papa was back in the master bedroom complaining to Mama. Fully dressed, she lay atop the bed-clothes clutching a windup alarm clock with double brass hemi-spheres on top, registering its hypertensive ticktock like the pulse of a mechanical hummingbird. The shutters were closed, and a ceiling fan stirred the indolent flies that patrolled the honeycombed vol-umes of space in redundant sorties.

"Who does he think he is, strolling around practically naked out there, leering at good Muslim girls?" he demanded, as if Mama had been complicit in the foreigner's lechery.

Mama drew a breath as if to speak, but did not.

"Look at him, guzzling beer in front of the girls. And at this hour. That's what these infidels are like. I've warned you and the girls about foreigners, and you laughed at me. And now you all can finally see with your own eyes. A man like that would gladly take advantage of you." This last statement he directed toward the living room, where the girls stood, afraid to sit or retreat to their room. "You can see the kind of people they are. Nakedness, drunkenness, lechery."

Finally Mama's eyes turned to him with such loathing that an at-tentive person would take a hint and leave her alone. "Why don't you go beat him up, then?"

He did not notice the sarcasm. "If he keeps it up, I might do it, God willing. But I'll tell you something: The girls are not going out on the beach while he's there."

"Papa, we can't stay indoors all day in the summer," Nadia said. "It's forty-three degrees today."

"You've got better things to do, anyway. Go listen to a tape and im-prove your mind."

The girls sat in their room—on the west side of the house, across the walkway from the foreigner's place—and listened to the preacher's warnings about women, who were weak by nature and, were it not for the teachings of the Prophet—God's blessing and peace be upon him—and the supervision of their fathers and husbands, would give in to the sins of gossip or flirtation or jangling their finery under their

166

robes, generation upon generation, always the same. For when the Prophet went to hell did he not see more women there than men? The preacher illustrated the sermon with an incident he had witnessed in Giza: a young hussy boarding a bus wearing a black dress that bared her forearms and her legs from the knees down—so exposed was she that one gust of the dun western wind had been sufficient to reveal certain garments to those boarding behind her, and when the good men and women of the bus reproved her and said there were places where people knew how to deal with the likes of her—through stonings, honor killings, cutting off noses, and suchlike—this defiant young harlot was reduced to tears and retorted that she was an Egyptian citizen and they had no right to tell her she should take the veil if she did not elect to. But who knows? Perhaps these good people had planted the seeds of repentance that would save her from the unquenchable fires of hell, God willing, for the Almighty was Oft Forgiving and Most Merciful. This woman interested Nadia, but the preacher moved on to a denunciation of similar transgressors, such as a tramp who stood in the doorway of her apartment openly talking with a male clerk from the Energy Ministry who had come to collect the electrical bill, or the woman who did not bother to put on her head scarf, but merely a baseball cap, when she went out to hang the laundry from the balcony of the mud-brick apartment where she lived, oblivious, apparently, to the longing eyes of teenage boys nearby, or to the possibility that she might distract even—say—a devout man who might happen to be sitting at a window across the courtyard, tearing him away from his reflection on God's Holy Book—for are we not all human and corruptible if we do not exercise vigilance?

The tape went on for a long time. Nadia peeked though a crack between the drawn curtains and glimpsed, in the space between the cottages, the foreigner's leg hanging over the wall. Sometimes his hand—holding his cup, a cigarette, or both—rested on the leg. "I'll tell Papa you're looking," Ghaada said, but the threat was entirely idle: the consequences would have been so dire—a firestorm of wrath that could end in the beating of both girls—that it could not be taken seriously.

The afternoon grew hotter, but even without the presence of a foreigner, another swim would have been out of the question, for there was dinner to prepare, and Mama could not go to the market because visible waves of nausea were smutting her vision. The girls walked up the road by the flat-roofed stucco houses. Most women they saw wore the hijab, like Nadia and Ghaada, but a few saintly sisters ghosted by in black chadors, their eyes flitting to take in the portion of the world allotted to them, as if through a slot in a steel door. Two Coptic girls, in jeans and T-shirts that read LIMASSOL WINE FESTIVAL 2002 and ALL THE CATS OF CYPRUS, strolled along chattering as they licked ice-cream cones. Farther on, a group of teenage boys in shorts and T-shirts and floppy beach hats were wrestling with each other on the sidewalk, but they stopped when the Awar sisters approached. Near the mosque were a number of bearded Islamists, wearing white skullcaps and short-sleeved outfits like nightshirts, through which the silhouettes of their legs and their underwear could be discerned. Scriptures droned melodiously from the loudspeaker in the minaret, and a drowsy policeman, dressed in a red beret and white uniform and black boots, guarded an automated teller machine with his Kalashnikov slung over his shoulder. A new photo lab had opened since the Awars were last in Arish, and the owner was crouching inside the display window, adjusting his portraits of newlyweds in gilded frames. But his own handiwork was dwarfed by posters of the gold-domed Noble Sanctuary, of the decapitated head of a martyr—just the head: his eyes smudges, his beard singed—lying in a supermarket amid a shambles of arms and legs and crushed cantaloupes and grapes and strollers. According to a caption, he had blasted himself straight through the gates of Paradise, God willing, while sending several infant Zionists and their mothers and a reserve soldier to hell. There was also a poster of a dead boy of eight or ten years lying in a coffin draped in a Palestinian flag, but when Nadia stopped to study it Ghaada said, "Let's go. I can't stand this." Along the market street the girls picked through the shops and side stalls selling dates, peanuts, cages of live chickens, Orbit gum, Crest toothpaste, Coca-Cola, packages of Abu Ammar potato chips decorated with a cartoon of President Arafat's gaping bespectacled face, Iranian soaps of a brand called Barf. When Ghaada had come home recently with a bottle of Barf dishwashing detergent, Mama laughed for the first time since before the day in February when they found her unconscious on the kitchen floor with an empty bottle of sleeping tablets beside her. "I don't know what this word means in Farsi," she said, "but in English it's what the cat keeps doing behind Papa's chair." Sides of beef and goat hung out in front of the butcher shops in the Sinai heat, but their colors were bad. Eventually the sisters found some fresh mutton. By the time they returned, the boys were gone.

That night after bedtime, Nadia peeked once again at the foreigner's place. His window was opposite the girls', and his lights were on. The curtains were of tulle, flimsy and translucent, and Nadia could see into the room where he was pacing about in blue shorts and his martyrs T-shirt, gnawing on a drumstick. The remainder of his dinner— the carcass of a chicken, an olive salad, some pita, a smear of hummus—was served on paper plates laid out on a tablecloth made of a copy of *Al-Abram*. "What are you doing?" Ghaada said.

Nadia shushed her with a scowl. For a time the foreigner was out of view. Then he returned and swept the remains and the newspaper into the trash and wiped down the table with a rag. Vanishing again, he left only his shadow on the wall, his arms working at something; then he came back drying his hands on his shorts. From a shelf nearby, he grabbed what looked like a billiard case and opened it on the table. He unpacked some steel rods and pipes and a pencil box and the padded end of a crutch, all of them black. With a glance at his watch, he fit them together rapidly, biting his lip. "Can you see him?" Ghaada whispered. He screwed the shoulder pad onto a rod, and fitted that to the pencil box. A thin pipe was attached to the other end. It hit Nadia that he was assembling a rifle—a sleek, lightweight weapon, nothing like the bulky Kalashnikovs shouldered by the police. He screwed on a silencer and rechecked his watch. Satisfied, he set the rifle on its mounts—an inverse V, with an I under the butt—and knelt behind the table, aiming in the direction of the beach. He peered through the scope and fingered the trigger.

"Pow," he said. Nadia could read his lips through the windows. "Pow."

Then he disassembled the rifle and cleaned it with rags and a long, thin brush.

"What's he doing?" Ghaada said.

"Nothing."

"I want to look."

"Hush. You can't."

"You're looking."

"He just put a rifle together."

Ghaada shoved her way to the window. The man sensed something and looked toward them, and the girls ducked.

After they deemed it safe to speak, Ghaada whispered, "We should tell Papa."

"Tell him what? That we were spying on a man in his room? You know what he'll do to us?"

"Maybe he's going to kill somebody."

"Why would a foreigner come to Egypt to kill somebody?"

When the stranger sprawled out on his patio a second day, the girls were again forbidden to swim. In the morning Papa alone ambled out, wearing trunks and a singlet, his skinny legs exposed, and belly-flopped into the lukewarm sea. Meanwhile, Nadia and Ghaada sat indoors, bored and quarrelsome, until Mama sent them to get some cayenne candies. The time in al-Arish was not all vacation for Papa; he was setting up another franchise here, so he left for the afternoon, and Mama remained in her room, sometimes lying facedown on the bed, sometimes sitting in a rocking chair and holding the clock. Nadia sat with her and held her hand and asked about the stories she already knew but which Mama used to like to recount. Once Grandpa, for example, had taken the entire family to Aswan when he was consulted on an important technical question concerning the dam. He was an engineer and a tender man, and his eyes always followed Grandma wherever she was in the room, even after she was old and liver-spotted, and she smiled modestly as if not wishing to flaunt her good fortune. Uncle Basel, who as a boy would chase Mama outside with the scarabs he found, ended up studying in Paris and stole a small marker that read JIM MORRISON from Pere Lachaise graveyard ("He wanted an unmarked grave: I read it somewhere," Uncle Basel had said), but then, in a fit of guilt, he tried to return it and was arrested. And later, when Mama was in university, a professor had told her that someday she would be interpreting for Egypt at the United Nations or in Washington or Sydney—her English was that good— but that was before she found a job at the translation service and met Papa, who needed help corresponding with an American corporation. Only after their wedding did he tell her, "You were not vouchsafed beauty, and you must admit that makeup doesn't improve your face. Be content with my accepting you as you are, with your plainness and your weight. I want you as God created you, with no artificial beautification. Second, you must terminate all contact with your workplace. You needn't submit your resignation; just quit showing up, without explanation. After fifteen days they'll fire you, in accor-

170

dance with the law. After all, who needs them?" Nadia also knew that all the relatives despised Papa and had urged Mama to leave him, but for some reason she had never found the courage to do so.

Today, however, Mama did not wish to talk. "I don't want to think about it. I just want to rest."

"Mama, stop looking at that." Nadia snatched the clock and set it aside.

"Time goes more slowly when you're aware of it. You savor it."

"It's not healthy. Tell me about that cruise to Lebanon when you were little."

But Mama picked up the clock again and said only, "Thirty-one years."

This was the amount of time she had been married to Papa.

When the foreigner sat outside on the third straight day, Papa decided to speak to him. Never mind the stranger's pretense that he did not comprehend Arabic; usually these people feigned ignorance, but you could see in their eyes that they understood. The girls sat on the couch by the open double doors in the living room, where they could crane and see what was going on.

"What are you up to in Arish?" Papa asked. "It's a long way from Giza and Luxor. Are you a spy?"

The foreigner raised his hands apologetically and replied in English. Nadia caught the words "sorry" and "Arabic." Papa had never permitted the girls to go to school, but they had learned to read at home. Mama also taught them English, and the exotic alphabet and words had excited Nadia, with their redolence of another world, of glass buildings and buttressed cathedrals and immobile beefeaters and black taxicabs crowding the snowy pavement and girls who sauntered the streets in tight jeans with their navels exposed, but Nadia found it impossible to master the language without the discipline of school.

Papa continued as if the man understood. "Or maybe you're just a libertine. You shouldn't drink in public. It's a disgrace. You want to go to hell, it's your choice, but don't set a filthy example for my daughters. We come to the beach and they're cooped up in the stuffy house all week because of your public drunkenness. Besides, you shouldn't stare at them. I know what's on your mind when you leer at Nadia that way."

The foreigner pulled out a packet of Dunhills and shook one out at

171

Papa. Flustered, Papa accepted. He lit his cigarette, then ignited the foreigner's.

"Well, that's all I had to say. No offense, eh? If you ever have daughters, you'll understand a father's concern. Ah, I used to smoke Dunhills, but I gave them up. The good thing about smoking Cleopatras is you cut back. They taste so wretched, I'm down to half a pack a day. That should add a few years to my life, God willing. You understand me?"

The stranger nodded on cue. It was obvious he did not.

"You know, smoke?" Papa puffed in an exaggerated manner; having suddenly taken it upon himself to teach an infidel the language of God. "Too bad my wife can't come out. She used to speak English quite well, and I'm starting to think you're an Englishman, eh? You seem to like our view. The sea? Ocean? Big water? It's lovely here, isn't it? Tell other foreigners to come, spend money. You are welcome to Egypt. But you must behave. If you must drink, keep it indoors. And the women: stick with your own kind. Our women are the most beautiful on earth, and once they marry they are lionesses in bed because they have been denied satisfaction so long, but they're not for you. You don't understand a word of what I'm saying, do you? Are you going to be here long? Long time? Many nights? Sleep?" He folded his hands under his cheek. The stranger laughed at Papa's antics, and Papa himself could not help chuckling. "Because if you are, I should find someone to interpret for me. You think I'm joking. This is serious."

That night Papa telephoned the imam for help. "The situation is rather awkward," he explained. "I'm not saying he's a bad fellow. I just need someone to tell him there are standards of conduct when you live next door to a good Muslim family." Within an hour a Mercedes taxicab clattered up in a cloud of smoke and two men came to the door. They were a mismatched pair: Ibrahim, a garrulous young Palestinian cabdriver, was clean-shaven and wore sneakers and jeans and a Chicago Bulls T-shirt, while his partner, who never stated his name, was a fat, gloomy, bearded man in a brown suit and a black-and-white kaffiyeh. When the visitors entered, the girls retreated to their room and listened through the vent in the door.

"I'm sorry about the problems you've been having," Ibrahim said. "We have already spoken to your neighbor, and he was mortified to learn he has offended you. He extends his apologies to you and your

172

elder daughter, whose chaste beauty he admits he admired." Nadia's heart was racing. Ghaada elbowed her. "Things are different in Ireland. Infidels. You understand. But listen to me: This guy is with us. He has work to do, God willing. You could have blown everything, blabbing around like that. Thank God the imam happened to call me because I speak English. I'm not blaming you. You didn't know. I'm just saying you must drop this. Discuss him with no one. Forget he exists, you and your family. We're serious."

"I'm sorry, I had no idea. I would never tell a soul. I'm of course thrilled that he wishes to join the struggle—" Papa hesitated, perhaps uncertain what struggle they were talking about, though logic suggested the one against the Zionist entity. He pressed on: "If he needs help, I have relatives in Gaza who can—"

"Listen. If you breathe a word to anyone, we'll cut your throat like a sheep's. Is that clear?"

"But I wouldn't—there's no need—" Papa faltered.

"Tell your family. It goes for all of you. Say nothing. To no one. Here or in Cairo. Ever. Till the day that you die. Forget you ever saw him."

That night a light through the window woke Nadia, and she thought, *He's up*. Ghaada was snoring, and Nadia checked her alarm clock: two-thirteen A.M. She lay there remembering Ibrahim's words: how the foreigner had admired her "chaste beauty"; how, when confronted with news of Papa's affront, he had extended his apologies like a gentleman. She wished she could express regret in turn for her father's boorishness. Nadia knelt on her bed and peeked through the curtains. The Irishman had just returned from a swim, and to her astonishment, he slipped off his trunks and stood there naked, toweling himself. She was shocked at how ugly a man's organs were. He had not removed the hair of his body, and it was of a darker red than that of his head. After tossing the towel aside, he absently tugged on his penis. Something prickled between her legs. She knew it was iniquitous to spy on a naked man, but she could not tear herself away. The foreigner vanished for a time, then returned, fully dressed, with his backpack and rifle case, which he propped against the table. Something popped in the walls, and Nadia started and lay down. Just the house contracting in the night air. Still, she dared not look out again. Deep inside something was ticking, and as she lay there, she brought the Irishman through the window into her room. In this fantasy Ghaada was elsewhere, back home in Cairo, away at a friend's. Nadia warned him, "Get out or I'll scream. My papa will kill you," but the Irishman only smiled and winked. His soft lips brushed hers. She would be naked, and trembling because in the moonlight he could make out the form of her body in her bed-clothes, and he peeled back the sheets and looked at her. He smoothed the gooseflesh of her shoulders and breasts, then his palms found their way to her abdomen, lingering on her belly, sliding to the prickly, shaven salient. At last his fingers moved within. "It's true: you're a lioness," he whispered. Something pulsed deep inside her and she gasped for breath. Sweat broke out, soaking her nightgown.

Gradually the ecstasy subsided into remorse. "Ghaada?" she whispered. Asleep. Nadia did not understand what had happened, but maybe it helped you have a baby, if a man was with you. She wished there was somebody she could consult—perhaps her older sister back in Cairo, who was married and would understand such things— but she knew she could never speak a word about it. Nothing. To no one. Ever. Till the day that she died. If she did, they'd cut her throat like a sheep's.

The next morning, the Irishman was gone, but his H-BLOCK MARTYRS T-shirt lay out on the chair on the patio. When there was no sign of him by noon, Papa let the girls go swimming. "I doubt we'll be seeing much of him after Ibrahim told him off," Papa said. "He said this Irishman was quite ashamed of himself. You see, even unbelievers can have a conscience when confronted by Muslim decency." Nadia stared, and Papa flushed. "Don't tell anyone about him, by the way," he added. "He's doing some important work. Top secret." Over time, the T-shirt flapped like a stingray to a corner of the patio and took refuge amid the broken glass and potato-chip wrappers. Nadia kept hoping the Irishman would return for it.

But on Sunday Papa came home waving a newspaper and announced, "Listen, girls. I've found our foreigner." He read aloud a story on page three. It seemed there had been a great victory in the occupied territories. A sniper, sitting on a hill near a Jewish settlement, had staked out the Zionist monkeys and pigs arriving for an evening school carnival and, in rapid succession, picked off two parents, five children, and a soldier while the Israelis scrambled to figure out where the shooting was coming from. Obviously, he was a professional: he had popped off exactly eight rounds, one for each enemy, then laid down his rifle and walked away. Every one of his so-called victims had died of head wounds, except for one Zionist kindergartner who was rendered, the report said, "a vegetable." Papa considered this, then nodded once and read on. The gunman nearly escaped, but the accursed Israelis, with their night-vision goggles, had found him fleeing and gunned him down. He was carrying an Australian passport, but the Zionists were investigating the possibility that he was connected to—"Get this," Papa said—the Irish Republican Army.

"An Irishman! I'm sure it's our neighbor. He was a little rough around the edges, but a decent young man nonetheless. Maybe he converted to Islam in the end, God willing. If so, today he's in paradise with seventy-two virgins."

That day Nadia retrieved the T-shirt, which still smelled of a man, and when the Awars left al-Arish she brought it with her. She often daydreamed about the Irishman, but at night she sometimes started awake, wondering what had become of the Zionist kindergartner, who lay in diapers in a hospital somewhere, unseeing, unthinking, unable to roll over in bed, day after day. Nadia kept the shirt for three years, until after her wedding to Taisir, her father's accountant. But Taisir resented the stories Papa whispered about this Irish martyr. How did they know he had converted? Were his head and body hair shaven when he died? Was he carrying prayer beads, a Koran? He was probably just a mercenary; an infidel could not become a martyr. The time had come for Nadia to throw the shirt away. Taisir also made her get rid of other frivolous possessions: letters from girlfriends, jewelry that tempted her to cupidity, an English language textbook, a map of London she had taken from her mother. He forbade her to work, but that was not really an issue because she could not get a job without an education. Nadia found ways to pass the time at home. Whenever her husband left for work, she turned the clock to face the wall, and she disciplined herself not to look at it until he returned. She did not wish to become like her mother.

Nominated by Zoetrope: All Story

SCATTERING MY MOTHER'S ASHES ON THE FAMILY PLOT AT HICKMAN, KENTUCKY

by DOUG ANDERSON

from CONNECTICUT REVIEW

Down into the black, flesh curdled dirt.
Down into the family charnel,
marinade in whiskey, with the murderers
and the soul-murderers
against whom you honed your tongue.
Down there with the starved
and yellow-fever-sickened,
with the beans-one-day-lard-the-next-
one-foot-in-front-of-the-other life.
Down in the river sodden mash
of sex smeared hate.
With the stained wall paper
peeled off the pale failing heart.
You burned for a while
against the cold dark and faded.
Let what continues on in the charred silence be
gentle as a baby's breath against your neck.

I wouldn't wish your life on anyone
and especially myself.
I sift the weight of you from my heart.
Take the hard words and the bloody welts
of fierce love with you.
Now that you are dead
I can get a word in edgewise
but I hate long eulogies
and therefore let me
make you one like a star that has collapsed
in on itself and is so dense it can hold
everything that is said
and everything that is unsaid.
I let the last of you drift with this
small wind that has made itself known
by moving the leaves as if to end this. Now.

Nominated by Wally Lamb, Connecticut Review

THE HURT MAN

fiction by WENDELL BERRY

from THE HUDSON REVIEW

WHEN HE WAS FIVE, Mat Feltner, like every other five-year-old who had lived in Port William until then, was still wearing dresses. In his own thoughts he was not yet sure whether he would turn out to be a girl or a boy, though instinct by then had prompted him to take his place near the tail end of the procession of Port William boys. His nearest predecessors in that so far immortal straggle had already taught him the small art of smoking cigars, along with the corollary small art of chewing coffee beans to take the smoke smell off his breath. And so in a rudimentary way he was an outlaw, though he did not know it, for none of his grownups had yet thought to forbid him to smoke.

His outgrown dresses he saw worn daily by a pretty neighbor named Margaret Finley, who to him might as well have been another boy too little to be of interest, or maybe even a girl, though it hardly mattered—and though, because of a different instinct, she would begin to matter to him a great deal in a dozen years, and after that she would matter to him all his life.

The town of Port William consisted of two rows of casually maintained dwellings and other buildings scattered along a thoroughfare that nobody had ever dignified by calling it a street; in wet times it hardly deserved to be called a road. Between the town's two ends the road was unevenly rocked but otherwise had not much distinguished itself from the buffalo trace it once had been. At one end of the town was the school, at the other the graveyard. In the center there were several stores, two saloons, a church, a bank, a hotel, and a black-

178

smith shop. The town was the product of its own becoming which, if not accidental exactly, had also been unplanned. It had no formal government or formal history. It was without pretense or ambition, for it was the sort of place that pretentious or ambitious people were inclined to leave. It had never declared an aspiration to become anything it was not. It did not thrive so much as it merely lived, doing the things it needed to do to stay alive. This tracked and rubbed little settlement had been built in a place of great natural abundance and beauty, which it had never valued highly enough or used well enough, had damaged, and yet had not destroyed. The town's several buildings, shaped less by art than by need and use, had suffered tellingly and even becomingly a hundred years of wear.

Though Port William sat on a ridge of the upland, still it was a river town; its economy and its thoughts turned toward the river. Distance impinged on it from the river, whose waters flowed from the eastward mountains ultimately, as the town always was more or less aware, to the sea, to the world. Its horizon, narrow enough though it reached across the valley to the ridgeland fields and farmsteads on the other side, was pierced by the river, which for the next forty years would still be its main thoroughfare. Commercial people, medicine showmen, evangelists, and other river travelers came up the hill from Dawes Landing to stay at the hotel in Port William, which in its way cherished these transients, learned all it could about them, and talked of what it learned.

Mat would remember the town's then-oldest man, Uncle Bishop Bower, who would confront any stranger, rap on the ground with his long staff, and demand, "Sir! What might your name be?"

And Herman Goslin, no genius, made his scant living by meeting the steamboats and transporting the disembarking passengers, if any, up to the hotel in a gimpy buckboard. One evening as he approached the hotel with a small trunk on his shoulder, followed by a large woman with a parasol, one of the boys playing marbles in the road said, "Here comes Herman Goslin with a fat lady's trunk."

"You boys can kiss that fat lady's ass," said Herman Goslin. "Ain't that tellin' 'em, fat lady?"

The town was not built nearer the river perhaps because there was no room for it at the foot of the hill, or perhaps because, as the town loved to reply to the inevitable question from travelers resting on the hotel porch, nobody knew where the river was going to run when they built Port William.

179

And Port William did look as though it had been itself forever. To Mat at the age of five, as he later would suppose, remembering himself, it must have seemed eternal, like the sky.

However eternal it might have been, the town was also as temporal, lively, and mortal as it possibly could be. It stirred and hummed from early to late with its own life and with the life it drew into itself from the countryside. It was a center, and especially on Saturdays and election days its stores and saloons and the road itself would be crowded with people standing, sitting, talking, whittling, trading, and milling about. This crowd was entirely familiar to itself; it remembered all its history of allegiances, offenses, and resentments, going back from the previous Saturday to the Civil War and long before that. Like every place, it had its angers, and its angers as always, as everywhere, found justifications. And in Port William, a dozen miles by river from the courthouse and the rule of law, anger had a license that it might not have had in another place. Sometimes violence would break out in one of the saloons or in the road. Then proof of mortality would be given in blood.

And the mortality lived and suffered daily in the town was attested with hopes of immortality by the headstones up in the graveyard, which was even then more populous than the town. Mat knew—at the age of five he had already forgotten when he had found out—that he had a brother and two sisters up there, with carved lambs resting on the tops of their small monuments, their brief lives dated beneath. In all the time he had known her, his mother had worn black.

But to him, when he was five, those deaths were stories told. Nothing in Port William seemed to him to be in passage from any beginning to any end. The living had always been alive, the dead always dead. The world, as he knew it then, simply existed, familiar even in its changes: the town, the farms, the slopes and ridges, the woods, the river, and the sky over it all. He had not yet gone farther from Port William than to Dawes Landing on the river and to his uncle Jack Beecham's place out on the Bird's Branch Road, the place his mother spoke of as "out home." He had seen the steamboats on the river and had looked out from the higher ridgetops, and so he understood that the world went on into the distance, but he did not know how much more of it there might be.

Mat had come late into the lives of Nancy and Ben Feltner, after the deaths of their other children, and he had come unexpectedly, "a blessing." They prized him accordingly. For the first four or so years of his life he was closely watched, by his parents and also by Cass and Smoke, Cass's husband, who had been slaves. But now he was five, and it was a household always busy with the work of the place, and often full of company. There had come to be times, because his grownups were occupied and he was curious and active, when he would be out of their sight. He would stray off to where something was happening, to the farm buildings behind the house, to the blacksmith shop, to one of the saloons, to wherever the other boys were. He was beginning his long study of the town and its place in the world, gathering up the stories that in years still far off he would hand on to his grandson Andy Catlett, who in his turn would be trying to master the thought of time: that there were times before his time, and would be times after. At the age of five Mat was beginning to prepare himself to help in educating his grandson, though he did not know it.

His grownups, more or less willingly, were letting him go. The town had its dangers. There were always horses in the road, and sometimes droves of cattle or sheep or hogs or mules. There were in fact uncountable ways for a boy to get hurt, or worse. But in spite of her losses, Nancy Beechum Feltner was not a frightened woman, as her son would learn. He would learn also that, though she maintained her sorrows with a certain loyalty, wearing her black, she was a woman of practical good sense and strong cheerfulness. She knew that the world was risky and that she must risk her surviving child to it as she had risked the others, and when the time came she straightforwardly did so.

But she knew also that the town had its ways of looking after its own. Where its worst dangers were, grownups were apt to be. When Mat was out of the sight of her or his father or Cass or Smoke, he was most likely in the sight of somebody else who would watch him. He would thus be corrected, consciously ignored, snatched out of danger, cursed, teased, hugged, instructed, spanked, or sent home by any grownup into whose sight he may have strayed. Within that watchfulness he was free—and almost totally free when, later, he had learned to escape it and thus had earned his freedom. "This was a *free* country when I was a boy," he would sometimes say to Andy, his grandson.

When he was five and for some while afterward, his mother drew the line unalterably only between him and the crowds that filled the town on Saturday afternoons and election days when there would be too much drinking, with consequences that were too probable. She would not leave him alone then. She would not let him go into the town, and she would not trust him to go anywhere else, for fear that he would escape into the town from wherever else she let him go. She kept him in sight.

That was why they were sitting together on the front porch for the sake of the breeze there on a hot Saturday afternoon in the late summer of 1888. Mat was sitting close to his mother on the wicker settee, watching her work. She had brought out her sewing basket and was darning socks, stretching the worn-through heels or toes over her darning egg and weaving them whole again with her needle and thread. At such work her fingers moved with a quickness and assurance that fascinated Mat, and he loved to watch her. She would have been telling him a story. She was full of stories. Aside from the small movements of her hands and the sound of her voice, they were quiet with a quietness that seemed to have increased as it had grown upon them. Cass had gone home after the dinner dishes were done. The afternoon had half gone by.

From where they sat they could see down into the town where the Saturday crowd was, and they could hear it. Doors slammed, now and then a horse nickered, the talking of the people was a sustained murmur from which now and then a few intelligible words escaped: a greeting, some bit of raillery, a reprimand to a horse, an oath. It was a large crowd in a small place, a situation in which a small disagreement could become dangerous in a hurry. Such things had happened often enough. That was why Mat was under watch.

And so when a part of the crowd intensified into a knot, voices were raised, and there was a scuffle, Mat and his mother were not surprised. They were not surprised even when a bloodied man broke out of the crowd and began running fast up the street toward them, followed by other running men whose boot heels pounded on the road.

The hurt man ran toward them where they were sitting on the porch. He was hatless. His hair, face, and shirt were bloody, and his blood dripped on the road. Mat felt no intimation of threat or danger. He simply watched, transfixed. He did not see his mother stand and put down her work. When she caught him by the back of his

182

dress and fairly poked him through the front door—"Here! Get inside!"—he still was only alert, unsurprised.

He expected her to come into the house with him. What finally surprised him was that she did not do so. Leaving him alone in the wide hall, she remained outside the door, holding it open for the hurt man. Mat ran halfway up the stairs then and turned and sat down on a step. He was surprised now but not afraid.

When the hurt man ran in through the door, instead of following him in, Nancy Feltner shut the door and stood in front of it. Mat could see her through the door glass, standing with her hand on the knob as the clutch of booted and hatted pursuers came up the porch steps. They bunched at the top of the steps, utterly stopped by the slender woman dressed in mourning, holding the door shut.

And then one of them, snatching off his hat, said, "It's all right, Mrs. Feltner. We're his friends."

She hesitated a moment, studying them, and then she opened the door to them also and turned and came in ahead of them.

The hurt man had run the length of the hall and through the door at the end of it and out onto the back porch. Nancy, with the bunch of men behind her, followed where he had gone, the men almost with delicacy, as it seemed to Mat, avoiding the line of blood drops along the hall floor. And Mat hurried back down the stairs and came along in his usual place at the tail end, trying to see, among the booted legs and carried hats, what had become of the hurt man.

Mat's memory of that day would always be partly incomplete. He never knew who the hurt man was. He knew some of the others. The hurt man had sat down or dropped onto a slatted green bench on the porch. He might have remained nameless to Mat because of the entire strangeness of the look of him. He had shed the look of a man and assumed somehow the look of all things badly hurt. Now that he had stopped running, he looked used up. He was pallid beneath the streaked bright blood, breathing in gasps, his eyes too widely open. He looked as though he had just come up from almost too deep a dive.

Nancy went straight to him, the men, the friends, clustered behind her, deferring, no longer to her authority as the woman of the house, as when she had stopped them at the front door, but now to her unhesitating, unthinking acceptance of that authority.

183

Looking at the hurt man, whose blood was dripping onto the bench and the porch floor, she said quietly, perhaps only to herself, "Oh my!" It was as though she knew him without ever having known him before.

She leaned and picked up one of his hands. "Listen!" she said, and the man brought his gaze it seemed from nowhere and looked up at her. "You're at Ben Feltner's house," she said. "Your friends are here. You're going to be all right."

She looked around at the rest of them who were standing back, watching her. "Jessie, you and Tom go see if you can find the doctor, if he's findable." She glanced at the water bucket on the shelf over the wash table by the kitchen door, remembering that it was nearly empty. "Les, go bring a fresh bucket of water." To the remaining two she said, "Get his shirt off. *Cut* it off. Don't try to drag it over his head. So we can see where he's hurt."

She stepped through the kitchen door, and they could hear her going about inside. Presently she came back with a kettle of water still warm from the noon fire and a bundle of clean rags.

"Look up here," she said to the hurt man, and he looked up.

She began gently to wash his face. Wherever he was bleeding, she washed away the blood: first his face, and then his arms, and then his chest and sides. As she washed, exposing the man's wounds, she said softly only to herself, "Oh!" or "Oh my!" She folded the white rags into pads and instructed the hurt man and his friends to press them onto his cuts to stop the bleeding. She said, "It's the Lord's own mercy we've got so many hands," for the man had many wounds. He had begun to tremble. She kept saying to him, as she would have spoken to a child, "You're going to be all right."

Mat had been surprised when she did not follow him into the house, when she waited on the porch and opened the door to the hurt man and then to his friends. But she had not surprised him after that. He saw her as he had known her: a woman who did what the world put before her to do.

At first he stayed well back, for he did not want to be told to get out of the way. But as his mother made order, he grew bolder and drew gradually closer until he was almost at her side. And then he was again surprised, for then he saw her face.

What he saw in her face would remain with him forever. It was pity, but it was more than that. It was a hurt love that seemed to include entirely the hurt man. It included him and disregarded everything else. It disregarded the aura of whiskey that ordinarily she would have resented; it disregarded the blood puddled on the porch floor and the trail of blood through the hall.

Mat was familiar with her tenderness and had thought nothing of it. But now he recognized it in her face and in her hands as they went out to the hurt man's wounds. To him, then, it was as though she leaned in the black of her mourning over the whole hurt world itself, touching its wounds with her tenderness, in her sorrow.

Loss came into his mind then, and he knew what he was years away from telling, even from thinking: that his mother's grief was real; that her children in their graves once had been alive; that everybody lying under the grass up in the graveyard once had been alive and had walked in daylight in Port William. And this was a part, and belonged to the deliverance, of the town's hard history of love.

The hurt man, Mat thought, was not going to die, but he knew from his mother's face that the man *could* die and someday would. She leaned over him, touching his bleeding wounds that she bathed and stanched and bound, and her touch had in it the promise of healing, some profound encouragement.

It was the knowledge of that encouragement, of what it had cost her, of what it would cost her and would cost him, that then finally came to Mat, and he fled away and wept.

What did he learn from his mother that day? He learned it all his life. There are few words for it, perhaps none. After that, her losses would be his. The losses would come. They would come to him and his mother. They would come to him and Margaret, his wife, who as a child had worn his castoff dresses. They would come, even as Mat watched, growing old, to his grandson, Andy, who would remember his stories and write them down.

But from that day, whatever happened, there was a knowledge in Mat that was unsurprised and at last comforted, until he was old, until he was gone.

Nominated by The Hudson Review

MY BROTHER, ANTONIO, THE BAKER

by PHILIP LEVINE

from FIVE POINTS

Did the wind blow that night? When did it not?
I'd ask you if you hadn't gone underground
lugging the answer with you.
Twenty-eight years old, on our way home
after a twelve-hour shift baking Wonder Bread
for the sleeping prisoners in the drunk tank
at the Canfield Station dreaming of a breakfast
of horse cock and mattress stuffing.
(Oh, the luxuries of 1955! How fully we lived—
the working-classes and the law abiding dregs—
on buttered toast and grilled-cheese sandwiches
as the nation braced itself for pate and pasta.)
To myself I smelled like a new mother minus
the aura of talcum and the airborne, acrid aromas
of cotton diapers. Today I'd be labeled
nurturing and bountiful instead
of vegetal and weird. A blurred moon was out,
we both saw it; I know because leaning back,
eyes closed on a ruined sky, you did your thing,
welcoming the "bright orb" waning in the west,
"Moon that rained down its silver coins
on the darkened Duero and the sleeping fields
of Soria." Did I look like you, my face
anonymous and pure, bleached with flour,
my eyes glistening with the power of neon light

or self-love? Two grown men, side by side,
one babbling joyfully to the universe
that couldn't care less, while the other,
practiced for middle age. A single crow settled
on the boiler above the Chinese restaurant,
his feathers riffling, and I took it for a sign.
A second sign was the couple exiting
the all-night pharmacy; the man came first
through the glass door, a small white sack in hand,
and let the door swing shut. Then she appeared,
one hand covering her eyes to keep
the moonlight at bay. They stood not talking
while he looked first left, then right, then left
again as flakes of darkness sifted upward
toward the streetlight. The place began to rumble
as though this were the end. You spoke again,
only this time you described someone humble
walking alone in darkness. I could see
the streetcar turning off Joy Road,
swaying down the tracks toward us,
its windows on fire. There must have been a wind,
a west wind. What else could have blown
the aura of forsythia through the town
and materialized one cross-town streetcar
never before on time? A spring wind
freighted with hope. I remember
thinking that at last you might shut up.
An old woman stood to give you
her seat as though you were angelic
or pregnant. When her eyes spilled over
with happiness, I saw she took your words
to heart as I never could. Maybe she recalled
the Duero, the fields asleep in moonlight,
maybe the words were music to her,
original and whole, words that took her home
to Soria or Krakow or wherever,
maybe she was not an old woman at all
but an oracle in drag who saw you as you were
and saw, too, you couldn't last the night.

Nominated by Grace Schulman, Richard Jackson, Len Roberts

THE SPEED OF MEMORY

by BRAD K. YOUNKIN

from RIVER TEETH: A JOURNAL OF NONFICTION NARRATIVE

THE MAN WHO RAPED MY MOTHER may not have been from Indiana, and he may have never lived there, but he drove through there. He carried a switchblade knife in the front pocket of his jeans where he could access it easily. He drove a small red car. He had brown hair, a bit disheveled, but had nice-looking features and seemed nice. He wasn't very tall. He smiled. Sometimes he wore a red flannel shirt, or at least did so once, when he drove U.S. Highway 41 in southwestern Indiana toward Vincennes. He drove behind a black four-wheel-drive Chevrolet Blazer that was pulling a brown horse trailer. He followed the Blazer and drove into the lane beside it. His windows were down. It was summer, warm and clear, late morning. From the left lane he motioned and got the attention of the woman in the Blazer, and he was saying something to her and pointing toward the back of the horse trailer.

"Like there was something *wrong*," my mother said. My father, my sister, and I had met her in the kitchen; she had just returned home, it was evening, already dark. She had told us the trip was fine, and sat down at the table, still in her boots, her purse still on her arm. "There was something *weird* that happened, though. I mean *weird*. This guy in a little red car drove up beside me and started waving at me and he kept pointing at the back of the trailer, like there was something *wrong*."

"You didn't stop, though?" my father said.

"No. I wasn't going to stop, I just kept driving. But it was so weird. After that he dropped back for a while, and a few minutes later he drove up beside me again. It was scary. And it was so bizarre—the man didn't have any *pants* on." She soaked up our reactions and told us that she'd sped up, that she drove over ninety miles per hour, that the man in the little red car finally dropped back and took an exit, and that she didn't see him again.

I was eleven when my mother told this story, the first lie I remember her telling, and the first of many more she would have to tell to uphold it. I stood by her that night listening, confused about the man in the red car, his nakedness, about her awed and almost smiling disposition as she spoke. I couldn't understand—why a man would do that, what he felt he could gain by it, or why a woman would tell of it the way my mother did, her story hopelessly unfinished, her body language mismatching her words.

When my mother and father were children, they both loved horses without ever owning one, and both resolved to raise horses when they reached adulthood. My father was a self described "city boy," raised in small towns in southern Illinois by his father, a Pentecostal preacher, and a stern, often unfair stepmother. He enlisted for Vietnam so he could leave home, and after a year of duty he chose to stay six more months instead of returning to his family. My mother grew up on a farm in Massac County in southern Illinois, the youngest of four children. Most snapshots of her show her in the yard with animals: dogs, chickens, goats, a pet squirrel, a duckling. She was a tomboy, preferring to work outside with Grandpa, in the garden, with the cattle and hogs, than inside helping Grandma with household chores. She hunted and fished with Grandpa. One time she fired twice and shot four ducks flying from a pond. When she was twelve, one of her brothers saw her bathing in the metal tub in the shed and made fun of her to schoolmates and she hit him in the head with a brick; Grandpa gave her a spanking she still remembers. She was fourteen when they got indoor plumbing. Though she was an aggressive tomboy, she was also thin and sickly, with allergies and a picky appetite. High school classmates called her "Bones" for her skinny frame, and she finished school with a rather disinterested efficiency, earning good grades without much engagement, with an unlikely notion that she'd like to be a nurse someday, and after graduation she married the young man she'd dated for two years, a drummer in a country band, and wouldn't meet my father for another two years.

189

Her first marriage produced my sister, but otherwise failed. Just before the divorce was final, she met my father while selling lingerie at a Sears in Paducah, Kentucky. He worked across the aisle selling men's suits and soon synchronized his break schedule with hers. He used the time to get acquainted, angle for a date, deflect her insistence that she didn't want a date, that she instead wanted time for herself and her baby. He was undeterred, confident, charming, kind, and she gave in. No one supported their relationship: my father's Pentecostal family called her "the devil's daughter" for having divorced and for wearing long pants and makeup; Grandpa said my dad needed to be castrated. But two years into their marriage, I was born.

It would require many more years—switching jobs, relocating, visiting family, sending and receiving birthday and Christmas cards—until their parents' criticism abated and at last stopped. Any disapproval was pointless now. When I was six Dad took a job in Paducah and we moved to Massac County onto a hill on twenty acres of cow pasture, part of Grandpa's will intended for my mother, bequeathed early. They wheeled in and anchored down a double-wide mobile home amid cow paths and cowpiles, built a barn, put up fences for horses, and settled down across the gravel road from my grandparents' farm where their cattle, displaced by our new home, stood grazing and flipping their tails.

On this horse farm, our lives were woven according to the needs of the horses, the needs of the farm, and we lived in a rhythm—daily, monthly, yearly—of work intended to keep the horses healthy and productive and marketable; and so when, in 1983, Mom came home the night after being raped and told us about her trip, business went on as usual. I don't remember when she started to waver; the rhythm for a while held her up, kept her and everyone else busy, until she couldn't find a way to weave her life into it anymore, and her life, outside of that rhythm, began to unravel.

She had driven into Indiana, bound for Vincennes, to drop off a friend's stud for a surgery. She turned north onto Highway 41, a four-lane divided highway, around midmorning. After a while, the small red car drove up beside her with the man inside waving, motioning toward the trailer. She saw him and tried to ignore him. She shook her head, as if to say, no, I'm not stopping. He dropped back behind her and drove in that manner for a time, before driving up beside her again and continuing motioning. She was scared, both of this stranger, and of the idea that perhaps something *was* wrong, either with the trailer, or, worse, the horse inside. She slowed down and drove onto the shoulder and stopped.

She stayed in the driver's seat, the Blazer's engine running. She rolled down her window. In the side mirror she saw the man get out of his car. He put up a hand.

"Good morning," he said. "You got some trouble back here."

She stepped out. "Trouble?"

"Something's wrong here with this window. It's banging around."

She walked toward the trailer. She wondered how anything could be wrong with the back window; she tried to recall closing it. When she got to the back she looked at the window, which was closed, and then at the man. He raised his switchblade in one hand and drove his other forearm under her chin, pinning her against the trailer, the blade at her face.

"You'll be dead by morning," he said.

He opened the left side of the trailer, the vacant side, and pushed her down inside it. On his knees, he unclasped and pulled down her jeans and opened his own. An occasional car may or may not have passed by, but it's unlikely either of them knew for certain; they both struggled. When it was over he leaned back and sat just behind the trailer, facing her, and looked up at the sky. He may have been un-guarded for only a second, maybe two. In this moment, with her jeans to her knees, she kicked the man in the crotch, pulled up her jeans, and ran.

He lay there for a moment, writhing, buckled, reaching out. The Blazer was still running and she climbed in. Before she could shift to drive, he had almost reached her. She pushed the button for the window to rise and pressed the accelerator, and as she pulled away his fingers were stuck in the window, and he dragged along a few feet, his fingers cracking, before he fell alongside and she drove away. In the side mirror she saw him climb to his feet and run stumbling to his car.

Perhaps a year or so later, but long before we knew the truth, Bobby Knight, basketball coach for the Indiana University Hoosiers, said: "If rape is so inevitable, why don't women sit back and enjoy it?" My family watched the story on the evening news. Bobby Knight didn't try to defend himself in a hastily arranged damage-control press con-

191

ference; he apologized and pleaded that his words were out of context, although he didn't adequately explain what that context might have been.

"How could somebody say that?" Mom said.

"It's pretty stupid," Dad said.

"How could somebody even *think* that?" She shook her head, awed.

"Rape is awful. It's a horrible thing, and to even think that is ridiculous, it's insane."

Dad and my sister and I agreed.

Mom said, "Remember last summer when that weird guy drove up beside me in Indiana and didn't have any pants on—that man could have raped *me*."

This was a stunning and perplexing possibility, and we were frightened and agreed that Bobby Knight was a fool. Connie Chung, while discussing the comment with a guest or with a co-anchor, said Knight's statement sounded like something an old grandfather would say, which further angered old grandfathers everywhere and which would lead her to publicly apologize for offending *them*. Mom said, "Grandpa would never, *ever*, say something like that. Would he?" We told her he would never say that.

It wasn't long after this that Mom became depressed periodically. She'd get sick. She wouldn't eat supper, but would instead stay in bed all night. When she left the bedroom late in the evening she'd wear her robe and move slowly down the hall. She'd move like a statue on wheels, across the kitchen floor to fill a glass of water. She'd step into the living room where we were watching television and wave to us sadly and say good night and go back to her bedroom. Her depression would last a couple weeks and subside.

One day Mom came home from shopping in Paducah.

"I just had the strangest experience," she said to me and my sister. "I was in Readmore, and this guy walked up to me; he was a young person, in his twenties, probably. He looked at me and said, 'Excuse me, ma'am. I just wanted to say that you look very . . . healthy. You really look healthy.' I didn't know what to say, so I just said, 'Thanks.' Isn't that weird? What does that mean—'You look healthy'? Healthy?"

We didn't know, but whatever it meant, or whatever the man and

192

his strange compliment meant to our mother—it sent her falling, soon after, into another depression.

After my mother was raped, she sped away on Highway 41 with her left trailer door swinging and the rapist's red car trailing her, visible in the side mirror, moving closer. She drove faster. The Blazer had a full-size eight cylinder engine, and soon she approached one hundred miles per hour and the red car faded.

She didn't slow down, even after she couldn't see the red car and didn't know where it had driven to. Little time had passed when she drove by an Indiana State Police cruiser, which immediately chased her with full siren and lights.

She pulled over. After a few long moments, the police officer approached. He looked in her window and asked if she knew how fast she'd been going. Mom said, "I was raped back there. A man in a red car raped me. I got away from him and he's still out there chasing me. He's still on the road."

The police officer looked at her. He was silent for a moment, and no cars passed and nothing seemed to be happening. He looked up and then down the highway. It was bright and still and quiet.

"Look," he said. "Just slow it down, lady."

He turned and walked back to his patrol car; in a few seconds he turned off his pursuit lights and drove away easily.

During Mom's depressions, we were all confused, perhaps no one more than my father. He would spend long hours sitting at her bedside talking to her, whispering, trying to locate the problem, asking her why she was feeling so bad, hoping to hear it articulated. Their bedroom was adjacent to mine, and instead of sleeping I would often put my ear to the wall. Now and then I listened through a wet glass, which seemed to amplify tiny sounds more clearly. Sometimes, in the living room, Dad would tell me, "Your mother and I are going to talk," and he'd ask me to go to my room. I would crouch in the hallway and listen. He asked her many times, in many different phrases: Why? He didn't know that she saw the rapist's face in any place at any time: while driving, eating dinner, taking a bath, walking to the barn, glancing out a window or into a mirror. He didn't know what she had to ignore and overcome when they made love. He didn't know how fast her memory had to run to elude the rapist before she

193

could settle her mind enough to fall into restless sleep. He didn't know how heavy a burden her guilt had become, that when she looked at her family she saw people she loved who were hurt by what she considered an inability on her part to cope with pain, which made her feel more guilty—guilt on top of guilt—until the pain and inability shook her down and, indeed, coping became impossible.

For almost two years, she openly blamed money problems for her depression. The horses drained their budget, for certain. Other times she said she worried about my teenage sister, who had become disenchanted with many things and made it known through various means: lying, smoking pot, dodging family events, ignoring school work. Other times Mom simply said she was feeling sick, tired, or plain sick and tired, or worried about various friends who were having problems. Yet the extremity of her reaction, her depression, never seemed consistent with the causes she offered, and Dad couldn't understand and he finally told her so. I couldn't understand either. My sister was troubled by it and often displayed her confusion through harshness. "I don't know what her problem is," she said once. "Why does she act like that?" This was a question we all asked. Dad would tell us, "Mom is just worried—a lot of it has to do with money problems. She doesn't want you all to feel bad or have a hard time. She's a kind and caring person and she's worried about us. It's in her nature to worry. She feels things more deeply than most people." I couldn't make sense of it. All I could do was file the experiences away without examination, without processing them, without thinking about them productively at all. There were times I heard her say to Dad, "I just want to die," or "I wish I could die," and I wouldn't know what to feel, or what to do differently, and even today I can't remember what I felt, beyond an open emptiness or despair and an almost tangible frustration that made me want to go to her and touch her shoulder and ask her to tell me why she would rather die than be with us, with me—what was it that made her life with us worse than death?

Before she told us about the rape, we went to a weekend horse show in Louisville in early October. My fourteenth birthday fell on that Sunday. It was an important show, held for yearlings and two-year-olds. We hoped to show well and sell a horse. My sister stayed home. During the weekend there was an enormous flea market, and I slipped away now and then to buy baseball cards from the various dealers with tables there.

On Sunday morning before the show Mom started acting strangely. Her speech was slurred, her movements uncoordinated, her words seemed to make little sense. She said a man backed his horse into her and knocked her down on purpose. We knew this was ludicrous, but she cursed him, said he worked for Larry Watson, a horseman who they knew. She lay down in the backseat of the Blazer and we had to leave her there with the doors locked when it was time for our class. I had to go with Dad.

I don't remember if we won or lost, but afterward we went back to the trailer and Mom was gone. We took turns looking for her while the other waited at the Blazer. Three hours passed. At midafternoon, I was searching around the flea market, moving quickly from one building to the next. It was crowded. Over the intercom I heard, twice: *Terry Younkin and Brad Younkin please report to the nurse's office in Assembly Hall.* I learned where to go and ran there, expecting she might be dead, expecting at least an ambulance. I suppose my expression gave away these fears; the woman outside the nurse's office saw me and said, "Are you Brad? Your mother's okay. She's in the office with your dad."

Mom was lying down on a table in the office. She had been found by a guard in a golf cart; she had been rolling, crying, in the middle of one of the streets of the fairgrounds, saying that someone was trying to kill her. They determined she was incoherent and took her to the nurse, who gave her a mild tranquilizer and found out from her who to page to pick her up.

Back at the trailer Mom was insisting that a man with brown hair and a red shirt with a brown jacket who worked for Larry Watson backed his horse up and knocked her down on purpose. Dad said that was ridiculous, that no one would do that, that someone working for Larry wouldn't do that, but Mom shook her head and insisted. "He meant to *hurt* me," she said. "I want you to go to him and tell him he's a son of a bitch."

"There's no way I'm going to do that."

"Tell him he's a son of a bitch. If you don't do it I will. He is a son of a bitch."

"You're not going to do that," Dad said. "He didn't do it on purpose."

"I want you to tell him. If you don't do it I will."

They stared at each other. The trailer and Blazer by now had been packed and we were ready to leave. They looked like two gunfighters about to draw pistols.

Dad pointed at her. "I'll find Larry," he said, "and find out where this guy is, and I'm going to tell him he's a son of a bitch. It's not right, and you're crazy, you know that? I'm going to do this and we're leaving." Dad walked away. Mom went to the backseat of the Blazer and lay down. I sat in the passenger seat, with a sunken feeling, knowing, as Dad did, that there was no positive solution to this problem. If he didn't do what she insisted, she would implicate him, blame him for taking the wrong side, even though he knew it was wrong. Going along with her seemed to be the only path to choose.

In fifteen minutes, he came back, and we left. After a few minutes of not speaking, we were on the interstate toward home. Dad said, "I told that guy he was a son of a bitch, and he didn't know what I was talking about. He never did anything wrong." Dad's voice was weakening and now he was crying. "If I thought," he said, "that you did this on purpose—I'd want to kick your ass." Nothing more was said for the rest of the four hours home; Dad and I would try vainly to figure out what had made her behave as she did. We would not know for another year that the man wearing a red shirt and working for Larry Watson had simply buttoned up his own misfortune. He had reminded her of another man.

When the police officer drove away from Mom and left her on the shoulder of the road, she was left with an immediate and horrible fear that the rapist would return. She hurriedly got out and closed the trailer door and drove away. The environment in the Blazer offered a heinous sense of normalcy: a plastic cup of iced tea, directions to the vet in Vincennes, her purse, a cinnamon roll, a George Jones cassette. She drove, frantic and dismayed and scared to death. The idea of disease came to her. She stopped at a convenience store, pulled up and parked, afraid to get out, afraid that he would be there, working the counter, hiding in an aisle, hiding in the bathroom, afraid that he would appear out of nowhere. She got out, locked the doors, and inside the bathroom tried to clean herself. She hurried back to the Blazer, looked inside, looked in the trailer, and then drove away, constantly trying to compose herself, always checking the side mirrors and the opposite lanes, her heart leaping at that color of red, remembering the neat fingernails and wide knuckles of his fingers clutching her window as it tried to close on them, and when she arrived in Vincennes her eyes darted about the pedestrians in an ongoing search for a man in red flannel, a young man with nice features who seemed nice, and she pulled up at the veterinarian's and took a deep breath.

She told Dad about the rape three years after it happened, in their bedroom, around 11 P.M., a Friday night. I heard it through the wall. She said, "I was raped." She told him it happened in Indiana. She told him she shouldn't have stopped, but she thought something was wrong with the horse. She said, "He had a switchblade knife, and he forced me into the trailer and raped me. He said I'd be dead by morning." She told him how she kicked him and escaped, and how she was pulled over, and how the police officer had said "Just slow it down, lady." She said later, "I couldn't tell you. I thought you would try to find him and you'd want to kill him. You'd have gone to jail. And I couldn't tell the kids. I just couldn't hurt them like that. I couldn't tell Daddy. I couldn't hurt him like that. He wouldn't understand." I listened longer, but I don't remember much more.

The next afternoon I was in the barn working and Dad said he needed to talk to me. He set up two folding chairs. I sat facing him; I was guilty for knowing the truth. He summarized her cycles of depression and suggested to me that there was a reason for them, and reminded me that Mom loved my sister and me very much and that she was a strong person, a good person, who never intended to hurt any of us or anyone else—I nodded and said that I agreed. He was crying. He said, "Three years ago, your mother was raped." He said the last word carefully. "It happened in Indiana." He asked if I understood, and I nodded that I did. He said it wasn't her fault. "She didn't do anything wrong. It was violent; it was wrong. And your mother tried to get over it on her own. She didn't want to hurt any of us. Your mother is a strong person, probably the strongest person I've ever known." He said a rape could happen to any person, that even a man can be raped, and that it can affect a person for years. He said that Mom would need our help, our support. The decision was made to not tell Grandpa, and to handle it ourselves.

After she told us the truth, things were better. There was a palpable sadness, but with it an understanding. We at least understood the facts, the reasons. We conducted ourselves with an optimism, probably unaware how overwhelmed we were by the truth, standing as if in the shadow of an enormous mountain, needing to climb it, our feet shackled. We knew why, when she again fell into a depression a few months later, but we knew of no means to help her through it, no words to say, no system to initiate to handle her particular needs. We let her know we understood, that it was okay, and that provided some comfort, but when she again became depressed, and then again after that, we grew tired of making the same appeals that didn't work well enough, and she likely tired of hearing them.

She became bitter. One night before supper, she and I were outside feeding the horses. In about thirty minutes she cussed twenty-one times, over anything: a horse, the barn door, the temperature, a bird on the rafter. When we were inside eating I was thinking, *twenty-one cuss words in thirty minutes.* Sometimes she would cry in the kitchen, behind the barn, sitting in her recliner, all evening, alone, in her bed; other times she would become nauseous and throw up. Viruses lasted for weeks. Arguments would flare up over small things: the way I said something, something my sister decided to do, some criticism Dad raised. She would sometimes stare at one of us for minutes on end without saying a word. Though I knew better, her expression looked like one of hatred. One time, I offended her—I don't remember how—and she demanded that I apologize. I knew I'd done nothing wrong, but as she stared with that look like hatred and disgust, I could think of nothing better to say.

"I'm sorry," I said.

"Do you mean that?" she said.

"Yes," I lied. It may well be that all of us—Mom, Dad, me, and my sister—looked at each other with some genuine resentment during this time. Everyone knew the truth and the reasons for Mom's behavior, and we tried to modify our actions around them without any sustainable success. There was no fine line between tough love on our part and soft compassion. Everything we tried didn't work in exactly the same way. She regarded us at times with love, with an apologetic and sorrowful sadness, but at other times with that look of disgust; we knew the truth, and confronting us meant confronting the truth that she was raped. It's no wonder that she resented such a regular threat, a regular reminder that, yes, she was raped, and no, she wasn't dealing with it. Our hopefulness for her recovery, probably visible on our faces, translated into something unrealistic and unfair. She was left more vulnerable yet, unable to appreciate anything we, or she, did to try to help, the chemicals in her mind swarming about in dangerous mixtures, stupefying her every three months or so, and for a couple weeks she behaved, as my sister pointed out, "like a zombie."

One summer, on a Saturday, she drove away in Dad's work truck to buy strawberries at a U-pick farm. She spun out of our driveway and down the hill and onto the road. After an hour or less, a strange car drove up and Mom got out of the passenger side. She was bruised on her face and her legs and arms were bleeding. She had driven too fast on a curve on a washboarded gravel road. The pickup was light in the rear and flipped easily; wearing no seat belt, she was tossed into dense weeds at the edge of a thicket. The truck was totaled and she was lucky not to have been killed. After being driven home, she walked from the car to the house without thanking the driver or speaking to anyone, stumbling, shrugging off the details of her accident, as if drunk, as if nothing was a big deal at all.

Something gave her the idea to drink vodka one afternoon in May while my sister and I were at school and Dad was working. She rarely drank, and I had never seen her drunk, but she found an old bottle of vodka and drove away in the Blazer.

She drank as she drove, turning down roads that seemed to suggest themselves. The roads she chose became progressively more rural, until she turned finally onto a tractor path that led into a farmer's field. It had rained recently, and she wound up in a low valley of heavy mud that stuck the Blazer.

I had gotten home from school, surprised to find Mom gone, but unaware of any problem until Dad came home and didn't know where she was. He made some calls but no one knew anything. Around 6:30 the Pope County sheriff's office called. Mom was drunk, in jail in neighboring Pope County, charged with a D.U.I.

Her license was revoked for two months, and because the arrangement was so unusual and obvious, we had to tell Grandpa about the D.U.I. He was already aware of her depressions, probably more than we realized. We told him she was worried about money and about other things, but we said nothing of the rape. He seemed to take in the information quietly and sympathetically and without judgment.

I drove Mom around for the two months. She was ashamed, yet

thankful for my understanding and help. We talked during the drives, and I learned the streets of Paducah quite well, and Mom seemed to enjoy the shared time. She had reached a low point, and seemed stoic about it; for those two months it seemed as if she might only go up from there.

Later that autumn, my sister's life, like my mother's, began to twist away from the rest of the family's. She had settled down and given up much of her teenage rebellion, and after graduating high school took a year and one-half of classes in a nursing program. She was working steady, studying well, and was in a two-year relationship with a likable young man. Over a two-month period beginning in October she inexplicably ended her relationship and began a new one, dropped out of college, quit her job, got married, and moved away to Chicago, leaving behind much of her belongings and a dumbfounded family.

It's unlikely that my sister's trouble was the ultimate cause of Mom's drifting back into periodic depression, but it didn't help. There was one less warm body in the house, one less person whose presence Mom could think about as she lay in bed in the evening, and one less person whose arrival she could anticipate during a long afternoon of worry and sadness.

My sister's problem, unavoidably, became the family's, but Mom had much more difficulty dealing with it. Because people tend to recall difficult times when difficult times are happening, Mom, depressed, began reliving pain, sorting through decisions she'd made that she wished to change, finding herself in the Blazer at one hundred miles per hour, sitting in the Pope County jail, hiding her face from her family, finding herself, like anyone depressed, wrestling with her memory and losing, wanting to find a kind thought, a soft hand, a hope to help her out of bed and elicit from her a smile, and finding herself without the energy or means to do so; depression made her thin, barely a thumbprint on an enormous pane of glass, an alien in her own body.

One afternoon Grandpa called Mom from his house across the road. He knew she was home, but there was no answer. After a few minutes, he called again without getting an answer, so he drove over. He found her in the backyard, lying on the ground, crying. She got up and insisted she was okay, only a little sad. He said it just wasn't right for a person to act that way, that she needed to get better or, if she

200

couldn't get better, get help. There was no way for her to adequately explain her behavior without telling him of the rape, so he left after a while, not understanding his daughter, knowing something in her had spun out of control.

The next January was cold. Mom had been steadily feeling worse since the holidays. One night she was in her bed while Dad and I watched television in the living room. One of our mares was in the barn, due to bring a colt any day. At 7:30 Mom walked down the hall and stepped into the living room, wearing her long blue robe and slippers.

She said, "I'm going to go check on Amber." She waved to us weakly and stood for a moment, waving, and turned into the utility room. I heard the back door open and close.

Just before eight o'clock Dad got up. "It's been a while. I'm going to go check on Mom." He went down the hall and returned after a couple minutes, carrying a note. "Brad, come here." He put the note on the counter in the kitchen. "We have to go find Mom. She's taken sleeping pills and run off." He held up an empty prescription bottle. "Get your boots on."

He and I put on boots and coveralls, and he got two flashlights. "Put a watch on," he said.

"Mom didn't wear her boots," I said, and I pointed to her boots, still there. "She's out there in her house-shoes," I said. On our way to the barn I said, "That's a suicide note?" He said it was.

Outside was a damp cold and a coal black sky with a bright moon. The barn was still and lifeless except for Amber dozing in her stall, standing under the orange glow of her heat lamp. Asleep, her bottom lip hung down like a cup and her ears fell sideways. Dad flipped on the security light in front of the barn and it flickered to a steady hum.

Dad said, "You go check the back pasture and the back woods and I'll get the Blazer and drive into the front pasture and down by the road. Come back here in thirty minutes."

I went into the back pasture. I shone my light around and now and then I ran a few yards, particularly when the shadows of the moon tricked me, when I thought I saw something lying in the thick weeds and fescue of the pasture, something that made a shadow; but when I ran to it I saw that it had been nothing but pasture. I picked my way into the woods. I imagined her propped against or lying at the base of every tree, alongside every log, partly underneath every briar

201

or bush. Many times in the silver light I was afraid that I had actually seen her, the patterns of the cold bark of a tree trunk suggesting her image, sitting with her eyes closed, wearing her blue robe, her arms hanging down and her mouth open, with pieces of leaves and grass caught in her hair. But when I held the light on the spot I only saw the blank face of a tree.

I was in the barn when the thirty minutes had passed. Dad had just driven back.

I said, "You didn't see anything?"

"No."

"I thought I did a few times but my eyes were playing tricks."

We split up again. I checked in the neighbor's pasture and Dad looked across the road on Grandpa's land. When this turned up nothing after thirty more minutes, Dad called for help from the police, who said they'd come out and bring the volunteer fire department.

"We're going to have to call Grandpa," Dad said.

He called Grandpa. I stood nearby in the tack room and looked at her note. It was scrawled in mostly heavy letters, sharp lines and long curves, literally tear-stained in places. It was a message of love and sorrow and pain; dying seemed to be the only good thing she had the courage to do, the only thing she could do to make our lives easier. She said I was her pride and joy, that Dad was a wonderful loving husband. References to my sister were scattered and confused, much like my sister herself—depression had gnarled my mother's life and rendered it unrecognizable.

I stepped out in front of the barn. I told Dad I was scared and I cried, uncontrollably for a moment. Grandpa's truck was moving down his hill. It turned onto the road and moved along slowly, like a knob, silently. Turning into and climbing our driveway, the lights of his truck sliced and cut a long arc out of the dark. Grandpa got out of his truck and approached us without speaking.

When he reached us, Grandpa said, "What's wrong?"

"Carol's taken a bottle of sleeping pills, and she's run off. We've got people coming to help us look for her. She left about 7:30."

"Taken off?"

"She was depressed."

"She's been that way."

"There's a good reason," Dad said, and he took one deep breath and told Grandpa everything. Grandpa watched Dad without judgment. His glasses were dark in the cold. He shook his head and looked down and then back at Dad. "Well—you tell me where to look and let's find her."

We went searching again a few minutes before help arrived. At least ten vehicles, and up to twenty men. The deputy sheriff came with a German shepherd search dog that responded to German commands. Everyone dispersed. There were walkie-talkies and orders made and received and thoughtful speculation over where she might be and many sympathetic and optimistic comments like: *I'm sure sorry we've got to do this*, and *Don't you worry, we're gonna find your Mom*. The night wore on and midnight approached and passed. Nearing three o'clock, Dad and I stopped in the kitchen to call the deputy. I got a glass of water and felt guilty and out of line for taking a sip of it. I told Dad there was one more place I wanted to look, though I doubted she could have gotten that far. The bridge over the creek, where I sometimes hiked to, where I liked to spend time alone; the water was heavy and dark under the bridge, with a false echo when a rock was flung into it. That was the last place I could think she might have reached, and beyond that I couldn't imagine any other possibilities; beyond the bridge the possibilities became too innumerable and daunting to know where to begin. Just as Dad and I were discussing this, the deputy called. They had found her lying in a ditch beside the bridge over the creek, alive, cold, and incoherent, wearing her robe and a jacket.

We got there as they loaded her in an ambulance on a stretcher. At the hospital they pumped her stomach and stabilized her. We were told she would be fine, and I went home for sleep.

I got to the hospital at nine o'clock in the morning. She had been moved to an open area behind a sliding curtain. Before I stepped around it, I was powerless to imagine what I would see or how it would affect me. Would she still be depressed, or ashamed of herself? Would she be incoherent? Would she be physically scarred, somehow damaged by pills or by the long night of cold? Would she be feeling okay or sick? Would she be able to speak? Would she recognize me, or even want to? I set my sights optimistically at okay. I hoped, realistically, for no change: nothing worse, certainly, but I could hope for nothing better, and I stepped around the curtain with my heart dangling.

She smiled.

I have tried, now and then over nearly fifteen years, to talk to my mother about her smile in the hospital that morning. My first attempt was when I went with her to Paducah for counseling after her suicide attempt. Her therapist, Bill Draper, asked me what I felt in the moment when I saw her smile.

"It was like the clouds moved away and the sun came shining through," I told him. He smiled too, as if he knew exactly what had happened. But he couldn't have known; neither could Mom have known, sitting in a chair beside mine, both of us facing Bill. If I could have known then what her smile meant to me, and had the words to describe it (I'm not sure I have them now), I might have added, *I felt as if we had reached bottom and were finally looking up, and we both knew it. We had nowhere to go but up, and, as hard as it might be, we could only move up, and we would be in control of things, and things would get better and easier.*

A week ago I visited Mom and Dad and my sister and her growing family, and while I was there I drove Mom to an acupuncture appointment. She wasn't scheduled for another week, but recently the pain from degeneration in her spine had flared up and she needed the needles. She and the doctor knew each other well, and he scolded her mildly and said to me, "She needs to stop pushing herself so hard and take it easy, doesn't she?"

She took her shoes and socks off and pulled up her pant legs and lay down on the examining table. The doctor opened a package of needles, Starting at her face, he tapped the needles in and gave each one a little twist and a push, finishing with several on her feet and toes. Over twenty in all. He picked up a handheld device that would send electricity through her body, and wired the machine to two needles on her neck, clamping onto them like tiny jumper cables. He turned it on and raised the electricity level until she said, "Okay. Let's try that." He turned off the light and left us alone. We would have about twenty minutes.

My eyes were adjusting to the dark. "Can you see this?" she said. "On my neck?" I stood up and saw the clamped needles. "Look at them twitch. I must really be hurting; it's usually not this bad."

She said after a few moments, "Brad, I've been thinking lately, and I want to tell you something: I'm sorry that things were hard for you growing up."

"You don't need to be sorry for anything," I said.

She said she was sorry anyway. "There's so much about what happened I'm not proud of." The needles on her neck were twitching.

"It took so long," she said, "And it's been so long. I should have found help sooner. I wish I'd have told you all sooner."

I told her my childhood, in spite of anything, was wonderful.

"You know," she said, "one of the strangest things about it, and one of the hardest things, was the fear. I remember being so scared, sometimes for no reason at all. Even when I was working and things were going better, I used to have this irrational fear." She had gotten a job at the *Metropolis Planet* while going through counseling. She put together advertisements for local businesses and arranged her counseling sessions around her work schedule and volunteering for Rape Victims' Services in Paducah. After a couple years of working at the *Planet*, she went to school and received, as my sister had, an LPN license. "One night I got off work and walked to my car. It wasn't dark yet, and the parking lot was small and it wasn't far to walk, but on my way to the car I was absolutely terrified. I started walking faster, and when I finally got to the car I was so scared I actually jumped inside so fast I hit my head—right on the door frame, I hit my head. *Hard*." The needles on her neck continued to twitch. Soon a nurse would return and remove them. "It took so long to get past it. There's a lot about it I'm not proud of." She lay in silence for a moment. "But the fear," she said. "I hit my head so hard that night it made a huge knot. There wasn't anything to be scared about but I was—I was scared to death. Some nights I would lie in bed, scared. I would think someone was outside in the yard, looking in the windows. It was hard. That fear really never went away." She was silent. She smiled. Lying flat, her body needled and unmoving, her eyes turned in my direction, she said, "But I don't get it as much anymore."

Nominated by Riverteeth

HORSEFLIES

by ROBERT WRIGLEY

from THE IDAHO REVIEW

After the horse went down
    the heat came up,
and later that week
    the smell of its fester yawed,
an open mouth of had-been air
    our local world was licked
inside of, and I,

the boy who'd volunteered at twilight—
    shunts of chawed cardboard
wadded up my nostrils
    and a dampened bandana
over my nose and mouth—
    I strode then

into the ever-purpler sink
    of rankness and smut,
a sloshful five-gallon bucket of kerosene
    in my right hand,
a smoking railroad fusee
    in my left,
and it came over me like water then,

into my head-gaps and gum
    rinds, into the tear ducts

and taste buds and even
      into the last dark tendrils
of my howling, agonized hair
      that through the windless half-light
hoped to fly from my very head,

and would have, I have no doubt, had not
      the first splash of kerosene
launched a seething skin
      of flies into the air
and onto me, the cloud of them
      so dense and dark my mother in the distance
saw smoke and believed as she had feared

I would, that I had set my own
      fool and staggering self aflame,
and therefore she fainted and did not see
      how the fire kicked
the other billion flies airborne
      exactly in the shape
of the horse itself,

which rose for a brief quivering
      instant under me, and which for a pulse thump
at least, I rode—in a livery of iridescence,
      in a mail of exoskeletal facets,
wielding a lance of swimming lace—
      just as night rode the light, and the bones,
and a sweet, cleansing smoke to ground.

Nominated by David Baker, Joan Swift, Bob Hicok, Claire Davis

THE CORE

fiction by JACK HERLIHY

from NEWS FROM THE REPUBLIC OF LETTERS

DAD AND I WERE REGULARS at the Funeral Parlors, though our shared time in them was over before I turned seven.

"They're glad she's gone," Dad once whispered about one dead woman who lacks a name in my memory. "You can tell. No restraint. Crying like this," he looked behind us at two women in black, their sobs near moaning, "is for show or when the dog dies." This was at a Funeral Parlor we sometimes attended when his mortician friend Tobin had nothing scheduled at his place on our night out. We were on our knees almost every Friday night that year, in between the recently deceased and their audience.

"Look," Dad said, pointing with his brow, "either the family went nickel and dime or the casket has been switched with a floor model. See the little scratches. And look at the uneasy way she's set, poor woman." Sometimes he gave me a moment for study, then leaned close enough again for me to smell the citrus residue of his shaving cream and lime cologne. "Maybe they dropped her."

He would say a silent prayer then make an air cross between his head and shoulders before getting up to greet the sorrowful family. He could be a little remote with the more dramatic mourners, unless they were the known poor or clients of Jimmy Tobin.

His family and the Tobins had been friends back in Ireland long before my father was born. They had been farmers and neighbors for generations before moving, one after the other, to the States. My Dad was only eight years old when his father died. After that the Tobins half-raised him as one of their own. They fed him at their table and played with him through their rooms while my grandmother worked for them as a cook. They fostered in him an appreciation of the funeral trade while he was still too young to work at it. He grew up seeing its worldly opportunities for contacts and gentility and probably anticipated a sponsored future in the Tobin's family business. Then he met my future mother and, eventually, he asked her to marry him. Maybe he should have been more explicit with her sooner, regarding his career plans. When he eventually did explain them, she said that she would not share a house with the dead or live with a man who touched them. She told him that he had to make a choice between undertaking and her. I don't think he ever got over it.

During our time at the Parlors, I understood the concept of death but never emotionally considered the nearby deceased as really gone. Their condition struck me more as a sort of severe disability that made them somehow inaccessible in their displayed flesh. Except for their prone postures and closed eyes, most didn't look very different from anyone else. As an easily distracted boy, I knew how hard it was to stay still, and half-expected corpses to fidget with the strain. That was probably due to the mortician's skill. The dead did not discomfort me nearly as much as the undertakers did. I saw them as a kind of spooky escort service, accompanying the deceased to some mysterious destination. That was before I acquired a more practical view of the trade both from attending my grandfather's funeral, my mother's father, and from listening to Dad. He was a close judge of the craft but rarely spoke of this particular interest in front of my mother.

My attendance at wakes began after my sister Meg was born, in the spring of my sixth year. Friday nights had always been Dad's own, to "stretch his legs" he said, without expense, despite having worked all week as a custodian at City Hall. He was on his way out one Friday night, as Ma was clearing the dishes, when she told him, "Take Patrick."

"Why?" he asked.

"He's your son."

He stood quietly for a few seconds, chewing his gum and watching her at the sink. "It's my night off."

"And tell me," she said, her scrubbing picking up speed, "when my night off is. If I got paid by the hour, never mind nights, holidays and Sundays."

"Go to the bathroom and wash up," he told me, interrupting her, with a peeved look, like the whole thing was my idea.

So we began our Friday night walks. In the beginning, he had a grouch on about it. There were no stops and little conversation unless he picked up a coin he found. He had a great eye for loose change.

"See that," he would say showing me the nickel, dime or quarter pinched between his thumb and forefinger, "that's because I pay attention," and put it in his pocket. He never picked up pennies.

We often chewed spearmint gum, a half-stick for me and a whole one for him. When I needed to, he let me take a discreet pee behind someone's bushes while he walked ahead. Strangers beeped their car horns at us. Dad returned their greetings with a quarter-circle wave of his arm. When I tried this he said, "Stop that," but he kept doing it. We kept along our common route for several uneventful weeks before he decided to take a chance on me.

The second Friday was the same as the first, aimlessly strolling around the city. The third Friday it rained, to my relief. I was bored. On the fourth Friday following we stopped across from a big white house on High Street. There were lots of cars out front and a lighted sign on the lawn. This was at the time of day, in late spring, when the neutral light evokes everything without shade or glare. The moon was barely a white scratch under a pinking band of cloud. We stood beneath a broad maple tree while Dad twisted out his cigarette under his shoe. We looked at one another as he took a folded black necktie out of his jacket pocket and started to arrange it around his upturned collar.

"I want you to be a good boy and do what I tell you," he said. "Can you do that?"

I nodded. He finished the tie to his satisfaction, took my hand in his and we crossed the wide street.

On the other side he led me down the front walk and up the steps past three men smoking who greeted my father by name, "Michael." No one ever called him Mike. Past the front door was a short hall with a thick red and gold carpet. There were the sounds of many people talking softly like company after bedtime. I looked at the sudden brightness above us and pointed straight up at it as we walked underneath. Hanging over our heads were what looked like three hoops of shining diamonds, their circles tapering smaller in descension.

Dad followed my finger directing upward. "Chandelier," he said. "Don't point."

There was a large open room on either side of the hall. Both had entrances wide enough so that four or five people could have entered abreast. We looked in one crowded room, then the other. There was little furniture, no television nor family pictures on the walls. I couldn't see much else or hear anything distinctly in the polite murmur of strange voices. We walked ahead, past the knobby white spindles of a staircase banister that climbed away from us, to a swinging door at the end of a hall. I heard men laughing.

"Wait here," Dad said, pointing his finger at me, "don't move," and positioned me under the stairs. He went through the door into a room gray with smoke and someone called, "Michael," sounding happy to see him.

Behind me was a closed door with gold letters on it. I looked out at the diamond light again. A man walked into the hall from one of the side rooms so I stepped back, listening for footsteps, scared until Dad came out and took me by the hand. We left the way we came, out past the smoking men who told us goodnight. Dad held on to me all the way down the tarred walk and only let me go after we had crossed through traffic and continued on our way.

The last daylight was fading fast so that the insides of occupied homes were becoming brighter than the out-of-doors. Families revealed themselves at evening meals and motionless before the pale illuminations of their televisions. It surprised me how many people watched theirs without a lamp on, which my mother told me was a shortcut to blindness.

Flowers bloomed from trellises and pots that hung in porticos and deeper porches shadowed with screens. Dogs charged out from their yards to bark behind us, or to yap along fence lines before they retreated, suddenly indifferent. I lagged behind, distracted by the sight of a family eating a late dinner with their white cat wandering over the tabletop. Our cat chewed off the heads of birds and pawed dead mice across the linoleum. The thought of a cat's breath and feet so near a family's food gave the supper I had eaten earlier an uncomfortable turn. I jumped when Dad gripped my shoulder and reset me ahead of him. My feet began to catch more of the brick sidewalk's unevenness, causing me an occasional small lurch as I resisted looking into any more houses for fear of another dining pet, though I could think of nothing else.

211

"Come here," my father motioned me toward him with his hand.

I turned and he was squatting six steps behind me, his tie gone and his shirt collar open again.

"Come on," he motioned me forward with his hand.

I stepped closer to him. His thin face was calm.

"See what I found?" There was an upright quarter in his fingertips. "This is good luck," he said and held it out for me.

I looked at the coin.

"Go on, take it."

I did and examined it on both sides.

"We can do this again," he cocked his head back the way we just came, "but it has to be our secret. Understand?"

I nodded.

"Good." He stood up and we started to walk side by side. I first thought that he just wanted me to carry the coin for admiration, then realized, as we went on, that he meant for me to have it.

"Your mother wouldn't approve and the baby is taking enough out of her," he said. "We'll keep it to ourselves."

I wasn't going to tell any of it, not a word about the quarter, the table cat or his abandoning me under the stairs. We walked the rest of the way home in silence. I felt the round money turn from cool to warm in my fist and moisten so that I had to wipe it on my shirt. I looked up at him several times and caught his eye once. He didn't look any different but I took the coin as a sign of his pleasure, even if I didn't understand why he gave it to me. We arrived home after dark and just before he opened the door he laid a finger to his lips. I nodded my agreement then ran in the house to hide my fortune.

The next Friday we went back to the white house with the sign on the lawn. He walked in, and down the hall, where he held me in place with one hand under the stairs again, while he pushed the swinging door open and looked inside. I saw two men in dark suits, smoking cigarettes and sipping from coffee mugs as they leaned against a black soapstone sink. They saw us and lifted their heads in greeting. Dad let the door close and directed me, by my shoulder, back down the hall and into the large room on our right. The diamond hall light was dimmer than I remembered and I felt disappointed.

There were not as many people as the week before so it was much quieter. The room, lit by lamps and a single candle on a stand, was larger than any in our house and had a ceiling I could not have reached on my father's shoulders. Underfoot was a thick dark blue carpet bordered in gold tassels. Dark blue drapes, taller than a grownup, covered the windows, leaving a bar of cream window shade showing between them. The white ceiling had no lights hanging from it but showed raised blocks of curved teardrop designs you sometimes saw on men's ties and women's scarves.

I looked back down when we stopped walking and there at my eye level was an old man with white hair and an oily looking tan, lying on his back in a dark wood paneled box. He wore a brown suit and tie with his hands clasped above his gut giving him a restful, satisfied appearance.

Dad knelt down so I did too, finding a padded kneeler. We made the sign of the cross and waited, watching the man closely. Through no specific instructions I could recall I knew that he must be dead but I was still afraid of disturbing him.

Dad leaned down toward me and whispered, "His name was Victor. I used to work with his son." He straightened and we stayed quiet for a minute, watching Victor. "Finished?" Dad asked.

I stared at him and him at me.

"Good boy," he said and touched my back before we crossed ourselves and got up. I immediately walked into the rear of his legs. He put his big dry hand behind my neck and steered me over to an old woman dressed in black and sitting in a folding chair against the wall. Her skin was butterscotch colored and very wrinkled except for a smooth patch under each eye where the folds below stretched the flesh above. Standing next to her was a man who looked as Victor might have at my father's age. Dad shook the man's hand and the woman rested her bony fingers on the men's grip.

"He looks good," Dad told them. They all let go of each other's hands.

"You don't think the makeup is too much?" asked the woman, pointing a limp hand at her face but looking to the casket. The four of us turned towards Victor then back at one another.

"No." Dad looked back again. "No. How's Annie?" he asked the man.

"Home with the kids. She was here last night." We waited. "Bigger turnout last night."

"Much bigger," the woman said. There was no one else present except for the four of us.

"I don't know what's wrong with people," Dad told her.

"He was so looking forward to it, toward the end," she said and sighed. "Thank-you for the Masses."

"He deserved more," Dad said and glanced at me.

"It was enough."

Dad looked around the room. "God rest him. I'm sorry." He shook the man's hand again.

The woman told us, "Bless you." She smiled at me and her teeth were the same color as her skin. I stayed pressed against my father's side as we left, almost tripping him at the threshold of a smaller adjoining room.

"God Almighty," he said, pulling me clear of him. "Will you please try and walk straight." We passed through the smaller room lined on both sides with coat hangers bunched on long hanging bars and pushed through a swinging door into a long brightly lighted kitchen with entrances at the four corners. Five men stood around with their suit coats unbuttoned, drinking coffee and smoking cigarettes that wraithed upwards into gray waves over their heads. Dad set me on a chair, gave me a cookie from a jar on the counter, then stepped away and turned his back to me. He said something private to three of the men. They shook their heads. He took a mug from a cabinet above the sink and poured himself some coffee from a pot on the stove. Without a spoken request or permission he held the mug out and one of the others tipped a brown decanter over it until Dad said, "That's good." The men looked at me but there was no introduction.

"It's a shame to take his life out on the family," said the tallest.

"A real shame," added the shortest.

"He wasn't the worst sort," said the tallest.

"No, not the worst," said the shorter. My father and the middle one shook their heads.

"It was the drink that made him mean," the tallest one said.

"Sure he showed up at the polls drunk and belligerent as a dime store Santa," Dad said, "but he was a good Democrat."

"God have mercy," said the short one and the four tapped their mugs together all at once.

I could not get the woman's teeth and the dead man's greasy skin out of my head. My gut got uneasy and loose-feeling. We couldn't have been there that long because Dad was suddenly reaching for one of my hands and I was looking at my unbitten gingersnap in the other.

"Didn't you like your cookie?" he asked. When I looked up at him

I still recalled the woman's teeth and skin so I said nothing. He took my hand and said our goodbyes. By the time he released me on the sidewalk outside, to keep up on my own, I had almost recovered from the widow's smile.

The daylight was sliding out, just a rouged glow at the sky's edge. Summer was coming on but the nights could still be cool. I should have taken off my sweater while I waited inside the warm kitchen. I was getting a chill.

"What happens when you die?" I asked.

"Your family calls the mortician and he takes the body to the funeral home."

"What's a mortician?"

"He prepares the body."

"How?"

"He cleans it."

"What else?"

"I don't know that you're old enough." He made up his mind in two strides. "Then they take the body to the cemetery for burial."

"In a grave."

"That's right."

I knew a little about graves from visiting where Dad's dad was buried. I tried to picture a space in the ground from the bottom up. "How deep is a grave?"

He watched me for several paces. Whether he thought I was having a breakthrough or if he was regarding me with some caution, I don't know. He looked ahead again. "About this deep," he made a flat-handed motion in the air as if to chop his own throat.

I pictured the empty shadowed place in the ground, too deep to reach the top if you died young. I soon thought about it no more in words. Rather I felt it as a drift of apprehension that inspired in me the image of looking up from the bottom of a narrow hole. I started to walk in a distracted zigzag. When I came closest to my father in this pattern he rested his hand near the back of my neck to guide me toward home.

The following week we viewed the client Eleanor Ward, a local taxi driver. I had never heard anyone refer to her as Miss Ward or Eleanor. It was always the full Eleanor Ward except for us neighborhood children who, amongst ourselves, called her Hiss for her tendency to string out words ending in s when she spoke. She only dressed in black or navy-blue and had never married. Adults mentioned this almost every time someone gossiped about the great variety of cats that sunned or kept watch from all the windows of her house. In her defense someone would inevitably say, "Well, she never married," and everyone would nod. Her voice was deep and she had a few long wiry chin whiskers that I found disturbing. She had lived around the corner from us so, as a neighbor, Dad knew her better than his peers did.

"She was a lovely person," he told them while I kept an eye on her. It was my experience by then that nearly everyone was lovely, misunderstood or an ideal example once they were dead. She didn't look much different than she did in her cab except for being horizontal with her eyes closed.

"Always a hello, how are you," he continued. We patronized her taxi because neither of my parents drove and she was always prompt and the least expensive in town.

"Always willing to chat or keep still. Never heard her speak ill or harm and very clean too, despite the animals. Neither she nor the cab were ever unpleasant or untidy."

After visiting the body to say a prayer, we went back into the kitchen. Dad gave me a cookie and sat me in a chair again. It was like most kitchens except there was no refrigerator and the black cast iron stove burned wood, something no one else we knew was doing anymore. The matching black sink was flanked by long white countertops with dark-stained cabinets over and under them. There was a large round globe of light in the center of the ceiling that made me see spots if I stared at it.

The room was all men roughly my father's age, six in all counting Dad. Three wore suits with baggy trousers, well used but not shabby. They turned out to be the barber Kelly, Twomey who ran a local coffee shop, and my Dad.

The other men wore newer looking suits with narrower pants and thin lapels. These were the proprietor James Tobin, whom we knew well enough to call Jimmy, Reardon the lawyer, and Burke the realtor. In time I learned that all six went to our church, were Democrats and Knights of Columbus. All six were familiars since childhood and all their parents had come over on the boat together. As a group they referred to themselves as The Core. Any one of them could be heard to remark, "You can always count on The Core Jimmy," when no one else showed for the wake of some aged customer without family.

I was six and bored by their conversations unless they swore exotically or gossiped about someone I thought I knew. I remember my attention returning to them from some reverie I was having; probably the residue of a television movie involving explosions and blood nobly spent, feeling their eyes upon me. My father was telling them part of the same thing he told me to be quiet about.

He finished by looking at me and saying, "How deep is a grave?"

Red Burke shook his head. "Makes you wonder what they're teaching in school these days." They nodded at his comment and sipped from their cups to better appraise me. I took from the mixed review of their faces that I was a disappointment in the making so I studied my second cookie with great care.

Red was the man Dad admired most in the Core, after Jimmy. Every chance Dad had he would tell mourners, "Did you know Red was almost a priest? Went to the seminary."

Red was the shortest among them, wore wire rim glasses and kept his red hair crew cut. Years later I learned that he had gone straight from high school to study for the priesthood. The choice had been a source of pride for his father and against his mother's wishes. When he came home for visits she gave him money and sent him out in her car, told him to have fun and be quiet if he got in late. Soon he was visiting more frequently but only to say hello and to take her car for the weekend. It was not many months after when he announced that he was leaving the seminary. The story goes that his father exploded, demanding that he go back before the news shamed the family. It was too late. Red was in love for the first time and the community thought it was scandalous. His reputation healed during the war when he eventually married a lovely girl from Wales who was at least a Catholic.

My father and these other men admired Tobin as they had his father before him. They enjoyed the Tobin generosity with a small cabinet of decanters available as a courtesy every wake, rich or poor. Men tipped these bottles over their coffee cups the way Dad used milk at home, though I never saw milk or cream in a funeral home kitchen. On the slowest nights with the fewest visitors, after three cups or so, they might share nostalgia for a harder bygone life as if those past sufferings, rather than their present circumstances, were the rewards of their heroic age.

"My poor Ma," Kelly told us one night, "married at seventeen, some said to get out of the shoe shops, had six children and a still birth the first ten years. Her legs were roped with varicose veins. She could knock the straw out of you with either hand, slapped my sister Rita hard of hearing in one ear for stealing peaches from a neighbor's yard. Drank as hard as the old man and died of consumption before she was forty."

The others stood around in a polite breather.

He sniffed and sawed a finger under his nose. "We adored her," he said, his voice wobbling, and we all looked down or away. When Kelly spoke again, he said softly, "It was the Depression and hard times." Everyone stirred.

"Hard times," Reardon started. "Sure they were, with me and my four brothers waiting in line at the Public Assistance warehouse for handouts like someone's old trousers that might not even fit. At least with brothers, you knew someone could use them." Anything about the Depression charged them and they would fill their cups for another round.

They always found time near the end of the night to praise the master's work. They tended to bunch in the kitchen doorway for a view, refreshments in hand, often led by my father.

"That's what I call a gentle repose, and the skin tone, perfect. Believe me," Dad said looking down at me and speaking in his lesson voice, "these things are a comfort to a family when they're staring at a loved one laid out for three days and fixing that last image in their sorrowful memories."

I don't remember many of the client's names, probably never knew them, but I can still picture the flesh-tan makeup caked along the seams of their faces and the occasional finger of rouge far back near the jaw, though never on one of Tobin's clients. Maybe six times that year we patronized other establishments when Dad had known the deceased and nothing was on at Tobin's. We never stayed long.

Some nights, after we got home, Ma would put an arm around my father's waist, kiss him on the chin and ask where we had been.

It was still an accepted decency at that time that a father could take a walking child into any of the private clubs in town where he was a member and sip among familiars. Obvious drunkenness in the company of your children invited intrusion.

I let Dad do the talking.

"We've been to the Boat Club," he answered and put his mouth in her hair. This was not really true but not wholly false. We had been to the Boat Club before but never on a Friday. Ma couldn't protest what she didn't know. I doubt that she wanted to risk giving Dad re-

218

course through discussion about our nights out, willing to let well enough alone.

Dad's concerns for his friend's business sometimes came up and never cleared the skirmishes at home. He had the habit of editorializing aloud as he read the paper, which Ma appeared to largely ignore with nods and shakes of her head that were enough for him. Now and then he did slip and let his momentum carry him into the obituaries.

"Teddy Flynn died."

"Who?" Ma asked.

"Teddy Flynn. We went to school together. He's going to be waked at Rourke's. I wouldn't let Gene Rourke bury the cat."

"I doubt your friend cares now."

"He must have been delirious."

"Must you always be morbid. He's past changing his mind."

"That's not the point. Teddy Flynn was a sensitive boy and Rourke can be . . . indelicate."

"Indelicate. That's a good accusation from someone who has a junkman's shrine for a yard."

"Can I read my paper?"

"And I don't know what you're planning with the old tires that you've been painting white in the basement but you can forget it."

"They're going to be planters and you've ruined the surprise." He was quiet for a few seconds then made a great noise of his breath. "Is it too much for a man to expect a little peace with his paper."

"And what possessed you to tack up a rodent's tail on the side porch? Are you out of your mind? Where's your pride?"

"It's a squirrel's tail."

"Still a rodent."

"Is one goddam moment of peace too much?" he would shout and slam his newspaper into his chair as he rose up.

"Don't swear at me. You could clean the yard. Throw something away. The neighbors must think we're savages."

By then he would be on his way to his refuge in the basement where he would curse to the end of his temper and play the radio loud as he dared. This is where he fixed, or promised to, the broken appliances and toys he picked from other people's sidewalks on trash nights. I almost never went downstairs without him because then I was the suspect for anything missing, guilty or not. I thought it was the most interesting space in the house, more than just a place for

219

tools and broken furniture. Outdated political posters and calendars bearing pictures of saints and snow-covered farmhouses covered the walls. I remember a huge freestanding red and white cigarette pack as tall as I was then. His workbench had a line of dusty cologne bottles in the shapes of animals and a clear blue bust of President Lincoln.

Once in a while Dad took me downstairs with him, gave me a piece of scrap wood, with nails and a hammer.

"What's that racket?" my mother would call down the stairs. It was kind of a game between us.

"I'm making you a chair," I used to holler. I would bang away until I had bent and smashed the nails down into hammer moons that split the wood. When I got bored or tired I gave the hammer back to Dad with the pieces. He lifted his chin and tilted his head back to inspect the thready pulp of my labors, turning the sticks in his hands.

"Done," he would say. "Now go find your mother."

Around the house my father and I continued to live lives of normal routine over our secret. It was not an easy cover for me. Funeral Home attendants, morticians and staff, would sometimes see me with my mother at the grocery store or on the street and greet me warmly by name.

Ma would nod hello on my behalf and ask, "Who's that?"

I would shrug, hoping that she would think they were Dad's work chums. It was not easy to lie to her because she was my favorite, his too, and our judge. Sweets, medicine, whatever you needed including hot food and clean clothes, came through her. She was the ruler in our home, and her idea of what was right went for father and son alike. In a tender way, we were afraid of her.

I knew most of my father's acquaintances from busy nights in Funeral Homes where I drank condensed milk flavored with coffee at my father's side. When attendants came back into those kitchens they usually dropped their glum looks and told stories, often about the clients. They gave me quarters and dimes. Their shared time at Tobin's may have been a mock secret to some of their families. It was not unusual, on the nights they gathered, that the kitchen phone would ring. Whoever answered would say "Just a moment please," then press the receiver against his chest before calling one of the others by name and asking, "You here?"

The sought person's part in the game was to shake his head no and check his watch, I guess so as not to over-abuse the trust of his lie.

The rest of us did not speak or move, in sympathetic stealth, until the phone was back in its cradle.

Friday nights became a comfortable ritual I looked forward to, feeling a part of something. I was one of them until February the following year.

We were at one of those one-night-wakes that Jimmy did for the poor. Jimmy was a State Representative and these discount affairs were good promotions, earning word-of-mouth praise and goodwill of the public. I didn't know that night's deceased woman by name but I remember how enormous she was, mounding up in her casket so that it looked a challenge to ever close the lid with her still in it. She must have been alone in the world because, when she left it, she didn't draw a single caller. The Core all took turns kneeling beside her to offer a prayer and then retired to the kitchen where they passed the hat for flowers, as was their habit for those without.

I was standing next to the black cast iron stove enjoying the heat and listening to Jimmy loosen up with time on his hands. His voice sometimes slipped into a bit of a lilt after a cup or two.

Addressing his fans he said, "Sad that she let herself go so, getting that big. She's three hundred if she's a pound. And . . ." He paused to tap a forefinger beside his nose. "She had a glass eye."

Everyone took a step toward the intervening door to peek at her lying in state two rooms away.

"No," Joe Twomey protested, "I knew her all my life."

The Core moved to the second doorway in the cloakroom, for a closer appraisal of the dead woman surrounded by four lighted candles, courtesy of the house.

"It's true," Jimmy said, "I washed it in the work sink myself."

"Hard to believe," said Red, leading the others back around Jimmy, "that in her youth she was a gorgeous creature, much appreciated." He was smiling as he said this then noticed me and gave up the smile. "For her convexities," and nodded toward me for the benefit of the others who nodded in return as the phone rang behind them.

An arm in a yellow sweater reached through the door from the stairwell that led to the Tobin living quarters and pulled the receiver through the open space.

"Yes," said a male voice. "Yes. Yes. Yes. You're very welcome. Good-bye." The arm hung up the phone and the rest of the person emerged. It was Jimmy's brother Buster, twelve years my senior and home from college. He put his hands in his pockets and smiled easily, as if he were one of us.

"Who was that?" Jimmy asked.

"Mrs. Burke."

"My wife?" asked Red.

"Yes," Buster told us.

"Is everything all right?" Jimmy kept after him.

"Yeah, sure. She just asked if her husband was here and if the client was someone he knew."

Red lowered his cup hand from his chest to his waist. "What did you tell her?"

"I told her yes to both questions. I was on my way down and couldn't help overhearing what you said. You knew her, right?"

Red straightened and his face looked in an excited way. "You couldn't have spoken to me first? You couldn't have been a little more considerate?"

"She asked me."

"She asked you." Red stuck his head forward. "She asked you?" He spoke slowly, staring at Buster, his eyes going wide. "It's not the way things are done."

"I don't see what the big deal is," Buster said.

"Excuse me Jimmy," Red looked to him briefly then back at Buster, "but you've no appreciation of protocol, and no knowledge of history."

"History?" Buster made an inquiring face.

"Don't interrupt," Jimmy told him.

"I was just saying . . ." Buster tried.

"You've a lot to learn," Red interrupted, his voice rising on the last word. "If this is your generation's way, it pains me to see the troubles ahead for all your hard working family's accomplishments." He looked away from everyone, saying, "Bad for business Jimmy," got his coat then started out the back, turning to face us at the door. "Brother against brother," his voice was almost at a whisper as he shook his head. "Merciful Lord Almighty, we're living out the Book Of Revelations." With this he drained his blue cup, slammed it on the soapstone counter top and left.

Jimmy and Buster exchanged disagreeable looks and Buster left too, going the way he came in. The kitchen was quiet and we sheepishly looked to Jimmy.

"Well," he said, "I'll talk to them both," and the room relaxed a little.

It didn't help me because I was still uneasy about the eye. I had never heard of such a thing. I tried not to picture Jimmy fingering it from her socket, rolling it in his hand under the faucet's rush, then pushing it back in, spinning it straight with his thumb. My head grew warm. Sensations prickled upon it the way small bubbles pop after rising in a glass of soda. I felt as if my skin was getting thick and gauzy. The room was quiet again except for the crackling in the stove.

"I'll straighten out Buster," said Jimmy, sounding distracted "and give Red a call in the morning." He hesitated, and then tried to go on with his story, though in a less enthusiastic tone. "As I was saying, she's three hundred if she's a pound, and full of fluid." He stared at the floor. "We had to wrap her in plastic to keep her clothes dry."

At this my sensibilities felt drawn upward to a point above my head, like the taper of a flame. I may have blinked once or twice and my awareness blew from the room to a quick nothing.

I came back slowly, a little confused, hearing voices up through a sore brightening redness, and opened my eyes under a circle of men's faces it took me a moment to recognize. Dad was dabbing my head with a damp hankie. The attentions of the rest embarrassed me. I tried to get up and got woozy for it with a sharp pain in my brow.

"Easy," someone said and I rested back against my father's arm. My face felt flushed and my body clammy in my clothes.

"There, he's all right," said Jimmy, "hit his head on the stove. Must have been too close to the heat."

"Can you stand?" Dad asked.

I nodded and got up with him pulling me by one arm. We stood there a long moment, the center of attention.

"Water?" Someone offered a red mug with clear drops clinging to the outside. I shook my head and the pain kept moving a bit, after I stopped.

"Maybe a spoon of brandy," Reardon suggested.

"No," said Dad, "we better be on our way," and there were nods all around. Someone handed my coat to me. The spirit seemed out of them as we left by the back. Dad guided me outside and down the walk with his hand between my shoulders.

"You all right?" he asked.

"Yes," I said softly, embarrassed and afraid that I had embarrassed him too.

"Does your head hurt?"

I nodded.

"You were never a crier."

We started for home, our warm breaths whiting behind us. The frost-heaved sidewalks were frozen over with blackened snow, sandy in places, and packed hard from many feet. The cold air felt concentrated at the pulsing corner of my head. I couldn't bear to pull my knitted hat over the front. The clamminess I felt at Tobin's had turned into a chill. I wasn't thinking clearly. We were quiet for a while.

"Am I going to die?" I asked.

"What?" he asked to my question, the word coming out with the short white plume of his breath.

"Am I going to die?"

He looked down at me, ahead, down at me again and then blew a long trail of his air that I turned my head to watch fade behind us as he spoke. "When? You mean now?"

"Someday," I said softly because the effort to speak made the pain sharper. I stumbled and paid more attention to my steps.

"Don't talk foolish," he sounded out of breath. "You've got sixty or seventy years, God willing. Don't go wasting time getting ahead of yourself."

My leather bottomed shoes slipped in unison on a slick spot and I bumped into him.

"Mary and Joseph. Will you try to walk like a human being. If you paid more attention you wouldn't always be falling into things."

It was a long walk home. My aching head felt foreign over my untrustworthy feet and I watched my steps the rest of the way. We were quiet until we reached our street. He stopped us at the corner and bent from the waist to speak to my face, giving one of his hands a single shake in the air without menace.

"Say nothing to your mother. Call goodnight and go straight to bed. I'll do the talking."

He must have cleared his throat two or three times on the way to the house. When we got there he gently opened the aluminum storm door, hesitated and peeked through the inside door's window. He pushed that open and motioned me in with his head toward the stairs directly ahead. I crossed the threshold just as my mother entered the living room from the dimly lit kitchen. I must have earned an impressive bump because when she saw me, her eyes and mouth opened in alarm.

"What have you done to him?" she demanded rushing to me. She gave my head a two second examination then pulled my face to her stomach. Her rough hug hurt my sore forehead on contact. "What happened?"

"God now," Dad said, "he fell down, he's all right."

"How's he all right?" she asked him before turning back to me, her eyes with the same fierce glint they got whether she was protecting or punishing. She took my face in both her hands and asked me, "Where did you fall?"

I wanted to look at Dad but I couldn't move my face in her grip. "Against the stove," I said, my pledged loyalty to him withered before the ready temper in her face.

"Gee-zus," muttered my father.

"What stove?" she kept on. Dad was already on his way to the basement.

"Tobin's," I said, too terrified to think of a lie. Maybe I could have held out if I only could have seen his face. I wanted to run to him as apology but ashamed by my confession, I felt, even if she released me, that chance was somehow past.

She watched me for some long seconds. "Tobin's Funeral Home?"

I tried to nod.

"And what were you doing there?" She asked this right before her own answer bunched in her face. By this time Dad was on his way down the cellar stairs. Ma led me to the bathroom where she washed and put Mercurochrome on my head. I went to bed without hearing or knowing any further outcome. Ma never followed him into the basement and I doubt that he came up that night, before she was asleep.

Nominated by Joseph Hurka, News from The Republic of Letters

GOD'S PENIS

by JEFFREY HARRISON

from THE SOUTHERN REVIEW

As usual, I had my zealous eye
on Nancy Morris, the object both of my desire
and my envy: Professor Schneider's pet
in Seminar on Jewish Mysticism,
the one he'd stop his lectures for to offer
some private suggestion about her thesis.
Her seriousness masked her blonde, smooth beauty
in frown lines I'd been trying to read between
all term: was she a Goody Two-Shoes
or the sensualist I sometimes thought I glimpsed,
in the way, for instance, she was sucking
on her pen cap that day? I couldn't take
my eyes away, or keep my errant mind
from unbuttoning her cashmere cardigan.
But she, as always, had her blue-eyed attention,
her whole rapt being, focused on Schneider.
Was she in love with this hunched homunculus
older than his fifty years, almost a mystic himself,
who whispered quotations from Hassidic sages
in a German accent as thick as his gray beard?

During a lull in our discussion of the Kabbala
Schneider mentioned in passing an article
he'd seen in one of the scholarly journals
on God's penis. None of us had ever heard

anything crude pass through his oracular lips,
and before we knew whether to snicker
or take him at his startling word, his chosen pupil
gasped violently and bolted up like someone
suddenly possessed, with a force that sent
her chair clattering backwards. Everyone stared,
but she was speechless, grabbing at her neck.
"Are you choking?" I asked, remembering the pen cap,
and, as if this were a desperate game of charades,
she pointed at me—her first acknowledgment
of my existence. "Heimlich maneuver!"
someone shouted, and Schneider lurched across the room,
and then he was doing it to her, hugging her from behind,
his hands clasped together under her snug breasts
and his pelvis pressing into her blue-jeaned ass,
closing his eyes and groaning with the exertion.

If it is true what Buber says, that no encounter
lacks a spiritual significance, then what
in God's unutterable name was this one
all about? Their long-awaited intimacy
nightmarishly fulfilled, or some excruciating twist
on "the sacrament of the present moment"?—
a phrase I remembered but couldn't have told you
where in the syllabus of mystic intimations
it came from. I couldn't have told you
anything: there was nothing but their dire embrace
wavering with the luminous surround
of a hallucination—and something inside me
rushing out toward them, silently pleading,
"God, don't let her die!" The answer came,
torpedoing through the air and ricocheting
with a smack against the framed void of the blackboard.
Relief and embarrassment flooded the room
like halves of the Red Sea while the girl who had choked
on God's penis looked around astonished,
as if returning from a world beyond our knowing.

Nominated by Robert Cording, William Wenthe, Ted Deppe, B.J. Ward, Joyce Carol Oates

DEATH IN NAPLES

fiction by MARY GORDON

from SALMAGUNDI

I T WAS WONDERFUL OF JONATHAN to have invited her. How many sons, her friends kept asking, would include their mother on a vacation with their wives? You could see it, her friends had said, if there were children: invite granny—a built in baby sitter. But there was nothing in it for Jonathan and Melanie but pure goodness of heart. How fortunate she was, her friends all told her, to have a daughter in law she was fond of.

And she was fond of Melanie, really she was, although she wasn't a person Lorna felt she could relax with. Certainly she was admirable, the way she dealt with everything: her job as a stock broker, keeping their apartment beautiful, regularly making delicious meals. And she always looked splendid; she kept her hair long, done up in some complicated way that Lorna knew must take time in the morning. Braids or curls or a series of barrettes or clips. And beautifully cut suits and beautifully made high heeled pumps. Lorna remembered when she had worn heels that high, and remembered how she'd loved them. But she remembered, too, how uncomfortable they had been and what a blessed relief, a consolation even, it had been to kick them off at the door. To give them up for something softer, slippers or loafers or tennis shoes. But Melanie didn't kick her heels off at the door. She kept them on even to cook her careful dinners. It occurred to Lorna that she'd never seen her daughter in law in slippers. She assumed that she must have a pair, but Lorna couldn't imagine what they might look like.

Lorna could be of use to them on their holiday in that she had some Italian and they had none. Don't overestimate my ability, she warned them: I'm not very good and I'm easily flustered. And when I'm flustered I lose the little proficiency I've had. Possibly, had she started younger, or lived in Italy for extended periods, her Italian would have been quite good.

That was what Richard kept telling her. They traveled to Italy every year the six years before his death. His death that was brief, composed, a line that completed itself effortlessly. He'd slipped into his death as a letter slips into an envelope, and is sent off, or as a diver, seen from a distance, enters the dark water, and swims into a cove from which he can't be seen again. Like the letter or the swimmer Richard had, she was sure, reached some proper destination. Only she could not name it or locate it. But she was sure there was such a place.

When they were in Italy, he was terribly proud when she could talk to waiters, and said it was nothing, nothing, when failures of comprehension occurred on either side. When a fruit vendor would say *"come"*, scrunching his face up when she had said perfectly clearly, she had thought, *uove* or *pere*, when she would have to say *"mi dispiace, no ho capito"* after someone had told her the directions to a museum, or when an Italian, losing patience, would lapse into English, Richard would say, "Relax, you're doing great." She knew she wasn't doing great, and even though Richard was right to tell her that no one in their conversation group could do half so well, she wasn't comforted. She knew that when real situations arose, she often failed.

The Italian conversation class was one of the things she and Richard did together after Richard's retirement. They'd hired an Italian student from the university to teach a group of them, four retired couples, or rather four retired men and their wives, because none of the women had ever worked. They'd planned to study all year and then travel, four couples, to Italy in the spring. The study had continued; the travel happened only once. For in reality the other couples hadn't really enjoyed themselves in Italy, had behaved dutifully rather than joyously and were unable to conceal their real joy at returning home to Cincinnati. To their own bathrooms, their own beds.

But Richard and Lorna had gone back every spring for six springs. They had not been able to wean themselves from Tuscany, landing in Florence, spending a week there in the same hotel, where, after the fourth year, and because they were never there in high season, they were given a room with a view of Piazza San Marco. She was grateful that Richard didn't mind driving in Italy; she could never have; the speeds on the *autostrade* terrified her. So they visited Siena, Civietalla, Pisa, Lucca. Gentle weeks during which they could digest the beauty they had seen in Florence, avoiding what she had read in a guidebook was called Stendhal syndrome. The novelist had suffered a nervous breakdown, overwhelmed by the pressure of having to assimilate so much greatness, so much human achievement in so short a time.

During the long wet winters in Cincinnati, she would regularly place a postcard of something they'd loved next to Richard's breakfast plate: Donatello's saucy David in his feathered hat, Michaelangelo's evening languidly waiting for something to be played out.

And then Richard had died, and she hadn't been back to Italy since. Six years, could it have been? She was seventy-four now, unarguably an old lady. Some women she knew, but no one she knew well, traveled alone at her age. A friend of a friend had made, at seventy-five, a trip to Thailand on her own. She envied such women, wished she could be like them, but she was not. She kept her life full; she wouldn't sell the house or get help with the garden, she was a docent at the museum; she kept up with her Italian and her women friends—widows and divorcees. The couples had, somehow, stopped including her. But she met with her friends, regularly, to cook elaborate meals. They swam together at the health club. Three times a year, she traveled to Chicago to see Jonathan and Melanie, staying only a few days at a time, going to the Art Institute, to the symphony, to see some experimental theater, priding herself on keeping out of their way and not staying too long. She believed them when they said they were sorry to see her go; she believed their friends when they told Jonathan how lucky he was to have a mother who was so "low maintenance." Low maintenance. It amused her how many phrases had become common that hadn't existed when she was young—or even ten years later. That was the world, that was language: it was a product of change. Change was a good thing; when you stopped believing that, you'd got old, you might as well chuck the whole business.

After a deprivation of six years, the prospect of seeing Italy with Jonathan and Melanie was particularly delightful. They were young and vigorous and full of curiosity. How strange that neither of them had been to Italy. Melanie had never been abroad. But Melanie's life, before she'd met Jonathan, had been difficult. Her parents had been killed in a car crash just after she started college; they'd seemed to leave her nothing. Lorna respected Melanie's reticence about her late parents; she saw her unwillingness to talk about them as an attractive fastidiousness—she was always uneasy at the modern tendency to reveal too much. She'd been surprised when, just before the wedding, Jonathan had said to her and Richard: "Melanie wants me to talk to you about what she's going to call you. She just doesn't feel comfortable calling you Mom and Dad; she says that's what she calls her own parents in her mind. Is it OK if she just calls you Richard and Lorna?" Lorna had never expected that Melanie would do anything else; she wondered what that suggested about Melanie's background, but as she thought there was no way of knowing, and as she was moved by Melanie's protectiveness of her parents' memory, she warmly agreed that Melanie should go on just as she had, calling them by their first names.

So it wasn't surprising that Melanie had never been to Europe; she had no indulgent parents to treat her; she'd had to augment her scholarship with a series of menial jobs. She'd gone to work at a bank a week after graduation. And Lorna and Richard had often remarked to each other that going to Europe, the whole idea of Europe, didn't mean to Jonathan's generation what it had to theirs. She and Richard had gone to Paris on their honeymoon, saving up a year for it, feeling that on the rumpled sheets of their left bank hotel, scene of so much illicit, such artistic love making, they could legitimate their sexual union without its losing its allure. Jonathan and Melanie had gone to St. Bart's for their honeymoon. They both worked so very hard. Eighty-hour weeks sometimes. Who could blame them for wanting to lie on a beach, rest up in the sunshine.

Jonathan hadn't been to Europe since college; she and Richard had taken him to the South of France for a pre-graduation gift. It hadn't been a success; Jonathan didn't seem to enjoy it as they did; Lorna thought he missed his friends. But now he'd be with Melanie; they were so perfectly matched; she knew that when Jonathan was with his wife, he felt no need for other company. She only hoped she wouldn't be in the way.

"We want to take you back to the old haunts, your old haunts with Dad, they're new for me and Mel. But we thought it would be fun for us to see something new to all of us. I've booked us into Naples, and from there, we'll tool around the Amalfi coast."

"Marvelous," said Lorna. "And maybe we can take a side trip to Pompeii."

"Archaeology's not Mel's thing," said Jonathan.

Lorna told herself it didn't matter that she'd miss Pompeii; they'd have more than enough to see.

For three months, she read and re-read guidebooks, trying to select a few things that would spark for Jonathan and Melanie the love that she and Richard had felt. Not too much, not too much, she kept saying to herself, cutting back her plans as she would prune a vine or a bush that could choke out fragile life with its over-effulgence. One beautiful thing a day, we'll see what we see, they're young, they'll come back. She would leave them to themselves in the afternoon; she remembered the sweet sleepy afternoons of lovemaking with Richard in Italian hotels, in beds that weren't really double beds at all but twin beds pushed together, a sheet stretched tight over the top. And of course, they worked so hard, they'd need their afternoon siesta. One beautiful thing a day, she said, pleased at her own modesty—they'll have love, and rest, and delicious food as well.

She'd never traveled business class before; the luxury quietly delighted her. She knew Jonathan was uncomfortable about being thanked for upgrading her fare; he seemed impatient that she should think it was anything to mention. "Mom, for heaven's sake, everyone flies business class. It's no big deal. Mel and I have so many miles we don't know what to do with them. She's the queen of the upgrade, my wife, aren't you babe."

"Jesus, yes," said Melanie. She reached into the tapestry bag at her feet and shyly handed Lorna a box wrapped in violet paper with a teal ribbon. "This is your survival kit for the airplane," she said. Lorna opened the box; there was an inflatable neck pillow, a set of earplugs, a lavender sachet that went over your eyes like a mask-sized pillow—it was supposed to induce a gentle sleep. There were Victorian tins of pastilles: one black current, one lemon, with pictures of little girls holding parasols. Tears came to Lorna's eyes at Melanie's thoughtfulness—all the more touching because she seemed so uncomfortable at being thanked. She put her lavender sachet—hers was a paisley print of dark blue and magenta—over her beautiful gray eyes. She'd taken a sleeping pill.

"She's also the queen of the sleepers. Just watch, five minutes, she'll be dead to the world."

Dead to the world, Lorna thought, what a terrible expression. If you were dead to the world, what, then, were you alive to? She opened her map of Florence. She'd left map reading to Richard and she was afraid she'd forgotten everything, and Jonathan and Melanie were depending on her to lead them around.

She watched the young people sleeping. Beautiful, she thought, their health, their wholeness. They shared a kind of sleep that she and Richard had never shared, because she had never worked as hard as Richard. Melanie and Jonathan were together in feeling they had earned their rest, that it was equally hard won, equally precious, because rare, to both of them. She thought of Jonathan's sleeping body when he'd been a little boy, how nothing had given her the pure peace and joy of holding her child's sleeping body. He was hers then. And now he was—what? The world's? Melanie's?

Melanie woke cranky; everything made her impatient. Their room in the hotel wasn't ready. Gingerly, Lorna suggested a coffee at a café in Piazza San Marco.

"What options do I have?" she asked.

"Chill out, babe," said Jonathan.

"Jonathan, I'm wondering what could possibly make you think that was a helpful comment," she said, snapping shut the lid on her blusher.

Jonathan and Melanie drank their coffee silently. Melanie kept looking at her watch. The girl at the hotel desk had said the room would be ready in half an hour. Melanie crossed and uncrossed her legs. Lorna noticed that her brown boots were very beautiful. She supposed Melanie would want to shop for shoes.

She took a sip of cappuccino. Her eyes closed with pleasure. "Isn't it wonderful, isn't it wonderful," she wanted to say, "isn't the coffee delicious, aren't the waitresses' uniforms charming, isn't the chandelier elegant." But Melanie was elaborately, ostentatiously making fanning gestures in front of her face.

"Haven't they ever heard of a non-smoking section," she said.

"I'll bet there's no Italian word for second-hand smoke," said Jonathan.

"Unbelievable," said Melanie, and they moved closer together, united, a couple once again.

The bellman showed them to their rooms. Melanie didn't even open the shutters. "Don't wake me for lunch," she said.

"I think it might be better if you just took a short nap, and tried to get on Italian time," Lorna said.

"Look," said Melanie, in a way that Lorna knew was more polite than her impulse. "I'm just not up to it."

"I'm with you, Mom. I'll just snooze for an hour, then we'll meet for lunch and do some sightseeing."

"Whatever suits you, dear," Lorna said.

"One o'clock then, it's a date," Jonathan said, cocking his hand like a gun.

It was February, off season. They had said it to each other time and time again, congratulating themselves for their cleverness— warning themselves in advance about disappointing weather and doors seasonally closed. But Lorna's heart was entirely light when she said the words to herself—off season—approaching Capella San Marco, home of the Fra Angelico frescos. She dreamed that she and Jonathan would have the place to themselves. The silvery disc of sun that fell onto the flat leaves of the plane trees did not have to pass through throngs of tourists or buses; the square wasn't empty, but the traffic seemed normal, native, workaday. There were no lines at the ticket window and no one was ahead of her on the dark staircase that culminated in the famous fresco of the Annunciation.

She hadn't said anything to Jonathan about it; she wanted him to be taken entirely by surprise as she had been—could it have been half a century ago—when she'd seen it for the first time. Nothing had prepared her for it; no one she'd known had spoken to her of it, perhaps because no one she knew well had ever seen it. The sweet- ness of the virgin's face, the serious blue of her skirt, the vibrant expectant lunge of an angel, as if he'd only just landed, as if he hadn't given over yet, completely, the idea of flight. And those miraculous wings: solid, sculptural, wings the colors of fruits or jewels, peach, emerald, rust red, the shade of blood but with no hint of blood's liquidity. Tears came to her eyes, as they always did when she saw the fresco. She was not a religious woman, nor a tearful one, but always when she saw it, she wanted to thank someone, she did not know whom. When she and Richard were together they would squeeze each other's hands.

But Jonathan was yawning when she looked back at him with what she hoped was not too expectant a smile.

"Great colors, Mom," he said. "You don't see something like this every day."

Now she must try not to make her smile disappointed. What had she wanted him to say? She wondered if it would have been better if he'd said nothing. And the guards chattered so that it was noisy: the place might as well have been full of tourists. She remembered the Italian word for chatter, which had pleased her for its onomatopoeia. *Chiacchiera*. But now the word didn't seem pleasing; it suggested restless, pointless busyness—not the atmosphere she wanted for Fra Angelico. Jonathan was walking down the corridors, stopping only seconds at each cell, each of which had its own fresco. At the opposite end of the corridor from her, she could see him stretching, doing exercises to loosen the tension in his neck.

Melanie complained that the room was noisy, that the beds were hard and the towels were thin. And Lorna told herself that all Melanie's complaints were justified and wondered why she hadn't noticed. It wasn't that she hadn't noticed, of course she'd noticed, but it hadn't mattered. Be honest with yourself, she said, it's not that you don't understand why it didn't matter to you, you can't understand why it would matter to anyone when there was so much out there, so much of beauty, of greatness. Why would it matter that the beds were hard, the towels thin. She simply couldn't understand.

Melanie would eat only grilled fish and salad. She said the vegetables were drenched in oil. "I wouldn't touch them with a ten foot pole." Lorna tried not to be irritated as she ate her *farro*, the thick Tuscan soup she and Richard always enjoyed. She wanted to hold the bottle of olive oil to the light and ask Jonathan and Melanie to share her pleasure in its greenness. She wanted to have wine with lunch, but she felt she couldn't because she didn't want to appear a drunkard or a glutton to her daughter in law, so slender, so chic, with her long legs and complicated braid.

"Florence is supposed to be a great place for leather. Where's the best place to look for bags?" Melanie said.

Lorna felt that, in confessing that she didn't know where to shop for bags, she was letting Jonathan down, revealing herself as provincial, dowdy, and out of touch. But she didn't remember having shopped when she and Richard were in Florence.

And she didn't remember that, at this time of year, the Piazza del Duomo was so crowded with tourists. In summer, yes, at Christmas or at Easter, but they had purposely avoided those times; it was February now. Why was the square so full of buses? And wasn't this a new kind of tourists, a new kind of Americans, people in their sixties, abashed couples dressed in matching leisure suits in various shades of blue, new white sneakers dragging themselves across the cobble stones. Were there always so many of the nearly elderly? she wondered. She had read that people were retiring earlier now. Were they traveling because they had too much time and too much money and didn't know what to do with either? Had they always been here and she just hadn't noticed them? Or was it that they were younger than she was now, but seemed older? Herded through the Duomo, the Uffizi, they looked stunned, like oxen that had been struck with a mallet. They weren't seeing anything, they looked miserable; they made stupid jokes to each other. Melanie was right; they did spoil Botticelli's Venus, Michaelangelo's David.

"Jesus, Americans are unbelievable," Melanie said. "The obesity is epidemic. Look at them, men and women, they all look like they're in their third trimester of pregnancy."

Lorna wondered if Jonathan and Melanie would have a child. She rather thought they wouldn't.

On the morning of the third day, Jonathan knocked on Lorna's door.

"Mom, we've had some bad news. One of Melanie's clients is losing his shirt. You know how all the dot coms are tanking. Mel's got to leave immediately and see what can be salvaged."

"Of course," Lorna said.

236

"Sweetheart, can you manage here alone? She wigs out when she's stressed. I need to be with her."

"Of course," Lorna said.

Dot coms are tanking, wigs out when she's stressed. The words made pictures her mind had to ingest; there were entities, ideas she'd never had to know about that she now had to try to understand. Talking to her son made her feel old. And crotchety. I am becoming a crotchety old lady, she told herself. So she was extra careful to make it clear to Jonathan and Melanie that she'd be just fine on her own, that they mustn't think about her.

"Mom, you're a great sport," Jonathan said.

Go with God, she wanted to say, which she thought odd. It was a thing she never before would have thought of saying.

She told herself it was a blessing in disguise that Jonathan and Melanie had to leave. It was the kind of push that did a person good, particularly a person of her age. What kept a person young was doing new things; what aged a person was giving into the fear of the unaccustomed. Now she would be traveling alone, like the women she'd admired but had feared to be. Now she would be going, entirely on her own, to places she hadn't been with her husband. And how generous Jonathan and Melanie had been. Jonathan had put an envelope on her bed, full of lire. Fifteen hundred dollars it would come to. And the hotel bill had been taken care of.

It was not the kind of hotel she and Richard would have chosen: the art-deco grandeur would have made them feel, as a couple, fearful and at sea. Her room was larger than any she'd ever stayed in with Richard; it was larger than their bedroom in Cincinnati. She looked over all the rooves of Naples. Vesuvius crouched in the distance, and if she stood by the window, the blue slice reminded her that she was near the sea. No, not the sea, she told herself, the bay. The bay of Naples.

It would have been Richard who would have read the history of the place they were visiting, but she had done that part too. He would have learned about the dynasties, the wars, the politics. Now it was her responsibility; she hoped she hadn't skimped. But if she had, what difference would it make now? Who would know? And if something was missed, there was no one to judge her. The loss was only hers.

From her bed she could push a button that opened and closed the blinds. Another turned the lights on and off, a third started the television. She kept mixing them up, and she tried to laugh when, attempting to close the blind, she brought into her room the Simpsons in Italian. She supposed she could learn something from watching it, but she didn't want to. She wanted the darkness. The bed was overlarge; she had not been sleeping well.

On the Neopolitan streets, she had to work very hard not to lose her way. Every few seconds she would look down at her map, then look up at the street signs, saying to herself if Via Chiara is to my left, if left is west, then I am all right, I am not lost. But it was very tiring, this kind of concentration, and she felt as if the part of her brain that had the words for things was being taken up trying to find her way. She felt she could either get lost or remember the words for things, and she was more afraid of being lost than being speechless. But it alarmed her that the simplest sentence seemed beyond her now; what she would once have found easy now seemed to her impossible.

She kept telling herself that she wasn't disappointed in Naples, not really, that the weather was really bad luck, that was it, that was what was keeping her heart from its Italian soaring. She very much admired what she saw in the great Baroque churches; she was charmed by the majolica cloister of Santa Chiara, there was a fresco in San Domenico Maggiore that came near to the Giottos in Santa Croce for the freshness of its blues. And beside it was a Magdalene, her gold hair covering her rosy flesh—it was miraculous, really miraculous. She was more tired than she remembered being anywhere else in Italy, and there seemed to be fewer cafés to rest in. She liked that it was a real city, a working city, not some hopped-up showcase for tourists. She remembered a poster in Florence protesting the banning of cars in the city center: "This is our home, not your museum," the poster said. And she had understood. But Naples wasn't Florence; it was a place where people went about their business, and their business was not tourism.

It was wonderful that she hadn't seen a single American in the streets, hadn't heard a word of English spoken. It made her feel proud of herself that she was negotiating this really foreign territory. She ordered her meals competently. On the street of the *presepii*, where figures for elaborate nativity scenes were sold, she had no trouble getting the sellers to show her the pieces that she wanted. Her trouble came in choosing; she was attracted to the elegantly costumed bisque angels hanging on wires from the ceiling—but what difference did it make whether she chose the peach one or the teal, the one in the coral robe with the serene expression, the one with the striped wings and impish grin? And did she really need a fancy Christmas ornament? Who would see it? They weren't expensive; they were lovely, every one one of them had its own appeal. Leaning her head back to look up at them had made her dizzy. All the angels seemed to swim into each other, and blur into a wave of indistinguishable colors, features. She left the street of the *presepii* having bought nothing.

One waiter in a restaurant had been kind to her, telling her with a gruff paternalism that she had to have dessert, it was customary, and she needed her strength. She had probably overtipped him, but when she went back the following night she was glad she had. He took her arm and escorted her to her table and told her she must leave the ordering to him. She enjoyed his kindness as she enjoyed the pasta with mussels and clams, but by the time she was back in bed the pleasure of both had worn off, and she felt her body rigid, a supplicant for sleep which did not come. Was she becoming one of those people she and Richard had secretly condemned: people like Jane and Harry, or Albert and Jean, who could only sleep in their own beds? She must get over this. She was in one of the places history had marked as great; she would get the good of it, she would expend herself, test her limits. For once, she was doing what no one she knew had ever done. No one she knew well had been to Naples. She realized that for her whole life, she had walked in the footsteps of others. Now she would be breaking her own trail.

At 3 A.M. there was a terrifying clap of thunder. You are perfectly safe, she told herself. Nothing can happen to you here. Yet the sight of Vesuvius, which she had only to prop herself on her elbows to see, suggested that the idea of safety was the most fragile of illusions. Flashes of silver lit the heavy mountain with what she thought was a capricious show of force. Then the mountain would hide itself behind gray and become invisible. It was easy to see its malevolence, its carelessness. She thought of the Pompeii mummies, turned to stone embracing, or foolishly trying to run. But was that so bad? What would be lost if she met her end in this way rather than some other? Why not be crushed by a huge, indifferent fist, squashing her insignificance? The idea of her insignificance didn't bother her; she found it comforting—the notion that she would not be very much missed. Richard had gone before her, and Jonathan—well, Jonathan had Melanie. He would grieve her passage, but his grief would not leave much of a mark.

The next day it was cold and rainy; she decided on a visit to the Archaeological Museum; she didn't need good weather for that. She rented a taped guide to the museum, a thing she ordinarily would not have done, but her guidebook had warned her that the museum might be overwhelming, and she felt that, as she was alone, she didn't want to be overwhelmed. But the machine confused her; she seemed unable to find what the voice told her was in the rooms; the spoken descriptions seemed to match nothing before her eyes. Reliefs, vases, tiles: what people had lived with and amongst before their lives were extinguished in a blink—none of it seemed connected to any human experience she could understand. After a while she realized that for half an hour she'd been walking up and down the same corridor, in and out of the same rooms. She sat down on a stone bench in front of a showcase displaying drinking vessels and she wept. There is nothing I understand, nothing I understand, nothing I understand, nothing I will ever comprehend, she heard her own voice saying. She put on her sunglasses, hailed a taxi in the freezing rain, went back to the hotel and went to bed. She kept pressing buttons trying to close the blinds; she didn't want to see Vesuvius through the rain. But every button that she pressed was wrong; the lights went on and off; the television blared. She got out of bed and tried to pull the blinds shut, but only a button could effect a change, and she couldn't make the buttons work. She got back into bed, covered her head with blankets, and listened to the outlandish beating of her heart.

She had two days left in Naples. There were many enjoyable things to do. But if she were honest with herself, they didn't seem enjoyable enough to justify the effort. Everything seemed too difficult. Life itself was too difficult, not just life but what life had become. Buttons and audio guides and dot coms tanking. And travel so comparatively cheap and easy, and people with too much money and too much time. Things that used to be simple seemed too taxing now. Taxing. Tax. What was the tax that was paid, what was the rate, and what the currency? And to whom was the payment made? Was it flesh or blood or spirit that was demanded? She thought of Caravaggio's St. Matthew in the church of S. Luigi Francese in Rome. The last time she and Richard were there, even seven years ago, they had had to worm their way into a knot of tourists, all of whom looked bored and oppressed to be there. St. Matthew was a tax collector. He gave it all up to follow Jesus. What was it he was giving up, and what was it he was following? She remembered the mysterious light coming through the window, and Matthew's expression of shocked surprise at being called. She remembered her own joy at the painting, a joy that made her heart beat hard, perhaps dangerously so for someone of her age. There were many Caravaggios in Naples. Tomorrow she would begin in earnest to seek them out.

But the next day was Monday. The Caravaggio *Flagellation* was in the *Museo di Capidomonte*, and it was closed on Mondays. Well, she would look elsewhere. The guidebook said that the Seven Mercies of Caravaggio was in a still active charitable institution, the Pio Monte de Misericordia. The sun seemed weakly, tentatively, to be coming out. She would take a taxi to Piazza Jesu and walk down the Via Tribunali. She hadn't been getting enough exercise; at home she swam three times a week. Perhaps that was the reason for her low spirits.

She walked down the Via Tribunali, her money pouch tucked inside her coat, her collapsible umbrella in her pocket. It was a shopping street; it could have been in any minor city in the world. But not a great city; there was no place that lifted her heart with displays of unattainable beauty. She passed a section that specialized in bridal gowns. But all the lace on the dresses had an unfresh look, as if it had been worn before, but in the recent, ungenerous past, by an unsavory groom and unfortunate bride. Everything seemed made of cheap-looking synthetic material, surely not the right thing for a girl's

241

great day. The mannequins seemed squat and fat and middle aged. She could only imagine that shopping in such stores would be a lowering experience for the girl herself, and surely for her mother. And there was something about store after store of bridal gowns that made the possibility of uniqueness seem out of the question. People got married, as they were born and died; the species must be propagated and the ceremony insuring the propagation must be marked by something that was meant to be special but, by virtue of its very frequency, could not be. She remembered her own wedding; she'd worn a navy blue suit; it had been a morning in November, a small wedding, but the day had been very happy. Jonathan and Melanie's wedding had been lavish; they'd taken over the Spanish consulate in Chicago; they had paid for everything themselves, it had cost, they told her later, fifty thousand dollars. No synthetic lace for Melanie. It had been, she remembered, quite a happy day. Except that Melanie had lost her temper at the photographer, and had burst, quite publicly, into tears. Richard had settled things somehow, and Melanie had collapsed into Lorna's arms. She'd been touched by the glimpse of the child in Melanie; the orphan child, gamely coping on her own for much too long. For the first time, she wished the young people were with her. She would spend time looking for a postcard that would please them both.

She came to the Pio Monte de Misericordia. The heavy oak door with its embossed studs was fastened shut. *Chiuso*, a sign said, unnecessarily. The guidebook had said it was a functioning charitable institution. But the place seemed so tightly, so permanently shut, it was impossible to imagine anything functioning inside there in the locatable past.

She walked back up the street, as quickly as she could, not wanting to look at the bridal dresses. She wasn't hungry, but she made herself have an early lunch.

The day was warmish now, with a weak sun. A few people were eating at outdoor tables. This seemed such a good idea, here in the land of sun, the mezzogiorno. She ordered an *insalata caprese*. The cheese was good, but the tomatoes were unremarkable. She wondered why she thought it would be good to order fresh tomatoes in March. Over coffee she caught the eye of a woman near her age at another table. The woman's formal dress pleased her. She was wearing a royal blue woolen suit, a white blouse that tied in a bow at the neck, plain black pumps, gold earrings. Her hair was pulled back in a French twist. Lorna didn't think that the new informality—dressing down it was called—had been successful. She wondered why everyone liked it so much. Didn't this woman look lovely? Wasn't it better that people should take this kind of trouble than that everyone wear sneakers? She thought with pleasure of her own outfit; her charcoal pants suit, pink silk shirt, black Ferragamo oxfords. She hoped that her appearance pleased the woman as the woman's had pleased her.

"Enjoying Naples?" the woman said, in an English accent.

"Oh, yes, very much," said Lorna. When she told the woman what she had actually seen, it seemed so scant that she felt ashamed. Yet she wouldn't make excuses for herself, for in doing that she'd have to express her disappointment in Naples, her annoyance that so many things had been closed. And she didn't want to do that.

"You must see the monastery of San Marco. Splendid cloisters, spectacular views, a great collection of eighteenth century *presepii*. A glimpse of that particular Neapolitan mix of elegance and tenderness. And you must take the funicular to get there. You'll see the Neapolitans at their most natural. And you'll think of it whenever you hear the song Funiculi, Funicular, which is written about it." Lorna wondered if the woman would begin singing, which she did not. She was a little sad that the woman, who had seemed to be taking her under her wing, did not invite her home for a cup of tea. She could imagine her apartment. It would be large and dark; there would be a cavernous sitting room with shabbily elegant, uncomfortable sofas and chairs; the light would be dim; on the walls would be etchings of 19th Century Neapolitan street scenes, darkish oils depicting the *campagna*. A small, silent servant would bring them coffee in small, gold-rimmed cups. If she were honest, she was more than a little sad that the woman had left without her. She wondered what would happen if she ran after her, caught up with her, started a conversation as they walked. You mustn't do that, she said to herself. The woman would think you were very peculiar if you did that. She ordered another coffee so that she would be sure not to get up, follow the woman, pretend to bump into her by accident. But the loss of the apartment she had conjured in her mind made her feel outlandishly bereft.

The sun disappeared again; she felt drowsy as she walked to the funicular. Had she ever, she wondered as she walked, visited another city where it was so difficult to cross a street? She felt it was entirely possible that the cars would not, in the end, stop for her. The scooters put their brakes on inches from her feet. She waited for the light to turn, hyper-alert, as if she were waiting for the shotgun blast to signal the beginning of the race. She thought the light was very long. As she stood waiting for it, a boy on a scooter passed in front of her, carrying a sheet of glass over his head. His hands held the glass; he balanced on the scooter without holding on. Cars veered around him; annoyed at having to slow down, even a little, they honked their horns. His hair was dark and curly and he showed his beautiful white teeth in his smile of defiance and pleasure at this risky task. Delivering a pane of glass through the city of Naples on a motor scooter. Suddenly she saw how it would happen: a car would not stop for him or would stop too fast, the glass would break and then, as if a line had been drawn across his neck, he would be beheaded. His beautiful head, the curls blood-stained, would lie in the street and cars would drive around it. She would have to pick it up, cradle it in her arms. And then put it where? What would she do with this treasure of a beautiful severed head?

She was trembling as she waited for the funicular. The boy was far away now, she would never know if he'd made his destination safely. Don't think of it, she said, or think of him delivering the glass, think of him sitting with his girl, having a *caffe*. But she could not stop thinking of herself holding the beautiful head.

The funicular started up with a frightening grind. Her eye fell on a mother and a child. The child was lively, unusually fair, she thought, for this part of the world. The mother was much darker. Her frizzy hair looked unclean; her skin was marred by blackheads; she wore rings on each finger, several with large stones; her nails were bitten and her cuticles were raw.

It seemed to Lorna that she talked to the child strangely, as if she didn't know her very well. No, Lorna thought, as if she were pretending to know her well, as if she wanted everyone on the funicular to believe she knew the child well. She could not be the child's mother. She had kidnapped the child, but the child didn't know it yet. She thought she was being brought back to her real mother. But Lorna knew that she would not be brought back. She imagined the dark room where the child would be taken; a bucket would be given to her so that she wouldn't have to go to the toilet; she would be given crackers, warm soda in cans, stale candy bars to eat. How could Lorna tell someone what she knew to be the case? The woman and the child got off. Lorna knew she had left the child to her fate, as she had left the boy on the scooter to his. She had left them to their fate because she had no other choice.

She thought of the beautiful child, the beautiful boy. Left to their fate, left to their fate, kept going through her head. And she could do nothing but get off the funicular, walk to the museum.

It had been a wealthy monastery, closed in the eighteenth century, a museum for thirty years. She bought her ticket, asking for the directions to the *presepii*, excited at the memory of the English woman's words.

"*Chiuso*," said the guide, a somber blonde, clicking her silver fingernails, as if Lorna's request had been ridiculous.

"*Chiuso perche?*" Lorna asked.

"*NON SO*," said the girl. "*Forse in ristauro.*"

It would be ridiculous to go back to the hotel, although that was what she wanted to do, go back to her room, close all the blinds, lie in her overlarge bed with the lights turned out. Sleep for a while, then read her book on the Bourbons and order dinner from room service. But this was her last day in Naples, her last day in Italy for who could tell how long. Perhaps the rest of her life. The English-woman had said the cloisters were extraordinary, the views spectacular. She had obviously been a person of taste.

She walked around the cloisters saying to herself, "I am an old woman now. I will never come back to this place."

The Englishwoman was right, it was a beautiful cloister, but it was beautiful in a way that seemed to Lorna wrong for a cloister. A cloister should be in relation to something growing at the center, grass, or roses, or something lively, natural: the water splashing in the central fountain. But this was a cloister whose referents were classical. The

245

walls were gray, the borders white, the statues were not fragmented saints but white ivory reliefs of heroes. It reminded her of the Place des Vosges in Paris, which she had loved, because it seemed a tribute to geometry, to lines, angles, and plains. But a cloister shouldn't feel like that; a cloister should be a place of prayer. She felt as if she'd put her lips to a child's forehead and had felt cold stone. She pulled her coat closer around her, but she knew that she hadn't dressed warmly enough for the weather, and that nothing she could do right now would make her warm enough.

The guidebook said the chapel was a triumph of the Baroque, that there were paintings by Ribera and Pontormo. But she couldn't find them. The paintings were too high up, too far from their labels. She couldn't tell which paints went with which label, and none of the paintings seemed distinguished enough to be immediately identifiable as a masterpiece. She knew it was the genius of the baroque to suggest movement, sweep, but she wasn't swept up, she was overwhelmed. Now her coat was too hot; the colors on the wall—mostly reds, were too hot and her head pounded. She nearly ran out to the courtyard, to the open air. She would go and sit on the terrace, where there was the spectacular view of the bay.

But she couldn't find the door that led to the terrace She kept walking through rooms of maps, none of which had any meaning for her. None of the doors seemed to lead to the open air. Finally, not knowing how she did it, she was back in the cloister. One of the doors of the cloister led to the terrace, the guidebook had said.

She took door after door. None of them led anywhere but to dark rooms. Rooms of maps, of antique silver, of eighteenth century carriages. She asked the guards for the terrace, and they answered politely, but she had lost all the Italian she once had and their words meant nothing to her. She knew they kept watching her walk into the wrong doorways, come back to the central passage, and take another wrong doorway. She couldn't imagine what they thought. Finally one guard took her by the hand and led her to the terrace.

She thanked him, she tried to laugh, to pass herself off as a silly old woman who couldn't tell her right from her left. But it was true, she seemed unable to tell her right from her left. She was grateful for the white marble bench, where she could sit, where she need choose nothing, make no decision. She looked out over the marble balustrade. Nothing was visible. There was no bay, no city, only a sheet of mild, dove gray.

The rain fell softly on her tired face, on her abraded eyelids, her sore lips. It was cool; the coolness was entirely desirable. This gray was what she wanted: this offering of blankness, requiring no discernment. Nothing demanding to be understood. She leaned over the railing. A moist breeze wrapped itself around her like a cloak. She leaned further into it. It was so simple and so comforting, and as she fell she knew that it was what she'd wanted for so long, this free and easy flight into the arms of something she would find familiar. A quiet place, a place of rest, where she would always know exactly what to do.

Nominated by Salmagundi

from THE FACE

by DAVID ST. JOHN

from PLOUGHSHARES

XXVII.

The voice, a woman's, says, "You self-absorbed prick!" & I swear
Every man in the place looks up, assuming in a heartbeat, &
   probably not
Without reason, that he's the one—& I include myself here—that
   this bullet
Is clearly meant for. But then we can see her, because she stands up
   beside
The table, looking down at him the way a gargoyle surveys the filth
   below,
& then of course we notice him, wickedly handsome, beautiful
   really,
Late-forties with jet-black dyed hair slicked back & though of
   course it's
Unfair, you hear the whole restaurant decide together, all at once,
Well, she's probably got a point . . . He's pure Eurotrash, your
   standard
Rodeo Drive chauffeur-cum-gigolo-cum-male model, all grown-up
& burnt out, & it's hard not to feel just a little sorry for him
As she raises her steak knife to her shoulder & buries it in the back
   of his
Left hand, flattened—now pinned—against the starched white linen
   tablecloth.
She looks at the knife & slumps into her chair. He looks over at her,
   with what

Seems enormous tenderness, & it's easy to believe, in fact, that
  we've got it
All wrong. As the waiter comes over with an ice pack & the first-aid
  kit;
As the several doctors in the house compete with their cell phones
  & advice;
As the lake of blood deliberately advances toward her . . . well,
  looking at the two
Of them looking at each other, it's hard not to admit they must be in
  love.
I mean, really *really* in love—

Nominated by Marvin Bell, Katrina Roberts, Ralph Angel, Diann Blakely, Mark Irwin

BULLET IN MY NECK

by GERALD STERN

from THE GEORGIA REVIEW

I AM SO USED to having a bullet in my neck that I never think of it, only when the subject comes up and someone—full of doubt or amazement—gingerly reaches a hand out to feel it. It is a memento of the shooting on an empty road on the edge of Newark, New Jersey, when Rosalind Pace and I got lost on the way from Newark airport to a conference of poets in Bethlehem, Pennsylvania. We made the mistake of stopping at a red light and were cornered immediately by two boys, sixteen or so, dressed in starched jeans and jackets and sporting zip guns. Before we could reason with them, or submit, or try to escape, they began shooting through the open windows. The boy on Rosalind's side pointed his gun, a .22, directly in her face, a foot away, but it misfired. The boy on my side emptied his gun, hit-ting the steering wheel, the window, and the dashboard. One bullet grazed my right shoulder, and one hit my chin then buried itself in the left side of my neck, less than a half inch from the carotid artery.

Everything in such a situation takes on a life of its own, and the few seconds it took me to realize I wasn't going to die seemed like a much longer stretch of time, and though my neck swelled up and blood was pouring out, my only thought was to get out of there as quickly as possible. My memory was that I fell to the floor, pushed the gas pedal down with one hand, and with the other put the gear into drive till Rosalind took over and drove us out of there. All the time I was screaming at her not to lose control, that she had to save our lives. It was Friday night and we were someplace in downtown Newark, and it was 1986 or 1987. No one would give us directions to

the hospital; it seemed as if everyone was drunk or high. I kept jump-
ing out of the car to stop cabs, but when they saw the blood they
rushed off. Then, by some fluke, we found ourselves driving up a
lawn to the back entrance of Beth Israel where, after a crazy alterca-
tion with a ten-dollar-a-day rent-a-cop with a noisy beeper, we drove
over another lawn to the emergency entrance where, thanks to the
fake cop, two doctors were waiting to rip my clothes off and save my
life. I'd told the fake cop that if there wasn't someone waiting I
would crawl back and kill him, even if it was the last thing I did in
this life—I think I said "with my bare hands" for, after all, I was in
the midst of a great drama—and that may have awakened him.

The one thing the doctors, the nurses, and the police lieutenant,
who came later, said over and over was that it was a mistake to stop at
the red light. "Why did you stop at the red light?" I was asked. "No
one stops at that light!" I felt guilty, as if I myself were the perpetra-
tor. It was as if Newark lived by a different set of rules. Certainly it
was a battle zone and probably more intensely so in the mid-eighties
than it is now in the twenty-first century, at least at this point. There
is rebuilding and there is talk about rebirth. But the burning and the
racial wars and the final flight may have been too much, and New
Jersey may have lost its only true city.

Rosalind has written an essay about the event. Some of the differ-
ences in our memory are striking, particularly in details, but what in-
terests me is the emotional difference, what we make—or made—of
the shooting. She remembered the boys as eleven or twelve years
old—I thought they were a little older; she remembers the one on
her side as wearing a sweat shirt—I remember them both in freshly
ironed matching jacket and jeans, almost like uniforms; she remem-
bers us going up a drive, at the hospital, into an entrance—I remem-
ber us driving across the lawn. We could either be right, or neither,
and it makes little difference—it is how we received the event in our
lives, how we absorbed it and located it. For her the initial emotional
response was a mixture of shock, disbelief, and fear. Later, it was
more anger, mixed with guilt, sadness, and frustration. My initial re-
sponse was also disbelief and fear, though later it was mostly grief—
and almost no anger. I don't mean to make an odious comparison; if
anything, I am perplexed at my lack of anger, and if I comment on
my own feelings it is not by way of either denigrating or elevating
Rosalind's. I may have been only concealing or converting my anger;
furthermore it is a quite decent and quite useful emotion—anger—

one which I make use of all the time, and I get furious at soft-spoken cheek-turners who smile lovingly at the slaps, however their eyes are wet with pain, rage, and disappointment. It just didn't happen for me here. Also, Rosalind's experience was different from mine in two ways: she was driving and therefore felt responsible, and she wasn't shot, and I was. It was more than guilt, her pain; it was agony.

I know that I was more "accepting" of the event than she was. I never argued with the circumstances or raged against the gods. Nor, for a second, did I blame her. We did make a wrong turn off the highway, we did stop at the red light, we didn't leave ten minutes earlier—or later. That's that! If anything, I felt lucky. The bullet didn't kill me, the gun on her side misfired. There were angels watching over us and they had a hell of a time leaping from side to side of the car, deflecting and stopping the shots as well as they could, keeping enough blood in my body, helping us out of there, guiding us to the hospital. If anything, I am grateful, and I love and kiss everyone and everything involved. I regret Rosalind had to go through this. I'm sorry for her suffering. But I don't hate the boys and I'm not angry with them and I don't hold it against Newark. In a way, once it happened I was glad it did, which doesn't mean I wouldn't prefer that it didn't. I suffered a few months from a stiff jaw and swollen neck, but there's no permanent damage except for the bullet that lodged in my neck and was never removed and, as I say, I forget it's there unless I'm telling the story to someone and press his or her amazed finger to the center of my neck, a little to the left of the windpipe.

When I describe my "state" after I was shot I say I was totally alert and responding in a manner to save both of our lives. I'm certain I argued a little but after the bullets started coming I had the usual rush of adrenaline and reverted to the fight or flight pattern, however it's described medically or physiologically. I didn't go into shock, in spite of the loss of blood and the trauma, though when we got to the hospital a certain "forgetfulness" set in, maybe when I was released of responsibility and was under care and protection.

I do remember the doctors waiting for me at the entrance, that they cut my shirt off, laid me down, stopped the bleeding, and examined the wound. I remember there was a long consultation, a discussion, and I was a part of it. The question was whether to remove the bullet or not, given how close it was to the artery, since there was always the danger of the instrument slipping. I don't know whether we took a vote or what, but the choice was against operating. Apparently, there had been some problems in Vietnam. My dear friend, Alex Greenberg, a head surgeon and poet, told me he would not have hesitated to remove the bullet, but all ER doctors are not like him. A surgeon was called and he agreed with the others.

In the emergency room I was attached to a half dozen machines and instruments and my face—which I saw in a mirror—was covered with blood and my neck—black, yellow, purple—was swollen grotesquely. I asked Rosalind about my poems, in an old leather briefcase, which she set down beside me. For the next two hours, while I was undergoing tests, I was busy orchestrating the immediate future. I directed Rosalind to telephone the conference leader— it was the middle of the night—to explain what happened, and to reschedule my appearance for Sunday, but the shithead said he couldn't change the schedule until Rosalind, under my direction, battered him into submission. I told Rosalind that it was extremely important for me to attend a part of the conference and to read and talk. I didn't care, as such, for the conference itself, nor for the measly bucks they were probably giving me; what I cared about was being there, going back to my life, not letting the shooting defeat me. And Rosalind drove me there—Sunday afternoon, a day and a half after I'd been shot. I gave a talk on Gil Orlovitz—one of the lost poets—and read some of my own poems. I must have been a pretty sight, on whatever stage they were using, neck of three colors, rotten clothes, wild eyes. Rosalind, dear supporter, says I was "clear, spontaneous, coherent, witty, profound, and brilliant as usual." I don't remember who the other writers were. Friends, I know, but they were—some of them—resentful and embarrassed when I appeared. They had learned I was shot, I'm not sure when, and had a reading of my poems in absentia: a memorial service. Then I appeared, a blood-swollen ghost, to interrupt the order of things. I wanted to apologize to them, but I had to quickly demythologize and locate the shooting, to put a skin around it just as my body eventually put a skin around the bullet, so I could go on with my life's work.

Orlovitz, a native of Philadelphia, died on the sidewalk in front of his apartment building on the Upper West Side. He was a poet, novelist, and playwright, who had published over a hundred poems— most of them sonnets—in major and minor periodicals, but never had a serious book publication. At his best, he was a powerful and

253

original writer, but he is virtually unknown today. He is probably re-membered by writers in their seventies and beyond, but younger than that only by severe scholars and devouring readers. He popped pills and drank unmercifully and died at fifty-four in 1973. He was incredibly well-read, passionate, and generous. I lent him money, read his poems, and got him a couple of readings. I'll never forget him descending from the bus for his reading at Rutgers. He wore a stylish suit, a black tie, and an overcoat. He was modest and self-assured, a beautiful reader. He drank gin straight, with a bit of chaser from time to time.

As for Rosalind, it was crazy not to do something for her in the hospital. They should have given her a sedative, talked to her, maybe offered her a bed, let her undress and take a shower, see if she could or could not drive home. I remember her washing the blood out of her coat and my jacket in a tiny sink. She describes how her hands were plunged in red water and the padding came out of the shoulder of my jacket where a bullet had lodged. She was more or less ignored and had the fear and pain—and boredom—of waiting, and going over and over again the events of the evening. She describes herself trying to sleep on a couch somewhere in the hospital, of a nurse giv-ing her a blanket, of waking up to the cold morning with the sudden knowledge of what happened, of confronting the car, blood on the windshield, rearview mirror, door handle, seats, and windows, bullets embedded in the steering wheel and the dashboard, and a two-hour ride home, alone in the car, weeping, screaming, pounding her head, pounding the steering wheel. She said she screamed for two hours.

Me they treated well—almost like a guest rather than a patient. They seemed to have a collective guilt, as if I were mistreated on their watch. I was mistreated, but it was surprising to me that they assumed anything like responsibility. I had to reassure them, tell them how conscientious they were, even kind. They were ashamed of their city. It may be that they were acknowledging class. I was ed-ucated, a college professor; they were professionals. In a city that had exploded fifteen or so years before over race, poverty, redlining, cor-ruption, brutality, injustice, I got the treatment that doctors give to each other or to the privileged. Moreover, the hospital never charged me, and I don't feel it was an accident. I don't mean my Blue Cross (from Iowa) covered the whole thing. There was no paperwork, no processing, no bills, no ER charges, no statement that said at the bottom "this is not a bill," no surgeon's fees, no giant profit on Band Aids and tap water. It was as if the hospital itself was ashamed.

When I was being wheeled into the intensive care unit, I joked with the doctors, reciting the names of famous people in history who had been shot—presidents, kings, and the like. For some reason, I couldn't remember the name of Emma Goldman's lover, whom she sent off to Pittsburgh to shoot Henry Frick. He arrived at Frick's office in the early evening while he was still at his desk and shot him with a little revolver that barely wounded the bastard. Frick stayed at his desk till the accustomed time and Berkman—his name was Berkman—was thrown in jail for a couple of decades, then deported to Russland, home of the pink and the brave. Berkman was a good anarchist, but a poor marksman. Red Emma didn't want anything to do with him when he finally came home; I think he disappointed her.

Later, when I got to my room and finally lay down on the coarse sheets, I alternated between pure joy and grief. Joy at being alive; at having escaped the way I did; at having such amazing luck—and grief that there was such malice, such willful indifference to life in the world. I kept saying to the nurses, to Rosalind, to my callers, "I can't believe one person would do that to another." And I wept over it uncontrollably.

I thought of two things. I know that because I have kept track. One was the 1942 shooting of Bruno Schulz by the German officer he encountered on the street in front of his house, after he had brilliantly and devotedly painted the officer's nursery for his children. The other was the malicious destruction of a small animal, a frog, by a friend of mine when we were both about twelve. He had stuffed a bullfrog into a no. 2 Mason jar, screwed the lid on, and threw him from the third floor onto the sidewalk in front of our apartment house. A bullfrog is not a Jewish slave, let alone a gifted and famous one, but the state of mind—of heart—may have been the same in those two murderers. I thought about the frog for years. I rushed downstairs and he was still alive with large pieces of glass embedded in his body. I had to kill him before I went back upstairs to beat the shit out of my friend. As for the murder of Schulz, that beautiful writer—and painter—it has become for me, as I know it has for others, a symbol of capricious and perverse human behavior. And it is the method of killing, a casual shot to the head, almost as an after-

255

thought, or a preprandial bit of exercise, that horrifies me. I understand that in Byelorussia, during the war, German pilots shot Jews in the same way when they came back from their bombings and dogfights. As a sort of celebratory act.

I have taken up the trade of poet in part because of the difficulty in understanding—and the need to "explain"—just that willful, capricious, perverse behavior. It's as if there's no other way. Auden says that "wild Ireland" drove Yeats into poetry. Easily—if beautifully—said. I was driven into it by nearsightedness and unforgivable innocence. What I learned I learned with a vengeance even if it came late. And quickly enough I got used to my learning. When the two boys stood at the two sides of our car, whether engaged in an initiation rite or a robbery or just to see what it felt like to kill someone, I wasn't at all surprised, even if later I was grief-stricken.

There was one other book that came to my mind as I lay there—Thomas Mann's *Doctor Faustus*. And it was only when I reread it that I realized how direct the connection was. The pact with the devil itself occurs during a small afternoon nap of the "hero," Adrian Leverkühn. The narrator, one Serenus Zeitblom, a high school Latin teacher, is nominally writing a biography of Leverkühn, a boyhood chum and a musical prodigy who studied theology and then went back to music, but it may as well have been a critical history—a kind of allegory—of Germany in the first half of the twentieth century. Leverkühn became a great, little known, deeply experimental composer, a cult figure and a recluse. His last composition was a symphonic cantata titled—naturally—*The Lamentation of Dr. Faustus*; brutal, pure, formal, expressive, "the most frightful lament ever set up on this earth." Leverkühn made the pact with the Destroyer, and so did Germany and even Zeitblom, with his flabby middle-class piety and his righteous scholarship, though he was both witness and spokesman, even if seen through Mann's irony and scorn. The year was 1944 when *The Lamentation* was released, just before the landing at Normandy. It is an ode to sorrow, the reverse, the opposite, the negative to Beethoven's "Ode to Joy"; in a way it is the revocation and there is a chorus of grief to match Beethoven's chorus. The whole book—very German in this—is based on opposites, the daemonic, the dark, the uncanny, versus the humane, the enlightened, the civilized; the irrationalism of the "folk" versus reason, dignity, culture, science; the Nazi state versus the democratic. It's not a simple matter. It's not as if Zeitblom represents one side and

Leverkühn the other. There is a hopeless mixture, and there is the limitation of language and of knowledge.

The most moving scene in the novel is the one where the divinely beautiful little Echo, Leverkühn's five-year-old nephew, first enchants the household in Leverkühn's country retreat with his goodness and innocence and then is suddenly struck down by cerebrospinal meningitis and suffers days of unmitigated agony. The child, whose name is Nepomuck, shortened to Nepo, calls himself Echo, quaintly skipping the first consonant, and speaks of himself in the third person. Overcome with convulsions, vomiting, and skull-splitting headaches, his neck rigid, his eye muscles paralyzed, he pleads with the powers. "Echo will be good, Echo will be good." I first read the novel—I remember—in Scotland, so the year would be 1953. Echo, and his cry, I never could forget. It compares to Lear, and there is the additional fact that my own sister, my only sibling, twelve months older than I, was struck down by the same disease when she was nine years old. I sometimes imagine her hydrocephalic shrieks, her heartrending moans, dear Sylvia.

It took me two, three months to recover from the wound. The physical pain was greater than I thought it would be. I couldn't lift my chin up so I didn't shave. My neck was so swollen that I couldn't turn it. I slept ten hours a night—five, six more hours than I normally do. I was exhausted all the time. But emotionally I recovered quickly, which surprised me. Growing up in a brutal time, in a brutal city, I was always alert to vicious, unexpected, and insane behavior. I learned early not to be astonished at the undeserved and outrageous. I was a warrior, alas, and my one task was to preserve dignity and honor the human, though I didn't know such words yet. It was a sad way to be nudged out of one world into another and to achieve thereby not only a small kinship with the brutalized but an understanding of brutality itself.

It's ironic about the two worlds, isn't it? Sometimes the brutalized is brutal, the oppressed is oppressor. It's an agony to think of it, though sometimes it's a comedy. We can be both at once; we can even split the difference. Maybe only Diogenes was not oppressive. But who knows what his wife would say? And wasn't his dour, puritanical, and fearless message itself oppressive? Ah lamb! Ah, your slit throat and the blood flowing on your white chest! Why are you here? Are you sheep or shepherd? Apocalypse would have it that the slaughtered lamb, albeit with seven horns and seven eyes, was the one who took up the book, and the one who sat on the throne. He was slaughtered, and yes he was a judge. Or was he a butcher, this lamb?

> all those who worship the beast
> and his image and receive a mark on his forehead
> even those humans will drink
> the wine of the wrath of God, which is poured
> undiluted into the cup of anger
> of their God, and they will be tormented
> in fire and in sulfur before the holy angels
> and *before the lamb*. The smoke of their torment
> will rise forevermore, and there's no rest
> day and night for any who worship the beast
> and his image or wear the mark of his name.
> Such is the endurance of the saints, who keep
> the commandments of God and faith in Yeshua.

It's not that I imagine a world without butchers and it's not that I ever forget the horrors of the century we have just gone through. My friend Jerry Ostriker, an astronomer and spokesman for the universe, says that it is entirely indifferent to this minute speck of dust we call earth. In the dining room of his house in Princeton he has a "map" of that universe which we can study as we sit there eating. I tell him that, after all, we have invented the universe, and the dust is supremely important. We both make light of our dilemma. A little gallows humor in both of us. The height of stubbornness, and loyalty.

I hope the two boys are all right. If they survived the life in Newark, if they aren't dead yet, they would be in their thirties. They could be in prison, or they could have made a breakthrough. Maybe one of them went to college, is in computers, selling cars, studying law. I want to apologize for turning them into symbols, or vehicles. They weren't pernicious, though what they did was unjust and stupid. And I want to remember how small was my brief "suffering" compared to thousands of others', what cruelty, absurdity, insanity, maliciousness they were forced to experience, how the lamb itself was twisted and pulled in a thousand ways, how it wept for itself at last, just as it wept for others—and continues to do so.

Nominated by Ron Tanner, The Georgia Review

WHEN DEAN YOUNG

TALKS ABOUT WINE

by TONY HOAGLAND

from WHAT NARCISSISM MEANS TO ME (Graywolf Press)

The worm thrashes when it enters the tequila.
The grape cries out in the wine vat crusher.

But when Dean Young talks about wine, his voice is strangely calm.
Yet it seems that wine is rarely mentioned.

He says, Great first chapter but no plot.
He says, Long runway, short flight.
He says, This one never had a secret.
He says, You can't wear stripes with that.

He squints as if recalling his childhood in France.
He purses his lips and shakes his head at the glass.

Eighty-four was a naughty year, he says,
and for a second I worry that California has turned him
into a sushi-eater in a cravat.

Then he says,
                This one makes clear the difference
between a thoughtless remark
and an unwarranted intrusion.

Then he says, In this one the pacific last light of afternoon
stains the wings of the seagull pink
                    at the very edge of the postcard.

But where is the Cabernet of rent checks and asthma medication?
Where is the Burgundy of orthopedic shoes?
Where is the Chablis of skinned knees and jelly sandwiches?
with the aftertaste of cruel Little League coaches?
and the undertone of rusty stationwagon?

His mouth is purple as if from his own ventricle
he had drunk.
He sways like a fishing rod.

When a beast is hurt it roars in incomprehension.
When a bird is hurt it huddles in its nest.

But when a man is hurt,
                    he makes himself an expert.
Then he stands there with a glass in his hand
staring into nothing
                    as if he was forming an opinion.

Nominated by David Rivard, Charles Harper Webb, Laura Kasischke,
Wesley McNair, Barbara Hamby

GOD LIVES IN
ST. PETERSBURG

fiction by TOM BISSELL

from MCSWEENY'S

GOD, IN TIME, takes everything from everyone. Timothy Silver-stone believed that those whose love for God was a vast, borderless frontier were expected to surrender everything to Him, gladly and without question, and that those who did so would live to see every-thing and more returned to them. After college he had shed America like a husk and journeyed to the far side of the planet, all to spread God's word. Now he was coming apart. Anyone with love for God knows that when you give up everything for Him, He has no choice but to destroy you. God destroyed Moses; destroyed the heart of Abraham by revealing the deep, lunatic fathom at which his faith ran; took everything from Job, saw it did not destroy him, then returned it, which did. Timothy reconciled God's need to destroy with God's opulent love by deciding that, when He destroyed you, it was done out of the truest love, the deepest, most divine respect. God could not allow perfection—it was simply too close to Him. His love for the sad, the fallen, and the sinful was an easy, uncomplicated love, but those who lived along the argent brink of perfection had to be watched and tested and tried.

Timothy Silverstone was a missionary, though on the orders of his organization, the Central Asian Relief Agency, he was not allowed to admit this. Instead, when asked (which he was, often and by every-one), he was to say he was an English teacher. This was to be the pry he would use to widen the sorrowful, light-starved breach that, according to CARA, lay flush across the heart of every last person in the world, especially those Central Asians who had been cocooned within the suffocating atheism of Soviet theology. "The gears of history have turned," the opening pages of Timothy's CARA handbook read, "and the hearts of 120 million people have been pushed from night into day, and all of them are calling out for the love of Jesus Christ."

As his students cheated on their exams, Timothy drifted through the empty canals between their desks. His classroom was as plain as a monk's sleeping quarters; its wood floors groaned with each of his steps. Since he had begun to come apart, he stopped caring whether his students cheated. He had accepted that they did not understand what cheating was and never would, for just as there is no Russian word which connotes the full meaning of *privacy*, there is no unambiguously pejorative word for *cheat*. Timothy had also stopped trying to teach them about Jesus because, to his shock, they already knew of a thoroughly discredited man who in Russian was called *Hristos*.

Timothy's attempts to create in their minds the person he knew as Jesus did nothing but trigger nervous, uncomfortable laughter Timothy simply could not bear to hear. Timothy could teach them about Jesus and His works and His love, but *Hristos* grayed and tired his heart. He felt nothing for this impostor, not even outrage. Lately, in order to keep from coming apart, he had decided to try to teach his students English instead.

"Meester Timothy," cried Rustam, an Uzbek boy with a long, thin face. His trembling arm was held up, his mouth a lipless dash.

"Yes, Rustam, what is it?" he answered in Russian. Skull-clutching hours of memorizing rows of vocabulary words was another broadsword Timothy used to beat back coming apart. He was proud of his progress with the language because it was so difficult. This was counterbalanced by his Russian acquaintances, who asked him why his Russian was not better, seeing that it was so simple.

After Timothy spoke, Rustam went slack with disappointment. Nine months ago, moments after Timothy had first stepped into this classroom, Rustam had approached him and demanded (actually using the verb demand) that Timothy address him in nothing but English. Since then his memorized command of English had deepened, and he had become by spans and cubits Timothy's best student. Timothy complied, asking Rustam "What is it?" again, in English.

"It is Susanna," Rustam said, jerking his head toward the small blond girl who shared his desk. Most of Timothy's students were black-haired, sloe-eyed Uzbeks like Rustam—the ethnic Russians able to do so had fled Central Asia as the first statues of Lenin toppled—and Susanna's blond, round-eyed presence in the room was both a vague ethnic reassurance and, somehow, deeply startling. Rustam looked back at Timothy. "She is looking at my test and bringing me distraction. Meester Timothy, this girl cheats on me." Rustam, Timothy knew, had branded onto his brain this concept of cheating, and viewed his classmates with an ire typical of the freshly enlightened.

Susanna's glossy eyes were fixed upon the scarred wooden slab of her desktop. Timothy stared at this girl he did not know what to do with, who had become all the children he did not know what to do with. She was thirteen, fourteen, and sat there, pink and startled, while Rustam spoke his determined English. Susanna's hair held a buttery yellow glow in the long plinths of sunlight shining in through the windows; her small smooth hands grabbed at each other in her lap. All around her, little heads bowed above the clean white rectangles on their desks, the classroom filled with the soft scratching of pencils. Timothy took a breath, looking back to Rustam, unable to concentrate on what he was saying because Timothy could not keep from looking up at the row of pictures along the back wall of his classroom, where Ernest Hemingway, John Reed, Paul Robeson, and Jack London stared out at him from plain wooden frames. An identical suite of portraits—the Soviet ideal of good Americans—was found in every English classroom from here to Tbilisi. Timothy knew that none of these men had found peace with God. He had wanted to give that peace to these children. When he came to Central Asia he felt that peace as a great glowing cylinder inside of him, but the cylinder had grown dim. He could barely even feel God anymore, though he could still hear Him, floating and distant, broadcasting a surflike static. There was a message woven into this dense noise, Timothy was sure, but no matter how hard he tried he couldn't decipher it. He looked again at Rustam. He had stopped talking now and was waiting for Timothy's answer. Every student in the classroom had looked up from their tests, pinioning Timothy with their small impassive eyes.

"Susanna's fine, Rustam," Timothy said finally, turning to erase the nothing on his blackboard. "She's okay. It's okay."

Rustam's forehead creased darkly but he nodded and returned to his test. Timothy knew that, to Rustam, the world and his place in it would not properly compute if Americans were not always right, always good, always funny and smart and rich and beautiful. Never mind that Timothy had the mashed nose of a Roman pugilist and a pimply face; never mind that Timothy's baggy, runneled clothing had not been washed for months; never mind that once, after Rustam had asked about the precise function of "do" in the sentence "I do not like to swim," Timothy stood at the head of the class for close to two minutes and silently fingered his chalk. Meester Timothy was right, even when he was wrong, because he came from America. The other students went back to their exams. Timothy imagined he could hear the wet click of their eyes moving from test to test, neighbor to neighbor, soaking up one another's answers.

Susanna, though, did not stir. Timothy walked over to her and placed his hand on her back. She was as warm to his touch as a radiator through a blanket, and she looked up at him with starved and searching panic in her eyes. Timothy smiled at her, uselessly. She swallowed, picked up her pencil and, as if helpless not to, looked over at Rustam's test, a fierce indentation between her yellow eyebrows. Rustam sat there, writing, pushing out through his nose hot gusts of air, until finally he whirled around in his seat and hissed something at Susanna in his native language, which he knew she did not understand. Again, Susanna froze. Rustam pulled her pencil from her hands—she did not resist—snapped it in half, and threw the pieces in her face. From somewhere in Susanna's throat came a half-swallowed sound of grief, and she burst into tears.

Suddenly Timothy was standing there, dazed, rubbing his hand. He recalled something mentally blindsiding him, some sort of brainflash, and thus could not yet understand why his palm was buzzing. Nor did he understand why every student had heads bowed even lower to their tests, why the sound of scratching pencils seemed suddenly, horribly frenzied and loud. But when Rustam—who merely sat in his chair, looking up at Timothy, his long face devoid of expression—lifted his hand to his left cheek, Timothy noticed it reddening, tightening, his eye squashing shut, his skin lashing itself to his cheekbone. And Timothy Silverstone heard the sound of God recede even more, retreat back even farther, while Susanna, between sobs, gulped for breath.

Naturally, Sasha was waiting for Timothy in the doorway of the teahouse across the street from the Registan, a suite of three madrasas whose sparkling minarets rose up into a haze of metallic, blue-gray smog. Today was especially bad, a poison petroleum mist lurking along the streets and sidewalks and curbs. And then there was the heat—a belligerent heat; to move through it felt like breathing hot tea.

Timothy walked past the tall, bullet-shaped teahouse doorway, Sasha falling in alongside him. They did not talk—they rarely talked—even though the walk to Timothy's apartment in the Third Microregion took longer than twenty minutes. Sasha was Russian, tall and slender with hair the color of new mud. Each of Sasha's ears was as large and ornate as a tankard handle, and his eyes were as blue as the dark margin of atmosphere where the sky became outer space. He walked next to Timothy with a lanky, boneless grace, and wore blue jeans and imitation-leather cowboy boots that clomped emptily on the sidewalk. Sasha's mother was a history teacher from Timothy's school.

When his drab building came into sight Timothy felt the headachy swell of God's static rushing into his head. It was pure sound, shape-less and impalpable, and as always he sensed some egg of sense or insight held deep within it. Then it was gone, silent, and in that mo-ment Timothy could feel his spirit split from his flesh. *For I know*, Timothy thought, these words of Paul's to the Romans so bright in the glare of his memory they seemed almost indistinct from his own thoughts, *that nothing good dwells within me, that is, in my flesh. I can will what is right, but I cannot do it.*

As they climbed the stairs to Timothy's fifth-floor apartment, Sasha reached underneath Timothy's crotch and cupped him. He squeezed and laughed, and Timothy felt a wet heat spread through him, ani-mate him, flow to the hard, stony lump growing in his pants. Sasha squeezed again, absurdly tender. As Timothy fished for the keys to his apartment door Sasha walked up close behind him, breathing on Timothy's neck, his clothes smelling—as everyone's clothes here did—as though they had been cured in sweat.

They stumbled inside. Sasha closed the door as Timothy's hands shot to his belt, which he tore off like a rip-cord. He'd lost so much weight his pants dropped with a sad puff around his feet. Sasha shook his head at this—he complained, sometimes, that Timothy was getting too skinny—and he stepped out of his own pants. Into his palm Sasha spit a foamy coin of drool, stepped toward Timothy and with the hand he spit into grabbed his penis. He pulled it toward him sexlessly, as if it were a grapple he was making sure was secure. Sasha laughed again and he threw himself over the arm of Timothy's plush red sofa. Sasha reached back and with medical indelicacy pulled himself apart. He looked over his shoulder at Timothy, waiting.

The actual penetration was always beyond the bend of Timothy's recollection. As if some part of himself refused to acknowledge it. One moment Sasha was hurling himself over the couch's arm, the next Timothy was inside him. *I can will what is right, but I cannot do it.* It began slowly, Sasha breathing through his mouth, Timothy pushing further into him, eyes smashed shut. What he felt was not desire, not lust; it was worse than lust. It was worse than what drove a soulless animal. It was some hot tongue of fire inside Timothy that he could not douse—not by satisfying it, not by ignoring it. Sometimes it was barely more than a flicker, and then Timothy could live with it, nullify it as his weakness, as his flaw. But without warning, in whatever dark, smoldering interior shrine, the flame would grow and flash outward, melting whatever core of Timothy he believed good and steadfast into soft, pliable sin.

Timothy's body shook as if withstanding invisible blows, and Sasha began to moan with a carefree sinless joy Timothy could only despise, pity, and envy. It was always, oddly, this time, when perched on the edge of exploding into Sasha, that Timothy's mind turned, again, with noble and dislocated grace, to Paul. *Do not be deceived!* he wrote. *Fornicators, idolaters, adulterers, male prostitutes, sodomites—none of these will inherit the kingdom of God. And this is what some of you used to be. But you were washed, you were sanctified, you were justified in the name of Lord Jesus Christ and in the Spirit of our God.* It was a passage Timothy could only read and reflect upon and pray to give him the strength he knew he did not have. He prayed to be washed, to be sanctified in the name of Jesus, but now he had come apart and God was so far from him. His light had been eclipsed, and in the cold darkness that followed, he wondered if his greatest sin was not that he was pushing himself into non-vaginal warmth but that his worship was now for man and not man's maker. But such taxonomies were of little value. God's world was one of cruel mathematics, of right and wrong. It was a world that those who had let God fall from their hearts condemned as repressive and awash in dogma—an accurate but vacant condemnation, Timothy knew, since God did not anywhere claim that His world was otherwise.

A roiling spasm began in Timothy's groin and burst throughout the rest of his body, and in that ecstatic flooded moment nothing was wrong, nothing, with anyone, and he emptied himself into Sasha without guilt, only with appreciation and happiness and bliss. But then it was over, and he had to pull himself from the boy and wonder, once again, if what he had done had ruined him forever, if he had driven himself so deeply into darkness that the darkness had become both affliction and reward. Quickly Timothy wiped himself with one of the throw pillows from his couch and sat on the floor, sick and dizzy with shame. Sasha, still bent over the couch, looked back at Timothy, smirking, a cloudy satiation frosting his eyes. "*Shto?*" he asked Timothy. *What?*

Timothy could not—could never—answer him.

The next morning Timothy entered his classroom to find Susanna seated at her desk. Class was not for another twenty minutes, and Susanna was a student whose arrival, on most days, could be counted on to explore the temporal condition between late and absent. Timothy was about to wish her a surprised "Good morning" when he realized that she was not alone.

A woman sat perched on the edge of his chair, wagging her finger and admonishing Susanna in juicy, top-heavy Russian. Her accent was unknown to Timothy, filled with dropped Gs and a strange, diphthongal imprecision. Whole sentence fragments arced past him like softballs. Susanna merely sat there, her hands on her desktop in a small bundle. Timothy turned to leave but the woman looked over to see him caught in mid-pirouette in the door-jamb. She leapt up from his chair, a startled gasp rushing out of her.

They looked at each other, the woman breathing, her meaty shoulders bobbing up and down, her mouth pulled into a rictal grin. "*Zdravstvuite,*" she said stiffly.

"*Zdravstvuite,*" Timothy said, stepping back into the room. He tried to smile and the woman returned the attempt with a melancholy but respectful nod. She was like a lot of women Timothy saw here—bull-necked, jowled, of indeterminate age, as sexless as an oval. Atop her head was a lumpen yellow-white mass of hairspray and bobby pins, and her lips looked as sticky and red as the picnic tables Timothy remembered painting, with his Christian youth group, in the parks of Green Bay, Wisconsin.

"Timothy Silverstone," she said. *Teemosee Seelverstun*. Her hands met below her breasts and locked.

267

"Yes," Timothy said, glancing at Susanna. She wore a bright, bubble-gum-colored dress he had not seen before, some frilly, ribboned thing. As if aware of Timothy's eyes on her, Susanna bowed over in her chair even more, a path of spinal knobs surfacing along her back.

"I am Irina Dupkova," the woman said. "Susanna told me what happened yesterday—how you reacted to her . . . problem." Her joined hands lifted to her chin in gentle imploration. "I have come to ask you, this is true, yes?"

Her accent delayed the words from falling into their proper translated slots. When they did, a mental deadbolt unlocked, opening a door somewhere inside Timothy and allowing the memory of Rustam's eye swelling shut to come tumbling out. A fist of guilt clenched in his belly. *He had struck a child.* He had hit a boy as hard as he could, and there was no place he could hide this from himself, as he hid what he did with Sasha. Timothy felt faint and humidified, his face pinkening. "Yes, Irina Dupkova," he said, "it is. And I want to tell you I'm sorry. I, I—" He searched for words, some delicate, spiraled idiom to communicate his remorse. He could think of nothing, entire vocabularies lifting away from him like startled birds. "I'm sorry. What happened made me . . . very unhappy."

She shot Timothy a strange look, eyes squinched, her red lips kissed out in perplexion. "You do not understand me," she said. This was not a question. Timothy glanced over at Susanna, who had not moved, perhaps not even breathed. When he looked back to Irina Dupkova she was smiling at him, her mouthful of gold teeth holding no gleam, no sparkle, only the metallic dullness of a handful of old pennies. She shook her head, clapping once in delight. "Oh, your Russian, Mister Timothy, I think it is not so good. You do not *vladeyete* Russian very well, yes?"

"Vladeyete," Timothy said. It was a word he was sure he knew. "Vladeyete," he said again, casting mental nets. The word lay beyond his reach somewhere, veiled.

Irina Dupkova exhaled in mystification, then looked around the room. "You do not know this word," she said in a hard tone, one that nudged the question mark off the end of the sentence.

"Possess," Susanna said, before Timothy could lie. Both Timothy and Irina Dupkova looked over at her. Her back was still to them, but Timothy could see that she was consulting her CARA-supplied

Russian-English dictionary. *"Vladeyete,"* she said again, her finger thrust onto the page. "Possess."

Timothy blinked. *"Da,"* he said. *"Vladeyete.* Possess." For the benefit of Irina Dupkova he smacked himself on the forehead with the butt of his palm.

"Possess," Irina Dupkova said, as if it had been equally obvious to her. She paused, her face regaining its bluntness. "Well, nevertheless, I have come here this morning to thank you."

Timothy made a vague sound of dissent. "There is no need to thank me, Irina Dupkova."

"You have made my daughter feel very good, Timothy. Protected. Special. You understand, yes?"

"Your daughter is a fine girl," Timothy said. "A fine student."

With that Irina Dupkova's face palled, and she stepped closer to him, putting her square back to the doorway. "These filthy people think they can spit on Russians now, you know. They think independence has made them a nation. They are animals, barbarians." Her eyes were small and bright with anger.

Timothy Silverstone looked at his scuffed classroom floor. There was activity in the hallway—shuffling feet, children's voices—and Timothy looked at his watch. His first class, Susanna's class, began in ten minutes. He moved to the door and closed it.

Irina Dupkova responded to this by intensifying her tone, her hands moving in little emphatic circles. "You understand, Timothy, that Russians did not come here willingly, yes? I am here because my father was exiled after the Great Patriotic War Against Fascism. Like Solzhenitsyn, and his careless letters. A dark time, but this is where my family has made its home. You understand. We have no other place but this, but things are very bad for us now." She flung her arm toward the windows and looked outside, her jaw set. "There is no future for Russians here, I think. No future. None."

"I understand, Irina Dupkova," Timothy said, "and I am sorry, but you must excuse me, I have my morning lessons now and I—"

She seized Timothy's wrist, the ball of her thumb pressing harshly between his radius and ulna. "And this little hooligan Uzbek thinks he can touch my Susanna. You understand that they are animals, Timothy, yes? *Animals.* Susanna," Irina Dupkova said, her dark eyes not leaving Timothy's, "come here now, please. Come let Mister Timothy see you."

In one smooth movement Susanna rose from her desk and turned to them. Her hair was pulled back into a taut blond ponytail and lay tightly against her skull, as fine and grained as sandalwood. She walked over to them in small, noiseless steps, and Timothy, because of his shame for striking Rustam before her eyes, could not bear to look at her face. Instead he studied her shoes—black and shiny, like little hoofs—and the thin legs that lay beneath the wonder of her white leggings. Irina Dupkova hooked Susanna close to her and kissed the top of her yellow head. Susanna looked up at Timothy, but he could not hold the girl's gaze. He went back to the huge face of her mother, a battlefield of a face, white as paraffin.

"My daughter," Irina Dupkova said, nose tilting downward into the loose wires of Susanna's hair.

"Yes," Timothy said.

Irina Dupkova looked over at him, smiling, eyebrows aloft. "She is very beautiful, yes?"

"She is a very pretty girl," Timothy agreed.

Irina Dupkova bowed in what Timothy took to be grateful acknowledgment. "My daughter likes you very much," she said, looking down. "You understand this. You are her favorite teacher. My daughter loves English."

"Yes," Timothy said. At some point Irina Dupkova had, unnervingly, begun to address him in the second-person familiar. Timothy flinched as a knock on the door sounded throughout the classroom, followed by a peal of girlish giggling.

"My daughter loves America," Irina Dupkova said, ignoring the knock, her voice soft and insistent.

"Yes," Timothy said, looking back at her.

"I have no husband."

Timothy willed the response from his face. "I'm very sorry to hear that."

"He was killed in Afghanistan."

"I'm very sorry to hear that."

"I live alone with my daughter, Timothy, in this nation in which Russians have no future."

Lord, please, Timothy thought, make her stop. "Irina Dupkova," Timothy said softly, "there is nothing I can do about any of this. I am going home in three months. I cannot—I am not able to help you in that way."

"I have not come here for that," she said. "Not for me. Again you do not understand me." Irina Dupkova's eyes closed with the faint, amused resignation of one who had been failed her whole life. "I have come here for Susanna. I want you to have her. I want you to take her back to America."

Struck dumb had always been a homely, opaque expression to Timothy, but he understood, at that moment, the deepest implications of its meaning. He had nothing to say, *nothing*, and the silence seemed hysterical.

She stepped closer. "I want you to take my daughter, Timothy. To America. As your wife. I will give her to you."

Timothy stared her in the face, still too surprised for emotion. "Your daughter, Irina Dupkova," he said, "is too young for such a thing. *Much* too young." He made the mistake of looking down at Susanna. There was something in the girl Timothy had always mistaken for a cowlike dullness, but he could see now, in her pale eyes, savage determination. The sudden understanding that Susanna's instigation lay behind Irina Dupkova's broke through Timothy's sternum.

"She is fourteen," Irina Dupkova said, moving her hand, over and over again, along the polished sheen of Susanna's hair. "She will be fifteen in four months. This is not so young, I think."

"*She is too young*," Timothy said with a fresh anger. Again he looked down at Susanna. She had not removed her eyes from his.

"She will do for you whatever you ask, Timothy," Irina Dupkova was saying. "Whatever you ask. You understand."

Timothy nodded distantly, a nod that both understood but did not understand. In Susanna's expression of inert and perpetual unfeeling, he could see that what Irina Dupkova said was right—she *would* do whatever he asked of her. And Timothy Silverstone felt the glisten of desire at this thought, felt the bright glint of a lechery buried deep in the shale of his mind. *My God,* he thought. *I will not do this.* He was startled to realize he had no idea how old Sasha was. Could that be? He was tall, and his scrotum dangled between his legs with the heft of post-adolescence, but he was also lightly and delicately haired, and had never, as far as Timothy could tell, shaved or needed to shave. Sasha could have been twenty-two, two years younger than Timothy; he could have been sixteen. Timothy shook the idea from his head.

"I have a brother," Irina Dupkova was saying, "who can arrange for papers that will make Susanna older. Old enough for you, in your nation. It has already been discussed. Do you understand?"

271

"Irina Dupkova," Timothy said, stepping backward, both hands thrust up, palms on display, "I cannot marry your daughter."

Irina Dupkova nearly smiled. "You say you cannot. You do not say you do not want to."

"Irina Dupkova, *I cannot do this for you.*"

Irina Dupkova sighed, chin lifting, head tilting backward. "I know why you are here. You understand. I know why you have come. You have come to give us your Christ. But he is useless." Something flexed behind her Slavic faceplate, her features suddenly sharpening. "*This* would help us. *This* would save."

Timothy spun around, swung open his classroom door, poked his head into the hallway and scattered the knot of chattering children there with a hiss. He turned back toward Irina Dupkova, pulling the door shut behind him with a bang. They both stared at him, Irina Dupkova's arm holding Susanna close to her thick and formless body. "You understand, Timothy," she began, "how difficult it is for us to leave this nation. They do not allow it. And so you can escape, or you can marry." She looked down at herself. "Look at me. This is what Susanna will become if she remains here. Old and ugly, a ruin." In Irina Dupkova's face was a desperation so needy and exposed Timothy could find quick solace only in God, a mental oxbow that took him to imagining the soul within Susanna, the soul being held out for him to take away from here, to sanctify and to save. That was God's law, His imperative: *Go therefore and make disciples of all nations.* Then God's distant broadcast filled his mind, and with two fingers placed stethescopically to his forehead Timothy turned away from Irina Dupkova and Susanna and listened so hard a dull red ache spread behind his eyes. The sound disappeared.

"Well," Irina Dupkova said with a sigh, after it had become clear that Timothy was not going to speak, "you must begin your lesson now." Susanna stepped away from her mother and like a ghost drifted over to her desk. Irina Dupkova walked past Timothy and stopped at his classroom door. "You will think about it," she said, turning to him, her face in profile, her enormous back draped with a tattered white shawl, "you will consider it." Timothy said nothing and she nodded, turned back to the door, and opened it.

Students streamed into the room on both sides of Irina Dupkova like water coming to a delta. Their flow hemmed her in, and Irina Dupkova's angry hands fluttered and slapped at the black-haired heads rushing past her. Only Rustam stepped aside to let her out,

272

which was why he was the last student into the room. As Rustam closed the door after Irina Dupkova, Timothy quickly spun to his blackboard and stared at the piece of chalk in his hand. He thought of what to write. He thought of writing something from Paul, something sagacious and unproblematic like *We who are strong ought to put up with the failings of the weak.* He felt Rustam standing behind him, but Timothy could not turn around. He wrote the date on the board, then watched chalkdust drift down into the long and sulcated tray at the board's base.

"Meester Timothy?" Rustam said finally, his artificial American accent tuned to a tone of high contrition.

Timothy turned. A bruise like a red-brown crescent lay along the ridge of Rustam's cheekbone, the skin there taut and shiny. It was barely noticeable, really. It was nothing. It looked like the kind of thing any child was liable to get, anywhere, doing anything. Rustam was smiling at him, a bead of wet light fixed in each eye. "Good morning, Rustam," Timothy said.

Rustam reached into his book bag, then deposited into Timothy's hand something Timothy remembered telling his class about months and months ago, back before he had come apart; something that, in America, he had said, students brought their favorite teachers. It got quite a laugh from these students, who knew of a different standard of extravagance needed to sway one's teachers. Timothy stared at the object in his hand. An apple. Rustam had given him an apple. "For you," Rustam said softly, turned and sat down.

Timothy looked up at his classroom to see five rows of smiles. Meester Timothy will be wonderful and American again, these smiles said. Meester Timothy will not hit us, not like our teachers hit us. Meester Timothy will always be good.

Woolen gray clouds floated above the Registan's minarets, the backlight of a high, hidden sun outlining them gold. Some glow leaked through, filling the sky with hazy beams of diffracted light.

Timothy walked home, head down, into the small breeze coming out of the Himalayan foothills to the east. It was the first day in weeks that the temperature had dipped below 38 C., the first day in which walking two blocks did not soak his body in sweat.

Sasha stood in the tall doorway of the teahouse, holding a bottle of orange Fanta in one hand and a cigarette in the other. Around his waist Sasha had knotted the arms of Timothy's gray-and-red St.

Thomas Seminary sweatshirt (Timothy didn't recall allowing Sasha to borrow it), the rest trailing down behind him in a square maroon cape. He slouched in the doorway, one shoulder up against the frame, his eyes filled with an alert, dancing slyness. Sasha let the half-smoked cigarette drop from his fingers and it hit the teahouse floor in a burst of sparks and gray ash. He was grinding it out with his cowboy-boot-tip when Timothy's eyes pounced upon his. *"Nyet,"* Timothy said, still walking, feeling on his face the light spume of rain. *"Ne sevodnya,* Sasha." *Not today, Sasha.* Timothy eddied through the molded white plastic chairs and tables of an empty outdoor café, reached the end of the block and glanced behind him.

Sasha stood there, his arms laced tight across his chest, his face a twist of sour incomprehension. Behind him a herd of Pakistani tourists was rushing toward the Registan to snap pictures before the rain began.

Timothy turned at the block's corner even though he did not need to. In the sky a murmur of thunder heralded the arrival of a darker bank of clouds. Timothy looked up. A raindrop exploded on his eye.

Timothy sat behind his workdesk in his bedroom, a room so small and diorama-like it seemed frustrated with itself, before the single window that looked out on the over-planned Soviet chaos of the Third Microregion: flat roofs, gouged roads that wended industriously but went nowhere, the domino of faceless apartment buildings just like his own. The night was impenetrable with thick curtains of rain, and lightning split the sky with electrified blue fissures. It was the first time in months it had rained long enough to create the conditions Timothy associated with rain: puddles on the streets, overflowing gutters, mist-cooled air. The letter he had started had sputtered out halfway into its first sentence, though a wet de facto period had formed after the last word he had written ("here") from having left his felt-tip pen pressed against the paper too long. He had been trying to write about Susanna, about what had happened today. The letter was not intended for anyone in particular, and a broken chain of words lay scattered throughout his mind and Timothy knew that if only he could pick them up and put them in their proper order, God's message might at last become clear to him. Perhaps, he thought, his letter was to God.

Knuckles against his door. He turned away from his notebook and wrenched around in his chair, knowing it was Sasha from the lightness of his three knocks, illicit knocks that seemed composed equally of warning and temptation. Timothy snapped shut his notebook, pinning his letter between its flimsy boards, and winged it onto his bed. As he walked across his living room, desire came charging up in him like a stampede of fetlocked horses, and just before Timothy's hand gripped the doorknob he felt himself through his Green Bay Packers sweatpants. A sleepy, squishy hardness there. He opened the door. Standing in the mildewy darkness of his hallway was not Sasha but Susanna, her small nose wrinkled and her soaked hair a tangle of spirals molded to her head. "I have come," she said, "to ask if you have had enough time to consider."

Timothy could only stare down at her. It occurred that he managed to let another day go by without eating. He closed his eyes. "Susanna, you must go home. Right now."

She nodded, then stepped past him into his open, empty living room. Surprise rooted Timothy to the floorboards. "Susanna—" he said, half reaching for her.

After slipping by she twirled once in the room's center, her eyes hard and appraising. This was a living room that seemed to invite a museum's velvet rope and small engraved plaque: Soviet Life, Circa 1955. There was nothing but the red sofa, a tall black lamp which stood beside nothing, and a worn red rug that did not occupy half the floor. Susanna seemed satisfied, though, and with both hands she grabbed a thick bundle of her hair and twisted it, water pattering onto the floor. "We can fuck," she said in English, not looking at him, still twisting the water from her hair. She pronounced it *Ve con foke*. She took off her jacket and draped it over the couch. It was a cheap white plastic jacket, something Timothy saw hanging in the bazaars by the thousand. Beneath it she was still wearing the bubble-gum dress, aflutter with useless ribbonry. Her face was wet and cold, her skin bloodless in the relentless wattage of the lightbulb glowing naked above her. She was shivering.

Timothy heard no divine static to assist him with Susanna's words, only the awful silent vacuum in which the laws of the world were cast and acted upon.

"We can fuck," Susanna said again.

"Stop it," Timothy said.

"We can," she said in Russian. "I will do this for you and we will go to America."

"No," Timothy said, closing his eyes.

She took a small step back and looked at the floor. "You do not want to do this with me?"

Timothy opened his eyes and stared at the lamp that stood next to nothing. He thought that if he stared at it long enough, Susanna might disappear.

"I have done this before with men."

"You have," Timothy said—it was a statement—his throat feeling dry and paved.

She shrugged. "Sometimes." She looked away. "I know what you think. You think I am bad."

"I am very sad for you, Susanna, but I don't think that."

"You will tell me this is wrong."

Now both of Timothy's hands were on his face, and he pushed them against his cheeks and eyes as if he were applying a compress. "All of us do wrong, Susanna. All of us are bad. In the eyes of God," he said with listless conviction, "we are all sinners."

A knowing sound tumbled out of Susanna. "My mother told me you would tell me these things, because you believe in *Hristos*." She said nothing for a moment. "Will you tell me about this man?"

Timothy split two of his fingers apart and peered at her. "Would you like me to?" he asked.

She nodded, scratching at the back of her hand, her fingernails leaving a crosshatching of chalky white lines. "It is very interesting to me," Susanna said, "this story. That one man can die and save the whole world. My mother told me not to believe it. She told me this was something only an American would believe."

"That's not true, Susanna. Many Russians also believe."

"God lives for Russians only in St. Petersburg. God does not live here. He has abandoned us."

"God lives everywhere. God never abandons you."

"My mother told me you would say that, too." From her tone, he knew, she had no allegiance to her mother. She could leave this place so easily. If not with him, she would wait for someone else. She shook her head at him. "You have not thought about marrying me at all."

"Susanna, it would be impossible. I have a family in America, friends, my church . . . they would see you, and they would know. You are not old enough to trick anyone with papers."

"Then we will live somewhere else until I do." She looked around, her wet hair whipping back and forth. "Where is your bed? We will fuck there."

"Susanna—"

"Let me show you what a good wife I can be." With a shoddy fabric hiss her dress lifted over her head and she was naked. For all her fearlessness, Susanna could not anymore meet Timothy's eye, her xylophonic ribcage heaving, the concave swoop of her stomach breathing in and out like that of a panicked, wounded animal. She hugged herself, each hand gripping an elbow. She was smooth and hairless but for the blond puff at the junction of her tiny legs. She was a thin, shivering fourteen-year-old girl standing naked in the middle of Timothy's living room. Lightning flashed outside—a stroboscope of white light—the room's single bright light bulb buzzing briefly, going dark, and glowing back to strength.

His bedroom was not dark enough to keep him from seeing, with awful clarity, Susanna's face tighten with pain as he floated above her. Nothing could ease the mistaken feeling of the small tight shape of her body against his. After it was over, he knew the part of himself he had lost with Sasha was not salvaged, and never would be. *I can will what is right, but I cannot do it.* He was longing for God to return to him when His faraway stirrings opened Timothy's eyes. Susanna lay beside him, in fragile, uneasy sleep. He was drawn from bed, pulled toward the window. The beaded glass was cool against his palms. While Timothy waited—God felt very close now—he imagined himself with Susanna, freed from the world and the tragedy of its limitations, stepping with her soul into the house of the True and Everlasting God, a mansion filled with rooms and rooms of a great and motionless light. Even when Susanna began to cry, Timothy could not turn around, afraid of missing what God would unveil for him, while outside, beyond the window, it began to rain again.

Nominated by McSweeny's

THE REAL ELEANOR RIGBY

fiction by ALICE FULTON

from THE GETTYSBURG REVIEW

E DNA LIVINGSTON was the loneliest girl in North America. She was the only Catholic High student who subscribed to *Zen Teen: The Journal of Juvenile Macrobiotics* published by the Youth in Asia Foundation (Euthanasia! Someone should point out the unhappy homonym), the only member of the Sodality of the Blessed Virgin who'd read *Tropic of Cancer*. Once when she mentioned Henry Miller, the entire group thought she was referring to the amiable, goateed host of the popular TV show, *Sing Along with Mitch*.

Arthur Miller maybe, but Mitch!

In a weak moment Edna had joined her school's chapter of Up with People, the moral rearmament choral group. She'd performed with them once or twice, but she was asked to leave after taking liberties with the windshield-wiper waves. Now she spent her weekends immured in her room, cataloging items in *BeatleLuv Unlimited* magazine and *IshMail*, the Melville Society newsletter.

"John, Paul, George, and Herman!" her mother said. "If you ask me, *Moby Dick* is one dull book. Where's the romance, the love interest? If you ask me, Herman was a fink."

Edna felt deeply misunderstood. Like Melville, she wanted to ship out to Liverpool.

No one shared her obsessions except Sunny Metzger, a Lutheran who attended Troy High. The two girls were desperate virgins, isolated by their attraction to the non-Troy and exotic. Edna had heard all about Sunny's brief fling with an Estonian boy who wanted her to eat borscht while he snapped Polaroids. She heard how one famished night, Sunny agreed, and afterwards during the sad, postculinary intimacy, the boy drove her to Albany Airport to watch the planes take off. They had sat in the car outside the runway's chainlink till Sunny's hair smelled like jet fuel, a musky residue of adventure that Edna envied, though the Estonian boy never called again.

Every night Edna fell asleep with her transistor radio under her head like a renunciate's stone pillow. The local station was always holding contests. Their call letters, WTRY, stood for Troy, but in their elastic ID jingles, she heard the command *to strive*. Third caller, try again, fifth caller, try again, the deejay would say. One lucky midnight she became the ninth caller and won a pen touched by the Beatles. It arrived by mail a week later.

"It's a second-class relic," Edna said, placing the sealed envelope in the middle of the kitchen table. Her mother was ironing nearby. Sunny was sipping a Diet Rite.

"Well, I call it pretty chintzy. At least they could give you a first-class prize," Mrs. Livingston said.

"C'mon, Ma. First-class relics are rare." First-class relics were taken from the body or any of its integrant parts, such as limbs, ashes, and bones. How many times had she explained? But her mother was an Easter-duty Catholic. What could you expect.

"Well, I still say it's pretty darn cheap."

"A third-class relic, now that would be cheap," Sunny offered. "A third-class relic is anything that's touched a first- or second-class relic. You can't take a relic like that theriously." Sunny lisped when she got excited. Sometimes she stuttered. "Hey, Ed. Now we can make our own third-clath welicths," she said. "We could thell them."

They had learned about relics during a special weekend retreat taught by a foreign priest full of discouraged Catholic lore. Sunny had sat in the back, and the visiting cleric did not recognize her as an interloper. His presentation was part show-and-tell, part autopsy. He explained how a particle extracted from a saint had been placed in a locket, covered by crystal, bound by red thread, and sealed with the insignia of office. Then he opened the back cover of the locket and showed them a swatch of red wax that looked like a hundred-year-old heart, wizened and dripping with antiquity.

Sunny raised her hand. "Father, I know a second-class welic is an object that has come in contact with a living saint, like the instruments wherewith a martyr has been tortured, the chains by which he was bound, the clothes he wore, or objects he used. But what about Saint Peter's shadow or a saint's bray-bray-braces? I mean, it's just a high-high—" A couple of boys snickered, and Brew Thudlinsky, the school bully, belched derisively—"hypothesis, Father, but what class would a saint's con-con-contact lenses be?"

And though the priest spoke perfect English, he had sighed in Spanish. "For the sake of simplicity, let's stick with the bones," he said.

The pen the Beatles touched was enrobed in a red plastic pencil case. Edna eased the zipper back. As the tiny metal fangs gave way, a faint gas, a perfume of petroleum products, essence of black vinyl and steel strings, escaped, and there it was: an instrument of monastic plainness nestled in the scarlet darkness. A cheap black ballpoint. A new warmth possessed her. Hope, the thing with feathers, was perching in her soul.

"Are you sure it's not the albatross like in that other poem?" Sunny asked.

A relic might be *coronse spinse D.N.J.C.*, taken from the crown of thorns, or *de velo*, from the veil. It might be *ex parecordi*, from the stomach or intestines; *ex pelle* from the skin; *ex capillus*, from the hair; *ex carne*, from the flesh. It could be *ex stipite affixionis*, from the whipping post, or *ex tela serica quae tetigit cor*, from the silk cloth that touched the heart.

"Or maybe it's the liver. That extinct bird Liverpool was named for."

"This is Hope," Edna said. "You'll know it when you feel it." Hope felt like a summer clearance when the worn merchandise was offered up and whisked away.

Her mother hung up a blouse with a vehemence that made the hangers shriek. "It doesn't take much to make you girls happy, does it?" she said.

"Knock, knock!" Mrs. Livingston had yelled on the day Herman Melville entered Edna's life. She was sequestered in her bedroom, which resembled a clipping service run by a poltergeist. The floor was a brittle strudel of back issues and loose paper. Narrow paths had been cleared between the door, bed, and stereo.

"What a booby trap," her mother said, walking the plank of carpet.

"It kind of makes you glad paper has only two sides." She placed two books on the bed next to Edna. "Old junk from the Phoenix." The Phoenix, an old residential hotel, had belonged to Edna's father. He had died a year ago.

Typee: A Peep at Polynesian Life by Herman Melville, Edna read. New York, Wiley and Putnam, 1846. Volume I popped like an arthritic knuckle when she opened it, and a dank, riverish smell rose from the pages.

"*Typee* is a cookbook and a sex manual," she told Sunny during their nightly phone call. "It's a hunger novel."

Melville's book told the story of two starving pals, Tommo and Toby, on their perilous journey into the heart of the Marquesas. The infinite care with which these deserters parceled out their sea biscuits, the division of a little sustenance into less, worked upon Edna's imagination. Every night she gave Sunny a synopsis. *Tommo and Toby have been captured by natives! Toby has escaped, but Tommo is being treated well! Today the island girls gathered a thimbleful of salt. They spread a big leaf on the ground, dropped a few grains on it, and invited Tommo to taste them as a sign of their esteem.* "From the extravagant value placed upon the article," Edna read, "I verily believed that with a bushel of common Liverpool salt, all the real estate in Typee might have been purchased."

"I verily believe it, too," Sunny said.

The girls passed *Typee* back and forth, reading and rereading. They went to the Troy Public Library and checked out everything on Herman Melville. One night Edna called with a major discovery. "Herman wrote *Typee* in Lansingburgh. He was living on 114th Street, near the Phoenix Hotel." The next day, she called the Lansingburgh Historical Society, and they gave her the phone number of a ninety-year-old man named Tim Brunswick, whose father was rumored to have actually known Herman Melville.

"I'd like to meet him," she told her mother.

"I wish you could find someone your own age."

"Don't you mean *from* my own age?" Edna said.

When Mrs. Livingston realized the girls were determined to visit the ancient Melville expert, she offered them a ride. Tim Brunswick lived in a trailer on the banks of the Hudson River. He met them at the door with a quivery little dog in his arms. A toy poodle? Sunny asked.

"A Maltese," said Tim Brunswick. "Name of Blimey." He led them into a tiny parlor lined with gray file cabinets. A picture window showed a dismal river view, and a saxophone gleamed dully in one corner like the esophagus of a golden beast. The room shivered when the wind blew, as if it might lunge into the Hudson at any minute. Edna felt a little seasick.

"Did your father really know Herman Melville, Mr. Brunswick?" Sunny asked.

"Everybody in the 'burgh knew him. Dad went to school with his kid brother, Tom. Those boys worshipped Melville." Blimey buried his tiny nose in his master's shirt, and Tim Brunswick peered at Mrs. Livingston over his bifocals. His eyes were a vibrant baby blue. "I also knew your husband, Sammy Livingston. He was a serious person. Quiet, but accommodating."

"That's why he needed me." Mrs. Livingston crossed her legs and started swinging the top one with aggressive abandon. "I was fun-loving as all get-out."

"Lansingburgh was quite a place in his day. It has quite a history." And Tim Brunswick told them how the first Dutch settlers had named the village Steen Arabia and how in Melville's time, the 1840s, peach trees and willows had grown along the Hudson, which was then a busy shipyard. "Melville and a local girl, Mary Parmalee, used to stroll on the riverbank, reading Tennyson to each other. 'Far on the ringing plains of windy Troy. I am a part of all that I have met—' "

"Mary Parmalee!" Edna's mother interrupted. "What a pretty name! How did I wind up being plain old Annie Livingston?"

"What was Herman like?" Sunny asked eagerly.

"Like a real sailor, Dad said. Suntanned. And he walked with this racy kind of swagger, what they called the sailor's roll. It was considered very suggestive in his day."

"Yeah?" Sunny smiled encouragingly.

"Yeah. Melville walked like he was on a rocking boat, kind of bow-legged like—" And Tim Brunswick set the dog down on his chair and lurched around the table, demonstrating. Then he came to a halt and swayed tipsily above the little Maltese.

"Blimey!" exclaimed Sunny.

"You betcha!" said Tim Brunswick. "The ladies love a sailor. All the belles of Lansingburgh were after Herman Melville. Ladies led sheltered lives in those days, and he was a man of the world, swashbuckling, like Errol Flynn. He was what we'd call a sex symbol today."

"I don't understand symbolism, do you?" Mrs. Livingston appealed. "That's why I don't understand *Moby Dick*." She shifted restlessly on the narrow love seat. "It's full of symbolism."

"Some books you have to read twice to understand," Edna said.

"And some you'd never understand if you read till time immortal. *Gone with the Wind!* Now there was a book."

Edna handed Tim Brunswick her copy of *Typee*. "This was in my father's safe at the Phoenix Hotel."

He opened volume one and examined it. "You'd better take good care of this, young lady. This is a first edition. It might even be an association copy."

"Wow!" Sunny said. "What's that?"

"A book Melville owned himself. He might have given it to the innkeeper in payment for his drinking tab."

"You mean Herman touched *Typee*? That makes it a thecond-clath welic."

"Say again?"

"An object rich with spiritual electricity," Edna translated. "An object made luminous by contact with a radiant being."

As they walked to the car, she looked for evidence of peach trees by the Hudson. She felt the past must exist behind, beside, inside, or under the present. The problem was time. Time came between things, shutting them off in loneliness and ignorance. And time had dimension. It wasn't flat like paper. Time had substance, yet it was invisible, like all important things.

"All the lonely people!" Sunny exclaimed.

Edna had long believed she had the power to pull things toward her with her mind. Now she sensed something desirable approaching, and she urged it on, envisioning a limo with dark windows, a single-masted schooner. A yellow submarine.

A week later Mrs. Livingston came running upstairs in a state of high emergency. "The Beatle Buggy's outside!" she said. "It looks like a Ford Fairlane. Hurry!"

WTRY was giving away tickets to see the group at Shea Stadium. The winners also would attend the junior press conference in New York. Edna and Sunny had sent in a hundred entries with "Jay Blue is sexy!" scrawled all over them. They'd found the deejay's name in the phone book under *Blue, Jay* and called to say they admired his jingles. Now he sat in her mother's living room, a palpable absence of

284

sound taking shape around him. His quietude felt lifeless, as if uttering inanities at the speed of light for a living drained him of élan vital. Maybe he's a mild-mannered mortician by day and a swinging deejay by night, Edna thought. "It'll be a gas," Jay Blue said in the forced baritone that was his air voice. He scratched his head and his mod-style toupee, said to be made of genuine mink, slipped down and touched the top of his sunglasses. Then he stood up and handed Edna the tickets, and Mrs. Livingston burst into applause. "Since her father died, she's hardly left her room. Maybe this will get her out of the house."

"Say, that's a good idea," said Jay Blue.

Edna held the receiver at arm's length after telling Sunny. "We have to stop screaming and think," she yelled into the mouthpiece.

"Thop threaming and think!"

"We need a way to get close to them. We need the perfect gift."

The usual offerings—gum wrappers woven into an eighteen-foot strip, a life-size portrait of Ringo made entirely of uncooked elbow macaroni—would not do. All that chewing and plaiting and dying and gluing did not reflect well upon the giver. They'd have to come up with something unique. Something the Beatles might actually want. The perfect gift could open doors. It must be something that would not melt or die on the bus to New York, something that could be carried while sprinting in a miniskirt.

"For the man who has everything," Edna continued, "a relic would make a very special present."

"Why would the Beatles want a pen they touched?"

"Not that, Hairspray Brains! *Typee*."

Sunny squealed in shock. "If we give them *Typee*, what are we going to re-re-read?"

"There are other books in the world, you know." Edna affected a supercilious tone. "We could read *Billy Budd*. Or *Moby Dick*." In fact, she was tired of second-class relics. If she could get close to the Beatles, she might achieve the hands-on, naked knowledge that came from touching a primary source.

"Why not give them uth," Sunny suggested.

"Give them us?"

"Remember Regina." This cousin of Sunny's had lost her virginity at Jose's Deli, and her description—the really amazing pain, the counter boy's commands to open wider—made sex sound like a terrible trip to the dentist. Now Sunny said she thought they could do better. Since Herman was unavailable, she thought the Beatles might be equal to the task. Try the best, then try the rest, she said, and the concept appealed to Edna's perfectionism.

And so over the next few weeks, they set about starving their bodies into bodies the Beatles could want: model bodies, twiggish and ravishingly thin. Sometimes at the end of a meal, Sunny would pick up her plate and lick it clean. She was so hungry!

"Zen cookery uses four yangizing factors to achieve change," Edna said. She and Sunny were eating their usual dinner of brown rice with brown rice. "Heat, time, pressure, and/or salt."

"You girls need more variety in your diet," her mother remarked. "You need more color. 'A bright color on a brown gruel is like a song in the heart.' I made that up myself."

"Was Jay Blue anything like his image, Mrs. Livingston?" Sunny asked.

"No. In real life he's dead timber. Not my type." She took another bite of Irish stew.

"Who's your type, Ma?"

"Tyrone Power. He had bedroom eyes. And Sam, your father, liked Kay Francis." Her mother set dishes of pink pudding before them.

"I don't want any," Edna said.

"Sam was the only one who thought I was swell." Her mother sighed. "He was the only one who liked my cooking. Though when I was a visiting nurse, I had admirers. I once had a patient change her name to mine, you know."

Edna rolled her eyes. "This patient changed her first name *and* her last name," she told Sunny.

"I know it!" crowed her mother. "She became Annie Monahan. That was before I became Annie Livingston, of course."

"Did she change her name to Livingston when you did?" Edna asked.

"Huh?" her mother's mind was back in the 1930s. "We'd lost touch by then. Who knows, she might have. She thought very highly of me, that's for dang sure."

"Well, I like your cooking, Mrs. L.," Sunny said.

Mrs. Livingston gave another martyred sigh. "I eat to live, I don't live to eat."

"The body is water, but the mind is sea," said Edna. "The body—"

"The body is water, but the mind is at sea! What's that supposed to mean?" Mrs. Livingston interrupted.

Since earliest childhood, whenever Edna tried to speak, her mother's voice had drowned her out. Rather than compete for conversational space, she had become a seriously silent person. Her father had mistaken her reticence for arrogance. He'd accused her of caring more for John Lennon than her parents. And what could she say? The Beatles are my Polynesia?

"The ripe raw breadfruit can be stored away in large underground receptacles for years on end," Edna quoted from *Typee*. "It only improves with age." They were sitting at a card table in the cellar of her house. The cellar, fusty with oilcloth and light-absorbing knotty pine, reminded them of the Cavern, where the Fab Four had begun. Now that school had ended for the summer, they spent much of their time there, playing the one folk song they knew over and over on their warped guitars. "Danger water's coming, baby, hold me tight," they sang in loud, flat voices.

"Were it not that the breadfruit is thus capable of being preserved for a length of time, the natives might be reduced to a state of starvation."

"If I could get my hands on a breadfruit, I'd know what to do with it," Sunny said. But breadfruit was not available at the local supermarkets, and when they asked after it, the produce managers became churlish and depressed.

"What was Jay Blue like?" Sunny asked.

"He was like—nothing. He seemed kind of lonely."

"Troy must be the loneliest place on Earth. I bet we're one of the only places on Earth without a sister city."

"One of the only! That's a redundancy," Edna said.

"Wow!" Sunny dropped her guitar with a metallic boom. "Herman's first voyage was to Liverpool, right? And he was living in Lansingburgh then, right? Well, it's obvious. We'll start a petition to make Lansingburgh and Liverpool sister cities, and we'll ask the Beatles to sigh-sigh-"—her voice sounded as if she'd been breathing helium—"sign it!"

"We can't do that! It'll ruin our image. They'll think we're fans." Edna fluffed her hair near the crown to give it more height. "Anyway, it's so—municipal."

"Your mother can do the embarrassing part, asking for their autographs." Since the girls were only fourteen, Mrs. Livingston insisted on accompanying them to New York. "We need more than one idea," Sunny said. "We shouldn't put all our begs in one ask-it."

"Wouldn't we have to get somebody's approval, like the lord mayor of Liverpool or at least the mayor of Lansingburgh?"

"If the Beatles sign, do you think those guys will say no? They're politicians! They know which side their butt is breaded on!"

And Edna didn't argue. *Do I dare to eat a peach?* she often asked herself. Lately, more often than not, the answer was yes.

On August 22, Edna, Sunny, and Mrs. Livingston took the bus to New York City. The girls were using years of baby-sitting savings to pay for a room at the Warwick, where the Beatles were staying. They spent the hours before the junior press conference donning their Beatle girlfriend costumes: hip-hugger skirts, net stockings, paisley shirts with white cuffs and collars, ghillie shoes of golden suede. Do I look like a fan? No, do I? they asked each other.

The press conference was held on the second floor. Girls waited outside, trying to insinuate themselves to the front of the pack, and at last the doors swung open. As the crowd trampled past, Edna was stabbed in the clavicle by someone's JOHN IS GOD button. She hugged her copy of *Typee*, which she planned to present at a suitable moment. An aide appeared and said, "The Beatles are about to enter. Would those in front please kneel?" All the girls sank like barn animals on Christmas Eve. "I mean," he amended, "so those in back can get their picture. Make room." Edna and Sunny were pressed against an emergency exit when suddenly it opened, hurtling them back into the hall. A long, navy blue arm reached over their heads and slammed the door, stranding them outside.

"We won passes!" Edna wailed.

"Win some, lose some," the policeman said.

"You're supposed to be a community helper," Sunny scolded.

"I'm helping those rich fairies stay alive." He patted his gun holster. "If you ask me, those guys are a little light in their loafers."

"Nobody asked you," Sunny snapped. Muffled munchkin squeals erupted from within the room, followed by deeper, foreign inflections that flipped up at the ends. Edna and Sunny pulled their hair and groaned in frustration. When the doors opened they rushed in, but the Beatles had been whisked away. We've been cheated! they told each other through disbelieving tears.

"Yes, they do that to your mother, too," Mrs. Livingston remarked, when they returned to the room. "But I don't let them get away with it."

The girls were prostrated in shock on the bed. "They're above us right now," Edna said. "Just one floor up." And they listened to the footsteps on high, trying to guess their identities.

"C'mon," her mother said, putting on her pumps. "Let's meet the Beatles and get it over with. Then we can go out and have some fun."

As soon as the girls had repaired their eyeliner, Mrs. Livingston hustled them onto the elevator. When the doors opened at the eighth floor, a guard blocked their exit. Edna peered into the corridor and spied the Beatles' road manager. "Neil As-As—" Sunny called, as the elevator door slammed into her side. "—Aspinall!" The road manager paused, and Edna told him how they'd missed the press conference. He asked her age. Eighteen, she lied, and for once her mother didn't contradict her. Follow me, Neil said. When he saw Mrs. Livingston was with the girls, he hesitated. Then he unlocked a door, and with a sweeping gesture, bade them enter.

Four dove-gray suits with plum-red stripes lay draped across the bed, gleaming in the lunar light of the TV. Edna reacted like a Geiger counter sensing uranium nearby. Her teeth began to chatter, and she had to suppress high-pitched trills of impending revelation. "If you wouldn't mind doing us a favor," Neil said. "These have to be ironed before the show tomorrow." He pointed to an ironing board in the corner. "I'll be back," he promised.

"Always leave the door ajar when you're in a strange man's hotel room," Mrs. Livingston instructed, propping it with the telephone book. She examined the suits. "What elegant tailoring! You have to take everything out of the pockets, or they won't lie flat. Oh, name tags."

The girls exchanged thrilled looks. "Which one do you want?" Edna asked.

"Paul, of course," Sunny said. "Paul is All!"

"Is he the single one?" Mrs. Livingston inquired.

"He's the Cute One," Edna said dismissively. "I want John, the Sexy One."

"Paul's had a very hard life, you know," Sunny told them. "His mother died when he was fourteen."

"John's mother died, too," said Edna. "And his father deserted him. He's an orphan."

Mrs. Livingston sighed. She'd been born near an orphanage, and as a student nurse she'd worked in the New York Foundling Hospital. "Poor motherless boys! At least they're young and healthy."

"Oh no," Edna informed her. "Ringo had peritonitis as a child, and George had nephritis. They're actually kind of sickly." She knew her mother had sympathy for physical ills, though disturbances of the mind only made her irritable. Mrs. Livingston respected reality and those who kept in touch with its firm facts. Now she sat on the bed, watching TV, while Edna and Sunny took turns ironing. John Lennon came on the screen, apologizing for saying the Beatles were more popular than Jesus. The report that followed said the group had been nearly crushed to death in Cleveland, picketed by the Ku Klux Klan in Washington, D.C., and almost electrocuted in St. Louis. They'd received death threats in Memphis, where someone tossed a bomb on stage, and today two fans had promised to leap from the ledge of a New York hotel unless they met the Beatles.

"Silly girls!" Mrs. Livingston frowned. Edna and Sunny were caressing the suits as if they were alive. They ran the zippers up and down, unbuttoned the waistbands, rubbed their faces against the lapels. "Don't be getting lipstick on their outfits. And there's another thing I won't stand for."

Edna held her breath.

"I won't have you throwing things at those boys while they're trying to play their music. They have enough trouble."

"The only thing I want to throw at them is myself," Edna said. She ironed lasciviously, stopping to inhale the faint scents—shaving crème and sweat, patchouli and dry cleaning fluid—liberated by steam and heat. She felt delirious. "How many pleats go in each leg?" she asked.

"Give me that iron," her mother said, pushing her aside. "I can't believe we came to New York for this. This is just like home."

At last the suits were finished, but there still was no sign of Neil Aspinall. "That dress manager of theirs. He has what are called 'craggy good looks.' Do you girls know what that means?"

"Like Frankenstein might have looked if Frankenstein had been good-looking?" Sunny suggested.

Suddenly fragments of song—"Summer in the City"—burst from a room at the end of the hall, a door slammed, and voices came lilting along the corridor. Edna, Sunny, and Mrs. Livingston rushed to the threshold in time to see a fantasia of flowers and paisley, polka dots and stripes, mossy velvets and sun-bright satins levitate down the hall. Then the mirage vanished in a Beatle-scented breeze. Edna and Sunny grabbed each other. Did you see them? Did you see them?

" 'Had a glimpse of the gardens of Paradise been revealed to me, I could scarcely have been more ravished with the sight,' " Sunny quoted from *Typee*. "Didn't they look—mythical?"

"Mystical, yes," Edna said. She had expected the Beatles to sense their intimate bond with her and stop. How could they have mistaken her for a stranger?

"If you knew that was them, why didn't you speak up? You missed your chance," her mother said. "Here comes their handsome valet." Mrs. Livingston showed Neil the ironed suits. She pointed to a little heap of Beatle detritus on the dresser. "That was in their pockets."

"Oh, you can keep those things." The road manager's eyes looked dreamy and glazed. "As souvenirs."

"When do we meet the Beatles?" Mrs. Livingston asked.

"The boys are tired. They've had a hard week."

"Listen, we kept our part of the bargain." Mrs. Livingston folded her arms across her chest, preparing for battle. "These girls have come a long way. They've waited a long time."

"Okay," Neil said reluctantly. "All right." He extracted three red press passes from his wallet and handed them out. "Come by the suite tomorrow around four, and you'll meet the Beatles."

At the appointed hour the next day, they showed their passes and joined the line extending from the Beatles' suite. Edna spotted Jay Blue just ahead of them, talking into a cassette recorder and punching the air for emphasis. She clutched *Typee* with clammy fingers. On this day of days, her bangs were wrinkled, her hair full of flyaway, her Beatle girlfriend ensemble disheveled from dress rehearsals. And how could she meet the Beatles with her mother tagging along? She wanted to be back in her room, copying their song lyrics with the patience of a scrivener. Last year she'd ordered some bromeliads from Florida, and when she opened the carton, the pots were swarming with centipedes. She had shrieked and thrown the shipment away before her mother, always disgusted by forays into the strange, could find out. Now she felt the same hysterical alarm. "You go, I'll wait here," she said.

"The heck you will," her mother said, pulling her through the door.

The Beatles' suite was crawling with gifts. It's like Christmas morning in here, Edna thought. *Your riches taught me poverty.* What she had to offer seemed shabby in comparison. By the time they'd edged near enough to see the group, everyone else had been ushered out except Jay Blue. The Beatles were holding court from the sofa. There was a gritty orb before them on the cocktail table, and they were staring at it as if it might hatch.

"Is that egg really one hundred years old?" Jay Blue asked.

"No," John Lennon said. "The Chinese only call it that so ignorant Westerners will think they'll eat anything."

"Say, that's a good idea!" said Jay Blue.

The Beatles seemed disgruntled, almost crotchety behind their granny glasses. Apathy poured off them, and joyless waterfalls of worry. Edna yearned to make them happy, if only for an instant. Five minutes, their press agent called. "There's no time like the present," her mother hissed, nudging the girls forward. Edna knew Sunny would not speak for fear of stuttering. She wanted to be introduced as a mute painter who spoke only in watercolors of a halcyon refinement.

"Hi," Edna whispered.

The Beatles went on talking all at once and only with each other above the insect whir of the recorder. They seemed to be discussing the hundred-year-old egg. . . . "Looks like snot I suppose you could wear a blindfold whilst eating it my son please don't use the word 'snot' in my hearing snot nice I deplore having used it smells disgusting take it to the loo if you must burn incense," they said.

"Hey, fellas!" Mrs. Livingston interrupted. "These girls have brought you a special present."

The Beatles nodded and mumbled sleepily. George Harrison yawned. Edna and Sunny had decided they must return everything they'd taken from the suits except one relic too precious to relinquish. Now they stepped forward and emptied their purses onto the table before the group. Out tumbled guitar picks, chewing gum, half a cigarette, a little box of perfumed incense papers, a ballpoint pen, and a sticker that said "I Still Love the Beatles."

"It's from your pockets," Edna said.

"Are you thieves or magicians?" George Harrison asked. He lit one of the incense papers, and they began talking about the explosion during their Memphis show.

"You know how George is the Quiet One, I'm the Bigmouthed

One, etc.," John Lennon told Jay Blue. "We were looking around to see who was going to be the Dead One." And Jay Blue told them about a friend of his in the music business who'd been shot in the heart. Doctors had removed half the bullet and left the other half in his chest, and now he was fine. He just had some tear duct problems.

"Perhaps we shouldn't have called our album *Revolver*," George said, twiddling his thumbs.

"You know the old saying. Those who live by the song, die by the song," Mrs. Livingston put in.

John Lennon looked up, aware of her for the first time.

"My husband was musically inclined," Mrs. Livingston continued. "He was shot in the arm during Prohibition."

"Has Prohibition ended?" John asked.

Mrs. Livingston chose that moment to produce the Sister City petition. The quartet picked up pens, and John was about to sign when the TV began to report on anti-Beatle demonstrations in the South. "They're burning my book," he said.

"Shame on them!" Mrs. Livingston seized the "I Still Love The Beatles" sticker, licked it, and pressed it onto the petition folder. "There! That'll show them!"

John blinked slowly. Edna thought it might have been the first time he'd blinked in several years. He said something to the others in a dialect that even she, with her scholarly knowledge of the Scouse language, could not translate. Then Paul McCartney hit the stop button on Jay Blue's recorder, and they all started to speak in a rich mishmash of code that seemed to be their native tongue. Their press agent, sensing a change in atmosphere, came charging over. "Get Brian," John told him. And the Beatles fell silent.

"Well, a lot of people still love you," Mrs. Livingston assured them. "It's not just us."

George, Paul, and Ringo lowered their eyes demurely. John gnawed delicately at his index finger. At last Ringo spoke. "We're very fond of you, too," he said, and with his words some hidden signal seemed to pass between the four, a vibration more enigmatic than a glance. Yes, we loove you too, they insisted. We loove you too!

"That's good," Mrs. Livingston said, grabbing the petition. "It was nice meeting you fellas, but we don't want to wear out our welcome—"

"No!" the Beatles shouted, and the force of their voices almost knocked Edna's contacts off her eyes.

"What's your name?" Paul McCartney inquired gently of her mother. "Yes, which one are you?" John Lennon added.

"Annie. I'm the sensible one, and these two—" she nodded toward Edna and Sunny—"are the dreamy ones."

"And what can the Beatles do for Annie and the Dreamers?" John asked, with a pleasant smile. "Yes, what can we do, would you like a cup of tea?" the others echoed. And it was as if they'd morphed from petulant pop stars into solicitous male nurses, custodians of perfect love.

"Well, if we're staying, could somebody make these girls a peanut butter and jelly sandwich?" Mrs. Livingston said. "They haven't had a thing to eat all day." Edna tried to kick her mother discreetly.

"Would you care for some macadamia nuts?" Paul McCartney said, tearing the cellophane from a gift basket piled high with exotic produce. Their manager, Brian Epstein, arrived then, looking impeccable yet flustered. He asked them to wait in the vestibule while he conferred with the boys.

"Gosh, Mrs. L., you've got the Beatles wrapped around your little finger," Sunny gasped as soon as they were alone.

"Listen to this," Edna said, opening *Typee*. " 'The natives, actuated by some mysterious impulse . . . redoubled their attentions to us. Their manner towards us was unaccountable. . . . Why this excess of deferential kindness, or what equivalent can they imagine us capable of rendering them for it?' " She gave them an astonished glance.

"I was kind of surprised myself," her mother admitted, "by how grateful they were that we still love them. I guess everyone needs a kind word. Then they all started speaking in Gaelic or Liverpuddle or something—"

Brian Epstein returned. His eyebrows met in a furrowed point. He cleared his throat and said there had been a slight mishap. Apparently some medicine of John's had been affixed to the back of the "I Still Love The Beatles" sticker that Mrs. Livingston had licked. This medicine, lysergic acid diethylamide, was used to enhance creativity. Thus it could have disquieting effects. One could expect to feel rather odd. One could expect visions, hallucinations—

"You mean it's like someone put a Mickey in my drink?" Mrs. Livingston interrupted.

"Rather."

Nothing scared Edna's mother more than an unquiet mind. "Listen, I'm not the creative type," she said. "I've never had a vision in my life! I don't believe in visions." Then all her bluster faded. She clutched her throat with a trembling hand. "I'm a registered nurse, and I never heard of any medicine being administered on a stamp."

"But you haven't practiced in thirty years," said Edna. "Times change."

"Quite," said Brian Epstein. "This drug makes one highly suggestible. Whatever your companions suggest becomes your reality. But you mustn't fret. You are amongst friends. The boys and I would like you to join our entourage tonight so that you might be in the safest, indeed the happiest, indeed the most—" he searched for the ideal hyperbole—"fabulous place on earth."

"Where is that, Mist-Mist-Mr. Epstein?" Sunny wondered.

"The Beatles' dressing room." And his eyes fluttered briefly, involuntarily, heavenwards. "Please." He adjusted his cravat. "I implore you. Do not share this with reporters."

"Don't be a snitch, that's my motto," Edna's mother said. "Nobody likes a tattletale."

"Quite."

"Is this drug habit forming?" she asked.

"On the contrary." And Brian Epstein smiled benignly, glad to be the bearer of good news at last. "You might wish never to take it again."

And so they had been driven by limo to Shea Stadium, escorted to the locker room, and abandoned in that windowless bunker. The lockers were painted gunmetal gray; a few benches and folding metal chairs were the only furnishings. "Are we buried alive?" Mrs. Livingston asked.

Edna was distraught. The Beatles had terrified her. Their godlike confidence brought out her awkwardness. She'd been crushed by their surliness, confused by their kindness. Worst of all, they'd been too busy doting on her mother to notice her existence. She missed the cell-like safety of her room. Yet she could not quit until she had given them her gift. This might be her only chance to achieve the metaphysical-physical contact of her dreams.

"Are you all right?" she asked her mother. Mrs. Livingston looked a little wild eyed.

"This must be the dreariest place on earth," her mother said.

Edna browsed through *Typee* in search of a soothing passage. " 'When I looked around the verdant recess in which I was buried, and gazed up to the summits of the lofty eminence that hemmed me in, I was well disposed to think that I was in the 'Happy Valley,' and that beyond those heights there was nought but a world of care and anxiety—' " Footsteps. Her pulse quickened. Her contacts were dirty. She was seeing everything through the oily shimmer her optometrist called spectacle blur. When the Beatles came sprinting in—day of daze!—each was haloed by his own greasy rainbow.

"How are you feeling, all right?" Paul asked her mother.

"I'm feeling kind of—" The Beatles leaned forward, attentive. "Creative. I want to hold your—" She paused, distracted by their raised eyebrows.

"Hand?" Paul said hopefully.

"Guitar," her mother said, and he obligingly extended his Hofner bass. "No, not that little one. I want to hold that big one," she said, pointing to a sunburst Epiphone Casino in the corner. George brought it over and began trying to teach her a chord. "Are you the Orphaned One?" she asked. "No, I'm the Lonely One," he told her. His guitar made an empty thunking sound when she strummed it. "Gee, this is harder than I thought. Don't you fellas have to practice?"

"All we have to practice is smiling," John said. He took a long drag on a hand-rolled cigarette.

"Are those roofers you're smoking?" The air was thick with rank, weedy fumes. Before he could answer she said, "Do you know these girls are your biggest fans?" Edna froze, her shame revealed.

"No, but hum a few bars and I'll fake it," said John.

"That's an old one."

"We're old at heart." He rubbed his sideburn reflectively.

"You do seem kind of tired for young fellas."

"We had to perform twice on Sunday," Paul explained. "In Cincinnati and St. Louis. We had a contract." And he squinched his face into a frown.

"Well, don't be making any more contractions," Mrs. Livingston commanded. "Take a rest."

"Say, that's a good idea!" Paul said in a fine imitation of Jay Blue. Once again some unspoken agreement buzzed between the four, and they fell into a pensive silence.

"Cheer up, boys!" Mrs. Livingston said, springing to her feet. Then, to Edna's horror, her mother began to do the dance they called her routine: a high-spirited cancan with kicking Rockette variations performed to her own sung accompaniment. Edna knew it well.

"Mom, stop," she pleaded. But the Beatles were yielding little

296

ironic smiles. Ringo started clapping, and George began to play along. "Julia," Paul said. Julia was John's mother who'd died when he was a teenager. Every fan knew that. Edna felt sullen with envy. She wanted to rise into the Beatles' consciousness, if only for a minute, but even in close proximity it seemed impossible. Her mother kept getting in her way.

At last Mrs. Livingston stopped prancing, out of breath. "Now why don't you sing to us?" she asked.

"They can't," Edna said quickly. "They can't sing now."

"Course we can sing," said Paul. "Don't believe everything you read."

John wearily picked up an acoustic guitar. He strummed the first chords of "Anna," an oldie about a girl who'd come and asked him to set her free. He changed the name to Annie, in honor of Mrs. Livingston, and sang that all his life he'd been searching for a girl to love him, but every girl he ever had broke his heart and left him sad, what was he supposed to do? And the other Beatles chorused "like his mum," "I deplore," and "drink my sweat." After a verse or two, John forgot the words, and the song broke down.

"It's now or never," Sunny whispered. *Typee.* George was closest, so Edna thrust the book at him. "It's about sailors held captive by a group of man-eating cannibals," she said.

"The fans would devour us if they could." He nibbled on his guitar pick. "It's because they love us. And it's the thought that counts."

"This is a first edition. It belonged to Herman Melville." She paused for effect. "You can have it."

"I don't want it," he said, handing it back. "It'll only get lost or left behind. It'll only get ruined." The room whirled. Her fears were realized, her gift rejected. "Try John," George added quickly. "His father was a sailor."

The walk across the room to John Lennon seemed long and fraught with obstacles. "This book is set on a remote island where there's no religion or possessions, no greed or hunger," she began. He listened to her ragged exegesis with half-closed eyes, impassive as a Buddha. Then he opened *Typee* and read aloud. " 'Her manner convinced me that she deeply compassionated my situation, as being removed from my country and friends, and placed beyond the reach of all relief.' " He stopped and stared off into space.

"Can I ask you something?" Edna said. Everyone else was across the room, admiring her mother's earrings.

"Sure," he said. "Shoot."

"What would you do if you were in love with someone who didn't know you were alive?"

"Love really tears us up, doesn't it?" He paused. The pause was delicious, eloquent. "But we always get another chance."

The other Beatles were taking their stage suits out of the lockers. They called John over, then George spoke up. "We have to turn off the lights so we can change," he said. For a second Edna imagined them assuming another identity, like Gregor Samsa becoming a bug. "You won't be upset now, will you? We won't be long. Just stay put." He asked her to work the lights, and she nodded, feeling a new sense of power.

The Beatles hummed and whistled like a human meadow as they dressed, and the darkness amplified their chirping and rustling. They shouted reassurances—we still loove you, Annie!—and in no time at all, they called for the lights. But Edna must have lost her bearings because she could not find the switch. She stroked the cinder blocks and shuffled to the left, groping blindly. Then she tripped over a guitar cord and crashed against a texture she knew well. A suit of summer wool, now sculpted into three dimensions. Her previous experience of the Beatles had been so flat, so limited to pictures and screens, that the depth and breadth of this actual body felt almost wrong. She clung like a barnacle nonetheless. Now that she had him, she would not let him go. And instead of pulling away, he stood patiently, perhaps resignedly, in an attitude of forebearance, emitting an aura of—was it possible?—understanding. His face felt gritty as a beach, and through his shirt she heard the rock-solid four/four of his heart and an ambient hum like damaged nerves. "Let there be light!" her mother called. "Quick, before I have a vision!" His hair sifted through her fingers then like salt dissolving, silky with escape. And she let him go.

She found the switch, and by the time her eyes adjusted, the Beatles looked perfectly composed. John, Paul, and George had assumed their guitars like shields. Only Ringo had nothing to hide behind. "How do we look?" he asked.

"Like stars," Mrs. Livingston said with satisfaction. "Like brothers. Like you should."

John, meanwhile, was searching his pockets. Now he held up an "I Still Love The Beatles" sticker for all to see.

"Mine is missing," Paul said. "And there was nothing funny about mine."

"You mean—she didn't take that drug?" said Edna.

"Looks like your trip is over before it's begun," George told her mother.

Then Neil flung the door open, and a noise like a force of nature rushed in. John gave *Typee* to the road manager for safekeeping. The PA system boomed "Now . . . The Beatles!" And they were gone. Edna, Sunny, and Mrs. Livingston hurried out onto the field to watch them play. Flashbulbs splashed the night as John launched into "Twist and Shout," his legs braced like a sailor's on a tossing ship. Brian Epstein stood near second base, nervously chewing gum on the downbeat. Edna was struck by how solitary the Beatles looked on stage, on their private island of fame. If a string broke or an amp exploded, if they needed a drink or felt unwell, there was no one to help them. They were at the mercy of the fans and police. For thirty minutes the Beatles were the loneliest people on earth.

One of Mrs. Livingston's earrings fell off, and she pitched it at the stage. Sunny, meanwhile, was screaming Be-Be-Be-Beatles! Rah-Rah-Rah-Ringo! Edna had kept one item from their pockets, a scrap from a cigarette pack. Now she dug this second-class relic from the depths of her purse. "Rich Choice" was printed on one side, a set list of songs handwritten on the other. She crushed it and tossed it toward the stage like an offering, a flower over a burial at sea.

"Those Beatles work a short shift, don't they?" Mrs. Livingston said. The parking lot was covered with tickets like fallen leaves. Sunny spotted a taxi with a model of a yellow submarine secured to its roof, and the driver said he'd take them to the city as soon as he had a full cab. He had one other passenger already, an older girl with a Beatle haircut, wearing a dress made from the Union Jack. A pin identified her as PaulMichelle, a stringer for *Teenbeat*. "Enjoy yourselves, ladies?" the cabbie asked.

"We had the time of our lives," Mrs. Livingston said. "The Beatles autographed our petition."

"No," Edna corrected. "John never signed."

"Well, you gave him your book," her mother said proudly.

The driver checked the moorings of the yellow sub on his roof. "I want to shake the hand that shook the hand of John Lennon," he said to Edna.

"Gosh, Ed, your hand's become a second-class relic," said Sunny.

"We didn't shake hands."

"But he sang to us. And George let me play his guitar," her mother boasted.

The *Teenbeat* stringer looked skeptical.

"It's true, PaulMichelle," Sunny said. "The Beatles really liked her. They thought she was—"

"Swell," Mrs. Livingston interrupted. "The Beatles thought I was swell. And they were nice, too. I felt like I'd known them forever."

"So what are those guys really like?" the driver asked.

"Not what you'd expect," Edna's mother said. "They seemed old as the hills. Believe me, those boys are century plants. Those boys were born old."

"But what were they *like*?" PaulMichelle persisted.

"Real regular and down-to-earth. They were so ordinary! That's what I loved about them."

"Ordinary!" Edna scoffed. "Little do you know." Was it possible to love someone, with the love the Beatles sang in their close harmonies, without ever knowing that person?

"Well, I know one thing," her mother asserted. "Paul explained the hidden symbolism of that Eleanor song to me."

" 'Eleanor Rigby!' What is it?" Sunny asked.

"I—uh—I can't remember. It was very hidden. But he told me, he explained it all."

"C'mon, Ma. Try to remember. It's important."

"It was something about lonely people. Where they come from, where they belong. There's a priest in it, a loner who never connects with Eleanor. They never get to know each other, then she dies, and it's too late. They're like two ships that pass in the night."

"That's not hidden," said Edna. "That's really obvious."

Then PaulMichelle started talking about a relative of hers who had emigrated to Liverpool many moons ago and met the real Eleanor Rigby. This relative had revealed the secret meaning of the song to her. In fact, PaulMichelle considered herself an expert on the boys, for she had traveled with the tour since Boston, almost a week, and Neil had given her two of John's guitar picks, which she'd had made into earrings, see? And she shook her head to make them swing.

"Who was your favorite, Mrs. L.?" Sunny asked.

Edna felt her mother weighing her answer. "George," she said finally. "I liked George Harrison best."

"But George is the Spiritual One," Edna argued. "He's not your type at all. What about the two motherless boys? What about John and Paul?"

"George has a mind of his own. He calls a spade a spade, and I admire that. George was my favorite Beatle. But my favorite guy is Neil. Neil has dreamboat eyes."

"John, Paul, George, and Neil!" Edna exclaimed in disgust.

"Who did you like the best, Hon?" Mrs. Livingston asked Sunny.

"Paul's her favorite," Edna said quickly.

"Paul is All," agreed PaulMichelle.

But Sunny twirled a strand of her long dark hair. "There was something about Ringo."

"Paul," Edna said firmly.

"Remember when the others put on their guitars, and Ringo had nothing but his drumsticks? He looked so unprotected. I guess that's when I fell for him. And now that I've met him," Sunny continued, "I think Jay Blue is kind of cute."

"I don't get you," Edna said. Stars were easier to understand, celebrities on elevated stages illuminated by giant lights, who could be resurrected anytime at will within your head.

"Who was *your* favorite, Ed?" Sunny asked.

Headlights from buses pierced the warm August darkness. Edna saw Jay Blue standing alone by the WTRY Beatle Buggy, dabbing at his eyes under his sunglasses.

"I'm not sure," she said. Her favorite was the one who'd understood her wish for contact in the dark. But if she lived to be a hundred, she'd never know for certain who that was.

She felt her mother scrutinizing her. "Those fuzzy blonde hairs under your chin," Mrs. Livingston said. "I never noticed them before. I have those, too. My own!"

And she seized Edna in a bone-crushing hug. It was the first maternal embrace Edna could remember, and she endured it stoically, amazed to be touched by this stranger, her mother.

Nominated by Ed Falco, The Gettysburg Review

ECTOPLIMANIESSENCE

by HAYDEN CARRUTH

from THE AMERICAN POETRY REVIEW

For two years and several months now, since
the medicolocrats opened my chest with a little
buzz-saw—but not so little as to be unrecognizable—
well, what the hell, I've been unable to walk upstairs
to my room,
or to my lover's room
which is soomwhut paragorical, as Vermonters say,
because I'm eighty-one and three months and eight days
old.
    I'm not Methuselah, thank heavens. But I ain't
Shirley Temple either.
    The point is that I sleep downstairs in the room that
has no reasonable designation in our house
but which for convention's sake and because it
is located between the kitchen and the bathroom
we call the living room.

    Tell me, is language still language when the words
don't mean anything?

    I have a little cot,
    on which I lie a lot
    and meditatively plot
    my escape. From what?
I'm a frookin salamander if I know.

But from my spot each night all night I see a shadow
cast by no light and laid against no wall or other surface,
like a holograph, or so I've heard the optitechnics say,
a woman leaning toward her left with her right arm
extended, as if to hold her from leaning farther—very
graceful, and beautiful. No light, no surface, but extremely
beautiful, the epitome of a non-species, for she is no myth,
Diana and Athena can't touch her,
    there in the air, *absolutely irreproachable*. What an
extraordinary apparition.
    I have investigated on my wobbly knees and inflamed
ankles. She is the shadow of the vacuum cleaner, her body the
tank and her extended arm the hose. But still no source of light,
no surface on which her tantalizing image reposes.

    But this is crazy. She is she. Lovely and compassionate. So
much the better if she is a shadow. And every
night she visits
    an aged invalid in his narrow cot.

Nominated by Donald Revell, Maura Stanton

FANTASTIC VOYAGE

by EMILY FOX GORDON

from SALMAGUNDI

I

THE PREPARATIONS for my husband's colonoscopy were more un-
pleasant and elaborate than we would have thought, but he followed
his doctor's printed instructions to the letter. He fasted from lunch-
time onward the day before and spent the evening swallowing three
and a half liters of a nauseating cherry-flavored solution of mineral
salts in eight-ounce increments every ten minutes, sucking on quar-
tered lemons to kill the taste. The explosive purgation began on
schedule, and before long what came out was nearly as clear as wa-
ter. But we saw that a few shreds of what the instructions called
"solid matter" still floated in the bowl, and in spite of my assurances
that he had done as much as could reasonably be expected, my con-
scientious husband forced himself to swallow the final half liter. He
spent the hour that followed struggling not to vomit. Teeth clenched
and shoulders hunched, shivering, he paced the floor of our bedroom
while I lay watching late night comedians on TV.

Neither of us got much sleep, so we were both groggy and irritable
as we pulled into the hospital parking lot just before dawn. I had
slowed down our departure by taking my time drinking my coffee—
he wasn't allowed any—and my husband spent most of the half-hour
car trip complaining about that. I countered by pointing out that we
were ridiculously early, and would have to sit in the waiting room for
at least forty minutes before he was called.

But we were not the first to arrive at the hospital that morning.

The lot was nearly full, and as we made our way, squabbling quietly, through the hospital grounds and along a walkway that separated its two pavillions, we saw that we had joined a loose procession. In groups of two and three and four, people were approaching. An obese woman, noticeably lame, wearing khaki pedal pushers and a nautical jersey, pushed a wry-necked adolescent boy in a wheelchair. Two other women brought up the rear: perhaps they were sisters of the wheelchair-pusher, aunts to the boy. Two husky, laughing young men with sketchy goatees supported a frail old woman between them. A pair of elegantly dressed WASPS in late middle age walked together, their long strides matched, their facial expressions neutral. They seemed to be united in an intention to dispose of an unpleasant errand with verve and dispatch. Impossible to tell which of them was the patient, unless you guessed from the magazines in the woman's leather carryall that it was the man, but this would not have been a safe inference. She might have brought them to occupy herself during her own hospitalization, or even carried them for him, to read while he waited for her to undergo some procedure. These two had a long-married look, and it was anyone's guess what arrangements had evolved between them.

The lobby was a big, humming, low-ceilinged rotunda, and everyone in it moved as if according to a preestablished harmony. The light was indirect and timeless, but the day was evidently well advanced: a flight of newly discharged patients in wheelchairs, their belongings bagged in plastic and stashed in their laps, were rolled out to waiting cars while a fast, steady traffic of nurses and orderlies and delivery men pushing loaded dollies crisscrossed the space diagonally. My husband and I found our way to a desk in a shadowy alcove, where a hospital functionary asked him questions about his insurance coverage. He sat down in a chair across the desk from her, but I chose to stay on my feet, hovering over him a little to assert my proprietary status.

I had been thinking that I envied the lives of the hospital workers—the way their time was caught up and regularized by the rhythms of the institution. How cheerful the nurses and doctors and orderlies seemed as they crossed the lobby in pairs—the small Pakistani walking with the big, raw-faced blonde, both wearing pale blue scrubs and surgical moonboots, both taking swigs from water bottles and smiling brilliantly at some shared joke. To a writer who works alone, and struggles to observe a self-imposed schedule, the prospect seemed attractive. But looking at the middle aged woman with whom my husband was disputing the amount of his deductible, I revised that judgment. Unlike the freeranging nurses and orderlies, this person was a fixture, rooted to a desk in front of a jointed, fabric-covered panel that concealed the financial heart of the hospital. The light at her desk was most unflattering; it illuminated her face from below, making powdery floodlit caverns of her nostrils. A hand-shaped shadow reached from the crown of her cap of bleached hair down to her cheekbones, obscuring her eyes.

We rode the elevator to the third floor, arriving at the endoscopy waiting room. I noticed that the handsome WASP couple were already seated at the far end. The man had put on his bifocals and was reading the New York Times. The woman was simply waiting, one spare, exemplary knee crossed over the other.

How old were they, those fast walkers? Early sixties, I guessed. Only one actuarial notch past us—my husband is 58 and I'm 53—but they had a dry settled dignity the two of us will never achieve. The thought actually left me with a moment's relief, a sense that by failing to be severely handsome, my husband and I had cleverly escaped the common fate. But then, of course, I realized I'd gotten caught up in an aesthetic non sequitur. Whether or not our aging becomes us, we are aging, and will continue to do so.

But even so, I also felt sure that we'll continue to experience ourselves as juicy; not yet dry. At least we'll feel ourselves to have juicy centers. For us, the problem is not so much resistance to the inevitability of aging as it is a sense that we're being slow to catch on to its ways.

But then the fast walkers probably feel juicy too; to feel juicy is to feel alive. People in their seventies say they feel thirty; they find the sight of themselves in mirrors unrecognizable. This is one of the few observations about the subjective experience of aging I can think of that has become a commonplace; apart from complaints about stiffness and dimming vision and the alarming acceleration of perceived time, there really isn't a lot of lore handed down from the old to middle-aged initiates like my husband and me. Aside, I mean, from upbeat magazine articles about the refusal of the elderly to accept the limitations of aging, their insistence on continuing, or beginning, to sky dive and tap dance and go to medical school—articles which miss the point entirely.

Just the other day, my husband and I had been asking ourselves why nobody had ever pointed out to us that for the aging each step along the continuum is always an advance into unknown territory—that growing old is a matter of constantly encountering the new? Which offers a partial explanation, I suppose, for the rarity of dispatches from the old. Each age cohort—and the time periods they encompass grow shorter as age advances—awaits briefings from the one just ahead, until by turns each goes over the cliff, unenlightened and unable to enlighten.

Youth is full of norms; age is anarchic. Youth is a round-up; age is a dispersal, a proliferation of paths by which everyone reaches the same end. How many of these sessions of brooding about age have ended with a sudden rush of mortification at the almost ungraspable banality of my thoughts? Time is running out. Death approaches. Well, duh!

The waiting room was huge, the size of a stockyard, and chilly, and rapidly growing crowded. One roped-off section was reserved for families with children; a few picture books had been flung into a corner, and a partially assembled plastic playhouse lay on its side. I counted five children, but only one was doing anything that could be described as playing. Three sat huddled on the floor, watching a closed circuit TV program about the prevention of osteoporosis. The fourth was a tiny wide-eyed Mexican toddler who sank into her mother's skirts, sucking two fingers.

I turned to my husband. "How are you doing?" I asked, and patted his knee. He looked up from the professional journal he was reading and smiled, then shrugged. "Well as can be expected?" I asked. He smiled and shrugged again. I knew this response; he was acting like an adolescent boy with an over-solicitous mother. I also knew that he found it gratifying to behave this way. What had just transpired between us was an apology from me for having been less attentive than I should have been and an acceptance of that apology from him, along with an implicit bid for further sympathy. He was nervous, of course. In his place I would have been even more so—so much more so that in fact I wouldn't be here at all.

Nothing scary had precipitated my husband's decision to undergo what he jokingly called a "fantastic voyage." There had been no pain, no blood in his stool. He was simply following the screening protocol recommended by the A.M.A. He was sensible enough to be willing to lie down and be put into a stupor—I couldn't rid myself of the image of a drooling anesthetized tiger I once saw on a show about the care of zoo animals—so that the walls of his bowels could be explored by a long probe with a camera on one end while his doctor followed its sinuous progress on a TV monitor.

All morning I had been feeling small spasms of primitive resentment toward him. He's so good, I was thinking, as I've thought many times in the course of our nearly thirty-year-old marriage. As a child he kept a log of every book he took out of the library. All his life he's been disciplined, rational, well-organized, prompt, truthful—most of all, prudent. Once again, I found myself toying with a question that my husband, who happens to be a professional philosopher, has never been able to answer to my satisfaction: why should prudence be counted as a virtue?

He comes from a long line of careful people, my husband does. When an airline lost his mother's suitcase, she was able to produce an inventory of everything she had packed, and the original sales slip for each item. A triumph, said a therapist I once told this story to, of compulsiveness.

My resentment was colored by an admixture of superstitious dread. I could not shake the irrational sense that by subjecting himself to a screening test like this, my husband was tempting fate. And added to my faint resentment and fainter dread was a certain envy. He was the one who had made himself pure and ready, while last night's furtively eaten supper of leftovers rotted invisibly in my own unexamined colon. He was the one who would walk into the waters of anesthesia this morning; he was the one who would emerge on the other side while I remained in this anteroom, fully dressed and conscious, a fugitive from medical justice.

Assured of the health of his lower intestinal tract, he would enjoy a brief respite from his chronic anxiety, or at least a respite from this particular anxiety—a part which for a week or so would stand in for the whole. A temporary palliation, but still an enviable one. And besides, for the rest of the day at least, he'd have a legitimate claim on everyone's attention and solicitude, especially mine.

II

Keeping up an aggressively cheerful line of sports patter, a wiry black attendant in purple scrubs led us across the hall and through a set of swinging double doors into another long chilly room, this one windowless and lined with rows of cubicles hung on three sides with drapery. It was a space so big and white and undifferentiated that it made me think of a tent city on the Siberian steppes. Or it would have, if it hadn't been for the glimpses I caught in passing of the patients and families through gaps in the curtains—the gleams of pink or brown flesh, the flashes of colored cloth, the quick impressions of recumbent and bending bodies.

The attendant ushered us into our own drapery-nook, which contained a chair and a hospital bed, both on wheels, and monitoring equipment bolted to the wall. "You the designated driver?" he asked me, and handed me a hospital gown. "Get him out of his clothes and into this. He needs to take it all off except his socks. The nurse'll be along in a moment."

I sat down on the chair while my husband removed his shirt, belt, pants, undershirt and underpants, and finally his shoes, handing me each item. I tried to help him into the hospital gown, but he put an arm into the head-hole at first, and when he got that right, I snapped it up wrong, so that it hung down too low on one side and I had to unsnap it and start over again. My husband had not eaten for more than twenty hours now. He stiffened and sighed as I fussed over him.

This was an old story between us: in all our years together we have yet to learn how to cooperate when puzzling out a thing like a hospital gown. But I felt particularly stung on this occasion because my husband's shivering nudity made him seem so vulnerable, and I had been feeling so tender toward him. I was just about to tell him to do it himself when the nurse flung open the curtains. "Having a little trouble?" she asked, and smoothly remedied the problem.

The nurse was a woman of action; her movements were whippet-quick. In what seemed one continuous motion, she pushed my husband gently onto the bed, popped a thermometer into his mouth and clapped a blood-pressure cuff around his left arm. She ripped open a foil pouch and pulled out an IV needle; after a brief exploration of the back of his hand, she settled on the crook of his elbow as the site for insertion. I looked away, and as I did so I remembered my own stay in the maternity ward twenty years ago when our daughter was born. Every morning, a technician appeared at my bedside to draw blood. "I love coming to this floor," she told me once. "You new moms have such nice big veins."

When I turned back, the nurse had finished, and was securing the

309

needle with a band-aid. "I think he's a little chilly," I ventured. "Don't you want to keep his wallet and keys in your purse?" she replied. "We can't be responsible for items like that." Lying on his back, my husband looked up at the nurse with perfect trust. His eyes were wide, his breathing calm. "Are all those teeth yours?" she asked him, and covered him from his beard to his feet in an insulated blanket. The hands and arms of a second nurse introduced themselves into the cubicle, and my husband slid past me on his high rolling bed. "He'll be an hour or so," said the first nurse, turning back to give me something that looked like a high-tech childrens' toy. By the time I'd identified it as a pager—exactly the kind of device I'd been handed recently while waiting for tables in restaurants—my husband had been wheeled past the nurses' station into the shadows at the far end of the room. "Goodbye," I called out, and then, inappropriately, "Good luck!"

III

Where to? The cafeteria was the natural place, and I had had no breakfast, but perhaps I would be out of range of the pager there. Still, I had an hour before I could expect it to go off. But what if I was needed? But why on earth *would* I be needed?

Should I find somebody to ask? I stood, irresolute, in front of the double doors until I realized I was blocking traffic. The attendant in purple scrubs swept by me with another party in tow, strutting and swivelling his shoulders, hamming it up for my benefit as well as for the family he was escorting. I knew this because as he passed me, he winked. The way time was reckoned in the Endoscopy service, it seemed I was already an old hand.

I was beginning to be uncomfortably hungry, and I remembered that I had a box of raisins in my purse, but I also remembered a sign on the waiting room door: no food or drink. Could I eat my raisins standing casually by the elevator? Too busy there. I'd feel foolish. Instead, I went into the ladies' room and ate them sitting in a stall. Ten years ago I would have smoked a cigarette in the bathroom at a time like this; now I was furtively stuffing raisins into my mouth. With time, it seems, more and more becomes less and less permissible. When I stood up, the toilet flushed itself.

Back in the waiting room it appeared that every seat was taken. They must set aside a single day each week for endoscopy, I was

310

thinking; how otherwise could they fill a space like this? I took a walk around the perimeter. The room contained, I discovered, four distinct areas, each a square carpeted in a different color, each with its own eye-level aquarium and television. I looked for the fast-walking couple, but they were gone. I looked for the Mexican mother with the wide-eyed daughter, but she was nowhere to be found.

I was tempted to picture the waiting room as a refugee camp, or a ship's steerage compartment, but that would have been a romanticized vision. There was a lot of humanity in this place, but nobody was dirty or obviously wretched or suffering openly. Actually one person was—a tall, emaciated, unshaven character with a startled-horse expression and metal braces on his legs. He was talking loudly, in Greek, I thought, and groaning. A young woman I took to be his daughter was shushing him gently and patting his hand. Something about her manner made me guess that his agitation was chronic and not specific to this place and time.

Apart from him, the crowd was conspicuously docile, and that made sense. Many of these people were here, I assumed, to be tested for prudential reasons, like my husband. At his desk by the door, the attendant in purple scrubs barked out a name every few minutes, enunciating each syllable with military precision. From the other end of the room came an occasional softer directive—"Rodriguez family, please come to the nurses' station." This was an efficient operation. Patients walked in, got processed, were rolled out in wheelchairs and decanted into waiting cars, went home.

But what if—I could not help but ask myself—what if, in the course of the explorations of bronchial tubes and esophagi and gastrointestinal tracts that were conducted in the off-limits place where my husband was even now lying on his side under "conscious sedation," something bad was discovered? Better it should be known about: that was the conventional wisdom.

Well yes, if it was a little polyp or discoloration or suspicious spot—something just beginning to make itself known. But what if, in some particular case, a stitch in time had failed to save nine? What if what was discovered during one of these routine procedures was a big fat blossoming out-of-control tumor? What if someone's body had been rude enough to ignore the rules of the screening protocol, which seem to offer a nearly automatic negative result to the patient virtuous enough to observe it? What if, like a drunken party guest who responds to a polite query about his wife with a shocking and unwelcome confession of adultery, this body were to embarrass its host by disclosing a gross pathological secret? What then? Would that throw a spanner into the smoothly functioning works of the Endoscopy service?

This question had been swimming around latently in my mind all morning, but no sooner had I brought it fully into consciousness than I witnessed a little scene that answered it. Three official-looking people, one of whom was a doctor—or so I took him to be: he was wearing a white coat and a stethoscope—trooped into the room and surrounded a small Asian woman. It was like an annuciation scene: two of them actually knelt at her feet. Sad news, it seemed, was gently imparted. The woman wept. The committee rose and departed. A nurse led the the woman away, presumably to the tent city, where the stricken one lay waiting. The whole thing lasted perhaps forty five seconds. Now I saw that the functioning of the Endoscopy Service was no more impeded by the breaking of bad news to a family member than the dinner service at Bennigan's is interrupted when the waiters gather to sing "Happy Birthday to You" to a customer.

I found an empty seat opposite an aquarium. Two big silver carp were doing rounds; each time they took a corner, rows of scales caught the light and flashed sequentially. A beautiful many-fronded creature like an exploding apricot souffle hung high in the water. At the bottom of the tank a black bewhiskered scavenger lay absolutely still, its belly submerged in pebbles.

The aquarium was the size of a bathtub, the water inside it clear as the air in the room. I had read somewhere recently that the contemplation of fish is a cost-effective way to lower blood pressure, and it was true that as I watched them I could feel my pulse rate slowing. The fish were tranquilizers for the masses. Perhaps they were meant to represent a parallel, idealized existence. Be like them, the hospital was telling us. They worry not; neither do they think.

But what if the team of three made another entrance, and what if this time it was my feet at which they knelt? (Was it possible that I had invented a meaning to explain that scene? And had the small Asian woman actually wept, or had I imagined it?) What if I was the one led by the nurse back to the place where they were keeping my husband?

He would be coming out of anesthesia, still too groggy to be alarmed. His doctor would be in attendance, and as I entered the curtained-off cubicle, he would turn to me and take my hand in his. His head cocked, a rueful wince wrinkling his forehead, the doctor would look into my eyes, squeeze my hand, and tell me the news. I'm afraid we have a problem, he would say, and while he was explaining his findings and the likelihood that the biopsy would prove positive, and that immediate surgery would be necessary, I would absorb only a fraction of what he was saying. My husband would have propped himself up on his elbows by now. Comprehension would be dawning, and early terror.

Soon enough I would be sitting at my husband's bedside in a real hospital room with solid walls, offering him post-operative sips of apple juice from one of those little foil-topped plastic tubs with flexible straws. I'd settle into a hospital routine, reading aloud to him when he woke, dozing when he slept. I'd roam the halls in search of the elusive nurse. I'd step outside to get myself a sandwich in the cafeteria, call his mother and brothers and colleagues at the university, but only when I made trips home to sleep for a few hours, take a shower and change my clothes, would I register how tired and frightened I was.

I could imagine the consolations that caring for my husband at the hospital would offer me. I would feel a shameful joy at the prospect of relinquishing my writing ambitions in the service of his care. Everyone would marvel at my capacity for self-sacrifice. After thirty years of running behind, I would take the lead in the who's-a-better-person competition, or so it would seem to outsiders. Only I, and my husband, would need to know that to me, certain kinds of self-abnegation come all too easily.

And then, before I was ready, he would be discharged. Clutching a semi-deflated balloon bouquet, he would be waiting in the regulation wheelchair at the patient pick-up dock when I brought the car around. When we got home, the house would be dusty and cluttered, unfit for an invalid. He would complain, and for the first time since his diagnosis, irritation would flare up in me. I would find that the mobilizing adrenaline that had transformed me into an angel of forbearance and efficiency in the hospital had run low.

My husband would be waking fully to his fear, and I to my loss— not to the unimaginable loss of him to death, but to the more immediate loss of his companionship. Illness would undo and reveal as incompatible two of the intertwined elements of marriage. In caring

313

for him, in dealing with him instrumentally rather than mutually, I would lose him as my friend—my closest, really my *only* friend. He would become, full-time, the querulous recipient of my care he had been since yesterday, a dwindled being, incapable of full reciprocity.

Once, when we were younger, my husband confessed that some-times he thought about what it would be like to have an affair. He concluded that it would be exciting and fun, but then he remem-bered that he would not be able to tell me about it, and that realiza-tion turned the fantasy desolate. If my husband became ill and I became his caretaker, there would be no "telling about" in that case either. Our sessions of intimate, freewheeling, playful talk would come to an end. Our fast-walking days would be over.

What had promised to shape up as a gratifying reverie about my-self as a caretaking martyr had for some reason changed its nature in midflight and become a grimly plausible imaginative probe of the idea of loss. It was all too real, but then so was the Endoscopy wait-ing room. I found myself wishing I'd been allowed to wait in the tent city, which had somehow become a real tent city in my mind's eye, a wintry settlement under a starry sky where families huddled around central fires on earthen floors.

This waiting room was humane enough, in a minimalist kind of way, but it made no provision for imaginative transcendence. The drama of mortality had been reduced here to a matter of risk reduc-tion. There were no grand prospects, no long perspectives—no sight lines, even. I looked around again and saw rows of anxious compliant patients and their designated drivers.

How could all these people remain so calm in the face of what they were awaiting? How could they allow themselves to be "put un-der" and be seen in that unguarded condition by strangers who would insert camera-eyed snakes into their orifices in order to learn the secrets of their mortality—all in the name of prudence, and with-out the compensation of fantasy?

IV

All through our married life, my husband has played the cautious ant, storing up food against the winter, while I've taken the role of the improvident grasshopper, lounging around in the high grass and playing my fiddle.

The analogy breaks down almost immediately, of course. In the fable the ant and the grasshopper are not married to each other; the grasshopper has no legitimate claim on the ant's foodstores, and the ant is under no obligation to feed the grasshopper. And besides, it's a fable, not a novel. It captures the ant and grasshopper as one-dimensional exemplars, not as complex protagonists. It makes no allowance for the ant's nervous admiration of the grasshopper's style, or the grasshopper's stealthy emulation of the ant.

What happened to all that time? How is it that next summer we will have been married for thirty years? Once again, I'm stunned into banality.

We spent those years together—very much together, more so than most of the couples we know—but it was two different kinds of time we were spending. My husband's life has been lived according to ant time, by which I mean the careful piling up of day plus day plus day plus day plus day, each one marked by steady, devoted effort.

My husband has held a university affiliation for over thirty-five years, but he's no scholar. In the parlance of the profession, he "does" philosophy. He does it by writing, and he's done that nearly every day of the week since I've known him. Though his pace was sometimes agonizingly slow, he has amassed a large and impressive body of work. The doggedness of his attack has concealed the spirit of adventure he has brought to it, the daily brinksmanship of a thinker who lives by his wits. A modest, curious, unassuming man, enthralled by intellectual inquiry, he has become an important senior figure in his field. As he's grown older, his work has become steadily bolder, more complex, more original.

My life has been lived according to grasshopper time, marked not by the passage of days, but by long, irregularly spaced eras. I've made a mess of time, like a person who wastes wrapping paper by cutting too big or too small a square to fit the present. Usually too big, I suppose: I took twenty years to complete two college degrees, and I drew out the care of my daughter far longer than anybody seemed to think was necessary. I spent thirty years getting ready to write, but only the last ten writing. Like my husband, I've had a success at it, but it's been a thinner one than his and I'm afraid it may already be over, a rise and fall that feels steep only because it has been compressed into one late decade.

But to say I made a mess of time is to concede too much to the ant's way of reckoning it, and thus to disguise the radical difference between my husband and me. To me, time has never been something to make one's life out of, but rather something to travel through.

It seems I was operating under a half-realized imperative; the idea was to submit myself passively to time, and to wait until further notice was somehow given to me. My life has been like the changing views of open fields and woods and urban rooftops that flash by a passenger in a train. Time has never seemed like an accumulated or accumulating thing to me—not until recently, that is, when I've looked back to see that I've left what looks like an undifferentiated heap of it behind me.

Hard to imagine a union of opposites more extreme than ours, or one with more potential for conflict. In our bitterest fights—they're mostly behind us now, but every time I say so we have a relapse—I accused my husband of living a willfully monotonous, blinkered life in the service of his ambition, of selfishly putting his writing ahead of me and our daughter. He, in turn, accused me of laziness and parasitism, of demanding that he compensate me for the failure of my own life project.

There were years when a conflagration would burst out of a single word: heightened. It became a code for the ant/grasshopper conflict. What do you mean, "heightened?" my husband would demand. What do you mean, you need things to be *heightened*? As he grew frantic in his incomprehension I turned stony in my mysterious knowledge. These scenes ended with shouting and door-slamming, or worse.

Once I marched into his study and swept an entire shelf of philosophy journals, arranged by date and title, off the shelf and into a heap on the floor. While my husband stood over me, his hands flung up in helpless horror, his face contorted like a Yiddish actor playing Lear, I fell to my knees and scrambled the pile of journals, deliberately destroying any vestiges of order that might have survived the original act of sabotage.

Interestingly, though a number of therapists have tried to recruit my husband and me individually, none has been willing to take the two of us on together. I like to think our combined intellectual power intimidated them, but it's more likely that they saw how readily we would unite in the face of a therapeutic intrusion. No doubt they

316

judged us to be hopelessly "enmeshed." There'd be no clean way to separate us; we'd both come away with bloody pieces of the other hanging off. But then I really don't believe that therapy can heal and restore a marriage. I believe time can—lots of time, that is.

For most of my life I've liked to think that I'm a nihilist at heart, one of those people who feel that they can only profit from a new roll of the dice. I've been fascinated by cataclysm, eruption, abrupt reversal, the dire glamor of life-changing diagnoses, the "heightened" life that my husband has always insisted he doesn't understand.

But I think now that I haven't given myself adequate credit. My attraction to nihilism has always had an element of false bluster—what nihilist stays married for thirty years? It was a face-saving distraction, behind which I was slowly preparing myself to write. But it was also a byproduct of my frustrated ardor for meaning, of my impatience with waiting. My mistake was to confuse meaning with the sensation of meaning; meaning itself is not something that can be experienced. It's a slow, impalpable drip and the evidence it leaves of its workings can be assessed only in retrospect.

From within the safety of my marriage I've displayed a swaggering, swashbuckling contempt for caution. My husband has enjoyed and applauded this performance; even though it has amounted to an assault on him, he's found it diverting. I think perhaps he has even drawn strength from it. But recently, since my long, secret apprenticeship has come to an end, I've arrived at a late conversion, I've come to appreciate the impulse of the ant—the desire to protect and maintain, to keep a careful vigil over what one values. The therapists were right: it was a collusion all along.

So now we find ourselves in deep middle age, survivors of our own long, loyal, close, angry marriage. How can I convey the regret I feel at the years we wasted in fighting? And how can I also convey the satisfaction I feel at the strength of the friendship that those years have forged between us? We're like two boxers who've fought so many rounds together that we've decided to forego the late ones in favor of an extended, exhausted clinch.

Or perhaps it's not the depletion of energy I'm talking about, but its diversion. For the past ten years especially, ever since I've become a practicing writer, we've found a new ease and harmony. Under the terms of our writing truce, we've established a number of treaties and reciprocal agreements. Routine, which was oddly lacking in our marriage for the first twenty years, has become important to our writing life. We talk in the mornings over our coffee, and then adjourn to our respective studies. We read and edit one another's work. My husband has tirelessly encouraged my writing and taken real delight in my successes. I've come to understand the strictures that writing imposes on a writer's life, the need to keep it regular and calm.

And during those years, while we were busy writing, our marriage built itself around us like a house, its walls strong enough to withstand the force of any internal explosion—unassailable, even by me. I wish I had known, twenty-five years ago when we were in the worst of it, how the passage of time can turn a marriage into an edifice, a great house almost indistinguishable from all the other great houses of long marriage. Aging is a dispersal, but one of the works of time is the slow conversion of anomaly into universality; the years are a comb tugging ceaselessly at the knot of singularity.

People tend to conflate time and aging, but they are separate influences, with separate spheres. Aging disintegrates the body, but time is a conservator. As it rubs away at the organic, it reveals meaning and pattern.

Even so, I still don't understand why prudence is a virtue. All I understand is that it's prudent to be prudent. Still, I can't deny that the ant's way makes sense for the years immediately ahead of us, because these will be the years in which almost any change will be a change for the worse.

V

But now the pager was dancing in my hand, flashing red and green. I made my way out of the Endoscopy waiting room, back across the hall and past the elevators, through the swinging doors and down the central corridor of the tent city. Once again I caught glimpses of human color and movement through gaps in the white.

Halfway down the room I sighted the fast-walking couple. It was the woman who was the patient, and I received the sudden, strong impression that she was very ill. I saw it in the yellow, waxen soles of her feet, which seemed to jut out of the cubicle into the passageway, and in the stiff disorder of her long white hair, sprung free of the neat chignon she had been wearing in the waiting room. Dressed in her tweeds she had looked enviably lean, but in the hospital gown

318

she showed herself to be painfully thin, just on the edge of emaciation. Her bed had been raised to a sitting position, but her eyes were half-closed and her head lolled to one side. I was shocked by the way she seemed to have come undone; it was as if a large floppy doll loosely stuffed with rags had been propped up in her place. A nurse stood behind her, adjusting a monitor, while her husband sat calmly at her side, reading aloud to her from *Town and Country*.

But it wasn't only the woman's appearance that conveyed the impression of chronic illness. It was also the curtain left carelessly open, an apparent indifference to the reactions of others suggesting that these two were veterans of a long siege.

Even so, I might have been wrong. My husband has often criticized me for my habit of drawing conclusions on the basis of insufficient evidence. The woman might have been very ill or quite well, just coming to from the anesthesia after a routine screening test. I simply didn't know.

At the nurses' station I handed in my pager and asked to be directed to my husband. A pudgy young woman in flowered scrubs led me back down the corridor, past the fast-walkers' cubicle, where the curtain had been pulled shut. We found my husband lying on his back, his eyes wide open. This was a familiar attitude; many times I've turned over in bed to find him looking just like this, instantly alert after waking, already at work in his mind on the problems of his current writing project.

The nurse closed the curtain behind her and stood leafing through what I took to be my husband's chart. Conscious of her expectations, but also suddenly full of feeling, I leaned down to kiss my husband on his forehead. The nurse discreetly smiled her approval and gestured me toward the chair. "He'll be here a little while, while we monitor him," she said, and I saw that he had been hooked up to a gently beeping machine, and that the waves of his heartbeat were calm and regular. I sat down and took his hand.

This nurse had a sweet dimpled face. A few of her molars were missing on the upper left side. I liked her much better than the hyperefficient nurse who had prepared my husband for the procedure. "He did fine," she said, looking up from the chart. "Nothing in here to worry about." I registered a tiny transient thrill of disappointment. The nurse cranked my husband's bed into a sitting position and continued to page through his chart, jotting down notes.

The nurse put down the chart and left the cubicle. She returned with three tubs of juice, offered one to me and two to my husband. He took the two apples, I the remaining grapefruit. She unhooked my husband from the monitor, and the atmosphere in the cubicle turned quietly festive. I was reminded of the happy half hour my husband and I spent in the recovery room after the birth of our daughter, holding her and marveling while medical personnel bustled peacefully around us. There was the same sense then that the unremarkable was being celebrated; things had gone as they should and usually do; all was well.

While we waited for the doctor to arrive, the nurse told stories about patients who made embarrassing disclosures under the anesthetic, patients who screamed during the procedure and boasted afterward that the whole thing had been absolutely painless. "Did I do anything like that?" my husband asked. Oh no, said the nurse. Not you. You did just fine.

Once again, the nurse excused herself. Left alone, my husband and I listened to the limping rhythms of a chorus of monitor beeps in the cubicles around us. My husband turned on his side and confided to me that he was enjoying lying here with me to keep him company, excused from his labors for a little while by medical directive.

I could see by the slow delight dawning on his face that something interesting was occurring to him. He told me that he retained a hazy memory of seeing the probe on the monitor just as it was introduced. But before that, even before the "conscious sedation" drug had begun to do its work, he remembered being advised by the nurse that while he would experience the procedure, he would remember nothing of it. He found himself, he told me, in the odd position of wondering whether or not to dread what was about to happen to him. How, he had asked himself, could he fear something that he would not remember?

The doctor, a comedian, made a flying visit to our tent. He told my husband that everything was normal, though there was some early evidence of the diverticulosis that is almost inevitable with age. The only thing really abnormal about my husband's colon, he told us, was its spectacular length. "A few more feet," he said, spreading his arms wide, "and I would've run out of scope."

My husband got up and put on his clothes as methodically as he had taken them off. Purple Scrubs was waiting outside the curtain with a wheelchair. I took my husband's briefcase, and the three of us rode down the elevator together. While I walked to the parking lot to find the car, getting briefly lost in the process, they waited by the hospital entrance. I pulled up to find the two of them wreathed in smiles and high-fiving one another.

But only when he had opened the car door for my husband would the attendant allow him to get out of the wheelchair; even then he took him by the elbow and solicitously helped him into the front seat. As we drove away, my husband explained that he and the man in purple scrubs had discovered that they were exactly the same age, and that this lively, punctilious, theatrical person who had been shepherding him back and forth all morning had undergone quadruple-bypass surgery just six weeks earlier.

We took the local route home, and that got us embroiled in traffic for half an hour, but even so it was only noon by the time we reached our neighborhood. My husband and I both remarked on how much of the day remained, and how remarkably energetic and alert the procedure had left him. We stopped for lunch at his favorite barbecue stand, and after that he asked me to drop him off at his office, where he would make use of the afternoon by catching up on some work.

Nominated by Richard Burgin

ANYWAYS

by SUZANNE CLEARY

from SOUTHERN POETRY REVIEW

for David

Anyone born anywhere near
        my hometown says it this way,
                with an *s* on the end:
                        "The lake is cold, but I swim in it anyways,"
                "Kielbasa gives me heartburn, but I eat it anyways,"
        "(She/he) treats me bad, but I love (her/him) anyways."
Even after we have left that place
        and long settled elsewhere, this
                is how we say it, plural.
                        I never once, not once, thought twice about it
                until my husband, a man from far away,
        leaned toward me, one day during our courtship,
his gray-green eyes, which always sparkle,
        doubly sparkling over our candle-lit meal.
                "Anyway," he said. And when he saw
                        that I didn't understand, he repeated the word:
                "Anyway. *Way*, not *ways*."
        Corner of napkin to corner of lip, he waited.
I kept him waiting. I knew he was right,
        but I kept him waiting anyways,
                in league, still, with me and mine:

Slovaks homesick for the old country their whole lives
who dug gardens anyways,
and deep, hard-water wells.
I looked into his eyes, their smoky constellations,
and then I told him. It is *anyways*, plural,
because the word must be large enough
to hold all of our reasons. *Anyways* is our way
of saying there is more than one reason,
and there is that which is beyond reason,
that which cannot be said.
A man dies and his widow keeps his shirts.
They are big but she wears them anyways.
The shoemaker loses his life savings in the Great Depression
but gets out of bed, every day, anyways.
We are shy, my people, not given to storytelling.
We end our stories too soon, trailing off "anyways. . . ."
The carpenter sighs, "I didn't need that finger anyways."
The beauty school student sighs, "It'll grow back anyways."
Our faith is weak, but we go to church anyways.
The priest at St. Cyril's says God loves us. We hear what isn't said.
This is what he must know about me, this man, my love.
My people live in the third rainiest city in the country,
but we pack our picnic baskets as the sky darkens.
We fall in love knowing it may not last, but we fall.
This is how we know *home:*
someone who will look into our eyes
and say what could ruin everything, but say it,
regardless.

Nominated by Dan Masterson, Arthur Smith

CLAIRE

fiction by STEVEN BARTHELME

from THE YALE REVIEW

BAILEY LONG had borrowed five hundred dollars from Claire the month before and so the day he came back to borrow another thousand he was a little touchy. He was standing around in her big white apartment with the dusty hardwood floor looking at what she called "Jersey DNA"—a hunk of chrome in a spiral she had found beside a highway.

"Look," he said, "if you don't want to lend it to me don't lend it to me. Don't do things you don't want to do." He always tried to give some advice while he was sponging, to maintain the advantage he had once had over her.

Claire was sitting at a table by a window, watching him. "Well," she said, "I'm sorry, Bailey, but I just don't have it. I can give you three hundred. But I'll need it all back, say a week? When do you figure to get it back?"

Bailey nodded, casually, trying to affect an air of not caring, taking little fractional steps toward the door of her apartment, fidgeting as if he had business, some place to go. He was a small man, but well built and good-looking, or had been before he'd gotten middle-aged, which is what he looked now. "Nevermind," he said. "I didn't know you were tapped."

"Don't be silly," she said, and took a pen from a can of pens on the bright windowsill. The can had once held some kind of fancy fruit from Poland or someplace and the label was striking, green, blue, black. Claire had always found things like that, nice things that Bailey overlooked, didn't notice, couldn't see, on his way to some obvious choice, some thing he had read about in a magazine. Her unerring eye, the ease of it, had always been mysterious to him. She shrugged and settled at the long oval table off the kitchen to write out a check. "You need the money. I have the money."

Claire was more beautiful now than she had been in college and in college she had always drawn a crowd. Stop a clock, Bailey thought. Her hair was shorter now and she was given to skirts and loose cream-colored silk blouses instead of t-shirts and jeans, but age had made her thin face and her gaudy brown eyes more heart-stopping than they had been, and she wasn't foolish any longer, the way she had had to be foolish to carry on an eleven-year love affair with Bailey, living in trashy apartments and making her own clothes and surviving on cheese sandwiches, rice cakes in picante sauce, and beer. Sometimes she seemed like the only thing that had ever happened to him in his whole life.

"Here you go," she said, tearing out the check. "I'd like you to come back tomorrow night, for dinner. I want you to meet my intended. I want to hurt your feelings." She smiled broadly and closed the big checkbook. "How is the store? You a vice-president yet?" She stood up and swung her long skirt around her legs as she turned to hand Bailey the check. "Dinner, tomorrow."

"Don't you want to know what I need the money for?"

"Blackjack?" she said, and smiled. "Isn't it? He's just like you. His name is Dave. You'll hate him."

"Dave? I hate him already. Isn't this like stuff people do in movies?"

Her expression went hard. "Exactly. Yes, exactly like that, jerk. But it's the price of your loan." She pointed at the check. "Okay, sweetie? Tomorrow, around eight."

Bailey nodded, leaving. After he had cashed the check, what could she do about it? He'd be all right with this, a little something scrounged off credit cards, maybe a few hundred on the line of credit at the casino, although that made him nervous. They weren't the kind of people you wanted to write bad checks to, really. Start with this, maybe get on a roll, he thought.

When he got to the parking lot in front of the apartments, he saw something move inside his car as he approached it, and his heart started to race. When he got to the car and looked in, a cat, black with blue eyes, was lying on the back seat. What the hell? he thought, and looked around. The parking lot was almost empty. Trees shivered lightly in a gentle wind. He pulled open the rear passenger door. "C'mon," he said. "Get out, stupid."

The black cat, emaciated and hostile looking, sat staring at him, curled on the back seat like a furry black shrimp. Bad luck, Bailey thought.

"C'mon. Get out of the car. C'mon, kitty. I don't know who put you in here, but time to get out." The cat watched him. Bailey reached carefully in over its head and took hold of the scruff of the neck and lifted the cat out of the seat. "Jesus," he said. "You're just bones. You haven't eaten in a month. Easy now." When he carried it to the grass, it curled its back legs up like a kitten. He set it down on the lawn and then stepped backward, away. "Go on," he said, but the cat didn't move, lying the way Bailey had deposited it, head up and tail hidden under its body. It let out a sharp, sudden yowl that sounded as though it had just remembered something, an afterthought, and then it blinked.

"Okay," Bailey said. "Just a second."

He shut the back door of the car and opened the front one, reached in and shook a chocolate bar and a crumpled bag of Cheetos out of a brown paper bag onto the seat. He opened the chocolate bar, broke off a brown corner, and took it to the cat. The cat looked, looked away. "Try it. Here, watch," he said, and took a bite from the bar himself. He nudged the broken-off piece closer to the cat, which recoiled slightly, and the chocolate slipped down between blades of grass.

"Twit," Bailey said, and walked back over to his car, finishing the candy bar, glancing back a couple of times. He sighed, and reached in for the Cheetos and uncrumpled the bag. Caught in the bottom were a few scraps of Cheetos, which Bailey emptied onto his palm. He walked back over. The cat yowled again. An old man in wool pants and a brown shirt had come out of his apartment and stood watching them from fifteen feet away.

"Your cat?" Bailey said.

"I like dogs," the old man said. "That looks sick."

Bailey crouched down and opened his hand. The cat jerked forward and cleaned all three Cheetos in one bite. "Hey," Bailey said, and pulled his hand back as the cat tried to lick orange dust from his palm.

"You better get rid of it," the old man standing on his doorstep said. "No pets here."

"It's not mine," Bailey said. He glanced back down the walkway, hoping Claire would come out of her apartment and neutralize this old man somehow.

"You're feeding it," the man said. "Just put it back in your car, boy. Take it to the SPCA, they know what to do with trash animals. Go on."

"Why don't you shut the hell up?" Bailey said. When he looked back down, the cat had slipped away underneath his car. "God damn it."

A blond boy standing on the other side of Bailey's car waved to the old man. "Hey, Mr. Keys, what's going on? Is there a problem?" He looked across at Bailey.

Bailey knelt beside his car. "Shh, go away, I'm stealing a car." He reached under and pulled the cat out.

"This man's trying to ditch his cat here," the old man said.

"Yeah, but Mr. Magoo here caught me," Bailey said, again holding the squirming cat by the scruff of the neck.

"You're kind of sarcastic?" the boy said, coming around the car. He was fair, muscular, wearing an expensive t-shirt and tailored khaki shorts. A weird, hairless-looking gray dog walked up as the boy stopped halfway between Bailey and the old man.

The dog sat on its haunches for a millisecond before it saw the cat, which had already shaken loose from Bailey's grip. The cat landed upright, looked hastily right and left, and then disappeared backward under the car again while the dog hit the open passenger's door and fell, bounced up again. The dog was snarling, its long, fetishy muzzle reaching under the car. "Get this damn dog," Bailey yelled, kicking at it.

"Hey," the boy said. "He won't hurt him." He and the old man were walking over.

"He'll scare the poor little fucker to death, Kato, what're you talking about," Bailey said. He affected a childish, mocking voice: *"He won't hurt him."*

The dog jumped back, yelling, a weird, twisting cry that began in a growl and then raced into something higher pitched and plaintive. It backed away from the side of the car, looking confused, blood all over its face.

The boy was beside it, kneeling down to it, checking the dog's eyes, talking, soothing it with his voice. He looked up at Bailey. "I've got a Magnum in my car," he said. "You better get that fucking cat out of here, 'cause I'm gonna kill it." The dog started growling again.

"None of that," the old man said, frightened. "None of that now, Davey. You're not supposed to have that dog, you know? I haven't said anything, but—"

"Go inside, Mr. Keys," the boy said, his hand in the dog's collar, restraining it.

"All right," Bailey said. He slammed the passenger door shut and started around the car, then stopped and made a slow sweeping motion with his hand. "All right. Just get the dog away."

The cat, under the far side of the car, lay limp on the blacktop, fast breaths heaving in its gaunt sides, you could see its lungs. Bailey dragged it out as gently as he could, opened the car door and set the cat on the back seat. "Way to go," he whispered, getting into the car.

The blond boy shook his head and sneered. Bailey let the car roll backward out of the parking lot and drove away, thinking he would drop the cat on the next corner, and the next, and the next. But he didn't; he took it home and locked it in his extra bathroom with an ancient can of tuna fish and a plastic dishpan full of newspaper as a litter box.

The next day Bailey called in sick at work and went back to sleep until late afternoon. After a shower, he cashed Claire's check at her bank and went by an ATM to squeeze what he could from seven credit cards, then got a soft drink at a drive-through and rolled out of town, headed for the coast casinos with a little over five hundred dollars. He had won sometimes, it wasn't always losing, but even quitting while you were ahead took a discipline that he couldn't seem to maintain once he got inside the places.

Don't eat ice, Bailey told himself, chewing. His teeth were cracked already, lines running up and down every one he looked at when he leaned in close to a mirror, which he did on occasion. It meant you were orally fixated, too, which meant something—you wanted to suck a tit, you were childish, or something. Got that right, Bailey thought. But a quarter of the population smokes cigarettes, which means the same thing supposedly, so it's not so bad, being childish. If you weren't oral, you were anal, was that any better? No way.

He tilted his cup up for more ice. No way, he thought. He had been in the car an hour now, and had another hour's ride. Twilight was rising up ahead of him, orange and dark, reminding him of a place he and Claire had had once, a tiny apartment on one side of a lake with hills on the other side. The apartment had a balcony where they'd sit and watch the sun set behind the hills. One afternoon she said, "I bet there's a pile of big orange suns lying around over there somewhere."

Bailey laughed, raised his cup. He would stop in Gulfport, eat a comp steak at that fancy restaurant, then drive down the beach highway to Biloxi. He liked the dealers better there. Maybe I'll make a couple grand and return her money the very next day, he thought. Here, baby, I appreciate the loan. In fact I'm buying you dinner. Bring what's his name.

He had first come down here for a stupid sales education conference that he didn't need, didn't want, and a waste of two weeks of his time and two thousand dollars of the store's money. The "rotunda concept" was what they were big on that year, get the stiffs walking in a circle, merch to the right, merch to the left. . . . Most of the great merchandising concepts were equally sly. He shook his head. The first time he had come down here he had won eight hundred dollars, like it was easy, like it was meant to be. He even won two hundred on a slot machine. Patterson was unhappy when he found out about it, but it had been the old man's idea to send Bailey to the dumb sales conference.

They found out about everything. He remembered when he was hired, how he had been surprised that they knew Claire's name, where she lived, what she did, how long they'd been together. They even knew that girl's name—Dashy—that Bailey was fooling around with when he and Claire split up. "What're y'all running, a department store or the CIA?" he'd said, and none of them had laughed. They actually had a department called "Intelligence." Patterson himself wasn't so bad, just nosy. He paid well, and had done well by Bailey, shooting him up to the second spot in marketing in less than three years, him without even a business degree. Then when they sold the chain to a bigger chain, Patterson had become some kind of token figure, ceased to matter, near as Bailey could tell.

Then he'd started gambling, which was more interesting. It was a department store, who could stay interested in that? It was dull, although he liked the people who worked on the floor, all the clerks and stock people and the tech crew, the people that built displays, moved stuff around. The people who ran the place were horrible, piously stabbing each other for dimes and for the old man's favor. The smart alecks and old drunks at the casinos were far better company. And you never knew, you might make a killing some day, and bye-bye, nine to five. Pay off all the damn blood-sucker credit cards.

He had his free dinner at the steakhouse on top of one of the casinos, and then drove down to Biloxi to another to play. Two and a half hours later, even betting cautiously and not drinking, he was into his line of credit for a thousand dollars, with about half that left, twenty green chips lined up in front of him.

The dealer was some girl, not anyone he knew, lots of brown hair, very good-looking, looked like a magazine girl, with a magazine girl's indifference. She looked about eighteen but she had two kids, and she was twenty-four. Bailey was thinking about trying another table, when she said, "Press," quietly, and then, when he gave her a doubtful look, reassumed her indifferent expression. She hadn't said more than a dozen sentences in an hour. Bailey stacked the chips, all he had, in one tall stack the way he had seen people do. It was always jerks who did it, but they always won. He pushed the stack onto his spot, and got two face cards and doubled his money. "Black out," she called out for the pit boss, and gave Bailey black hundred-dollar chips. He left it all on the spot and doubled it again. And again. And again. She was paying him in purple chips, five hundred dollars apiece. "Wait," Bailey said, and reached out and settled his hand on the chips. The object, he thought, is to get out of this fucking place with some of their money.

The pit boss was standing sort of sideways behind the dealer, watching. Bailey looked up at the girl, who was waiting for his bet, her hand poised over the shoe, her eyes gently blank as if her whole consciousness was pulled back somewhere well behind them. "I don't have the nerves for this," Bailey said. Still nothing.

A Vietnamese man walked up to the table, set some bills down in front of him, looked at Bailey's hand still resting on his chips, then at his face, and picked up the bills and walked away. The pit boss smirked, a chubby guy with stiff permed gray hair and a name tag that said "Lucky." "You're on a roll," he said. "Let it ride." It was a dare, a taunt.

Bailey, sweating, looked at his utterly indifferent dealer again. "Bets," the girl said. Okay, he thought. Once more. He shook his head and stacked all the chips on the round spot on the felt in front of him. "Be nice," he said, and she dealt out the cards. He got a thirteen, an eight and a five, and she dealt herself a deuce. She looked at him.

"Dealer's ace," Lucky said. "Glad that's not my eight grand." He laughed, and glanced away, over at each of the other tables in the pit, as if this game were already over. "She could still break," Lucky said, doubtfully, and laughed again.

Just a stupid thing everybody says about deuces, Bailey thought, but he didn't like that the pit boss had counted his chips, or counted them so accurately. Or maybe they had it fixed. Players' paranoia, he thought. Can't mean anything. The dealer was waiting for him to play. Not this, he thought, shaking his head. It's twelve against a three you're supposed to hit. But he tapped the felt with his index finger twice, asking for a hit. She laid down a card, a three, now he had sixteen. The pit boss rocked, smirking. Bailey lifted his hands in a gesture of surrender, took a breath, rocking, too, a little, forward and back, he couldn't stop the movement. "I'm good," he said, and waved his hand flat above his cards. "I'll stay. Turn it up."

She turned up her down card, a queen, spades.

"That's a start," the pit boss said. "That's a good start."

The girl dealt herself another card, a deuce, and then a third deuce. It was taking forever. "Sixteen," she said, and stopped, and a hint of a smile slipped over her face. Why wasn't she dealing it? Bailey thought. Do it. "Twenty-six?" she said, and flipped out another card, another queen.

"Twenty-six," Bailey said, breathing out, and he shook his head sharply as he felt tears rising in his eyes. "It's twenty-six. Dealer busts."

"Misdeal," Lucky shouted. And then, when he saw the look on Bailey's face, "Little jokie." And then he wandered away to a telephone and a computer at a stand in the middle of the pit.

"Color these up," Bailey said, pushing his chips toward the dealer. "I can't—" He shrugged. "—do this."

He watched, wondering if he had figured it right, trying to recount his stacks himself as she counted up his chips and made stacks from hers, all purples, sixteen thousand dollars. Lucky was back, watching. "Sixteen thousand," the girl said.

"Sixteen thousand," Lucky said. "Okay."

When she had pushed the chips across to Bailey, he took one and slid it across the insurance line to her and slipped the rest of them

331

into his shirt pocket. "Thank you, ma'am," he said. His hands were shaking.

The girl took it blankly. "Thank you, sir," she said, then called out, "Dropping five hundred for the dealers, for the boys and girls," and slipped the chip into the toke box by her right hand. The dealers at the other tables turned to look.

Get out, Bailey thought, checking his pocket. Cash it all in. Don't look at the slots. Don't think. Walk to the cashier, he thought, and headed that way. At the main cage he asked for twelve thousand in a check and the rest in cash. The IRS would hear, anything over ten. It only took a few minutes, but getting the chips cashed in felt like landing an airliner. He looked this way and that. Suddenly all the casino patrons looked like sleazy bit actors on *NYPD Blue.*

It wasn't until he was in the car on the highway with the dark pine trees and bare fields passing by outside that he began to breathe easy again, and even then he kept patting his pocket for the fold of hundreds and the twelve-thousand-dollar check they'd given him. And then he started laughing, quietly, to himself, but that made him self-conscious so he just shook his head a little.

He drove straight to Claire's, but he didn't get there until after midnight, and the windows of her apartment were all dark. Then he remembered the dinner he had been supposed to come to. Whoops, he thought. Well, I never said I'd be there. I'll take her to dinner tomorrow, he thought. Take some roses, too. *Really* piss her off. So he pulled out of the parking lot and drove back to his own apartment.

He had completely forgotten the cat, which started yowling the moment his key went in the door lock and didn't let up until he opened the bathroom door. "Jesus," Bailey said, "shut up. You aren't winning any friends that way." The cat sat on the edge of the bathtub, looking up.

Bailey let it follow him into the kitchen, where he shuffled through the cabinets looking for something to feed it. "Looks like you're out of luck, Slick," he said. "That was my only can of tuna fish." He took down a plastic bag of chocolate chip cookies and ripped it open.

"Here," he said, and dropped a cookie on the linoleum in front of the cat, which looked at it. "Moist and chewy," Bailey said. "And don't give me any twaddle about this, as until yesterday you've been eating out of the garbage unless I miss my guess. I'll get some Cheetos tomorrow." He dropped another cookie beside the first one, and the cat set himself down to dinner. "That's better," Bailey said.

He went into the living room and lay back in the big chair, watching the kitchen doorway, waiting for the cat to come in and start hassling him again. He turned on the TV, but left the sound muted, and thought about the money that was still in his shirt pocket, touching it every once in a while. It came to him that Claire wouldn't care about it, not at all. She'd be happy to take her loan money back, but that's all. He hadn't done anything at all, the way she saw it. Just didn't matter to her. He ran through some channels on the TV, settled on some talk show, set the control down. He touched his pocket, looked toward the kitchen. "God-damn it," he said, "get in here, you pest."

It was a little after four in the morning when he went out and got in his car and started back over to Claire's apartment. He wasn't drunk. He'd had a couple beers to try to mellow out, but it hadn't worked. There was no way he was going to be able to sleep with all that brand-new money. There was something disappointing about it, anyway. It was like being a kid and doing something really spectacular about which no one cared, like getting all the way home through the woods without ever touching the ground, or hitting a home run in an empty ballpark, when it didn't count.

Maybe they could try again, him and Claire. He didn't feel about new women the way he had felt about her, that it mattered, that it could end well, that it might not end. You met a woman and even if you had more than fifteen minutes' worth of talk in common, even if she could say something interesting or funny, you were thinking, when do we find out what's wrong with her, what's wrong with me that she can't tolerate, how long before we find out. But he didn't feel about Claire the way he felt about them, either, that weird sort of hunger for them, for their faces, for their eyes. Claire's eyes were beautiful but it wasn't the same. You know me, you don't know me, look, don't look, don't look away.

The place was all dark when Bailey got there, and he sat in his car out front, trying to think of a way to put it, something to say to her, looking at the still, sleeping apartment building. But what did he want to say? The small lights in glass at the corners of the building, marking the ends of the three walkways into the interior courtyard, seemed friendly, almost like living things. He turned the key part way in the ignition to get the dashboard clock to light. 4:24. This is not normal behavior, he thought. This is the way I used to behave, before I got a job. Marketing.

On the concrete walk, he stepped as lightly as he could, making his way into the courtyard and then past a half-dozen doors to hers. His knock was stuttering, and waiting, he glanced quickly up and back the walk, afraid to see a light come on in some other apartment. Claire's door swung open a few inches, and she stood blinking her brown eyes at him, holding her shoulders. Air-conditioning floated out around her.

"You're late, Bailey," she said, and frowned. "You're way late." She was dressed in an aluminum-colored negligee edged with lace, and floppy white socks. She was wearing her glasses, and Bailey felt suddenly as if he had accidentally touched her, bumped into her. It seemed unfair that he was so close to her and she should look like this, like she had a life, preoccupied. It wasn't what he had expected, although he hadn't really expected anything. But it was as if they had agreed ever since their final separation to meet in a certain way, relaxed, not formal, but not en dishabille either, not personal.

"For dinner, I mean," she said. "I was asleep."

"I brought your money back," Bailey said. "All of it." It sounded pathetic, but everything else he could think of seemed wrong.

She began to laugh, sleepily, and then nodded, more to herself than to him, and opened the door. There was a gray dog standing beside her. The apartment's white walls looked faintly yellow in the moonlight. "By all means, then," she said. "Come in."

Bailey stood staring at the dog, the same dog from yesterday afternoon, or its twin brother. He was shaking his head, trying to sort it out, trying to separate the scene in the parking lot and Claire, Claire and the dog, four o'clock in the morning and—

"Come in," she said again, emphatically. Behind her, standing in the tiny hall at the doors to the apartment's bathroom and bedrooms, was the boy who owned the dog. He was holding a pair of slacks in one hand, barefoot on the wood floor, wearing boxer shorts and brushing his ninety-dollar haircut back with his hand, looking at Bailey, who didn't really know what to do.

Bailey stepped inside and the air conditioning hit him full force. The dog loped back to the blond boy. The boy put his pants on.

Claire, having added a pale blue oxford shirt, tried to shake off Bailey's stare, looked away, looked back, then again, the same gesture, and failing, started talking.

"Oh stop. It's the middle of the night and you have come to my place ostensibly to return some money at—" She checked the clock

334

on the microwave on the kitchen counter, squinting. "—at four forty-five a.m., which is not really banking hours, you know, after failing to appear at a dinner at which you agreed to appear and which was bought and cooked as per agreement, if you know what I mean. So stop fucking staring at me."

"I think you'd just better go," the boy said.

"Dave," Claire said, and shot a glance at him.

"Okay," he said.

"This is Bailey Long," she said. "My old flame. Love of my former life. Bailey, Dave Boyette, my fiancé." She slid up on a barstool beside the counter.

"Hi," Bailey said, and then to Claire, "We ran into each other yesterday." *Davey*, he thought, still trying to assemble the pieces of the situation into something coherent. The old man called him "Davey." "Somebody put a cat in my car," he said, and then he thought, She won't get that, that doesn't make any sense at all. "It's a long story," he said. "This kid carries a gun, did you know that? It's in his car? It's one thing to hang around with teenagers, but *armed* teenagers?"

"Look—" Dave began, but this time Claire only had to look at him. He sighed. "Okay," he said.

"Bailey, this is Dave Boyette. My fiancé," she said, and wiggled her toes in her sock, pointing. "The one I told you about."

"Yeah, but I didn't take you seriously," Bailey said.

"You probably should have," the boy said, advancing into the front room for the first time, passing between Bailey and Claire and walking around the counter into the kitchen, taking a new tack. "Do you want a beer or something? Pepsi?" His dog came with him, shy of Bailey, settling on a throw rug near Claire's feet.

She slid off the bar stool. "Well, if we're going to have . . . conversation," she said, "I'll feel more comfortable with some clothes on. I'll be a minute. You boys can start over, how about?" she said, and walked back into the bedroom.

"She's a great lady," Dave said, breaking the silence. "You want something?"

"Beer. A beer," Bailey said. He sat at the table off the kitchen by the front window and took the money out of his shirt pocket, set the roll in front of him and counted off eight hundred-dollar bills, his debt. "Listen, I'm sorry about the other afternoon. It really wasn't my cat."

"So you're the big gambler," Dave said. He handed a bottle over to Bailey and took a chair across from him. "I go down there sometimes."

"No, I'm a department store salesman who plays too much blackjack," Bailey said, looking around for Claire.

"What's all that?"

"Money," Bailey said.

"I could tell that much." Dave sat back in his chair. "You're making this harder than it has to be, you know? I'm trying to get along, and I really don't have any reason to."

Bailey settled his head in his hand and shook it gently. This must be what it comes to, he thought. Sitting here sick at your stomach, getting advice about life from a teenager. This is how you pay for rank stupidity, for slovenliness, for falling a little short at everything your whole life long.

He looked across at Dave. "Sorry. I didn't mean to be making it hard. That's money I owe Claire, some of it is, which I am paying her back, which she lent me." He looked over his shoulder toward the back of the apartment. "Sorry I woke you up. When is it you're getting married?"

"December," Dave said. "I wanted to do it right away, but Claire wanted to wait. Her parents are in Fort Worth—but I guess you know them."

Bailey nodded. He heard a whistle from outside the window, and then again. That's a bird, he thought. That's morning. He looked toward the window, but the sky hadn't begun to light. "What do you do for a living, Dave?"

"Now you sound like her parents," the boy said. "I'm second year at the law school. I was managing Bechtold's—the restaurant—but you know, I needed to make—"

Bailey looked up, then followed the boy's glance to Claire, who had apparently been watching. "That's better," she said. Now she was wearing white jeans and a shirt of her own, white, a short, sleeveless tunic.

"A Snapple?" Dave said, standing and reaching for the refrigerator door. She smiled, his answer.

Bailey looked at the table in front of him. "I guess I'll go," he said. "Sorry to barge in, I don't know what I was doing. No, I know what I was doing. I just won sixteen grand and I had to tell somebody, I guess." He picked up his money and stuffed it into his pocket.

"Here's the eight I owe you," he said and handed Claire the hundreds he had taken from the roll.

She took the money and kissed him, laughing. "You really won sixteen thousand dollars? That's great, Bailey. Aren't you happy? You're going to quit now, I hope?"

Dave let the refrigerator door fall closed and handed her a bottle of what looked like pink lemonade. "Jesus," he said. "That's a lot of money."

"Bailey?" Claire said.

"I gotta go," he said, and nodded to Dave. "It was good to meet you."

Dave stood to shake hands. The dog got to its feet. "Good to meet you," Dave said.

"I'll walk you out?" Claire said. She took a drink of lemonade and set the bottle on the table beside the hundreds, but then thought better of it and picked the bottle up again and walked out the door, leaving Bailey and the boy standing there.

"Goodnight," Bailey said and turned and followed Claire outside.

He found her sitting with her lemonade beside her on a low concrete wall at the edge of the property, near where his car was parked. It was still not quite morning, although the air was wet and birds were already chirping and whistling all around.

"I wanted to show you all this dumb money," Bailey said, taking it out of his pocket in a ball, staring at it. "Isn't that pathetic?" He settled beside her on the concrete wall, shaking his head slowly back and forth. "You're busy doing the watata with the sweetheart of Sigma Chi." He shrugged. "Sorry. I didn't mean that." He threw the money on the grass.

Claire laughed. "And you accuse *me* of making movie gestures?" she said, and slipped off the wall.

"Okay," Bailey said, "Right. Give me that back. Make sure the ink isn't running on that damn check."

She handed him the dewy money, yawning.

"All the good gestures have been gestured," he said, replacing it in his shirt pocket. "So, I mean, what are you thinking? Breeding stock? It's not only that he's not me, he's not even *like* me."

"You'd like that better?" Claire said, sipping lemonade. The glass bottle clanked when she set it back down on the wall.

"No, I guess not. But he has a dog. He has a gun. He's a goddamn norm. He's the enemy."

337

"He wants to have children."

"Oh, Jesus, it *is* breeding stock." Bailey caressed the concrete wall absentmindedly, then realizing it, lifted his hand to touch his forehead with the tips of his fingers, then clapped his hand on his jeans above the knee. "Look, marry me. We'll have children, tomorrow, or Friday. I'd like to have children. Can we use a Skinner box? We have these gahunga cat carriers for dogs at the store—perfect for children. Claire?"

She was watching a police car cruising up the street and past the apartments. The cop, a kid wearing sunglasses even though it had barely gotten light, gave them his best stare as he passed. "Only you are good enough for me, is that it?" she said.

Bailey's heart sank a little. That was it. It occurred to him for the first time that maybe it wasn't true, or that maybe the whole notion of "good enough" didn't have anything to do with it. "No," he said, weakly. "Don't be silly."

"We're in love," Claire said. "Whether we meet your specifications or not."

"I got a new cat," Bailey said. "Somebody here put it in my car Monday while I was talking to you. When I came out, it was in the car. I tried to leave it here. Then your precious boyfriend drove up and offered to blow it away with his big pistola. I guess he's a dog person." He feigned a smile. "I keep trying to figure out when my life ended. It wasn't when we split up, it was before that. It was when I got that goddamn job, I think. I just didn't notice because the job itself was distracting. Anything can be interesting for a while. And then you dumped me. It's like, this money, this sixteen grand? I stopped caring about it ten minutes out of Biloxi. What good is it? I can pay off credit cards."

"You had another girl," Claire said. "Did you forget? She was about twenty and very tall, if I remember correctly." She laughed, then stopped as abruptly as she had started and rubbed her chin, a weird, mannish gesture. "I remember every damn thing about her. She had a stupid name. Dashy. One of her charms, I guess."

"You don't feel like your life ended? Really? I don't mean when we split up." Bailey looked at her, looked away. "Like what you're doing now is just so much busy work?"

In her white outfit, in the soft morning light, she didn't look so much uncomprehending as horribly indifferent. She shrugged. "I got older."

Bailey stood up. "All that time, when we were together, when I was a lowlife, a slacker, every goddamn day, it was electric. Something wonderful was coming. I remember how wonderful stuff at the grocery store was, those Rubbermaid things and the little hardware display and funny vegetables. Then I got a job and a nice fat salary." He turned his palms up and gave her a puzzled look. "All gone," he said.

"Bailey, I don't—"

"No," he said sharply, suddenly afraid. "Nevermind. Sorry to bother you with this rot." He smiled, a quick fake. Who knows what she might have been about to say, he thought. It was okay that she was intending to marry some perfectly ordinary young blond boy and go off to believe with him in everything that in the past they together had not believed in. It was even okay to no longer believe in the things that they had believed in together. But he didn't want to hear that it had never happened, that he had understood it wrong, that he had in fact been alone then, too.

The idea of it made him shudder. She put her arm around him, leaning in, as if to kiss him, and hesitated. "Bailey?"

"Anyway, this cat is skinny," he said, "looks like he hasn't eaten since the Bicentennial. You'll come to see him sometime. He's black, looks a little like Otto." He glanced vaguely out into the damp morning air, closed his eyes, and shuddered again. "Still like cats, don't you?" he said, waiting, urgently, for her kiss.

Nominated by Ben Fountain III

339

TOUR DAUFUSKIE

by TERRANCE HAYES

from PLEIADES

In that small coastal town
in the last century
during one of its tropical storms

people tied to the necks
of pine trees drowned

when the wires and whips
and webs and ropes of
rain covered their bodies

so that when our small golf cart crept
along the dirt back roads

and we paused to
photo the AME church
and one room schoolhouse
and small shacks of
the black folk of Daufuskie

no voices trailed us
or floated out to greet us.

Sometimes now
the trunk of a tree

340

resembles the waist
of a black body;

sometimes your naked waist
still and rooted before me,
smells thick and sweet
as the freshly cut meat of a pine.

Woman, Woman, Woman, when I knock
against you, it is like swimming
from the world

out to the small island of Daufuskie
in the witching hour of a storm,
like drowning in the arms of a tree.

Nominated by Toi Derricotte, Eleanor Wilner

THE POISON THAT

PURIFIES YOU

fiction by ELIZABETH KADETSKY

from THE GETTYSBURG REVIEW

> *I dreamed that the beloved entered my body*
> *pulled out a dagger*
> *and went looking for my heart*
>
> —Rumi

JACK IS WALKING THROUGH CONNOUGHT PLACE. The area is laid out in several concentric circles with a park in the middle. He has noticed that the closer to the park you get, the more you are hassled. Near the perimeter a man selling colorful stuffed puppets from Rajasthan attaches himself to Jack. "Pretty doll you buy sir for pretty daughter?"

"*Meri beti nahin,*" Jack responds bluntly, keeping his hands in his pockets. This is decent enough Hindi for "I have no daughter." A few words of Hindi are usually enough to discourage a hustler, but this one persists, in his bad English.

"For cousin sir. Little girl like little doll sir." The man tails Jack for several yards, until the duo is intercepted by a young couple from, probably, France. The woman has a maternal way about her that the vendor seems to sense as well. "Madam pretty doll for pretty daughter." She pauses long enough to gaze at the puppet. *Her first misstep,* Jack chuckles to himself as he separates from the vendor. It will take her hours to shake him.

342

Closer to the center Jack pauses to sip from his water bottle. He's thirsty enough, but he also thinks of the water as an antidote to the air around him, which is black with ash and exhaust. He lowers it from his mouth and keeps walking, holding the cap in one hand, the bottle in the other. In a few paces he will stop to take another sip, only he doesn't get there. A slight man with a close beard and prominent cheekbones, wearing black trousers and loafers, cuts him off. "Excuse me sir," he says. This man's diction is closer to standard English. Still accented, it suggests a better comprehension of words than the doll hawker's. "You know there are ten million microbes per cubic centimeter of air in Delhi," the man begins.

Jack looks at him dumbly.

The man is gesturing to Jack's water bottle.

"Really it is a health hazard, this."

Jack wants to know what *this* is, but he's wary of giving the man the impression he actually wants to have a conversation. Up to now the interaction has been solely a matter of one man assailing another. Until he gives a sign of consent, he is not actively taking part. Jack has not been a willing interlocutor with anyone in Connought Place, ever. He has only been hustled. He's glad that he's never given in, but as of this morning, he's also decided maybe he should give in sometimes, too.

He made the decision at the Ankur Guest House, where he is staying for five dollars a night near Delhi Station. There are no sheets or towels. He sleeps on a mattress in a room with no natural light, right on the mattress cover. This has given him pause. After five months in India, Jack now believes that comfort is a misnomer. Sleeping on a mattress cover is not uncomfortable. It only requires you to imagine your relationship to the people around you differently. It requires you to allow them closer to you, in every way. Raw and unwashed, the uncovered mattress connects you to the person who was here before you. And by association, it allows you closer to all of Delhi.

Sleeping at the Ankur last night, Jack imagined that his body and the mattress were like two continents buffing against each other. Exposing the continent of his body to the continent of the mattress caused them to join slightly, the contours of one shore interlocking with the contours of the other. He wanted the sand of the far shore to make its way into his own skin, to make it darker and tougher, better prepared for danger.

Jack woke up with the realization that only in this skin with its bigger pores could he engage in an honest relationship with India. He wants to become a part of this continent, to experience a true interchange before he gets on a plane back home—whenever that is. This has become the single precondition for his return, in fact; forging an enduring alliance with this place, and its people, will inure him to the sterile California roadways that await him—their clean yellow lines, their sidewalks freshly scrubbed, the bushes at their shoulders so green, so free of grime and soot they seem to have been painted onto the landscape. He will stay in India longer, as long as it takes to erase this painted landscape from his memory. He will let India deep inside him. The squalor of India will become a part of him, so much so that it will have lost the power to make him feel dirty.

The hustler's open face peering at him, his hand gesturing neatly toward his water bottle, reminds Jack that this very man could be one of the Delhi-ites who has slept on his mattress. The impression of this man's very body could be sunk inside of it. If Jack is willing to sleep on canvas cast in the shape of this man's body, or a body *like* his body, he might at least talk to him.

Jack clears his throat. "What's *this?*" He is aware that his tone might seem mildly threatening.

"You should never leave the top off of the water container, you see." The man pauses, as if Jack should follow his logic effortlessly, which he doesn't. "Delhi is the second most polluted city in the world, see, according to the *India Today*. So you see."

"Actually I don't."

"The microbes. They will fall from the air into your container. And when you sip, you will drink the microbes. Foreign bellies are not constructed to drink microbes. A missing enzyme or something like this. Really you must put on the top. Now. Really sir. Now exactly. It is actually quite imperative." The man is making fluttering gestures with his fingers, so they impersonate butterfly-like creatures dropping from the sky. He looks at the bottle with an alarmed expression. It seems to Jack that even if the man is a hustler, his anxiety about the continuing exposure of his water to the air is genuine.

Jack gazes at the mouth of the bottle and lifts it to his lips. "But I'm drinking."

"Please sir, you must only drink inside. If you don't mind. Could I invite you?"

The heat outside is enormous. Peering back at his bottle, Jack realizes he's drunk a third of it in just the time it took to walk here from the Ankur. This means that right now there's about a half-liter of water moving by gesture of peristalsis into his bladder, and he has to pee. A café, with a toilet, is certainly in order.

With the same neat movement of his hand, the man points to a café on the rim of the park. "I buy you coffee. Western man likes Indian coffee nah? Very sweet. Too sweet."

Jack nods, following.

The café is one of those brightly lit chrome and Formica spaces that in the States would look glaring and uninviting. Here, the layers of grit subdue the harsh tones. The toilet is suitably foul. In India Jack has gotten in the habit of washing his hands before rather than after he pees, for salutary reasons. As expected there's no soap. He pulls a miniature bar from his fanny pack and unwraps it; he bought it for five rupees this morning with the water, at the *paniwalla's*. There is no urinal or squat toilet, only a Western toilet, de rigueur at Connought Place, gathering place for foreigners. The toilet seat is speckled with the requisite drops of urine. Jack considers whether he should risk touching the urine to lift the seat with his hand and thus pee straight into the bowl; leave the seat up and probably wind up adding his own pee to the drops; or clean the toilet seat so as to avoid touching the urine when lifting it. He chooses the latter, allowing that it works against his new resolution about the mattress. He pulls a tissue from his fanny pack as he meditates on the many shades of meaning between *sanitary* and *salutary*.

The man's name is Rohit. He tells Jack about his upbringing shuttling between London and Delhi, and what brought him back to this nation of "wretchedness and dross," as he puts it. Jack considers whether Rohit's diction is that of someone who's lived half his life in London; until now he assumed Rohit was overstating the Western side of his story.

He also realizes that Rohit is a very beautiful man. He has slender wrists with a light covering of long and shiny black hairs. The skin on his face is a deep olive and so smooth that it, like the hairs on his arms, seems to shine. This glow makes it hard to guess Rohit's age. He looks like he's in his twenties, but Indian skin lies. His sharp cheekbones, outlined by the few strands of cheek hair growing down to meet his short beard, create dark shadows on his face, suggesting greater seriousness and age. He guesses Rohit is approximately ten to fifteen years younger than he himself. There is a delicate quality to everything about Rohit, not just his skin and the hairs on his cheeks and forearms, but his body, which looks neurasthenic inside his loose-fitting trousers. Jack imagines that Rohit is someone who was well cared for by his mother at one time, which is what Rohit is telling him now, in so many words.

"My mother's parents loved me very much, but mostly just from the photographs. I met them one time here in India when I was eight and went to visit the ancestral village. This was a dusty old place with quite an illustrious past. My family were Brahmins, see, and they once owned the entire village. The government took the village from them in the 1970s to give it to the poor—they fancied themselves the Robin Hoods of India, of course. This was bad. Very bad. All over India this transpired. The villages became very poor as a result, because the Brahmins had been managing the land. Now the Brahmins had no jobs—they went to work as clerks in the government, working for the very factotums who'd taken their land away."

Factotums? Jack is impressed with Rohit's diction. "Factotum?"

"Yes. You know. Apparatchik."

"Apparatchik?"

"So sorry. You see here in India we have so great a bureaucracy we have several words to describe it. The Eskimos in your country have ten words for snow. We've borrowed a word from every language for *bureaucrat*."

"Yes. So the factotums? Or would that be *factoti?*"

Rohit's eyes smile at Jack, and Jack lets his make the same.

"The Brahmins were unhappy everywhere working in these offices, but in my mother's ancestral village, the poor people were unhappy too, and they asked my mother's family to come back to take the land. It was really a very benevolent situation. You have to forget, please, this paradigm that India is divided between possessed and dispossessed, ruler and ruled, oppressor and oppressed. Disregard this entirely, if you please."

Jack continues to be impressed with Rohit's speech, even if he pronounced the g in *paradigm* hard, so the word sounded like "para-dig-em." This is actually the first Jack has heard about the politics of land distribution in India. It's all a little fuzzy to him. He read Marx in college, but poetry was his major. He was thinking more about Rohit's particular way of telling the story than class conflict. He just wants the details to fall in place. "So your family took the village back?"

"Spot on. Then it is sad but everyone in my family has died. Mother father grandmother grandfather. My grandfather just now."

"I'm sorry."

"Yes thanks. So they have left the village to me. I own the village."

"What's it called?" Jack isn't sure he believes Rohit. If Rohit stumbles in coming up with the name, he's probably lying.

Rohit has an easy answer. "Saharanpur."

"Never heard of it."

"No, you wouldn't have. You'd like to come maybe? For luncheon. There is a very kind family there that treats me like their son. I show you a typical Indian family. Not Brahmins. Kshatriya caste actually."

Kshatriyas are the traditional warrior caste. They are the caste that has always intrigued Jack most in India. He doesn't know much about them, but in his imagination they ride bareback on elephants or tigers as they vanquish invaders—Aryans, Muslims. He's read about a seventeenth-century Kshatriya warrior in his *Lonely Planet* travel guide, Shivaji, who fought off the brutal Mughal conquerer Aurangzeb. "Kshatriya is fine," Jack says. He is aware that his tone might have sounded more condescending, more colonialist, than he would have liked. He meant to be ironic, so to show this in retrospect, he adopts his smile face. He's relieved when Rohit returns it. "Like Shivaji," Jack adds to soften the irony.

Rohit pauses before responding, the way someone does when they don't understand but haven't decided yet whether to admit it. At first this confuses Jack, because there's no way an Indian Hindu could not know about Shivaji. From what Jack gathered from the *Lonely Planet*, Shivaji is as revered among Hindus as Gandhi, maybe even more. Gandhi cooperated with Muslims, after all, while Shivaji fought them. And Jack has never, not once, seen a store selling, say, sheets named after Gandhi. But there are plenty of Shivaji Sheets, Shivaji Sinks, Shivaji Sweets. Given these facts, Jack decides he's misread Rohit's reaction. He peers into the Indian's face and feels a small physical thrill at the idea that between Rohit and himself lies a whole potential universe of missed cues, crossed signals, misinterpreted cultural nuances. Rohit is a mystery indeed.

"Like Shivaji," Rohit says, smiling.

In the dream, Rohit is so delicate, Jack is afraid he'll crush him. He embraces him with all his might nonetheless. He wants to consume Rohit. He is smooth and warm, like sweet Indian tea. Jack kisses him hard on the lips, but the lips respond by staying soft and slippery. They taste of almonds and have the same oily quality. He kisses Ro-

347

hit's torso, first his nipples, which have only a thin down growing at their circumference and in a thin shiny line at the midline of his chest. His abdomen is flat. His member is large, like the god Shiva's. Jack has seen statues at Mahabalipuram depicting Shiva sitting cross-legged with a lingam the size of a small building growing out of his lap. Jack arranges Rohit in this seated position and puts his mouth on his great lingam. It is warm and smooth, and he worries that he will give it abrasions when he rubs his cheek, coarse with stubble, against it.

When Jack wakes up he's sweating profusely, and he's hard. He rocks from side to side on the mattress, pulling at himself until he comes. He tries to keep his come on his abdomen, but a glob drops onto the mattress. Because of the sweat, it proves hard to clean with a towel; he rubs the stain hard with water, but this only creates a solution of come and sweat, its precise chemical composition suiting it perfectly to the act of seeping deep into the stuffing of the mattress.

Rohit is waiting as arranged outside the café on Connought Circle, wearing the nondescript Delhi garb of trousers, a button-down poly-ester shirt, and sandals. Jack is wearing shorts, Birkenstocks, and a long Indian *kurta* top cinched at the waist by his fanny pack. Rohit embraces Jack's forearms warmly with both hands. The physical closeness embarrasses Jack. His penis stiffens slightly as he returns the gesture. "Come come. My friend has got the vehicle," Rohit is saying as he leads Jack through the late-morning chaos of Connought Place. "This drive it is ninety kilometers, something like this. We shall arrive promptly in time for luncheon. Promise promise."

Jack has never walked this quickly in this kind of heat. It occurs to him that the brisk movement might have a homeopathic effect against the heat, like drinking hot tea to stay cool the way they do in south India. Walking at this speed, on the heels of an Indian, also has a repellent effect on the usual retinue of Indian hustlers. Jack and his companion move swiftly through the obstacle course.

Another young man, whom Rohit introduces as Vikram, is waiting in a Land Rover. Vikram and Rohit talk in fast Hindi as they gesture for him to step into the backseat. The Indians take the two front seats. It all seems to go by too fast for Jack to consider. Inside, he can only pick up a word of Hindi here or there—numbers, the words for *right* and *left, road, distance, kilometers, the American*. Vikram doesn't address Jack directly, probably, figures Jack, because he doesn't speak English. The Land Rover pulls out into the street at a point where traffic funnels straight into a daisy wheel. He finds the way the vehicles move through the circular space mesmerizing; they intercept each other so that if each were trailing a piece of string, the threads would interlock to create a complicated braid of rope.

The car winds through miles of city, one scrappy block after another. Socialist realist apartment structures with tilted, laundry-clad balconies give way to store-lined blocks that then shift back to apartments. Signs in Devanagari and Roman script dominate a street front broken only intermittently with signs in Urdu, in the Persian script. Jack tries to parse snatches of Hindi writing, but the car moves too quickly for him to read anything but small chunks, syllables or two-syllable combinations that he sounds out in his head. The act reminds him of learning to read as a six-year-old; he has an image of his first grade teacher pronouncing vowel-consonant combinations written on a blackboard. "*Ab, ah, la,*" he mouths in a low voice.

The Roman script is mostly Hindi and Sanskrit words. Gurukula Apartments; Chapatis Vishnu; Laxshmi Banking; Shivaji Housewares. It amuses Jack to imagine that the Urdu signs, so exotic and lovely in their arabesque shapes, advertise items equally charming and camp: Sheikh Iqbal's Internet, perhaps, or Masjid Mosquito Netting.

They pass a sign reading Santosh Kuti. *House of happiness*, Jack translates to himself. He realizes he doesn't even have a picture in his head of this house in the village that he is visiting, and as he scans his memory for an image of a hut—a *kuti*—in an Indian village, he sees himself lying on a mattress on the floor of a dirt lean-to, a paisleyed Indian tapestry covering the entryway. The tapestry parts, and Rohit walks in—wearing only a *lungi* bound around the waist. The *lungi* hangs low, giving Jack a generous view of the line of hair stretching from Rohit's navel to his groin. He wonders if he will sleep with Rohit, if Rohit knows how to read the hidden give-and-takes of Jack's lovers' calls. If Jack were to look deeply into Rohit's eyes, would his meaning be any clearer to Rohit than Rohit's was to Jack when he stumbled over the name Shivaji?

During the five months he's spent in India, Jack has had several encounters with Indian men, but none that was ever consummated. Once, a dark-skinned south Indian Christian named Michael chatted with Jack in a pizza parlor until late. Jack invited him to sleep over.

They walked to Jack's hotel together like schoolboys, holding hands, joking, teasing, jabbing each other in the ribs. This continued when they got to Jack's room, until, innocently enough, Michael announced he was tired and proceeded to make a bed for himself on Jack's balcony. Jack was dumbfounded.

Another time, Jack developed a great friendship with an Indian banker. They shared details about their parents, their pasts, their dreams, catching lunch or dinner together every day without fail for two weeks. One night the banker asked Jack to meet him at a disco. The disco was the closest thing to a gay bar Jack had seen in India. In dim light, men danced together, holding hands, whispering into each other's ears while standing close. There were women too, but they mostly sat alone or in dour groups. The man arrived late, showing up with a woman he introduced as his wife. She was large and unhappy looking, rounding out her capacious Punjabi *kameez* and bloomer pants. Like the other women, she kept to the sidelines. Despite the presence of his wife, the man was unrestrained on the dance floor with Jack. They touched hands, hips, whispered. They were touching shoulders, front to front, when the man's wife broke it up. Broke in, like in any proper waltz. Then Jack saw the man and his wife arguing bitterly, and Jack left without ever again seeking contact. That night he paid for an expensive hotel with fine linens, seeking desperately to close the cavern inside of him, to build a bridge connecting home to here, the past to now.

When Jack looks up again, he realizes they've made it out of the city. The landscape is now rough and desertlike, arid except for occasional outposts of shanties with animals and children running in front. On a particularly barren stretch of road, Vikram slows the vehicle. Jack makes out two men standing by the side of the road. Rohit stretches across the back of his seat to break the silence with Jack. "Just some guys," he says. "Just some guys we're giving a lift." Rohit's voice is languid, his body limber as it curls over the seat back.

Jack watches the guys approach, walking to either side of the rear. It seems strange. One gets in either back door, so they are sitting on either side of Jack. Rohit begins speaking with them in Hindi, but even though Jack can understand only a word here or there in the conversation, he has the sense that the conversation is wrong. It's as if they already know each other. Jack feels prickles on the back of his neck and remembers the way the dark boys in his high school used to slap the white boys on the backs of their necks to give them red necks. The man on his right interjects the word *"Amriki."* It seems like Rohit and this man are arguing. From behind, Jack can see the back of even Rohit's neck flushing.

"What the fuck's going on?" Jack's voice says. It seems to be speaking on its own. He notices that it sounds more American than it did before, when he made an effort to pronounce each syllable so Rohit could follow. "Who the fuck are these people? Rohit, tell me the fuck what's going on."

Rohit arches back over the seat and then slides down so he's peering between the two front seats straight above Jack's lap, which is now positioned in the center of the backseat. Rohit gently takes Jack's forearms with the same gesture he used to greet him at the park this morning. "I'm sorry friend." Rohit is looking deep into Jack's eyes. At the precise moment that Jack feels cold against the skin of his neck, he senses Rohit's eyes latching onto something inside his own. It's this, only this, that keeps Jack from swinging at the gun like a spastic. He feels strangely calm.

"I'm sorry friend. American friend," Rohit says. "Keep your hair on please. You are kidnapped, for the cause of Kashmiri freedom."

The man on Jack's left takes out a large swath of brown embroidered cloth and slides it over Jack's head. It is the kind of thing Muslim women wear to cover their heads and bodies, only this one covers Jack's eyes as well.

He hears Rohit's voice again from the other side of the cloth. "I'm sorry friend."

Sitting in the safe house, surrounded by the four Indian men and a small artillery of heavy weapons, Jack tries to make lists of things to keep himself calm. There were at least three false notes in Rohit's self-presentation. First, if he is a Kashmiri militant, he is not a Hindu at all. He is a Muslim, and this explains his ignorance about Shivaji. Second, if he's Muslim, he hasn't been speaking Hindi at all, but Urdu, its Muslim stepbrother. And third, his name, Rohit, which is a Hindu name, is not his name at all. The guys are calling him Johnny now, but it's probably really something like Omar or Mustafa.

The hood is off now, and Jack is sitting on a cheap, uncovered floor mattress, chained by his wrists to a pole. The four men from the

Land Rover have fed him dal and vegetables. It was certainly not the luncheon feast Jack was expecting but no more simple than the five-rupee *thalis* he's been subsisting on through his travels.

Jack watches his captors as if from the other side of a camera lens. Two new men have arrived; the men from the car are less languid in their presence. With their wiry bodies they seem jacked up, like schoolboys whose hours of play have been interrupted by a stern mother. The new men are of a completely unrelated type from the kidnappers. Rohit and his posse are frail in loose-fitting trousers, with watery eyes and new beard hairs on their cheeks. The two new men are portly, with thick, full beards and loafers rather than sandals. Rohit seems to be the go-between, but Jack can't make out Rohit's speech—he swallows his words and says little, looking away when he addresses the new men. The words of the new men, too, blend into each other, like so much street Hindi at Connought Place. There seem to be many accents and languages, with many words that cross over like bridges between the languages. *Amriki, American. Sheikh. Thug. Badmash.* The familiar yet distant quality of the words makes Jack feel like a child learning to attach loose meanings to approximate sounds. His comprehension, likewise, feels no more sophisticated than a child's.

A sudden movement jolts Jack out of his stupor. One of the portly men has backhanded Rohit. Rohit, who has only about 66 percent body mass to the big man's, stumbles backwards. He looks back at the man, blinking, and then says something odd and confusing to Jack. "Bugger! What kind of a berk are you? Have you gone barking mad?"

Barking mad?

It strikes Jack like the answer to an obvious math problem that what made Rohit so hard to understand was the incongruity of the fact that he has been addressing the men in English all along—and not just impeccable English but a slang obscure to even Jack. "It's not quite cricket then, is it?" Rohit is saying now. "We've nabbed your Nancy boy and it wasn't for jam at all you know," Rohit goes on. He's speaking queen's English. Or is it cockney? "This is all hideous."

Hideous?

Rohit has preserved none of his earlier awkward Indianisms, the dropped articles, the dangling modifiers. Jack thinks of the old Harvard joke. He used to toss it around with his ex, a Harvard grad: *You know where the library's at, asshole?*

Jack realizes his knowledge of language now—Hindi, English, anything—is too rudimentary to parse any single one of these men's identities. He wishes he knew more about London, that he could place "Johnny's" accent in a particular neighborhood or social class, but unfortunately his knowledge of the colonial seat is far less extensive than his understanding of India, England's "jewel in the crown."

Rohit/Johnny is a jewel. This Jack still believes. There is a gemlike quality about him. He's shiny—that impression hasn't faded. Is to be a gem to be a subject? Jack can only take the train of thought so far. Then his mind starts to mist up, and he feels confused and emotional and angry.

He falls into a deep sleep. He dreams that he is back at the Ankur, Rohit lying under a thin sheet on the far side of his mattress. While Jack sleeps, Rohit masturbates. In the morning there is a large brown stain on Rohit's part of the sheet. His come is brown, like a dark ruby.

Jack shakes awake. As in the dream Rohit is next to him on a mattress—now the mattress at the safe house. Everyone else is gone. Rohit is stretched out so only his head and shoulders rest against the wall and his spine is in the shape of the top of a ski. Rohit was half asleep himself. He looks at Jack quizzically but not with the incomprehension of the day of their first meeting—the incomprehension of a man less in control of the common language than his interlocutor—but of a man lumbering back to consciousness through gelatinous layers of sleep.

"It's hideous," Rohit says, slicking back his hair.

"Hideous?"

"What we've done to you. It's all gone squiffy. I'm sorry, brother. Truly sorry. These activities have got to seem absolutely extremist to you."

Squiffy?

"You'll be thinking *I've kissed the Blarney stone,* but we had no intention of harming you. We needed one American, a Sherman Tanks the likes of you, to bring the atrocities in Kashmir to the limelight."

Sherman Tanks?

"The sum of my activities in the past was fund-raising," he goes on. "But we must open eyes. Bosnia. Chechnya. The treatment of Muslims everywhere is atrocious. We have resorted to drastic measures. Sorry for the pig's breakfast." Rohit chews on a fingernail, pushes

353

back another stray lock of hair. "I have sacrificed my career. This will not go to waste if the government will address Kashmir." Rohit fixes Jack with a stare. Jack believes this is an honest stare, that this is the real Rohit—or Abdullah or whatever his name is. He feels that somewhere within the treacherous Rohit there is a kernel of integrity, and he himself has found the pathway to get there.

"Your career?" It had never occurred to Jack what Rohit might do for a living. He supposes he imagined him as a truck driver or a hustler. Or better, probably unemployed.

"I went to a private school, a very beautiful place, in East London. Forest School. You know it?"

Jack looks at him dumbly. He's not used to hearing British English, and it's taking him longer than it should to assimilate his captor's phrases. It's no easier than Hindi. The signposts in Rohit's monologue have likewise left Jack feeling lost and unmoored. He's never heard of the school, could find neither Bosnia nor Chechnya on a map, and knows nothing about Kashmir except that it is, indeed, Muslim, and that because of a contested border, it is at the center of a power struggle between India and Pakistan. This he read in *Lonely Planet*. He has also heard it spoken of in the context of a breakaway struggle for independence. There his knowledge ends.

"I remember one hydrangea bush."

Hydrangea?

"So lovely. We are quite educated, my family. My sister is at Oxford. I myself am enrolled at the London School of Economics. Statistics. And what college is it you attended?"

"UCLA. Poetry."

The longest relationship Jack has ever maintained was with his Harvard ex. Talking with Rohit, Jack remembers several instances where his boyfriend's Ivy snobbery offended him. He often had the same feeling he has now, that there was a code he'd never been given that was essential to understanding the dialogue. Inside references acted as rungs by which to hang onto a conversation. There were cocktail parties where a profusion of disconnected details fused with a self-conscious Boston argot to the point where Jack felt his brain turn to so much twisted rope. He could no longer make out words or meaning at all. He feels that way now.

"You've heard of Convoy of Mercy?"

Jack stays quiet.

"Sending supplies to Bosnia. Bosnia. Now that, friend, is where Muslims must unite. We must fight for our brothers."

Rohit's expression suddenly turns feral. No one has hit him this time, but the abrupt shift in his eyes is as dramatic. "In London we will rise. Rise. Men like you," he adds, now fixing Jack with a look not unlike that of a trapped possum, "you're no better than brown bread. Dead. You're in a Barney, friend."

Jack's relationship with the man from Harvard ended unexpectedly. One day the man didn't show up at their usual meeting time and place. He's had no contact with him since. The loss of Rohit's solidarity is the closest thing he can remember to his feeling of heartache during the days after his boyfriend's disappearance. It's as if a mentally imbalanced, cold-blooded, and militant killer has kidnapped Rohit himself.

Rohit has uncurled himself so that instead of a ski, his body is angled into a taut upright sitting position from which he lunges forward to look straight into Jack's face. Now he stands as if to start pacing, but after just one step, he flings his body in a full circle so he is facing Jack again. Then, as if personifying a strange, genderless demon, he strikes a pose—arms up, fingers pointed and gazelle-like so that Jack can imagine them extended by long painted fingernails. *Voguing,* is what Jack thinks—like the drag queens of Santa Monica Boulevard. Then Rohit begins swiveling his hips in a grotesque gesture accentuated by a circular movement of his wrists. Rohit is doing a dance, a lurid and suggestive belly dance. He puts his hands, fingernails pointing downwards, over his abdomen and slowly begins pulling them up so the very tips of his fingers lift his shirt slightly, exposing his belly. The trail of hairs. The low hang of his trousers.

Rohit stops just as instantly, bringing his face close to Jack's again. He has reverted to the fierce militant. How Jack longs for the person two cycles back—the cultured Muslim university student—or three, even—the obsequious Hindu secular.

"We have asked for a prisoner exchange. One hundred and fifty Kashmiri men have been jailed in Indian prisons under the most untoward, the most brutal conditions. We will accept their release in exchange for you and three others. In your poetry education you undoubtedly learned arithmetic. The algebra of the human soul, it is then. You see your value in this equation. One to forty, is it? You have forty times the value of a Kashmiri then, is it? Our Sherman Tanks.

Hamari Amriki." Rohit marches more furiously, spinning on his heel now like a parodic soldier from a World War II sitcom.

"Your family will scour the streets of Delhi looking in every ditch, behind every railway track. They will find pieces of you scattered about the slums of this city where Muslims toil in their abject lives. Like the droppings of nightingales, your body will decompose in the streets, in the sewers. Your family will mourn your death like the thousands of Kashmiri mothers and sons crying over our lost martyrs. No one can find you here. Friend."

As Jack watches Rohit fly across the room, he feels himself falling back into the dissociated state of watching his surroundings through a lens. Jack is dropping off to sleep against his will, and for all his efforts to dive back through the lens, he is caught in a thick layer of gelatin through which he cannot plunge back. As his eyes mist over, the last image he catches is of Rohit smacking the walls with his fists and then kicking.

When Jack's eyes close there is still an image of Rohit warring with the wall, only now he is climbing it, then standing with his feet on the ceiling, then pummeling the contours of the room with every limb of his body.

Jack dreams he is in a zoo. Rohit is inside a cage, hanging by claws from its chain-link ceiling and making a terrible shattering sound as he shakes its wall with his bare feet. Jack walks up to the metal wiring and grips it with both hands, pushing his face up to the metal to get as close to Rohit as he can. He wants to offer him a way out. Then Jack looks up and sees that there is cage metal above him as well, and when he looks back to Rohit again, his captor is dressed in a sharp, loose-hanging blue suit and tasseled loafers. He is watching Jack from a spectator's bench with a cool, detached stare. Jack rattles the walls of the cage and silently makes a pleading gesture with his eyes. *Let me out.* He no longer has language. Rohit returns the stare coldly.

When Jack shakes awake the first thing he sees is the back of Rohit's neck. Rohit has come back to the mattress and has been sleeping alongside Jack. It is an oddly intimate posture for a man who a short time ago was subjugating a wall in a fit of rage.

To the constant disgruntlement of his mother, Jack was exceptionally wild as a child. He has several fond memories, though, of lying in

356

bed deep in the night with his mother seated next to him stroking his hair. "Even the rottenest boy is an angel when he sleeps," she used to say. Looking at the sleek hairs growing on the back of Rohit's neck, Jack has that same wistful feeling now. Jack always wondered how his mother was able to marshal such deep reserves of forgiveness for her raucous son. But Rohit, vulnerable in sleep, inspires that tenderness in Jack; it's a feeling he doesn't recognize.

Rohit stirs awake and turns, so that now the two men are face to face. The gun is lying next to Rohit, in easy reach for Rohit but not for Jack, who is still shackled to the wall. Rohit sits up, lies against the wall in the ski position again, and fingers the silencer on the gun. "Tell me friend, how are the birds in America? Girls?"

Girls? Jack wonders if, finally, he is beginning to understand. When Jack was young, when he had his first fumbling adolescent sex, it always began with talk of girls: two boys, snuggling together, talking about girls. It was so commonplace an initiation into adolescent homosexuality that, later, Jack came to assume that male talk of women axiomatically stood for gay sex. Fill in the blank: How do you like girls? How do you like *men?* How do you like *sex?* How do you like *me?*

Jack pauses. "They're, I don't know, girlish."

"In London, brother, they're nutters, you know, tough."

"Do you like poetry?" Jack recovers. Fill in the blank: *Do you like poetry do you like sex do you like me?*

Rohit cites some words of verse in a language that is not Hindi—or even Urdu, Jack thinks he's sure. Then he translates. " 'She hides behind screens calling for you, while you search and lose yourself in the wilderness and the desert.' "

Rumi. Rohit has uttered the unmistakable verse of Rumi. Jack wrote his thesis at UCLA about Rumi, worshipper of a delectable and godly object of passion whose name was Shams. A man. Jack's kidnapper is quoting Rumi. He is quoting Rumi in Persian. No one has ever quoted Rumi to Jack in Persian. It comes like a wash of cold, immersing him in the bright, fresh quality of his earliest sensual memories, when words articulated the sparkling internal sensations of his body. " 'The flames of my passion devour the wind and the sky,' " Jack recites in response.

Rohit picks up: " 'My body is a candle, touched with fire.' "

Jack feels calm. " 'Let me feel you enter each limb, bone by bone.' "

" 'There are no edges to my loving now.' "

"Rumi," Jack says.

Rohit's eyes dance.

"I knew a bird once—" Rohit says.

"For Rumi the love of a woman was an incomplete love, a less than perfect completion of the circle of desire," Jack responds, or deflects.

Rohit nods. "For Rumi the love of a woman was certainly platonic. A metaphor, really, for the true heights of passion a man could achieve."

"A woman's body could never contain the full weight of a man's actual desire," Jack volleys back.

Rohit looks at Jack long with his watery eyes. "We truly understand each other, friend. 'The beloved is all, the lover just a veil.' " He lies back onto the mattress with his hands behind his head, and staring at the ceiling, he begins to hum. Rohit's hum escalates slowly to a chant. It is a gorgeous melody sung in a thin and sinewy high-pitched voice, flowing through the room like the trickle of a drought-choked stream. The chant grows louder, seeming to rebound now around the corners of the room, to flood it with its echo. Jack recognizes it as a thread of Qur'anic chanting—not unlike the melodies mosques broadcast from their towers at daybreak. Rohit is suddenly lost to Jack, lost in a prayer, devotional and otherworldly.

Jack leans back, and listening to the sinewy phrases, feels himself dropping back again behind the lens. With his eyes closed he imagines the water of Rohit's choked stream gurgling over his face. " 'The water that pollutes you is poison, the poison that purifies you is water,' " he recites to himself. The stream turns into a rush of water, and then Jack feels he is suffocating as it enters into him, through his lungs, coursing through his own body, as if he is part of the room, a receptacle for Rohit's devotion. Grasping for breath, he swings his arm in front of him to find Rohit on top of him. The Indian is lying above him, the full weight of his body crushing Jack's chest, the kidnapper's hands covering his face.

Rohit is whispering something in Jack's ear. " 'You sit on top of a treasure,' " his breath says. " 'Yet in utter poverty you will die.' Friend. In utter poverty. You will die."

Nominated by The Gettysburg Review

ELEGY FOR THE SAINT OF LETTING SMALL FISH GO

by ELIOT KHALIL WILSON

from THE SAINT OF LETTING SMALL FISH GO (Cleveland State University Poetry Center)

I.

You too might step into a puddle of fire,
or splash through a stream of glowing lava
where only moments before you were barefoot
in your kitchen after a late night of too much wine
and, nearly naked, frying bacon at the stove.

A burn like this is a different thing the doctor said
and I can believe it. I was a different thing.

I was a man with an unquenchable oil well fire on his feet
that would blaze up as the medicine ebbed.
And the skin curled over, brown-red,
too much like the meat I was cooking in the pan that I dropped
—an irony not lost on even the youngest of nurses
drinking and bacon don't mix
she kidded as I healed.

Yet had my wounds burned like Vulcan's forge
they'd be a distant fire in light of the child
behind the glass in the opposite bed.

II.

Where were you saints when the fire first licked his hands?
Hadn't he in living prayed to you?

I want the saint of ice cream trucks
to turn off the carnival, climb down, and explain it all—
         account for all the betrayers—
The saints of reachable branches and bank envelope lollipops,
the saints of his mother's cool arms, of new basketball shoes, and
professional wrestling,
The saints of tree forts, pocket knives, and stadium food.
The saints of waffles and eyebrows and box turtles.
The saint of jam.
The saint of his own bed.
Where were you saints of wheelies and rodeo clowns and rockets?

III.

I was at home when the sepsis took him
and they wheeled him to that all-light room
and when they covered his face.

Yet I had seen his grafts and debridements,
the twice daily baths and dressings,
and the shock at that last turn of gauze
—how the fire bit at his summer legs and arms—
black skin, blacker still, and red.

I was there to see the lost mother
who would live in fire for the child she had known.
There to see all who entered shake their heads
as if wondering as I wondered
how so small a thing can carry such pain
—pain that pushed through the morphine push—
—pain that conquered even those numbing Nordic gods—
Vicodin, Ativan, and Tylox.

It is not my place.
He was not my child,

360

and I could never speak to him,
but hold him out of the fire.
I would not have him burned again.

Give him back to rocking water,
to pendulum down through the fingers of the sun.
Let the ocean run his veins and heart—
        full, then empty, then full again.

Or return him to the folding ground,
face up to the sky.
A boon for dreamlessness,
this petty thief of time.

Nominated by Cleveland State University Press

SHUNNED

by MEREDITH HALL

from CREATIVE NONFICTION

Even now i talk too much and too loud, claiming ground, afraid that I will disappear from *this* life, too, from this time of being mother and teacher and friend. That It—everything I care about, that I believe in, that defines and reassures me—will be wrenched from me again. Family. Church. School. Community. There are not many ways you can get kicked out of those memberships. As a child in Hampton, New Hampshire, I knew husbands who cheated on their wives. Openly. My father. I knew men and women who beat their children. We all knew them. We all knew men who were too lazy to bring in a paycheck or clean the leaves out of their yards, women who spent the day on the couch crying while the kids ran loose in the neighborhood. We knew who drank at the Meadowbrook after work each day and drove home to burn Spaghetti-Os on the stove for the children. We even knew a witch. We called her Goody Welsh, as if her magic had kept her alive since the Salem days. But this was 1966. All these people were tolerated. More than tolerated; they were the Community. The teachers and ministers' wives and football players and drugstore owners. They lived next to me on Leavitt Road and Mill Road and High Street. They smiled hello when I rode my bike past their clean or dirty yards, their sunny or shuttered houses.

Then I got pregnant. I was 16. Family, church, school—each, which had embraced me as a child—turned its back. Shunning is supposed to keep bad things from happening in a community. But it doesn't correct the life gone wrong. It can only expose the transgression to a very raw light, use it as a measure, a warning to others that says, "See? That didn't happen in *our* home. Because we are Good. We're better than that." The price I paid seems still to be extreme. But I bet it was a while again before any girl in Hampton let herself be fucked in the gritty sand by a boy from away who said *love*.

A friend once told me that when he was in seventh grade, he and his best friend, Nathan, fought. Nathan got everyone in school to ignore my friend the next day, incited them to the silent treatment. It only lasted until noon. One by one my friend drew his friends back, outmaneuvering Nathan. But still my friend remembers the impotent shame he felt for those four hours. The injustice. It didn't last because my friend was a boy, a boy who knew how to fight back, a boy who believed that he could interrupt the current and draw his world back into order. It didn't work because he felt powerful, after all, worthy of those friends and their loyalty.

And it didn't work because there was no moral to be exalted, no messy failure to be feasted upon. But pregnant in 1965: If this could happen to Bobbie's daughter, then, like contagion, it could happen to anyone's girl. Unless we scared them so much they would never spread their legs again. Injustice. It had to be unjust. It had to be electrifying to work.

I have often wondered whether the grown-ups I went to church with, who had made sandwiches for me and their children on dreamy, summer days, who praised me year after year for my A's and my manners and my nice family, who paid me extra for watching their babies so well—I have wondered if they had to tell their children to shun me, or if the kids slid into it on their own. The motives of the grown-ups seemed quite different from those of my peers. When Diane and Pepper and Debbie and John and Stephen stopped speaking to me, when they started to cross the street in tight, hushed groups, when they left Tobey's Rexall, their cherry Cokes unfinished because I walked in—had they been told to steer so clear of me? Did they understand that if shunning is to work, it must be absolute? No soft heart to undermine the effect? Or did they find their own reasons to cast me out? "I never liked her, anyway" or "She thinks she's so smart." "Her father left, you know." Maybe I was simply too dangerous. If they did not abruptly turn away, they would be judged, by association, for being as dirty as I was.

This sort of shunning has the desired effect of erasing a life. Making it invisible, incapable of contaminating. I suddenly had no history with these kids. I had started school with them at Mrs. Winkler's kindergarten, in the basement of her husband's dental office. First grade, fifth, eighth, 10th—Mrs. Bean and Mrs. Marcotte and Mr. Cooper—24 kids moving together year after year. We all knew each other's parents and brothers and sisters and whether they went to the Congregational or the Methodist or the tiny Episcopal church. We knew who practiced piano after supper and who lived with a grandmother and who read secretly in the field behind Pratt's barn.

No one in our class was bad. We believed we were good children, and were. The 1950s still breathed its insistent, costly calm through our childhoods. When we said, "I'm in sixth grade," we meant, *I belong with these boys and girls; we are bound in inevitable affection.* The grown-ups reinforced for each of us this sense of our lives being woven together, sticky strands of a resilient web. We liked each other as a matter of course; idiosyncrasies and conflicts, like broken rays of the whole, were quickly corrected, the flaw made invisible and forgotten.

I still can tell you that Kenneth had a funny, flat head. That fat Jimmy surprised us in eighth grade by whipping out a harmonica and playing country ballads. That he also surprised us that year by flopping on the floor in an epileptic fit. That Jill, an only child, lived in a house as orderly and dead as a tomb. That I coveted her closetful of clothes. That Patty's father had to drag our muddy, sagging dog back every few weeks from hunting in the marshes; that he apologized politely every time to my mother, as if it were his fault. That in kindergarten Jay wanted to marry me and that I whipped him a year or two later with thorny switches his father had trimmed from the hedge separating our yards. That his father called me Meredy-My-Love, and I called him Uncle Leo. That Heather's grandmother, Mrs. Coombs, taught us music once a week, the fat that hung from her arms swinging wildly just offbeat as she led each song.

I still can tell you that Linda wouldn't eat the crusts. I thought she was spoiled. That Sharon smelled and was supposed to be pitied, not ostracized. That Bonnie wore my old skirts and dresses, found in the Clothes Closet in the church vestry, and I was never to mention anything to her, as though everyone had not seen those same clothes on me all the previous year. That Bev was Mr. Fiedler's pet, that her mother made cookies for the Brownies every Wednesday when we sat like grown women, gossiping while we sewed aprons and washcloth slippers for our mothers and grandmothers at Christmas. That Johnny was a flirt and liked to kiss girls, and he would come to no

364

good, although he came to something better than I did. That Sheila's mother sold us eggs. That Bill was almost as smart as I was, but he was a boy and never got all A's. That I followed the rules and craved praise, that I was cheerful and a pleaser, a leader who was headed somewhere.

These are myths, of course. We children touched ourselves in the dark and stole money from our mothers' purses and listened at night to our parents screaming obscenities. But the myths worked; none of those secrets were visible. There was a silent hierarchy based in part on social class but also on something less tangible—an unswerving sense of who came from a "good" family. They didn't need to have money. But the good family must protect its secrets. No grandparent could be a public drinker or an atheist. If Dad walked out, Mother must become a saint.

Lucky for me I came from just such a family. I was a good girl, the darling of teachers and chosen as a friend by these 24 kids I knew as if we were cousins.

I have a very small box containing everything that survives that childhood—a perfect-attendance pin from Sunday school; my Brownie sash; a jet-and-rhinestone pin given to me by a crazy old woman up the street; my toe shoes, the pink satin worn through; one Ginny doll, her hair half gone, and a few clothes my mother and I sewed for her; a silver dollar my first boyfriend gave me for Christmas my sophomore year; my prayer book, signed in the front by my mother, "To my beloved daughter"; and a class picture, titled "My Class," from 10th grade.

I don't ever look at this photo and should throw it out. I loved My Class. I loved belonging. I loved the promise I thought I heard, that they would become my past, my history. It is as if there was a terrible death and they were all lost to me, abruptly and all at once. But nobody died. The loss was only mine, a private and interior devastation.

Robin and I walked to school together every day until the day I was kicked out. I heard from her suddenly 10 years ago—24 years after I walked home alone at 11:30 in the morning with the green slip of expulsion in my book bag, my secret let loose and starting its zinging trip mouth to mouth—when her mother, my mother's best friend, Margie, was dying of Alzheimer's. Now when Robin and I get together, she tells me the stories of my own life that I have had to forget. Like an artist painting in the details of a soft charcoal sketch, she fills in the forgotten, the high-school years that I cannot afford to carry. She says, "*You* remember, Meredy. MaryAnn lived on the corner of Mill Road. You used to spend the night at her house a lot." I don't remember. Maybe a certain flip of dark hair or a faint laugh. But I vanished in my own mind, along with all the comfortable, small facts of my life, on that day of expulsion in 1965. Shunned, made invisible, I became invisible to myself. The photo of "My Class" is a record of the history I do not share.

I suppose they all get together every few years for a reunion. They were the class of 1967. I am certain that the space I occupied in the group for 16 years closed in as fast as the blooms on a shrub when one flower dies or is pinched out. I wonder what they would say if my name came up. I wonder if they ever think of me. I sometimes imagine that I will somehow find out where they will meet for the next reunion. I will arrive looking clean and successful and proud. But what would I say to them? That this thing, this shunning, this shaming is an eraser, a weapon that should never be wielded?

Last year I had a student from Hampton in my writing class at the state university. I knew from her last name that she must be the daughter of Timmy Keaton. I told her that I had known her father all through my childhood. I didn't tell her that we weren't really friends, that I was important in class and he was one of those peripheral members no one ever really noticed. She came back the next Monday for a conference. To make conversation—or maybe, 30 years later, to reclaim some of my purged identity—I asked if she had mentioned my name to her father. She looked embarrassed, and I realized right away my misstep: I could not have a student knowing my dark and secret past. But she said, squirming in her chair, "He couldn't really remember your name. I tried to describe you, but he couldn't remember you."

Mrs. Taccetta played the small organ softly as I followed my mother and sister to seats up front. My shy brother was lighting candles on the altar with a long wand, his face shiny with embarrassment. This used to be Johnny Ford's house, a big colonial, gone to seed, between my house and uptown. The Episcopal church had originally met upstairs in the Grange hall, my mother and Mrs. Pervier and Mr. Shindledecker setting up folding metal chairs and restacking them each Sunday morning for six years. Finally those pioneers, seeing some crucial and mysterious distinction between themselves and the Congregationalists and Methodists, raised the funds to buy Johnny's house and turn his living room and dining room into a chapel. The kitchen stayed, but my mother donated our old refrigerator; I could still smell our potatoes in the old-fashioned flip-out drawer in the bottom. The fridge gave me a sense of ownership in the church. So did my mother's role as president of the women's auxiliary. Exotic, deeply embroidered stoles and altar cloths hung in her closet, carefully washed, starched and ironed and laid over my absent father's wooden coat hangers. My mother walked up to the church each Saturday afternoon to set up, arranging flowers and replacing the grape juice and communion wafers.

I felt important there, and loved. I heard every Sunday as we walked into church, "Oh, Bobbie, you have raised such wonderful children." My mother told us we were special, a family united by the trauma of my father's going, and made stronger for it. Church allowed us to parade our family's bravery and fortitude. Smiling, slim and tan and absolutely capable, my mother led us into the gaze of our congregation. I was proud. When Mrs. Palmer and Mrs. Zitrick and Mr. Keniston and Crazy Lulu and Reverend Andrews nodded and smiled their hellos, I felt the light of adoration shine on me. In the pew, in the little chapel she had helped to build, my mother held my hand, and I was a child of grace.

I was kicked out of school on the day we returned from Christmas vacation. I was a junior, 16 years old. My mother had watched me with cool suspicion as I refused to eat breakfast. Five months pregnant, a slim dancer, I had zipped my wool skirt over my hard, round belly and prayed for one more day of hiding.

In gym class that morning, we had used the mats for tumbling. Over and over, Miss Millett had made us practice running somersaults, kips and splits. When my turn came to do a move called the fish-flop—a backward somersault, legs held high for a pause in the follow-through, and an arched-back slide down onto the chest and belly—I balked. I was starting to understand that what had ended my periods, what made my belly grow, was not just a terrifying threat, an ominous messenger telling me that I was doomed; it was becoming a life—a child, curled inside me in, perhaps—why not?— the same dread and fear of its future that I carried every minute. Suddenly, watching the girls ahead of me slamming back down onto the mats, I felt a confused and ferocious protectiveness and a giving-in, two of us too tired to hide anymore. The class watched as I ran out of the gym into the girls' locker room.

My best friends, Kathy and Chris, followed me. "What's wrong?" they asked earnestly. I hadn't showered after gym class for a month, but they had bought my excuses about not having time before biology class. This time I turned and faced them in the clammy room. "I'm pregnant," I said. I remember now that they both visibly drew back, sucking in air, suspended. Maybe not. Maybe they just stared for a minute. Maybe they looked at me and considered how to react. But I was surprised, after all the months of rehearsing the scene in my mind, to see them turn silently to their lockers, fumble with their clothes, and leave together without saying a word to me. If I hadn't understood during those five terrified months that everything I had ever been, everything I had ever believed in and dreamed of was gone, I understood it at that moment.

Miss Millett may have called Mrs. Zitrick, the school nurse and my mother's helper on the women's auxiliary at church. Or maybe Mrs. Zitrick watched me one day too many as I ran up the steps of the cafeteria into the bathroom to vomit lunch, my skirt stretched tight. Maybe she saw the change in my face, the darkness of fear and aloneness underlying the charade of walking and talking and sitting. She called me to her office. She was surprisingly tender as she handed me the expulsion slip.

"Do you want me to call your mother at work?" she asked.

"No, thank you," I answered. "How will I take my midterms?"

Mrs. Zitrick sat back in her chair. "You understand that you may not return to this school?"

I left my books, left my notes, my notebooks, with my childish penmanship of looping phrases and doodles and who-loves-whom, on her desk. I walked down the silent, polished hallway to my locker, put on my jacket and mittens, and walked alone through the White wing, past the office staff staring at me through the big window, and out the door. The first phase of outcasting was done.

"Well," my mother said that night after work, sitting on the couch across the room in her trim wool dress and heels. "Well. You can't stay here."

The second phase.

I was supposed to move to my father's house the next morning. I asked my mother if I could wait until Sunday so I could go to church.

She looked surprised. "Haven't you figured anything out?" she asked. "You can't go to church like that. They won't want us anymore." I don't believe my mother ever went to church again. When she died my brother and sister and I argued about whether she would want a minister at her grave. I believed that she would; I knew my own ambivalent heart. Finally we asked a nice man from the Unitarian church to come, a neutral voice who was delicate in referring to a benevolent God.

No one from church ever called or wrote to me after I left Hampton. The silence made me feel as if I had never been part of their Christian body. The beloved smells of leather prayer books and wax and old women's perfume, the swish of Mr. Andrews' robes, the sweet wheeze of the organ, Mrs. Taccetta's tiny feet in stubby, black heels pumping the pedals; the voices of the church rising together, proclaiming God's mercy and forgiveness; the refrigerator humming in the kitchen; my mother's hand wrapped around mine while we stood to sing and knelt to pray; Mr. Spellacy or Miss St. Germaine smiling at me during the long sermon; the permanence and comfort of the affection of grown-ups. The radiant, bored peace of church. All this evaporated when word got out.

Last Easter I finally succeeded in getting my grown sons to accompany me to a service in the local Episcopal chapel. They had never been in a church, and I had not been in one, except for funerals, since I was 16. "Come," I said. "Easter is a joyous time in the church. Let's go sing about the rebirth of the Earth." They liked it. I sang by heart every word of "Christ the Lord is Risen Today" and gave the responses to the Nicene Creed like a believer. I wasn't. But I was home—the sublime faces and the murmurings and the music and the candles and the lilies. The warmth felt deceptive, though, and seductive. Dangerous. My old defenses rose up again instinctively, and I defied the beautiful place and the pious hearts and the father on the altar to catch me again.

I hadn't spent time with my father since he had remarried six years before. He and Dorothy lived in a large, old colonial in Epping, 15 miles from home. They were renovating the house themselves, and Dorothy was a terrible housekeeper, so it was crowded with sheetrock panels and five-gallon buckets of plaster and boards and crushed boxes of nails and screws and tiles for the bathroom and old magazines and piles of mail and clothes strewn over chairs. The kitchen was greasy, and mounds of dirty dishes filled the sink. My father and Dorothy both traveled for their jobs and were seldom home. Dorothy told me to keep the thermostats at 64; she bought cottage cheese and pineapple so I would stay thin and not "lose my shape." I had never slept alone in a house before.

I was not formed yet, not a decision-maker about my life. I was not yet born to consciousness. But here, suddenly, I was facing the results of *being* in the world. In those empty, slow, lonely days, I had to be born into my next life, as I lost my old self in a kind of death.

My stepsister, Molly, was still on her winter vacation from Deerfield Academy. The morning before I arrived, she was moved from her home to her grandmother's house in western New Hampshire. We were told to stop writing letters to each other; my father explained that Molly was still only 15 and they didn't want her exposed to "things like this." I was forbidden to go outside because no one in town was told that I was there and pregnant. Once after a deep, comforting snow, I shoveled the driveway and walks, thinking that my father and Dorothy would be happily surprised when they came home the next day. They were angry and reiterated that I must never go outside again.

I spent long, silent days and nights in the house. When my father and Dorothy were home, they often had dinner parties. I was sent up to my room early with a plate of food and told not to make any noise. I didn't dare go to the bathroom down the hall, afraid that someone would come up the stairs. So I lay under the covers in my frosty, gloomy room, holding my pee, waiting. The laughter rose in bursts from the room below, voices from lives lived on another planet.

The winter was very long and very cold and very gray. The house, my room were large and cold and gray. I waited for calls from Karen and Chris, from friends at school who would be missing me, and then stopped waiting. Once I got a letter from a boy named Bill, a kind letter referring obscurely to my trouble and asking me to write back. It was a moment of tenderness that threatened to break my new, tough heart. I could not afford to cry and could not figure out what I—a dirty pregnant girl hiding upstairs in a cold, lonely house— could say to a handsome boy who still went to history class and shoveled driveways on Saturday mornings. I never wrote back.

I know now that what happened that winter was a deep and scarring depression. Despair and a ferocious, watchful defiance saturated my young life. I was formed largely in those four months, those months that isolated me from any life, from any belief, from any sense that I belonged to anyone. I was alone. My fear and grief burned like wildfires on a silent and distant horizon. I watched the destruction day after day, standing by my bedroom window, staring out over the snow-covered fields that belonged to my father.

My mother finally called in March. My birthday was coming, and she wanted to bring me home for dinner. I was pushed to excitement. I missed my mother badly, the mother of my childhood. I missed my bedroom and my cat. I missed that life, that girl, and wanted to reclaim her for a day.

I was exchanged between my parents' cars on the Route 101 overpass at noon. My mother stared at my large belly and didn't hug me. We drove in silence to Hampton; I wished I had not agreed to come. Being near her, being in our car, which belonged now to *before*, approaching my town on roads as familiar as my own body had once been, all agitated the deep, deep sense of loss that I had struggled so hard to kill. When we turned onto Lafayette Road near town, my mother told me to get down on the floor of the car. I didn't move. "We might see someone," she explained. I squeezed my baby and me onto her floor and watched my mother's faraway face staring straight ahead as we drove home.

My bedroom was a museum of another life. It was pink and soft and sunny and treacherous. I sat all afternoon on my bed, fingering the white chenille bedspread and stroking my purring, black cat. I called up my numbness. A white lace cloth, one I had ironed when I was a child in this house, covered the bureau. The blue plastic clock whirred quietly. Cars slid silently down High Street, carrying people I knew: Mrs. Shindledecker and Corky Lawrence and Sally and Mr. Palmer. They were in a movie, and I watched from beyond the screen.

I don't remember my birthday dinner, at 17 years old and seven months along. I am sure my mother gave me something nice. I hid on the floor of the car in the dark and was relieved to return to the empty obscurity of my father's house.

I had a keen sense of my baby and me being outcasts together. My father and mother had decided immediately that "we" would give the baby up for adoption. I didn't fight; I understood with absolute clarity that I would have no one helping me, that I had held one summer job in a candy store at the beach, that I could never return to high

371

school. That we would be loved and protected nowhere. My sister and brother "knew," but no one else in the family had been told. I still don't know where my grandparents thought I was that year. I do know they were not there telling me that families don't give babies away.

The sense that I had a foreign and threatening force inside me had given way to an intense feeling of connection, of being lost together. We spent the dead-quiet hours alone, our heartbeats measuring together the passage of time, the damage, the unexpressed grief. We would be separated forever in two more months. We shared time in a strange and intense and encompassing sorrow.

My sister, six years older and longing since she was 10 to have a baby of her own, said to me, "This is a baby. A baby is growing inside you." I could not afford it with her.

"I hate this baby," I said to her, scaring her away.

I could feel his small heel or an elbow pressing hard against the inside of my belly as he rolled. I spent the days doing nothing but thinking, learning to live in my head, my arms wrapped under my belly, my baby absorbing my stunned sadness. He had hiccups in the night. I lay in the deep, cold emptiness of the house, the night shared with another living being. My blood flowed through him. Tenacious threads joined us outside the world. I could not feel loved by him, ever. But we were one life, small and scared and alone.

"You have got to let this baby go!" the doctor roared at me. He smelled of cigarettes. We had been there a very, very long time. "You cannot hold this baby inside you," he said angrily. "Push!" My baby was born on Memorial Day, 1966.

Four days after the birth, my mother drove me to High Mowing, a small boarding school on a mountaintop in western New Hampshire, for an interview to enter in the fall. That morning she had found me crying as I squeezed milk from my impacted breasts into the bathroom sink.

"Oh, Sweetheart," she had said. "My poor Sweetheart."

I whipped around and hissed at her, "Get out." They were the first and only tears I had shed throughout the pregnancy and birth and the terrible, terrible drive away from the hospital. We had moved beyond mother and daughter forever. Whatever she felt, watching me cry, could not help me now.

She was cheerful and talkative on the way to the school. "This is a time to regroup," she told me, "to get back on track." She didn't look at me as she drove. "You need to forget these difficult months and make a new start," she said.

My belly was empty and soft. I had stuffed handkerchiefs in my bra to soak up the milk that spilled and spilled from my breasts. I felt old. The fierce sense of aloneness intensified. My other being, my baby who shared life with me, who was alive in me when everything else had died, was left alone someplace on the third floor of the hospital, the absolute outcast, a castaway.

"I'm relieved," my mother said, "that this whole ordeal is over." She reminded me again that some of her friends had dropped her when they heard about me; she had paid a big price, she said. I was lucky she had found this school, the only one that had agreed to consider me. She talked on and on while we drove toward my next life.

Mrs. Emmet met us in the living room of the old farmhouse. She was 83, a wealthy eccentric and educator who carried her ideas from Germany and Austria. I felt at home; this was a world away from Hampton and Epping and my school friends, who had become cardboard cutouts from someone else's past. If I did not get in here, I would have to go to work without a diploma. I had always imagined I would go to Smith or Wellesley, the first generation. Now I hoped this old woman would let me finish high school in her strange little school for fuckups.

She said I could come, even though I had "run amok." I had to promise I would never talk to any of the girls about what I had done; I would have the only single room, to isolate me from the possibility that the need to talk would compromise my promise. In September, ancient and so diminished I barely felt alive, I joined 80 children for a final year of school. I graduated in 1967, the same year my old class finished up in Hampton.

For several years after that, I occasionally went "home." I slowly grew bold and defiant and would walk uptown and into the familiar stores. I always saw someone I knew. Inevitably they stared and then turned away abruptly. If two were together, they bent together in whispers and walked away from me. Patty, who had been for six years the only other member, with me, of an experimental, accelerated class, refused to sell stamps to me at the post office. Mrs. Underwood stayed busy in the back of the five-and-10, folding and refolding clothes until I left. Once as I got out of the car in my mother's driveway, Diane drove by with three girls from my class. They whipped around in the next driveway and stopped in front of my house. Diane leapt out of the car, smiling at me. "Is it true—" she asked loudly, grinning back at my old friends, "Is it true you got knocked up?"

I have not been to my father's house for 30 years. There are many things and many places that speak to me of what has been lost. I long, in an odd way, for my gray and forsaken bedroom in that lonely house, where someone lay close to my heart.

✿   ✿   ✿

There are other truths, of course, behind this history, glimmers and flickers of understanding that underlie these memories. I was not the do-good child I thought myself to be. For example I know now that I hated school. I was bored and arrogant, clamoring for more from better teachers. I once told the principal to go to hell. I offered to replace Mr. Belanger as French teacher when he couldn't answer my questions. My brother was a day student at Phillips Exeter, and I was jealous.

I think I was a skeptic—actually a cynic—by the time I was in high school. I was outspoken, with strong opinions—even defiant. I was intolerant of ignorance or injustice. I read the daily paper and Atlantic Monthly and knew that people suffered terrible inequities. I laid blame passionately around me—the battle was between the haves and have-nots. I believed in the Truth, in what was Right, and must have been righteous. I tended to be a loner; I had lots of friends, but they knew, I think, that I always reserved some elemental piece of myself. I imagined myself always on the outside, by choice on the days I felt loved and by some fated flaw on those other days. I carried a deep sadness, a melancholy that belied my cheerfulness.

I did love my church. But when at 14 I attended confirmation class, I grew increasingly frustrated with the lack of answers to my questions. I perceived this as a failure on the part of the minister and the church to own up to its limitations and hypocrisies. I challenged Mr. Andrews; he appeared to tolerate my confrontations, but I left confused and agitated each Wednesday evening. Two years before my expulsion, I realize now, my beliefs in God and my church had already started to fray.

It is true that my mother might not have continued in the church after I left. But she had met Paul the year before. He was a jazz mu-

374

sician, a writer, a thinker. I remember going to church alone for a while, probably during that year of tumultuous changes in my mother's own life. She became a radical, started keeping a journal, sketched faces on the phone pad. She worked for Paul at a new job with a small, artsy magazine. After work they joined friends at the house Paul rented at the beach for long nights of drinking and talk and cigarettes and music. That was the summer I got pregnant. Leaving the church may actually have happened for my mother months before my outcasting. Of course I believed completely that she was a nearly perfect mother and any trouble I found was born in my own reckless, selfish heart.

It is true that my shunning was a message from our community to my mother, also: *Bobbie Hall thought she was so high and mighty, but she couldn't keep her husband, and now she hangs out with beatniks at the beach. And don't even mention her youngest. You get what you deserve.* Her rejection of me was a measure of the humiliation she felt. She believed until her death that I caused her to lose her friends and her stature in our town.

I struggle to reckon with my own silence, my lack of fight. I allowed my family and community to abandon me while I was drowning. Worst of all I allowed my baby to be abandoned. I abandoned my baby. I never said a word. Sometimes my own failure of courage feels like the most hideous kind of cowardice, a flaw in me that confirms my unworthiness for love. Sometimes, rarely, I get a flicker of understanding about other realities and feel a powerful protectiveness of that stunned and desperate girl.

These various truths sometimes collide with memories I have used to reconstruct the puzzle, but they cannot alter the perfect truth I carry of having been turned out.

It is a function of shunning that it must eliminate the shunned completely. It feels like a murder and is baffling because there is no grave. No hymns were sung to ease my going or to beg for God's blessing on my soul. Shunning is as precise as a scalpel, an absolute excision, leaving, miraculously, not a trace of a scar on the community body. The scarring is left for the girl, an intense, debilitating wound that weeps for the rest of her life. It's quite a price to pay for having sex, scared sex, on a beach on a foggy Labor Day night.

The shunning has created a deep shame that infuses my life. It makes me feel wildly vulnerable. I struggle still to claim a permanent

WALKING AFTER DINNER

by PATRICIA STATON

from MID-AMERICAN REVIEW

We head out the levee road
to where three gray donkeys
hold down one corner of a pasture,

their croaky voices anthems
tugging us across the rocky landscape.
Lulled by the half-light I think

the older one has reached the bottom of things.
It sways me the way their ears hang
out. In the field of weeds

blamelessness lies everywhere.
How their feet don't get tangled
where the barbed wire is down.

It isn't grief that curves toward us.
It is a kind of mercy.
Stepping into the opening

we scratch their available necks,
raising slow clouds of dust.
They let us,

standing dopey-eyed in their beggar sleeves.
In the rise and fall I think even this
is a kind of survival.

It's a consolation
the way they stand in the light,
gold clinging to the air around them.

Nominated by Marvin Bell

GINA'S DEATH

fiction by CHARLES BAXTER

from TIN HOUSE

A SQUIRREL SQUATTED IN THE BIRDBATH. Another squirrel was ·
hanging by its claws onto the bird feeder. The girl, looking out her
bedroom window at the back yard, cleaned her fingernails halfheart-
edly with the nail file and thought of the end-of-the-world that didn't
happen on January 1, 2000, and the one that did happen twenty-one
months later, and then she wondered why, if there was a word, "ruth-
less," that was often applied to enemies of the USA, then what hap-
pened to its opposite, its lost positive, "ruth," which would have to
mean "kind," but didn't mean anything because no one used it? We
had ruthless enemies but no ruth friends.

If some people were "unruly," then who was "ruly"? Nobody.
When her room was messy, her mother said it was "unkempt," but
when it was clean, it was never "kempt" because the word didn't ex-
ist—everybody had a word for the wrong thing but silence prevailed
for the right. When her room was clean, it wasn't anything you would
put into words. It was wordless.

Early in the morning, just after the sun was up, the squirrels
looked like boys, somehow, she couldn't say why. Maybe because of
the way they moved, skittering and chasing each other, twitching. Or
maybe it was the fur. Something.

Her name was Gina, she was sixteen years old, and it was Sunday,
Family Day. After staring at the squirrels, she remembered to feed
her guinea pig his breakfast food pellets. Wilbur squeaked and
squealed softly as she dropped the pellets down the cage bars into
the red plastic tray. It didn't take much to make him happy.

On the other side of her room was a picture of Switzerland her mom had put up years ago. The picture had a lake in it, which was ruthlessly blue. Gina felt funny when she looked at this picture, so she didn't look at it very often. She couldn't take it down because her mom had given it to her.

Family Day. The plan was, her dad would show up and take them—her brother, her mom, herself—to the beach. Gina threw on a T-shirt and a pair of jeans. She grabbed her flute and went into the basement to practice for the school marching band, of which she was a member.

• • • • • • •

Ten minutes later she heard the thud of the morning newspaper flung against the front screen door. Gina put her flute on top of her dad's workbench (he had never bothered to move it to his apartment after he moved out) and went upstairs to read the headlines. The news consisted of Iraq (bombs), Cuba (jails), Ireland (more bombs), and then there was something about Gordy Himmelman.

Gordy Himmelman! He had shot himself. To death. It was permanent. Why hadn't anyone called her about it?

She had been in classes with Gordy Himmelman since kindergarten, but he was in a class by himself, and she hadn't seen much of him since he had dropped out. He muttered and swore and blew his nose on notebook paper, and he talked to himself in long strings of garble and never had any friends you could show in public. You could feel sorry for him, but he would never notice how sorry you felt, and he wouldn't care. Pity was lost on him. It was a total waste of time. In third grade he had brought a penlight battery into school and, standing next to the monkey bars, he had swallowed it during recess to attract attention to himself. The battery was only a double-A, but even so. He had black-and-blue marks all over him most days. His breath smelled of dill pickles that had gone unfresh. You couldn't even talk to him about the weather because he never noticed it—it didn't make any difference to him what the sky was doing or how it was doing it. He had this human-junkyard don't-mess-with-me look on his face and would kick anyone who got in his way, though he did have one comic routine: slugging himself in the face so hard that his head jerked backward. He had bicycled to that teacher Mr. Bernstein's house, where he had blown his brains out in the yard, in front of a tree, in the morning, a matinee suicide. On the front page of the paper was a picture of the tree. It was a color picture, and you could sort of see the blood if you looked closely.

There hadn't been a suicide note. A suicide note would have been like a writing assignment. Way too hard. He would have had to get his aunt to write it for him.

Gina felt something stirring inside her. She was kind of interested in death. Gordy was the first person she'd ever known who had entered it. He had gone from being Mr. Nothing to being Mr. Something Else: a temporarily interesting person. She sat at the kitchen counter eating her strawberry Pop-Tart, wondering whether Gordy was lying on a bed surrounded by virgins, or eternal fire, or what.

It was sort of cool, him doing that. Maybe the smartest thing he'd ever done. Adventuresome and courageous.

If you didn't have a life maybe you got one by being dead.

• • • • • • •

Her dad was late. Finally he showed up at eleven-thirty in his red Durango, saying, "Ha ha, I'm late." He and Gina's mom were divorced, but they were still "friends," and her dad had never really committed himself to the divorce, in Gina's opinion. He was half-hearted about it, a romantic sad sack. They had cooked up this Family Day scheme two years ago. Every weekend he'd come to pick up Gina and Bertie, her little brother, and their mom—Gina envied most divorced kids who went from their moms to their dads, without the cheesiness of Family Day—and then they'd do bowling-type activities for the sake of togetherness and friendliness, which of course was a total fraud since they weren't together or friendly at all. Usually Saturday was Family Day but sometimes Sunday was. Today they were going to the beach. Wild excitement. She had meant to bring a magazine.

• • • • • • •

In the car, Gina studied her father's face. She had wanted to drive, but no one trusted her behind the wheel. For once she had been allowed to sit up front: semi-adult, now that she had filled out and like that, so they gave her front seat privileges sometimes, occasional woman-privileges. Her mom and Bertie were in the back, Bertie playing with his GameBoy, her mom with her earphones on, listening to music so she wouldn't have to hear the plinks and plunks of the GameBoy, or talk to her ex, Gina's dad, the driver, half committed to his divorce, an undecided single man, driving the car. He would fully commit to the divorce when he found a girlfriend he really liked, which he hadn't, yet. Gina had met one of the girlfriends whom he had only half liked, a woman who tried way too hard to be nice, and who looked like a minor character on a soap opera who would eventually be hit by a rampaging bus.

Gina had mentioned Gordy Himmelman to her dad, and her dad had said yeah, it was way too bad.

She was interested in her father's face. Because it was her father's, she didn't know if he was handsome or plain. You couldn't always tell when they were your parents, though with her friend Gretchen Mullen you sure could, since Gretchen's father looked like a hobgoblin. At first she thought her own father had a sort of no-brand standard-issue father face; now she wasn't so sure.

He was possibly handsome. There was no way of knowing. Her dad was a master plumber. Therefore his hands often had cuts or grease under the fingernails. Very large hands, made big by genetic fate. His hair was short and brown, cut so it bristled, and near his temples you could see a change in color, salty. On his right cheek her dad had a crease, as if his skin had been cut by a knife or a sharp piece of paper, but it was only a wrinkle, a wrinkle getting started, the first canal in a network of creases-to-come, his face turning slowly but surely into Mars, the Red Planet. His teeth were very white and even, the most Rock Star thing about him. His eyes were brown and spaced wide apart, not narrow the way teenage boys' eyes are usually narrow, and they drilled into you so that sometimes you had to turn away so you wouldn't be injured by the Father Look. Her father's beard line was so distinct and straight, it looked put in with a ruler and was so heavy that even if he shaved in the morning, he usually needed another shave around dinnertime. That was interestingly bearlike about the masculine father-type. His nose was exciting. His breath had a latent smell of cigarettes, which he smoked in private. You couldn't find the boy in him anymore. It wasn't there. He was growing a belly from the beer he drank at night and weekends, and most of the time he seemed comfortable with it, though it seemed to tire him out also. He didn't smile much and only when he had to. He had once told Gina, "Life is serious."

On winter weekends he watched football on television speechlessly.

He looked like a plumber on a TV show who comes in halfway through the program and who someone, though not the main character, falls in love with, because he's so manly and can replace faucet washers. He would be the kind of plumber who wise-cracks and makes the whole studio audience break up, but he would be charming, too, when he had to be. But then sometimes at a stoplight or when he saw a car pull in front of him, her dad's face changed out of its TV sitcom expression: suddenly he grimaced like someone had started to do surgery on him right over his heart without anaesthetic, and he was pretending that nothing was happening to him even though his chest was being opened, bared to fresh air. And then that expression vanished like it had never been there. What was that about? His pain. His secret squirrel life, probably.

Still, there was no point in talking to him about Gordy Himmelman.

• • • • • • •

At the lake they settled in on their beach towels. Bertie, who was oblivious to everything, went on playing with his GameBoy. Gina's mom stretched out on her back in an effort to douse herself with lethal tanning rays. Her dad carried the picnic basket into the shade and started to read his copy of *Car and Driver*, sitting on the picnic table bench. Gina went to the concession stand to get herself an ice cream cone, which she would buy with her own money.

The stand itself had been constructed out of concrete blocks, painted white, covered overhead by a cheap corrugated roof. Under it, everything seemed to be sun-baking. Behind the counter was a popcorn machine with a high-intensity yellow heat lamp shining on the popped kernels in their little glass house, making them look radioactive. The sidewalk leading up to and away from the stand, stained with the residue of spilled pink ice cream and ketchup, felt sticky on the soles of Gina's feet. The kid who worked at the stand, selling snack food and renting canoes, was a boy she didn't recognize, about her age, maybe a year or two older, with short orange hair and an earring, and he stood behind the counter next to the candy bar display, staring with pain and boredom at the floor. He was experiencing summer job agony. He had a rock station blaring from his battery-operated radio perched on top of the freezer, and his body twitched quietly to the beat. When Gina appeared, the boy looked at her with relief, relief followed by recognition and sympathy, recognition and sympathy followed by a leer as he checked out her tits, the leer followed by a friendly smirk. It all happened very fast. He was like other boys: they shifted gears so quickly you couldn't always follow them into those back roads and dense forests where they wanted to live with the other varmints and wolves.

Raspberry, please, single scoop. She smiled at him, to tease him, to test out her power, to give him an anguished memory tonight, when he was in bed and couldn't sleep, thinking of her, in the density of his empty, stupid life.

Walking back to the sand and holding her ice cream cone, she started to think about Gordy Himmelman, and when she did, the crummy lake and the public beach with the algae floating in it a hundred feet offshore in front of her, she felt weird and dizzy, as if: what was the point? She kept walking and taking an occasional, personal, lick at the ice cream. There weren't too many other people on the sand, but most of the men were fat, and their wives or girlfriends were fat, too, and already they had started to yell at each other, even though it was just barely lunchtime.

She kept walking. It was something to do. Nobody here was beautiful. It all sucked.

The lake gave her a funny feeling, just the fact that it was there. The sky was sky blue, and her mother had said it was a perfect day, but if this was a perfect day, if this was the best that God could manage with the available materials, then . . . well, no wonder Gordy Himmelman had shot himself, and no wonder her mother had put up that picture of Switzerland in her bedroom. Gina saw her whole life stretched out in front of her, just like that, the fifty-two deck of cards with Family Day printed on one side, like the picture of the lake in Switzerland that she could barely stand to glance at, vacuuming her up. Why couldn't anything ever be perfect? It just wasn't possible. This wasn't perfect: it was its opposite, fect. A totally fect day. Just to the side, off on another beach towel, somebody's mom was yelling at and then slapping a little boy. Slapping him, wham wham wham, out in public and in front of everybody, and of course the kid was screaming now, screaming screaming screaming screaming.

Everybody having their own version of Family Day.

Gina carried the ice cream cone to the water's edge.

Right there, she saw herself in the algaed water, walking upside down holding a raspberry ice cream cone, and, next to her own water-image, another water-image, the sun this time. Gina walked into the water out to where the algae dispersed, staring first at her diminishing reflection and then at the sun. It'd be interesting to get blind, she thought, people and Seeing Eye dogs would take care of you and lead you through the rest of your life forever. You'd be on a leash. The dog would make all the big decisions. Then she noticed that when she walked into the water her images were sucked into it. As the water got deeper, there was less of you above it, as if you had gone on an instant diet. Okay, now that her legs had disappeared, she didn't have to look at her legs, because they weren't there anymore. Well, they were underwater, but the water was so dirty she couldn't see them as well as she could see her reflection at the surface: of her waist, her head, her chest, the ice cream cone. She wished she were prettier, movie pretty, but walking into the water was a kind of solution, watching your girl-image get all swallowed up, until there was no image left, just the water.

She held the ice cream cone above the water and then after another lick let it go as she went under.

Under the surface she held her breath as long as she could, and then she thought of Gordy Himmelman, and, sort of experimentally, she tried breathing in some water, just to see what it was like, and she choked. She felt herself panicking and going up to the surface but then she fought the panic when she imagined she saw somebody like Gordy Himmelman, though better looking, more like her dad, under the water with her, holding her hand and telling her it was better down here, and all the problems were solved, so she tried to relax and breathe in a little more water. She registered little thunderbolts of panic, then some peace, then panic. Then it was all right, and Family Day was finally over, and, because she wasn't a very good swimmer anyway, she began to sink to the bottom, though there were all those annoying voices. She would miss Wilbur, the guinea pig, but not much else, not even the boys who had tried to feel her up.

She drifted down and away.

Her father and the lifeguard had seen the cone for the raspberry ice cream floating on the surface of the lake at the same time. They both rushed in, and Gina's dad reached her body first. He pulled her up, thrashed his way to the beach, where, without thinking, he gave his daughter a Heimlich maneuver. Water erupted out of her mouth. Gina's eyes opened, and her father laid her down on the sand, and she said, "Gordy?" but what she said was garbled by the water still coming out of her lungs into her mouth and out of her mouth into the sand. As she came around, her hair falling around her eyes, she seemed disarrayed somehow, but pleased by all the fuss, and then she smiled, because she had seen her father's face, smeary with love.

Nominated by Margaret Luongo, Tin House

TO TELL THE

LITERAL TRUTH

by STEVE KOWIT

from TRIPLOPIA

is the trick by which poetry, Rico was saying,
anchors itself to the actual world (I
had been rash enough to suggest that
in art the literal truth doesn't matter
a bit), when a rattler, a good four feet of her
stretched in the heat on the ill-marked
Moorfred Rivercrest trail we'd been hiking,
startled us out of our chatter.
We didn't breathe, gave her a wide berth,
& were safely past, when Zoly,
our Aussie companion, who'd just gotten back
from a month-long dig in the outback
pits of Rodinga—Zoly, who cares not a whit
for epistemological theory—did
something I'll never forget: in one motion
swiveled, bent & grabbed for her thorax,
the other hand closing above that whiplash
of rattles, then, with a grin, rose to his feet.
The creature writhed in his hands, its hideous
rattlers buzzing while she hissed
with her godawful tongues & tried to break free.
Rico & me, we jumped back in terror. Zoly,

holding her out for us to admire, said
"Western Diamondback. Marvelous specimen, no?"
I could care less what it was called. I
took another step back. Zoly strode to an outcrop
of boulders a few yards away, & gently
as setting a kid in its crib, & with only
the tiniest flourish—the sort a jaunty
conductor or close-up magician might make—
tossed the thing free. Instantaneously
it vanished, slithering into the rocks,
I took a deep breath & relaxed.
From where we stood, on that rise, you could
make out the Salton Sea, far to the east,
& the undulant floor of the desert a long
drop below, endless & dreamlike.
"Amazing!" Rico mumbled under his breath,
lifting his Padres cap & rubbing the sweat
from his brow. But whether he meant the vista,
or snake, or how quickly it vanished,
or what Zoly had done, or the whole
delectable drift of the thing, god only knows.
Listen—In art, the truth—in that sense—
doesn't matter. I made the whole story up.
The Aussie. The outback. The snake.
Even the name of the trail. All but the part
where two friends & I argue over the poet's
complex relationship to the literal fact.
Everything else in this poem is a lie.

Nominated by Triplopia

THE APOLOGY

fiction by BROCK CLARKE

from NEW ENGLAND REVIEW

W YATT AND DAVE were in Wyatt's attached garage, searching for a croquet set Wyatt insisted he had bought, once, long ago, and that had to be in the garage *somewhere*, and while they were looking they got to talking, idly, about the weather, baseball, the status of their job searches, and the conversation took a surprising turn or two and soon Wyatt and Dave discovered that they had both been abused by Catholic priests when they were boys.

Once that was out in the open, Wyatt and Dave forgot all about croquet. From the mouth of the garage they could see their wives— Susan and Rachel—smoking Merits under the last remaining mature oak in Shady Oaks, which was the name of their subdivision. Wyatt's two sons were playing a complicated game involving a Frisbee, a dog, a detached piece of rusty gutter extension, and someone's hat. They all of a sudden seemed very far away, as if they were someone else's wives and children, as if Wyatt and Dave were very far from the selves they now were. Wyatt could smell the chemicals from the slow-burning charcoal fire he'd set earlier. As was the case with every barbecue he hosted, Wyatt had already made a big speech about cooking with charcoal and not propane. But now that he and Dave had ripped open their chests and revealed their tortured hearts, he felt very far from the man who had been so adamant about the superior taste of ground beef cooked over charcoal, too.

As for Dave, he felt something different. His and Rachel's baby son had died just two months earlier. He had died of crib death. The doctor had told them that it happened more often than people think, but news of its surprising frequency did not make Dave or Rachel feel any better. The doctor had also asked them if they had put their son to sleep on his stomach or his back. "He liked to sleep on his side," Dave said. The doctor had nodded sadly, as if sleeping on one's side were the problem, which pretty much ruined what was left of Dave to ruin. Every night Dave had sneaked into his son's room to watch his son sleep on his side and in doing so had begun to feel the blossoming of his own loving, fatherly self. Now that he and Wyatt had told the truth to one another about their abuse, he could start thinking about that and stop thinking about his dead baby.

But he didn't say any of this. Instead, he said, "I don't want to be like one of those guys on TV." He was talking about the many other men who'd been sexually abused by Catholic priests in their youths, those legions of sad, wide-eyed men you see on TV who told their stories in public for reasons—money? attention? forgiveness? peace of mind? the well-being of other would-be victims?—that seemed mysterious, even to them. No, Dave didn't want to be one of those men, didn't want what they wanted.

"But what do we want?" Wyatt asked.

"We want an apology," Dave said.

He was right. They simply wanted an apology. So Dave and Wyatt abandoned the garage and set off for St. Anthony's.

Rachel and Susan were finishing their cigarettes when they noticed their husbands walking down the street, away from the garage and the smoldering charcoal briquettes and their chirping children and their smoking wives.

"Dave, where are you going?" Rachel asked.

"We're going to St. Anthony's."

"What for?"

"To demand an apology," he said, and then they kept on walking.

This was not the first time Dave and Wyatt had demanded an apology. Dave had demanded an apology from his bank for sandbagging him with hidden withdrawal fees. Wyatt had demanded an apology from his children's teachers for making assumptions about how much time Wyatt did or did not spend with his sons going over their homework after school. Dave and Wyatt had both demanded apologies from Lance Paper Company for transferring them from jobs in Utica, New York, and Worcester, Massachusetts, respectively, to Clemson, South Carolina without giving them a real say in the matter, and then they demanded an apology from their new bosses in South Carolina for laying them off not even six months after they'd uprooted themselves and their families. When Dave and Wyatt were done demanding their apologies, they had apologized to their wives for not getting the apologies they felt they deserved, or for getting the apologies and then being disappointed that those apologies didn't make the sun any brighter or the grass any greener or their lives any happier.

So Dave and Wyatt had demanded other apologies. But this was the first time they had walked out to demand one. It was a longer walk than they'd reckoned. For one, Dave and Wyatt never walked anywhere anymore, a fact their physicians couldn't say enough about vis à vis Dave's and Wyatt's hanging bellies and high blood pressure and diminishing life expectations, and every quarter mile or so Dave and Wyatt had to pretend to look at a bird or something so that they could stop and catch their breath. For another, Shady Oaks didn't have sidewalks. Plus, theirs was one of those pick-up truck subdivisions and the S-los roared by all the time, going well above the posted thirty mph limit and sending Dave and Wyatt diving into the open sewers their taxes had been raised for. Wyatt—whose belly was bigger than Dave's and whose blood pressure was higher—even raised the possibility of turning back and just driving to the church in their own S-los, or maybe just making the trek some other time, when the sun wasn't so high or the heat so oppressive or the traffic so heavy, and when he and Dave were in better physical condition. But Wyatt's suggestion didn't have much conviction behind it and Dave knew it was just nervousness talking. Because they knew they were doing what they had to do, and as Dave pointed out, that they were walking instead of driving was a testimony to their seriousness of purpose. Besides, Dave said, there was something biblical and symbolic about their walking, and Wyatt agreed that he couldn't really imagine Moses driving around the desert for forty years in a detailed truck with running boards and cupholders.

They kept walking. It took Dave and Wyatt over an hour before they got to St. Anthony's. In fact, they almost walked right past it, because neither of them was an actual member of the church or had even attended mass there and they had really only had a vague idea of where it was located. Besides, it looked nothing like the churches they'd been abused in—nothing like Sacred Heart in Utica with its spire reaching up five stories and the cross at its peak reaching another story; nothing like Our Lady of Assumption in Worcester, which was made of native granite and which took up a whole city block and was so grand and massive that it seemed like even God wouldn't be able to destroy it when the day finally came. No, St. Anthony's was more or less a brick ranch house, and they would have missed it entirely had Wyatt not said, "Hey, there's a crucifix over the front door of that brick rancher," and he and Dave turned around, gathered themselves, and then knocked on the church's front door.

Who knows why they didn't just go right in instead of knocking? Why is a vampire in the movies unable to enter a house unless he's been invited? Even a vampire wants to feel wanted. They knocked and knocked, and finally, a priest opened the door. He wasn't wearing a collar or even those black casual clothes priests wear: he was wearing jeans and flip flops and the kind of collarless button down shirt that makes you think of a rich person on vacation. But Dave and Wyatt knew he was a priest—because of course he had answered the church door, but mostly because he looked remarkably like the priests who had abused them: he had a full head of curly reddish-brown hair and a cautious fatigued smile and raised eyebrows and Dave and Wyatt both took a step back, because the priest looked much like both of their abusers, as though they had summoned those priests to appear before them in a single body.

"Can I help you?" the priest asked. His voice was tired, resigned, as if he knew the answer to the question before he even asked it.

"Yes," Dave said and explained how he and Wyatt had been abused by Catholic priests in their youth and now they wanted an apology.

Dave and Wyatt really had been abused. Their abuse had run the gamut. Dave had been fellated on retreats, and the same priest had also more-or-less innocently and chummily draped his arm over Dave's shoulders during church school's discussion of the Virgin Birth and didn't remove the arm until the lesson was through. Wyatt had been fondled in empty church gyms after CYO basketball games, and the same priest, in front of Wyatt's parents, had simply remarked that Wyatt was a "good-looking boy." Dave and Wyatt had been forced to do some things that they couldn't talk about, even now, even with each other. They sometimes still woke up in the middle of the night yelling, "It hurts, it hurts," and had to be comforted by Rachel and Susan, who thought their husbands were merely having garden-variety nightmares.

Wyatt hadn't told Susan about his abuse, but he'd told his three previous wives. His first wife had wondered immediately if the abuse had turned Wyatt homosexual, or if it had happened because he had already been homosexual. Wyatt's second wife had used the abuse as a trump card, and if their checking account was empty when it came time to pay the mortgage, or when Wyatt accidentally spilled wine on the white lace tablecloth his second wife had had in her family centuries before they'd immigrated from Donegal, the second wife said, "Don't worry about it, Wyatt. It's nothing compared to what that son-of-a-bitch priest did to you." Then there was Wyatt's third wife, who had been purely supportive when he first told her. She'd said, "It's better that you told me. It can't hurt you anymore. Life will be different now." But their marriage turned out to be something less than the happy, healthy thing she thought it would be, and whenever Wyatt drank too much at dinner parties and took long, loud stands that were somehow both offensive and boring, or whenever he failed to get the raise or promotion that he felt sure he would get, Wyatt would say "I'm sorry, I don't know what happened, it's not really my fault," until finally, his third wife accused him of subconsciously using the priest's abuse as an excuse for all his subsequent failures and shortcomings. Wyatt hadn't told Susan, his fourth wife, which seemed to Wyatt the only smart thing he had ever done.

Dave hadn't told Rachel, either, and didn't think he ever would, for exactly the reasons that Wyatt had had four wives to his one, and for exactly the same reason that he never, ever talked about his baby son's death, either. In the case of both the abuse and his son's death, Dave was afraid that once the truth was out there in the open it would be promptly lumped in with other unpleasant truths and its importance would be diminished; and he was also afraid that it wouldn't be lumped in with all these other truths, that it would dominate the others and that once it was visible no one, not even Dave, could ignore it if he wanted. Dave was afraid too that he'd be accused of using his abuse and his son's death as an excuse, and that, at some level, there would be some truth to the accusation.

So Dave told no one about the abuse and he never talked about his dead son either, not even with Rachel. They instead talked idly. They had so many conversations about the weather that Dave had begun to feel the same way about Rachel that he did about the television weatherwoman—sometimes she wore clothes that were understated and flattering, sometimes garish and unbecoming;

sometimes he found her encyclopedic knowledge of tornadoes fascinating, sometimes dull. But he did not feel love for Rachel anymore, which before their son had died had been pretty much the only thing he'd felt for her. But at least he didn't talk to her about their dead son, at least she didn't make him admit to his terrible, true feelings—that the only thing that mattered anymore about their son was that he was dead; and not once did Dave tell her or anyone else about being abused, until he told Wyatt, and then the priest at St. Anthony's.

The priest listened, head down like a man in deep thought or deep regret, and when Dave and Wyatt were done he said, "I see," and then said, "It doesn't sound like either of you was abused in this church, though."

"Even so," Wyatt said. "We'd like an apology."

"Can you come back tomorrow?" the priest asked. "Or maybe later in the week?"

"No," Dave said. "We've waited twenty-five years already. We want it now."

"Okay." he said. "But I'll have to talk to the bishop first. He'll have to talk to the cardinal. Lawyers will have to be consulted. It might take a little while."

"That's fine," Dave told him. "We have plenty of time."

And it was true that Dave and Wyatt had plenty of time. They could have waited there all night and into the morning for their apology. Because even though the next day was Monday, Dave and Wyatt had no jobs to go to. They hadn't looked for work since they'd been laid off six months earlier, even though they both had new houses and crushing mortgages and Wyatt had children who would eventually have to get their teeth straightened and go to college. Dave and Wyatt weren't old, either; they were still in their late thirties; they had the relevant college degrees; they could have gone out and found something: there were paper companies everywhere, and someone needed to work for them. But Dave and Wyatt didn't even bother looking. It was as though they had lost their will to do something about anything. It wasn't that they were lazy, exactly; it was that they felt that being ambitious wouldn't amount to much. Besides, Wyatt had the kind of oversized garage designed to accommodate the speedboat Wyatt talked about buying but knew he never would. Wyatt and Dave liked to set up folding chairs in the garage and leave the country music channel playing softly on the transistor radio and not talk and watch Wyatt's grass seed wash away in the warm, monsoonal spring rains. The rain made a nice, fat, bonging sound on the garage's tin roof; it was comfortable in the garage, safe. Why would they want to go and look for work when they could stay in the garage?

Wyatt's and Dave's abuse at the hands of their priests might have had nothing to do with this lethargy. This was yet another thing they were afraid of: that they wouldn't know what was the product of abuse or what was simply part and parcel of being a normal thirty-eight-year-old American man disgruntled and living far away from his true home with no job, not even one he disliked. They would never know what was connected to the abuse and what was not. They would never be sure. This was another thing they would demand an apology for.

The priest made them wait in the church basement. Wyatt griped about this at first. The basement was carpeted and the carpet smelled of something wet and long dead and the glaring overhead fluorescent light kept flickering and if it were to go out Dave and Wyatt would be in complete darkness, because there were no windows and no other lights that they could see. Wyatt said, "After all we've been through, we deserve better than to be stuck in a church basement." Wyatt hadn't been in a church in ages, and spoke longingly of the seed-oiled wood pews, the stained glass, the votive candles, the towering pipe organ, the holy water, the veined marble pulpit, and the stations of the cross. "I wouldn't mind waiting so much," Wyatt said, "if we could only wait in the church itself."

But Dave said, "No, it's better that we wait in the basement. It's better this way," and the subject was dropped.

They waited. They waited a very long time. They did not speak to each other. Wyatt breathed heavily through his nose, then began whistling in the distracted manner of a person unaccustomed to introspection. Dave was crying softly, so softly that Wyatt couldn't hear it over the white noise of his nose breathing and whistling.

Dave was crying because he had started thinking about the apology—how satisfying it would be to get it finally after all these years and how maybe he could then forget about the priest, the retreats, everything, how maybe once the apology was tendered he could then start living his life—and then he realized that he had never asked anyone to apologize for his son's death. It had simply never occurred

394

to him. He had demanded apologies from everyone and for every-thing imaginable, and yet he had not demanded one for what had happened to his son. It was yet another way he had failed his son: he had failed to keep his son alive, and he had failed to demand an apol-ogy for his death. This was why he was crying; he cried for what seemed like hours, until the crying exhausted itself. You couldn't cry forever, Dave knew this from experience; and once you stopped cry-ing, you had to do the only thing you were capable of doing. The only thing Dave was capable of doing was to wait for the priest's apology, and that apology would have to double for the apology he should have gotten for his son.

Just then Wyatt and Dave heard voices. The basement door opened; there was the sound of someone walking down the stairs. They both rose to their feet without realizing that they had risen to their feet. They expected it to be the priest, of course, apology in hand. But it was just Rachel and Susan, their wives.

Wyatt was glad to see Susan, because he had begun to think his and Dave's mission was a big mistake: they had begun the quest for their apology together, on the same page, but they were not on that same page anymore. There was something about Dave's gloominess Wyatt could not penetrate. Wyatt knew about Dave's son, of course, and was very grateful that nothing bad had happened to any of his three boys, but he had not realized until now how much greater Dave's pain was than his. It had not occurred to Wyatt that all pain is not equal, and that one's pain didn't give one a greater insight into someone else's. Dave's and Wyatt's abuse had brought them together, but it could not do so completely, or forever, and so while Wyatt felt sorry for his friend, his best friend, he also felt estranged.

As for Dave, he wasn't thinking about Wyatt now; he was thinking about Rachel, how beautiful she was with her hair swept back in the messy ponytail that would always make her look like a twenty-year-old girl just back from the beach, how she was much too lovely to be in this musty basement, how her beauty didn't make him feel any better and in fact made him even more sad because the beauty didn't matter to him anymore, and how he wanted her to leave im-mediately.

"What are you doing here?" Dave asked them.

"We're here to get both of you to come home," Susan said. "The kids are waiting in the van. We saved some hamburgers for you back home."

"Is the priest up there?" Dave asked.

"Yes," Rachel said.

"What's he doing?"

"He's just sitting in a pew, staring into space. When we asked him where you were, he put his face his hands and said, 'Basement.'"

"He seemed a little freaked out," Susan said.

"Good," Dave said.

"Dave," Rachel said, "what are *you* doing here?"

Dave shot a look at Wyatt, who sighed his big man's sigh and nodded, and so Dave told the story. He spoke for himself and for Wyatt, looking at his feet the whole time. When he was done telling the story, he didn't look up.

"I'm sorry," Wyatt said to Susan. He knew his history, and could see the end of their marriage looming in the distance like an abandoned factory.

Susan shrugged and said, "That's okay," because she was more than a decade younger than Wyatt, and her generation was relatively comfortable talking publicly about the bad things that had been done to them. "No big deal," she said. "I still love you."

"Do you know what I hate?" Rachel said to Dave.

"What?" Dave said. But she didn't answer him back until he lifted his head to look at her.

"I hate when I tell people that Nick died of crib death, and they ask 'Where did it happen?'"

Dave smiled then, he really did. But when Rachel said, "I want you to come home," he shook his head, and the smile disappeared and he said, "No, I'm going to wait for this apology."

"I miss him, too," she said. "And I'm truly sorry about what that priest did to you. But I want you to come home."

"I can't," he said.

"I wish you'd come home with me right now," she said, very slowly, as if speaking to someone addled or retarded. "Because I don't think I'm coming back to get you." They looked at each other for a while, their gazes steady, unblinking. It was the way people stare at each other not when they're in love, but afterward, when they finally realize all the many horrible and beautiful things locked up within that love. But Dave didn't move, and Rachel finally broke the eyelock and ran up the stairs, two at a time.

Wyatt was on his feet; he was already thinking of how lucky he was to have this younger fourth wife and his spacious garage and his kids and suddenly the apology didn't seem so urgent anymore: he had waited so long, he could certainly wait a little longer. And even if Wyatt never got his apology, then maybe that was all right, too; it seemed to him that he had gotten what he wanted, somehow, without getting what he wanted, and he marveled to himself about how resilient the human animal is and thought that he might even work on his resume when he got home, maybe check the employment ads in the morning.

"I'm going home, buddy," he said to Dave. "You should, too."

Dave shook his head. "It's all right," he said. "I'll catch up with you later."

They shook hands, then Wyatt took Susan's and they walked up the stairs, closing the door behind them.

When they were gone, Dave turned off the light and lay down on the rug. He was thinking of the future. His wife and friends were gone; it was undoubtedly too dark to walk home, and besides he didn't want to go there anyway. But maybe he could stay in the basement. It wasn't as nice as Wyatt's garage, but overall it didn't seem such a bad place to stay. There was an old Frigidaire humming in the corner. There was a bathroom with an exhaust fan. He could conceivably stay in there forever. Maybe he would ask the priest if that were possible. Maybe he could attach it as a rider to the apology. Dave fell asleep, rolling over on his side in the fashion of his dead son, and his last thought before falling asleep was that he would waive his demand for apology if God would just let him die in his sleep, just as God had let his son die in his sleep, just as God had let so many other things happen.

But Dave didn't die in his sleep; he woke up when he heard a door open at the top of the stairway. He got up and walked to the foot of the stairs. The priest was standing there, illuminated from above by the chandelier in the vestibule. The priest saw Dave, but he didn't move, and neither did Dave. It seemed possible that they would stand staring at each other forever; and that was fine with Dave. Because there was nothing left for him to do but wait for his apology, which was the only thing standing between the life he had lived up until now, and the life to come.

Nominated by Antonya Nelson, New England Review

397

CAN'T YOU HEAR THE WIND HOWL?

by FRANK X. GASPAR

from THE GEORGIA REVIEW

I'm shivering here with Coleman Hawkins and cup of gin
and no idea what hour of the night it is—feeling ashamed
of how time passes when everyone knows I should be the
responsible party and put a stop to all this waste: What good
is a night if there's a dawn always lurking somewhere in the future?
How can I ever be completely certain of the stars if they fade
so easily before such cheap theatrics? When will I learn, as all
my betters have, to live in the moment? Out in the alley there's
a possum looking for a home. Out in the city lights there's an
alley looking for a street. You can hear the wind blowing
all along the window screens. It's singing to the voices in my head,
it's saying, *Quiet!* It's saying, *Shooo!* Coleman Hawkins isn't
saying a word. He's occupied with some friends. He's living
in the moment among certain characters with names like Dizzy
and Django and Pee Wee and Cozy. He ain't going nowhere,
he is all past *and* future, if you know what I mean. I don't have
the nerve to say my heart is aching—not with *that* crowd all
around me, not with that bass line shaking the books and their
cracked spines and rocking the pens and pencils. Am I wrong?
Am I wrong to let Cicero rest awhile and to let Sappho, in her
tatters, sleep under the seven sisters, and to breathe in deeply
and to breathe out deeply? And to let the ice in my blue cup bark
in its quiet cataclysms and let the brown air blow down a hundred
   miles

398

from the deserts because I have no choice in these matters? Now
let me tap my foot in a certain way. In a certain way because there
was a machine once that could cull every kind of music from a room
and save it for a while, unharmed. Can't you hear the wind howl?
Here, all around my feeble senses. Here, in the iron lung of the
    night.
Here it comes again, all teeth in the palm leaves, looking for a
    home.

Nominated by Philip Levine

THE SQUEEZE

by BARBARA HURD

from ORION

MY FIRST ATTEMPT AT CAVING ten years ago began in inspiration and ended in terror. I'd been teaching creative writing at an environmental camp for middle school students who were scheduled to take a field trip to a nearby cave. For two days before the trip, I primed them with stories about Mohammed in the cave, Plato's cave, why caves so often symbolize rebirth. It's a hidden space, I told them, an unexpected, inscrutable space. I didn't anticipate trouble. I didn't mention claustrophobia or the guide's warning we'd need to belly-squirm down the initial passage. We all loved outdoor adventure, and on the day of the expedition, two guides, eleven students, and I fastened the chinstraps of our helmets in anticipation and climbed down a rope ladder into a muddy pit, at the bottom of which was the mouth of the cave.

One guide explained the sloping first passage, how to get through it, what lay beyond. Head first, he said, and then scooch with your elbows. At the far end, he explained, the tunnel opens up on a ledge and then you squirm down into a big room where you can stand and stretch.

I bent down and peered into the chute's entrance. It was, by any caver's standards, an extremely easy passage, fairly round, maybe two feet high. It actually looked tidy, a railroad tunnel in some miniature train layout. I stood up and watched as the kids kept disappearing down it. They'd lean over, stick their faces in, and then lie down and start squirming. The last I'd see of them was their feet wiggling, the toes of their boots shoving against the hole's interior floor, and then nothing. My heart started to pound a bit.

400

"Ready?" the last guide asked me. We were the only ones left in the pit. I was supposed to go, and then he'd bring up the rear.

"Yep," I said. And stood there.

"You okay?" he asked.

"Yep," I replied and got down on my hands and knees, down on my elbows, and looked in again. My headlamp threw a small circle of light into what no longer looked tidy, looked, in fact, like something gouged open, the interior walls jutted and slimy. The guide waited. I lowered my upper body and then my hips to the cave floor and dragged myself forward on my elbows, pushing with my right hip and then left, right boot and then left, the tunnel growing darker and muddier, my light smaller and smaller. And then something was moving toward me, not stone, not anything I could see, maybe sound, maybe wind, and then something else: the Mack truck that barreled into my cousin's car moments before his death. I felt it as clearly as if I'd been in that silent car with him, windows rolled up, both of us speechless as an impossibly large pair of headlights, steel bumper, and grille loomed into the side-view mirror, bore down on our watery bodies of burnable flesh, only I wasn't there, I was here in a dark tunnel and couldn't see what I felt, knew only that I was about to be flattened by the thing that moves inside stone, the thing that was hurtling up that tiny tunnel toward me—who was by now scratching and clawing my way backwards.

When I came back toward him, rear-first, knees bumping in reverse, frantic, I heard the guide scramble out of my way and felt him catch my shoulder as I turned to scurry up the ladder and out of the pit. "Just wait for a few minutes," he said. "It'll pass. You can try again." I looked at him steadily. My voice was eerily calm. "No," I said, one foot on the first rung.

"Absolutely not." Something had been suddenly siphoned out of my mind and all that remained was what I knew not to do: not to try again, not to even look back. He urged again but I shook him off and climbed out of the pit and into the sunshine.

But slowly I did try again. Something drew me, some curiosity about that unexpected terror and a lifelong love of stones. As children, my friend Jeanne and I had created endless small-stone dramas in the woods behind my house, built hospitals for injured stones, nursed them back to health. We'd gone on to college together, signed up for two semesters of geology, mostly because we'd heard that in the labs you got credit for rubbing and licking stones. We loved geodes and the rock exposed when road-building crews dynamited away the side of a mountain—anything that let us look at what's been concealed for thousands of years. How could I let one afternoon of terror keep me from the ultimate intimacy with stone: to go inside it?

It's April in West Virginia, season of tender green and the cows out in the meadows at last after a winter in the barn. I've explained to the two leaders what I want: to crawl around in the dark, to try another tight spot, to be helped through any panic that might follow.

The entrance to this cave is in a cliff on the other side of a stream that divides a meadow. Walking across the new green grass, I look up at the mountain and though I can't see the opening itself, I can see where the stone gets more convoluted, the folds and crevices deeper, the shadows more suggestive. We scramble up a bouldery slope, inch sideways across a ledge, and suddenly there's the entrance, a rather wide entrance, maybe four feet high. Easy, I think. Three of the others go in immediately. Debbie, Kathy, and I sit outside a while. They describe the passage, how it narrows a bit fairly soon but not for long, and ask me how I want to do it. Do I want them in front or behind me? How close? Someone else nearby?

It's an odd experience, being calmly asked how you want to get through a fear that might be about to squeeze you breathless. I think of friends who've helped one another through difficult times. What is it we can offer each other? An unruffled presence, maybe a map of good handholds, words of encouragement. But mostly, perhaps, the obvious demonstration that someone else has been through this and lived. In the middle of a divorce, you want someone nearby who's done it before, who can describe the landscape ahead. When your dog dies, nobody's better than the friend with the most recent dog death in the family. And now, when Jeanne, my childhood friend and stone-loving compatriot, is slowly dying, I want Ann, who survived her sister's death. "Here," your friend says, "put your hand here, your knee over there, find your body's sense of balance, now push with your foot." You're in unfamiliar territory, a landscape where you could get lost, wander, or grieve forever. You need, more than anything, the willingness to be instructed. I want Debbie in front of me, I tell her, close enough so I can touch the heel of her boot. And Kathy behind me, three feet back, her light aimed as far ahead as possible. I'm amazed how easy it is to tell them what I need.

We squat and duck-walk a short while and then have to get on our hands and knees. Daylight from the entrance fades. The darkness is broken only by the small lights on our helmets. Debbie and Kathy banter a bit as we crawl, as if we were all sitting around someone's kitchen table. It soothes me, though I keep reaching out my hand, making sure I can touch Debbie's boot. We keep our heads low. The walls aren't muddy here but close enough that if I turned my elbows out as I crawled, they'd scrape against stone. I keep my eyes fixed on Debbie's boots. She doesn't have to push with her feet here and so the boots simply follow her knees, one after the other in a steady pistonlike action I find comforting. I adjust my pace to match hers. When her right knee moves forward, mine does too. Same with the left. First one, then the other. I study the soles of her boots, feel our movements synchronized, as if we're hooked to the same pulley system, ratcheting ourselves forward together in the darkness, until I begin to relax a bit, comforted by our steady movement, and am able to swing my head to the side for a second and look at the small circle of the tunnel wall lit up by my headlamp.

It's fairly dry, pebbly almost, gray-brown, and pocked. And irregular, as if a drunken plasterer had crawled in and slathered mud, which then dried in a haphazard pattern of chunks and swipes and small ridges. I'd forgotten how hard stone is, the bony patella of my knees scraping directly on it. Sound is harsh here, too, unmuffled, our boots grating, pants crinkling, water bottles sloshing in the otherwise great silence of a cave. And then the others' voices and the ceiling suddenly rise and I look up. Though it's pitch-black except for our six small lights, I can tell this room is fairly large, twenty by twenty, perhaps, high ceilings and sloping floor. The others have been poking around, waiting for us, eager to move on. I want to hug everyone, to toast my own feat. I lean against a wall and look at what I've just crawled through. I don't know what's ahead. I do know that's the only way out.

What's immediately in front of us is a fairly smooth passage, an easy walk. I shine my headlamp on the irregular walls, the sloping ceiling. I want to see everything and don't yet have the experienced caver's ability to construct a passage in the mind, to see without aiming a light into every nook and cranny. Their heads are fairly steady on their necks: mine wobbles and bobs like a lollipop on a soggy stick as I swing my light everywhere I can. The passage soon brings us to a breakdown, a section strewn with fallen boulders.

Breakdowns occur because limestone fractures easily. It also dissolves easily, which explains the development of the cave in the first place. Limestone is a sedimentary rock formed in shallow seas where millions of shells dropped to the ocean floor, were crushed under the weight of millions of other shells, compacted and pulverized, and finally pressed into stone. Layers and layers of limestone, lifted and folded by tectonic-plate action and mountain-building forces, rose above those ancient seas and now lie beneath topsoils all over the world. Because groundwater is laced with a mild carbonic acid, when it seeps underground it slowly, almost imperceptibly, dissolves bits of the highly soluble limestone, creating tiny fissures, which channel more and more of the water. After millions of years, the fissure becomes crevice becomes tunnel and then cavern, a whole subterranean system of streams that continues to widen and dissolve.

Eventually, if water drains completely out of the cave or walls are later undercut by streams, the cave ceiling may lose its support, and the limestone begins to crack and fracture and the roof then collapses. The result is a breakdown, a pile of debris that can be scattered over a hundred yards or heaped into fifty feet, debris that can range in size from tennis balls to houses. Of course in the dark you can't see them all at once. We turn and sweep the narrow beacons of our headlamps over the boulders in the middle of this cave passage, our half-dozen small ovals of light sizing up the obstacles ahead. The chunks of debris are angular, tilted, propped against one another, some with knife-ridges, others flat as altars.

We move through the breakdown slowly, carefully. Each foot is placed deliberately, the next move already determined. Debbie leads me, calling out directions, showing me how to hoist my body, how to use my knees, how to lean into a boulder and inch sideways. Constantly aware of the fragility of my body, I work these stones like a slow motion, 3-D hopscotch, searching out the safe foothold, the wide-enough ledge, the handhold that will keep me from falling. I forget that I'm deep inside a mountain. I forget about everything but the next move. And the next and the next, and a crawling, scrambling, exhilarating, exhausting hour later we have worked our way through. My legs are trembly, my knees ache, and I'm sure that underneath my overalls, my skin has begun to bloom into bruises.

We pause for water, and Kathy says we have a choice to make. We can take a shortcut through a very narrow passage or continue on the longer, easier way. Two of the guys, Debbie, and Sue choose the shortcut. I want to look at it first. Kathy leads me around a corner and shines a light toward an impossibly small opening. It's irregular, a cleft between an old jumble of rocks, maybe fourteen inches high. It twists around in there, Kathy explains matter-of-factly. It's best to go head first and there's a bit of a downward slope at the end.

It's what cavers call a flattener, a squeeze, the kind that can take the buttons off your shirt and the skin off your cheek. Every eighth of an inch matters, which might mean taking your pack off, sometimes your helmet, maybe even your clothes. The most notorious squeezes have names: the Gun Barrel, Jam Crack, the Electric Armpit Crawl, Devil's Pinch. You can even train for them by buying a product called a squeeze box. It's essentially a play torture chamber for cavers, a wooden box, about thirty by thirty inches, open on the two ends. You set it up in your living room, get down on your hands and knees, and crawl through it. The box has adjustable sides and top. You loosen the bolts, lower the lid, slide the sides closer, crawl through again. You keep doing this, keep shrinking the interior space, until you find your "zone of comfortable passage." Or, as another caver puts it, your "too-tight threshold."

I stare at the narrow slit at my feet. Choosing this route could mean five minutes of panic-stricken thrashing against stone. But choosing the long route around means an extra hour of climbing and butt-sliding, a sure strain on my already trembling limbs. Suddenly I want sunshine, a paved intersection with a stoplight and green arrow, oldies on the radio station, and not this dark, silent world in which neither choice appeals.

Attempting to sail home, Odysseus approached a narrow passage of water that runs between the cave of Scylla and the whirlpool of Charybdis. Circe had warned him about the strait, that on one side, the sea swirls and sucks down black water and three times a day swallows whatever comes near it. That on the other, a six-headed cave monster with rows of hideous fangs preys on whoever passes by. The story has become idiom: to be caught between Scylla and Charybdis is to be squeezed between two dangers. Avoiding one means exposing yourself to the other. How many times do we find ourselves having to choose between two risks? Possible death to the entire crew or certain death to six men? Loneliness or hostility? Unkindness or dishonesty? What to do?

Taking the long route means adding an hour not just to my time, but to Kathy's too, as she will not leave me alone in the cave. Taking the short route might mean the others have to calm a panicked novice. I squat down and look closer, try to imagine sliding my body into that stony hole. I tell Kathy I need to take the long way round.

Lunch is where we meet up again, a half-hour of rest and squashed peanut butter sandwiches and the story of Sue's moment of panic in the shortcut. Not more than a couple of yards from the end, one arm extended, the other pinched to her side, her head turned sideways to fit through, she'd been seized by claustrophobia. It lasted only a few seconds, and she was able to laugh about it over lunch. I was oddly relieved. Here was an expert caver who'd gone underground all over the world and she could still have such moments.

Mine was coming.

After another hour of climbing and crawling, we split into two groups, Kathy and I staying behind to poke around more leisurely while the others scrambled off to find a further passage. Kathy wants to show me some small rimstone pools just up a small incline. Miniature dams on a miniature terraced hillside, they look like an aerial scene from a film of the Indian countryside. A little farther up the incline I see a cleft in the stone. A tight passage, Kathy says, but short, maybe fifteen feet. You're on your belly but there's still a good four inches above your head. I want to try it, I tell her. Away from the others, Kathy's calm presence nearby, I want to do it. Kathy hesitates and then leads me up, describes it again, pointing out that if she goes first I'll see her light on the other end. It'll be something clear to scooch toward. She wiggles through in fifteen seconds with no trouble. I start through.

I get a third of the way in. I'm on my belly, arms stretched out ahead. I can move my head, lift it slightly to look for the end, lay it sideways on the floor, inch forward with my hands and elbows, but I have to stay flat on my belly. I can't sit up or draw my knees up close to my chest, which is what I suddenly want to do.

How to explain it? Some curtain falls, blocks off your ability to be rational. I stop where I am, head turned sideways, staring at the passage wall. I'm pretty sure Kathy's talking to me but my heart's begun to race, its pounding far louder than her calm voice, which sounds muffled now, trying to get through to me, halfway out of a nightmare, the sheets wrapped around my face, the air thick with dread, only these sheets are made of stone and I can't claw them away from my face, can't even get my hands close to my face. My body's instinct to escape is suddenly distended, swollen, flooding every available place in my mind. A reckless instinct, incapable of negotiation, completely oblivious to the tiny part of my shrunken mind that sends out one last gasping word of restraint—*wait, wait*—it sweeps wildly through the body, which wants immediately to heed the new command: *run, run*. I try to bend my right leg, as if readying for a sprint, but my knee smashes immediately into the wall. It's as if I'm in a full-body straightjacket shoved headfirst into a too-small casing inside solid stone.

I think Kathy's still talking to me. I can see her headlamp, but it's not the welcome light at the end of a tunnel; it's a train light too far into the tunnel to stop and it's barreling toward me, who is blocking all the space with my body. The stones have begun to edge closer, the ceiling to lower, and I look at Kathy again and miraculously, I hear her say, "Take a deep breath." She says it in the same tone she might offer me orange juice, a poached egg for breakfast. I close my eyes and breathe, picture the air filling my lungs, feel my chest expand and then drop, imagine the exhaled air keeping the walls at bay. I breathe again.

The best advice for managing a squeeze comes from Buddhism. The squeeze, Buddhists say, is the unbearable place. The place that makes us want, more than anything else, to be elsewhere. The uncomfortable, embarrassing place where the irrational, the fearful, the panicking parts of ourselves want out, to jump ship, to leave. Buddhists are talking, of course, about mental squeezes, when one part of the mind presents us with irrefutable evidence of something another part of the mind absolutely will not acknowledge. What to do? The usual reaction is to suppress one part and carry on as if it doesn't exist, meaning something in us shrinks, gets smaller. It's a strategy we resort to often. Getting a little smaller, after all, means gaining a little more wiggle room. Now maybe we can squirm another inch, sidle sideways, slip out of the crack. But if we're in the grip of a real squeeze, denial doesn't work anymore and all the evidence becomes palpable: you can't live with him and you can't live without him. There's no more forward and there's no backward. There's a rock in front of your face and there's a rock digging into your back.

Study the rock, the Buddhists say. Open your eyes and study the rock that's pressing into your nose. Look at its color. Note the variations in texture. Breathe. If you can get your glove off, feel it. Muddy? Sandy? A bit of slime? What, exactly, is pressing into your back? Is it ridged or smooth or lumpy? Where, exactly, does it press? Into your shoulder blades, your bum, your ribs? These are impossible tasks, and exactly what a Buddhist would recommend to someone caught in a squeeze. Study the place. Watch how your mind leaps to absurdities. Watch the way panic looms and recedes. You're not going anywhere at the moment, so you might as well be curious about where you are.

I open my eyes. In front of me is a damp wall of bedrock. Dark brown, grayish, a thin skim of viscous mud. A few inches up, the wall's pebbly surface shows through. Small craters and crust, a little more tan, speckled. This is limestone, I know, the primary rock in which caves form. I'm lying in a small tunnel, I tell myself, in which the stone has been dissolved, so what's left here, crowding me, has to be less soluble than what's gone. I try to see the tunnel itself and the room behind me that we've just left, try to picture the breakdown we crossed through before lunch, the ceiling above it, the mountain above that, the valley we drove through to get here, the sinkholes and disappearing streams so typical of karst, this landscape of pocked and riddled limestone. A book I have at home flashes through my mind—photographs of karst landscapes all over the world, in England and New Zealand, in China and New Mexico, their deep pits and sunken bowls and, underneath, their caverns and tunnels, like this one I'm frozen in. I turn my head sideways on the floor to rest. I breathe, I hear Kathy's voice, I hear Rilke's voice: *everything close to my face is stone.*

Odysseus lingered at the entrance to the passage. In the end, he did as Circe had advised: he passed through on Scylla's side of the strait. Scylla saw them coming, of course, twisted her six heads down to the ship and plucked six men from the deck. Odysseus did what commanders-in-chief do in every major battle, what each of us does in large and small decisions a dozen times a year: he chose the certain deaths of a few over the probable deaths of many. We do it all our lives. We reject small parts of ourselves, which then die—unexpressed dreams, secret longings, the hopes we say were minor once we've chosen to discard them.

The Odyssey is the quintessential Western hero's story, full of agonizing choices and ordeals. The hero makes all the right moves and eventually gets home again. His adventures teach us about the indomitable human spirit, about courage, perseverance, and the need to make hard choices. I raise my head. My helmet bangs immediately against the ceiling. A warning, I think, lowering it slowly. Odysseus couldn't avoid the Scylla vs. Charybdis passage entirely; it was way too late to turn around and find another route home. But I want to know how Western thought would have been different if Odysseus had lived a little later, been able to read a bit of Buddhism before he set sail. Caught between two dangers, what if he'd heeded the Buddhist advice, lowered his sails, and studied the passage between them? Why couldn't he have waited, spent a few days timing Charybdis's thrice-daily thrashings? It seems he could have charted the pauses, understood the pattern, and then steered his boat to that side of the passage during a lull and avoided Scylla altogether.

The trouble with a squeeze, Odysseus knew and I know, is that it imparts a certain urgency. We think we can't stand being caught between a rock and hard place, can't stand it one more second, and so we flail our way out, bruised and panicky. To resist the panic, to wait until the mind can consider more carefully, just to wait at all, in fact, requires patience and a tolerance for boredom, neither of which makes for the high drama of legends.

A diagram in a cave rescue document flashes through my mind. It shows a caver caught in a vertical crevice. Her left arm is stretched up, as if reaching toward the rescuer at the top who leans over, shines his light down into the crack. Her right arm is pinned to her side, straight down. Her head is turned to the side. The two crevice walls squeeze her the whole length of her back, her rear, her knees, her chest. She can't breathe well. Her feet dangle. There's nothing below them. Her only possible course of action is to stay calm and completely still while others work their ropes and harnesses. To squirm at all is to risk slipping further down. In fact, any movement on her part will only jeopardize her position. I'm suddenly grateful for the stone my body's stretched on. I lift my head carefully, turn it to the right, wiggle the toe of my right boot a bit, feel how firm the cave floor is beneath me. Breathe.

Ten years ago, about to enter a cave for the first time, I might have read the wrong things to my young creative writing students. Or to myself. Instead of myth and metaphor, maybe we should have studied mud and rock, studied the literal in front of our faces for a while, let the figurative emerge on its own. It does. It will. I might have avoided panic, gotten through that squeeze, been able to follow my

THERE

by EAMON GRENNAN

from THREEPENNY REVIEW

All his life, we're told, Chardin struggled *to overcome his lack of natural talent,*
So I begin to look again at his olives and peaches, at that cut-open cantaloupe
With its orange innards on show, or that orange from Seville he kept giving
A bit part to—to burn softly in its given space, to weight the picture in a newly
Luminous way. Or how the dead rabbit's fur is a dry gleam of white at the heart
Of warm browns, or the way each feather in the dead red partridge is a live thing—
The bird's life stilled to this final exposure of itself. The struggle you see is with
The facts themselves, and with some knowledge he kept hidden from our eyes, some
Unspoken sense of how *there* these bodies are, and nothing can say it the way it is—
Only you look again, stretch your hand, dip the bristles, risk again the failing stroke.

Nominated by Lucia Perillo

VIRTUOSO MIO

fiction by KAREN PALMER

from THE KENYON REVIEW

PERLA RAMIREZ IS CAT-FACED AND SULLEN, foul-mouthed and resentful, and at twelve she is already a vandal, a pickpocket, a sneak, and a snitch. The entire neighborhood hates her. Does she care? It seems she does not. "Ay, Perla!" rings at her back wherever she goes, but she returns every curse with a violent "Fuck!" of her own, continuing unstopped on her furious way, spilling trash cans, breaking windows, spying on lovers, stuffing her pockets with candy bars, lipsticks, and CDs for the Walkman she pinched off a drunk.

Perla lives with her mother, Sonni, and baby sister, Lani, in three rooms on the sixth floor of a walkup on 137th Street in New York. The skinny railroad-style flat is piled high with junk: stacks of old newspapers, tattered furniture, dead appliances. In the kitchen a closet behind the breakfast table houses the john. A pea-green bathtub stretches along one entire wall, clear to the window ledge; filled, the tub looks like a lake. Hinged to its back edge, a heavy sheet of unpainted plywood serves as a makeshift countertop. Here Perla's mother stores their dishes, their bowls and glasses and plates. Because it is such a chore to clear everything off, the three Ramirez women bathe together just once each week, every Saturday morning at six. And since today happens to be Saturday, Perla, still half asleep, sits huddled in tepid water, scowling at the weak winter sunlight that forces its way through the window's coating of soot. Sonni laughs, and Perla shifts her aggravated attention to the other end of the tub, where her mother lolls with baby Lani laid out in her lap. Famously beautiful all over their neighborhood, Sonni at twenty-nine looks barely nineteen. Her skin is unblemished, smooth as syrup; her arms are round, hairless, and soft. Her eyes are the color of wet maple leaves. She has dimples and curls, red lips, and even white teeth. At the Café Reál, where she works as a waitress with three of her girl-friends, Sonni is considered the sexy one, her looks a calling, almost, and she smiles all the time, as if waiting for someone to take her picture.

Perla, on the other hand, never smiles. She has her reasons, among them the fact that last year Maxie Otero threw a beer bottle at her and knocked out two teeth, his explanation being that Perla looked weird. Now she looks weirder still. And although Sonni keeps making promises that she'll take her daughter to the dentist to see about the hole in her mouth, she never does. They never have any money; but in Perla's opinion, that's no excuse.

The chestnut tips of Sonni's breasts poke through the bubbles. Perla hisses. She crosses her arms over her own scrawny chest. Humming, Sonni soaps Lani's hair with a slivered white bar and Perla slips down till she is submerged to the eyeballs. She opens her mouth and lets it fill with water, then rears up and spits across the lake. The stream hits her mother right in the face.

"Ay, Perla!" Sonni squints one-eyed. "What's the matter with you?"

There is no good answer to that question.

Baby Lani looks as if she might cry.

"Maybe," Sonni says, "you should go hear music at Carnegie Hall." She's talking about the concert this afternoon. Mrs. Davis, the director of the Youth Center, is taking a bunch of kids downtown to a piano recital. It's a gift from the city, an afternoon of culture for the underprivileged. *Classical music*. Fuck that, Perla thinks. She likes hip-hop, Aceyalone and Wu-Tang Clan and Krayzie Bone. She likes the way the angry voices vibrate inside her skull, and in her chest, too, a feeling that pushes against her skin from the inside. Sonni says, "It's that Italian kid, eh, Perla? What's his name? Luigi something something something."

Perla is too smart for that. The flyer is right there on the kitchen table and if Sonni wants to know, all she has to do is look.

"I can still get Rita to watch the baby," Sonni says.

Perla hunches forward. The idea of ditching Lani is very tempting. She wouldn't even have to make the concert, she could go wherever, do whatever. But there is a hopeful eagerness in her mother's face she feels she must squash.

413

"I hate that Davis bitch," Perla says, though really, Mrs. Davis is mostly OK, with her kinky gray hair and a gap-toothed smile Perla can identify with. Mrs. Davis lets Perla drink black coffee on cold days, and once gave her a pair of Nikes with lights in the heels that a grandson had outgrown.

Sonni cups a palm over Lani's eyes. She reaches over the side of the tub, fingers grazing the linoleum to retrieve a plastic cup. Carefully, she rinses the baby's hair. Lani, squealing, hits the water with the flat of her palm. Waves splash to Perla's end of the tub. The baby looks sly, as if seeking applause. Lani is fifteen months old and has a different father from Perla, a white guy that passed on his papery skin and light hair. Perla hates it that the baby is so fucking sweet, that kisses fall on Lani like soft summer rain. Each night, the girls camp out in the living room—Sonni claiming the only bed in the apartment's only bedroom—toe-to-toe on the orange Abortion Couch, so-called because wicked steel coils stab up through the weave; and sometimes, very late, when Perla can't sleep for wanting something, she doesn't even know what, she throws off the covers and flips around and crawls to her sister's side. She fits the earphones from the Walkman over Lani's little pink ears. She puts her cheek against Lani's hot little temple. Then she twists the volume, the tinny threads raveling from the radio's heart, the sound growing louder and louder—she can't help herself, she has to do it—until the baby wakes with a scream.

Sonni leaves for work.

There is nothing to do.

Perla digs through the newspapers in the living room, dredging up old comics to read. She spreads them out on the floor. Lani swats at the print, laughing when Perla pushes her hand aside. "You're such a baby," Perla says. Lani scrunches the paper up in her fist. She could play this game till the day's bitter end, but after twenty minutes, Perla is bored.

She heads for Sonni's bedroom. She wants to try on her mother's clothes. Short dresses, bright tops, jeans that fall straight from Perla's hips. But as soon as each item is on, she can't wait to take it off. Sonni has a red silk kimono that Perla rips accidentally-on-purpose, stepping on the hem. The heap of discarded clothing grows. Lani watches from the floor, open-mouthed. She drags a garment from the pile and waves it like a flag.

Wearing a flowered sundress cut so low that her nipples peek out, Perla wanders into the kitchen, Lani toddling after. Perla skirts the breakfast table and squeezes into the john. She opens the medicine cabinet and hunts, looking for something, she has no idea what. She sees: mouthwash and toothpaste, deodorant, tampons, lotions and potions, a cache of makeup. Perla lifts a plastic compact. She opens the lid and wets the small brush with spit, as she's seen her mother do. She lines her eyes thickly with black, then steps back and winks at herself in the mirror. Then she grimaces; she looks like a fucking vampire. Lani, holding on to Perla's legs, bounces energetically and puckers her tiny lips. Perla bends down to apply fuchsia gloss. The baby smacks, not sure she approves of the taste.

Sonni has devoted an entire shelf to plastic bottles that contain various pills. Perla makes a random selection. She shakes a few red capsules into her hand, lines them up on the tip of her tongue. She studies herself again in the mirror. The pills look like little canoes. The baby sits down hard on her diaper and starts to whimper and Perla picks the pills off her tongue and pitches them into the toilet. She helps Lani up, guiding her hands to the seat for support. The baby grips as Perla flushes. They watch the water circle, the pills riding the whirlpool, a gay fleet on a luckless rendezvous.

Lani is making a lot of noise now and Perla realizes the baby's hungry; they both need to eat. Back in the kitchen, Perla dumps Lani in her high chair. "Pea-buh," Lani says, so Perla makes peanut butter and jelly sandwiches. She leaves the dirty stuff out. Sonni can do the dishes herself.

Perla sits at the table and chews her sandwich and looks out the window. The building across the alley looms, abandoned, awaiting the wrecking ball. Some of the flats have busted windows, some are boarded over. A ragged black dress hangs from a forgotten clothesline. Perla runs her eyes along the inside of the window frame, coming to rest on a screw placed loosely in a hole in the sill—Sonni's idea of a security system. Perla pulls the screw. She opens the window and the curtain floats in a blast of cold air. It feels good; the super keeps the heat way too high. Perla sticks her face out, and her arms. Then she climbs out onto the fire escape. Perla grabs the railing. The icy metal burns her hands, and she wonders about that, how cold can also be hot. Six floors below, the yard is a garden of cardboard boxes and soda cans and liquor bottles. A patch of sky shines, very white. There's a wet taste to the air. Flatfooted, Perla jumps a few times, enjoying the metallic clang and clatter. Next she climbs down three rungs and threads her legs through to sit. She can just see into her own window from here, Lani waving from the high chair, bottle raised in her fist. Perla lets herself fall backward, slowly, trying not to bang her spine against the steps. The blood rushes instantly to her head; her ponytail sweeps the fifth-floor balcony. From this position she has a good view into the kitchen below, and she sees at once that Victor Boccard is home. He's hanging out naked, getting a blow job from his girlfriend, who kneels on the linoleum. Upside down, it looks really weird, but Perla is interested so she watches for a while. The girlfriend has on a short T-shirt and pink underpants. She looks sweaty and uncomfortable, mechanically compromised, hand and mouth working at odds. Meanwhile, Victor is running fingers idly over his chest, playing with his hair. His eyes are bleary, unfocused. During the week, he works as a meter maid, and Perla has a sudden picture of him writing tickets, wearing nothing but a frilly apron. She stifles a laugh. Victor stares right at her. Perla lashes her arms and moans theatrically. The pressure in her head makes her feel as if her eyes are bleeding. It takes Victor another half a minute, but finally he yells, "Perla! You little shit!" Perla hauls herself up. She untangles her legs and climbs the two steps, then scrambles across the platform and over the window ledge and back into her own apartment. Swooping past Lani, she makes a run for Sonni's bedroom. Perla slams the door. She sinks down onto the floor, panting, listening.

She hears Lani babbling to herself in the kitchen.

Perla sits and sits.

There is nothing to do.

Perla decides to take the baby for a walk. She dresses Lani in her plastic snowsuit and boots, puts on her own winter coat over the flowered sundress. She adds a pair of baggy green corduroy pants and black high-tops. She drops a few subway tokens into her shoe and gets the stroller from the hall closet and belts Lani in. They bump down the six flights of stairs, pausing only for Perla to groan orgasmically outside Victor Boccard's front door.

Out on the street, Perla picks a direction at random. The wind is brisk and her eyes water. She ducks her head as she walks and wheels, turtling her neck into the coat's scratchy collar. Soon enough, she finds herself at the Youth Center. Perla peers through the dirty storefront. Inside, bookshelves line one wall. There are a few desks and scattered artwork, a waste bin filled with deflating basketballs. Mrs. Davis is standing alone at a chalkboard. Banks of fluorescent lights flicker; her hair looks like a pulsating halo. She wears a brown skirt, patterned knee socks and sandals, and a red shirt, too large, with a rip under the arms that displays a crescent of pale flesh as she writes.

Mrs. Davis steps back to assess her handiwork. She presses a fist into the small of her back and stretches and turns, catching sight of Perla through the window. Mrs. Davis grins wildly. She rises up on her toes, as if she can't rein in her enthusiasm sufficiently to remain on this earth.

Perla spits on the sidewalk.

Mrs. Davis comes to the door. She swings it open, a bell tinkling inside. "Come in, Perla!" she says. "Come in! You're very early, dear."

"Early for what?" Perla says.

Mrs. Davis looks temporarily confused. She steps outside, where the traffic is heavy and she must raise her voice. "Why, for the virtuoso!"

The word makes Perla mad. "Who?" she says.

"Why, Luigi Marchieri dei Sonatello."

"*Who?*"

Mrs. Davis cries, "Beethoven, dear!"

Perla scowls.

Mrs. Davis says, "The program says the Waldstein is last. Such a difficult piece. And for such a young fellow. All those trills!" Mrs. Davis purses her lips and warbles, sounding just like a bird. A man pushing a shopping cart loaded with black plastic bags stops to stare. He digs in the pocket of his filthy black coat, coming up empty-handed.

"I hate that shit," Perla says.

Mrs. Davis says, "You do not! You've never even heard it." Her cheeks are pink and Perla thinks of Victor's girlfriend, her face all caved in at the mouth. In the stroller, Lani kicks her heels. Mrs. Davis crouches. She tickles Lani under her chin, setting off a waterfall of giggles. "Girl or boy?" she asks.

"Boy," Perla says.

"Your baby brother?"

"No way," Perla says. She hears the twangy *thwoc* of a ball bouncing against a metal fence. The Youth Center is across the street from a park. A break in the traffic, and Perla sees a kid on a bench hand something off to a middle-aged man. "I found this baby," she says to Mrs. Davis, "in the park. Just now, in fact. But I'm gonna get rid of him. He's a fucking pain in the ass."

Mrs. Davis folds her hands primly. "You know, dear," she says, "the little one can't come to Carnegie Hall. It's not allowed."

Perla kicks at the stroller's wheel. The brake isn't set, so the stroller does a little sideways jump, then rolls about a foot. Mrs. Davis lunges at the handle. Lani twists in her seat, looking for Perla, who ducks into the Youth Center's doorway. The baby's face screws up into a knot. A piercing wail escapes. Mrs. Davis looks at Lani incredulously. She sticks a finger in her ear. Turning to Perla she says, "Perhaps, dear, you can go another time."

Perla doubts it. There won't *be* another time. She draws back her foot, taking aim at Mrs. Davis's shin. The rubber toe of her hightop connects.

Mrs. Davis yelps like a dog.

Perla grabs the stroller and takes off running. She can hear Mrs. Davis calling after her, but the words are drowned out by other voices, and by wind, by squealing brakes and honking horns, and the blood that pounds in Perla's ears, sounding doom.

There's a plywood barrier in the middle of the next block. It runs alongside the sidewalk for several yards. Behind the barrier there used to be a building, but it's been torn down. The plywood is papered over with posters that advertise a play at a theater downtown, a bunch of elegant white people standing around looking famished. Someone has drawn breasts and a mustache on one of the women, an enormous hairy penis on one of the men. Farther down, there's a taped flyer about a missing tabby cat. *Fuzzy*, it says. *De-clawed. 13 lbs.* Perla trails her fingertips on the wall, pretending each ragged nail is a red-hot razorblade.

At the point where the barrier should butt up tightly against the building next door, she stops. There's an unexpected break about a foot wide. Perla gets Lani out of the stroller and stands her on the sidewalk. She folds the stroller, and shoves it through the opening, squeezes herself in, then reaches back and drags Lani through.

They are alone on the other side. There is rubble everywhere, glass and rebar and broken concrete, and in the middle of the lot a giant hole. Wind funnels between the buildings and bites the girls' cheeks.

418

Perla sticks Lani back in the stroller and belts her in. The baby protests. Perla searches until she finds a piece of stiff red cellophane, like the stuff that's wrapped around flowers at the grocery. Lani takes the cellophane in her fists and plays it like an accordion.

Perla studies the excavation. The sides are steeply sloped, but she guesses she can run it easy enough. She moves the stroller so that Lani can see, then she slips and slides down into the hole.

At bottom, Perla can no longer hear the traffic. She begins to search the dirt floor, every square inch, the sound of her footsteps oddly deadened. Perla is looking for something, she doesn't know what. But she's found a lot of neat shit by keeping her head down. Old postcards, videotape, a claw hammer with some rusty stuff on it that looked like dried blood. Once she found a ring she was sure was a diamond, though Sonni said it was glass. Here, she sees piles of cigarette butts, and loose newsprint that looks like it's been used as toilet paper. Charred cardboard—she wishes she had her Bic, she'd like to start a fire down here—the remains of a cookout. An unopened bottle of Seagram's V.O. stands like a lone bowling pin. And then something small catches her eye, something shiny and white. She bends down and plucks a seashell from the dirt. Quickly, she closes it in her palm. Perla knows someone dropped the seashell, and not that long ago, but still it gives her the weirdest feeling, as if it had been here before the city was built.

She looks up at Lani. The baby has tossed the cellophane and is sucking her thumb and looking solemnly down on Perla. The dirt sides of the hole appear steeper and taller from this perspective and Lani seems far away, on another level in more ways than one. The hole feels like more than a hole. Perla is reminded of the day Sonni walked her miles down Broadway. A blue afternoon, the air so sharp it hurt her chest to breathe. Sonni wanted Perla to lift up her head, to look at the signs in the second-story windows, the banners and flower boxes. It's a whole 'nother life, she said, and we don't even know. Perla didn't get what that had to do with her. But Sonni's always saying this kind of stuff. In Perla's opinion, her mother is dumber than rocks.

Now, standing here, she thinks about how she might scream murder at the top of her lungs and no one but Lani would hear. Perla drops the seashell. She kicks dirt over it, hiding the shine.

*　*　*

419

The Café Reál is an old-style American diner, with gold-flecked Formica countertops, swiveling metal stools, vinyl booths, a jukebox, and a milkshake machine. Painted on the bricks above the front door is a faded street scene: merchant graffiti from the turn of the century. Once the lunch counter of a prosperous five-and-dime, the diner has long since been partitioned down to its current size. The specialty now is Caribbean food. Burgers and fries are still on the menu, but there are better things to eat here.

Perla barges in, crashing the stroller into the deserted hostess's podium. The café is crowded, noisy with the tail end of the lunch hour crush. Waitresses rush about, platters balanced on the insides of their forearms. Perla smells roasted pork, rice and beans in sofrito, fried plantains seasoned with garlic. Her eyes sweep the room. It's mostly workers, men in flannel shirts and jeans and steel-toed boots. Salesclerks who toil in the shops farther downtown. A guy Perla knows for a neighborhood pimp sits alone at a table for six, whispering into his cellular phone.

One of the waitresses is Sonni's best friend, Jess, a great big fatso who in Perla's opinion puts the lie to jolly. Jess lumbers toward an elderly couple, slams their plates onto their table. The old man is holding one of the old woman's hands in his own, and some of the hot food bounces onto their arms. They don't seem to notice. On the way back to the kitchen, Jess catches sight of Perla and frowns and shakes her head. Perla makes a few understated pig noises and sticks out her tongue. Then she sees her mother.

Sonni is standing behind the counter, one hip thrust forward. She is listening with intense concentration to a man seated on a swiveling stool. There's an empty next to him, so Perla makes a beeline. She parks the stroller so that it blocks the flow of traffic, then huffs and puffs through a show of getting Lani out of her seat. Perla flops down on the stool, the baby perched in her lap. Over the top of Lani's head, she checks out Sonni's talker, who has yet to come up for air. The guy has wavy brown hair, a pocked red neck. He gestures extravagantly as he speaks. His hands look older than the rest of him, freckly and loose-skinned.

The guy is saying, "—and if I can get enough investors, everyone stands a chance of striking it rich."

"Uh-huh," Sonni says.

Up close, Perla can tell Sonni isn't quite as enthralled as she first thought. Sonni's chewed off every bit of her lipstick, and she keeps rubbing her arms, as if she's freezing. Perla grabs the edge of the counter and lifts her feet and gives herself a spin. She holds on tight to Lani as the seat twirls around twice. The baby squeals with delight.

"I mean," continues the talker as if they aren't there, "why should the fat cats get it all every time? It's time the little guy stepped up to the plate. It's time—"

"*Perla*," Sonni interrupts. "What are you *doing* here?" Perla spins again and Sonni says, "Stop that."

Perla drops her feet. The talker turns sideways to stare at the two girls. "Yours?" he asks Sonni.

"What do you want?" Sonni says to Perla.

There is no good answer to that question.

Perla bats her eyes at the guy. "You marry Mama," she says earnestly, "me and Lani'll call you Daddy."

"Ay, Perla!" Sonni says.

The guy says to Sonni, "You don't look anywhere near old enough."

Asshole, Perla thinks.

The guy cocks his head. "That baby's a little doll," he says. "She's got a future, that one."

"Hi, hi," Lani says.

Perla wants to throw up. She squeezes Lani and the baby burps. Instead of being disgusted, the guy laughs.

Perla gives Sonni the evil eye. Her mother returns the favor. They hold each other's gaze. But there is something in Sonni's expression that Perla can't read. Fear, or anticipation, maybe, as if Sonni wants something from her daughter she knows she can't have.

But Sonni says only, "What's that on your face?"

Perla puts a hand to her cheek.

"Your *eyes*," Sonni says.

Perla remembers now. Sonni's eyeliner, looking on Perla like shit.

"Go to the Ladies and wash it off," Sonni says.

"Fuck you," Perla says.

"Ay, Perla!"

"Hey!" the guy protests. "Don't speak to your mother like that."

"Fuck you, too," Perla says.

"Go home now," Sonni says in a voice flat with warning. "The baby needs a nap. Put her down right away. OK, Perla? OK?"

Perla sits there.

"*Now*," Sonni says.

Perla packs Lani none-too-delicately in the stroller. She stomps off, headed for the door. She passes the table where the old couple sat. They're gone now, but their plates haven't been cleared. Perla stares at untouched mounds of cold beans and rice. She wonders why they did not eat their food.

At the threshold, she turns and glances back at her mother. Sonni is leaning against the counter now, bent forward so that her cleavage spills from the top of her uniform. The guy says something to her and Sonni throws back her head, offering him her long throat.

Jess waddles up to the table and begins stacking plates. She throws the silverware ringing on top. She looks at Perla, then at Sonni, then at Perla again. Shrugging, she says, "Everybody's good at something."

Twenty minutes later, back at the flat, Perla watches her little sister sleep. The baby lies flat on her back on the Abortion Couch. Her chest rises and falls. Perla takes a step away from the couch and Lani sighs. A bubble of spit pearls between her lips. Perla takes another step. Lani lies motionless. And now Perla is walking slowly backwards, moving first through the living room, then Sonni's bedroom, then the kitchen. She opens the door to the sixth-floor landing. She takes a deep breath, and closes it, carefully, and quietly.

The long line in front of Carnegie Hall is comprised of children from all five boroughs, snaking west on 57th Street, from the box office to the end of the block, then around onto Fifth Avenue. In no way is this line orderly; kids shout, punch each other, dash back and forth, jump, fuss, fidget, giggle, cry. The few adults are pathetically outgunned. It takes Perla a couple of passes to locate Mrs. Davis and the others from the Youth Center, losers she wouldn't be caught dead with under other circumstances. Mrs. Davis is holding forth on some aspect of proper concert hall behavior and Perla takes the opportunity to sidle into line. Maxwell Otero, princely young beer-bottle-throwing shit that he is, jabs Perla with an elbow, contorting his features into a mask of disgust. He holds his big nose. Perla says, "Fuck you, Maxie," and Mrs. Davis stops her lecture. "Perla, dear!" she cries. Instead of being mad, she looks unaccountably cheered. "You made it! Just in time, too."

Perla shrugs. But it's true, the line is starting to move.

At the box office, Mrs. Davis sorts out their admission, and then they all file into the lobby. They march up a short flight of steps and enter Recital Hall. There are paneled cream-colored walls and row after row of plush red seating. Mrs. Davis herds everyone down the aisle toward the stage. They stop at the twelfth row: they have excellent seats. Perla stares up at the tiers that curve around the sides of the hall, running lights like on an ocean liner.

Mrs. Davis takes Perla's arm. She shoos the group down the row, then scoots in herself, settling into the seat second from the end. She gestures for Perla to take the aisle. "So you can see his hands, dear," she says.

When the lights finally go down, a chorus of shushing ensues. Perla squirms. But she's finally noticed the enormous piano up on the stage. The instrument is polished to a high shine, the lid yawning wide. It looks like a huge black bird on the wing. Then a man in a tan windbreaker and chinos strides out from behind the curtain and the drone of young voices comes to a halt. The man steps to the edge of the stage, raises a hand to his eyes and comments on his inability to see the audience. He waggles a finger, indicating that perhaps the invisibles are up to no good. Then he veers off into a speech about the beneficence of the City of New York, the gracious management at Carnegie Hall. Soon the kids are shifting restlessly. Perla wonders why she bothered to come. She begins to tear up her program. She puts little rolled pieces into her mouth and shoots spitballs down the aisle. Mrs. Davis is yanking the program from Perla's hands when the man in the windbreaker abruptly exits. A long, expectant minute passes. Then Luigi Marchieri dei Sonatello walks onto the stage.

Perla's first thought is: he's just a little boy. Mrs. Davis has told her charges that dei Sonatello is thirteen, but he looks much younger, lost and lonely in his black tie and tails. A pouf of black curls falls over his ears, onto his neck. His face is ghostly pale, the black brows slanting dramtically. Dei Sonatello makes his way to the piano. Turned now to face the audience, he places one hand on his belly, the other on the instrument. He bows deeply, then seats himself at the stool. After making an adjustment to its height, he raises his arms. He lowers his hands to the keyboard.

Dei Sonatello begins to play.

And Perla, who has never in anyone's memory ever sat still, is frozen in place. For an hour and more she can't move. The music is unlike anything she's ever heard. The sound is everywhere, thrown into every corner of the hall, but it's as if the piano speaks to Perla alone, in a language incomprehensible yet absolutely complete. From the first note, she's caught on the verge of crying. And Perla never cries. She stares at the boy's hands, feeling the lightning fingers like knives at her throat. The power is *there*. It's like what she hears in Krayzie Bones's songs; but it's different, too; or maybe it's just a matter of discovering what the connection might be. One thing Perla knows: she wants this power for herself. Dei Sonatello plays a slow piece, then a fast, then a series of things that make Perla think of foxes dancing. A moment of silence follows, dei Sonatello visibly composing himself. Mrs. Davis leans over and whispers to Perla, "Now comes the Waldstein, dear!" Dei Sonatello repositions his hands. He nods his head once. A persistent thud sounds, very fast and low on the keyboard, and then the music takes off. It is running away with Perla. The notes build a solid vibrating wall. The boy plays and time races forward while also standing utterly still, until at last the notes begin to rise, higher and higher, like bells pealing from a mountaintop or water cascading from a break in the clouds. And all at once it's over. The audience stands. The hall fills with applause. The young virtuoso stands also, and bows. Perla leans out into the aisle, trying to see. Clapping thunders around her. The man in the chinos and windbreaker trots out from the wings, a microphone in his hand. Dei Sonatello says something into it. His voice is liquid, rollingly soft, but Perla can't hear through the applause. It sounds as if he's talking about seas—or seats, maybe. *Seeds*. Perla mimics the movement of his lips, which twist as he speaks. She sticks the tip of her tongue into the empty sockets left by her missing teeth, and concentrates. But she still can't understand. The words come too fast. It's *Italian*, she realizes. She has a brief sensation of fullness, then of a rushing wind that sweeps everything clean. In the next moment, she remembers the open window in the kitchen at home, the curtain floating. With frightening clarity, she sees the rusty screw on the kitchen table. She sees Lani awake, toddling through the flat, looking for Perla. She sees Lani crawling out onto the fire escape.

Perla bolts out into the aisle. She runs toward the back of the hall, into the lobby, and through the front doors. Outside, snow is falling heavily on 57th. Perla stops to stare at the huge flakes that blanket the pavement in white. There is so much snow in the air she can't see the buildings on the other side of the street. Then Mrs. Davis clamps a hand at the back of Perla's neck, grabbing her coat. "What on earth!" she cries.

"I have to *go home*," Perla says.

Mrs. Davis's grip is surprisingly firm. "What's the matter with you?

What happened in there?" And then a dreadful comprehension seems to dawn. "You don't mean—" Shocked, she covers her mouth with her hand. And Perla can't stand it. Mrs. Davis knows she's left Lani alone. Perla is embarrassed; she's *ashamed*. She sags a little and Mrs. Davis's hold on the coat weakens and Perla wriggles free. She tears off, wearing nothing but Sonni's flowered sundress and the baggy green cords. But the cold can't touch her. The street is cloaked in silence and her footsteps are muffled, erased behind her as she goes. "Fuck," Perla says. *Fuck, fuck, fuck, fuck, fuck.* She repeats it all the way into the subway station, while waiting for the train and on the train, too, running from car to car, trying to shave a minute or two off her time. By the time she emerges again out into the world, the word has become useless, just another sound.

Streetside, the world is buried under inches of snow. In the course of the final few blocks, Perla is covered. When she stands, finally, before the door to the flat, melted droplets fall around her like tears. Trembling, Perla takes the key from under the mat. She straightens. She opens the door and steps inside, into the kitchen where she sees that, yes, the window is open, the curtain is fluttering. The rusty screw sits where she left it on the table. Broken glass sparkles by the bathtub. Three cans of tinned beans lie on their sides, rolled up against the refrigerator. Perla shudders from the cold. She toes the shards of glass. She kneels and, thick-fingered, sets the cans to rights. On her feet again, she decides to bypass the fire escape, advancing instead to Sonni's bedroom. There the discarded pile of clothing has exploded, shirts and dresses dragged into every corner. But a definite trail leads into the living room. *Seeds*, Perla thinks. She moves forward slowly. In her head she hears music. The odd individual note leaps, and she is flooded with an optimism she knows she doesn't deserve.

And for once, Perla is lucky, so very lucky. Because here is Lani, fast asleep on the couch. Sonni's red silk kimono is tucked under her cheek. Dirty tear tracks streak her face and she's soaked with pee and smells bad. Legs buckling, Perla lowers onto her end of their bed. Lani's eyes pop open. The baby glares fiercely at Perla, then smiles.

Nominated by Joyce Carol Oates, The Kenyon Review

GEOGRAPHERS AT MARDI GRAS

by ANDREI CODRESCU

from TURNROW

An Address to the American Geographer's Association Annual Meeting in New Orleans, March 4, 2003

I hope that you haven't lost any geographers to Mardi Gras
it may be years before they are found—
Who can blame them?
Some of them may not want to be found again
as a way to expiate for the sins of geography
—today is Ash Wednesday after all—
so I thought that instead of lecturing to you today
I would go around the room and ask each one of you
to confess a cardinal sin of geography
or even a mortal one and then I will give you poetic penance
by erasing the cross you all bear
namely NSEW—
Poets, my friend Ted Berrigan used to say,
should endeavor to make at least four directions
in their poems: Up and Down and Sideways
and that's a cross
the rest of the dimensions will take care of themselves—
When my friend and colleague Kent Matthews approached me

to speak to you people I wasn't too sure.
I wasn't too sure what geographers were
I looked it up in the OED and it said something like
Geographers study physical boundaries
but then the secondary definition said that people boundaries and
economic ones were involved too
but obviously not very much because that would be anthropology
and economics
which kind of reassured me because that's just like poets
who get to study everything but not enough to call it anything else
Though—to tell you the truth—many poets today don't really care
   what you call what they do as long as they get to do their best
   thinking about whatever it is in the most provocative language
   available—
Maybe geographers are like that now—
But then to go back to the question of sins and Ash Wednesday
I don't think poets have as many sins as geographers—
But maybe I'm wrong so maybe I should just point out some differ-
   ences
that may be only a layman's prejudices:
   1) Geographers are people who know where everything in the
      world is and cause maps to be made that—if you know how to
      read them—let you also know where you are
   2) Poets are people who have no idea where anything is so they
      rethink wherever they are because they don't trust maps which
      they suspect of some unspeakable original sin
   3) Geographers know north from south and east from west and
      teach this to generations of children like myself who learn to go
      against the grain of their common sense
   4) Poets have an obscure but stubborn compass that makes them
      resist the classification of direction just as they have resisted
      the Linnean classifications after thousands of years of associat-
      ing patterns and colors; I'm not saying that we are right—I'm
      just pointing out a difference
   5) Geographers are people who generation after generation filled
      in the terra incognitas until the only blank spaces left on maps
      were ones that had the misfortune—or good sense—to change
      their locations—or at least their names—after natural or
      man-made cataclysms—On the other hand, the constant intru-

sions of nature on the topography of a changing earth and the intrusions of history on what's there one minute and gone the next like let's say Masuria, a country between Poland and Germany that exists now only in a book by a writer named Siegfried Lenz—is what keeps geographers in business—the boundary lines made by men over those of nature and the migratory life that follows or goes against nature's lines but also the intrusions as well of our ontological and psychological understanding of where we are at any given moment with or without maps

6) and that's the business of poetry, too but with the proviso that for us maps go against common sense and that we suspect that even the most skilled readers of maps know that they are performing an unnatural act that is in itself an intrusion on the natural and human world and that the makers of maps already know this and the venality that lies at the base of all that codified exploration and so-called "discovery"—and that the ethics of mapping unlike those of (some) poetry are highly suspect if one "follows the money" as good journalists do, and not the rhetoric which is what (some) professors used to do and some still do and that geographers must be like Mormons always endeavoring for accuracy and precision in order to correct some egregious flaw in the founding and that this is good on the one hand because it makes you energetic and restless
     people buffetled by the storm of profound dilemmas brought
         about by shaky beginnings
         and not so good if you do not on the other hand question
     those fundaments—

My own beginning was shaky
born in a place drawn and redrawn after every war
a ping-pong region batted about by great powers
settled at the time of my birth inside the fish of Romania
"Our country looks like a fish," my geography teacher said
with an indescribable irony that carried in it some unspoken curse
of something slippery, silent, ready to be hooked by the many
fishermen hovering above us with various maps spread before
     them
I made my own maps

pirate maps leading to treasures
secret maps for our gang's secret places
maps for getting to my house
and escape maps in case of a bad oedipal storm
I realized then that the treasure map and the escape map
          were ur-maps
the first drawn to point the location of loot
the second intended to escape the armed looters
and that the fine humanist sentiment of discovery
was mostly an ode-for-hire to legitimize
the taking of treasure and the necessity of escape
I knew this even at ten because I wanted to go to new places
and discover worlds unknown to me
just like all the poetry said
but I was principally motivated by the desire to escape
the tight borders of my walled-in childhood in a walled-in country
in a walled-in continent and a walled-in prison planet
and there is surely a book to be written and many have
on the imaginary geography of childhood
and imaginary geography before the age of physical discovery
and the rise of instrumentation
I still have notebooks full of detailed description
of places on my imaginary maps

Which brings me to one of the points of this talk
which is that imaginary geography is still the prime mover
of human beings now when all that can be seen and measured
has been seemingly mapped seen and measured
and that far from being exhausted or literary
this particular imagination is reshaping our world
making it necessary to re-envision its mapping according to desire

And there is no better time for discussing this mapping of desire
than the day after Mardi Gras in New Orleans
          where I'll just say with Homer that the "wine-dark sea" has
          more wine in
it than elsewhere
          which is the defacto reality of our American Venice
a city that refuses to conform to anything that is known about it
and has had its geography redrawn and reimagined

430

first as a creature of the lower Mississippi
a river that has no intention of conforming and never has
to the designs of those that'd fix its course and propensities
a city founded against common sense in a hostile swamp
then fought over by the great powers of Europe
the subject of countless imprecise descriptions and claims
a city where geographical directions such as NWSE are not part of
      the natives' map
who give directions as either "away" or "toward" the river
and whose boundaries and life have been re-imagined many times
by the life-forms that stubbornly thrive here
waging a guerrilla-war against definition and conclusive mapping
and will continue to do so until the city is either taken back or
      abandoned
              by the river
a knowledge of finitude that is intimately woven into our psyches
and that urges us to live intensely before the assured cataclysm
a tenuous and time-bound existence that gives an infinite license
      to the imagination
the infinite available by the way only to the tragic sense of
      existence
      we are all wine-dark kierkegardians here—
my own sense of where we are is helped by four investigative
  methods,
namely:
The proprioception or Charles Olson's Poetics
Mysteries
Surregionalism
& TAZ

That is:

Proprioception or Olson's poetics, as developed by Olson in his
long poem, "Maximus," and his essays on Melville, The Human Uni-
verse, and Projectivist Verse, at the end of the 1950s.

Mysteries as revealed in *The Mysteries of New Orleans* by Baron
von Reizenstein, completed in 1853, translated and edited by Steven
Rowan, The Johns Hopkins University Press, 2002.

Surregionalism, as coined by the philosopher Max Cafard in an essay first published in *Exquisite Corpse, a Journal of Life & Letters* in 1997.

& TAZ, Temporary Autonomous Zones, coined by the Sufi scholar and poet Hakim Bey who discussed TAZ in a number of essays, including a slim volume published and reprinted several times by Autonomedia in the mid-90s.

Charles Olson's vision of American space was embodied by his hometown of Gloucester, Massachusetts, and was a simultaneous cosmic, geological, human, economical, political, psychological, and literary exploration of Gloucester by means of a poetic method he called "projectivist verse," driven by proprioception, which is a synesthesic drive to compress and push forward all that one knows and intuits in that knowledge as well as in imagination. Olson envisioned Gloucester as a becoming out of known facts, a journey that the poet undertakes as a 20th century Odysseus who has been schooled in everything since Homer.

Of course, that's an epic undertaking that can be overwhelming, as Olson himself acknowledged:

"What did happen to measure when the rigidities dissolved? . . . What is measure when the universe flips and no part is discrete from another part except by the flow of creation, in and out, intensive where it seemed before qualitative, and the extensive exactly the widest, which we have also the powers to include?"

This post-modern vision looks to me exactly like the Mississippi River seen both before and after "discovery," a great natural force that is best intuited—using both the sensual fact of the river itself and the immense history and literature that sprung from it, beginning with geology, Native American ritual and commercial interaction, on to La Salle and the whole modern age, Mark Twain included.

The intuitive project (and the ongoing necessity for it) comes out of a profound mistrust toward the official readings of one's habitation. As a poet, Olson was not satisfied by any reading of Gloucester proceeding from either Marx or Freud because, while these gave a certain coherence to its economic and psychological existence, they

432

produced equally dogmatic and official readings of their own that did not open the space of Gloucester (or of thought, or of the Mississippi) to the unknown, but enclosed it instead within their own logics.

Olson may have even coined the term "post-modern"—and pointed out the way to a revisioning of place through a high-temperature poetic rethinking of contradictory readings. Olson was difficult to read until recently, because a reader schooled in text might have felt claustrophobic inside "Maximus"—Olson knew too much and he laid it all out in a cinematic sort of way that only the hippest movie buffs can truly enjoy—used as they are now to film-editing, quick cuts and montage. Now he's easier to read—provided you're a movie buff.

The Mysteries of New Orleans

Baron von Reizenstein, a young German aristocrat, was sent to New Orleans by his parents in the mid-19th century in the hope that he wouldn't get mixed up in Germany's revolutionary ferment. So, instead of becoming a European radical, he came to pre-Civil War New Orleans and found a place that was in a state of ferment way beyond the anti-oedipal socialism of Germany—it was putrefact, in fact, fermenting both literally and metaphorically. It was a multi-cultural, decadent mix of the new and old world, a psychological laboratory, a wide-open port. A thriving German community supported two German-language newspapers, a Bohemian one and a proper one. The young Baron wrote *The Mysteries of New Orleans* in German as a serial in the Bohemian paper. By 1850, the genre of "The Mysteries Of . . ." was well-established in the New World by German writers; there were already *The Mysteries of Cleveland*, and *The Mysteries of Pittsburgh* . . . The genre itself was born of Eugene Sue's *The Mysteries of Paris*, a brilliant re-envisioning of one's own city as an exotic locale. Sue, who was too poor to travel, turned an awed gaze to the familiar and gave his readers a city they would recognize but which hid a poetry far from the familiar. Von Reizenstein saw New Orleans as a great unwritten and continually unfolding experiment. He described, daringly and possibly for the first time, lesbian and homosexual love, and gave every street in the city an essential character and a stage for activities that were only partly imagined and that are true to this day. His contemporary readers doubtlessly recognized

433

their city and, because of it, they stayed when Reizenstein took them abruptly into a world of magic and horror that had its source in the yellow fever epidemic and introduced characters with super-human powers. The Yellow Fever itself was spread through the seeds of a psychedelic plant found at the source of the Red River. A magical weave of African ritual and Christian superstition superimposes its geography on that of the "real" New Orleans. Reading von Reizenstein now one is seized suddenly by the certainty of the existence of this magical geography in our time. I certainly was, because, long before reading *The Mysteries of New Orleans*, I wrote a book called *Messiah*, which takes place in this city and introduces a magical cast and a mystical geography that coincides more than eerily with Reizenstein's one hundred years earlier. Many writers, in fact, have stumbled in the same way on the mysteries of New Orleans—a vibrational reality that lies like gossamer over the city's physical features and per-meates even the most casual visitor with a strange sense of something invisible.

Right after I had typed, "The Yellow Fever itself was spread . . . ," there was a knock at the door and UPS delivered a box. I opened it and found *A River and its City: the Nature of Landscape in New Orleans*, by Ari Kelman, California University Press, a new book, and I opened it at random and read this: "Yellow fever emptied some spaces and filled others, redefining the way New Orleanians used and viewed their public landscapes." The author goes on to write: ". . . cities and surroundings should not be seen in opposition to each other. Instead we find the built and the natural mingling as part of the complex narrative of New Orleans' urban-environmental history." (P. 117)

And, I might add, its super-natural history.

Reizenstein co-authored the mysteries of New Orleans with the Yellow Fever, the city itself, myself, Ari Kelman, the UPS man, and hundreds of other writers of "the complex narrative."

What this means to me is that: 1) New Orleans has specific Geniuses of the Locus, local deities present in the geography before its founding, who grew and grow increasingly more specific in place and time, neither one of which stands still,

434

and 2) New Orleans is imaginable, hospitable to the geography of desire that anyone can project imaginatively on it, finding the appropriate receptors without much difficulty.

What does this mean to Frommer's or the Planet Guides?

That it's a party town.

I once had a tour of Chicago from the historian Tom Frank who took me to all kinds of vacant lots where significant moments in Chicago's labor history had occurred, such as the massacre by the Pinkertons of 100 striking workers at Republic Steel, the REAL site of the Haymarket riots, etc, none of these places commemorated by markers and, indeed, not on any map. In fact, the South Side of Chicago where some of these sites were, was not even shown on the tourist maps of Chicago!

My number three text for geo-imaginative practice is:

Max Cafard's Surregionalism. Max Cafard, by the way, is the pseudonym of a philosophy professor here in New Orleans, who wrote me a note in connection with this talk, and reminded me that today is the 40th anniversary of the death of Joseph Stalin, one of the founders of modern geo-politics. So we have another reason for celebrating. Anyway, I quote, from the "Surregionalist Manifesto":

"Where is the Region anyway? For every Logic there is a Region. To mention those of particular interest to us, the Surregionalists: Ecoregions, Georegions, Psychoregions, Mythoregions, Ethnoregions, Socioregions, and Bioregions.

Regions are inclusive. They have no borders, no boundaries, no frontiers, no State Lines. Though Regionalists are marginal, Regions have no margins. Regions are traversed by a multitude of lines, folds, ridges, seams, pleats. But all lines are included, none exclude. Regions are bodies. Interpenetrating bodies. Interpenetrating bodies in semi-simultaneous spaces. (like 'Strangers in the Night.')"

In Surregionalism we have a vision of New Orleans as a place both emptied by its geography and history to accommodate new bodies and reimaginings, and a creative matrix that is a near-perfect rhizome, an uber-potato.

Mardi Gras, carnival itself—*carne vale*—farewell to the flesh—is one of those paradoxes, a street festival that goes against the grain of the general paranoia promoted by Homeland Security—and always has, by allowing the mob to rule the streets in a (still) unmediated explosion.

Which is not to say that we are not threatened here like everyone else in the world. But before there was this generalized threat that is now attempting to turn the whole American continent into a suburban police station, artists were already feeling threatened by boundaries imposed by "economic development," overpriced real estate, and strict "community standards." Because of this threat, we have resorted to fast-moving, nomadic vehicles called **TAZ, or Temporary Autonomous Zones**. TAZ are communities of imaginative souls that don't care much for appearing on official maps, especially tourist ones.

New Orleans is now, at its margins, the most TAZ-hospitable city in America, but TAZ are only successful as long as they are nomadic. They take root in poor areas of cities or the unincorporated countryside where space is plentiful and there are mixed cultures. Tazzerites thrive in racially and culturally diverse environments from which they draw the strength to grow, but then they are noticed, and this eventually draws scouts, geographers, and zoning, followed by land-development, rising real-estate prices, city planning, preservation societies, law enforcement, and art simulacra. The lifespan of TAZ used to be decades-long until the last quarter of the 20th century when TAZ destruction accelerated, making TAZ short-lived and prone to extinction, but also smaller, faster, and harder to spot.

Tazzerites draw their territorial lines through song and dance like the native Australians; they use local concepts of time and space that they activate with found materials, speak a variety of hipster lingoes, and use advanced technology to communicate. The "objects" they make are temporal and ephemeral but they transcend time and space to link both vertically through history and horizontally through geography with all TAZ past and present. They are connected to each other across the globe and often merge when one of them is destroyed.

I call the TAZ of New Orleans Narcississipi, because it is in Louisiana cradled by the Mississippi. For the time being, and especially in the Carnival season Narcissipians man the night-shift in this surregion.

I hope that I have succeeded in getting you at least a little lost. Thank you kindly.

Nominated by Turnrow

THE FLAYED MAN

by NADINE MEYER

from GULF COAST

After Juan de Valverde's 1560 anatomy text, Anatomia del corpo umano.

He has flayed himself for our inspection, pressed
his knife through the dermis of his large right toe,
run its tip along the base of his foot, splitting left
from right, up the back of his calf and thigh, carefully,
the way a woman runs the seam of her stockings
up the midline of each leg, and slipped his muscled
and gelatinous body from its casing. As one slices
the skin from an apple in a long spiraling similitude,
he has kept, where possible, his ghostly likeness
intact. In one hand he holds it out to us, a testament
to what he has done, and in the other he holds
the knife. Martyr for science, he stands, each muscle
overdeveloped, numbered for the anatomist's study
as if it were possible to slit this human casing, slip
from one's integument, and go on living
in the delicate inner flesh. What then is beauty
when the skin has been shucked? The marbling of muscle
and fat, the patterning of veins and arteries, tenderness
of disease? Complicit, a participant in his own dissection,
the Flayed Man brandishes his life: without regard
for his soul, he offers this oblation, his own decorticated
corpus, to Medicine and Anatomy. For over a thousand

years, for fear that to dissect the body is to impede
the soul's chrysalis, its incorporeal unfurling, the study
of anatomy had virtually stopped, but now
the Flayed Man, his jaunty disregard, his terrible
theatrical privation, the outstretched offering
of his own skin as if to say, *all this, I have done for you.*

Nominated by Gulf Coast

.

JUAN THE CELL PHONE SALESMAN

fiction by DEB OLIN UNFERTH

from NOON

It was a holiday which means the woman in question went home. And this included an encounter with the mother of the woman in question, and the mother's questioning of the woman upon her arrival. The woman questioned waited for her special box on the go-round and endured.

That same evening, over chicken and lemonade, the mother made a strange statement: She had pinpointed on this earth the Perfect Man for the woman in question. Actually she had found two. But one perfect man was out of town so luckily there was another.

The second Perfect Man had a name and a career and those were Juan and cellular phone salesman respectively. The mother and the little sister showed the woman the phone he had touched and sold them and explained how its presence had transformed them into a super-efficient mother/daughter tag team. Team of two, that is, until today, happily, now three, if only momentarily, now that she, older sister, woman in question, was home.

A cell phone salesman, said the woman. This is who you want your daughter to plan her future with.

How, said the mother, did my daughter come to be such a snob.

The woman questioned was slipping through thin fingers as she phoned Juan the cellular phone salesman on mother's cellular phone, phone to phone, phoned because when the woman at first refused,

440

mother said that she was deliberately ruining Christmas for everyone.

Several hours if not a whole day had elapsed by this time. And then there were several more hours, if not a whole day, while the woman and mother and sister waited for Juan to pick up his cellular and phone their home. Which he didn't. The mother carried the cellular phone from room to room, set it next to her as she pinned balls to the tree, and said, Where is he? Where could he be? Maybe she should call again. How did she know he'd even gotten the message, those cell phones are so unreliable and she should call again.

Obediently, foolishly, the woman in question did call again, while meeting eyes with the younger sister and noting a note of sympathy in them because everyone knows that according to the social rules and regulations we have agreed on, to leave two messages for a stranger is a bit untoward. But she left it, then retreated to her bedroom like the old days.

Sure enough, he still didn't call, and sure enough, the mother was like a bride left at the altar. How dare he not call. She walked through the house, checking the phones one by one. He had said he'd like to take her out and she had shown him the nicest picture and now why would he lie, the bastard. Slowly, slowly, the mother circled around and around with the cellular phone. She tried to be casual, the mother, tapping on the door, Hey let's call Juan! like it was a forgotten invitation to a party. But the woman—woman, yes, not a little girl of nine—would not be fooled and even the sister agreed that three times was two times too many but when the mother began to get the swirled crazy eyes, the woman grabbed the phone and phoned again. This time though she lost all patience and dignity and said onto his voice mail the devastating: Hello Juan, my mother would like to go out with you.

What happened next happened fast, which is why the mistake about the off button was made. When mother grabbed the phone from the woman, she screamed a word that wasn't very nice about the woman in question, screamed it before she realized about the off button, that nobody had pressed it, and everybody stood horrified for one long moment before mother ran from the room.

That afternoon the sister and the woman in question had fun with the phone, shouting desperately into the cellular, *Juan, we miss you, Juan!* or sternly, *Juan, you're ruining Christmas for everyone,* or sadly, *Juan, please call us, Juan, and leave us a little message,* or angrily, *It's over for good this time, Juan. Don't ever call us again!* And the woman in question felt, well, pleased with her sister, but also a bit unwomanly as she stuck herself under her thin blanket that evening.

This part is miraculous: Juan phoned the next day. He phoned while the woman was showering.

He phoned and I nearly dropped the receiver, said the sister, which would not have been good. These little phones are delicate creatures.

He phoned and he spoke charmingly, said the sister. He, as always, asked many interesting questions.

Which is impossible, of course, to even say such a thing because how long is always if you've only spoken to him twice?

It's the kind of man he is, insisted the sister. The kind who asks questions and listens and asks more questions.

Like a talk show host, said the woman. What a treat. Still she will go out with him on this very night. And for the next several hours the three, they are a three, yes. Look at them, they sew and unclutter, they pin hair and dresses. How womanly they are, how sisterly, how motherly, daughterly.

And now here is the climax. Look how they stand in the mirror, the three, and joke and apply lipstick for the Coming Juan, the cell phone salesman. The sister says she almost wishes she could go in her place and the woman in question says she doesn't see why she shouldn't, who cares if she's only sixteen, the sister and she could simply swap names. Or better yet they could both go and say they have the same name and are, in fact, doubles. And the sister and the woman practice in the mirror saying her name over and over, in unison and separately, and the mother joins in like a song. This is a nice moment.

The next moment is not so nice. It will be a few hours later and Juan will be very drunk and unable to drive the woman in question home. She will also be drunk and having an unpleasant time with Juan who can be a little mean. And she will—by this time she is in his apartment, an unsavory detail—phone mother on Juan's cellular phone at three in the morning, and mother and sister will come to retrieve her, minus one shoe which she will never recover, and it will be at this moment that Juan will utter the only statement anyone anywhere will ever remember him making, and he will roar it as he lifts his head from between two couch cushions: "Get your drunk sister out of here!" he will say and that will be his great contribution. Thank you, Juan.

The very last part is this: We are in the front seat without any lipstick on, me and mother and sister. It is dark and late. We aren't talking about Juan.

Nominated by Pat Strachan

TO THE SURGEON KEVIN LIN

by W.S. MERWIN

from POETRY

Besides these words that are made of
breath and memory with features
of both and are only mine as
    I address them to you

what do I owe to that steady
fire I watched burning behind your
glasses through the dire spelling-out
    when we met that first day

and to the passion of the boy
from Taiwan and the sharp knowledge
it burned a way to until it
    stood before the open

red cavern and between pulses
was sure how to do what came next
had it not been for that would I
    have been here this morning

at home after a night's rain as
the first sunlight touches the drops
at the tips of the leaves I owe
    you the sight of morning

Nominated by Tony Quagliano, Judith Hall

AVIAN NIGHTS

by SHERMAN ALEXIE

from NEW LETTERS

Starlings have invaded our home and filled
Our eaves with their shit-soaked nests. Rats with wings,
They are scavengers we pay to have killed
By the quick exterminator who sings

In Spanish as he pulls three baby birds,
Blind and mewling, from the crawlspace above
Our son's bedroom. Without a word,
The exterminator uses a thumb

And finger to snap the birds' necks—*crack, crack,*
Crack—then drops their bodies to the driveway
Below. For these deaths, I write him a check.
This is his job. He neither loves nor hates

The starlings. They just need to be removed.
Without guilt, the exterminator loads
His truck with dead birds and the tattered ruins
Of nests: twigs, string, newspapers. It is cold

When he drives away and leaves us, mother
And father of a sick son, to witness
The return of the father and mother
Starlings to their shared children, to their nest,

All of it gone, missing, absent, destroyed.
The starlings don't understand synonyms
As they flutter and make this terrible noise:
The *screech-screech-screech* of parental instinct,

Of panic and loss. We had to do this,
We rationalize. They woke up our son
With their strange songs and the beating of wings
Through the long, avian nights. Then, at dawn

The babies screamed to greet the morning light.
What could they've been so excited about?
What is starling joy? When a starling finds
A shiny button, does it dance and shout?

Do starlings celebrate their days of birth?
Do they lust and take each other to bed?
Are they birds of infinite jest, of mirth
And merry? How do they bury their dead?

We will never know how this winged mother
And father would have buried their children.
Our son almost died at birth. His mother
And I would have buried him in silence

And blankets that smelled like us. These birds
Don't believe in silence. They scream and wail.
They attack the walls. We have never heard
Such pain from any human. Without fail,

The starlings mourn for three nights and three days.
They fly away, only to carry back
Insects like talismans, as if to say
They could bring back the dead with bird magic,

As if their hungry children could cheat death
And suddenly appear with open mouths.
At birth, our son suffocated, his breath
Stolen as he swallowed his own shit. Faith

In God at such time seems like a huge joke.
To save our son, the doctors piped the blood
Out of his heart and lungs, then through his throat,
Via sterile tube, via smooth cut

Of his carotid, then sent his blood through
The oxygen machine, before they pushed
The red glow back into him. This was new
Technology, and he lived, though he crashed

Twice that first night, and spent the next five weeks
Flat on his back. His mother and I sat
At his bedside eighteen hours a day. *Screech-*
Screech-screech. We cawed and cawed to bring him back.

We attacked the walls of the ICU
With human wings. *Screech-screech-screech.* Grief can take
The form of starlings, of birds who refuse
To leave the dead. How much love, hope, and faith

Do these birds possess? They lift their faces
And scream to the Bird-God while we grow numb.
The starlings are odd, filthy, and graceless,
But if God gave them opposable thumbs,

I'm positive they would open the doors
Of our house and come for us as we sleep.
We killed their children. We started this war.
Tell me: What is the difference between

Birds and us, between their pain and our pain?
We build monuments; they rebuild their nests.
They lay other eggs; we conceive again.
Dumb birds, dumb women, dumb starlings, dumb men.

Nominated by New Letters

ROMAN EROTIC POETRY

by ALBERT GOLDBARTH

from THE GETTYSBURG REVIEW

It was a young male griffin in its first plumage. The front end, and down to the forelegs and shoulders, was like a huge falcon. The Persian beak, the long wings in which the first primary was the longest, and the mighty talons: all were the same, but, as Mandeville observed, the whole eight times bigger than a lion. Behind the shoulders, a change began to take place. Where an ordinary falcon or eagle would content itself with the twelve feathers of its tail, Falco leonis serpentis *began to grow the leonine body and the hind legs of the beast of Africa, and after that a snake's tail.—T. H. White*

There was a discomposure about his face, as though his features got on ill together: heron's beak, wolf-hound's forehead, pointed chin, lantern jaw, wash-blue eyes, and bony blond brows had minds of their own, went their own ways, and took up odd postures, which often as not had no relation to what one took as his mood of the moment.—John Barth

1.

This seems to be the summer of com-, recom-, and uncombining.

Once a week I do (or "undergo," if she's steaming away her angst at some ferocious power speed) a walk around (and around and around) Hill Park with Martha. Arthur's just moved out of the house this month, supposedly to "reconnect with himself" and reconsider the marriage. "Albert, today I think"—but *really* what she means is "this five minutes I think," and then she pre-rejects it—"or maybe not." I've been alongside Orthodox rabbis studying the yolks of eggs in search of the telltale pinpoint of blood that would render the meal unfit for a kosher plate. I've seen crew tekkies fussily inspect the engines of film set stuntmobiles before a dangerous chase, but *nobody* comes close to the atoms-parsing exactitude of Martha dissecting her marriage's strife. "He *might* be thinking. . . ." Tolkien, even, couldn't explore so many finely realized imaginary worlds.

And then again there's Sweet and Danny. Can't *they* see it? Everyone else can see it. Every day he passes her desk, and she passes his desk, and they pass by "chance" in the mailroom, and the building— all ten stories of it—seems to realign itself in generous accord to the complicated physics of human attraction. *Say something* already, one of you. Go on, do it! That nonchalance is sheerer than the negligee on the cover of the current *Frederick's* catalog, and the breathy yearnings under it are all too clear. Look, we're rooting for you, but help us out! There are bets on this. They circle closer, then break away. Then circle again: a little tighter in, this time. Tomorrow? Look at her goo-blue, Lake-of-the-Ozarks eyes! His chin with its first goatee! What are the odds being quoted this afternoon by the Sweet and Danny pundits for tomorrow?

But tomorrow I'm also having lunch with Ed, whose life has been hurtfully empty of anyone, or any possibility, for three or four years. And then I'm supposed to drop by Yancy's: you know, Yancy, who spent an hour randily experimenting with Gal Pal 3 as Gal Pal 5 was lazily driving around the block, awaiting her turn for his Buddha talk and beautifully broken-in prizefighter face.

This seems to be the summer, all right.

And that's not even mentioning Mister J and George, my two gay friends who have been a stable couple for as long as I've lived in this city. "Stable . . . but gay. The unwanted ten percent." (And Mister J chips in, "In *this* city? Maybe about, oh, zero-point-five.") "So even the best of days, there's always this sense of an outside chemistry that intrudes. A joke, a look. And it could even be a well-intentioned look, but *it's always there*." And an image from Mister J: "It's like we're just two cars with their hoods up, side by side, attempting to jump each other's engines. See? But there's traffic all around: the other ninety percent. Gawking, honking, offering advice. It makes it more tough to get charged."

I'm telling you now what I hope to do in the sections that follow: simply show how friends of mine have often inspired long thought on the subject of sexual pairing; how that one thought organized everything else I considered and did in the summer of the year 2003.

"Long thought . . . ," "organized . . ."—it sounds so arid and geometric. But these are my friends. The "thought" is salted, from out of

449

their eyes and night sweats. And the "organization" is their continuous leaving and finding and missing and entering one another: lines that extend out into the world from a starting point in our DNA.

2.

Fifty-six, in the standard editions.

That well-known and knowingly scurrilous poem of Catullus's, in which he comes across a young man "jerking off." The youth 1) is a slave in the house of Lesbia (a lover of Catullus's, who was known for her bedroom appetites) and 2) is, we assume, her on-call sex toy, currently supping on Lesbia's favors with a frequency that Catullus himself can only frustratingly dream of (in the Oxford translation by Guy Lee, "slave" is more winkingly rendered as "boy pet"). What Catullus does at this opportune conjunction is approach from the rear and "bang him with my hard"—thus simultaneously enjoying a serendipitous homoerotic quickie *and*, through this very literal fucking, metaphorically "fucking over" his all-too-promiscuous ladylove. "A funny thing," he calls it, "worth chuckling over."

Only a prig would not see the humor involved, much of it arising from the way form is wedded to function here. Just as the agendaless sexual lark and the agenda-ridden act of petty vengeance are a tidily compacted act, seemingly over in one swift jab (which is why, perhaps, the David Mulroy version opts for "spear" instead of "hard"), the poem itself lasts correspondingly only seven lines from setup to conclusion. It bears the lightning smack of a comically good vaudevillian half-a-minute.

But thinking about it afterward is liable to be discomforting. The ethically fastidious will be squeamish over the callous yoking of sex and spite. And there's also the question, how welcome is the speaker's attention? Rape?—could we credibly say this is rape? But the tone is so high-spirited! And the implication is that this horny, self-pleasuring boy may be surprised by Catullus's entry, yet not distressed. And *could* he even be surprised? The nearing, step by step; the lusty raising of the garment's hem; the business of fleshly adjustment . . . surely the boy could have skipped away easily enough *sometime* during all that finessing? Although . . . what are the rights of a slave in ancient Rome? Of course, he isn't *Catullus's* slave in the first place. . . . So much is lost in a cross-millennial and bilingual fog. My two-book selection of variant Catullus translations attests to the slipperiness of certainty, "hard" and "spear" as just one instance. Another: "jerking off" in Guy Lee's edition is given as "wanking" in Mulroy. However, even if we could prove it was consensual and nothing but a bright, midday caprice for its participants amid the hurly-burly of Rome in 56 A.D. (or thereabouts), as one was leisurely making his way on behalf of his owner to the market, and one was off to the baths . . . the problem remains that same-sex union is abhorrent to many (to you? to that guy over there? to me?). As Mister J once said, "It doesn't matter how decent George and I might be as individuals. As a couple, we give 'em the willies."

So: what is and what isn't a proper coupling? We could say that the definition of those two states is what a culture exists for. It's not proper for a mortal to mate with a god (although it happened in ancient Greece: Leda looks wildly fletched from head to toe as she rises to meet the violent, otherwordly wingbeat of the great swan). Nor should the gods disport among *themselves*, if codified prohibitions exist. In Ovid, when Venus seduces Mars (adulterously: she's married to Vulcan), the poet passes unmediatable censure: "It was wrong." *And* consequential: "Then Vulcan's mind went dark. He dropped his work and at once began crafting revenge." So it turns out even the Olympians are assumed to be delimited in their choices!

To marry across the lines of caste in traditional Indian culture is strenuously forbidden; a Brahmin-Nayar pair would be as grotesque as some 1950s monstrosity out of a Hollywood one-week wonder: a lizard-ape or a gorilla-panther rampaging about in its ill-fitted halves. In Shakespeare too; between the tangled worlds of Montague and Capulet, a chasm intervenes, so deep and wide across that the bodies of both sides' children will plummet helplessly into its shadows and be broken on the rocks at the bottom. Ask the Pope in 1633 if Galileo has permission to conduct the marriage of Earth and sky: the answer is no; the answer is that *some* possible combinations of human material and human spirit are always going to be on the "forbidden" list, in the interests of keeping ever intact the *sanctioned* combinations of a culture; the answer is simply that, to kill his vision, this fine old man with the astronomical truth in his head will be threatened, very persuasively, with torture (say, "correction") in the dungeons of the Inquisition. Some marriages are so dangerous, the fright they create in the cultural authority is immediately translated into loathing, before the fear can be consciously registered.

And high among these is homosexual marriage. What else so direly lays siege to mainstream gender roles in the majority population and implicitly undermines its basic structural unit, the hetero nuclear family? In the first code of laws for Plymouth Colony in 1636, "sodomy" and "buggery" (along with murder and "solemn compaction with the devil by way of witchcraft") take their place on a list of "capital offenses liable to death." Most often "buggery" referred to the act that we would term bestiality. In 1642 Love Brewster's seventeen-year-old servant Thomas Granger was hanged on the gallows for committing this pollution with (in William Bradford's account) "a mare, a cow, two goats, five sheep, two calves and a turkey" and, before the noose was snugged around that young man's neck, "first the mare and then the cow and the rest of the lesser cattle were killed before his face, according to the law, Leviticus XX.15. And the cattle were all cast into a great and large pit that was digged of purpose for them, and no use made of any part of them." Even the flinty Bradford finds the outcome "very sad."

And in 1641 in Puritan Massachusetts Bay Colony, a servant "of twenty or under" was charged with sodomy and duly hanged. If that's the standard, then John Alexander was lucky—in 1637 he appeared before the court with Thomas Roberts, the both of them "found guilty of lewd behavior and unclean carriage one with another, and often spending their seed one upon another." For this "the said John Alexander was therefore censured by the Court to be severely whipped, and burnt in the shoulder with a hot iron, and to be perpetually banished from the government of New Plymouth." Because such heathenish adjoinment is an affront in the eyes of the Lord, and is of a foulness in the nostrils of Our Maker, and is an abomination of which the After-life awaits for ever and aye with an eternal torment of flames and the stench of brimstone.

Although the truth is—for me this week, this summer—it's Martha and Arthur who seem to be schlepping their lives through the ravenous fires of hell.

3.

Or Marthur and Artha, as some of us had taken to saying, they always seemed *so right* for each other, so in-blended.

"*Now*, though . . . I don't know. We'll have to wait and see." Martha's voice somehow imparts to even these empty words a gravid expectation.

Her hair is a burgundy shade of auburn, descending in great cascades on either side: it frames her face like opened theater drapes. This is appropriate enough, since these days Martha's conversation appears in her face with all of the immanence, the up-close physicality, of puppets acting out the rapidly alternating highs and lows of this difficult time.

"He said he'd call this morning, but he didn't. Should *I* call *him*? I mean, would that be intrusive?" Before I can answer—"Or maybe he'd see that I cared, if I called. Unless he purposely didn't call to test me. Or maybe. . . ." This is a woman who, a couple months ago, would fancifully wonder if the universe were infrastructured, "from even before our species evolved," according to laws of beauty, "but even supposing the answer is yes, would it be a sort of beauty we'd recognize," and was it even possible (although horrible) that "our suffering is part of a larger, inhuman beauty that *uses us* as factors in its equations," arguing all of this with deft allusion to Keats, to the choreography of Twyla Tharp, to Greek myths. Now we huff our way through Hill Park incessantly testing the edges of Arthur-this and Arthur-that, a finite deck of Arthur cards with infinite architectural potential, and what-does-Albert-think?

The changing Hill Park prospect sometimes suns her face and then, just seconds after that, tree-shadows it—like her hopes and her fears in their puppetry show. And Albert wishes, *dearly* wishes, he knew what he thought, but he doesn't, and what he *suspects*, in his gut, is a slow-building bolus of dismal news.

In a kindly intended review of one of my books, St. Louis poet Richard Newman said, "The author comments throughout his characters' heartbreak, discussing our culture's failed marriages with the experience of a marriage counselor [and now my favorite part] without the psychobabble." Ah, yes. If only friends *were* characters, whose lives abide by authorly rules of beauty and whose suffering could, at the very least, be explained away in those acceptable terms. But I'm at a loss for advice, now, here, in the park, as the light and the branches deal out the scenery of our friendship.

We pass a few kids playing. "Albert . . . is there a helium balloon that's going to lift me out of this quicksand?" Who would have thought the classically minded Martha G. would one day be talking to me in images from a cliché Walgreens Valentine card? Who would have thought that Arthur's emphatically ink-black hair could one day leave the stylist's in a ring of yellow spikiness, so looking as if his head

453

were on fire, as if he couldn't think clearly until some mental baggage—call it the "old life," maybe the old life including Martha herself—had been surrounded and burned away?

And who would have predicted seven years ago when they first arrived, to open a small art gallery (that specialized in installation pieces), Off the Wall—a gracious, urbane, and completely in-synch young couple—that they would be so frayed on a future day? I remember the night when Nettie found some of us having a drink at The Tin Cup, sat down, ordered a first wheat beer, and said, "Wow. I just went down to the gallery, it was closed, but I looked through the window in back. . . ." *Yeah? And?* "Well they were there, sure enough. From now on, I'm calling it On the Floor."

And really: *isn't* it crazy that these two joined halves have come undone? We have reason now to believe that there was effective, and even commonly ho-hum, mating between Neanderthals and those Pleistocene people the paleoarchaeologists are wont to call "anatomically modern humans"—us. Across that amazing genetic and physiological divide . . . and out of what had to have been the obvious species-species suspicions and competition for game . . . one specimen, "Lagar Velho 1, from 25,000 years ago, bears a combination of Neanderthal and modern human traits that could have resulted from only extensive interbreeding"—*and my friends from the same undergraduate college, Martha and Arthur, can't maintain a cohesive, functioning unit?* "In a single late-twentieth-century decade, veterinarians learned how to use the uterus of one species to carry the embryo of another"—*and Martha and Arthur, who vote the same way, and dance the same way, and rumor has it like the same position for intercourse, can't bond in a lasting polymer?* The "Feejee Mermaid" that Barnum started successfully displaying in 1842 (to a profit of almost a thousand dollars a week) . . . although "the upper half was a monkey and the lower half a fish" (undetectably joined together with elfin nimbleness by its anonymous Japanese coastal village fisherman originator), several gaga university naturalists and a slew of newspaper editors proclaimed it upon examination a single, supple creature of the sea—*and Martha and Arthur are incapable of stitching themselves back together? Can't they just kiss and make up?*

I'm thinking of Brancusi's *The Kiss*, that brick of stone so minimally but eloquently yinned and yanged. But people aren't stone, and an unscentable though real human musth can drive us wild at times. It simmers inside and presses against the forehead from be-hind, and then invisible but undeniable psychological chancres open all over our skin and fill us with needs for which there may not be therapy terms yet. The Neanderthals surely knew this, whatever "knowing" meant to them, and the knowledge hasn't changed over millennia. It goes back to the battle that was fought out in the caves, between our earthy, remnant brain stem and the upward aspirations of our overlayering neocortex: *it isn't easy, this being a hominid.* So, no, I *can't* say if Martha and Arthur are going to reinstate themselves . . . and after a recent visit at Arthur's, I am *not* aglow with hope.

I don't want to cast him as villain in this. He has his own Arthury versions of things, and they have their own Arthury, loopy way of sometimes sounding loopily right. I'm sitting with him one afternoon in the backyard of his new place. Two or three beers each. Some lazy, cagey chitchat . . . chummy but always carefully easing away from the raw lip of the troublous spot. So long as we don't stray over that line, everything is up-tempo from him. I've seen his new bed and his new bold, floral shirt and his new bold, floral acrylic painting, and in sixty minutes I've heard his cell phone beep him into seven brief but mys-terious and smile-making conversations carried out in a hushed voice in the next room, and I've heard him tell me repeatedly how "every day is a new adventure," skimping on the sandwich fixings, figuring out the bank account: boom! awesome, enthralling, new adventures! I let my eyesight's edges loll about the house for signs of a woman . . . none. (Am I disappointed? Relieved?) But neither does he ask, not once from noon to five, *how's Martha coming along,* or wax nostalgic for a single halo'd molecule of the air they shared so long so well. I think the ring of vibrant yellow tufting dyed around his hair is a magic circle, intended to keep the past at bay—the marriage-past that needs to die in order for "new" to be born.

Thinking all that, I'm lost in wishing I *did* possess a trove of psy-chobabble into which I could dip—when Martha (who never grows breathless on these walks, as I do) asks me, "What was that mytho-logical animal?"

"Huh? Which one?"

"That's what I'm asking. The one that was made up from half-parts of other animals."

"The basilisk."

"No . . . another one."

Centaur? Manticore? Pegasus? Griffin? Pan? . . .

"The griffin. I was thinking about how a marriage is really a crea-
ture fashioned patchily out of other lives. Like Frankenstein—"

"He's the doctor. You mean his monster."

"—or the minotaur or the griffin. Wasn't it something like a lion
and a serpent?" and before I can answer—"*Something* like that. I
was thinking how it all depends on whether the two parts stay to-
gether over time . . . who knows? A horse and bird wings—*stupid*.
But look at any illustration, and Pegasus is this gorgeous, airborne,
exalted thing. Like a breath with muscles. Then again, those freaking
flying monkeys in *The Wizard of Oz* are sorry beasts. And Franken-
stein turned out pretty altogether godawful shitty."

"His monster."

I don't think it's my mild correction that suddenly has her weep-
ing, stopping under one tree's overarching arms and weeping
ashamedly into her own two hands, it isn't me who's caused this alto-
gether godawful shitty mess, and it isn't me who has the hoodoo to fix
it. I'm only a friend who's standing next to a woman in peril. No last-
minute balloon. And how can I look at that quicksand and hand her
my small stone of foreboding?

4.

If Catullus does offer a single incontrovertible view of marriage, it
escapes my novice reading of that poet's oeuvre. If anything, the
beast we call "monogamy" turns out to be—as the pages turn, and
the cast of Catullus's characters go about their pleasures and mis-
eries—as cobbled together as any griffin: sometimes contented and
steadfast; often gusted by lust into treachery of one kind or another;
and sometimes sing-the-blues conflicted over being so pied a beauty
in a world of so many similar pinto-spotted, checkered, and mongrel
attempts to be lifelong wedded for better or worse.

Poems 61, 62, and 64 are three of the lengthiest in the Catullus
canon and three of the most ornate and delightful: even their jests
are not so rough as those in his other poems, and their immediate oc-
casions (again, as opposed to those of the other pieces) are grounded,
the way that starlight is, in the constellated figures of gods and the
implications of timelessness. All three concern marriages. Sixty-one
serves well as their representative: here, in a choral piece of 225 lines
(created in celebration of an actual wedding, Junia Aurunculeia to
Manlius Torquatus), the speaker welcomes the overpresiding god of

weddings, Hymen ("He brings us Venus the good; he is love's uniter"); lushly compliments the bride and groom on their beauty and on the fitness of their match; emboldens their spirits, should they be prone to the jitters; and reminds them that their days of lightweight love affairs are over, that a new, more important, and nourishing commitment is upon them now.

The erotic is admitted, yes, and its heats are even stoked ("Don't weep, Aurunculeia! Whoever wants to count the many thousand games of desire that will fall into your nights . . . let him first try to number Africa's sands!"). The poem is attitudinally *way* removed from being a paean to abstinence. But theirs will be a "virtuous passion," validated by family, by tradition, by the poet's own witnessing presence, and by the approval of the participants' deities. There is no irony here. Clearly Catullus intends his poem to honor the idea of formal nuptials: and he means us to see that sincerity, fidelity, and a durable mutuality flower out of this moment. These are, he tells us, "sacred rites."

Elsewhere (and more typically) in Catullus's poetry: fucking; sucking; and shucking off old lovers for new with a conscienceless ease. Sexual shenanigans—complete with deceit and depravity—abound, indeed are the steaming entrée. This is the start (the First Triumvirate) of the darkly scandalous decades. A "well-known noblewoman invited three hundred orgiasts to a banquet" and was carried into the dining hall, nude, on a queenly platter, graped at her breasts and figged at her crotch and intended to be the main feast. A Calpurnius Bestia stood accused "of killing his wives—how many, not stated—by smearing a fast-acting poison on their vaginas as they slept." This is the field in which Catullus's poetic invention grazes and romps.

The beloved referred to, or addressed, in most of the poems is Clodia Pulcher, code-named Lesbia, an aristocrat and "enthusiast of sexual license." In this, she arrives with a pedigree: her father, Publius Clodius Pulcher, "is most often remembered as the young man who sneaked into an all-female religious festival, disguised as a flute girl, for an illicit meeting with Julius Caesar's wife." It was rumored that Lesbia and her brother were incestuous lovers. Another rumor: her husband Metellus Celer died by poison at her hand. Since she was adulterous as a wife (and Catullus would have been only one name in her schedule-book of dalliances), it's no surprise that she became, as Mulroy phrases it, "a merry widow with an insatiable appetite for young men." In 58, one of his spiels of spite, the poet reports that Lesbia, "loved by Catullus more than he loved himself or all of his kin," is spending her time in the nooks of alleys skinning back the foreskins (and he doesn't mean for medical exams) of a series of sleazily-come-by partners. Nor was *he* Mr. Faithful: "his poems imply unseemly extra-Lesbia entanglements with girls named Ipsithilla, Ameana, and Aufilena. In addition to this, he was infatuated with a boy named Juventius."

And so we have, at once, a body of poems in which the speaker can—with an articulate, genuine ardor—morosely observe how the gods have abandoned humankind ("Our mad confusion of everything fair with everything foul/ has driven away their righteous and forgiving thoughts. They do not deign to visit any longer") *and* can glory at a face slobbered into some bodily crack like a truffle pig at work. Today, with Martha on my mind, this *is* a literary version of the griffin's composite anatomy, and it raises similar questions about how fated any alliance is; how pasted together with tissue paper and spit; how able to wake the next morning with ashes in its mouth and in the corners of its eyes and, like the phoenix, rise up anyway; how granite; how elastic; how bohemian; how cleaving to a norm. When do its differences know to yield to a greater good—and when do they squabble, slammingly pack their bags, and drive away to widely separated zip codes?

5.

The hoofprint of a deer in snow: a perfect kiss.

The trail of such prints: a trail of perfect kisses, left by what we think of as a perfect creature, sleek and fleet, enabled in its leaps by some angelic oil suffusing its bones, a creature of one smooth piece, and of a piece with its surroundings.

But the griffin?—leaves the talon marks of an eagle; bears the hooked beak of an eagle, for a proud and ferocious prow of a face (*griffin* comes from *gryps*, Greek, "hooked"); has massively large, strong-tendoned wings; is partially feathered, black and cobalt and crimson—warrior colors; and has the torso of a lion, tipped by a lion's ears, a hint of mane, and a whipping tail . . . altogether an overpowering hodgepodge of an animal, albeit one known for a predator's strength and speed (in both running and flying): the tiger, the elephant, and the dragon will all succumb to the pounce of the griffin and its rending paws. It lays eggs. It constructs nests laced with threads of gold and protects this treasure most vigorously. It confounds and beguiles and terrorizes: it haunts the night beyond the shepherds' comforting circle of campfire light.

Some mystifying ancestral line of the griffin's must have been in our heads, in the back cave-dark of our own heads, from at least Neanderthal times. The recognizably classic griffin makes its first appearance in Central Asian visual art around 3000 B.C. and its first appearance in written texts around 700 B.C. Its amalgam body lends itself to a range of striking depiction—on brooches, on serving platters, about the bellies of bowls, on funerary caskets, as tattoos (a sign, for the Scythians, of lofty birth). It is particularly a staple of medieval bestiaries, there with the fox, and the boar, and the weasel, and the unicorn, and other real animals as described by the experts. Tenacious, it remains in these books of lore past Shakespeare's day. . . . and Dickens mentions a cynic who "in his hatred of men [is] a very griffin." Catullus presumably could have expected to see an example in one of Rome's newly founded *vivaria*, tethered for safety near the pit with the ragged tiger or by the column where the elephant was chained. The imperial gardens surely possessed one!

Classicist Adrienne Mayor posits that belief in the griffin was fueled by protoceratops remains, which "are so thick in that region, some researchers in the field regard them a nuisance. The prominent beak, large eyes and impressive claws . . . the body about the size of a lion's, the claws and long tail, the birdlike collarbone frill"—these are consistent with the anatomy claimed for the griffin. Plus, protoceratops laid eggs. "In many ways, the ancient people who came upon the bone fields of Central Asia were doing the same thing modern paleontologists do today—postulating unknown animals from ancient remains." Is it any less realistic than the platypus? (Than the couple next door, that devout fundamentalist kneeler-in-the-street and her atheist husband? Out of a skull filled with its superstition-powered hosts of devils and fluttering seraphs, and a skull filled with its one brisk whiff of a clear and rational ozone . . . comes this strange but functioning double-headed invention called "the neighbors." Try describing *that* in a bestiary across the page from the "cameleopard" or "cockatrice," and we'll see if it feels as credible.)

And in fact the griffin and all of its kin—all of the hybridized opposites, from real-life hermaphrodites to the fabled goat-footed people of northern Scythia and the dog-headed tribes of western Libya—hold a psychological value. They ease us through the horrors and astonishments of our dichotomized lives; all of us (from the oxy-

459

genating red cells in our pulmonary systems to those pumping, gushing organs of our greatest physical ecstasies) are the stuff of amazing weddings, some metaphorical, some literal.

"Hold a psychological value"—yes. In her smart and snappy essay "The Terrible Griffin," Mahalia Way reminds her reader "how important the preservation of conceptual dichotomies can be to a culture, how seminal they are to the way we understand the world to be ordered." Hesiod's account of the creation of the universe begins with Chaos, a word that first meant "undivided." Then division is made as in the Judeo-Christian tradition (and really *every* world mythology)—of light from dark, Earth from sky, land from sea—and by this act the universe is scaled to human comprehension, after which the divisions continue, people from animals, man from woman, etc. All of this may only echo the ur-division of Big Bang energy out of the primordial singularity-dot . . . and afterwards the original self-combining of that energy into elements.

Or in other words, one's culture is the child of a cosmos that itself was born of endless demarcation . . . so a culture will maintain the demarcation lines that clarify its values with the thorough-most of fervors. It will generate tales about the dangerous consequences of threatening essential distinctions (Eve and Adam, for instance, nearly "becoming like gods" by eating of the forbidden apple; ditto the overprideful labors behind the Tower of Babel). The culture will nurture myths about the taboo status of almost all trans-boundary beings (children produced by incestuous sex; the offspring of human-animal matings; all of the werewolves and vampires slinking nefariously through the nethertwists of our brains; think *octaroon* in nineteenth-century New Orleans, think *The Island of Doctor Moreau* and its menagerie . . . no, "man-agerie"). And the culture will fabricate legends that also show weird admiration for, or even honor, *some* trans-boundary beings (here the androgyne is a fine example, lauded in alchemical texts as an emblem of twofold knowledge: or as in the song by Joni Mitchell, "I've looked at life from both sides now / From all around and up and down").

In many cultures, there's one day a year when the rigor with which we emphasize the lines is officially loosened, and men will dress as women, women will parade about in the trousers of men, the madhouse gets unlocked, a fool in a dunce's cap is ushered into the mayor's sumptuous chair: these needs, these rich confusions, must be admitted. The rest of the year the sanctity of the lines is defended with every informal, religious, and legal muscle a culture can flex.

It wasn't uncommon in English villages of medieval times for pre-marital sex to be winked at by the authorities and, if anything, only lightly admonished. (The "legerwite" or lecher-wite, a fine for pre-marital sex, was once as low as three pence in the Huntingdon village of Elton circa 1300; it never rose above twelve pence throughout that era. And a jury in Elton was fined by the local lord in 1316, charged with having failed to levy a fine at all in five proved cases of premarital hotcha hotcha.) Among the reasons: often enough, those indiscretions were simply a prelude to marriage and (given fertility) to family . . . they resulted in a proper boundaried unit of the community. Adultery, on the other hand, was severely punished: for peasants, a whipping. Obviously adultery unpegs the squared-off corners of that same familial unit and leaves it flapping away like a crazed wing on the squally winds of disorder, among the eddying ghosts, the demons and imps, that populate the air of this time and place and that tempt the frail will of people.

Mahalia Way:

> Things that defy categorization exist. How is a culture to deal with them safely? Fascination with creatures who straddle dichotomies is itself a way of exploring and "feeling" these divisions. The griffin served this purpose. As a hybrid of bird and beast, it represented both Heaven and Earth, good and evil, God and Satan. It could be a mind-lessly vicious aggressor—or plundered victim; a rapacious, vigilant hoarder—or a selfless, generous protector; a symbol of scientific knowledge—or of the sacred. In fact, the griffin has a lot to teach us about the process of interpretation.

For example: even my slow, lay reader's journey through Catullus gets stuck at forks in the interpretative road. Where Guy Lee uses "nipples" in Catullus 55 (the civil version, the "Doctor Jekyll" version), Mulroy opts for "tits" (the "Mister Hyde" choice). These are tonal worlds apart, and surely *one* of these is closer to the Roman poet's intention, but . . . I can only fuddle and muddle and shrug. I've already mentioned the venomous poem wherein a whorishly active

Lesbia is "skinning" (i.e., rolling back the foreskins of) her alley clientele . . . or at least she is in Lee and Mulroy; Edith Hamilton, with only slightly more politeness, interprets "skinning" fiscally: Lesbia "on highways and byways seeks her lovers, strips all Rome's sons of money."

If my friend Martha is going crazy, generating variorum interpretations of Arthur-stuff and rumored Arthur-stuff and dreamed-up Arthur-stuff . . . if Marthat is sinking faster and with a more immediate woe on her lips than most of us . . . still, everyone I know has days (let's label them "interpretation days") when what they thought was solid ground below turns quicksand. As for all of those impressively credentialed claims for the widespread interbreeding of Neanderthals and *Homo sapiens:* "this interpretation has not gone unchallenged." Duarte (of the Portuguese Institute of Archeology in Lisbon) and Trinkaus (Washington University) say the child bones called Lagar Velho 1 "resulted from interbreeding." I've already told you that. However . . . Tattersall (the American Museum of Natural History in New York) and Schwartz (of the University of Pittsburgh) "argue that Lagar Velho 1 is most likely 'a chunky *Homo sapiens* child' " and only that.

More: in 1964, when Arno Penzias and Robert Wilson (radio engineers out testing a new, experimental antenna for satellite communications) stumbled upon the mysterious hiss we know now is the background radiation from the Big Bang, they were forced to eliminate all of the more expectably mundane causes, including "a white dielectric substance" they'd found sticking to the equipment. Meaning: "pigeon shit." We fall from tonal world to tonal world; we sink, then bobble to the top, then sink again.

And here it comes, our symbol for *all* of this, making its way through an anecdote from the life of that genius of hokum and flimflam, P. T. Barnum. He'd purchased the Feejee Mermaid, but "the public must be made receptive first. It required a build-up." So Barnum hired his old friend Levi Lyman to stir the public press a bit, in Montgomery, Alabama, and Charleston, South Carolina, and Washington, D.C. This finally resulted in Lyman's bringing the Feejee Mermaid to New York and Philadelphia while disguised as a dignified British representative of the Lyceum of Natural History in London. The editors ate it up! Their readers were thrilled and expectant! And the name that Barnum and Lyman concocted for their bogus

British duster-offer of stuffed exotic hummingbirds and arranger-by-size of old bones? *Dr. Griffin*.

6.

This summer Yancy is one bright chip in a kaleidoscope: along with other scintillant chips called Amy and Della and Elinore and Leslie and Raven and Nora (and more), he's part of an ever-morphing con-fettiesque flower bed of *amor*. (Hey, he's *my friend*. He's not "a predator upon women's affections," not "an opportunist." He's a salt lick in the wilds, and the deer draw near in a mesmerized queue. He's a dollop of pollen: the bees go nuts. He's a saint in blotchy sil-houette in the center of a tortilla, and the faithful flock from miles away to bake themselves in the rays of the One and Only True Tor-tilla.) There's a lot of midnight jasmine tea and bedspring-jounce at Yancy's house.

At Ed's house there's a lot of Ed. One night, when the echoes of loneliness are especially unbearable, Ed invites me over to share a recently purchased twelve-pack of beer and a two-gallon drum of Chocolate-Rum-Pistachio Fantasia ice cream, also a retro-trip through the groovy 45s of his adolescence ("My God!—The Associa-tion!!! *Cherish!*"). It's fun, or at least, it's the fun edge of desperation: *my* companionship isn't what Ed needs. What's the matter here? He's likeable. He's as tender as underdone veal. Aren't women *al-ways saying* that's what they're searching for? "Right. As they kick off their slingbacks and head out the door with Mr. Arrest Record." Ed drops into a fitful snooze around 3 A.M., and I let myself out. In the quiet of his driveway, I imagine I can hear (about . . . let's see now . . . seven miles away) a gentle duo of satiated snores from Yancy's bed-room.

Yes, but all of that is only a muffled murmur in the background of (as it's known in the office) The Soon-to-Be-Fateful Summer of Sweet and Danny. They're suddenly *everywhere*. Not as a couple, ex-actly: it's frustrating. An example—I'm chatting with Arthur in the parking lot of our neighborhood Stop-N-Go store: motor-rev, kid yowling, gas fumes, angry curses, a rising escalator of lady-laughter, breaking glass . . . the usual, and *boing!* here's Sweet with her weight-less field of corn-silk hair in the breeze that attends her, waving non-chalantly to me as she walks out with a twenty-ounce Summer Sipper cup of cherry punch. *Hey Sweet, hi, do you know Arthur, how's it go-*

ing, take care, and she slips her lusciously bare legs into the front seat of her low-slung and electrically scarlet speedster with the single thoughtless flip of a dolphin diving. As she turns the engine . . . Danny ("Just coincidence?" Sandi the secretary asks of me the following day, "or [here, a pencil drumroll on the desk] The Wheels of Destiny?") pulls into the lot three spaces away and waves to us all with a smile, and—as Sweet screeches out into noontime traffic—enters the store for his own cool drink. For me the whole thing squeaks like a narrative straining to break from its pupal case.

Let's roll, guys. Office memo to Sweet and Danny: *Tempus fugit, carpe diem.* One day last week they arrived at the office wearing the same style knit shirt (hers, a lavender; his, a Navy blue) and—the dopes—*they seemed oblivious to this portentous fact.* The rest of us weren't: all that day the pencil drumroll followed the travel of each of them through our office mazelet of desks. We've done our research, people: neither of you is "seeing anybody else." Let's step on the gas! Let's pop the first of the many potential sequential sexual questions! Let's rumble! They go about their workday in their independent sugar-spun fogs. . . . Let's rock! Let's make evolution happen!

Some afternoons I'm tempted to waylay Danny in the supplies room and unfold for him a lovingly detailed road map toward the Country of Sweet. *Albert "Cupid" Goldbarth. No Poor Shmo Too Hopeless, No Lothario Too Chock-Full of Success! A Free Service.* I'm tempted, but I don't. I'm tempted not only because these two were imprinted, each with the other's image, somewhere around the zygote stage, but also because I think (and it's unanimous) that Danny's . . . well, "a good guy," in the forthright words of Sandi, our office's Peerer into the Souls of Men. He's hunky, and yet he hasn't been tainted by locker-room garbage-talk. He's still a somewhat unformed lump of manhood, but the lumpen raw material is rich with the glints of an honest smile and steadfast gaze.

I think of him in the way Edith Hamilton thinks of the young Catullus. For almost every other commentator, the poems and the poet behind them mean a carnal capability for the nitty-grittier, demimondish side of our behavior. And maybe okay, he *did*, under Lesbia's wickedly appetitive tutelage, eventually embody that disposition. (She would have provided effective schooling.) But when he first arrived in Rome from Verona, "sent by a careful father to be cultivated and polished out of small town ways, [Catullus] was perhaps twenty or so. We must conceive him on his first entrance a very shy

464

young provincial, hesitating on the edge of [big city] company." For Hamilton his first response to Lesbia's attention was "the holy purity of a great love. A passion conceived of as eternally faithful has always been felt to be its own justification, and through his life Catullus loved Lesbia only." Ah . . . ! What if his emotions had been stirred by someone worthier, by someone like. . . .

Sweet ambles past with the boss's request for a jumbo box of paper clips in her hands. On empty afternoons I'm likewise tempted to waylay *her* and likewise drag her into the supplies room for a mini-lecture on love and Danny and ways godammit to be a little more directed, please, in her thus-far aimless floating amidst the birds and the bees.

I'm tempted, sure; but again I don't. In the first place . . . spotless soul though I am, you'd be surprised at how many coworkers of mine would cast a cynical eye upon that innocuous attempt to be alone with Sweet in the confines of the supply room. They're a drag-ass, mealy-spirited bunch, but still I understand: the air around her is as clear as fresh spring water . . . and as potent as booze. And anyway, in the second place, thirty-five years separate us. I don't speak Sweet-ish.

If I could I'd knock their silly heads together; the ensuant spark might profitably land in their tinder and lead to an appropriate conflagration. The weather is right for this; the wind is right; the conditions for this benevolent, righteous fire are at their likeliest. *Oh flame, oh flame, oh little itty-bitty knock.* . . . It's tempting, but I don't. It rarely works in the buttinsky's favor—everybody knows this. In Aston, Bedfordshire, in the late 1200s, the village records show that "Robert Haring and his wife Sybil fell to quarreling." Then, says *Life in a Medieval Village,* "a friend eating lunch with them tried to intervene as peacemaker, and"—let this be a lesson for one and all— "was slain by an axe blow."

7.

"Shotgun wedding": everyone knows the term. In the village of Elton in 1300 it would have been, I guess, a "pitchfork wedding." The sadness is always the same: the narrowing of the options in a life. Not that I advocate one's ditching the responsibility often born of a cautionless whoopee. Even so it's possible to recommend that one take up the burdens of his or her unasked-for and sudden, sullen adulthood—recommend it with a sanctimonious heartihood—and still understand how suffocating the grip of that circumstance feels. Springsteen has it just right in his song "The River": "Then I got Mary pregnant / And man, that was all she wrote. / And for my nineteenth birthday / I got a union card and a wedding coat." His raspy, almost choking voice and the music to match: yet another man and woman have entered the roll call of the living dead. The dulling factory job. The tonnage of laundry. A horribly long-term payment for a simple hour of pleasure.

But the genes don't care if we're miserable: the genes want more and better genes, and therefore want as many possible combinations of genes as they can force from us. They want that child. They want a cultural institution inside of which that child will grow to fulfill its own fate in the procreative nature of things. We live inside of these culturally inherited lines—at least most of us do—and we stare down their iron, unwavering train-track length to what we call the horizon, and see . . . well, you know what we see: at their end the tracks are so close together, they're going to squeeze us dry. And so we also understand (even if we don't recommend it) the gesture of fugitive celebration when one of Springsteen's other speakers leaps out of the lines, in "Hungry Heart": "I got a wife and kids in Baltimore, Jack. / I went out for a ride and I never went back."

Springsteen's speakers—the out-of-work and the out-of-wedlock, the flunkies and junkies, the part-time roofers, late-night diner waitresses, racetrack hustlers, red-eye flyers, experts in petty theft and broken dreams and stolen kisses—know (whether intellectually or out of hard-knocks experience) the power of cultural hierarchy. Lines: in "Atlantic City," the speaker—whose choices in life are all used up, who's betting his future against one last suspicious (and, as the listener comes to understand, doomed) favor for a friend—is a streetwise scholar of the importance of heeding categories: "Down here it's just winners and losers and don't get caught on the wrong side of that line."

When the lines between permitted and unpermitted foods were established in Deuteronomy and Leviticus, they were established (so far) forever: thousands of years in the future, my father would be helplessly gagging up his food in public and spitting it out, on discovering—some swallows too late—that pork was part of the recipe. (An old-time Woolworth's soda fountain counter remains my most embarrassing memory of such moments.) The aversions attaching to *kosher* run deep. My own first encounter with shrimp, at thirteen, left me retching in a men's room: *shrimp!*—those delectably meaty paisleys of the sea I've eaten since then *thousands* of times, in dozens, hundreds, of creative preparations, and always with gusto.

In *Purity and Danger*, Mary Douglas deconstructs the rationale behind the dietary rules—the rules of defilement and accordance in matters of food choice—as instructionally dictated in the Old Testament. "You shall not eat any abominable things . . . ," the camel, the hare, the rock badger, the swine, the buzzard, the carrion vulture, the stork, the mouse, the gecko, the weasel, the cormorant, and a "zoo who's who" of other prohibited creatures of every footed, finned, and bewinged stripe. Then a similar, smaller list of the properly edible: the ox, the sheep, the goat, the wild ibex, certain locusts (and yet not any locusts), the frog, the roebuck, and others. What *is* the principle here, so powerful that millennia later it toggled my father's gag reflex? In an earlier chapter Douglas has prepared us for the answer when she says, "Ideas about separating, purifying, and punishing transgressions have as their main function to impose system on an inherently untidy experience. It is only by exaggerating the difference between within and without, above and below, male and female, with and against, that a semblance of order is created."

Later she turns to the Deuteronomy and Leviticus strictures. First, she argues, they aren't primarily early guidelines for a healthy diet (the "tapeworm thesis"). Nor are they primarily an attempt at defining the Jewish tribe by contrast to neighboring peoples (*"they* eat such-and-so, those filthy-dick pigfuckers, but *we* eat so-and-such"). Instead, she says, it's a straightforward matter of realizing that "holiness" is defined for Biblical Judaism "as wholeness and completeness." Ideally every aspect of personal and social life would serve to reflect this principle of unity, and Douglas provides a number of examples.

Sacrificial animals must be "without a blemish." A priest of the tribe "may not come into contact with death"—his commitment to life must be one hundred percent. A warrior who experienced a nocturnal emission, a woman menstruating, are to be quarantined away from the population: in *our* language their bodies have ceased to be "closed systems" so have temporarily given up their natural perfection. A man who has started to build a house but not completed it, or planted a vineyard and not yet tasted the fruit of its wine, or wedded but not yet consummated the marriage . . . these are unfit to go into battle: they must first fulfill the earlier totality. "You shall not let your

467

cattle breed with a different kind; you shall not sow your field with two kinds of seed; nor shall there come upon you a garment of two bemixed sortings of cloth. Be holy [complete], for I am holy [complete]."

And the same for one's menu selection. "Holiness," says Douglas, "requires that individuals conform to the class to which they belong . . . and requires that different classes of things shall not be confused." So four-footed creatures that fly are imperfect members of a grouping and thus unfit for consumption. An animal that has two hands and yet still locomotes on all fours like a quadruped is unclean. And " 'swarming' is not a mode of propulsion proper to any [one particular] element; swarming things are neither fish, flesh nor fowl. Eels and worms inhabit water, though not as fish; reptiles go on dry land, though not as quadrupeds; some insects fly, though not as birds. There is no order in them." (In this formulation a badger isn't a mammal; it's a fraction of two discordant halves. Or in Marthan-and-Arthurian terms, its parts aren't wedded persuasively and coherently.) One by one Douglas ticks down the list, and every animal's status is explained in the light of her theory. And the bottom line? "The dietary laws would have been like signs which at every turn inspired meditation on the oneness, purity and completion of God."

Is this a case of overkill in response to unbearable knowledge? Is a people's God required to be so whole, and his people so unreservedly pledged to a mimetic wholeness, only because some last remaining lucid intuition-node in the back of the brain suspects that in reality the Creator of this universe could *only* be conflicted in his own wants and intentions? To suspect such a frightening thing is to need immediately to deny it, with every atom of our zealousness.

It is *this* God, the maker but also the breaker of covenants; the one who stands above all petty bickering but admits to being a jealous and vengeful Lord; the one who makes man in his image, and in so doing makes a creature bound to disappoint; the birther of us, and the smiter of us, the one who demands our trust and yet, untrusting, repeatedly tests us; the sexual prude for whom our profligate reproduction is a sign of his favor; the one who giveth and taketh away, who asks of us both love and fear, who demands to be known by us in all of his terror and glory and also to be *un*knowable . . . *this* is Jack Miles's God, in his book *God*, and it makes for a compelling (and somewhat scary) read. Essentially conflict occurs in our lives because of "the conflict of good and evil" in the character of God himself.

If this is true, is it any wonder we stumble though Springsteenian workplace days and desperate (or boozy, bluesy, spunk-and-fury-fueled) Springsteenian nights with feelings about the lines of our lives that—in the calmest of us, even—often appear as diagnosably bipolar? We yo-yo crazily from middle-class conformity to jailbreak rebellion and then back. We envy the family man. We envy the foot-loose wanderer. We keep our good-guy noses to the grindstone, and we keep our wise-guy eyes out for a piece of ass. We sing our hal-lelujahs in a great praise for "the ties that bind"; we sing in great self-pity of "the chains of love"—they are, of course, the same one thing but modulated according to whatever the zing of the moment is. We lullaby and ai-yi-yi and oy and okeydokey.

Is it any wonder we turn to each other and ask that our bodies sup-ply and receive some solace? (Or is that only what the genes would have us think, for their own reasons?) Just as someone, somewhere, knows how mortal flesh yearns to be mingled with the spirit . . . so do Springsteen's speakers know the urge of flesh to be jazzed up with a counterbalancing flesh, shuffled together, lost and found and com-bo'd out of themselves for a night or a lifetime and into a new thing.

On a bottle's label: Shake Well Before Using.

8.

The hill land pasture is higher than he's taken his sheep in a while. No practical reason brought him here this morning, just the increas-ingly wonderful lavender hues of the hill land itself, which deepened as he rose along the rocky trail, leading him on as if *he* were a sheep, leading him by the eyes, by beauty. "Shit Nose," and he snaps his fin-gers. Shit Nose (meant affectionately) is his dog—his herder dog, his more-to-him-than-his-own-right arm. The dog abandons its one es-pecially funkily gunked-up tuft of hill land weeds and gives him a look, the equivalent of "Huh?" "Shit Nose," and he moves his hand in a circle that means to admire the whole increasingly lavender vista, "this is . . . ," then he falls silent. Swept entirely into a momentary sublimity he may be, but his vocabulary—he's an ancient Scythian—is weak on words accommodating grandeur in Nature's showcase.

Indeed, for an ancient Scythian, Nodor is rather dreamy. The typ-ical Scythian is a badass slice-your-nuts-off guy, an up-yours momma. The men are not only fearless and accurate archers but are brutal as well: they attach thorns to their arrowheads and coat them in a po-tent mixture of rotting adders, dung, and putrefied blood. They tan the hides of vanquished enemies, then use them for clothing, towel rags, shield coverings; the cranium of an enemy makes a drinking vessel of stylish appeal. A woman must kill an enemy in battle as a prerequisite to marriage. I said the *typical* Scythians. Up in the hills are flocks (or is it prides?) of griffins, eager for meat (*these* hills, our Nodor realizes queasily, ending his reverie), and according to rumor, Scythian bandits, outlawed from the tribal units, still use these hills as a headquarters: what do *they* care for carnivore griffins!

So it's no surprise that Nodor's life is his shepherding. (*Some* person in this rough, nomadic culture has to do it—but no one of stature.) There are streaks of Scythian fierceness in him, certainly: both nature and nurture have seen to that. But these are counter-weighted, or more, by a tendency toward gentleness and a penchant for daydream. It wasn't an easy childhood; it's astounding that he *survived* childhood. In any case, his marriage didn't survive long past the oaths sworn over the ritual, shared drinking-skull. (In this formulation, a marriage isn't a unit of two people, but a fraction of two discordant halves.) Sometimes he feels as if there are two, or three, or ten (and here his counting ability ceases) Nodors, sewn together with only the coarsest of skill. And so we meet him up here, in the thinner hill land air, alone and thoughtful.

But it isn't only the height and the stone and the meadow flowers that give this lonely place its lavender coloration. It's also the hill land light which, quicker than Nodor's eye has realized, deepens into a dusky plum, and then a gray, and then an impenetrable obsidian. He won't be returning his sheep to the fold, it looks like, so he gets them loosely penned inside a natural circle of rocks he finds conveniently at hand, then lights a fire for himself, to push the chilly touch of that besieging obsidian a little farther away. "Here, Shit Nose." Out of the pouch, a dried rind for himself and one for his weed-exploring companion. And then: strange noises, faintly, from out of the surrounding mystery zone. Like claws on tile. Like grunts from an inhuman throat. A whine from Shit Nose now: alert and not entirely courageous.

It's a thickly Persian-lamb night sky. The darkness all around him is a thin black shell, and, yes, he's sure, there are sounds of . . . something. Something on the other side of that black shell, trying to break through. Nodor has a stick, his only weapon. He lifts it now, although without much confidence. He's never seen one of these dangerous beasts but grew up with their stories and their images, and he isn't

470

too heartened. Even so, with a dry-mouthed swallow he wills the battle-lust part of himself, the thirster for blood from a living body, up from its psychic hiding place.

More claw-click . . . thudding . . . a grunt rising into a howl. . . . And the black shell shatters, and horror itself steps through. There are three of them. Everything is fast, and flickered by firelight, and made a blur by fright, but he sees the savage beaks and the wings and the scourging tails . . . one of them clubbing Shit Nose into unconsciousness, another beginning to club the sheep, to splatter them into death. . . .

A *club?* And Nodor sees, in his panicked, shadowed, adrenalin-crazy version of seeing: the beaks descend from masks, the wings are strapped on, and the tails are parts of shabby, belted-on animal pelts. "Griffins are people," he thinks. He whirls, he ducks, he deftly jumps out into the darkness—now for a minute *his*, not *their*, enabler—and he runs, and then runs more, and he doesn't stop until his lungs seem emptied of the ability to inhale, and it's really only coincidence that by the time he falls in a heap to the dark dirt in the dark air of this dark night of his life, the frightening sounds of pursuit are long gone. He gives a few weak pukes, then lies there sobbing, doing a dead man's float on the ground. When the sobbing has wrung him dry, he blanks out. When he comes to, it's still up-the-asshole dark, but there's the slobbery nudge of Shit Nose all over his face, and some revivifying licking.

Shit Nose—is alive! And he, *he*, Nodor, is alive! And he really did handle himself with a fierce adroitness! Nodor the shepherd handled himself with a warrior adroitness! And before he blanks out for a final time, Shit Nose standing guard, he remembers saying, "—Or people are griffins."

There's a version of the legend of Theseus similar in its intent: another story of confrontation with a monster that leads to a moment of self-understanding. But in Theseus's case, the hero proves a disappointment.

Catullus zeroes in on Theseus's fall from our admiration in the longest of his pieces to have survived, the marriage poem we number 64 and which the poet himself may well have considered his masterpiece. An epyllion—in effect a miniature epic—of 408 lines, the poem imagines the wedding of Peleus and Thetis ("when the long-awaited light of this chosen day appears, the entire region of Thessaly throngs to the palace!"). If marital unions bridge the separation between two lives, and then combine their differences, *this* love-pairing out of Greek mythology is a paragon of the distance such a bridge can span: Thetis, a goddess, (sea-nymph daughter of Nereus, an ocean god) is going to swear her troth in marriage to Peleus, a mortal man. It's a doozie of a synchrony and a glorious occasion.

The poem, however, uses the marriage only as a framing device, devoting more space to other, interior narratives. For example, a vibrant tapestry arrayed upon "the nuptial bed of the goddess" is "embroidered with old-time human figures" enacting some of the history of Theseus and Ariadne. Whatever his reasons, Catullus chooses *not* to retell the moment of high adventure when Theseus triumphs over the savage man-bull Minotaur in its labyrinth down in the bowel of the world, and he *doesn't* (as would be appropriate for the blanket over a wedding night's explorings) let us linger on the early love of Ariadne and Theseus.

Instead Catullus has this coverlet show the scene, much later on, where Theseus abandons Ariadne on an island—she's of no use to him now—and sails alone into what he believes will be a golden future. Ariadne, "emerging from treacherous sleep," finds herself "on an empty beach, deserted"; "she sees what she sees, but she hardly believes that she sees it." Her hurt is immense ("her entire heart and soul and dissolving mind hung upon you, Theseus") and soon so is her anger ("a fire engulfed her entire frame, igniting the depths of her being, her innermost marrow"). What follows is her long-term, virulent cursing not only of that king-of-all-ingrates Theseus but of anyone forthcoming in his genealogical line: *nobody* does scorn and high dudgeon better than Catullus's Ariadne. "As my grievance is real and my tears are wrung from my heart, oh gods and goddesses, do not allow my sorrow to languish forgotten, but let the heedless mind of Theseus cause death and destruction to him and his kin!"

All this because—as she says in addressing the dot of his ship as it slips swiftly toward the horizon—"you raised up lying expectations in my piteous heart of married happiness, longed-for hymeneals . . . all of which, the winds have tattered now into nothingness." With all of Greek mythology at his disposal, this is a strange choice of Catullus's for a poem in celebration of a wedding. Unless he means it to serve as a kind of poetry lightning rod, a story to attract the gods' laments and censures, thus keeping the house of Peleus and Thetis safe from these. Or it's the necessary counterweight by which the unending delight of Peleus and Thetis will forever be able to measure itself. (The dirty question: is this the way Martha and Arthur work for the rest of us?) This makes some sense since the poet himself has been perpetrator and victim, lambkin, stalking wolf, destroyer and destroyed, on love's unstoppably revolving wheel of roles.

And so in the version of the adventure that I was referring to, Theseus—still of virtuous motivation and brave heart at this moment—stands victorious, panting, wounded, over the fresh corpse of that hideous conglomeration, the Minotaur, and witnesses in its dimming eyes . . . his own face mirrored back at him, with a sense *of its being at home there.* A premonition, perhaps. A glimmer of self-analysis, perhaps, and an admission of confusion. As if any action the beast could imagine, Theseus could imagine too.

One day Danny stays home with a cold. How can his undeclared devotion stand it, being away from her presence? How can *she* stand it? Everyone's invisible-but-capable curiosity antennae are erect and on their highest sensitivity settings. Will Sweet reveal, whether overtly or through scattered dozens of smaller clues, that she misses him? *That's* stupid; *of course* she misses him! All year they've been doing their pas de deux in pirouetted arabesques that sometimes swing them to opposite sides of the office, or even (when out on various errands) opposite sides of town, but always attached by gossamer strands that stretch to the point where they can't be seen, yet exhibit a tensile strength that won't allow the pairing to break apart. We *know* it! But will she admit it today, in little acts of this or that? Sandi: *yes.* Sean: *no.* Juanita: *yes.* Sweet is oblivious to this, as she makes her cream-and-honey way around the office, but she's a Rorschach test for the rest of us.

Heading back from a hurried lunch, I find her on the front steps, sipping dreamily out of a Styrofoam cup on coffee break alone and seemingly pondering something mesmerizing exposed in the tarry bottom of the cup. The sun is pleased to gleam on her bare legs; I can almost hear it congratulating itself on this good fortune.

"Hey, Sweet."

"Hey, Albert." So I sit down too, figuring that "Hey, Albert" counts as a heartfelt invitation. Some people *do* like talking to me—unburdening themselves. I may be of help here. I may even leave with something choice for Sandi or Ron or Shonika to chew on.

"What's up, Sweet?"

473

She doesn't answer right away. People pass by; a few clouds tease the sun and then give up on that game; a sparrow considers a cigarette butt, its head cocked over to one side with the serious tilt of an airport security guard who's just discovered an abandoned suitcase. She's thinking: how trustworthy am I? Will I laugh at her? (No.) Will I tell the others? (Well maybe.) She cocks her head too.

"I think I'm in love. Is that crazy or what?"

"Not crazy. Why shouldn't you be in love?"

"Or not in love, exactly. But I have to tell you: I have this big crush on someone. That's it: I'm in crush."

"Do I know him?"

"*Do* you! Remember that day at the Stop-N-Go? He's that friend of yours, what's-his-name. Flowery shirt. Art, right? With the thingy of blonde-tint spikes."

Arthur.

We are so royally screwed-up, we human beings.

9.

One week the rains come in, they *own* this city. They hose this city clean of everything else and fill it with only themselves. Every hour is rain o'clock. Gray ghosts of the rain leak through our basement walls. And then, in a day, it's gone. The sun takes over: the new regime, as bad as the last one. Everything bakes. A car is like a brick just out of the oven. Getting into a car is like entering the center of oven heat. Rain, sun, rain, sun, a story of how the president lied to us, a story of third-world people looking to better their lives by slitting our throats, day, night, drought, flood, a heartwarming story of child-A who was cured of fatality-Z, dark, light, stability, flux, the summer of com-, re-com-, and uncombining.

It's also the summer of *The Incredible Hulk*, that blockbuster special effects box office hoo-ha-ha of a hit. You know, the movie of the original Marvel comic book of the same name: milquetoast Dr. Bruce Banner is . . . something, what is it? Irradiated or something, caught in a comet's tail or something, and now whenever he grows angry— *wham!* He jolts beyond controlling into a green humongous rampaging thing, all vein-snaked sacks of muscle and teeth that want to chew rocks for practice before they get to the bad guys' throats.

Which is really a way of saying it's the summer of Robert Louis Stevenson's Jekyll and Hyde, redone in cartoon garishness. Stevenson predates Freud with his insight (that the bull-man of the labyrinth still roams the brains of all of us and waits to be let out, a violent, infantile, irrational genie: "don't rub me," the saying goes, "the wrong way"). But the marriage of human and animal predates Stevenson by millions of years, is present in the umbers and smoky blacks of the earliest representational art we know, in the caves, where stag and shaman, cow and fertility goddess, ox and Paleolithic hunter are made as one and perform their untranslatable rites.

"The marriage of human and animal"—*marriage*. You see? It's the summer of Martha and Arthur, who provide the major structuring image through which my hazy conjectures approach all things. Like reading a recent essay on Jung: "The integration of conscious and unconscious contents creates a balanced perspective known as the 'self.'" Is the "self" a marriage, then, of two distinct but binary-system partners? If so would a "centered self" (in the language of buzzword therapy) be the same as a "happy marriage" (in the language of Joe and Jill from down the block)? Is this metaphor helpful at all? The summer of Hulk, of Ed, of Yancy, the unending summer of Martha and Arthur.

Another brilliant understanding from popular horror storytelling comes (on lurching steps) when, in the original Frankenstein movie by director James Whale, the standard destructiveness-tenderness polarity is reversed, and instead of being reminded yet again that a monster resides in the souls of even the kindliest among us, we see the equally true opposite: the monster, newly risen from the laboratory table of his creation, raises his hands in an innocent wonder at the sunlight, trying to hold it, softly mewling. For all of his bolts and sunken glower, for all of the plain fact that his body is really a *scrimmage* of other bodies, he's as freshly formed as a butterfly drying its wings of the damp of its birth throes. Later we'll see his attempts to play with a little girl in the village, one of the movie's few other scenes where sunlight is allowed to touch the monster. (He's a child too, with a childlike need for community.) Is he "sensitive?"—in the second of Whale's Frankenstein movies, the monster sits, with a rapt and obvious fulfillment, through a violin rendition of "Ave Maria" (and in the novel, you'll remember, he has the desire and time to learn French).

And still he's doomed to become the murder-thirsty, lumbering thing implied by his grab-bag origins, his brain-from-here-and-liver-from-over-there parody of our own beginnings. "Lumbering," "murder-thirsty" . . . and desperately lonely. Wise in the ways of the mind, the novel exhibits how much of the monster's savagery is really a reaction to the institution of marriage (or to community of any sort) and his exclusion from it. (*"Everybody's* got a hungry heart," says Springsteen.) The promise of companionship arises when Victor Frankenstein begins work on a second of his odious fabrications—but "during a sudden attack of scruples, he destroys his handiwork, infuriating the monster" (Tropp), who runs off (actually, sails away across the Irish Sea) with this threat: "I shall be with you on your wedding night." True enough, the wedding night eventually comes around, and the monster is there to strangle Frankenstein's childhood sweetheart Elizabeth.

James Whale's movie version *also* tantalizes the monster with a vision of companionship. Most of us can readily picture Elsa Lanchester tilted up on her table ("She's alive! ALIVE!") and then unbandaged, giving us an eyeful of her electrodynamically frizzled wings of hair—the intended bride. And yet on seeing the intended groom, she recoils, as anybody would, and the monster can all too clearly read the leaping disgust in her eyes. In its way the scene is heart-rending. How could he have imagined being wedded to her, when his own self isn't a seamlessly unified entity? (I think of a poem from a student, Lindsay McQuiddy: "My face is sliding off of me, / a leaf of skin . . ."). His own bones, heart, lungs, skull, and pods of nerves are uneasy cohabitants, and some days they must feel as irreconcilable as a Brahmin (who "will not eat ginger or onion: for these are grown in the ground") and one of the same religion's *achuta*, "untouchables," whose work is to unclog raw shit from the sewers in Indian villages—by hand—or cremate the dead or sweep up the dung from the streets (one caste is called the Musshar, "the rat-eaters": you can imagine). There was a time within living memory when an untouchable would be beaten if his shadow touched a person from a higher caste. Now Frankenstein's monster looks in the mirror: his left eye and his right eye want to file for divorce.

Although ample evidence also exists that meldings of otherwise piecemeal portions *can* be truly incorporative and greater than the mere sum of their parts: can be a *marriage* in the sense that Martha means in her more dogged spates of optimistic thinking. Mahalia Way suggests one function of the griffin was to serve as—and *because of*, not despite, its multi-speciesness—a symbol of Totality: to that extent, it was paid reverence. The same is true of the pangolin—

an "actual" animal in Lele culture that fills the role of the mythological griffin. Mary Douglas:

> The pangolin or scaly ant-eater contradicts all the most obvious animal categories. It is scaly like a fish, but it climbs trees. It is more like an egg-laying lizard than a mammal, yet it suckles its young. And most significant of all, unlike other small mammals, its young are born singly, in the nature of humans. In its own existence it combines all the elements which the Lele culture normally keeps apart, and so suggests a meditation on the inadequacy of the categories of human thought. It achieves a union of opposites. It overcomes the distinctions in the universe.

She calls it a "benign monster."

Could *any* of this be of use to my friends? To Cissy and Will, who are just back from their road trip to the Smoky Mountains, "now that the kids are grown and out of the house"—and so are the flocks of spooks, suspicions, and selfishly yammering demands that filled their heads for the first two decades of their life together? To Cynthia, at the singles mixer "opera night?" (Not that "karaoke night" and "casino night" were successes.) To Ben, who's waiting for Reese to show up with his bail? Out of all of this, is there a gift I can bring to them, a clarity? The summer days accumulate; the summer nights are a sour, black murk on top. The summer of Martha and Arthur, still no closer to reconciliation *or* to a terminal split. The days are long; if light can have an echo, then these summer days are it, as they keep bouncing off the darkness with unwillingness to fade. Then finally the moon comes out, and it juggles even that leftover light. And the moon that we see in the river, which is a lie of a moon, also juggles *its* light accordingly: which is, I suppose, a version of truth. Tharur and Armtha, Athra and Marthur. The summer of griffins being reported everywhere, their bodies built completely of synesthesia, of all of your photographs of bygone lovers you tore one night and let the wind remix and marry. Who knows—what unfathomably expert chemist of human savors and human dreams will *ever* know —the extant combinations that can rain down from the potential-sphere, sinking into our little garden hearts and briefly flourishing there?

477

I only wanted to look at the simple question, "What is and isn't a proper coupling?" You read it so many pages ago. And when you did, you automatically clicked onto sidebars: Greek gods, P. T. Barnum, laws of *kosherkeit*, nostalgia rock. The DVD "director's cut" of a talk-filled walk through Hill Park. And for all of that . . . well, here we are, Tharma, Rathur, Mathrum, Amthur, trading our carbon dioxide for the oxygen of the Hill Park trees. It's the boggled-up summer of all this; and it all comes down, like a fine silt, to the delta of marital imagery. "I haven't called him in over a week" or "Why do I hear he's buying new shirts?" It's sunny out, and we go for our walk. It rains, we don our hooded, rubberized ponchos, and we go for our walk. We do what we can. We read great works. We ring our bells and buzzers.

The genes, the aether, the mystically charged gestalt, the elemental subparticles of the fire in the hearts of stars . . . we have to understand that we're arrangements of What's Out There, we're the way What's Out There comprehends itself and grows. We're temporary; we'll be rearranged—sometimes apparently for the better, sometimes not. But that we will be rearranged is certain. We will go to pieces and be repieced; this is inevitable. That we will rest, be stable for a while, in a shape that pleases . . . this can happen too, in its turn. Luck helps but isn't a guarantee. Intelligence helps but isn't a guarantee. Sometimes we're hammered into a thousand slivers, each with its pain. Sometimes we're still, and the world around us is still, and a small joy asks us if we want to break out of this stillness and dance. Who knows why, but sometimes it all works out.

One evening I visit Mister J and George out on their front porch. The moon is full; tonight it can juggle a thousand plates of light, or more, and not drop one. Since Mister J is known for his micro- (read here: *one-small-screened-off-portion-of-musty-basement*) brewery, we're enjoying a third apiece of his latest triumph in the world of malts and hops. The two of them seem so pleased, and I let myself feel complicitous in their pleasure. The sounds surrounding us are mainly those of a difficult city—slams of cars and howls of sirens and far-off factory rumblings—but the thinnest hum of cricket-mantra from out in back is like the application of a lubricant that allows these giant gears to engage. We've been talking tonight about dozens of things and dozens of people we know in common. Suddenly I find myself asking them, "How do you do it, stay together?"

George leans close with his secret juju wisdom. "It's because I've volunteered to take out the garbage on Wednesdays."

"Oh right," Mister J chimes in. "Like puffball here knows what it's like to hustle off of his little foofoo fairy-ass and *sacrifice*."

There's a second of silence. And then at once from both of them, with eventually my accompaniment, is the laughter of people lucky in love, that leaves us like an invisible keyboard trilling its music on up to the sky.

10.

Later that summer, I'm rehearsing for a fall undergraduate course that I teach on poetics. Sometimes the skeleton and the skin of a poem are inseparable from its subject—that's the best, I tell them. Think of a poem which is spoken to us by somebody in a straitjacket, and it's tightly rhymed, A-A, B-B. Or a long poem over-spilling its lines, spoken by a cokehead. I remind them of Catullus 56—the poem (as a student of rowdy intelligence once put it) where he stuffs it into Lesbia's slave's back hole—and then I read to them out of Ross King's book *Ex-Libris*, about "the lone parchment of the works of Catullus that had been found . . . bunging up a wine barrel in a tavern in Verona." Some metaphors won't let go. "There are many things I don't know," I say, "but trust me: I know how to recognize the marriage of form and content."

Nominated by Bruce Beasley, The Gettysburg Review

TRIPTYCH

by DICK ALLEN

from THE DAY BEFORE (Sarabande Books)

I
The lake beyond the two boys playing basketball
    does not shimmer. It's simply a gray wash
below a few unfocused hills
    so low and commonplace no one's yet named them,
and the house in the foreground, with the old
    Dodge up on blocks beside it isn't worth
even a glance. Why enter it? Inside,
    the mirrors will be dusty, the furniture a few
dark pieces scattered on some thin gray rugs,
    nothing that would make you climb the stairs
to the bedroom in back, its single window
    facing the lake, beneath it an old half-rotted
picnic table salvaged from a dump, the circular
    clothesline in a square of ragged bushes. . . .
Yet this isn't poverty. The boys are fed
    sufficiently, and loved. The roads
you can't see joining other roads
    are passable, the cities at their ends—
thick airstrips leading off to Vietnam,
    Nicaragua hot beneath the moon—
no dream. All reaches and is reached from here,
    even on this day my father stands outside
and lifts his Kodak, takes his undistinguished
    photograph of house and car and lake and bare
tree branches cluttering, haphazardly, the white

November sky. And like an afterthought
or because they happened to be there,
    too small and distant to be waved away,
two boys.

II
            What were his thoughts? What were
my mother's thoughts outside her magazine
    ambitions for her sons? *Gray Saturdays.*
The radiator cat. Schoolboy friends
    killed at Normandy. The never-ending wish
and want! When the lake froze over
    we'd walk a mile across it toward the dark
and gutted icehouse. "Listen!" my father would shout
    into a broken window. *Listen, listen . . . listen*
his voice would echo. Then retracing
    our snowcrust path, we made our way out on
the lake again, ice booming, and the mist
    of slight wind-scattered snow so gossamer
we'd lift our mittened hands to part it constantly.
    White eyebrows and hot cocoa and the game of Clue
my mother always won. All reaches. All is reached
    from here. Chernobyl. The fattened goosenecked cloud
of the Challenger. Nixon waving. Dallas.
    Press of fingers on computer buttons.
The Chinese horns and hellgates of Korea.
    Hiroshima. Dresden. "The Eyes and Ears of the World."
The Holocaust. . . . You touch my arm
    to bring me out of it. Dulled, dazed,
approaching sixty with my hands still balancing
    a basketball, knees bent, my eyes
sighting to the hole in space above the rim,
    I fire. The world arcs up. My father fires. . . .

III
            Listen, listen . . . listen
his voice would echo. But for what? For why?
    Not even half a century has passed since I
first heard him shouting in those charred-wood rafters
    and the booming of the ice, the fleck, fleck

481

of dry snow scraped by boots—and one day for an hour
    with my Gilbert microscope upon the picnic table,
I tested the hypothesis of no
    snowflake shaped the same—and in that world
of crystal symmetry, found such elegance
    and mystery I thought I might reach God
through search, not prayer. Mistake. How blurred
    was my belief. . . . In the photograph
two edges and one chimney of the cottages
    whose lots touched ours; a section of the fence
around the village's cracked tennis court;
    a streetlamp that will soon come on,
the boys will stand beneath. They'll toss
    the basketball, bounce-pass it, dribble it
until their hands are raw. No one will take
    their picture at this hour—soon not even they
remember what they say: passing the ball, brilliantly
    catching it behind their backs and whipping it
away, away. Up to the moon. Up to the stars,
    away, away. . . . When they're gone
perhaps it rains or snows. Ice freezes
    on every twig and branch, catching the streetlamp's glow
in such a way a web of light is spun
    around it until dawn. No color in the frame.
November day, then night. . . . Two boys playing ball.

Nominated by Joyce Carol Oates, Philip Levine

LOST VICTORIES

fiction by WILLIAM T. VOLLMANN

from CONJUNCTIONS

> *And then, as I smoked a cigarette with a tank crew or chatted with a rifle company about the overall situation, I never failed to encounter that irrepressible urge to press onward, that readiness to put forward the very last ounce of energy, which are the hallmarks of the German soldier.*
>
> —Field-Marshal Erich von Manstein (1958)

1.

IN THE SLEEPWALKER'S TIME, we took back our honor and issued Panzergrüppen in all directions. But when I finally got home, the advance guard of the future had already come marching through the Brandenburg Gate, with their greatcoats triple-buttoned right up to their throats, their hands in their pockets, and their eyes as expressionless as shell craters! According to my wife, whose memory isn't bad when she confines herself to verifiable natural events, some of our lindens were in bloom that May, as why wouldn't they be, and the rest were scorched sticks, so she refers to that time as the "Russian spring," which proves that she can be witty, unless of course she heard that phrase on the radio. Anyhow, we got thoroughly denazified. Our own son, so I hear, threw away his Hitlerjugend uniform and sat on the fountain's rim, listening to the United States Army Band day after day. Next the wall went up, so half of Germany got lost to us, possibly forever, being magically changed into one of the new gray countries of Europe Central, and all our fearfulness of death came back. An old drunk stood up in the beer hall and tried to talk about destiny, but somebody bruised his skull with a two-liter stein, and down he went. When I reached home that night my wife was standing at the foot of the stairs with her hand on the doorjamb, peering at me through the place where the diamond-shaped glass window used to be, and I must have looked sad, because she said to me in a strange soft voice like summer: Never mind those lost years; we still have almost half the century left to make everything right, to which I said: Never mind those eight years I spent in Vorkuta, when they knocked my teeth out and damaged my kidneys, to which she replied: Listen, we all suffered in the war, even me whom you left alone while you were off raping Polish girls and shooting Ukrainians in the ditches; it's common knowledge what you were up to; besides, you're a middle-aged man and, and look at all the beer you swill; your kidneys would have given out on you anyway.—Having reconnoitered her disposition (as my old commanding officer would have said; he died of influenza in some coal mine near Tiflis), I fell back, so to speak; I withdrew from the position in hopes of saving something. I retreated into myself. Let her talk about destiny all she wants, I said to myself. At least *I'm* not tainted by illusions!

As it happened, I'd been saving up a little treat for myself; I'd hoarded it beneath the cushions of my armchair. Right before I went to the hospital, Athenaum-Verlaug released the memoirs of my hero, Field-Marshal von Manstein. Although I don't consider myself a bookish person, it seemed befitting to show my support, so to speak, especially since the poor old man had recently gotten out of jail, fourteen years early if memory serves—the only favor I'll ever thank those "Allies" for. For four years I couldn't get to it, on account of the shell splinter in my head, but finally the thing stopped moving, so I got some peace, and there he was, right there on the dust jacket in all his gray dignity, wearing his Iron Cross and his oak leaves. The title of the book was *Lost Victories*.

I've always been of the opinion that had Paulus only been permitted to break out and link up with von Manstein's troops, we could have won the war, and I've proved it to quite a few people, even including one of the Russian guards at Vorkuta. Von Manstein really could have saved us all.

Whenever I think about what happened to Germany, or my own miserable life, or the way my fourteen-year-old niece died, burned to death by the Americans in Dresden, I get so emotional that I start grinding my teeth, and then my wife tells all her friends: *He's in one of his moods again.* She never cared for my brother the former engineer, who's now imprisoned behind the wall of that so-called German Democratic Republic, repairing sewer mains for the Communists and earning almost nothing, my poor brother whom I'll never see again (although he can still telephone me); he's another victim of our former High Command's deeply echeloned illusions. *She says* he didn't welcome her into the family. As if that were the point! Well, I could go on and on. But von Manstein was going to take me out of my funk. Von Manstein was going to show me how it should have been done! And I knew from the very first page that he would stand up for the German army, too. You see, another thing that really pisses me off is the way the whole world condemns "German militarism," as if we hadn't been fighting simply for enough living space to survive! What would, say, the French have done if they'd lost the last war, and been forced to pay in blood, soil, and money, year after year, while all the neighbors sharpened their knives and got ready to carve off another piece of France? They say we went too far in Poland. Well, the Poles would have annexed Germany all the way to Berlin if they could! Von Manstein makes exactly this point in his book, which I really do recommend. He exposes the aggressive power politics of the Poles. Anybody who reads him will never feel the same way about Poland; this I guarantee. To get right down to it, von Manstein knows what's what! The victors may try as hard as they like to bury him, but that only makes me admire him all the more. As a great German said, *The strong man is mightiest alone.*

Well, I hadn't gotten very far in his book, really. I was only about halfway through the Polish campaign. But I could already tell that my faith in von Manstein wouldn't be disappointed, because as soon as the starting gun went off he exploded that lying slander that we meant the Poles any harm; he said—let me find the page—aha, here is how he put it: *When Hitler called for the swift and ruthless destruction of the Polish army, this was, in military parlance, merely the aim that must be the basis of any big offensive operation.* And how about all those so-called atrocities we committed in the process? (Anybody who complains that our army behaved, relatively speaking, incorrectly ought to spend a few years in Vorkuta!) We brought matters to an end as quickly as we could. The capitulation of Poland, again in von Manstein's words, *in every way upheld the military honor of an enemy defeated after a gallant struggle.* And that's all any good German needs to say about it.

485

So then what happened? Then those degenerate "Allies," who hanged our leaders for aggressive conspiracy, declared war on *us!*— Well, we did our duty. My best friend, Karl, who was with von Richthofen's Eighth Flying Corps and who never in his life told a lie, wrote me in a letter that an eagle flew beside him, just outside the cockpit window, on every sortie against Sedan. I'm not a sentimentalist, but that anecdote does make a person think. Well, Karl got shot down over Stalingrad. He was bringing food and medicine to the Sixth Army. Everything wasted! But he wouldn't have wanted my pity. The point is that we followed the only correct line, and our policies remained as generous as they could have been under the circumstances.—Just as a burst or two of light machine-gun fire will usually clear a road of partisans, so von Manstein utters a line, and all objections get blasted away! For instance, *as a result of the impeccable behavior of our troops,* he writes, *nothing happened to disturb our relations with the civil population during my six months in France.* Von Manstein's word is gold. If he says a thing is so, case closed. And yet they punish us for "crimes" against France! That's why sometimes I wake up in the morning all hungover and thinking, what's the use?

My wife was angry again, this time because I'd clogged up the drain by shaving, so her indictment ran, but I bunkered myself down, because right after that part about military honor, *Lost Victories* became especially interesting. I've always had a taste for theoretical issues. In Vorkuta I used to ask the guards how it all would have turned out if Stalin had died instead of Roosevelt; that question cost me those two top front teeth. So you can imagine how excited I felt when von Manstein began to raise theoretical questions, too. What should Poland have done to avoid defeat? To me it's a real exercise in open-mindedness to step into the enemy's shoes just for an eye blink, and then wiggle one's toes a little, so to speak; it's good preparation for *next time.* Yes, that's the correct way to go about it. And von Manstein, needless to say, had the answer in his ammo clip: Poland should have abandoned the western territories to save her armies from encirclement, then waited for the Allies to come. (Of course, they wouldn't have; they never did. What can you expect from those cowards? Look what Poland is now—a Russian satellite!) I wanted somebody on whom to try this out, but my son, who in the old days would have agreed with everything I said, hadn't shown his face all day; I suppose he was as close as he could get to the Tiergarten, hoping to cadge cigarettes from American Negroes. Anyhow, what would he have cared? When I got back from Vorkuta, he looked at me as if I were a monster. My wife tried to smooth it over by claiming that he didn't recognize me. Well, so what; *the strong man is mightiest* and all that. Next came the question I could really throw my soul into: what ought *we* have done to avoid defeat at Russia's hands? Needless to say, I had this more or less worked out, but only in general terms. So pay good attention, I told myself, because this is Field-Marshal Erich von Manstein speaking! He'd make me *see* the arrows on the maps, the spearheads, the long dotted trails, the ingotlike rectangles of our army groups! I was back there now, rushing through all those new states which so came into being on practically every page of *Lost Victories*, with their Reich Commissars preassigned by our sleep-walker himself while the Wehrmacht continued forward, its operational area ideally to be (see, I really do understand the theory behind this) not much deeper than the frontline itself, in order to avoid interference with our "Special Detachments" in the rear, and about those it's better not to say anything, because they're secret; what I'm trying to get across is that in *Lost Victories* Germany was on the march again, and the farther we went the stronger we got, until we were giants in a land of dreams. I'm a realist, but why can't I visit the past, especially when it's as sweet to me now as that smell of burned sugar that rose up when our bombers hit the Badayevski warehouses in Leningrad? About Leningrad, von Manstein says (and I agree with him), that back in '41 we could have taken the place if we'd just pushed a little harder, but the sleep-walker wouldn't let us; he demanded Moscow at the same time, which is why he got neither. (In retrospect, he does seem to have been—let's put it kindly—a bit starry-eyed.) We made another thrust in '42, but just when we were getting somewhere, Vlasov's Second Shock Army attacked us, then troops got diverted to the Caucasus; and no sooner had von Manstein straightened out *that* mess than Paulus got into trouble at Stalingrad! So, you see, it was just bad luck that we never got to roll into Leningrad. Burned sugar! I'll never forget that delicious smell. It was as if all the confectioners in Russia were getting busy, baking us a victory cake as big as a mountain; the frosting was all ready; I've always liked caramelized sugar.

Field-Marshal von Manstein closes the first chapter of his memoir: *From now on the weapons would speak.* Soon we would break through the Stalin Line. We would take Leningrad at last. And when we did, von Manstein would be there! He'd raise his Field-Marshal's baton to say *Germany*. At once there would come undying summer.

2.

Some of us in that open cage in Vorkuta, with our caps always on and our footcloths and anything else we could find wrapped around our faces against the cold, so that we resembled Russian babushkas, well, to pass the time we used to talk about politics, almost never about love, because that would have been too unbearable; it was almost as if we could already see those sleazy smiles on the faces of the Aryan girls we'd given our all for; now they were doing it with American soldiers just to get a little chocolate; when I got home and saw them flashing their teeth at the men who'd burned Dresden, I almost let them have it, I can tell you! As sad and sullen as most of us were at Vorkuta, the woman-crazy ones were the worst off. You can hum "Lili Marlene" like an idiot: you can fantasize about this lady or that until you're as black in the face as a hanged partisan, but you're still here and she's still *there*, beyond the barbed wire; still, even in the Gulag you can advance a theory or an opinion, and precisely because opinions feel, to get right down to it, less real than they do back home, in the barracks or even on the march, why not make the most of them? Headlamps in the forward trench, I always say! You might as well be speeding in dusty convoys of exultation beyond the steppe horizons, with that growl of tank treads comforting you all the way across the summer flatness; once you've heard that, you'll never stop wanting more. In that frame of mind you can pleasurably debate a question—for instance: was the Russian campaign aggressive or not? Von Manstein considers the Soviet troop dispositions to have been *deployment against every contingency*, which implies, at least as I see it, that Operation Barbarossa was arguably defensive. Moreover, he writes how on the very first day of the Russian campaign, *the Soviet command showed its true face* by killing and mutilating a German patrol. To me, that's conclusive (especially since von Manstein said it), but in any event you can argue something like that and polish your opinions until they're as fixed and perfect as diamonds, you might as well, since you're not going anywhere for years and years, if ever.

Right before the sleepwalker married Eva Braun and blew his brains out, he wrote his political testament, a copy of which my paraplegic friend Fritzi somehow got hold of last year. Good thing Fritzi was already denazified! Now, this document makes several statements which I can't entirely support; for example, in my opinion the man was too hard on the Jews, not that they don't need a firm hand. But what did impress me was that he'd made up his mind about everything—*everything!*—back when he was nothing but a hungry tramp in Vienna; in that testament, he insisted that he hadn't altered his conclusions about a single matter in the decades since then. Then he looked around him and said (so I imagine): What are we Germans going to be now? A rabble of syphilitic raped girls and legless men!— So he pulled the trigger. That takes guts. Paulus didn't have the courage to do it at Stalingrad. I would have done it in an eye blink, if that would have made any difference for Germany. Now, *that's* triumph of the will! So I do still respect him in a way, not least for the fact that he knew what he knew, whether it was true or not. (If only he'd allowed Guderian's mobile formations to do what Germans do best, instead of adopting that static defense which is more suitable to Slavs!) So why not pass the time deciding what you believed, then arguing for it, being true to it?

Even in those prison days, something in me was getting ready to feel a certain way, like a field gun zeroing in on the target; I wanted to become something once and for all; strange to say, Vorkuta came back to me as I sat so comfortably at home, reading von Manstein; and they weren't wasted years anymore; they were leading up to something. I wanted to clarify existence, if only for myself, to draw secret and perfect distinctions until my comprehension was a narrow spearhead. (Here's a distinction for you, free of charge: Russians opt for a massive artillery barrage before an attack, while we Germans prefer to trust in our own blood.) It was happening line by line, and I still had hundreds of glorious pages before me, like the Russian steppes in summer '42, stretching on perfectly golden and infinite like all our victories, our lost victories, I should say; and as I read I kept notes on the progress of our assault divisions.

3.

Don't think I haven't seen it all: the national enthusiasm, the pride, the successes thrown away contrary to the will of nature, the way our bigshots in their long gray coats used to lean backward and smile like sharks when some Polish dignitary or other would scuttle up to shake hands! In those days the sleepwalker could still dream of cracking Leningrad like a nut, making the Neva run backward, riding on the shoulders of the Bronze Horseman; while I for my part had all my teeth; my dreams swept east like silhouettes of German infantry marching up dusty summer roads. (For laughs we used to tune into Radio Leningrad, because all they broadcast was the ticking of a metronome.) Well, summer's long gone. But I don't care about that, for I've come to recognize something within my soul as titanic as the Big Dora gun which helped us reduce Sevastopol—yes, by now you'll have guessed: I served under *him*; I'm a veteran of von Manstein's Eleventh Army! And I hold the Iron Cross, First Class— no matter that the Americans have decreed that I can't wear it. So I read on and on, *knowing* that I did somehow have a thousand more years ahead of me; and the lindens were shimmering outside the window and German workmen were rebuilding everything. We live not far away from the Landwehrkanal, which was our primary defensive line during the battle of Berlin (it's also where that Jewish bitch Rosa Luxemburg got hers back in 1919). This is where our thirteen-year-old German boys came out in their black school uniforms to die in the struggle against Bolshevism. So much history all around me! And that day I really felt as if I were a part of it, I can tell you, sitting in my armchair finishing *Lost Victories*. Then I got to the part where von Manstein says that Hitler wasn't bold enough to stake everything on success; and that thing that I'd been getting ready for so long to feel, I felt it now. And it was this: *If only von Manstein had been our Führer. . . .*

Nominated by Conjunctions

HEDONISM

by DAVID BAKER

from AMERICAN SCHOLAR

Nothing under the black walnut. Nor where
our three hydrangeas share a mild shadow.
Nothing beside the limestone ridge, dry creek,
nor where cuttings from last year's fallen pine
—split in half by ice—freshened enough spores
to germinate a big crop of morels.
They're usually a perennial growth.
We depend on them thus for our pleasure,

cooked to our liking, sautéed with a spoon
of garlic over noodles, flash-fried in
egg batter like an omelet—but also
for the sheer delight of their springing up
in the soft humus, the leaf spoil of woods,
or near some new mayapples unfisting
so green they glow. So if we count on them,
does their absence account for a loss?

Legally yes. That's the way the lawyers
have added up the worth and shortfalls now
that the marriage is done. Not only what
we have, but what we would have had. Income,
children, happiness, and earth. Even sex
—sex we would have had—measurable
as money on a standard pro-rated
by expectation and level-of-life . . .

sex, whose absence is calculable, in-
curable, and called our "hedonic loss."
It's just that way this year, old-timers say.
The weather. Or the cycles. Or the fates.
Nothing by the apple trees. Nor where old
barns have crumbled into mulch and flowers.
Nothing is left but what is lost. And I
will go on missing you until I die.

Nominated by Marilyn Hacker, Grace Schulman, Katrina Roberts, Arthur Smith

READING IN HIS WAKE

fiction by PAMELA PAINTER

from PLOUGHSHARES

"AT LAST," MY HUSBAND SAID, when I had locked up for the night and come to bed.

"You knew I would," I said.

"But I didn't know when." Propped up in the recently rented hospital bed, he peered more closely at my chosen book. A novel by Patrick O'Brian. "Wait, no, no," he said. "You must begin at the beginning."

"But I like the sound of this one," I said, drawing out the swish of *The Mauritius Command*.

"Ah, but you want to be there when Aubrey and Maturin meet."

"I can always go back," I said, only slightly petulant, aware that at another time we'd never see again I would have been reading favorites, Trevor, Atwood, or Munro. Or tapping into the wall of biographies across from our beds, Rowley's Christina Stead, or Ellman's Joyce. Continuing through the poetry at the top of the stairs: Rivard, Roethke, Ruefle, Solomon, Szymborska.

His eyes gleamed. "But Aubrey and Maturin meet at such an unlikely place—especially to begin the series. They meet at a concert. Italians on little gilt chairs are playing Locatelli." He stopped, out of breath. "Never mind."

"So what's the first one?" If I was going to do this, give him this gift, so to speak, I must do it right. He named *Master and Commander*, and, ignoring the irony, I did as commanded and retrieved *Master and Commander* from his study next door. Carefully I settled in beside him, our old queen set flush to his new bed, and embarked. In

493

running commentary over years of hurried breakfasts and long dinners, he'd extolled to me Patrick O'Brian's sheer genius; how in the first novel he delivers to the reader in dramatic scenes of tense negotiation a detailed account of everything that Jack Aubrey must buy to outfit a ship circa 1859.

Four pages and an "introduction" later, I said, "I see what you mean. A most prickly meeting. Maturin delightfully pissy because a rapt Aubrey, from his seat in the scraggly audience, is audibly 'conducting' the quartet a half beat ahead."

"Don't forget their terse exchange of addresses as if for a duel," he said, laughing and coughing. I looked toward the oxygen machine, then at him. He shook his head.

Relieved, I slid the damp shoulder of his nightshirt into place. "Conflict on page one," I said, making us both happy.

Fifty pages later, when I murmured, "Mmmmmm," he said, "What? Tell me." He turned on the pillow with an effort and put aside his own O'Brian, *The Truelove*. So I read for him: *". . . the sun popped up from behind St. Philip's fort—it did, in fact, pop up, flattened sideways like a lemon in the morning haze and drawing its bottom free of the land with a distinct jerk."*

". . . distinct jerk," he repeated.

I said again *". . . drawing its bottom free of the land with a distinct jerk."* A shared blanket of satisfaction settled over us, and we went back to our books, companionably together, and companionably apart.

When I stopped reading to bring him a fresh glass of water to chase his myriad pills, he wanted to know where I was now. I slipped back into bed and tented the book on my flannel chest as I described how Mowett, an earnest member of the square-rigged ship's crew, is explaining sails to a queasy Maturin, and here my husband smiled wryly in queasy recognition of feeling queasy. I took his hand, and went on to describe how Maturin affects interest, although he is exceedingly dismayed to be getting this lesson at the appalling height of forty feet above the roiling seas. "Meanwhile, the reader is getting the lesson, too—and drama at the same time. Here," and I read, *"The rail passed slowly under Stephen's downward gaze—to be followed by the sea . . . his grip on the ratlines tightened with cataleptic strength."*

"It makes me want to start all over again," my husband said. Then, not to be seen as sentimental, he held up his book to show he'd just finished the most recent O'Brian. It slipped to the rug, and we left it there.

"You could read Dave Barry now," I said, acknowledging the only good thing about our new sleeping arrangement. My husband used to read Barry's essays in bed, laughing so hard the bed would shake, shake me loose from whatever I was reading. Annoyed, I'd mark my page and say, "Okay, read it to me." The ensuing excerpt was a tone change and mood swing one too many times, because I finally banished Dave Barry from the bed after his column titled "There's Nothing like Feeling Flush," which had my husband out of bed and pacing with laughter. In it, Dave Barry refers to an article published in a Scottish medical journal, "The Collapse of Toilets in Glasgow." Barry says, "The article describes the collapsing-toilet incidents in clinical scientific terminology, which contrasts nicely with a close-up, full-face photograph, suitable for framing, of a hairy and hefty victim's naked wounded butt, mooning out of the page at you, causing you to think, for reasons you cannot explain, of Pat Buchanan." We said it again and again. It answered everything: "for reasons you cannot explain."

"Do you want a Barry book?" I asked. He didn't answer. He was either sleeping or wishing I would shut up.

When we were about to leave for radiation, he was still bereft of a new O'Brian. I found him standing in his study, leaning on a walking stick from his collection, now no longer an affectation.

"The W's are too high," he said, stabbing the air with his stick. "It's Wodehouse I'm after."

"Why Wodehouse?" I said. Jeeves, the perfect valet and gentleman's gentleman, would be totally disapproving of how my husband's shirts went un-ironed and how his trousers drooped on his thinning hips. "I'm almost finished with Trevor's *After Rain*, it has that startlingly dark story about—"

"I think I'll read Wodehouse," he said, his jaw set. Out of breath, he slumped into his desk chair and pointed again. "But I can't reach him." On the shelves behind where my husband was pointing ranged the two hundred-plus books he'd edited at a Boston publishing house, and the four he'd written, the last novel, *A Secret History of Time to Come*, included by the New York Museum of Natural History in a time capsule that would outlast us all. "We have too many books," he said.

"That's what you always say," I said. Hitching up my skirt before the wall of English and European Fiction, I mounted the wobbly wooden ladder we swore at on principle every time we retrieved an out-of-reach book. Waugh Winterson Wodehouse. I called down three titles before he nodded at the fourth. *The Code of the Woosters*. "Why Wodehouse?" I asked again on my descent.

"Ah, you haven't read Wodehouse yet. Arch, mannered humor. You'll see." Then, as if anticipating my early mutiny against O'Brian in deference to Wodehouse, his eyes narrowed, and he instructed, "Keep with the O'Brians for now."

We left for the hospital, armed with our respective books. On the way, I mentioned that Raymond Chandler, also English, and Wodehouse had both attended the posh prep school Dulwich College. "Dul-ich, but spelled Dulwich," my husband said, surprised by Chandler.

Our bookish, competent doctor always wanted to know what we were reading. My husband waved the Wodehouse at him. "It has a blurb by Ogden Nash," he said, and read, *"In my salad days, I thought that P. G. Wodehouse was the funniest writer in the world. Now I have reached the after-dinner coffee stage, and I know that he is."*

"Woadhouse," the doctor said, making a note on his prescription pad.

"W-o-o-d. I hope he's still funny," my husband said, peering at the doctor over his glasses. "I'm way past the after-dinner coffee. I've reached the medicine stage."

A week later, we were again side by side, my husband's bed rising smoothly and electronically to a barely comfortable position I tried to match with pillows, despairing of the difference in height. I'd finished *Master and Commander* and put it in a safe place because the doctor had meticulously written his home phone number inside its cover. *Post Captain* was next. My husband's long fingers, thin and bony, were oddly free of books because he was listening to the tape of O'Brian's latest Aubrey/Maturin, *The Wine-Dark Sea*. His eyes were alertly closed beneath the Walkman's earphones curving over his new, silky growth of hair.

When he stopped listening to take his pills, I asked him to recall what he'd liked best about *Post Captain*. I closed my eyes against a hysterical welling up of water. And when he'd told me, I thought yes,

yes, after years of reading and rereading, arguing, damning, and praising, I knew now almost exactly what he would say. Although I didn't tell him this—but tested more. I badgered him about the repetition of one battle scene after another, asked him to name his favorite title in the series, asked him if Maturin ever dies. I moved on to Ford's *The Good Soldier*. Didn't the narrator's equivocation grate on his nerves? Yes and no. Who was Dante's best translator? Yes, yes. And what did he think of the poem in *Pale Fire*?

"Stop it," he said, his voice stronger than it had been in days. "Enough."

The next evening, when he had finished both sides of the first tape, he told me to look in his desk for a second Walkman. Why didn't matter. "Now, listen to this tape," he said.

"You're still seducing me with literature," I accused him.

He took the tape from his Walkman and inserted it into mine.

"No. No. I can't," I said. "I'll get the plots mixed up." Already I was awash in the unfamiliar world of sloops and frigates, admiring of royals, baffled by masts and yards, and dipping in and out of *A Sea of Words: A Lexicon and Companion for Patrick O'Brian's Seafaring Tales*, chastely beside me on the bed. In love again.

"Here," he said. "Listen."

I donned the earphones, and because he was watching, I closed my eyes. Across the tiny gulf between our beds, his hand found my hand as a calming voice began, *"A purple ocean, vast under the sky and devoid of all visible life apart from two minute ships racing across its immensity."*

Until my husband's hand slipped from mine, until his breath failed, until I called 911, until the ambulance arrived to provide our last voyage together, on that last evening I sailed precariously in two different seas, astride two listing vessels, keeping a third in view against a dark horizon, reading in his wake.

Nominated by Thomas Kennedy

THE GREEK SHIPS

by ROBERT BLY

from POETRY

When the water holes go, and the fish flop about
In the mud, they can moisten each other faintly,
But it's best if they lose themselves in the river.

You know how many Greek ships went down
With their cargoes of wine. If we can't get
To port, perhaps it's best to head for the bottom.

I've heard that the mourning dove never says
What she means. Those of us who make up poems
Have agreed not to say what the pain is.

For years Eliot wrote poems standing under
A bare light-bulb. He knew he was a murderer,
And he accepted his punishment at birth.

The sitar player is searching: now in the backyard,
Now in the old dishes left behind on the table,
Now for the suffering on the underside of a leaf.

Go ahead, throw your good name into the water.
All those who have ruined their lives for love
Are calling to us from a hundred sunken ships.

Nominated by Ed Ochester

from URBAN RENEWAL

by MAJOR JACKSON

from PROVINCETOWN ARTS

XVI.
What of my fourth grade teacher at Reynolds Elementary,
who weary after failed attempts to set to memory
names strange and meaningless as grains of dirt around
the mouthless, mountain caves at Bahrain Karai:
Tarik, Shanequa, Amari, Aisha, nicknamed the entire class
after French painters whether boy or girl. Behold
the beginning of sentient formless life. And so,
my best friend Darnell became Marcel, and Tee-tee
was Braque, and Stacy James was Fragonard,
and I, Eduard Charlemont. The time has come to look
at these signs from another point of view. Days passed
in inactivity before I corrected her, for Eduard was
Austrian and painted the black chief in a palace in 1878
to the question whether intelligence exists. All of Europe
swooned to Venus of Willendorf. Outside her tongue,
yet of it, in textbooks Herodotus tells us of the legend
of Sewosret (Seosteris I, II, or III), the colonizer of Greece,
founder of Athens. What's in a name? Sagas rise and
fall in the orbs of jumpropes, Hannibal grasps a Roman
monkeybar on history's rung, and the mighty heroes at recess
lay dead in woe on the imagined battlefields of Halo.

Nominated by Provincetown Arts

SPECIAL MENTION

(The editors also wish to mention the following important works published by small presses last year. Listings are in no particular order.)

POETRY

Ornithology—Lynda Hull (Brilliant Corners)
Ode to American English—Barbara Hamby (Boulevard)
Born Blind—Peter Cooley (North American Review)
The Old Liberators—Robert Hedin (WLA)
In the Parking Lot of the Muffler Shop—Richard Tillinghast
   (Hudson Review)
Ovid At Fifteen—Christopher Bursk (New Issues)
The Debtor In the Convex Mirror—Susan Wheeler (Boston
   Review)
Focus—Joel Brouwer (Ploughshares)
Downhill—Richard Frost (American Scholar)
Proverbs of Hell—Lorna Knowles Blake (Hudson Review)
Mailing A Letter: The Miserable Highways—Minnie Bruce Pratt
   (Bloom)
Verses for the Madonna of Humility With The Temptation Of
   Eve—Lynn Powell (University of Akron Press)
Bat Boy, Break a Leg—Julia Kasdorf (Shenandoah)
Anniversaries of Autumn—Alan Soldofsky (Gettysburg Review)
To A Sea-Unicorn—Deborah Greger (Raritan Review)
The Earth Without—Gina Franco (Black Warrior Review)
Aubade—Cecilia Woloch (*Late*, BOA Editions)
Prayer At The Gym—Patrick Donnelly (American Poetry Review)
The Box—Mark Turpin (*Hammer*, Sarabande)
Fearless—Tim Seibles (Cape Cod Voice)

FICTION

502

Chicken Man—Susan Jackson (North American Review)
The Future—Daniel Stern (Hampton Shorts)
Wild California—Victoria Nelson (Raritan)
Gaining Ground—Robin Black (Alaska Quarterly Review)
from *The Sleeping Father*—Matthew Sharpe (Soft Skull Press)
How To Lose 30 Lbs In 30 Days!—Elizabeth Wetmore (Black
   Warrior Review)
That Kind of Nonsense—Patrick Tobin (Agni)
Hypnagogia—Tama Baldwin (Fiction International)
The Last Member of the Boela Tribe—Cathy Day (Antioch Review)
Night Train—Thom Jones (Doubletake)
In the Garden—Kim Edwards (Ploughshares)
Second Hand—Chris Offutt (Iowa Review)
Svengali—Rick DeMarinis (Epoch)
The Drowned Boy—Jerry Gabriel (Epoch)
Social Discourse, 1944—Jane Eaton Hamilton (Missouri Review)
Trouble—Stacy Grimes (Five Points)
Visitors—Aimee Phan (Chelsea)
Cove—Nicholas Montemarano (Crazyhorse)
Help These Days—Linsey Trask (Alaska Quarterly)
Blue Night, Clover Lake—Mary Stewart Atwell (Epoch)
The Specialist—Alison Smith (McSweeney's)
Love And The Imitation Artist—Joan Alonso (Boulevard)
I'll Change Completely—Stephen Elliott (McSweeney's)
Bernard Jr's Uncle Luscious—Emily Raboteau (Missouri Review)
Strike Anywhere—Antonya Nelson (failbetter.com)
My Husband and Your Story—Robert Olmstead (Willow Spring)
Six Elogs Deep—Richard Lewis (Lynx Eye)
The Only Thing—Tom Pacheco (Words of Wisdom)
News From Nevada—Brian Bedard (Briar Cliff Review)
Far From Fight—Ben E. Campbell (Timber Creek Review)
Mother's Day—Kaylie Jones (Confrontation)
Belly Talk—Lee Martin (Southern Review)
Eating, Ohio—Imad Rahman (One Story)
The Taste of Penny—Jeff Parker (Ploughshares)
Death Care World Expo Reno, Nevada—Darrell Spencer
   (American Literary Review)
Give—James Salter (Tin House)
Pilgrim Girl—Mary Otis (Tin House)
The Turk And My Mother—Mary Helen Stefaniak (Epoch)

Breasts—Stuart Dybek (Tin House)
Ongehoma—Ryan Harty (Missouri Review)
The Shortest Distance Between Me and The World—Mark Kline
    (Missouri Review)
Quarterday—Ward Just (Five Points)
Looking For War—Douglas Unger (TriQuarterly)
Life Could Be A Dream (Sh-Boom, Sh-Boom)—Clark Blaise
    (Michigan Quarterly Review)
This Is For Chet—Jonis Agee (Descant)
Percussion—Valerie Miner (Prairie Schooner)
Kid Coole—M.G. Stephens (Witness)
The Revived Art of the Toy Theatre—Debra Spark (Agni)
The Opposite of Stone—Katharine Haake (Witness)
A Good Boy—Cynthia Morrison Phoel (Missouri Review)
Some Other, Better Otto—Deborah Eisenberg (Yale Review)
Recreational Biting—B. Lee Hope (Witness)
Honors—Jesse Lee Kercheval (Prairie Schooner)
Vines—Becky Hagenston (Fugue)
Kitchen Friends—Katherine Shonk (StoryQuarterly)
The Lackawanna Crawl—Roger Yepsen (Shenandoah)
Applause—Maura Stanton (River Styx)
Two Men Do Not Dream The Same Dream—Ewing Campbell
    (Georgia Review)
Murdering The Moonlight—Pete LaSalle (New England Review)
Burning Woman—Adam Desnoyers (Lit)
Down In The Jungle Room—Brent Spencer (Epoch)
The Pleasure of Man and Woman Together On Earth—Thomas E.
    Kennedy (New Letters)
The Deaf Musician—Katherine Haake (Iowa Review)
Two Stories—Brian Evenson (Conjunctions)
Stricken By Love—Suzanne Berne (Epoch)
In Bogalusa—Paul Maliszewski (Indiana Review)
Robert and His Wife—Richard Burgin (RBS Gazette)

NONFICTION

The Messenger—David Antin (Conjunctions)
My Yiddish—Leonard Michaels (Threepenny Review)
Exploding The Dog—Andrew Hudgins (American Scholar)

Calley's Ghost—Philip Beidler (Virginia Quarterly)
Renée—Carolyn Michaels (Missouri Review)
Diminished Things—Ginger Strand (Raritan Review)
Happiness—Jane Miller (Raritan Review)
Taming The Gorgon; My Mother Into Fiction—Lynn Freed
   (Georgia Review)
My Blue Cousin—Itzhak Kronzon (Bellevue Literary Review)
After The Snow—Paula Fox (Paris Review)
Graham Greene's Vietnam—Katie Roiphe (Tin House)
The Dog Gets to Dover: William Maxwell As A Correspondent—
   Michael Collier (Georgia Review)
Going South—Natalie Pearson (Bellevue Literary Review)
My Suicides—Merrill Joan Gerber (Salmagundi)
My Private Germany—P.F. Kluge (Kenyon Review)

PRESSES FEATURED IN THE PUSHCART PRIZE EDITIONS SINCE 1976

Acts
Agni
Ahsahta Press
Ailanthus Press
Alaska Quarterly Review
Alcheringa/Ethnopoetics
Alice James Books
Ambergris
Amelia
American Letters and Commentary
American Literature
American PEN
American Poetry Review
American Scholar
American Short Fiction
The American Voice
Amicus Journal
Amnesty International
Anaesthesia Review
Another Chicago Magazine
Antaeus
Antietam Review
Antioch Review
Apalachee Quarterly
Aphra
Aralia Press
The Ark

Art and Understanding
Arts and Letters
Artword Quarterly
Ascensius Press
Ascent
Aspen Leaves
Aspen Poetry Anthology
Assembling
Atlanta Review
Autonomedia
Avocet Press
The Baffler
Bakunin
Bamboo Ridge
Barlenmir House
Barnwood Press
Barrow Street
The Bellingham Review
Bellowing Ark
Beloit Poetry Journal
Bennington Review
Bilingual Review
Black American Literature Forum
Black Rooster
Black Scholar
Black Sparrow
Black Warrior Review

Blackwells Press
Bloomsbury Review
Blue Cloud Quarterly
Blue Unicorn
Blue Wind Press
Bluefish
BOA Editions
Bomb
Bookslinger Editions
Boston Review
Boulevard
Boxspring
Bridge
Bridges
Brown Journal of Arts
Burning Deck Press
Caliban
California Quarterly
Callaloo
Calliope
Calliopea Press
Calyx
Canto
Capra Press
Caribbean Writer
Carolina Quarterly
Cedar Rock
Center
Chariton Review
Charnel House
Chattahoochee Review
Chelsea
Chicago Review
Chouteau Review
Chowder Review
Cimarron Review
Cincinnati Poetry Review
City Lights Books
Cleveland State University Poetry Center
Clown War
CoEvolution Quarterly
Cold Mountain Press
Colorado Review

Columbia: A Magazine of Poetry and
    Prose
Confluence Press
Confrontation
Conjunctions
Connecticut Review
Copper Canyon Press
Cosmic Information Agency
Countermeasures
Counterpoint
Crawl Out Your Window
Crazyhorse
Crescent Review
Cross Cultural Communications
Cross Currents
Crosstown Books
Cumberland Poetry Review
Curbstone Press
Cutbank
Dacotah Territory
Daedalus
Dalkey Archive Press
Decatur House
December
Denver Quarterly
Desperation Press
Domestic Crude
Doubletake
Dragon Gate Inc.
Dreamworks
Dryad Press
Duck Down Press
Durak
East River Anthology
Eastern Washington University Press
Ellis Press
Empty Bowl
Epoch
Ergo!
Evansville Review
Exquisite Corpse
Faultline
Fence

510

Malahat Review
Mānoa
Manroot
Many Mountains Moving
Marlboro Review
Massachusetts Review
McSweeney's
Meridian
Mho & Mho Works
Micah Publications
Michigan Quarterly
Mid-American Review
Milkweed Editions
Milkweed Quarterly
The Minnesota Review
Mississippi Review
Mississippi Valley Review
Missouri Review
Montana Gothic
Montana Review
Montemora
Moon Pony Press
Mount Voices
Mr. Cogito Press
MSS
Mudfish
Mulch Press
Nada Press
Nebraska Review
New America
New American Review
New American Writing
The New Criterion
New Delta Review
New Directions
New England Review
New England Review and Bread Loaf
    Quarterly
New Letters
New Orleans Review
New Virginia Review
New York Quarterly
New York University Press

News from The Republic of Letters
Nimrod
9 × 9 Industries
Noon
North American Review
North Atlantic Books
North Dakota Quarterly
North Point Press
Northeastern University Press
Northern Lights
Northwest Review
Notre Dame Review
O. ARS
O. Blēk
Obsidian
Obsidian II
Oconee Review
October
Ohio Review
Old Crow Review
Ontario Review
Open City
Open Places
Orca Press
Orchises Press
Orion
Other Voices
Oxford American
Oxford Press
Oyez Press
Oyster Boy Review
Painted Bride Quarterly
Painted Hills Review
Palo Alto Review
Paris Press
Paris Review
Parkett
Parnassus: Poetry in Review
Partisan Review
Passages North
Penca Books
Pentagram
Penumbra Press

Pequod
Persea: An International Review
Pipedream Press
Pitcairn Press
Pitt Magazine
Pleiades
Ploughshares
Poet and Critic
Poet Lore
Poetry
Poetry East
Poetry Ireland Review
Poetry Northwest
Poetry Now
Post Road
Prairie Schooner
Prescott Street Press
Press
Promise of Learnings
Provincetown Arts
Puerto Del Sol
Quaderni Di Yip
Quarry West
The Quarterly
Quarterly West
Raccoon
Rainbow Press
Raritan: A Quarterly Review
Red Cedar Review
Red Clay Books
Red Dust Press
Red Earth Press
Red Hen Press
Release Press
Review of Contemporary Fiction
Revista Chicano-Riquena
Rhetoric Review
Rivendell
River Styx
River Teeth
Rowan Tree Press
Russian *Samizdat*
Salmagundi

San Marcos Press
Sarabande Books
Sea Pen Press and Paper Mill
Seal Press
Seamark Press
Seattle Review
Second Coming Press
Semiotext(e)
Seneca Review
Seven Days
The Seventies Press
Sewanee Review
Shankpainter
Shantih
Shearsman
Sheep Meadow Press
Shenandoah
A Shout In the Street
Sibyl-Child Press
Side Show
Small Moon
The Smith
Solo
Solo 2
Some
The Sonora Review
Southern Poetry Review
Southern Review
Southwest Review
Spectrum
Spillway
The Spirit That Moves Us
St. Andrews Press
Story
Story Quarterly
Streetfare Journal
Stuart Wright, Publisher
Sulfur
The Sun
Sun & Moon Press
Sun Press
Sunstone
Sycamore Review

Tamagwa
Tar River Poetry
Teal Press
Telephone Books
Telescope
Temblor
The Temple
Tendril
Texas Slough
Third Coast
13th Moon
THIS
Thorp Springs Press
Three Rivers Press
Threepenny Review
Thunder City Press
Thunder's Mouth Press
Tia Chucha Press
Tikkun
Tin House
Tombouctou Books
Toothpaste Press
Transatlantic Review
Triplopia
TriQuarterly
Truck Press
Turnrow
Undine
Unicorn Press
University of Georgia Press
University of Illinois Press
University of Iowa Press
University of Massachusetts Press
University of North Texas Press

University of Pittsburgh Press
University of Wisconsin Press
University Press of New England
Unmuzzled Ox
Unspeakable Visions of the Individual
Vagabond
Verse
Vignette
Virginia Quarterly
Volt
Wampeter Press
Washington Writers Workshop
Water-Stone
Water Table
Western Humanities Review
Westigan Review
White Pine Press
Wickwire Press
Willow Springs
Wilmore City
Witness
Word Beat Press
Word-Smith
Wormwood Review
Writers Forum
Xanadu
Yale Review
Yardbird Reader
Yarrow
Y'Bird
Zeitgeist Press
Zoetrope: All-Story
ZYZZYVA

CONTRIBUTING SMALL PRESSES FOR PUSHCART PRIZE XXIX

A

The Adirondack Review, P.O. Box 46, Watertown, NY 13601
Agni, Boston Univ., 236 Bay State Rd., Boston, MA 02215
Alaska Quarterly Review, Univ. of Alaska, 3211 Providence Dr., Anchorage, AK 99508
Alice James Books, 238 Main St., Farmington, ME 04938
Alligator Juniper, 220 Grand Ave., Prescott, AZ 86301
Always in Season, P.O. Box 380403, Brooklyn, NY 11238
Amaze, 10529 Olive St., Temple City, CA 91780
American Letters & Commentary, 850 Park Ave., Ste. 5B, New York, NY 10021
American Poetry Review, 117 S. 17th St., Ste. 910, Philadelphia, PA 19105
American Scholar, 1606 New Hampshire Ave., NW, Washington, DC 20009
Ancient Paths, P.O. Box 7505, Fairfax Station, VA 22039
Anthology, Inc., P.O. Box 4411, Mesa, AZ 85211
Antietam Review, 41 S. Potomac St., Hagerstown, MD 21740
Antioch Review, P.O. Box 148, Yellow Springs, OH 45387
Architectural Boston, 52 Broad St., Boston, MA 02109
Arctos Press, P.O. Box 401, Sausalito, CA 94966
Argonne House Press, 1620 Argonne Pl., NW, Washington, DC 20009
Arkansas Review, English Dept., P.O. Box 1890, State University, AR 72467
Arsenic Lobster, 1800 Schodde Ave., Burley, ID 83318
Artful Dodge, English Dept., College of Wooster, Wooster, OH 44691
Arts & Letters, Georgia College & State Univ., Milledgeville, GA 31061
Ashland University Poetry Press, 401 College Ave., Ashland, OH 44805
Atlanta Review, PO Box 8248, Atlanta, GA 31106
The Aurorean, P.O. Box 219, Sagamore Beach, MA 02562
Axe Factory, P.O. Box 40691, Philadelphia, PA 19107

B

The Baltimore Review, P.O. Box 410, Riderwood, MD 21139
Bamboo Ridge Press, P.O. Box 61781, Honolulu, HI 96839
Barnwood Press, P.O. Box 146, Selma, IN 47383
Bayou, Creative Writing Workshop, Univ. of New Orleans, New Orleans, LA 70148
Bayousphere, Box 456, Ste. 1239, Univ. of Houston, Houston, TX 77058

The Believer, 826 Valencia St., San Francisco, CA 94110
Belle Books, P.O. Box 67, Smyrna, GA 30081
Bellevue Literary Review, NYU School of Medicine, 550 First Ave., OBV 6-612, New York, NY 10016
Bellingham Review, MS-9053, WWU, Bellingham, WA 98225
Bellowing Ark Press, P.O. Box 55564, Shoreline, WA 98155
Beloit Fiction Journal, Box 11, Beloit College, Beloit, WI 53511
Beloit Poetry Journal, P.O. Box 151, Farmington, ME 04938
The Berkshire Review, P.O. Box 23, Richmond, MA 01254
Big City Lit, Box 1141, Cathedral Sta., New York, NY 10025
Birmingham Poetry Review, University of Alabama, Birmingham, AL 35294
Bitter Oleander Press, 4983 Tall Oaks Dr., Fayetteville, NY 13066
BkMk Press, Univ. of Missouri, 5101 Rockhill Rd., Kansas City, MO 64110
Black Warrior Review, P.O. Box 862936, Tuscaloosa, AL 35486
Blackbird, P.O. Box 843082, Richmond, VA 23284
Blink, P.O. Box E, Mississippi State, MS 39762
Bloomsbury Review, 1553 Platte St. (# 206), Denver, CO 80202
Blue Fifth Review, 267 Lark Meadow Ct., Bluff City, TN 37618
Blue Light Press, P.O. Box 642, Fairfield, IA 52556
Blue Monk Press, 3445 Seracedar St., Baton Rouge, LA 70816
Blue Unicorn, 22 Avon Rd., Kensington, CA 94207
BOA Editions, Ltd., 260 East Ave., Rochester, NY 14604
Boston Review, Bldg. E53, Rm. 407, MIT, Cambridge, MA 02139
Boulevard, 6614 Clayton Rd., PMB #325, Richmond Heights, MO 63117
bowwow, 2130 West Race, Chicago, IL 60612
Brain, Child, P.O. Box 5566, Charlottesville, VA 22905
The Briarcliff Review, 3303 Rebecca St., P.O. Box 2100, Sioux city, IA 51104
Brilliant Corners, Lycoming College, Williamsport, PA 17701
Broadstone Books, 418 Ann St., Frankfort, KY 40601
Buckle, P.O. Box 1653, Buffalo, NY 14205
Byline, P.O. Box 5240, Edmond, OK 73083

C

Caduceus, Yale Physicians Bldg., 800 Howard Ave., New Haven, CT 06536
Calyx, P.O. Box B, 216 SW Madison, Corvallis, OR 97339
The Canary, English Dept., Univ. of Alabama, Tuscaloosa, AL 35487
The Caribbean Writer, Univ. of the Virgin Islands, RR2-100000 Kingshill, St. Croix, U.S. Virgin Islands
    00850
Carve Magazine, P.O. Box 1212, Enumclaw, WA 98022
Center, 202 Tate Hall, Columbia, MO 65211
Chaffin Journal, Eastern Kentucky Univ., Richmond, KY 40475
Chariton Review, English Dept., Brigham Young Univ., Provo, UT 84602
Chatoyant, P.O. Box 832, Aptos, CA 95001
The Chattahoochee Review, 2101 Womack Rd., Dunwoody, GA 30338
Chelsea, Box 773, Cooper Sta., New York, NY 10276
The Children's Beat, 4321 Hartwick Rd, Ste. 320, College Park, MD 20740
Cimarron Review, 205 Morrill Hall, Oklahoma State Univ., Stillwater, OK 73409
Cinco Puntos Press, 701 Texas Ave., El Paso, TX 79901
Cleveland State University Poetry Center, 1983 E. 24th St., Cleveland, OH 44115
Coal City Review, English Dept., Univ. of Kansas, Lawrence, KS 66044
Colere, Coe College, 1220 First Ave., NE, Cedar Rapids, IA 52402
Colorado Review, English Dept., Colorado State Univ., Fort Collins, CO 80523
Columbia, Columbia Univ., 2960 Broadway, New York, NY 10027
The Comstock Review, 4956 St. John Dr., Syracuse, NY 13215
Confrontation, P.O. Box 10507, Longboat Key, FL 34228
Conjunctions, Bard College, Annandale-on-Hudson, NY 12504

Connecticut Review, English Dept., Southern Connecticut State Univ., New Haven, CT 06515
Connecticut River Review, P.O. Box 4053, Waterbury, CT 06704
Cottonwood, 400 Kansas Union, University of Kansas, Lawrence, KS 66045
Crab Orchard Review, English Dept., Southern Illinois Univ., Carbondale, IL 62901
Crazyhorse, English Dept., College of Charleston, Charleston, SC 29424
Creative Nonfiction, 5501 Walnut St., Ste. 202, Pittsburgh, Pa 15232
R. L. Crow Publications, P.O. Box 262, Penn Valley, CA 45946
Crucible, Barton College, Wilson, NC 27893
Cumberland Poetry Review, PO Box 120128, Ackten Station, Nashville, TN 37212
CutBank, English Dept., Univ. of Montana, Missoula, MT 59812

D

Daedalus, 136 Irving St., Cambridge, MA 02138
Dana Literary Society, P.O. Box 3362, Dana Point, CA 92629
John Daniel & Co., P.O. Box 2790, McKinleyville, CA 95519
Dark Animus, P.O. Box 750, Katoomba, NSW2780, *AUSTRALIA*
Denver Quarterly, University of Denver, Denver, CO 80208
Diagram, 60 Prospect NE #3, Grand Rapids, MI 49503
Diner, Box 60676, Greendale Sta., Worcester, MA 01606
Disinformation, 207 West 25th St., 4th fl., New York, NY 10001
Divide, Writing & Rhetoric Dept., Univ. of Colorado, Boulder, CO 80309
The DMQ Review, P.O. Box 640746, San Jose, CA 95164
D-N Publishing, 6238 Old Monroe Rd., Indian Trail, NC 28079
Dogwood, English Dept., Fairfield Univ., Fairfield, CT 06824
Double Room, 999 Park Ave., Rochester, NY 14610
DoubleTake, 55 Davis Sq., Somerville, MA 02144
Dream Horse Press, P.O. Box 640746, San Jose, CA 95164
The Drunken Boat, 5602 Tarry Terrace, Farmington, NM 87402

E

Eastern Washington University Press, P.O. Box 161236, Sacramento, CA 95816
Edgar, P.O. Box 5776, San Leon, TX 77539
Edge Publications, P.O. Box 799, Ocean Park, WA 98640
88, P.O. Box 2872, Venice, CA 90294
Ekphrasis, P.O. Box 161236, Sacramento, CA 95816
Elixir, P.O. Box 18010, Minneapolis, MN 55418
Epoch, Cornell Univ., 251 Goldwin Smith, Ithaca, NY 14853
Erosha, P.O. Box 185, Falls Church, VA 22040
Eureka Literary Magazine, Humanities Division, Eureka College, Eureka, IL 61530
Evansville Review, English Dept/.Univ. of Evansville, Evansville, IN 47222
Event, Douglas College, P.O. Box 2503, New Westminster, BC *CANADA* V3L 5B2

F

Facets, P.O. Box 380915, Cambridge, MA 02238
Failbetter, 63 Eighth Ave., Ste. 3A, Brooklyn, NY 11217
Fiction International, English Dept., San Diego State Univ., San Diego, CA 92182
Field, 10 N. Professor St., Oberlin, OH 44074
Fine Madness, P.O. Box 31138, Seattle, WA 98103

Finishing Line Press, P.O. Box 1626, Georgetown, KY 40324
Firewheel Editions, P.O. Box 793677, Dallas, TX 75379
The First Line, P.O. Box 250382, Plano, TX 75025
5 AM, Box 285, Spring Church, PA 15686
580 SPLIT, P.O. Box 9982, Mills College, Oakland, CA 94613
Five Points, Georgia State Univ., Univ. Plaza, Atlanta, GA 30303
flashquake, P.O. Box 2154, Albany, NY 12220
Flights, English Dept., Sinclair Community College, Dayton, OH45402
Flyway, 206 Ross Hill, Iowa State University, Ames, IA 50011
Folio: A Literary Journal, Dept. of Literature, American Univ., Washington, DC 20016
The Formalist, 320 Hunter Dr., Evansville, IN 47711
Four Way Books, P.O. Box 535, Village Station, NY 10014
Fourth Genre, Michigan State Univ., 229 Bessey Hall, East Lansing, MI 48824
Free Verse, M233 Marsh Rd., Marshfield, WI 54449
Frigg, 9036 Evanston Ave. N, Seattle, WA 98103
Frith Press, P.O. Box 161236, Sacramento, CA 95816
Fugue, 200 Brink Hall, Univ. of Idaho, Moscow, ID 83844
Future Poem Books, P.O. Box 34, New York, NY 10014
Futures Myrsterious, 3039 38th Ave., S. Minneapolis, MN 55406

G

Gargoyle Magazine, P.O. Box 6216, Arlington, VA 22206
The Gavis Press, P.O. Box 734, Mary Esther, FL 32569
The Georgia Review, Univ. of Georgia, Athens, GA 30602
Gettysburg Review, Gettysburg College, Gettysburg, PA 17325
David Godine, Publisher, 9 Hamilton Pl., Boston, MA 02108
Grand Street, 214 Sullivan St. (#6c), New York, NY 10012
Grasslimb, P.O. Box 420816, San Diego, CA 92142
Graywolf Press, 2402 University Ave. #203, St. Paul, MN 55114
Green Hills Literary Lantern, P.O. Box 375, Trenton, MO 64683
The Greensboro Review, English Dept., UNCG, Greensboro, NC 27402
Gulf Coast, English Dept., Univ. of Houston, Houston, TX 77204

H

the habit of rainy nights press, 104 NE 72nd Ave., Portland, OR 97213
Hampton Shorts, P.O. Box 3001, Bridgehampton, NY 11932
Hanging Loose Press, 231 Wyckoff St., Brooklyn, NY 11217
Happy, 240 E. 25th St., 11A, New York, NY 10016
Harp-Strings Poetry Journal, Box 640387, Beverly Hills, FL 34464
Harpur Palate, English Dept., State Univ. of N.Y., Binghamton, NY 13901
Harvard Review, Lamont Library, Harvard Univ., Cambridge, MA 02138
Hawaii Pacific Review, 1060 Bishop St., Honolulu, HI 96813
Hayden's Ferry Review, Arizona State Univ., P.O. Box 871502, Tempe, AZ 85287
The Healing Muse, 725 Irving Ave., Ste. 406, Syracuse, NY 13210
Helicon Nine Editions, 3607 Pennylvania Ave., Kansas City, M) 64111
Hobart, 9251 Densmore Ave. N, Seattle, WA 98103
Hogtown Creek Review, Marathonweg 84, 1076 TM, Amsterdam, *NEDERLAND*
Hotel Amerika, Ohio Univ., Ellis Hall, Athens, OH 45701
Hudson Review, 684 Park Ave., New York, NY 10021
Hunger Magazine, 1305 Old Rte. 28, Phoenicia, NY 12464
Hunger Mountain, Vermont College, 36 College St., Montpelier, VT 05602

I

Ibbetson Street Press, 25 School St., Somerville, MA 02143
The Iconoclast, 1675 Amazon Rd., Mohegan Lake, NY 10547
The Idaho Review, English Dept., Boise State Univ., Boise, ID 83725
IG Publishing, 178 Clinton Ave., Brooklyn, NY 11205
Illuminations, College of Charleston, 66 George St., Charlestn, SC 29424
Illya's Honey, P.O. Box 700865, Dallas, TX 75370
Image, 3307 Third Ave., W, Seattle, WA 98119
Indiana Review, 1020 E. Kirkwood Ave., Bloomington, IN 47405
Inkwell, Manhattanville College, 2900 Purchase St., Purchase, NY 10577
Iowa Review, Univ. of Iowa, Iowa City, IA 52242
Iris, Univ. of Virginia, Women's Center, P.O. Box 800588, Charlottesville, VA 22908
Isotope, English Dept., Utah State Univ., Logan, UT 84322
Italian Americana, 80 Washington St., Providence, RI 02903

J

Jabberwock Review, English Dept, Mississippi State Univ., MS 39762
James White Review, 290 West 12th St., Apt. 6C, New York, NY 10014
The Journal, English Dept., Ohio State Univ., Columbus, OH 43210
Journal of New Jersey Poets, Co. College of Morris, 216 Center Grove Rd., Randolph, NJ 07869
Jubilat, English Dept., Univ. of Massachusetts, Amherst, MA 01003

K

Kelsey Review, Mercer Co. Community College, P.O. Box B, Trenton, NJ 08690
The Kenyon Review, Kenyon College, Gambier, OH 43022
Kings Estate Press, 870 Kings Estate Rd., St. Augustine, FL 32086
Kyoto Journal, 35 Minamigoshomachi, Okazaki, Sakyo-ku, Kyoto 606-8334, *JAPAN*

L

Lake Effect, Pennsylvania State Univ., 5091 Station Rd., Erie, PA 16563
Land-Grant College Review, P.O. Box 1164, New York, NY 10159
The Laurel Review, 233 N. 8th St., Lincoln, NE 68588
Lean Press, P.O. Box 80334, Portland, OR 97280
Ledge Magazine, 78-44 80th St., Glendale, NY 11385
Lemon Shark Press, 1604 Marbella Dr., Vista, CA 92081
The Licking River Review, Northern Kentucky Univ., Highland Heights, KY 41099
LIT, 66 West 12th St., Rm. 508, New York, NY 10011
Lit Pot Press, Inc., 3909 Reche Rd., Ste. 132, Fallbrook, CA 92028
Literal Latte, 61 Fourth Ave., Ste. 240, New York, NY 10003
Literary Imagination, Classics Dept., Univ. of Georgia, Athens, GA 30602
The Literary Review, Fairleigh Dickinson Univ., 285 Madison Ave., Madison, NJ 07940
The Liturgical Press, St. John's Abbey, Collegeville, MN 56321
Livingston Press, Station 22, Univ. of West Alabama, Livingston, AL 35470
The Loft Literary Center, 1011 Washington Ave. S, Ste. 200, Minneapolis, MN 55415

Logan House Press, 1625 Pawnee St., Lincoln, NE 68502
The Long Story, 18 Eaton St., Lawrence, MA 01843
The Louisville Review, Spalding Univ., Louisville, KY 40203
Lynx Eye, 542 Mitchell Dr., Los Osos, CA 93402
Lynx House Press, Eastern Washington Univ., Cheney, WA 99004
Lyric Poetry Review, P.O. Box 980814, Houston, TX 77098
Luquer Street Press, 199 Luquer St., Brooklyn, NY 11231

M

Main Street Rag, 4416 Shea Lane, Charlotte, NC 28277
Malahat Review, University of Victoria, British Columbia, CANADA
The Manhattan Review, 440 Riverside Dr., #38, New York, NY 10027
Many Mountains Moving, Inc., 420 22nd St., Boulder, CO 80302
Manzanita Quarterly, P.O. Box 9289, Santa Fe, NM 87504
Margie, P.O. Box 250, Chesterfield, MO 63006
The Massachusetts Review, South College, Univ. of Massachusetts, Amherst, MA 01003
McSweeney's, 826 Valencia, San Francisco, CA 94110
Meredith Miller Internet Project, 4416 Fairview Ave., Newtown Square, PA 19073
Meridian, Univ. of Virginia, P.O. Box 400145, Charlottesville, VA 22904
Mid-American Review, Bowling Green State Univ., Bowling Green, OH 43403
Midnight Mind, P.O. Box 146912, Chicago, IL 60614
Midstream, 633 Third Ave., 21st fl., New York, NY 10017
Midwest Quarterly, Pittsburg State University, Pittsburg, KS 60762
Mindprints, Allan Hancock College, Santa Maria, CA 93454
MiPo Magazine, 9240 SW 44 St., Miami, FL 33165
MiPo-Print, 1100 Pedras Rd., Apt. G124, Turlock, CA 95382
Mississippi Review, Univ. of Southern Mississippi, Hattiesburg, MS 39406
Missouri Review, 1507 Hillcrest Ave., Univ. of Missouri, Columbia, MO 65211
Mizna, P.O. Box 14294, Minneapolis, MN 55414
The Montserrat Review, P.O. Box 391764, Mountain View, CA 94309
MS, 433 S. Beverly Dr., Beverly Hills, CA 90212
Muse's Kiss, P.O. Box 703, Lenoir, NC 28645

N

Nanny Fanny, 2524 Stockbridge Dr., #15, Indianapolis, IN 45268
National Poetry Review, P.O. Box 640625, San Jose, CA 95164
Natural Bridge, English Dept., Univ. of Missouri, St. Louis, MO 63121
The Nebraska Review, Writer's Workshop, Univ. of Nebraska, Omaha, NE 68182
Nevada Co. Poetry Series, P.O. Box 2416, Grass Valley, CA 95945
New England Review, Middlebury College, Middlebury, VT 05753
New England Writers, P.O. Box 5, Windsor, VT 05089
New Letters, see BkMk Press
New Orleans Review, Loyola Univ., New Orleans, LA 70118
News from the Republic of Letters, 120 Cushing Ave., Boston, MA 02125
NFG Magazine, Sheppard Centre, P.O. Box 43112, Toronto, Ont., CANADA M2N 6N1
Night Train, P.O. Box 6250, Boston, MA 02114
Nine Muses Books, 3541 Kent Creek Rd., Winston, OR 97496
96 Inc., P.O. Box 15559, Boston, MA 02215
Noon, 1369 Madison Ave., (PMB 298) New York, NY 10128

Northeastern University Press, 360 Huntington Ave., Boston, MA 02115
Northwest Review, Univ. of Oregon, Eugene, OR 97403
North American Review, University of Northern Iowa, Cedar Falls, IA 50614
Notre Dame Review, English Dept., Univ. of Notre Dame, Notre Dame, IN 46556

O

Octopus Magazine, 695 Northeast Ave., Tallmadge, OH 44278
One Story, P.O. Box 1326, New York, NY 10156
One Trick Pony, P.O. Box 11186, Philadelphia, PA 19136
Onearth, 40 West 20th St., New York, NY 10011
Ontario Review, 9 Honey Brook Dr., Princeton, NJ 08540
Opojaz, Inc., 6614 Clayton Rd., PMB #325, Richmond Heights, MO 63117
Osiris, P.O. Box 297, Deerfield, MA 01342
Other Voices, English Dept., Univ. of Illinois, 601 S. Morgan St., Chicago, IL 60607
Oyez Review, School of Liberal Arts, Roosevelt Univ., 430 S. Michigan Ave., Chicago, IL 60605
Oyster Boy Review, P.O. Box 77842, San Francisco, CA 94107

P

Pangolin Papers, P.O. Box 241, Nordland, WA 98358
Paris Review, 541 E. 72d St., New York, NY 10021
Passages North, English Dept., Northern Michigan Univ., Marquette, MI 49855
Paterson Literary Review, Passaic Co. Community College, Paterson, NJ 07505
Pathways Press, P.O. Box 2392, Bloomington, IN 47402
Pearl Editions, 3030 E. Second St., Long Beach, CA 90803
Penumbra, P.O. Box 115995, Tallahassee, Fl 32317
The Permanente Journal, 500 NE Multnomah, Ste. 100, Portland, OR 97232
Perugia Press, P.O. Box 60364, Florence, MA 01062
Phantasmagoria, English Dept., Century College, White Bear Lake, MN 55110
Phoebe, MSN2D6 George Mason Univ., Fairfax, VA 22030
Pleiades, English Dept., Central Missouri State Univ., Warrensburg, MO 64093
Ploughshares, Emerson College, 120 Boylston St., Boston, MA 02116
PMS, English Dept., Univ. of Alabama, Birmingham, AL 35294
Poems & Plays, English Dept., MTSU, Murfreesboro, TN 37132
Poet Lore, The Writer's Center, 4508 Walsh St., Bethesda, MD 20815
Poet Warrior Publications, P.O. Box 3175, Wayne, NJ 07474
Poetic Matrix Press, P.O. Box 1223, Madera, CA 93639
Poetry, 1030 N. Clark St., Ste. 420, Chicago, IL 60610
Poetry Miscellany, English Dept., Univ. of Tennessee, Chattanooga, TN 37403
Poet's Corner Press, 8049 Thornton Rd., Stockton, CA 95209
POOL, P.O. Box 49738, Los Angeles, CA 90049
Portland Magazine, Univ. of Portland, 5000 Willamette Blvd., Portland, OR 97203
Portland Review, Portland State Univ., P.O. Box 347, Portland OR 97207
Post Road, P.O. Box 590663, Newton Centre, MA 02459
The Powhaten Review, 4936 Farrington Dr., Virginia Beach, VA 21455
Prairie Fire Press, 423-100 Arthur St., Winnipeg, MB, CANADA R3B 1H3
Prairie Schooner, Univ. of Nebraska, P.O. Box 880334, Lincoln, NE 68588
Primavera, Box 37-7547, Chicago, IL 60637
Prism, Creative Writing Program, Univ. of British Columbia, Vancouver, BC CANADA V6T 1Z1
Prose Ax, P.O. Box 22643. Honolulu, HI 96823
Provincetown Arts, 650 Commercial St., Provincetown, MA 02657
Puerto del Sol, MSC 3E, P.O. Box 30001, Las Cruces, NM 88003

Q

Quarter After Eight, 12500 State Rte. 690. Athens, OH 45701
Quick Fiction, 50 Evergreen St., #25, Jamaica Plain, MA 02130
Quiet Storm Publishing, P.O. Box 1666, Martinsburg, WV 25406

R

Rain Taxi, P.O. Box 3840, Minneapolis, MN 55403
Raritan, 31 Mine St., New Brunswick, NJ 08903
Rattapallax, 250 Riverside Dr., #23, New York, NY 10025
Rattle, 12411 Ventura Blvd., Studio City, CA 91804
Raven Chronicles, 1634 11th Ave., Seattle, WA 98122
RBS Gazette, 49 Grove St., New York, NY 10014
Rearview Quarterly, P.O. Box 486, Sudbury, MA 01776
Red River Review, 2108 Stein Way, Carrollton, TX 75007
Redactions: Poetry & Poetics, 1322 S. Jefferson, Spokane, WA 99204
Revision, 1319 Eighteenth St., NW, Washington, DC 20036
Rhapsoidia Literary Magazine, 6570 Jewel St., Riverside, CA 92509
Rhino, P.O. Box 591, Evanston, IL 60204
Ridgeway Press, 10900 Harpes Ave., Detroit, MI 48213
Rivendell, P.O. Box 9594, Asheville, NC 28815
River King, P.O. Box 122, Freeburg, IL 62243
River Oak Review, 728 Noyes St., Evanston, IL 60201
River Styx, 634 N. Grand Blvd., 12th fl., St. Louis, MO 63103
River Teeth, Ashland Univ., 401 College Ave., Ashland, OH 44805
Rock Salt Plum Poetry Review, PSC 76, Box 4026, APO-AP 96319
The Rose & Thorn, 3 Diamond Ct., Montebello, NY 10901
Rose Shell Press, 15223 Coral Isle Ct., Fort Myers, FL 33919

S

Salamander, 48 Ackers Ave., Brookline, MA 02445
Salmagundi, Skidmore College, Saratoga Springs, NY 12866
Samba Mountain West, P.O. Box 4741, Englewood, CO 80155
Sandstar Publications, P.O. Box 181, Rockport, MA 01966
Santa Monica Review, Santa Monica College, 1900 Pico Blvd., Santa Monica, CA 90405
Sarabande Books, Inc., 2234 Dundee Rd., Ste. 200, Louisville, KY 40205
Schuylkill Valley Journal, 240 Golf Hills Rd., Havertown, PA 19083
The Seattle Review, Univ. of Washington, Seattle, WA 98195
Sentence, see Firewheel Editions
Sewanee Review, University of the South, 735 University Ave., Sewanee, TN 37383
Shenandoah, Washington & Lee Univ., Lexington, VA 24450
Sidereality, 19 Woodwind Ct., Columbus, SC 29209
Singles Network, P.O. Box 13, Springfield, VA 22150
Skidrow Penthouse Press, 68 East Third St., Ste. 16, New York, NY 10003
Skyline Literary Magazine, P.O. Box 295, Stormville, NY 12582
Slipstream, P.O. Box 2071, Niagara Falls, NY 14301
Slow Trains Literary Journal, P.O. Box 4741, Englewood, CO 80155
Small Beer Press. 176 Prospect Ave., Northampton, MA 01050
Small Town, 945 Taraval St., # 147, San Francisco, CA 94116
Solo, 5146 Foothill, Carpinteria, CA 93013

Southern Poetry Review, Armstrong Atlantic State Univ., Savannah, GA 31419
Southern Review, 43 Allen Hall, LSU, Baton Rouge, LA 70803
Southwest Review, Southern Methodist Univ., P.O. Box 750374, Dallas, TX 75275
Speakeasy, 1011 Washington Ave. South, Minneapolis, MN 53411
Spinning Jenny, P.O. Box 1373, New York, NY 10276
Spire Press. 532 LaGuardia Pl., Ste. 298, New York, NY 10012
Spoon River Poetry Review, Illinois State University, Normal, IL 61798
Spout, P.O. Box 581067, Minneapolis, MN 55458
Stone River Press, 2003 Corral Dr., Houston, TX 77090
Story-South, 3433 Portland Ave. S, #2, Minneapolis, MN 55407
The Storyteller, 2441 Washington Rd., Maynard, AR 72444
The Sun, 107 N. Roberson St., Chapel Hill, NC 27516
Swan Scythe Press, 2052 Calaveras Ave., Davis, CA 95656
Sweet Annie Press, 7750 Highway P24W, Baxter, IA 50028

T

Talebones, 5203 Quincy Ave SE, Auburn, WA 98092
Tatlin's Tower, 800 S. Vine St., Urbana, IL 61801
The Temple, P.O. Box 1773, 40 S. Colville, Walla Walla, WA 99362
Terminus. 1034 Hill St., SE, Atlanta, GA 30315
Terra Incognita, P.O. Box 150585, Brooklyn, NY 11215
Texas Review, Sam Houston State University, Huntsville, TX 77341
Thema Literary Society, Box 8747, Metairie, LA 70011
3rd Bed, 206 Franklin St., Brooklyn, NY 11222
Third Coast, Western Michigan Univ., Kalamazoo, MI 49008
Three Candles, 5470 132nd Lane, Savage, MN 55378
Threepenny Review, P.O. Box 9131, Berkeley, CA 94709
The Throwback, 1900 Eddy St., #15, San Francisco, CA 94115
Thunderbird Publishing, 935 Lighthouse Ave., #21, Pacific Grove, CA 93950
Timber Creek Review, 8969 UNCG Sta., Greensboro, NC 27413
Tin House Magazine, 2601 NW Thurman St., Portland, OR 97210
Tiny Lights Publications, P.O. Box 928, Petaluma, CA 94953
The Trilobite Press, 1015 W. Oak St., Denton, TX 76201
Triple Tree Publishing, P.O. Box 5684, Eugene, OR 97405
Triplopia, 6816 Mt. Vernon Ave., Salisbury, MD 21804
TriQuarterly, Northwestern Univ., Press, 629 Noyes St. Evanston, IL 60208
219 Press, P.O. Box 352, Perry, KS 66073
Tryst, 3521 Longfellow Ave., Minneapolis, MN 55407
Turnrow, English Dept., University of Louisiana, 700 University Ave., Monroe, LA 71209

U

Uccelli Press, P.O. Box 35394, Seattle, WA 98145
University of Tampa Press, 401 W. Kennedy Blvd, Box 19F, Tampa, FL 33606

V

Vallum Magazine, P.O. Box 48003, Montreal, Que., H2V 4S8 *CANADA*
Verse Libre Quarterly, P.O. Box 185, Falls Church, VA 22040

Verse Press, 221 Pine St., 2A3, Florence, MA 01062
Vestal Review, 2609 Dartmouth Dr., Vestal, NY 13850
Via Dolorosa Press, 701 E. Schaaf Rd., Cleveland, OH 44131
The Vincent Brothers Review, 4566 Northern Circle, Riverside, OH 45421
Virginia Quarterly Review, One West Range, Charlottesville, VA 22903

W

Washington Writers Publishing House, P.O. Box 15271, Washington, DC 20003
Watchword Press, 3288 21st St., #248, San Francisco, CA 94110
Water-Stone Review, Hamline Univ., 1536 Hewitt Ave., St. Paul, MN 56104
The Wayne Literary Review, Wayne State Univ., Detroit, MI 48202
Weber Studies, 1214 University Circle, Ogden, UT 84488
West Branch, Bucknell Hall, Bucknell Univ., Lewisburg, PA 17837
Western Humanities Review, English Dept., Salt Lake City, UT 84112
Westmeadow Press, P.O. Box 4338, Vineyard Haven, MA 02568
Wheatland Press, P.O. Box 18181, Wilsonville, OR 97070
Whistling Shade, P.O. Box 7084, St. Paul, MN 55107
White Pelican Review, P.O. Box 7833, Lakeland, FL 33813
Wild Earth, P.O. Box 455, Richmond, VT 05477
Willow Springs, EWU, 705 West 1st Ave., Spokane, WA 99201
Wind River Press, 254 Dogwood Dr., Hershey, PA 17033
Wisconsin Academy Review, 1922 University Ave., Madison, WI 53726
Witness, Oakland and Community College, Farmington Hills, MI 48334
The Worcester Review, 6 Chatham St., Worcester, MA 01609
Words, School of Visual Arts, 209 East 23rd St., New York, NY 10010
Words of Wisdom, 8969 UNCG Sta., Greensboro, NC 27413
Words on Walls, 18348 Coral Chase Dr., Boca Raton, FL 33498
Writer's Hood, 2518 Fruitland Dr., Bremerton, WA 98310
The Writer's Voice, 10900 Harper Ave., Detroit, MI 48213

X

Xantippe, P.O. Box 20997, Oakland, CA 94620

Y

Yale Review, Yale University, New Haven, CT
Yalobusha Review, English Dpt., Univ. of Mississippi, University, MS 38677

Z

Zoetrope, 916 Kearny St., San Francisco, CA 94133
ZYZZYVA, P.O. Box 590069, San Francisco, CA 94159

FOUNDING MEMBERS OF THE PUSHCART PRIZE FELLOWSHIPS

Renée Ashley
Ausable Press
David Baker
Jim Barnes
Dorothy Barresi
Barrow Street Press
Jill Bart
Ellen Bass
Judith Baumel
Ann Beattie
Madison Smartt Bell
Beloit Poetry Journal
Andre Bernard
Christopher Bernard
Wendell Berry
Stacy Bierlein
Mark Blaeuer
Blue Lights Press
Carol Bly
BOA Editions
Deborah Bogen
Susan Bono
Anthony Brandt
James Breeden
Rosellen Brown
Jane Brox
Andrea Hollander Budy
E. S. Bumas
Richard Burgin
Skylar H. Burris
David Caliguiuri
Janine Canan
Henry Carlile
Fran Castan
Chelsea Associates
Phyllis M. Choyke
Joan Connor
Tricia Currans-Sheehan
Thadious Davis
Edward J. DiMaio
Kent Dixon
John Duncklee
Elaine Edelman
Nancy Edwards
M. D. Elevitch
Irvin Faust
Tom Filer
Susan Firer
Nick Flynn
Peter Fogo
Linda N. Foster
Fugue
Alice Fulton
Eugene K. Garber
A Gathering of the Tribe
Emily Fox Gordon
Philip Graham
Eamon Grennan

Lee Meitzen Grue
Habit of Rainy Nights
Rachel Hadas
Jeffrey Harrison
Lois Marie Harrod
Healing Muse
Lily Henderson
Neva Herrington
Lou Hertz
William Heyen
Bob Hicok
Kathleen Hill
Edward Hoagland
Daniel Hoffman
Doug Holder
Richard Holinger
Rochelle L. Holt
Richard M. Huber
Brigid Hughes
Lynne Hugo
Illya's Honey
Mark Irwin
Beverly A. Jackson
Richard Jackson
Alice Jones
Journal of New Jersey Poets
Robert Kalich
Miriam Polli Katsikis
Meg Kearney
Celine Keating
John Kistner
Judith Kitchen
Stephen Kopel
David Kresh
Maxine Kumin
Babs Lakey
Maxine Landis
Lance Larson
Dorianne Laux & Joseph Millar
Donald Lev
Dana Levin
Rachel Loden
Radomir Luza, Jr.
Annette Lynch
Elizabeth MacKierman
Elizabeth Macklin
Leah Maines
Mark Manalang
Norma Marder
Jack Marshall
Tara L. Masih
Peter Matthiessen
Alice Mattison
TracyMayor
Robert McBrearty
Jane McCafferty
Jo McDougall
Sandy McIntosh

CONTRIBUTORS' NOTES

SHERMAN ALEXIE lives in Seattle. He is the author of the novels *Reservation Indian* and *Indian Killer* and the short story collection *Toughest Indian In the World*.

DICK ALLEN has received writing fellowships from The National Endowment for the Arts, the Ingram Merrill Foundation and others. His most recent book is *The Day Before: New Poems* (Sarabande).

DOUG ANDERSON is a Ph. D. candidate at the University of Connecticut. He lives in Willimantic, Connecticut.

DAVID BAKER is the author of nine books, most recently the poetry collection, *Changeable Thunder*. He lives in Granville, Ohio and is poetry editor of *The Kenyon Review*.

CATHERINE BARNETT's *Into Perfect Spheres Such Holes Are Pierced* was published by Alice James. She teaches at New York University.

STEVEN BARTHELME lives in Mississippi. He is a previous Pushcart Prize winner.

CHARLES BAXTER is the author of a book of essays, four books of stories and four novels, including the just issued *Saul and Patsy* (Pantheon).

WENDELL BERRY is the author of over forty books of fiction, poetry and essays, including *Citizenship Papers* and *That Distant Land*. He has farmed a hillside in his native Henry County, Kentucky for over thirty years.

TOM BISSELL lives in New York City. His collection, *God Lives In St. Petersburg*, is just out from Pantheon.

CHANA BLOCH's most recent book of poems is *Mrs. Dumpty* (Wisconsin, 1998), winner of the Felix Pollak Prize. Her new manuscript, *The Dark of the Day*, won the 2004 Alice Fay Castagnola Award from the Poetry Society of America.

ROBERT BLY lives in Minneapolis and is the author of many books of poetry and commentary plus translations from German, Spanish and Swedish.

ALISON CADBURY received both a Fulbright and an NEA fellowship. Her stories have appeared in *Ascent*, *The Missouri Review* and elsewhere.

HAYDEN CARRUTH has published twenty-nine books, most recently *Doctor Jazz: Poems 1996–2000* (Copper Canyon). He is past editor of *Poetry*, and *Harper's* and is an advisory editor of *The Hudson Review*.

BROCK CLARKE has published a novel, *The Ordinary White Boy*, and a collection of short stories, *What We Won't Do*. He has been a fellow at the Bread Loaf, Sewanee, and Wesleyan writers conferences.

SUZANNE CLEARY's *Keeping Time* was published by Carnegie Mellon in 2002. She teaches at SUNY, Rockland.

ANDREI CODRESCU is a frequent contributor to National Public Radio's "All Things Considered." Poet, essayist and anthologist, he teaches at LSU in Baton Rouge and is editor of *Exquisite Corpse*.

ALICE FULTON teaches at Cornell University. Her latest poetry collection is just out from W.W. Norton. Her fiction appears in recent issues of *Epoch*, *Georgia Review* and *Gettysburg Review*.

FRANK X. GASPAR won the Brittingham Prize for Poetry with his third collection, *A Field Guide to the Heavens* (Wisconsin, 1999). His next book is just out from Alice James Books.

ALBERT GOLDBARTH's latest book, *Budget Travel Through Space and Time*, was published by Graywolf. He lives in Wichita, Kansas.

EMILY FOX GORDON is the author of *Mockingbird Years*. Her essays have appeared in *Boulevard*, *Best American Essays*, and *The Pushcart Prize*.

MARY GORDON is the author of *Final Payments*, *The Company of Women* and other works. She teaches at Barnard College.

527

EAMON GREENAN's poetry has appeared in *The Threepenny Review*, *The New Yorker* and elsewhere. He teaches at Vassar College.

BENJAMIN SCOTT GROSSBERG has recent work in *Western Humanities Review, Paris Review, Malahat Review* and other publications. He teaches at Antioch.

MEREDITH HALL lives in Maine and teaches at The University of New Hampshire. She is at work on an essay collection titled "Without a Map."

JEFFREY HARRISON is the author of three books of poetry, most recently *Feeding the Fire* (Sarabande). His essay on Wallace Stevens appeared in *Pushcart Prize XXIII*.

TERRANCE HAYES is the author of *Hip Logic* (Penguin, 2002), which was a 2001 National Poetry Series selection and a finalist for the Los Angeles *Times* Book Award. *Wind In A Box* is due in 2005 from Penguin.

JACK HERLIHY lives near Boston. This is his first published story.

TONY HOAGLAND is the author of *What Narcissism Means to Me* (Graywolf), *Donkey Gospel* and *Sweet Ruin*. He won the James Laughlin Award from The Academy of American Poets and the Brittingham Prize in Poetry.

BARBARA HURD is the author of *Entering The Caves* (Houghton Mifflin), which includes this essay. She teaches at Frostburg State University in Maryland.

MAJOR JACKSON teaches at the University of Vermont. His recent poetry collection is *Leaving Saturn*.

ELIZABETH KADETSKY is the author of *First There Is A Mountain*, a memoir of India (Little, Brown 2004). She teaches at Columbia University.

DAVID KIRBY's *The House of Blue Light* was published by Louisiana State University Press. *The Ha-Ha* was just published by the same press. He teaches at Florida State University.

STEVE KOWIT, an American Jewish Buddhist, skeptic and anti-Zionist, founded the first animal rights organization in San Diego. He is the author of *In the Palm of Your Hand*, a book about writing, and *Dumbbell Nebula*, a poetry collection.

LANCE LARSEN's second poetry collection is due out from the University of Tampa Press. He teaches at Brigham Young University.

SYDNEY LEA, founding editor of *New England Review*, is author of eight volumes of poetry, most recently *Ghost Pain* (Sarabande Books). His 2001 collection, *Pursuit of a Wound*, was a 2001 Pulitzer finalist.

DANA LEVIN lives in Santa Fe, New Mexico. Her work has appeared in many journals nationwide.

PHILIP LEVINE's new book of poems is *Breath* (Knopf). He lives in Fresno, California and New York City.

YIYUN LI's stories and essays have appeared in *The New Yorker, The Paris Review* and elsewhere. She is the winner of The Plimpton Prize for New Writers from *The Paris Review*.

DONNA MASINI's new collection of poems, *Turning To Fiction*, is forthcoming from W.W. Norton. She teaches at Hunter College in New York.

ALICE MATTISON's novel, *The Wedding of the Two-Headed Woman*, was published in 2004. She is the author of three previous novels and short story collections, plus a book of poems. She teaches at Bennington College.

W.S. MERWIN lives in Haiku, Hawaii and is the author of many books of poetry, prose and plays.

NADINE MEYER is a Ph.D. candidate at the University of Missouri-Columbia. Her works appear in *Quarterly West, CutBank, North American Review* and *Pleiades*.

BRENDA MILLER is the author of *Season of the Body* (Sarabande Books, 2002). She has won three previous Pushcart Prizes, and her essays have appeared in *Fourth Genre, Georgia Review* and *Utne Reader*.

PATRICIA MONAGHAN teaches at DePaul University in Chicago. She is the author of recent books from Salmon Poetry and New World Library.

PAMELA PAINTER is the author of two story collections, *Getting to Know The Weather* and *The Long and Short of It*. She is a founding editor of *StoryQuarterly*.

KAREN PALMER is the author of two novels from Soho Press—*All Saints* and *Border Dogs*. She lives and works in Colorado.

ANN PANCAKE's collection of short stories, *Given Ground*, won the 2000 Bakeless Prize. Other awards include a Whiting Fellowship, and an NEA Fellowship.

DONALD PLATT is the author of two volumes of poetry from Purdue University Press. His poems have appeared in dozens of journals. He teaches at Purdue University.

DALE PECK is the author of *Martin and John, Now It's Time To Say Goodbye* and other works of fiction. He lives in New York City.

KAY RYAN received the 2004 Ruth Lilly Poetry Prize. She lives in Fairfax, California.

DAVID ST. JOHN's most recent poetry collections are *PRISM* (Arctos, 2002) and *The Face: A Novella In Verse* (HarperCollins 2004). He lives in Venice, California.

SUE STANDING's writing has appeared in many journals including *Africa Today, Agni, APR, American Scholar, Field, The Nation* and *Southwest Review*. Her most recent poetry collection is *False Horizon* (Four Way Books).

PATRICIA STATON has published in *Mid-American Review, Pleiades, Prairie Schooner* and elsewhere. She lives in Astoria, Oregon.

GERALD STERN's latest book of poetry is *American Sonnets* (W.W. Norton, 2002). Norton also published his book of essays which includes "Bullet In My Neck."

DEB O. UNFERTH's fiction has appeared in *Harper's, NOON, Fence, 3rd bed,* and elsewhere. She teaches at the University of Kansas, Lawrence.

WILLIAM T. VOLLMAN is the author of *The Rainbow Stories, Seven Dreams: A Book of North American Landscapes* and other volumes.

ELIOT KHALIL WILSON is a native of Virginia. He currently teaches at St. Olaf's College in Minnesota. *The Saint of Letting Small Fish Go* is his first book.

RUSSELL WORKING is a staff reporter for *The Chicago Tribune* and a former Iowa Short Fiction Award winner. His work has appeared in many newspapers and magazines worldwide.

ROBERT WRIGLEY's most recent poetry collection is *Lives of the Animals* (Penguin, 2003). He teaches at the University of Idaho.

BRAD YOUNKIN grew up on a horse farm in southern Illinois. He received an MFA degree from Southern Illinois University. This is his first published work. A gifted young writer, he was killed recently in a car accident.

529

INDEX

The following is a listing in alphabetical order by author's last name of works reprinted in the *Pushcart Prize* editions since 1976.

531

532

533

535

536

537

538

539

541

542

544

545

547

548

550

551

552

553

554

555

556

557

559

560